REA

Home and Beyond

Home and Beyond

An Anthology of Kentucky Short Stories

Edited By

Morris Allen Grubbs

With an Introduction by Wade Hall
and an Afterword by Charles E. May

THE UNIVERSITY PRESS OF KENTUCKY

Publication of this volume was made possible in part by a grant from the National Endowment for the Humanities.

Scholarly publisher for the Commonwealth,
serving Bellarmine University, Berea College, Centre
College of Kentucky, Eastern Kentucky University,
The Filson Historical Society, Georgetown College,
Kentucky Historical Society, Kentucky State University,
Morehead State University, Murray State University,
Northern Kentucky University, Transylvania University,
University of Kentucky, University of Louisville,
and Western Kentucky University.
All rights reserved.

Editorial and Sales Offices: The University Press of Kentucky
663 South Limestone Street, Lexington, Kentucky 40508-4008

05 04 03 02 01   5 4 3 2 1

Library of Congress Cataloging-in-Publication Data

Home and beyond : an anthology of Kentucky short stories / edited by
Morris Allen Grubbs : with an introduction by Wade Hall
and an afterword by Charles E. May.
    p. cm.
  ISBN 0-8131-2192-2 (cloth: alk. paper)
  1. Short stories, American—Kentucky. 2. Kentucky—Social life and
  customs—Fiction. I. Grubbs, Morris Allen, 1963-   .
  Title.
  PS558.K4 H66 2001
  813'.01089769—dc21
                                          00-012275

This book is printed on acid-free recycled paper meeting
the requirements of the American National Standard
for Permanence in Paper for Printed Library Materials.

Manufactured in the United States of America.

For my wife, Anissa

and in memory of
Delorah Jewell Moore
1961–2000

It's an old question—the call of the hearth or the call of the wild? Should I stay or should I go? Who is better off, those who traipse around or those who spend decades in the same spot, growing roots? . . . We're always yearning and wandering, whether we actually leave or not. In America, we all come from somewhere else, and we carry along some dream myth of home, a notion that something—our point of origin, our roots, the home country—is out there. It's a place where we belong, where we know who we are. Maybe it's in the past . . . or maybe it's somewhere ahead. . . . Maybe we'll never find what we're looking for, but we have to look.

BOBBIE ANN MASON, *CLEAR SPRINGS*

Writing is a search for truth. Sometimes, maybe, it is even a finding.

HOLLIS SUMMERS, INTERVIEW IN *THE KENTUCKY REVIEW*

Contents

Morris A. Grubbs ◆ Preface xi

Wade Hall ◆ Introduction xvii

1945–1960

Robert Penn Warren ◆ Blackberry Winter (1946) 3

Caroline Gordon ◆ The Petrified Woman (1947) 20

James Still ◆ The Nest (1948) 31

Jane Mayhall ◆ The Men (1948) 37

Elizabeth Hardwick ◆ Evenings at Home (1948) 43

Dean Cadle ◆ Anthem of the Locusts (1949) 51

Jesse Stuart ◆ Lost Land of Youth (1950) 58

Billy C. Clark ◆ Fur in the Hickory (1953) 66

Janice Holt Giles ◆ The Gift (1957) 71

A.B. Guthrie Jr. ◆ The Fourth at Getup (1960) 80

1960–1980

Hollis Summers ◆ The Vireo's Nest (1960) 89

Ed McClanahan ◆ The Little-Known Bird of the Inner Eye (1961) 101

Sallie Bingham ◆ Bare Bones (1965) 110

Robert Hazel ◆ White Anglo-Saxon Protestant (1967) 118

Jack Cady ◆ Play Like I'm Sheriff (1968) 145

Jim Wayne Miller ◆ The Taste of Ironwater (1969) 154

David Madden ◆ The World's One Breathing (1970) 162

Gayl Jones ◆ White Rat (1975) 179

Jane Stuart ◆ The Affair with Rachel Ware (1976) 186

Gurney Norman ◆ Maxine (1977) 194

Walter Tevis ◆ Rent Control (1979) 199

1980–2000

Bobbie Ann Mason ◆ Residents and Transients (1982) 209

Joe Ashby Porter ◆ Yours (1982) 217

Leon V. Driskell ◆ A Fellow Making Himself Up (1982) 222

Mary Ann Taylor-Hall ◆ Winter Facts (1983) 228

Richard Cortez Day ◆ The Fugitive (1984) 237

Sena Jeter Naslund ◆ The Perfecting of the Chopin
Valse No. 14 in E Minor (1985) 251

Pat Carr ◆ Diary of a Union Soldier (1985) 259

Wendell Berry ◆ That Distant Land (1986) 270

James Baker Hall ◆ If You Can't Win (1986) 279

Lisa Koger ◆ Bypass (1987) 287

Barbara Kingsolver ◆ Homeland (1989) 298

Normandi Ellis ◆ Dr. Livingston's Grotto (1989) 312

Guy Davenport ◆ Belinda's World Tour (1993) 323

Kim Edwards ◆ The Way It Felt to Be Falling (1993) 328

Chris Holbrook ◆ The Idea of It (1995) 341

Paul Griner ◆ Clouds (1996) 350

Chris Offutt ◆ Barred Owl (1996) 359

Dwight Allen ◆ Deferment (1998) 368

Crystal E. Wilkinson ◆ Humming Back Yesterday (1999) 384

Charles E. May ◆ Afterword 391

Preface

Kentucky, which sits between North and South, not quite in the East and not quite in the Midwest, is very near the heart of America. We are a microcosm of this nation, both what's best about it and what's worst.

BOBBIE ANN MASON, COMMENCEMENT ADDRESS,
UNIVERSITY OF KENTUCKY, 1994

Celebrating the modern American short story as penned by forty Kentucky writers, *Home and Beyond* offers us glimpses into the secret yearnings of the heart—and heartland. The stories collected here reflect life in later-twentieth-century Kentucky and America, but they spring from humanity's eternal questions: central among them, how do we balance our powerful homing instinct with the equally powerful journeying urge, the callings of home with the callings of the world? With this and other mysteries of allurement at their core, these stories are prime examples of the modern short story. Collectively they form a cyclical quest for identity, meaning, and wholeness in a turbulent and mutable world—an epic story of a people bound by the mysterious pull of their homeland.

Compiled for new and avid readers of the short story and for enthusiasts of Kentucky writers, this anthology brings together many of the finest literary short stories published in the last half-century. It is a descendent of *Kentucky Story*, a 1954 collection edited by Hollis Summers featuring stories that originally appeared between 1891 and 1951 by James Lane Allen, John Fox Jr., Elizabeth Madox Roberts, and twelve others. Like *Kentucky Story* and more recent state literary histories and interview collections, *Home and Beyond* defines a Kentucky writer as one who is connected to the state through birth or residence and whose Kentucky experience helped shape his or her identity. Within the broad sphere of Kentucky literature, writers have been selected because of the extent and reputation of their work in the short story genre. The state need not be a palpable presence for stories to have been considered for inclusion, though indeed nearly all of them included are either set in Kentucky or feature Kentuckians away from their native ground.

The writers in this collection at once embrace and transcend the Kentucky label: many of them have placed their stories repeatedly in national and international magazines and journals; more than half of them have had stories reprinted or cited in well-known prize annuals such as *Best American Short Stories*, *O. Henry*

Prize Stories, *The Pushcart Prize*, and *New Stories from the South*; and thirty-two of them have to date published short story collections. Although this is a gathering of regional fiction, the stories here are further proof that the universal is most powerfully expressed in the local, or as Summers says in his introduction to *Kentucky Story*, "The art of locality transcends geography. Its true concern is the neighborhood of humanity."

The word *Home* in this book's title is meant literally and metaphorically: it is the homeplace, the homeland, the familiar, the past, the longed-for future, family, security, felicity, Heaven. Thus the title's dichotomy of home and beyond extends to the known and the unknown, rootedness and rootlessness, faithfulness and infidelity, domestic entanglement and escape, homecoming and exile, local and mass acculturation, the past and the present, the present and the future. As writers from Homer to Wendell Berry have reminded us, life is a cycle of departures and returns: it is our nature to quest for what is beyond and to journey outward, and yet it is also our nature to long to come back, to turn homeward.

This cycle—home, beyond, and back again—is the basis for this collection's tripartite structure. Each of the three sections (1945 to 1960, 1960 to 1980, and 1980 to 2000) includes stories that share thematic traits. Most of the early post–World War II stories are characterized by a sense of impending loss. The home world is deeply rooted and insular, and the world beyond enters the frame of reference as an unknown, potentially disruptive, or formative force—intimations of the changes to come. Threatened by time and the world, and in the aftermath of war, the characters have a heightened appreciation of home; family, community, and memory are paramount. In contrast, many of the stories in the 1960s and 1970s are set in an urban or suburban world where home is mobile and characters are adrift. Separated from their heritage, no longer firmly rooted, and despite (or maybe because of) their freedom to roam, many of the characters are lonely or reveal a vague malaise. Other characters in the middle section experience a crisis of identity even within the gravitational pull of home. Finally, in the third section, characters are home again or are looking for a hearthstone, some meaningful and stable identity to act as an antidote to the malaise. Their relationship with home is more complex than ever, with home now permeated by mass culture and with individuals caught between conflicting worlds. Although some approach home with cautious reconciliation, nearly all are guided by a reinvigorated homing instinct—by the renewed desire to locate meaning in past or place.

Perhaps because Kentucky is such an intensely home-conscious state, the genre and the theme of home and beyond have found a common, fertile ground. The Commonwealth's degree of nativism and its percentage of people who leave and return are among the nation's highest. And the words to the official state song, "My Old Kentucky Home," resonate across America and beyond. But Kentucky, like the genre, is marked by ambiguity and paradox: the land was known both as a Dark and Bloody Ground and as a newfound Garden of Eden, both as a westward destination and as a westward passageway; later, the state was deeply divided in the Civil War, and in the twentieth century it became a noted region of social, political, and environmental contrasts. The genre naturally would flourish in a state of incongruity and among a people noted both for their love of place and their longing to escape. The Paradise myth—with its implications of contentedness and discontentedness, loss and gain—has remained a potent part of the state's character. America's famous frontiersman Daniel Boone has entered the realm of myth as a seeker of the Promised Land. His legacy endures in the Kentucky imagination. Janice Holt Giles once described Kentucky as "the land we hadn't come to yet—that far place of dreams where meadows were fair, forests were noble, streams were overflowing. It was always the land beyond—over another mountain, across another rolling river. It was the land God made just right and put in exactly the right place." As much a storied land as a land of stories, Kentucky is a confluence of the ideal and the real, a wellspring of an endless human story: the solitary and the collective search for home—for where the heart is.

In making selections I have tried to produce an anthology of diverse stories (with varied style, tone, point of view, etc.) as well as a short story cycle with underlying patterns of coherence. With the help of colleagues and students over a span of nearly four years, I have located and read—as many as could be acquired—the published stories by established and emerging Kentucky writers. As you might imagine, the field of such stories is immense, the crop dense, and for every story included here there are many others of similar merit by the same writer and by other Kentucky writers—a fact that has been both the reward and the rub of editing this anthology. In some instances, rather than choosing often-reprinted and widely available stories (such as Bobbie Ann Mason's "Shiloh"), I have chosen lesser-known but equally good—and fresher—ones. I have also tried to balance the stories' original reputations with their enduring appeal. My hope is that this anthology will stimulate further popular and academic interest in Kentucky short fiction. Readers may view it as a springboard for broader reading and further study; for example, students interested in the theme of initiation, perhaps best exemplified here by Warren's "Blackberry Winter," may want to read other stories of initiation by Kentucky writers, such as Sallie Bingham's "August Ninth at Natural Bridge," Gurney Norman's "Fat Monroe" and "Night Ride," and Wendell Berry's "Where Did They Go?"

Stories appear here because they reflect the umbrella theme of home and beyond and because they exemplify many of the characteristics of the modern genre, whose origins are in the mid-nineteenth-century Romantic tales of Nathaniel Hawthorne, Edgar Allan Poe, and Nikolai Gogol. In the late nineteenth and early twentieth centuries, the form further developed in the hands of realists, especially Anton Chekhov, James Joyce, Katherine Mansfield, Ernest Hemingway, and Katherine Anne Porter. Since World War II the genre has flowered in America through the stories of, for example, Eudora Welty, Flannery O'Connor, John Cheever, Grace Paley, Joyce Carol Oates, Raymond Carver, and many of the writers featured herein. Incidentally, during this short story renaissance many of the literary critics who helped shape the way the genre has come to be understood have been Kentuckians. Among the field's twentieth-century landmark texts are Robert Penn Warren and Cleanth Brooks's *Understanding Fiction* (1943); Caroline Gordon and Allen Tate's *The House of Fiction* (1950); Hollis Summers's *Discussions of the Short Story* (1963); and Charles E. May's several books on the history and critical theory of the genre, including *Short Story Theories* (1976), *The New Short Story Theories* (1994), and *The Short Story: The Reality of Artifice* (1995).

Although the modern short story resists a firm definition, and in fact its writers often defy convention and thwart expectation, the genre is characterized by a set of tendencies. Regardless of setting, good literary short stories strike universal chords, connecting us to the human condition. Among their core themes are loneliness, incommunicability, initiation, self-realization, and yearning. Modern stories tend to focus on epiphanic or defining moments, rely heavily on concrete detail to manifest meaning, thrive on a balance of revelation and concealment, and evoke—usually through their ambiguity or irresolution—a charged combination of satisfaction and frustration. Ultimately, their deceptively simple surfaces may belie their complexity and greater undercurrent of meaning. As Flannery O'Connor once said, "Meaning is what keeps the short story from being short." Thus the modern short story is a paradoxical, challenging, and rewarding form, beckoning the reader to act as a co-creator. These thematic and formal tendencies are present in varying degrees in classic short stories like Hawthorne's "Young Goodman Brown," Chekhov's "The Lady with the Dog," Joyce's "Araby," Hemingway's "Big Two-Hearted River," Welty's "A Worn Path," O'Connor's "A Good Man is Hard to Find," and Mason's "Shiloh"—all of which also portray the motivations for and the consequences of physically or spiritually journeying beyond home.

An anthology is the work of its contributors, so I am indebted to all of the short story writers whose imaginings and words form this collection; its strengths belong entirely to them. They also graciously reduced or waived their portions of publishers' or agents' permissions fees; without their generosity and assistance, this book would not have gone to press.

Librarians across the Commonwealth went beyond the call of duty to locate biographical information and acquire countless stories, especially Susan McDaniel in the Katie Murrell Library at Lindsey Wilson College, Claire McCann in Special Collections at the University of Kentucky, and Kate Black in the William T. Young Library at the University of Kentucky.

For encouraging my passion for the short story, I am grateful to Joseph R. Millichap at Western Kentucky University; David Durant, John Cawelti, Steven Weisenburger, Roger Anderson, and Stephen Manning at the University of Kentucky; Mary Rohrberger at the University of New Orleans; Susan Lohafer at the University of Iowa; and Charles May at California State University, Long Beach. I am especially grateful to Gurney Norman at the University of Kentucky, who is not only one of the great masters of the short story, but also one of the genre's greatest fans; our conversations over the last decade have deepened my understanding of the form and fed my own fanaticism.

For various assistance with this project, I thank Jane Gentry Vance, John Kleber, Charles Thompson, Jonathan Cullick, Clara Metzmeier, Jon Frederick, and Roger Rawlings. I am also indebted to James Alan Riley for his *Kentucky Voices: A Collection of Contemporary Kentucky Short Stories*, L. Elisabeth Beattie for her *Conversations with Kentucky Writers*, the late William S. Ward for his *A Literary History of Kentucky*, and Wade Hall for all of his wisdom and words.

Lindsey Wilson College funded a generous portion of the permissions fees, and numerous colleagues there supplied vital personal encouragement and editorial support, especially William B. Julian, Dorothy Julian, William T. Luckey Jr., Elise Luckey, Mark Dunphy, Delorah J. Moore, David Moore, Kerry Robertson, Carolyn Keefe, Tip Shanklin, Patrick Shaw, Tim McAlpine, Lillian Roland, George Kolbenschlag, Vonnie Kolbenschlag, Sylvia Ahrens, Sally Markle, Duane Bonifer, Phil Hanna, and Tina Nelson.

The Appalachian College Association and the Teagle Foundation Incorporated provided essential faculty-student research grants. In addition to funding a generous portion of the research costs and reprint fees, these grants allowed three senior English majors at Lindsey Wilson College—Greg Blair, Christy York, and Grant Young—to collaborate in the research, story selection, author correspondence, permissions acquisition, and typescript preparation. The students' contributions to this book were enormous.

Grant Young proved to be so helpful in shaping the entire project that I asked him—and he accepted despite great demands on his time—to serve as the book's assistant editor. He spent countless hours helping me read and ultimately choose stories, as well as compose biographical and critical headnotes. Our ongoing dialogue about short stories has led him to pursue the study of the short story in graduate school, and it has led me to affirm, broaden, and deepen my own beliefs about the genre. I am greatly indebted to him.

My deepest gratitude goes to my mother and father, Janette and James Edward Grubbs, and to my wife, Anissa Radford, for their examples and their loving encouragement. They have shown me, and kept me mindful of, the many meanings of home.

Introduction

WADE HALL

In this collection of short stories, Morris A. Grubbs has prepared a literary feast for readers of varied tastes. There are short short stories and long short stories. There are styles as complex as Faulkner, as plain as Hemingway, and as experimental as John Dos Passos. There are characters you will love and admire and those you will despise, some you will want to take home as permanent guests, and a few you'd like to have locked up.

These stories, published between 1945 and 2000, offer travels into the past, into fantasy, into geography. You will be taken on trips to the Kentucky mountains of James Still, the Louisville of Dwight Allen, the Port Royal country of Wendell Berry, and the Western Kentucky fields and flatlands of Bobbie Ann Mason. Trips are also offered to New York, Florida, and California, as well as a fantasy trip around the world. With Pat Carr you can time travel back to the Civil War, when Kentucky was a state divided against itself. With Hollis Summers you will witness the hilarious misadventures of the Artist's Colony of Kentucky, "the only non-alcoholic writers' center in the world," a workshop that is run, at least on the surface, like a Baptist retreat. You will meet people as common as dishwater and as mad as a hatter. You will suffer with boys and girls learning how to be adults, and you will shudder at adults who behave like children.

All in all, your odyssey through this collection will show you universal human comedies and tragedies with a Kentucky accent. You probably won't like all forty stories. Readers who like the great stories of Poe or Hawthorne don't necessarily like the great stories of Mark Twain or Henry James. But I guarantee that you will find in these pages enough stories to enrich your life.

You can open the book at random and read a story. Or you can start with the first story, "Blackberry Winter," by Robert Penn Warren, the greatest writer Kentucky has produced. Read this story set in 1910 about a nine-year-old boy who learns that life can be dangerous, even at home, with danger coming from both nature and man. Read this story and you will know what makes a great short story. Recalled by the man the boy became many years later are the early experiences that helped to prepare the boy for adulthood. It is one of many growing-up stories in this collection. Caroline Gordon's "The Petrified Woman" is also a memory story told by a woman about the summer when she was a girl and stayed with her grandmother and went to a nearby cave for a family reunion. This is a family with money and good breeding—and a dark underbelly. The girl, now a woman, remembers her pretentious relatives, and, in particular, the drunken man who falls in love (or lust) with Stella, a fake petrified woman in a cheap carnival.

Love, or its lack, is a constant theme. Janice Holt Giles's "The Gift" is a heartwarming story of a nine-year-old girl who falls in love with a handsome cowhand on her father's ranch. It is her first love, an impossible love; but her suffering is softened by the cowhand's "gift" to her, his affirmation that, though he is going to marry someone his own age, he loves her too. Set in the Southwest, this story is one of several written by writers who moved to Kentucky from other states. The list of Kentuckians-by-choice includes James Still and Sena Jeter Naslund from Alabama, A.B. Guthrie Jr., who grew up in Montana, Guy Davenport from South Carolina, and Leon Driskell from Georgia. Indeed, it was Kentucky that called forth the stories written by these adopted Kentuckians, even the stories about their native homelands.

Guthrie, who moved to Kentucky in 1925, juxtaposes Montana and Kentucky manners and mores in "The Fourth at Getup," which tells of four refined women from Kentucky who are touring the West and stop by Getup, Montana, to visit a friend. Their genteel manners are contrasted with the rough language and ways of Westerners celebrating the Fourth of July. Meanwhile, back in Kentucky, Billy C. Clark describes in "Fur in the Hickory" the initiation ritual of hunting that many Kentucky boys still learn. Clark shows us how a boy learns not only how to kill a squirrel without blowing him to pieces but also how to respect his elders. Another kind of initiation ritual is the leitmotif in Dwight Allen's "Deferment," which chronicles the efforts of a college sophomore to lose his virginity during summer vacation. Perhaps the most place-specific and class-conscious story in the collection, it is a delightfully humorous, slightly snobbish maturation narrative set in Louisville's upper middle class.

Another story about a student coping with family and personal problems is Kim Edwards's "The Way It Felt to Be Falling." Kate remembers that the summer she was nineteen and preparing for college everything and everyone seemed to fall apart—a recession had caused her father to go mad and her friend Stephen becomes suicidal. But she proves to be a survivor, even of a daredevil attempt at skydiving. Finally, the pain of growing up and falling in love is given a positive twist in Jane Mayhall's magical story, "The Men." She recalls three epiphanies stretching back to when she was an eleven-year-old girl in Louisville and went to her first ballet and became enchanted by the lead ballet dancer, a striking young man whose "insteps of his feet were so beautiful and alive that I fell in love with them at once." Her second revelation of love and happiness is sparked by a young male librarian at her high school, who has the sensuous grace and assurance of the ballet dancer. Her third blissful experience occurs after she has moved to New York and takes a Monday night class under an aging, gray-haired professor. Such moments of purity and wholeness may occur as well in New York, she suggests, as in her native city.

Family, home, flight, and return are themes common to most of these stories. As the boy in Warren's story learns, home and family do not always ensure safety. In "The Nest" one of the most eloquent voices of the Southern mountains, James Still, tells a stark tragedy about a six-year-old girl who must go to spend the night with her aunt over the ridge while her father and stepmother go to the bedside of her sick grandfather. On the way she gets lost and the freezing night forces her to make a temporary but vulnerable "nest" in a clump of broomsage. She is like a young bird untimely thrust from the nest and unable to find or build her own safe place before indifferent nature erases her. This gem of a story is told with the economy of a poet and the mystery and dimensions of a myth.

Many Kentuckians in life and in fiction have left home to find work and freedom outside the state. Sometimes they try to come back home. Happy Chandler, Kentucky's colorful former governor, once said about these exiles, "I never met a Kentuckian who wasn't coming home." In Chris Holbrook's "The Idea of It" a man whose family had fled Kentucky when he was a boy decides that he will return to his homeland to raise his son and unborn child. Instead of an idyllic Eden, he finds the spring water polluted by the runoff from a strip mine and an unstable mining economy prone to violence. A woman who had fled from the stultifying provincialism of her hometown in Elizabeth Hardwick's "Evenings at Home" discovers that her "fantastic manias" were distortions. Although she is still an outsider, she realizes that it is "comforting to have these roots"—and even a space "next to Brother" awaiting her in the family cemetery.

Bobbie Ann Mason's female narrator in "Residents and Transients" returns home to Western Kentucky from an academic sojourn of eight years ready to live there the rest of her life, "wondering why I ever went away." The exile in Chris Offutt's "Barred Owl" is fleeing a nasty divorce and winds up in Greeley, Colorado, where his car breaks down. There he meets another expatriate misfit, with whom he reproduces the speech and rituals of home (including "the ritual of tobacco"), the decorum of hospitality, and the skills required for skinning an animal for its pelt. "It felt right," he writes, "to sit with someone of the hills, even if we didn't have a lot to say." His friend's grotesque suicide makes him realize that he will not find a home like the one he left. Roscoe Page in Leon Driskell's "A Fellow Making Himself Up" spent the Depression bumming around the country and even made it to California, "God's country," some people called it. But not Roscoe, who says, "I didn't think their Hoovervilles beat the mountain shacks I knew back home."

The return of a native son to his Kentucky home and its family values is the theme of Wendell Berry's "That Distant Land." The story is centered around the death of the thirty-one-year-old narrator's grandfather. After "working in the city for several years," the young man brings his family home to the Kentucky River country of his youth. Despite his aged and declining grandparents, he is enthusiastic to be back. "My return," he says, "had given a sudden sharp clarity to my understanding of my home country. Every fold of the land, every grass blade and leaf of it gave me joy, for I saw how my own place in it had been prepared, along with its failures and its losses. Though I knew that I had returned to difficulties—not the least of which were the deaths that I could see coming—I was joyful." In Berry's story a good death is a gift, a natural part of life's cycles.

The pull of home and family are so strong on a network newsman in David Madden's "The World's One Breathing" that he will give up the opportunity to cover the Apollo 8 space flight to be at his dying mother's bedside, seeking her forgiveness and release. The newsman's return will be brief, but the exile in Jim Wayne Miller's "The Taste of Ironwater" hopes that he can leave Ohio and make a place for himself back in the mountains. Another exile's return is cause for a comic monologue in James Baker Hall's "If You Can't Win," in which an aging flower child of the '60s, now a doctor, comes back to Harrison County and finds herself saddled with a second husband, a filling station attendant (she has undermarried herself, she thinks), and a friend's overweight, simple-minded, candy-eating daughter Peggy, who is now stranded on the rooftop of the house.

The exile in "White Anglo-Saxon Protestant" by Robert Hazel lives and teaches in New York during the '60s, which he depicts as a hellhole of violence and death. The narrator himself is not very sympathetic. He is too smug, too clever, too self-satisfied, and too certain of his views. But he does realize that he is not living a good life and ends by trying "to imagine a time of love and goodness." New York is also the setting of Sallie Bingham's "Bare Bones," which shows the unraveling of a divorcee. She wanted her divorce until she got it. Now she realizes that she has been stripped to the "bare bones" and has no life and little hope left. Another flight into nightmare is the subject of Ed McClanahan's "The Little-Known Bird of the Inner Eye," the story of a college dropout artist who flees from Kansas to the surreal horror of a logging town in the Northwest. It is winter and he now waits "for spring to come and free me from this place."

There is no viable family life or safe place for Kentuckians at home or abroad in Gurney Norman's "Maxine." Norman's literary persona, Wilgus Collier, befriends his down-and-out, raw-talking, wine-swilling cousin Maxine, who has just returned from a failed trip to Detroit to rescue her pregnant, destitute daughter from her abusive husband. Wilgus has just finished college and plans a footloose trip to California and invites Maxine to go with him. She declines, saying, "I know what you're going to do. You're going to get out there to California and forget to come back. Homefolks'll never see you again." Maxine is trapped in the mountains and can only dream of escape. Wilgus's creator also went west as a young man, but Gurney Norman returned home to teach and to write.

The escape may be to California or New York or it may only be from a country community to the county seat. Set in the hill country of northeast Kentucky, Jesse Stuart's "Lost Land of Youth" is a poignant story of the failed return of a man to his rural community and the life he might have lived. He sees the land he might have farmed and hopes to see Mollie, the girl he might have married had he not moved away to town, climbed the ladder of success, and married the boss's daughter. Now a wealthy and unhappy widower, he finds only that he can't go home again.

Or the escape may be to Kentucky to flee a sour marriage. Mary Ann Taylor-Hall's "Winter Facts" portrays a thirty-five-year-old woman who leaves her husband in the city to come to the Kentucky countryside to take stock of her life and her future. Arriving in August to live in a house lent her by a friend, she prepares for winter and retreats into the house and kitchen, then plans for a spring garden and life without her husband. On her birthday she dances alone in the kitchen "not at all unhappy" while listening to George Harrison sing "Here Comes the Sun" on the radio.

In most Kentucky communities families are formed, blessed, and kept together by local traditions and institutions, in particular, the church. But in Dean Cadle's "Anthem of the Locusts" it is religion that keeps two young people apart. An Eastern Kentucky coal miner and his girlfriend are separated by her faith. During an emotional religious service, he continues to refuse her pleas to be saved and join her church; and she rejects him.

For couples who succeed in establishing families, they soon realize that marriage bonds are fragile. In "Rent Control" by Walter Tevis, a thirty-five-year-old couple learn that they can stop time by love-touching in their loft bed. Somehow they have tapped into eternity. Soon, however, they begin to resent their lives in real time when they continue to age. Finally, they withdraw completely from the world. The utopian dream of a perfect relationship becomes a meaningless life.

In her "Diary of a Union Soldier" Pat Carr returns to the Civil War to describe a new kind of relationship that is Platonic and eternal. A love-starved woman's life is changed when a wounded Union soldier staggers into her house from a nearby battlefield. She takes in the handsome Iowa soldier, binds his wounds, covers him with her company quilt, and keeps vigil over him during the night. As she prepares to wash his jacket and undershirt, a small diary falls out. After some hesitation, she begins to read the diary and to fall in love with him. She is unable to part with the diary after she discovers him dead the next morning and hides it in the folds of her wedding dress. This way she can secure his love forever in this kinder, gentler version of William Faulkner's Gothic chiller, "A Rose for Emily."

Indeed, despite legal and cultural guidelines, couples have always had to make their own modifications and definitions of marriage and family. In Jane Stuart's "The Affair with Rachel Ware," a writer of children's stories separates from his wife and moves south to Florida, where he has an affair with the bored wife next door. It is a temporary, somewhat vaguely satisfying relationship for both of them, but at least it is a reprieve from their isolation and loneliness. Normandi Ellis's protagonist in "Dr. Livingston's Grotto" discovers a respite from his overweight, card-playing wife when one summer afternoon in Bowling Green he steps through a sinkhole in his backyard into a cave. It is, he discovers, quite a wonderful place to be and he is reluctant to be rescued—particularly after his puzzled wife lowers him a blanket, a box of Kentucky Fried Chicken, and his saxophone.

Another satire on a dull, empty family life is Lisa Koger's "Bypass," which portrays a stay-at-home man who went to the local college, married a local divorcee with two daughters, and became a teacher at the local high school. He is almost forty and about to break out in the "middle-age crazies" as he realizes that all his romantic plans for life are dying. He makes a break one Friday, when he decides he's going to have home-fried chicken the way his mother used to cook it, even if he has to cook it himself. It's a modest rebellion, but it may also be the beginning of a new life. Or it may not.

Two Kentuckians find each other by accident in California in "The Fugitive" by Richard Cortez Day and form a sort of temporary family. A man from Hindman, Kentucky, meets a disabled woman from Dwarf, Kentucky, when her car breaks down and he takes her in for four days. In this short time she takes over his cabin and his life in her bossy way. When he first sees her, he is attracted by her "sweet Kentucky speech," which "reminded him of cool well water in a beechwood bucket, of the breeze in the willows by Troublesome Creek, back home in Hindman." After her car is repaired, she resumes her trip to see her sister in Oregon, leaving behind a man who has been changed by a relationship that was not about marriage and not even about sex but nonetheless meaningful.

Artificial families are sometimes created at conferences, especially if the participants are motivated by similar interests and objectives. The synthetic family created by Hollis Summers in "The Vireo's Nest" is a witty satire on writers' conferences and the various relationships that are formed. The Kentucky myth of the New Eden is turned inside out, with a comic cast of misfits and a snake to boot. The discovery of a moderately rare bird's nest upsets the writing routine of the colony and leads to a widow's catharsis.

The waning years of the twentieth century have made all sorts of new family groupings commonplace. And when you have new kinds of families, you have new kinds of break-ups. Joe Ashby Porter's "Yours" is about the break-up of a relationship (although the gender of the other partner is never specific). In the story a Kentuckian returns home to get his bearings, to find himself and "to suffer rebirth." While visiting Bardstown he writes a letter to the lover he's leaving and wanders around town, exploring his own life. An African American he meets on his walks offers a bit of positive advice. His wife has just died, he said, but "the onliest thing he looked forward to" was getting married again.

In Sena Jeter Naslund's beautifully mysterious story, "The Perfecting of the Chopin *Valse No. 14 in E Minor*," the family consists of a thirtyish woman and her phantom mother, who lived with her until her death. The opening sentence invites us into an enchanted world: "One day last summer when I was taking a shower, I heard my mother playing the Chopin *Valse No. 14 in E Minor* better than she had ever played it before." It was the same Chopin piece that she had heard her mother play thirty years before when she was a girl in Birmingham. The recitals continue throughout the summer, and each time the performance gets closer to perfection. The climax comes at an elaborate garden party in the fall, when her mother plays the waltz, with the assistance of Chopin himself, to perfection. Moreover, a rock in the garden that, according to the mother, had been placed "imperfect aesthetically" has finally moved "to the artistically correct place." It is the story of a relationship conceived in love that turns to madness and is sprinkled all over with the sparkling dust of magic. Likewise, Jack Cady's "Play Like I'm Sheriff" is another make-believe relationship. In Indianapolis a lonesome and troubled man meets a lonesome and troubled woman. They go to her house and pretend to be Norma and Johnnie. The story reads like an absurdist, existential play, with not-quite-real characters who are not quite real even to each other. But at least for one night they make a family and a home. Home is where you pretend it is. For such people as these two strangers, it's all they have.

Now we enter Guy Davenport's world of complete make-believe in "Belinda's World Tour," a fantasy trip around the world by a girl's lost doll and the doll's boyfriend. Here there is a home and a family, but it is only a fairy tale. Lizaveta has lost her doll Belinda in a park in Prague. Later, a guest who comes to tea, Herr Doktor Kafka, tells her that Belinda has met a boy ("perhaps a doll, perhaps a little boy") her age and is taking a trip around the world with him. Sure enough, Lizaveta begins to receive postcards from Belinda and her friend postmarked in England, Scotland, Denmark, Russia, Japan, Tahiti, and finally cities in the United States. At Niagara Falls they marry, leave for Argentina, and will presumably live happily ever after. After all, it's a fairy tale and anything can happen.

Strange things do happen in Paul Griner's surreal but believable "Clouds," which is about a wealthy, useless, dysfunctional family and the husband who develops an obsession with clouds—their names and shapes—after his wife suffers a miscarriage. He scours the world studying clouds, comparing and classifying them, and when his wife dies, he has her cremated. "I liked the idea of her smoke and ashes," he explains, "drifting up to the clouds."

Perhaps a passage from Robert Penn Warren's *World Enough and Time*, published in 1950, can serve as an epigraph for three stories about Native Americans and African Americans, two groups who have had their original customs and folkways almost destroyed by the dominant European invaders and enslavers. In order to survive, blacks and Indians have had to accommodate themselves to their conquerors, even if it meant denying who they were. Warren wrote:

> In the days before the white man came, the Indians called the land of Kentucky the Dark and Bloody Ground. But they also called it the Breathing Land and the Hollow Land, for beneath the land there are great caves. The Indians came here to fight and to hunt, but they did not come here to live. It was a holy land, it was a land of mystery, and they trod the soil lightly when they came. They could not live here, for the gods lived here. But when the white men came, the gods fled, either to the upper air or deeper into the dark earth. So there was no voice there to speak and tell the white men what justice is.

Barbara Kingsolver's "Homeland" is the inspiring story of our country's Indian legacy. Gloria Murray, a woman of mixed white and Indian blood, tells of her great grandmother (Great Mam), a Cherokee of the Bird Clan who married a white man, Stewart Murray, and rode with him on his horse from Tennessee to Morning Glory, in the Kentucky mountains, where their descendants have become coal miners. It is summer and almost time for Great Mam to die, so the family takes her back home to Tennessee in their old rusty Ford truck. Her homeland has changed so much she doesn't recognize it and she returns to Kentucky to die. Now her great granddaughter is honoring her memory by telling her story, a story of a great soul and spirit whose descendants would honor their mixed blood and heritage. It is a vision of beginnings and endings that unites all cultures. It is a new kind of family and home.

Finally, here are two stories by talented Kentucky African Americans that address the past and the future. Gayl Jones's "White Rat" is the powerful story about a black family from the Kentucky hills that is almost white but "claims nigger" and is now living near Lexington. It is related in a colloquial, run-on style by a forty-year-old African American who is blond-haired and light-skinned—like a white rat, he says—and thus is called White Rat. He is a man of mixed blood—too white to pass for African American, which he claims as his racial identity—and so he lives in a no-man's-land between the two races. For him there is no safe place, not even at home in Kentucky. And there is no place for him to go.

Crystal E. Wilkinson's "Humming Back Yesterday" is more optimistic and hopeful. Aberdeen Copeland is a young pregnant black woman with bad memories of an abusive stepfather. Now her loving husband, Clovis, and their newborn baby girl are the future. "The baby's face is that of a moon. Bright. Round. Clovis leans down, kisses Aberdeen's lips. Kisses the baby's head. Aberdeen smiles, says, 'You happy, Clovis?' adds, 'me too' before he has a chance to answer. She tries to look forward to tomorrow. Tries to keep yesterday from humming back." With justice finally on her side, perhaps there will be a bright tomorrow.

These three stories—original in style, structure, and language—are representative of the chorus of African American, Native American, Hispanics, gay, and other minority voices that are adding colors to the national rainbow. They are the leavening in contemporary American and Kentucky writing.

The Kentucky table of short stories is now prepared. Help yourself to some of the finest stories of our time.

1945–1960

There was loneliness in the dark hills when the wind stirred the withered leaves on the trees. It was music to me. It was poetry. It hangs to me better than a piece of clothing for it fits me well and will not wear out.

Jesse Stuart, *Beyond Dark Hills*

It was the fall or winter of 1945–46 just after the war, and even if one had had no hand in the bloodletting, there was the sense that the world, and one's own life, would never be the same again. . . . [W]hat had started out for me as, perhaps, an act of escape, of fleeing back into the simplicities of childhood, had turned, as it always must if we accept the logic of our lives, into an attempt to bring something meaningfully out of that simple past into the complication of the present. And what had started out as a personal indulgence had tried to be, in the end, an impersonal generalization about experience, as a story must always try to be if it accepts the logic of fiction.

Robert Penn Warren, "'Blackberry Winter': A Recollection"

Blackberry Winter

ROBERT PENN WARREN

Before Robert Penn Warren died at age eighty-four in 1989, he was considered by many to be America's greatest living writer. He was born in Guthrie, Kentucky, in 1905. After graduating from Guthrie School and Clarksville High School (in Tennessee), Warren entered Vanderbilt University, where in the early 1920s he was active in the Nashville group "The Fugitives." His first book-length publication, *John Brown: The Making of a Martyr*, appeared in 1929 and heralded a long and prolific career as a literary critic, novelist, poet, and short story writer. As a critic, Warren co-authored with fellow Kentuckian Cleanth Brooks the influential textbooks *Understanding Poetry* (1938) and *Understanding Fiction* (1943). Among his novels are *Night Rider* (1939); *All the King's Men* (1946), which won a Pulitzer Prize; *World Enough and Time* (1949); *Band of Angels* (1955); and *A Place to Come To* (1977). Among his many books of poetry are *Brothers to Dragons* (1953); *Promises* (1957), which won a Pulitzer; and *Now and Then* (1978), which won him a third Pulitzer. As a further testament to his greatness as a writer, Warren in 1986 was appointed America's first Poet Laureate.

Although three of his stories had earlier appeared in *Best American Short Stories* and two more would follow in the 1960s and 1970s, Warren in 1947 published what was to be his single volume of short fiction, *The Circus in the Attic and Other Stories*, containing two novellas and twelve short stories. Among them was "Blackberry Winter." Often regarded as a masterpiece of twentieth-century American short fiction, "Blackberry Winter" is a classic initiation story that has at its core the conflict between the security of a rural homestead and the threatening forces of time and the world.

◆

To Joseph Warren and Dagmar Beach

It was getting into June and past eight o'clock in the morning, but there was a fire—even if it wasn't a big fire, just a fire of chunks—on the hearth of the big stone fireplace in the living room. I was standing on the hearth, almost into the chimney, hunched over the fire, working my bare toes slowly on the warm stone. I relished the heat which made the skin of my bare legs warp and creep and tingle, even as I called to my mother, who was somewhere back in the dining room or kitchen, and said: "But it's June, I don't have to put them on!"

"You put them on if you are going out," she called.

I tried to assess the degree of authority and conviction in the tone, but at that distance it was hard to decide. I tried to analyze the tone, and then I thought what a fool I had been to start out the back door and let her see that I was barefoot. If I had gone out the front door or the side door, she would never have known, not till dinner time anyway, and by then the day would have been half gone and I would have been all over the farm to see what the storm had done and down to the creek to see the flood. But it had never crossed my mind that they would try to stop you from going barefoot in June, no matter if there had been a gully-washer and a cold spell.

Nobody had ever tried to stop me in June as long as I could remember, and when you are nine years old, what you remember seems forever; for you remember everything and everything is important and stands big and full and fills up Time and is so solid that you can walk around and around it like a tree and look at it. You are aware that time passes, that there is a movement in time, but that is not what Time is. Time is not a movement, a flowing, a wind then, but is, rather, a kind of climate in which things are, and when a thing happens it begins to live and keeps on living and stands solid in Time like the tree that you can walk around. And if there is a movement, the movement is not Time itself, any more than a breeze is climate, and all the breeze does is to shake a little the leaves on the tree which is alive and solid. When you are nine, you know that there are things that you don't know, but you know that when you know something you know it. You know how a thing has been and you know that you can go barefoot in June. You do not understand that voice from back in the kitchen which says that you cannot go barefoot outdoors and run to see what has happened and rub your feet over the wet shivery grass and make the perfect mark of your foot in the smooth, creamy, red mud and then muse upon it as though you had suddenly come upon that single mark on the glistening auroral beach of the world. You have never seen a beach, but you have read the book and how the footprint was there.

The voice had said what it had said, and I looked savagely at the black stockings and the strong, scuffed brown shoes which I had brought from my closet as far as the hearth rug. I called once more, "But it's June," and waited.

"It's June," the voice replied from far away, "but it's blackberry winter."

I had lifted my head to reply to that, to make one more test of what was in that tone, when I happened to see the man.

The fireplace in the living room was at the end; for the stone chimney was built, as in so many of the farmhouses in Tennessee, at the end of a gable, and there was a window on each side of the chimney. Out of the window on the north side of the fireplace I could see the man. When I saw the man I did not call out what I had intended, but, engrossed by the strangeness of the sight, watched him, still far off, come along the path by the edge of the woods.

What was strange was that there should be a man there at all. That path went along the yard fence, between the fence and the woods which came right down to the yard, and then on back past the chicken runs and on by the woods until it was lost to sight where the woods bulged out and cut off the back field. There the path disappeared into the woods. It led on back, I knew, through the woods and to the swamp, skirted the swamp where the big trees gave way to sycamores and water oaks and willows and tangled cane, and then led on to the river. Nobody ever went back there except people who wanted to gig frogs in the swamp or to fish in the river or to hunt in the woods, and those people, if they didn't have a standing permission from my father, always stopped to ask permission to cross the farm. But the man whom I now saw wasn't, I could tell even at that distance, a sportsman. And what would a sportsman have been doing down there after a storm? Besides, he was coming from the river, and nobody had gone down there that morning. I knew that for a fact, because if anybody had passed, certainly if a stranger had passed, the dogs would have made a racket and would have been out on him. But this man was coming up from the river and had come up through the woods. I suddenly had a vision of him moving up the grassy path in the woods, in the green twilight under the big trees, not making any sound on the path, while now and then, like drops off the eaves, a big drop of water would fall from a leaf or bough and strike a stiff oak leaf lower down with a small, hollow sound like a drop of water hitting tin. That sound, in the silence of the woods, would be very significant.

When you are a boy and stand in the stillness of woods, which can be so still that your heart almost stops beating and makes you want to stand there in the green twilight until you feel your very feet sinking into and clutching the earth like roots and your body breathing slow through its pores like the leaves—when you stand there and wait for the next drop to drop with its small, flat sound to a lower leaf, that sound seems to measure out something, to put an end to something, to begin something, and you cannot wait for it to happen and are afraid it will not happen, and then when it has happened, you are waiting again, almost afraid.

But the man whom I saw coming through the woods in my mind's eye did not pause and wait, growing into the ground and breathing with the enormous, soundless breathing of the leaves. Instead, I saw him moving in the green twilight inside my head as he was moving at that very moment along the path by the edge of the woods, coming toward the house. He was moving steadily, but not fast, with his shoulders hunched a little and his head thrust forward, like a man who has come a long way and has a long way to go. I shut my eyes for a couple of seconds, thinking that when I opened them he would not be there at all. There was no place for him to have come from, and there was no reason for him to come where he was coming, toward our house. But I opened my eyes, and there he was, and he was coming steadily along the side of the woods. He was not yet even with the back chicken yard.

"Mama," I called.

"You put them on," the voice said.

"There's a man coming," I called, "out back."

She did not reply to that, and I guessed that she had gone to the kitchen window to look. She would be looking at the man and wondering who he was and what he wanted, the way you always do in the country, and if I went back there now, she would not notice right off whether or not I was barefoot. So I went back to the kitchen.

She was standing by the window. "I don't recognize him," she said, not looking around at me.

"Where could he be coming from?" I asked.

"I don't know," she said.

"What would he be doing down at the river? At night? In the storm?"

She studied the figure out the window, then said, "Oh, I reckon maybe he cut across from the Dunbar place."

That was, I realized, a perfectly rational explanation. He had not been down at the river in the storm, at night. He had come over this morning. You could cut across from the Dunbar place if you didn't mind breaking through a lot of elder and sassafras and blackberry bushes which had about taken over the old cross path, which nobody ever used any more. That satisfied me for a moment, but only for a moment. "Mama," I asked, "what would he be doing over at the Dunbar place last night?"

Then she looked at me, and I knew I had made a mistake, for she was looking at my bare feet. "You haven't got your shoes on," she said.

But I was saved by the dogs. That instant there was a bark which I recognized as Sam, the collie, and then a heavier, churning kind of bark which was Bully, and I saw a streak of white as Bully tore round the corner of the back porch and headed out for the man. Bully was a big bone-white bulldog, the kind of dog that they used to call a farm bulldog but that you don't see any more, heavy-chested and heavy-headed, but with pretty long legs. He could take a fence as light as a hound. He had just cleared the white paling fence toward the woods when my mother ran out to the back porch and began calling, "Here you, Bully! Here you!"

Bully stopped in the path, waiting for the man, but he gave a few more of those deep, gargling, savage barks that reminded you of something down a stone-lined well. The red-clay mud, I saw, was splashed up over his white chest and looked exciting, like blood.

The man, however, had not stopped walking even when Bully took the fence and started at him. He had kept right on coming. All he had done was to switch a little paper parcel which he carried from the right hand to the left, and then reach into his pants pocket to get something. Then I saw the glitter and knew that he had a knife in his hand, probably the kind of mean knife just made for devilment and nothing else, with a blade as long as the blade of a frog-sticker, which will snap out ready when you press a button in the handle. That knife must have had a button in the handle, or else how could he have had the blade out glittering so quick and with just one hand?

Pulling his knife against the dogs was a funny thing to do, for Bully was a big, powerful brute and fast, and Sam was all right. If those dogs had meant business, they might have knocked him down and ripped him before he got a stroke in. He ought to have picked up a heavy stick, something to take a swipe at them with and something which they could see and respect when they came at him. But he apparently did not know much about dogs. He just held the knife blade close against the right leg, low down, and kept on moving down the path.

Then my mother had called, and Bully had stopped. So the man let the blade of the knife snap back into the handle, and dropped it into his pocket, and kept on coming. Many women would have been afraid with the strange man who they knew had that knife in his pocket. That is, if they were alone in the house with nobody but a nine-year-old boy. And my mother was alone, for my father had gone off, and Dellie, the cook, was down at her cabin because she wasn't feeling well. But my mother wasn't afraid. She wasn't a big woman, but she was clear and brisk about everything she did and looked everybody and everything right in the eye from her own blue eyes in her tanned face. She had been the first woman in the county to ride a horse astride (that was back when she was a girl and long before I was born), and I have seen her snatch up a pump gun and go out and knock a chicken hawk out of the air like a busted skeet when he came over her chicken yard. She was a steady and self-reliant woman, and when I think of her now after all the years she has been dead, I think of her brown hands, not big, but somewhat square for a woman's hands, with square-cut nails. They looked, as a matter of fact, more like a young boy's hands than a grown woman's. But back then it never crossed my mind that she would ever be dead.

She stood on the back porch and watched the man enter the back gate, where the dogs (Bully had leaped back into the yard) were dancing and muttering and giving sidelong glances back to my mother to see if she meant what she had said. The man walked right by the dogs, almost brushing them, and didn't pay them any attention. I could see now that he wore old khaki pants, and a dark wool coat with stripes in it, and a gray felt hat. He had on a gray shirt with blue stripes in it, and no tie. But I could see a tie, blue and reddish, sticking in his side coat-pocket. Everything was wrong about what he wore. He ought to have been wearing blue jeans or overalls, and a straw hat or an old black felt hat, and the coat, granting that he might have been wearing a wool coat and not a jumper, ought not to have had those stripes. Those clothes, despite the fact that they were old enough and dirty enough for any tramp, didn't belong there in our back yard, coming down the path, in Middle Tennessee, miles away from any big town, and even a mile off the pike.

When he got almost to the steps, without having said anything, my mother, very matter-of-factly, said, "Good morning."

"Good morning," he said, and stopped and looked her over. He did not take off his hat, and under the brim you could see the perfectly unmemorable face, which wasn't old and wasn't young, or thick or thin. It was grayish and covered with about three days of stubble. The eyes were a kind of nondescript, muddy hazel, or something like that, rather bloodshot. His teeth, when he opened his mouth, showed yellow and uneven. A couple of them had been knocked out. You knew that they had been knocked out, because there was a scar, not very old, there on the lower lip just beneath the gap.

"Are you hunting work?" my mother asked him.

"Yes," he said—not "yes, mam"—and still did not take off his hat.

"I don't know about my husband, for he isn't here," she said, and didn't mind a bit telling the tramp, or whoever he was, with the mean knife in his pocket, that no man was around, "but I can give you a few things to do. The storm has drowned a lot of my chicks. Three coops of them. You can gather them up and bury them. Bury them deep so the dogs won't get at them. In the woods. And fix the coops the wind blew over. And down yonder beyond that pen by the edge of the woods are some drowned poults. They got out and I couldn't get them in. Even after it started to rain hard. Poults haven't got any sense."

"What are them things—poults?" he demanded, and spat on the brick walk. He rubbed his foot over the spot, and I saw that he wore a black pointed-toe low shoe, all cracked and broken. It was a crazy kind of shoe to be wearing in the country.

"Oh, they're young turkeys," my mother was saying. "And they haven't got any sense. Oughtn't to try to raise them around here with so many chickens, anyway. They don't thrive near chickens, even in separate pens. And I won't give up my chickens." Then she stopped herself and resumed briskly on the note of business. "When you finish that, you can fix my flower beds. A lot of trash and mud and gravel has washed down. Maybe you can save some of my flowers if you are careful."

"Flowers," the man said, in a low, impersonal voice which seemed to have a wealth of meaning, but a meaning which I could not fathom. As I think back on it, it probably was not pure contempt. Rather, it was a kind of impersonal and distant marveling that he should be on the verge of grubbing in a flower bed. He said the word, and then looked off across the yard.

"Yes, flowers," my mother replied with some asperity, as though she would have nothing said or implied against flowers. "And they were very fine this year." Then she stopped and looked at the man. "Are you hungry?" she demanded.

"Yeah," he said.

"I'll fix you something," she said, "before you get started." She turned to me. "Show him where he can wash up," she commanded, and went into the house.

I took the man to the end of the porch where a pump was and where a couple of wash pans sat on a low shelf for people to use before they went into the house. I stood there while he laid down his little parcel wrapped in newspaper and took off his hat and looked around for a nail to hang it on. He poured the water and plunged his hands into it. They were big hands, and strong-looking, but they did not have the creases and the earth-color of the hands of men who work outdoors. But they were dirty, with black dirt ground into the skin and under the nails. After he had washed his hands, he poured another basin of water and washed his face. He dried his face, and with the towel still dangling in his grasp, stepped over to the mirror on the house wall. He rubbed one hand over the stubble on his face. Then he carefully inspected his face, turning first one side and then the other, and stepped back and settled his striped coat down on his shoulders. He had the movements of a man who has just dressed up to go to church or a party—the way he settled his coat and smoothed it and scanned himself in the mirror.

Then he caught my glance on him. He glared at me for an instant out of the bloodshot eyes, then demanded in a low, harsh voice, "What you looking at?"

"Nothing," I managed to say, and stepped back a step from him.

He flung the towel down, crumpled, on the shelf, and went toward the kitchen door and entered without knocking.

My mother said something to him which I could not catch. I started to go in again, then thought about my bare feet, and decided to go back of the chicken yard, where the man would have to come to pick up the dead chicks. I hung around behind the chicken house until he came out.

He moved across the chicken yard with a fastidious, not quite finicking motion, looking down at the curdled mud flecked with bits of chicken-droppings. The mud curled up over the soles of his black shoes. I stood back from him some six feet and watched him pick up the first of the drowned chicks. He held it up by one foot and inspected it.

There is nothing deader-looking than a drowned chick. The feet curl in that feeble, empty way which back when I was a boy, even if I was a country boy who did not mind hog-killing or frog-gigging, made me feel hollow in the stomach. Instead of looking plump and fluffy, the body is stringy and limp with the fluff plastered to it, and the neck is long and loose like a little string of rag. And the eyes have that bluish membrane over them which makes you think of a very old man who is sick about to die.

The man stood there and inspected the chick. Then he looked all around as though he didn't know what to do with it.

"There's a great big old basket in the shed," I said, and pointed to the shed attached to the chicken house.

He inspected me as though he had just discovered my presence, and moved toward the shed.

"There's a spade there, too," I added.

He got the basket and began to pick up the other chicks, picking each one up slowly by a foot and then flinging it into the basket with a nasty, snapping motion. Now and then he would look at me out of the bloodshot eyes. Every time he seemed on the verge of saying something, but he did not. Perhaps he was building up to say something to me, but I did not wait that long. His way of looking at me made me so uncomfortable that I left the chicken yard.

Besides, I had just remembered that the creek was in flood, over the bridge, and that people were down there watching it. So I cut across the farm toward the creek. When I got to the big tobacco field I saw that it had not suffered much. The land lay right and not many tobacco plants had washed out of the ground. But I knew that a lot of tobacco round the country had been washed right out. My father had said so at breakfast.

My father was down at the bridge. When I came out of the gap in the osage hedge into the road, I saw him sitting on his mare over the heads of the other men who were standing around, admiring the flood. The creek was big here, even in low water; for only a couple of miles away it ran into the river, and when a real flood came, the red water got over the pike where it dipped down to the bridge, which was an iron bridge, and high over the floor and even the side railings of the bridge. Only the upper iron work would show, with the water boiling and frothing red and white around it. That creek rose so fast and so heavy because a few miles back it came down out of the hills, where the gorges filled up with water in no time when a rain came. The creek ran in a deep bed with limestone bluffs along both sides until it got within three quarters of a mile of the bridge, and when it came out from between those bluffs in flood it was boiling and hissing and steaming like water from a fire hose.

Whenever there was a flood, people from half the county would come down to see the sight. After a gully-washer there would not be any work to do anyway. If it didn't ruin your crop, you couldn't plow and you felt like taking a holiday to celebrate. If it did ruin your crop, there wasn't anything to do except to try to take your mind off the mortgage, if you were rich enough to have a mortgage, and if you couldn't afford a mortgage, you needed something to take your mind off how hungry you would be by Christmas. So people would come down to the bridge and look at the flood. It made something different from the run of days.

There would not be much talking after the first few minutes of trying to guess how high the water was this time. The men and kids just stood around, or sat their horses or mules, as the case might be, or stood up in the wagon beds. They looked at the strangeness of the flood for an hour or two, and then somebody would say that he had better be getting on home to dinner and would start walking down the gray, puddled limestone pike, or would touch heel to his mount and start off. Everybody always knew what it would be like when he got down to the bridge, but people always came. It was like church or a funeral. They always came, that is, if it was summer and the flood unexpected. Nobody ever came down in winter to see high water.

When I came out of the gap in the bodock hedge, I saw the crowd, perhaps fifteen or twenty men and a lot of kids, and saw my father sitting his mare, Nellie Gray. He was a tall, limber man and carried himself well. I was always proud to see him sit a horse, he was so quiet and straight, and when I stepped through the gap of the hedge that morning, the first thing that happened was, I remember, the warm feeling I always had when I saw him up on a horse, just sitting. I did not go toward him, but skirted the crowd on the far side, to get a look at the creek. For one thing, I was not sure what he would say about the fact that I was barefoot. But the first thing I knew, I heard his voice calling, "Seth!"

I went toward him, moving apologetically past the men, who bent their large, red or thin, sallow faces above me. I knew some of the men, and knew their names, but because those I knew were there in a crowd, mixed with the strange faces, they seemed foreign to me, and not friendly. I did not look up at my father until I was almost within touching distance of his heel. Then I looked up and tried to read his face, to see if he was angry about my being barefoot. Before I could decide anything from that impassive, high-boned face, he had leaned over and reached a hand to me. "Grab on," he commanded.

I grabbed on and gave a little jump, and he said, "Up-see-daisy!" and whisked me, light as a feather, up to the pommel of his McClellan saddle.

"You can see better up here," he said, slid back on the cantle a little to make me more comfortable, and then, looking over my head at the swollen, tumbling water, seemed to forget all about me. But his right hand was laid on my side, just above my thigh, to steady me.

I was sitting there as quiet as I could, feeling the faint stir of my father's chest against my shoulders as it rose and fell with his breath, when I saw the cow. At first, looking up the creek, I thought it was just another big piece of driftwood steaming down the creek in the ruck of water, but all at once a pretty good-size boy who had climbed part way up a telephone pole by the pike so that he could see better yelled out, "Golly-damn, look at that-air cow!"

Everybody looked. It was a cow all right, but it might just as well have been driftwood; for it was dead as a chunk, rolling and roiling down the creek, appearing and disappearing, feet up or head up, it didn't matter which.

The cow started up the talk again. Somebody wondered whether it would hit one of the clear places under the top girder of the bridge and get through or whether it would get tangled in the drift and trash that had piled against the upright girders and braces. Somebody remembered how about ten years before, so much driftwood had piled up on the bridge that it was knocked off its foundations. Then the cow hit. It hit the edge of the drift against one of the girders, and hung there. For a few seconds it seemed as though it might tear loose, but then we saw that it was really caught. It bobbed and heaved on its side there in a slow, grinding, uneasy fashion. It had a yoke around its neck, the kind made out of a forked limb to keep a jumper behind fence.

"She shore jumped one fence," one of the men said.

And another: "Well, she done jumped her last one, fer a fack."

Then they began to wonder about whose cow it might be. They decided it must belong to Milt Alley. They said that he had a cow that was a jumper, and kept her in a fenced-in piece of ground up the creek. I had never seen Milt Alley, but I knew who he was. He was a squatter and lived up the hills a way, on a shirt-tail patch of set-on-edge land, in a cabin. He was pore white trash. He had lots of children. I had seen the children at school, when they came. They were thin-faced, with straight, sticky-looking, dough-colored hair, and they smelled something like old sour buttermilk, not because they drank so much buttermilk but because that is the sort of smell which children out of those cabins tend to have. The big Alley boy drew dirty pictures and showed them to the little boys at school.

That was Milt Alley's cow. It looked like the kind of cow he would have, a scrawny, old, sway-backed cow, with a yoke around her neck. I wondered if Milt Alley had another cow.

"Poppa," I said, "do you think Milt Alley has got another cow?"

"You say 'Mr. Alley,'" my father said quietly.

"Do you think he has?"

"No telling," my father said.

Then a big gangly boy, about fifteen, who was sitting on a scraggly little old mule with a piece of croker sack thrown across the sawtooth spine, and who had been staring at the cow, suddenly said to nobody in particular, "Reckin anybody ever et drownt cow?"

He was the kind of boy who might just as well as not have been the son of Milt Alley, with his faded and patched overalls ragged at the bottom of the pants and the mud-stiff brogans hanging off his skinny, bare ankles at the level of the mule's belly. He had said what he did, and then looked embarrassed and sullen when all the eyes swung at him. He hadn't meant to say it, I am pretty sure now. He would have been too proud to say it, just as Milt Alley would have been too proud. He had just been thinking out loud, and the words had popped out.

There was an old man standing there on the pike, an old man with a white beard. "Son," he said to the embarrassed and sullen boy on the mule, "you live long enough and you'll find a man will eat anything when the time comes."

"Time gonna come fer some folks this year," another man said.

"Son," the old man said, "in my time I et things a man don't like to think on. I was a sojer and I rode with Gin'l Forrest, and them things we et when the time come. I tell you. I et meat what got up and run when you taken out yore knife to cut a slice to put on the fire. You had to knock it down with a carbeen butt, it was so active. That-air meat would jump like a bullfrog, it was so full of skippers."

But nobody was listening to the old man. The boy on the mule turned his sullen sharp face from him, dug a heel into the side of the mule, and went off up the pike with a motion which made you think that any second you would hear mule bones clashing inside that lank and scrofulous hide.

"Cy Dundee's boy," a man said, and nodded toward the figure going up the pike on the mule.

"Reckin Cy Dundee's young-uns seen times they'd settle fer drownt cow," another man said.

The old man with the beard peered at them both from his weak, slow eyes, first at one and then at the other. "Live long enough," he said, "and a man will settle fer what he kin git."

Then there was silence again, with the people looking at the red, foam-flecked water.

My father lifted the bridle rein in his left hand, and the mare turned and walked around the group and up the pike. We rode on up to our big gate, where my father dismounted to open it and let me myself ride Nellie Gray through. When he got to the lane that led off from the drive about two hundred yards from our house, my father said, "Grab on." I grabbed on, and he let me down to the ground. "I'm going to ride down and look at my corn," he said. "You go on." He took the lane, and I stood there on the drive and watched him ride off. He was wearing cowhide boots and an old hunting coat, and I thought that that made him look very military, like a picture. That and the way he rode.

I did not go to the house. Instead, I went by the vegetable garden and crossed behind the stables, and headed down for Dellie's cabin. I wanted to go down and play with Jebb, who was Dellie's little boy about two years older than I was. Besides, I was cold. I shivered as I walked, and I had gooseflesh. The mud which crawled up between my toes with every step I took was like ice. Dellie would have a fire, but she wouldn't make me put on shoes and stockings.

Dellie's cabin was of logs, with one side, because it was on a slope, set on limestone chunks, with a little porch attached to it, and had a little whitewashed fence around it and a gate with plow-points on a wire to clink when somebody came in, and had two big white oaks in the yard and some flowers and a nice privy in the back with some honeysuckle growing over it. Dellie and Old Jebb, who was Jebb's father and who lived with Dellie and had lived with her for twenty-five years even if they never had got married, were careful to keep everything nice around their cabin. They had the name all over the community for being clean and clever Negroes. Dellie and Jebb were what they used to call "white-folks' niggers." There was a big difference between their cabin and the other two cabins farther down where the other tenants lived. My father kept the other cabins weatherproof, but he couldn't undertake to go down and pick up after the litter they strewed. They didn't take the trouble to have a vegetable patch like Dellie and Jebb or to make preserves from wild plum, and jelly from crab apple the way Dellie did. They were shiftless, and my father was always threatening to get shed of them. But he never did. When they finally left, they just up and left on their own, for no reason, to go and be shiftless somewhere else. Then some more came. But meanwhile they lived down there, Matt Rawson and his family, and Sid Turner and his, and I played with their children all over the farm when they weren't working. But when I wasn't around they were mean sometimes to Little Jebb. That was because the other tenants down there were jealous of Dellie and Jebb.

I was so cold that I ran the last fifty yards to Dellie's gate. As soon as I had entered the yard, I saw that the storm had been hard on Dellie's flowers. The yard was, as I have said, on a slight slope, and the water running across had gutted the flower beds and washed out all the good black woods-earth which Dellie had brought in. What little grass there was in the yard was plastered sparsely down on the ground, the way the drainage water had left it. It reminded me of the way the fluff was plastered down on the skin of the drowned chicks that the strange man had been picking up, up in my mother's chicken yard.

I took a few steps up the path to the cabin, and then I saw that the drainage water had washed a lot of trash and filth out from under Dellie's house. Up toward the porch, the ground was not clean any more. Old pieces of rag, two or three rusted cans, pieces of rotten rope, some hunks of old dog dung, broken glass, old paper, and all sorts of things like that had washed out from under Dellie's house to foul her clean yard. It looked just as bad as the yards of the other cabins, or worse. It was worse, as a matter of fact, because it was a surprise. I had never thought of all that filth being under Dellie's house. It was not anything against Dellie that the stuff had been under the cabin. Trash will get under any house. But I did not think of that when I saw the foulness which had washed out on the ground which Dellie sometimes used to sweep with a twig broom to make nice and clean.

I picked my way past the filth, being careful not to get my bare feet on it, and mounted to Dellie's door. When I knocked, I heard her voice telling me to come in.

It was dark inside the cabin, after the daylight, but I could make out Dellie piled up in bed under a quilt, and Little Jebb crouched by the hearth, where a low fire simmered. "Howdy," I said to Dellie, "how you feeling?"

Her big eyes, the whites surprising and glaring in the black face, fixed on me as I stood there, but she did not reply. It did not look like Dellie, or act like Dellie, who would grumble and bustle around our kitchen, talking to herself, scolding me or Little Jebb, clanking pans, making all sorts of unnecessary noises and mutterings like an old-fashioned black steam thrasher engine when it has got up an extra head of steam and keeps popping the governor and rumbling and shaking on its wheels. But now Dellie just lay up there on the bed, under the patchwork quilt, and turned the black face, which I scarcely recognized, and the glaring white eyes to me.

"How you feeling?" I repeated.

"I'se sick," the voice said croakingly out of the strange black face which was not attached to Dellie's big, squat body, but stuck out from under a pile of tangled bedclothes. Then the voice added: "Mighty sick."

"I'm sorry," I managed to say.

The eyes remained fixed on me for a moment, then they left me and the head rolled back on the pillow. "Sorry," the voice said, in a flat way which wasn't question or statement of anything. It was just the empty word put into the air with no meaning or expression, to float off like a feather or a puff of smoke, while the big eyes, with the whites like the peeled white of hard-boiled eggs, stared at the ceiling.

"Dellie," I said after a minute, "there's a tramp up at the house. He's got a knife."

She was not listening. She closed her eyes.

I tiptoed over to the hearth where Jebb was and crouched beside him. We began to talk in low voices. I was asking him to get out his train and play train. Old Jebb had put spool wheels on three cigar boxes and put wire links between the boxes to make a train for Jebb. The box that was the locomotive had the top closed and a length of broom stick for a smoke stack. Jebb didn't want to get the train out, but I told him I would go home if he didn't. So he got out the train, and the colored rocks, and fossils of crinoid stems, and other junk he used for the load, and we began to push it around, talking the way we thought trainmen talked, making a chuck-chucking sound under the breath for the noise of the locomotive and now and then uttering low, cautious toots for the whistle. We got so interested in playing train that the toots got louder. Then, before he thought, Jebb gave a good, loud *toot-toot*, blowing for a crossing.

"Come here," the voice said from the bed.

Jebb got up slow from his hands and knees, giving me a sudden, naked, inimical look.

"Come here!" the voice said.

Jebb went to the bed. Dellie propped herself weakly up on one arm, muttering, "Come closer."

Jebb stood closer.

"Last thing I do, I'm gonna do it," Dellie said. "Done tole you to be quiet."

Then she slapped him. It was an awful slap, more awful for the kind of weakness which it came from and brought to focus. I had seen her slap Jebb before, but the slapping had always been the kind of easy slap you would expect from a good-natured, grumbling Negro woman like Dellie. But this was different. It was awful. It was so awful that Jebb didn't make a sound. The tears just popped out and ran down his face, and his breath came sharp, like gasps.

Dellie fell back. "Cain't even be sick," she said to the ceiling. "Git sick and they won't even let you lay. They tromp all over you. Cain't even be sick." Then she closed her eyes.

I went out of the room. I almost ran getting to the door, and I did run across the porch and down the steps and across the yard, not caring whether or not I stepped on the filth which had washed out from under the cabin. I ran almost all the way home. Then I thought about my mother catching me with the bare feet. So I went down to the stables.

I heard a noise in the crib, and opened the door. There was Big Jebb, sitting on an old nail keg, shelling corn into a bushel basket. I went in, pulling the door shut behind me, and crouched on the floor near him. I crouched there for a couple of minutes before either of us spoke, and watched him shelling the corn.

He had very big hands, knotted and grayish at the joints, with calloused palms which seemed to be streaked with rust, with the rust coming up between the fingers to show from the back. His hands were so strong and tough that he could take a big ear of corn and rip the grains right off the cob with the palm of his hand, all in one motion like a machine. "Work long as me," he would say, "and the good Lawd'll give you a hand lak cass-ion won't nuthin' hurt." And his hands did look like cast iron, old cast iron streaked with rust.

He was an old man, up in his seventies, thirty years or more older than Dellie, but he was strong as a bull. He was a squat sort of man, heavy in the shoulders, with remarkably long arms, the kind of build they say the river natives have on the Congo from paddling so much in their boats. He had a round bullet-head, set on powerful shoulders. His skin was very black, and the thin hair on his head was now grizzled like tufts of old cotton batting. He had small eyes and a flat nose, not big, and the kindest and wisest old face in the world, the blunt, sad, wise face of an old animal peering tolerantly out on the goings-on of the merely human creatures before him. He was a good man, and I loved him next to my mother and father. I crouched there on the floor of the crib and watched him shell corn with the rusty cast-iron hands, while he looked down at me out of the little eyes set in the blunt face.

"Dellie says she's mighty sick," I said.

"Yeah," he said.

"What's she sick from?"

"Woman-mizry," he said.

"What's woman-mizry?"

"Hit comes on 'em," he said. "Hit jest comes on 'em when the time comes."

"What is it?"

"Hit is the change," he said. "Hit is the change of life and time."

"What changes?"

"You too young to know."

"Tell me."

"Time come and you find out everthing."

I knew that there was no use in asking him any more. When I asked him things and he said that, I always knew that he would not tell me. So I continued to crouch there and watch him. Now that I had sat there a little while, I was cold again.

"What you shiver fer?" he asked me.

"I'm cold. I'm cold because it's blackberry winter," I said.

"Maybe 'tis and maybe 'tain't," he said.

"My mother says it is."

"Ain't sayen Miss Sallie doan know and ain't sayen she do. But folks doan know everthing."

"Why isn't it blackberry winter?"

"Too late fer blackberry winter. Blackberries done bloomed."

"She said it was."

"Blackberry winter jest a leetle cold spell. Hit come and then hit go away, and hit is growed summer of a sudden lak a gunshot. Ain't no tellen hit will go way this time."

"It's June," I said.

"June," he replied with great contempt. "That what folks say. What June mean? Maybe hit is come cold to stay."

"Why?"

"'Cause this-here old yearth is tahrd. Hit is tahrd and ain't gonna perduce. Lawd let hit come rain one time forty days and forty nights, 'cause He was tahrd of sinful folks. Maybe this-here old yearth say to the Lawd, Lawd, I done plum tahrd, Lawd, lemme rest. And Lawd say, Yearth, you done yore best, you give 'em cawn and you give 'em taters, and all they think on is they gut, and, Yearth, you kin take a rest."

"What will happen?"

"Folks will eat up everthing. The yearth won't perduce no more. Folks cut down all the trees and burn 'em 'cause they cold, and the yearth won't grow no more. I been tellen 'em. I been tellen folks. Sayen, maybe this year, hit is the time. But they doan listen to me, how the yearth is tahrd. Maybe this year they find out."

"Will everything die?"

"Everthing and everbody, hit will be so."

"This year?"

"Ain't no tellen. Maybe this year."

"My mother said it is blackberry winter," I said confidently, and got up.

"Ain't sayen nuthin' agin Miss Sallie," he said.

I went to the door of the crib. I was really cold now. Running, I had got up a sweat and now I was worse.

I hung on the door, looking at Jebb, who was shelling corn again.

"There's a tramp came to the house," I said. I had almost forgotten the tramp.

"Yeah."

"He came by the back way. What was he doing down there in the storm?"

"They comes and they goes," he said, "and ain't no tellen."

"He had a mean knife."

"The good ones and the bad ones, they comes and they goes. Storm or sun, light or dark. They is folks and they comes and they goes lak folks."

I hung on the door, shivering.

He studied me a moment, then said, "You git on to the house. You ketch yore death. Then what yore mammy say?"

I hesitated.

"You git," he said.

When I came to the back yard, I saw that my father was standing by the back porch and the tramp was walking toward him. They began talking before I reached them, but I got there just as my father was saying, "I'm sorry, but I haven't got any work. I got all the hands on the place I need now. I won't need any extra until wheat thrashing."

The stranger made no reply, just looked at my father.

My father took out his leather coin purse, and got out a half-dollar. He held it toward the man. "This is for half a day," he said.

The man looked at the coin, and then at my father, making no motion to take the money. But that was the right amount. A dollar a day was what you paid them back in 1910. And the man hadn't even worked half a day.

Then the man reached out and took the coin. He dropped it into the right side pocket of his coat. Then he said, very slowly and without feeling, "I didn't want to work on your ———— farm."

He used the word which they would have frailed me to death for using.

I looked at my father's face and it was streaked white under the sunburn. Then he said, "Get off this place. Get off this place or I won't be responsible."

The man dropped his right hand into his pants pocket. It was the pocket where he kept the knife. I was just about to yell to my father about the knife when the hand came back out with nothing in it. The man gave a kind of twisted grin, showing where the teeth had been knocked out above the new scar. I thought that instant how maybe he had tried before to pull a knife on somebody else and had got his teeth knocked out.

So now he just gave that twisted, sickish grin out of the unmemorable, grayish face, and then spat on the brick path. The glob landed just about six inches from the toe of my father's right boot. My father looked down at it, and so did I. I thought that if the glob had hit my father's boot, something would have happened. I looked down and saw the bright glob, and on one side of it my father's strong cowhide boots, with the brass eyelets and the leather thongs, heavy boots splashed with good red mud and set solid on the bricks, and on the other side the pointed-toe, broken, black shoes, on which the mud looked so sad and out of place. Then I saw one of the black shoes move a little, just a twitch first, then a real step backward.

The man moved in a quarter circle to the end of the porch, with my father's steady gaze upon him all the while. At the end of the porch, the man reached up to the shelf where the wash pans were to get his little newspaper-wrapped parcel. Then he disappeared around the corner of the house and my father mounted the porch and went into the kitchen without a word.

I followed around the house to see what the man would do. I wasn't afraid of him now, no matter if he did have the knife. When I got around in front, I saw him going out the yard gate and starting up the drive toward the pike. So I ran to catch up with him. He was sixty yards or so up the drive before I caught up.

I did not walk right up even with him at first, but trailed him, the way a kid will, about seven or eight feet behind, now and then running two or three steps in order to hold my place against his longer stride. When I first came up behind him, he turned to give me a look, just a meaningless took, and then fixed his eyes up the drive and kept on walking.

When we had got around the bend in the drive which cut the house from sight, and were going along by the edge of the woods, I decided to come up even with him. I ran a few steps, and was by his side, or almost, but some feet off to the right. I walked along in this position for a while, and he never noticed me. I walked along until we got within sight of the big gate that let on the pike.

Then I said, "Where did you come from?"

He looked at me then with a look which seemed almost surprised that I was there. Then he said, "It ain't none of yore business."

We went on another fifty feet.

Then I said, "Where are you going?"

He stopped, studied me dispassionately for a moment, then suddenly took a step toward me and leaned his face down at me. The lips jerked back, but not in any grin, to show where the teeth were knocked out and to make the scar on the lower lip come white with the tension.

He said, "Stop following me. You don't stop following me and I cut yore throat, you little son-of-a-bitch."

Then he went on to the gate, and up the pike.

That was thirty-five years ago. Since that time my father and mother have died. I was still a boy, but a big boy, when my father got cut on the blade of a mowing machine and died of lockjaw. My mother sold the place and went to town to live with her sister. But she never took hold after my father's death, and she died within three years, right in middle life. My aunt always said, "Sallie just died of a broken heart, she was so devoted." Dellie is dead, too, but she died, I heard, quite a long time after we sold the farm.

As for Little Jebb, he grew up to be a mean and ficey Negro. He killed another Negro in a fight and got sent to the penitentiary, where he is yet, the last I heard tell. He probably grew up to be mean and ficey from just being picked on so much by the children of the other tenants, who were jealous of Jebb and Dellie for being thrifty and clever and being white-folks' niggers.

Old Jebb lived forever. I saw him ten years ago and he was about a hundred then, and not looking much different. He was living in town then, on relief—that was back in the Depression—when I went to see him. He said to me: "Too strong to die. When I was a young feller just comen on and seen how things wuz, I prayed the Lawd. I said, Oh, Lawd, gimme strength and meke me strong fer to do and to in-dure. The Lawd hearkened to my prayer. He give me strength. I was in-duren proud fer being strong and me much man. The Lawd give me my prayer and my strength. But now He done gone off and fergot me and left me alone with my strength. A man doan know what to pray fer, and him mortal."

Jebb is probably living yet, as far as I know.

That is what has happened since the morning when the tramp leaned his face down at me and showed his teeth and said: "Stop following me. You don't stop following me and I cut yore throat, you little son-of-a-bitch." That was what he said, for me not to follow him. But I did follow him, all the years.

The Petrified Woman

CAROLINE GORDON

Born in 1895 to a prosperous farm family in Todd County, Kentucky, Caroline Gordon was one of the grand women writers of the Southern Renaissance. Among her nine novels are *Penhally* (1931), *Aleck Maury, Sportsman* (1934), *None Shall Look Back* (1937), and *The Women on the Porch* (1944). She published two collections of short fiction, *The Forest of the South* (1945) and *Old Red and Other Stories* (1963), as well as her *Collected Stories* in 1981, the year of her death. In addition to her wide acclaim as a writer of fiction, Gordon was also well known for her essays and criticism. Her books of nonfiction include *How to Read a Novel* (1957) and *The House of Fiction: An Anthology of the Short Story* (1950), which she co-edited with her husband, fellow Kentuckian and Fugitive poet Allen Tate.

Gordon's stories are known for their controlled style, and several of them appeared in *Best American Short Stories* and *O. Henry Prize Stories*. In his introduction to *The Collected Stories of Caroline Gordon*, which includes "The Petrified Woman," Robert Penn Warren describes Gordon's stories as "dramatic examples of man in contact with man, and man in contact with nature; of living sympathy, of a disciplined style as unpretentious and clear as running water, but shot through with glints of wit, humor, pity, and poetry." "The Petrified Woman," which first appeared in *Mademoiselle* in 1947 and was reprinted the following year in *O. Henry Prize Stories*, shows this rare gift of the consummate story teller. In it Gordon takes us deep into the past to experience a family reunion charged with humor, pathos, and haunting significance.

◆

We were sitting on the porch at the Fork—it is where two creeks meet—after supper, talking about our family reunion. It was to be held at a place called Arthur's Cave that year (it has the largest entrance in the world, though it is not so famous as Mammoth), and there was to be a big picnic dinner, and we expected all our kin and connections to come, some of them from as far off as California.

Hilda and I had been playing in the creek all afternoon and hadn't had time to wash our legs before we came in to supper, so we sat on the bottom step where it was dark. Cousin Eleanor was in the porch swing with Cousin Tom. She had on a long white dress. It brushed the floor a little every time the swing moved. But you had to listen hard to hear it, under the noise the creek made. Wherever you were in that house you could hear the creek running over the rocks. Hilda and I used to play in it all day long. I liked to stay at her house better than at any of my other cousins.' But they never let me stay there long at a time. That was because she didn't have any mother, just her old mammy, Aunt Rachel—till that spring, when her father, Cousin Tom, married a lady from Birmingham named Cousin Eleanor.

A mockingbird started up in the juniper tree. It was the same one sang all night long that summer; we called him Sunny Jim. Cousin Eleanor got up and went to the end of the porch to try to see him.

"Do they always sing when there's a full moon?" she asked. "They're worse in August," Cousin Tom said. "Got their crops laid by and don't give a damn if they do stay up all night."

"And in August the Fayerlees repair to Arthur's Cave," she said. "Five hundred people repairing en masse to the womb—what a sight it must be."

Cousin Tom went over and put his arm about her waist. "Do they look any worse than other folks, taking them by and large?" he asked.

The mockingbird burst out as if he was the one who would answer, and I heard Cousin Eleanor's dress brushing the floor again as she walked back to the swing. She had on tiny diamond earrings that night and a diamond cross that she said her father had given her. My grandmother said that she didn't like her mouth. I thought that she was the prettiest person ever lived.

"I'd rather not take them by and large," she said. "Do we *have* to go, Tom?"

"Hell!" he said. "I'm contributing three carcasses to the dinner. I'm going, to get my money's worth."

"One thing, I'm not going to let Cousin Edward Barker kiss me tomorrow," Hilda said. "He's got tobacco juice on his mustaches."

Cousin Tom hadn't sat down in the swing when Cousin Eleanor did. He came and stood on the step above us. "I'm going to shave off my mustache," he said, "and then the women won't have any excuse."

"Which one will you start with?"

"Marjorie Wrenn. She's the prettiest girl in Gloversville. No, she isn't. I'm going to start with Sally. She's living in town now. . . . Sally, you ever been kissed?"

"She's going to kiss me good night right this minute," Cousin Eleanor said, and got up from the swing and came over and bent down and put her hand on each of our shoulders and kissed us, French fashion, she said, first on one check and then on the other. We said good night and started for the door. Cousin Tom was there. He put his arms about our waists and bumped our heads together and kissed Hilda first, on the mouth, and then he kissed me and he said, "What about Joe Larrabee now?"

After we got in bed Hilda wanted to talk about Joe Larrabee. He was nineteen years old and the best dancer in town. That was the summer we used to take picnic suppers to the cave, and after supper the band would play and the young people would dance. Once, when we were sitting there watching, Joe Larrabee stopped and asked Hilda to dance, and after that she always wanted to sit on that same bench and when he went past, with Marjorie Wrenn or somebody, she would squeeze my hand tight, and I knew that she thought that maybe he would stop and ask her again. But I didn't think he ever would, and anyway I didn't feel like talking about him that night, so I told her I had to go to sleep.

I dreamed a funny dream. I was at the family reunion at the cave. There were a lot of other people there, but when I'd look into their faces it would be somebody I didn't know and I kept thinking that maybe I'd gone to the wrong picnic, when I saw Cousin Tom. He saw me too, and he stood still till I got to where he was and he said, "Sally, this is Tom." He didn't say Cousin Tom, just Tom. I was about to say something but somebody came in between us, and then I was in another place that wasn't like the cave and I was wondering how I'd ever get back when I heard a *knock, knock, knock,* and Hilda said, "Come on, let's get up."

The knocking was still going on. It took me a minute to know what it was: the old biscuit block was on the downstairs back porch right under our room, and Jason, Aunt Rachel's grandson, was pounding the dough for the beaten biscuits that we were going to take on the picnic.

We got to the cave around eleven o'clock. They don't start setting the dinner out till noon, so we went on down into the hollow, where Uncle Jack Dudley and Richard were tending the fires in the barbecue pits. A funny-looking wagon was standing over by the spring, but we didn't know what was in it, then, so we didn't pay any attention, just watched them barbecuing. Thirteen carcasses were roasting over the pits that day. It was the largest family reunion we ever had. There was a cousin named Robert Dale Owen Fayerlee who had gone off to St. Louis and got rich and he hadn't seen any of his kin in a long time and wanted everybody to have a good time, so he had chartered the cave and donated five cases of whiskey. There was plenty of whiskey for the Negroes too. Every now and then Uncle Jack would go off into the bushes and come back with tin cups that he would pass around. I like to be around Negroes, and so does Hilda. We were just sitting there watching them and not doing a thing, when Cousin Tom came up.

There are three or four Cousin Toms. They keep them straight by their middle names, usually, but they call him Wild Tom. He is not awfully old and has curly brown hair. I don't think his eyes would look so light if his face wasn't so red. He is out in the sun a lot.

He didn't see us at first. He went up to Uncle Jack and asked, "Jack, how you fixed?" Uncle Jack said, "Mister Tom, I ain't fooling you. I done already fixed." "I ain't going to fool with you, then," Cousin Tom said, and he was pulling a bottle out of his pocket when he saw us. He is a man that is particular about little girls. He said, "Hilda, what are you doing here?" and when we said we weren't doing a thing he said, "You go right on up the hill."

The first person I saw up there was my father. I hadn't expected to see him because before I left home I heard him say, "All those mediocre people, getting together to congratulate themselves on their mediocrity! I ain't going a step." But I reckon he didn't want to stay home by himself and, besides, he likes to watch them making fools of themselves.

My father is not connected. He is Professor Aleck Maury and he had a boys' school in Gloversville then. There was a girls' school there too, Miss Robinson's, but he said that I wouldn't learn anything if I went there till I was blue in the face, so I had to go to school with the boys. Sometimes I think that that is what makes me so peculiar.

It takes them a long time to set out the dinner. We sat down on a top rail of one of the benches with Susie McIntyre and watched the young people dance. Joe Larrabee was dancing with Marjorie Wrenn. She had on a tan coat-suit, with buttons made out of brown braid. Her hat was brown straw, with a tan ribbon. She held it in her hand, and it flopped up and down when she danced. It wasn't twelve o'clock but Joe Larrabee already had whiskey on his breath. I smelled it when they went past.

Susie said for us to go out there and dance too. She asked me first, and I started to, and then I remembered last year when I got off on the wrong foot and Cousin Edward Barker came along and stepped on me, and I thought it was better not to try than to fail, so I let Hilda go with Susie.

I was still sitting there on top of the bench when Cousin Tom came along. He didn't seem to remember that he was mad at us. He said, "Hello, Bumps." I am not Bumps. Hilda is Bumps, so I said, "I'm just waiting for Hilda . . . want me to get her?"

He waved his hand and I smelled whiskey on his breath. "Well, hello, anyhow," he said, and I thought for a minute that he was going to kiss me. He is a man that you don't so much mind having him kiss you, even when he has whiskey on his breath. But he went on to where Cousin Eleanor was helping Aunt Rachel set out the dinner. On the way he knocked into a lady and when he stepped back he ran into another one, so after he asked them to excuse him he went off on tiptoe. But he lifted his feet too high and put one of them down in a basket of pies. Aunt Rachel hollered out before she thought, "Lord God, he done ruint my pies!"

Cousin Eleanor just stood there and looked at him. When he got almost up to her and she still didn't say anything, he stopped and looked at her a minute and then he said, "All right!" and went off down the hill.

Susie and Hilda came back and they rang a big bell and Cousin Sidney Grassdale (they call them by the names of their places when there are too many of the same name) said a long prayer, and they all went in.

My father got his plate helped first and then he turned around to a man behind him and said, "You stick to me and you can't go wrong. I know the ropes."

The man was short and fat and had on a cream-colored Palm Beach suit and smiled a lot. I knew he was Cousin Robert Dale Owen Fayerlee, the one that gave all the whiskey.

I didn't fool with any of the barbecue, just ate ham and chicken. And then I had some chicken salad, and Susie wanted me to try some potato salad, so I tried that too, and then we had a good many hot rolls and some stuffed eggs and some pickles and some coconut cake and some chocolate cake. I had been saving myself up for Aunt Rachel's chess pies and put three on my plate when I started out, but by the time I got to them I wasn't really hungry and I let Susie eat one of mine.

After we got through, Hilda said she had a pain in her stomach and we sat down on a bench till it went away. My grandmother and Aunt Maria came and sat down too. They had on white shirtwaists and black skirts and they both had their palm-leaf fans.

Cousin Robert D. Owen got up and made a speech. It was mostly about his father. He said that he was one of nature's noblemen. My grandmother and Aunt Maria held their fans up before their faces when he said that, and Aunt Maria said, "Chh! *Jim* Fayerlee!" and my grandmother said that all that branch of the family was boastful.

Cousin Robert D. Owen got through with his father and started on back. He said that the Fayerlees were descended from Edward the Confessor and Philippe le Bel of France and the grandfather of George Washington.

My father was sitting two seats down, with Cousin Edward Barker. "Now ain't that tooting?" he said.

Cousin Edward Barker hit himself on the knee. "I be damn if I don't write to the *Tobacco Leaf* about that," he said. "The Fayerlees have been plain, honest countrymen since 1600. Don't that fool know anything about his own family?"

Susie touched me and Hilda on the shoulder, and we got up and squeezed past my grandmother and Aunt Maria. "Where you going?" my grandmother asked.

"We're just going to take a walk, Cousin Sally," Susie said.

We went out to the gate. The cave is at the foot of a hill. There are some long wooden steps leading up to the top of the hill, and right by the gate that keeps people out if they haven't paid is a refreshment stand. I thought that it would be nice to have some orange pop, but Susie said, "No, let's go to the carnival."

"There isn't any carnival," Hilda said.

"There is, too," Susie said, "but it costs a quarter."

"I haven't got but fifteen cents," Hilda said.

"Here comes Giles Allard," Susie said. "Make out you don't see him."

Cousin Giles Allard is a member of our family connection who is not quite right in the head. He doesn't have any special place to live, just roams around. Sometimes he will come and stay two or three weeks with you and sometimes he will come on the place and not come up to the house, but stay down in the cabin with some darky that he likes. He is a little warped-looking man with pale blue eyes. I reckon that before a family reunion somebody gives him one of their old suits. He had on a nice gray suit that day and looked just about like the rest of them.

He came up to us and said, "You all having a good time?" and we said, "Fine," and thought he would go on, but he stood and looked at us. "My name is Giles Allard," he said.

We couldn't think of anything to say to that. He pointed his finger at me. "You're named for your grandmother," he said, "but your name ain't Fayerlee."

"I'm Sally Maury," I said, "Professor Maury's daughter." My father being no kin to us, they always call me and my brother Sally Maury and Frank Maury, instead of plain Sally and Frank, the way they would if our blood was pure.

"Let's get away from him," Susie whispered, and she said out loud, "We've got to go down to the spring, Cousin Giles," and we hurried on as fast as we could. We didn't realize at first that Cousin Giles was coming with us.

"There comes Papa," Hilda said.

"He looks to me like he's drunk," Susie said.

Cousin Tom stood still till we got up to him, just as he did in my dream. He smiled at us then and put his hand on Hilda's head and said, "How are you, baby?" Hilda said, "I'm all right," and he said, "You are three sweet, pretty little girls. I'm going to give each one of you fifty cents," and he stuck his hand in his pocket and took out two dollar bills, and when Hilda asked how we were going to get the change out, he said, "Keep the change."

"Whoopee!" Susie said. "Now we can go to the carnival. You come, too, Cousin Tom," and we all started out toward the hollow.

The Negroes were gone, but there were still coals in the barbecue pits. That fat man was kneeling over one, cooking something.

"What you cooking for, fellow?" Cousin Tom asked. "Don't you know this is the day everybody eats free?"

The fat man turned around and smiled at us.

"Can we see the carnival?" Susie asked.

The fat man jumped up. "Yes, *ma'am*," he said, "you sure can see the carnival," and he left his cooking and we went over to the wagon.

On the way the fat man kept talking, kind of singsong: "You folks are in luck. . . . Wouldn't be here now but for a broken wheel . . . but one man's loss is another man's gain . . . I've got the greatest attraction in the world . . . yes, sir. Behind them draperies of pure silk lies the world's greatest attraction."

"Well, what is it?" Cousin Tom asked.

The fat man stopped and looked at us and then he began shouting:

"Stell-a, Stell-a, the One and Only Stella!
Not flesh, not bone,
But calkypyrate stone,
Sweet Sixteen a Hundred Years Ago
And Sweet Sixteen Today!"

A woman sitting on a chair in front of the wagon got up and ducked around behind it. When she came out again she had on a red satin dress, with ostrich feathers on the skirt, and a red satin hat. She walked up to us and smiled and said, "Will the ladies be seated?" and the man got some little stools down, quick, from where they were hooked on to the end of the wagon, and we all sat down, except Cousin Giles Allard, and he squatted in the grass.

The wagon had green curtains draped at each end of it. Gold birds were on the sides. The man bent down and pushed a spring or something, and one side of the wagon folded back, and there, lying on a pink satin couch, was a girl.

She had on a white satin dress. It was cut so low that you could see her bosom. Her head was propped on a satin pillow. Her eyes were shut. The lashes were long and black, with a little gold on them. Her face was dark and shone a little. But her hair was gold. It waved down on each side of her face and out over the green pillow. *The pillow had gold fringe on it! . . . lightly prest . . . in palace chambers . . . far apart. . . . The fragrant tresses are not stirred . . . that lie upon her charmed heart. . . .*

The woman went around to the other side of the wagon. The man was still shouting:

"Stell-a, Stell-a,
The One and Only Stell-a!"

Cousin Giles Allard squeaked like a rabbit. The girl's eyes had opened. Her bosom was moving up and down.

Hilda got hold of my hand and held it tight. I could feel myself breathing. . . . But *her* breathing *is not heard . . . in palace chambers, far apart.* Her eyes were no color you could name. There was a veil over them.

The man was still shouting:

"You see her now
As she was then,
Sweet Sixteen a Hundred Years Ago,
And Sweet Sixteen Today!"

"How come her bubbies move if she's been dead so long?" Cousin Giles Allard asked.

Cousin Tom stood up, quick. "She's a pretty woman," he said, "I don't know when I've seen a prettier woman . . . lies quiet, too. . . . Well, thank you, my friend," and he gave the man two or three dollars and started out across the field.

I could tell that Susie wanted to stay and watch the girl some more, and it did look like we could, after he had paid all that money, but he was walking straight off across the field and we had to go after him. Once, before we caught up with him, he put his hand into his pocket, and I saw the bottle flash in the sun as he tilted it, but he had it back in his pocket by the time we caught up with him.

"You reckon she is sort of mummied, Cousin Tom, or is she just turned to pure rock?" Susie asked.

He didn't answer her. He was frowning. All of a sudden he opened his eyes wide, as if he had just seen something he hadn't expected to see. But there wasn't anybody around or anything to look at, except that purple weed that grows all over the field. He turned around. He hollered, the way he hollers at the hands on the place: "You come on here, Giles Allard!" and Cousin Giles came running. Once he tried to turn back, but Cousin Tom wouldn't let him go till we were halfway up to the cave. He let him slip off into the bushes then.

The sun was in all our eyes. Hilda borrowed Susie's handkerchief and wiped her face. "What made you keep Cousin Giles with us, Papa?" she asked. "I'd just as soon not have him along."

Cousin Tom sat down on a rock. The sun's fiery glare was full on his face. You could see the pulse in his temple beat. A little red vein was spreading over one of his eyeballs. He pulled the bottle out of his pocket, "I don't want him snooping around Stella," he said.

"How could he hurt her, Papa, if she's already dead?" Hilda asked.

Cousin Tom held the bottle up and moved it so that it caught the sun. "Maybe she isn't dead," he said.

Susie laughed out.

Cousin Tom winked his red eye at Susie and shook the bottle. "Maybe she isn't dead," he said again. "Maybe she's just resting."

Hilda stamped her foot on the ground. "*Papa! I* believe you've had too much to drink."

He drank all there was in the bottle and let it fall to the ground. He stood up. He put his hand out, as if he could push the sun away. "And what business is that of yours?" he asked.

"I just wondered if you were going back to the cave, where everybody is," Hilda said.

He was faced toward the cave then, but he shook his head. "No," he said, "I'm not going up to the cave," and he turned around and walked off down the hill.

We stood there a minute and watched him. "Well, anyhow, he isn't going up there where everybody is," Susie said.

"Where Mama is," Hilda said. "It just drives her crazy when he drinks."

"She better get used to it," Susie said. "All the Fayerlee men drink."

The reunion was about over when we got up to the cave. I thought I had to go back to my grandmother's—I was spending the summer there—but Hilda came and said I was to spend the night at the Fork.

"But you got to behave yourselves," Aunt Rachel said. "Big doings tonight."

We rode back in the spring wagon with her and Richard and the ice-cream freezers and what was left of the dinner. Cousin Robert D. Owen and his wife, Cousin Marie, were going to spend the night at the Fork too, and they had gone on ahead in the car with the others.

Hilda and I had long-waisted dimity dresses made just alike that summer. I had a pink sash and she had a blue one. We were so excited while we were dressing for supper that night that we couldn't get our sashes tied right. "Let's get Mama to do it," Hilda said, and we went into Cousin Eleanor's room. She was sitting at her dressing table, putting rouge on her lips. Cousin Marie was in there, too, sitting on the edge of the bed. Cousin Eleanor tied our sashes—she had to do mine twice before she got it right—and then gave me a little spank and said, "Now! You'll be the belles of the ball."

They hadn't told us to go out, so we sat down on the edge of the bed too. "Mama, where is Papa?" Hilda asked.

"I have no idea, darling," Cousin Eleanor said. "Tom is a law unto himself." She said that to Cousin Marie. I saw her looking at her in the mirror.

Cousin Marie had bright black eyes. She didn't need to use any rouge, her face was so pink. She had a dimple in one cheek. She said, "It's a *world* unto itself. Bob's been telling me about it ever since we were married, but I didn't believe him, till I came and saw for myself. . . . These little girls, now, how are they related?"

"In about eight different ways," Cousin Eleanor said.

Cousin Marie gave a kind of little yip. "It's just like an English novel," she said.

"They are mostly Scottish people," Cousin Eleanor said, "descended from Edward the Confessor and Philippe le Bel of France . . ."

"And the grandfather of George Washington!" Cousin Marie said, and rolled back on the bed in her good dress and giggled. "Isn't Bob priceless? But it *is* just like a book."

"I never was a great reader," Cousin Eleanor said. "I'm an outdoor girl."

She stood up. I never will forget the dress she had on that night. It was black but thin and it had a rose-colored bow right on the hip. She sort of dusted the bow off, though there wasn't a thing on it, and looked around the room as if she never had been there before. "I was, too," she said. "I was city champion for three years."

"Well, my dear, you could have a golf course here," Cousin Marie said. "Heaven knows there's all the room in creation."

"And draw off to swing, and a mule comes along and eats your golf ball up!" Cousin Eleanor said, "No, thank you, I'm through with all that."

They went down to supper. On the stairs Cousin Marie put her arm around Cousin Eleanor's waist, and I heard her say, "Wine for dinner. We don't need it." But Cousin Eleanor kept her face straight ahead. "There's no use for us to deny ourselves just because Tom can't control himself," she said.

Cousin Tom was already at the table when we got into the dining room. He had on a clean white suit. His eyes were bloodshot, and you could still see that vein beating in his temple. He sat at the head of the table, and Cousin Eleanor and Cousin Marie sat on each side of him. Cousin Sidney Grassdale and his daughter, Molly, were there. Cousin Sidney sat next to Cousin Marie, and Molly sat next to Cousin Eleanor. They had to do it that way on account of the overseer, Mr. Turner. He sat at the foot of the table, and Hilda and I sat on each side of him.

We usually played a game when we were at the table. It was keeping something going through a whole meal, without the grown folks knowing what it was. Nobody knew we did it except Aunt Rachel, and sometimes when she was passing things she would give us a dig in the ribs, to keep us quiet.

That night we were playing Petrified Woman. With everything we said we put in something from the fat man's song; like Hilda would say, "You want some butter?" and I would come back with "No, thank you, calkypyrate bone."

Cousin Marie was asking who the lady with the white hair in the blue flowered dress was.

"That is Cousin Olivia Bradshaw," Cousin Eleanor said.

"She has a pretty daughter," Cousin Robert D. Owen said.

"Mater pulcher, filia pulchrior," Cousin Sidney Grassdale said.

"And they live at Summer Hill?" Cousin Marie asked.

Cousin Tom laid his fork down. "I never could stand those Summer Hill folks," he said. "Pretentious."

"But the daughter has a great deal of charm," Cousin Marie said.

"Sweet Sixteen a Hundred Years Ago," Hilda said. "Give me the salt."

"And Sweet Sixteen Today," I said. "It'll thin your blood."

Cousin Tom must have heard us. He raised his head. His bloodshot eyes stared around the table. He shut his eyes. I knew that he was trying to remember.

"I saw a woman today that had real charm," he said.

Cousin Eleanor heard his voice and turned around. She looked him straight in the face and smiled, slowly. "In what did her charm consist, Tom?"

"She was petrified," Cousin Tom said.

I looked at her and then I wished I hadn't. She had blue eyes. I always thought that they were like violets. She had a way of opening them wide whenever she looked at you.

"Some women are just petrified in spots," Cousin Tom said. "She was petrified all over."

It was like the violets were freezing, there in her eyes. We all saw it. Molly Grassdale said something, and Cousin Eleanor's lips smiled and she half bent toward her and then her head gave a little shake and she straightened up so that she faced him. She was still smiling.

"In that case, how did she exert her charm?"

I thought, "Her eyes, they will freeze him, too." But he seemed to like for her to look at him like that. He was smiling, too.

"She just lay there and looked sweet," he said. "I like a woman to look sweet. . . . Hell, they ain't got anything else to do!"

Cousin Sidney's nose was working up and down, like a squirrel I had once, named Adji-Daumo. He said, "Harry Crenfew seems to be very much in love with Lucy Bradshaw."

"*I'm* in love!" Cousin Tom shouted. "I'm in love with a petrified woman."

She was still looking at him. I never saw anything as cold as her eyes.

"What is her name, Tom?"

"Stell-a!" he shouted. "The One and Only Stell-a!" He pushed his chair back and stood up, still shouting. "I'm going down to Arthur's Cave and take her away from that fellow."

He must have got his foot tangled up in Cousin Marie's dress, for she shrieked and stood up, too, and he went down on the floor, with his wineglass in his hand. Somebody noticed us after a minute and sent us out of the room. He was still lying there when we left, his arms flung out and blood on his forehead from the broken glass. . . . I never did even see him get up off the floor.

We moved away that year and so we never went to another family reunion. And I never went to the Fork again. It burned down that fall. They said that Cousin Tom set it on fire, roaming around at night, with a lighted lamp in his hand. That was after he and Cousin Eleanor got divorced. I heard that they both got married again but I never knew who it was they married. I hardly ever think of them anymore. If I do, they are still there in that house. The mockingbird has just stopped singing. Cousin Eleanor, in her long white dress, is walking over to the window, where, on moonlight nights, we used to sit, to watch the water glint on the rocks . . . But Cousin Tom is still lying there on the floor. . . .

The Nest

JAMES STILL

One of Kentucky's most beloved and enduring writers, James Still was born in 1906 in Lafayette, Alabama. He attended college at Lincoln Memorial University in Tennessee, where he majored in English and history and graduated with Jesse Stuart. He then attended Vanderbilt University for his M.A. in English and the University of Illinois for his B.S. in Library Science. While serving as librarian at the Hindman Settlement School in Eastern Kentucky, he began to write and submit poems and stories to leading publications, especially *The Atlantic Monthly*. In 1935 the *Virginia Quarterly* published "Mountain Dulcimer," generally considered his first mature poem, and in 1936 *Atlantic* published the short story "All Their Ways are Dark." After a three-year stint in the military during WWII, Still returned to live near Hindman at the forks of Troublesome Creek in Knott County.

Still's masterwork is the novel *River of Earth* (1940), whose title, as Jim Wayne Miller once noted, suggests a metaphor for the human condition. Among his volumes of poems are *Hounds on the Mountain* (1937) and *The Wolfpen Poems* (1986). His stories are collected in *On Troublesome Creek* (1941), *Pattern of a Man* (1976), *Sporty Creek* (1977; reissued 1999), and *The Run for the Elbertas* (1980). His work is remarkable for its ability to reflect the universal in the local. He is both a master of local idioms and folkways and a master stylist in the tradition of Chekhov. And his prose is known for its poetic and lyrical quality, similar to that of his friend and fellow short story writer Katherine Ann Porter.

Appearing originally in *Prairie Schooner* in 1948 and included in *The Run for the Elbertas*, "The Nest" is a prime example of his craftsmanship. In it Still takes us on a short but heart-rending journey beyond the safety of home. With his poet's eye, he puts us in direct contact with character and setting as Nezzie, whose mind keeps wondering back home, nestles in a womblike resting place in the natural world.

◆

Nezzie Hargis rested on a clump of broomsage and rubbed her numb hands. Her cheeks smarted and her feet had become a burden. Wind flowed with the sound of water through trees high on the ridge and the sun appeared caught in the leafless branches. Cow paths wound the slope, a puzzle of trails going nowhere. She thought, "If ever I could see a smoke or hear an ax ring, I'd know the way."

Her father had said, "Nezzie, go stay a night with your Aunt Clissa"; and Mam, the woman her father had brought to live with them after her mother went away, explained, "We'd take you along except it's your ailing grandpaw we're to visit. Young'uns get underfoot around the sick." But it had not been the wish to see her grandfather that choked her throat and dampened her eyes—it was leaving the baby. Her father had reminded, "You're over six years old, half past six by the calendar clock. Now, be a little woman." Buttoned into a linsey coat, a bonnet tied on her head, she had looked at the baby wrapped in its cocoon of quilts. She would have touched its foot had they not been lost in the bundle.

Resting on the broomsage she tried to smile, but her cheeks were too tight and her teeth chattered. She recollected once kissing the baby, her lips against its mouth, its bright face pucked. Mam had scolded, "Don't paw the child. It's onhealthy." Her father had said, "Women-folks are always slobbering. Why, smack him on the foot." She had put her chin against the baby's heel and spied between its toes. Mam had cried, "Go tend the chickens." Mam was forever crying, "Go tend the chickens." Nezzie hated grown fowls—pecking hens and flogging roosters, clucking and crowing, dirtying everywhere.

Her father had promised, "If you'll go willingly to your Aunt Clissa's, I'll bring you a pretty. Just name a thing you want, something your heart is set on." Her head had felt empty. She had not been able to think what she wanted most.

She had set off, her father calling after, "Follow the path to the cattle gap, the way we've been going. And when we're home tomorrow, I'll blow the fox horn and come fetch you." But there were many trails upon the slope. The path had divided and split again, and the route had not been found after hours of searching. Beyond the ridge the path would wind to Aunt Clissa's, the chimney rising to view, the hounds barking and hurrying to meet her, and Uncle Barlow shouting, "Hold there, Digger!" and, "Stay, Merry!" and they would not, rushing to lick her hands and face.

She thought to turn back, knowing the hearth would be cold, the doors locked. She thought of the brooder house where diddles were sheltered, and where she might creep. Still across the ridge Uncle Barlow's fireplace would be roaring, a smoke lifting. She would go to the top of the ridge and the smoke would lead her down.

She began to climb and as she mounted her fingers and toes ached the more. Briars picked at the linsey coat and tugged at the bonnet. How near the crest seemed, still ever fleeing farther. No more than half of the distance had been covered when the sun dropped behind the ridge and was gone. The cold quickened, an occasional flake of snow fell. High on the ridge the wind cried, "O-oo-o."

Getting out of breath she had to rest again. Beneath a haw where leaves were drifted she drew her coat tight about her shoulders and closed her eyes. Her father's words rang in her ears:

"Just name a thing you want. . . I'll bring you a pretty."

Her memory spun in a haste like pages off a thumb. She saw herself yesterday hiding in the brooder house to play with newly hatched diddles, the brooder warm and tight, barely fitting her, and the diddles moist from the egg, scrambling to her lap, walking her spread palms, beaks chirping, "Peep, peep." Mam's voice had intruded even there: "Nezzie! Nezzie! Crack up a piece of broken dish for the hens. They need shell makings." She had kept quiet, feeling snug and contented, and almost as happy as before her mother went away.

Nezzie opened her eyes. Down the slope she saw the cow paths fading. Too late to return home, to go meeting the dark. She spoke aloud for comfort, "I ought to be a-hurrying." The words came hoarsely out of her throat. She climbed on, and a shoe became untied. She couldn't lace it anew with fingers turned clumsy and had to let the strings flare.

And she paused, yearning to turn back. She said to herself, "Let me hear a heifer bawl or a cowbell, and I will. I'll go fast." The wind moaned bitterly, drafting from the ridge into the pasture. A spring freezing among the rocks mumbled, "Gutty, gutty, gutty." She was thirsty but couldn't find it. She discovered a rabbit's bed in a tuft of grass, a handful of pills steaming beside it. The iron ground bore no tracks.

Up and up she clambered, hands on knees, now paying the trails no mind. She came to the pasture fence and attempted to mount. Her hands could not grasp, her feet would not obey. She slipped, and where she fell she rested. She drew her skirts over her leaden feet. She shut her eyes and the warmth of the lids burned. She heard the baby say, "Gub."

The baby said, "Gub," and she smiled. She heard her father ask again, "You know what 'gub' means? Means, get a move on, you slowpokes, and feed me."

She must not tarry. Searching along the panels she found a rail out of catch and she squeezed into the hole. Her dress tore, a foot came bare. She recovered the shoe. The string was frozen stiff.

A stretch of sassafras and locust and sumac began the other side of the fence. She shielded her face with her arms and compelled her legs. Sometimes she had to crawl. Bind-vines hindered, sawbriers punished her garments. She dodged and twisted and wriggled a passage. The thicket gave onto a fairly level bench, clean as a barn lot, where the wind blew in fits and rushes. Beyond it the ground ascended steeply to the top.

Dusk lay among the trees when she reached the crest of the ridge. Bending against the wind she ran across the bit of plateau to where the ridge fell away north. No light broke the darkness below, no dog barked. And there was no path going down. She called amid the thresh of boughs:

"Aunt Clissa! Uncle Barlow! It's Nezzie."

Her voice sounded unfamiliar. She cupped her hands about her mouth: "Nezzie a-calling!" Her tongue was dry and she felt a great weariness. Her head dizzied. She leaned against a tree and stamped her icy feet. Tears threatened, but she did not weep. "Be a little woman," her father had said.

A thought stirred in her mind. She must keep moving. She must find the way while there was light enough, and quickly for the wind could not be long endured. As she hurried the narrow flat the cold found the rents in the linsey coat and pierced her bonnet. Her ears twinged, her teeth rattled together. She stopped time and again and called. The wind answered, skittering the fallen leaves and making moan the trees. Dusk thickened. Not a star showed. And presently the flat ended against a wall of rock.

How thirsty she was, how hungry. In her head she saw Aunt Clissa's table—biscuits smoking, ham fussing in grease, apple cake rising. She heard Uncle Barlow's invitation: "Battle out your faces and stick your heels under the table; keep your sleeves out of the gravy and eat till you split." Then she saw the saucer of water she had left the diddles in the brooder. Her thirst was larger than her hunger.

She cowered by the wall of rock and her knees buckled. She sank to the ground and huddled there, working at the bow of her bonnet strings. Loosening the strings she chaffed her ears. And she heard her father say:

"A master boy, this little'un is. Aye, he's going somewhere in the world, I'd bet my thumb."

Mam's sharp voice replied, "Young'uns don't climb much above their raising. He'll follow his pappy in the log woods, my opinion."

"If that be the case, when he comes sixteen I'll say, 'Here,' and reach him the broadax. He'll make chips fly bigger'n bucket lids."

"Nowadays young'uns won't tip hard work. Have to be prized out of bed mornings. He'll not differ."

"I figure he'll do better in life than hoist an ax. A master boy, smart as a wasper. Make his living and not raise a sweat. He'll amount to something, I tell you."

Nezzie glimpsed the baby, its grave eyes staring. They fetched her up. She would go and spend the night in the brooder and be home the moment of its return. And she would drink the water in the diddles' saucer. She retraced her steps, walking stiffly as upon johnny-walkers, holding her hands before her. The ground had vanished, the trees more recollected than seen. Overhead the boughs groaned in windy torment.

Yet she did not start down directly, for the pitch of the slope was too fearful. She tramped the flat, going back the way she had come, and farther still. She went calling and listening. No spark broke the gloom. The dogs were mute. She was chilled to the bone when she squatted at the edge of the flat and ventured to descend. She fell in a moment, fell and rolled as a ball rolls. A clump of bushes checked her.

From there to the bench she progressed backward like a crawdabber, lowering herself by elbows and knees, sparing her hands and feet. She traveled with many a pause to thresh her arms and legs and rub her ears. It seemed forever. When she reached the bench snow was spitting.

She plodded across the bench and it had the width of the world. She walked with eyes tight to shun the sting of snowflakes. She went on, sustained by her father's voice:

"Let this chub grow up and he'll be somebody. Old woman, you can paint yore toenails and hang'em over the banisters, for there'll be hired girls to do the work. Aye, he'll see we're tuck care of."

"He'll grow to manhood, and be gone. That's about the size of it. Nowadays . . ."

Sitting on a tuft she blew her nose upon her dress tail. Then she eased herself upon the ground with her head downhill. She began squirming left and right, gaining a few inches at each effort. She wallowed a way through briery canes, stands of sumac, thorny locusts. She bumped against rocks. Her coat snagged, her breath came in gasps. When snow started falling in earnest she was barely aware of it. And after a long struggle she pressed upon the rail fence. She groped the length of two panels in search of a hole before her strength failed.

Crouched against the fence she drew herself small into her coat. She pulled the ruffle of her bonnet close about her neck and strove against sleep. The night must be waited out. "Tomorrow," she told herself, "Pap will blow the fox horn and come for me. He will ride me on his head as he did upon an occasion." In her mind she saw the horn above the mantelpiece, polished and brass-tipped; she saw herself perched on her father's head like a topknot.

"What, now, is Pap doing?" She fancied him sitting by the hearth in her grandfather's house. "What is Grandpaw up to?" He was stretched gaunt and pale on a feather bed, his eyes keen with tricks. Once he had made a trap of his shaky hands, and had urged, "Nez', stick a finger in and feed the squirrel." In had gone her finger and got pinched. "'T'was the squirrel bit you," he had laughed. And seeing her grandfather she thought of his years, and she thought suddenly of the baby growing old, time perishing its cheeks, hands withering and palsying. The hateful wisdom caught at her heart and choked her throat. She clenched her jaws, trying to forget. She thought of the water in the diddles' saucer. She dozed.

"Nezzie Hargis!"

She started, eyes wide to the dark.

"I'll bring you a pretty. . . . Just name a thing you want."

She trembled and her teeth chattered. She saw herself sitting with the baby on her lap. It lay with its fair head against her breast.

"Name a thing . . . something your heart is set on."

Her memory danced. She heard her father singing to quiet the baby's fret. "Up, little horse, let's hie to mill." She roved in vision, beyond her father, beyond the baby, to one whose countenance was seen as through a mist. It was her mother's face, cherished as a good dream is cherished—she who had held her in the warm, safe nest of her arms. Nezzie slept at last, laboring in sleep toward waking.

She waked to morning and her sight reached dimly across the snow. An ax hewed somewhere, the sound coming to her ears without meaning. She lifted an arm and glimpsed the gray of her hand and the bloodless fingers; she drew herself up by the fence and nodded to free her bonnet of snow. She felt no pain, only languor and thirst. The gap was three panels distant and she hobbled toward it. She fell. Lying on the ground she crammed snow into her mouth. Then she arose and passed under the bars, hardly needing to tilt her head.

Nezzie came down the slope. She lost a shoe and walked hippity-hop, one shoe on, one shoe off. The pasture was as feathery as a pillow. A bush plucked her bonnet, snatching it away; the bush wore the bonnet on a limb. Nezzie laughed. She was laughing when the cows climbed by, heads wreathed in a fog of breath, and when a fox horn blew afar. Her drowsiness increased. It grew until it could no longer be borne. She parted a clump of broomsage and crept inside. She clasped her knees, rounding the grass with her body. It was like a rabbit's bed. It was a nest.

The Men

JANE MAYHALL

Jane Mayhall was born in Louisville in 1921, and following her public education there, she pursued a diverse range of study at colleges in the northeast and on the West Coast. In 1940 she married publisher Leslie George Katz and settled in New York City. She has taught at various universities and has served on the faculty of numerous writing workshops in Kentucky—including ones held at Morehead State University, Alice Lloyd College, and the Hindman Settlement School. Among her published book-length works are a verse play, *Ecologue* (1954); two volumes of poetry, *Cousin to Human* (1960) and *Givers and Takers* (1968); and an eclectic prose/poetry volume, *Ready for the Ha-Ha* (1966). Her short stories and poems have appeared in *Modern Language Quarterly, Paris Review, The Nation, Partisan Review, The New Yorker, The Hudson Review, Harper's Bazaar,* and many other venues.

"The Men" first appeared in *Perspective* in 1948 and was reprinted in *Best American Short Stories* the following year. Simultaneously candid and genteel, the story's tone is reminiscent of that of Eudora Welty. In an interview with *Contemporary Authors,* Mayhall explained her view of life as it is ideally represented through art: "What I look for, in viewing the world, is the uncompromising individuality; everybody has it, though people are always trying to live according to stereotypes . . . . Life is more interesting and complicated and I look for the revelation of that. [This] is never a state of rest, acceptance, adjustment—but is the precious lack of certainty that, as Keats intimated, is the necessity and the ground-soil for the creative act. I try to find this in poems and fiction."

◆

I remember when I was eleven years old and attended a ballet for the first time. It was held at the Memorial Auditorium, a large building in the town where I lived.

During the first group of dances, I sat up very high in the balcony with my family and the stage seemed too far away. It was a pretty show at such a distance, but the dancers with their bright dots of costumes appeared as small and no more alive than marionettes.

When intermission came, some friends of the family suggested that I sit down in the second row orchestra with them. This was probably because they considered me a "nice little girl," a point of view to which I had no objection.

The world of the second row orchestra was an immensely different one. The seats were softer and had slightly reclining backs. Here the members of the audience sat with much dignity, as if each had been appointed to a separate throne, I thought. A sweet flowery scent came from the ladies. As they settled into their places, one heard a faint sound of silk and fur.

Then the music began. Everyone leaned forward. The high arc of the curtain lifted as if moved by a hundred tiny unseen hands. The stage before us was a forest, bathed in willowy green light. The backdrop was splotched with painted leaves and gawk-headed birds whose artificiality seemed, for some reason, particularly exciting.

The dancers stepped forward, the make-up sharp on their faces.

But how near, how human they were! Their eyes moved, their lips smiled. Rising together and beginning to twirl on the tips of their toes, they were much more admirable from here than from afar!

It was a warm spring night. The sky appeared to reflect a pleasant tropical heat. Men wearing sky-blue jackets leapt to girls whose dresses ruffled like swans. Their smiles mingled, their arms embroidered the air with wonderful patterns. Several more dancers came forward, carrying garlands of green and yellow flowers into which they wove themselves. And all with such remarkable enjoyment. Surely something marvelous was going to happen.

And then it did.

Suddenly, the music stopped. The only sound to be heard was a thin, somewhat unsteady tone of a violin. The gaily costumed characters moved back silently and made way for someone.

A little flap in the backdrop pulled open. And a young man stepped forth.

The rest of the dancers departed and left him alone. The lights took on a whiter hue and one saw that the young man was very pale with dark-pencilled eyes. He was dressed in a light blousing shirt and tight breeches of cream-colored satin.

Stepping forward, with casual grace, he lifted his arms. He began to dance.

At first, all I could realize of him was the delicate-footed motion, the coolness and lightness of the figure. He wore soft close-fitting slippers and the insteps of his feet were so beautiful and alive that I fell in love with them at once. This will sound absurd of course, but I am ready to swear that every part, every gesture of that dancer became so immediately precious to me that to think of him even now is like re-counting a treasure one has once possessed. What created this strange effect of beauty, I did not know and certainly never questioned. He was small and perfectly formed, slender-hipped and probably quite typical of the ballet dancer. And perhaps there was something too mannered and too self-conscious in the face. His eyes were drawn to appear elongated, Oriental. The head was finely shaped, dark-haired. But the very self-conscious style of him seemed to add to the charm. What could equal the stance, the quick lightning movements of the body, or the severe control of its quietness?

But none of these features by themselves gave the full effect. The complete harmonious accord of the moment—there was no way to explain it.

When the ballet was over and the dancers were bowing outside the curtain, I felt a terrible childish sadness, the kind that is felt only after the accidental pleasure. It is a puzzling sensation, the regret for the loss of that which one had not—no, never—even hoped for in the first place!

The young man stood a little in front of the others, bowing. I noticed that his ears were beautifully pointed and his hair was sleek.

One by one, the dancers departed. He was the very last to leave the stage. When he had gone, the long velvet curtain rippled slightly, as if a door had been opened somewhere.

The lights in the auditorium went up. The orchestra began to play. The cello made a fat tweedledum and the piano plinked wittily. People put on their wraps and began to talk in matter-of-fact voices. But I was gravely occupied with the memory of the young man. Moving slowly, in the large arena of the Auditorium, I felt that I would never forget him. I listened dreamily to the music and watched the audience make its dignified parade to the rear exit. It seemed, to my impressionable mind, that everything existed only for the contemplation of him.

The crowd was pouring out into the night air. I met my family and, as our house was not very far from the Auditorium, we began to walk home. Around us automobile horns honked furiously and streetcars went by, their little jingling compartments of light swaying from side to side.

Another time, when I had become a high school student, I was studying for my senior examinations in the school library. I had been going to high school for three years but had not made much use of the school library because I preferred the Main Public Branch which had more books. However, during the three years and my few visits to the school bookshelves, I had become aware of the school Librarian who was a young man of about twenty-six years. He was an intelligent fellow and had a somewhat teasing nature. He always flirted with the girl students, patted them on the shoulder or jokingly pulled their hair. The girls appeared to enjoy these attentions. The library became quite a gathering place for young ladies interested in literature.

On this particular afternoon, I was sitting at one of the study tables, leafing through an ancient history book, trying to impress on my mind the names of cities and their conquerors. I remember looking up and noticing the strange light of the three o'clock sun. It came through the library windows at a curious angle, seeming to dissolve the walls and bookshelves into a golden gloom. The straight-backed book covers, lining the shelves, were wonderfully rich and vivid. The dark leaf greens, the library reds, the royal purples and blues, all had a depth of color I had not noticed before.

The soothing warmth of the sun, touching my neck and hair, produced in me a pleasant lethargy, a lazy feeling which was deepened by my reluctance to continue studying.

A sudden cascade of laughter awakened my thoughts.

The young Librarian was standing at his desk with two girl students. He was signing their autograph books. He held the books in the palm of his hand and inscribed them with exaggerated gestures. His expression was one of impertinent humor. The girls were prodding each other and shaking with uncontrollable giggles. Their little pink faces were screwed up in an agony of merriment.

As I looked up, the Librarian noticed my inquisitive glance and smiled at me. And in that flickering acknowledgment, I felt at once there was disclosed some remarkable secret. A quickening of the eyes, a slight movement of the mouth, here was expressed something—a frank sensuality!

And then slowly, as if I were perceiving the whole picture of the young man for the first time, I saw the beautiful contours of his head, the neck, the smooth lines of the neatly buttoned coat, the deft movements of the wrists, the supple fingers. He leaned forward, close to one of the girls. The motion was so earnestly desirous, so marvelously casual, I felt as if I were witnessing something quite as wonderful, as studied and perfected as the motions of the ballet dancer I had seen so long ago.

And—his teasing warmth was contagious! I looked at him with a sense of absorption and delight. And what if he had been different, say a little more vulgar? Or perhaps a little more refined? It would have mattered greatly. It was the full simple effect of him. The sun shone directly on his crisp, sedge-colored hair. I saw him lean more closely, his cheek almost touching the hair of one of the girls. His fingers brushed her bare elbow, seeming to taste all that a clasp or a kiss might.

Perhaps, for the first time, I felt an emotion which was quite natural and undemanding. It was not desire for *him* alone that held me. It was a more general gathering up of all the anonymous needs—which seemed, by his presence, to fly toward a momentary ecstasy. I looked with honest pleasure at the girls themselves. They were about my age. Their lips were soft and their eyes were of that calm brooding expression which children and animals have. They were talking in low voices.

The Librarian sat down at his desk. They bent over him, continuing to talk. Outside the school, a truck rattled by. There was the clear tweeting of a postman's whistle. From the grassy playground came the noise of a lawnmower. Each new item of sound appeared capriciously, then drifted into another. The sunlight was fading and its thin lustre had fallen to the floor.

The girls continued to talk, very softly now. The Librarian leaned back listening, a faint smile on his lips.

Later, I came to New York and worked as a secretary for a Chemical Company. And every Monday night I went, with a friend, to a well known New York university which offered evening courses for adults.

It was winter. There was no winter like the dark, chaotic cold of the city. Our apartments were not warm. Everywhere there was a wet chill which one must avoid.

And the cold streets seemed to be full of nothing but beggars and drunks, people who were trying to find something or people who were trying to escape something.

Sometimes one went to the movies, was conscious of the coughing restless audiences; sometimes one became sentimentally aware of the discrepancy between the midget-faced spectators and the giant silver screen folk. One came home with an uneasy feeling and stood by the window looking out over the ashen glow of the city. . . .

But on Monday nights we went to our class. We walked quickly through the streets, past the crowded apartment buildings, darkened warehouses and neon-lit bars. Then we passed a little scraggly park whose grounds were made up of dirt, gravel, and a few patient-looking trees which, by the light of a street lamp, stood revealed in all their winter's poverty.

A block from the park was the University. It was not a very beautiful building and in the daytime it looked about the same as the warehouses, except that the entrance way was more genteel.

But at night it was quite imposing, standing six stories high, windows twinkling against the bleak sky.

The classroom was warm. We settled down in the chair and leaned comfortably on the desk-shaped arms. Some younger student, about my age, began to talk to me.

Then the Professor came in. He was a gray-haired man of about fifty. His expression was thoughtful and naive; he appeared not to see us at all, but sat down and looked through his notes with great interest, as if he would discover something there he had not known before.

He cleared his throat. We waited.

We were all a trifle drowsy, ready to be bored. From far off we heard the traffic in the street below. A fire engine hooted in the distance.

The Professor was talking. He sat in a leisurely position, giving an occasional glance at his notes. We watched him idly. Having seen him so many times, we felt a certain intimacy with his face—although he had never spoken to any of us personally.

He had two different, but not really opposite, expressions. One was a bland, noncommunicative serenity. The other was a sudden, unforeseen smile which made him look like a big Chinese cat. He was a big man, with a strong width of shoulders and a fine heaviness of jaw. He might have been an athlete. But instead, here he was, wearing a small professorial bow-tie and speaking with a certain elegance.

Without realizing what he was saying, we began to listen. The sound of his voice was quiet, as comforting as rain. Then suddenly it seemed to me—

It seemed to me that something was happening to all of us. My friend, sitting to the left of me, leaned back and crossed his legs, put his thumbs in his buttonholes and exhaled reflectively. I noticed that the other people in the room were showing the same kind of strange unconscious pleasure. All of our clenched, abnormal city feelings were beginning to loosen. The tired certainty of boredom was being replaced with a fresh enlivened atmosphere—like happiness!

The Professor had put aside his notes and was speaking with that peculiar expression of expectancy people have when they are thinking deeply.

And I was overwhelmed by a sensation of memory. I remembered when I was eleven years old and attended a ballet for the first time. I remembered the wonderful young man, the cream-colored costume, the gay precise world of the dancers.

And too, I remembered the high school Librarian. . . .

What was there which gave such a quality of emotion to the scene? Only a bare classroom, the cleanly erased blackboards, the intolerable city darkness outside the windows. And above us, hanging from the ceiling, there was a round electric chandelier. Under that swinging bowl of light, everything appeared all too clearly—harsh and without illusion.

Nevertheless, I was in love with the room, the Professor and the timeless moment of the present. And I was aware that there was something about that gray-haired man in front of us, despite his alien breed of educator, there was something akin to the other two I had loved, so foolishly, momentarily, irrevocably.

And I felt that all other experiences had been fluid, colorless and of that perishable reality which could not even be recalled. But these three, the ballet dancer, the young Librarian and the aging Professor in front of me—they were of some unrelinquished magic, explainable perhaps by the very feelings with which I had come upon them. But the feelings themselves could never diminish. . . .

The Professor paused and let one hand fall palmwise across the wrinkled notepaper. He shrugged his shoulders and appeared to have completed the lecture. The woman in front of me stood up thoughtfully, took a notebook out of her bag and wrote there a sprawling sentence. The other people rose reluctantly.

When we left the building we realized that it had become colder. The cloudy sky reflected the reddish neon shadows from upper Broadway. There was a smell of snow in the air. Shivering, we buttoned up our coats and walked quickly. The professor was just ahead of us, on his way to catch an uptown bus. He walked with head bent, holding on to his hat to keep it from being whisked away by the wind.

Evenings at Home

ELIZABETH HARDWICK

Elizabeth Hardwick was born in Lexington in 1916 and graduated from Henry Clay High School. After earning an A.B. and M.A. in English at the University of Kentucky, Hardwick moved to New York City to pursue postgraduate studies at Columbia University. In New York she committed herself to writing, beginning a remarkable career which has now spanned over half a century. Her first novel, *The Ghostly Lover*, appeared in 1945. In 1949 she married poet Robert Lowell, and for the next ten years she focused primarily on short stories, the high quality of which earned her two inclusions in *O. Henry Prize Stories* and three (of six entries to date) in *Best American Short Stories*. A co-founder of *The New York Review of Books*, Hardwick has published two other novels, *The Simple Truth* (1955) and *Sleepless Nights* (1979); three volumes of criticism and reviews, *Seduction and Betrayal: Women and Literature* (1974), *Bartleby in Manhattan and Other Essays* (1983), and *Sight-Readings: American Fictions* (1998); and a biography, *Herman Melville* (2000).

Like the stories of Caroline Gordon and Jane Mayhall, Hardwick's early work differs in tone from the work of her male counterparts and heralds an emergence of the female voice in America, arising in part from the social restructuring precipitated by World War II. Her stories of the late 1940s and 1950s anticipate the direction the American short story was to take in the subsequent generation, as American men and women faced the need to reinvent themselves in a changing world where longstanding traditions would practically disappear in deference to temporary fashions.

"Evenings at Home," which appeared originally in *Partisan Review* in 1948 and was reprinted in *Best American Short Stories*, is an urbane and complex piece presented as very near stream-of-consciousness. Rather than be homesick, the narrator seems to have made the conscious decision to be sick of home, and internal conflict occurs as she confronts the contradictions of outer and inner realities.

◆

I am here in Kentucky with my family for the first time in a number of years and, naturally, I am quite uncomfortable, but not in the way I had anticipated before leaving New York. The thing that startles me is that I am completely free and can do and say exactly what I wish. This freedom leads me to the bewildering conclusion that the notions I have entertained about my family are fantastic manias, complicated, willful distortions which are so clearly contrary to the facts that I might have taken them from some bloody romance, or, to be more specific, from one of those childhood stories in which the heroine, ragged and castoff, roams the cold streets begging alms which go into the eager hands of a tyrannical stepmother.

I staggered a bit when I actually came face to face with my own mother: she carries no whips, gives no evidence of cannibalism. At night everyone sleeps peacefully. So far as I can judge they accuse me of no crimes, make no demands upon me; they neither praise nor criticize me excessively. My uneasiness and defensiveness are quite beside the point, like those flamboyant but unnecessary gestures of our old elocution teacher. My family situation is distinguished by only one eccentricity—it is entirely healthy and normal. This truth is utterly disarming; nothing I have felt in years has disturbed me so profoundly as this terrible fact. I had grown accustomed to a flat and literal horror, the usual childhood traumas, and having been away from home for a long time I had come to believe these fancies corresponded to life, that one walked in the door, met his parents, his brothers and sisters, and there they were, the family demons, bristling, frowning, and leaping at one's throat. I was well prepared to enjoy the battle and felt a certain superiority because I was the only one among us who had read up on the simplicities and inevitabilities of family life, the cripplings and jealousies, the shock of birth and brutality of parenthood. When I did not find these hostilities it was just as if the laws of the universe had stopped and I became wary and confused. It is awful to be faced each day with love that is neither too great nor too small, generosity that does not demand payment in blood; there are no rules for responding, no schemes that explain what this is about, and so each smile is a challenge, each friendly gesture an intellectual crisis.

I cannot sit down to a meal without staring off in a distraction and when they ask me what I am thinking I am ashamed to say that I am recalling my *analysis* of all of them, pacing again, in some amazement, the ugly, angry, damp alleys I think of as my inheritance. But now that I look around the table and can see these family faces—my father's narrow skull, the sudden valley that runs down my mother's cheeks from the ears to the chin, my sister's smile which uncovers her large, crooked teeth and makes one think for the moment that she is as huge as an old work horse, though she is, except for her great teeth, very frail—everything I see convinces me that I have been living with a thousand delusions. The simple, benign reality is something else. (I have only one just complaint and that is that the radio is never turned off.) But where are the ancient misdeeds and brutish insufficiencies that have haunted me for years?

My nephew, a brown-haired boy of three, disconcerts me as much as anything else. When I take him on my lap I feel he is mocking me for the countless times I have lamented that he should be doomed to grow up *here*. Since the day of his birth I have been shuddering and sighing in his behalf; I have sung many requiems for him and placed sweet wreaths on his grave; but often he looks at me, perhaps noticing the lines on my face and the glaze on my eyes, as if he were returning my solicitude.

At least one thing I anticipated is true and it makes me happy to acknowledge that I am bored. The evenings are just as long as ever, dead, dead, "nothing going on." I take a deep breath and yearn for the morning so that I can go downtown to see how the old place is coming along. And when I get on the streets I see vigorous, cheerful faces which, in spite of the dark corners and violent frustrations in small-town life, beam with self-love and sparkle with pride. These magnificent countenances seem to be announcing: Look! I made it! And the wives—completely stunned by the marvelous possession of these blithe, busy husbands. They sigh tenderly under the delightful burdens of propitious marriages and smile at the less fortunate with queenly compassion. Some wan, sensitive souls carry the dreadful obligations of being "wellborn" and do their noble penance by assuming an expert, affecting dowdiness, like so many rusty, brown, pedigreed dogs who do not dare to bark.

There is something false and perverse in my playing the observer, I who have lived here as long as anyone. Still these bright streets do not belong to me and I feel, not like someone who chose to move away, but as if I had been, as the expression goes, "run out of town." I can remember only one person to whom that disgrace actually happened and he was a dapper, fastidious little man who spoke in what we used to call a "cultured" voice and spent the long, beautiful afternoons in the park beside the wading pond in which the children under five played. No doubt he too went to New York, the exile for those with evil thoughts.

For the first week or so everything went well here and I was, during this sweet coma, under the impression that I might have a fine time. And suddenly a terrible thing happened. Just after dark I walked up to the mailbox, a few blocks away. On the way back home I passed a group of small, identical, red brick houses, four of them, each with a low concrete porch and a triangular peak at the top. In one of these houses I saw him, sitting alone on the porch, with a ray of light from the inside hallway shining behind his head. I stopped involuntarily and gasped because his face seemed with the years to have become much larger. It was incredibly ugly and brutal, a fierce face, rather like a crocodile's with wide, ponderous jaws, sleepy reptilian eyes, heavy, indolent features in horrible incompatibility with his fresh, pinkish skin. I walked on quickly without speaking, but my heart raced painfully, and I prayed I had not been recognized. When I reached my own house I was almost out of breath and rushed into the living room, believing I would ask what he was doing here in our neighborhood, what had happened to him in the last years. But I did none of these things. Instead I looked suspiciously at my mother, trying to decide why she hadn't mentioned him or if she had forgotten that I once knew him.

"You devil, you witch!" I thought, enraged by her bland face and even despising the dark blue dress she wore with a frill of chaste white organdy at the neck.

"What's the matter, sister?" she asked.

"Don't call me *sister*," I said, "it makes me feel like a fool. And if you want to know what's wrong, I don't like that dress you're wearing. It isn't good for you."

"How funny. I'm always getting compliments on it. But, I don't care one way or another."

The face on the porch belonged to a young man I had not seen for years, but whom I had once thought myself in love with. Had he always looked so sinister, so bloated with ignorance and lethargy? I tried to remember a younger, healthier face with some brightness or pathos that had appealed to me, some gaiety and promise; anything except that large, iron, insentient image on the porch. But I remembered nothing comforting, not even one cool, happy afternoon in which he was different from the dark, hateful person living out some kind of life a few steps away from me. It was not love I had felt, not *really* love, I assured myself, but simply one of those incomprehensible youthful errors.

"Mama," I said, "forgive me. The funny thing is that I honestly like that dress *better* than any you have."

"Make up your mind," she said with good humor. I said good night, but on the steps I turned around and saw my father looking at me, his blue eyes dark and strange with an infinite sadness. *He knows, he knows,* I decided. Men can sense these things. Let me die now.

I went to bed and in the darkness and stillness I felt the mere existence of the man I had seen to be sickeningly important to me. I was appalled by the undeniable fact that I had once been his slave, had awakened each morning with no thoughts except how I might please him. As two numb beasts we had found each other and created a romance. It was somehow better to believe that in him I had simply recognized an equal than to answer the shocking question as to why, if I was in any way his superior, I had been so violently attached to him.

It all came back to me: I had not only been in love with him, but he had required courage, daring, and cunning on my part. It had not been easy and I cannot excuse myself by saying we were "thrown together" when the truth is that every effort was made to tear us apart and only my mad-dog determination prevented that. And I began to hate my brother, my own flesh and blood, now dead, poor boy. It was he who started interfering and I can still see him, his face twisted with wonder and fear, saying, "How could you?" My brother's case was weakened, even in his own mind, by his inability to accuse my friend of anything except frightening, depressing stupidity. Oh, is *that* all? I must have thought victoriously, because I continued to make clandestine engagements and took no interest in anyone else.

I heard my parents coming up the steps—thump, thump, closer and closer—and then like the killer in the movies they passed by the one marked for destruction and went to their own rooms. But this is impossible, impossible, I resolved; I must face it. (Self-analysis, bravery, objectivity. Is anything really *bad*?) Yet it was so difficult to recall those old days, almost beyond my powers to see myself again. I couldn't even remember when I had first met that terrible creature. It seemed to have been in high school, some dull, immoral season, a kind of Indian summer romance. On the other hand, I had the weird and disturbing notion that I had known him since infancy, which is quite possible since he has lived off and on in our neighborhood or else we could not have gone to the same schools. In any case I remembered that he was literally not interested in anything, did his lessons with minimum competence and never became involved in anything he learned, never preferred one subject to another, since he was equally mediocre in all of them. He played sports but was not first-rate in any game, even though he was physically powerful.

A few other mortifying things flashed through my mind. His behavior had only two variations: he either went blindly through the days like a stupefied giant or then quite suddenly, as if bored by his own apathy, he would laugh at everything, burst forth in this rocking, strange sound as if some usually sluggish portion of his brain had flared up in a brief, dazzling moment. The laughter must have cost him great effort and he engaged in it only out of a rudimentary social instinct which at times told him that he owed the human race at least that raucous recognition. The other aspect of him I remembered was that, though he initiated nothing, things were always happening to him, one disaster after another. Violence erupted spontaneously in his presence and he was usually the victim. He was always either limping or wearing a bandage; he fell out of trees as a child, got shot in the leg when he was old enough to go hunting, lived through so many narrow escapes and calamities that finally shocks left no mark at all upon him.

But there must have been something else. What happened between us? No, no, merciful stars, not *that*! But yes, and on a gray, November afternoon, mad and dark, and as though I had just come into the world, an orphan, responsible to no one, magnificently free. Embraces and queer devotions, ironically mixed with that fine, beguiling notion of those years in which one thinks himself chosen from all people on earth for happiness. "I'll love you always! Nothing can separate us!" And it was true, for in his anarchic face, in his non-human, reckless force, I saw the shadow of something lost, some wild, torrential passion lived out years and years before in my soul. How shameful! What unutterable, beautiful chaos! Yes, it was he, he, image of all the forgone sin that forever denies innocence. Nothing can ever separate us.

How I regretted that walk to the mailbox to send a letter to New York. If I hadn't done that there is at least a good possibility that I might never have seen him again and might have been spared that long night in which I tried to account for humiliating days and emotions. I couldn't sleep at all and yet I didn't want the night to pass because it seemed to me that once morning came everyone in town would remember what kind of man I first fell in love with.

I looked up the dark street in the direction of his house and thought, suppose, great heavens, that I had married him. This idea completely unnerved me because I had wanted to marry him and would have done so if he had not violated one of those rigid, adolescent, feminine laws. I finally broke with him only because he went away for three days and didn't write to me on each of them. His infidelity crushed me and with real anguish I forced myself to say, "My heart is utterly broken. If you don't care enough for me to keep your promises. . . ." The thought of the risk I had taken chilled me to the bone. I might at this moment have been asleep in his house, my stupid head pressed against his chest, touching the stony curve of his chin.

At last I dozed off and when I awakened late the next morning there was great commotion downstairs. We were going on a picnic. I threw myself into the preparations so gleefully that my mother was taken aback and said, "If you like picnics so much I'm surprised you haven't mentioned them before."

Another week has passed and I have found the temerity to see some of my old friends. They are all somewhat skeptical of me but not for the right reasons. It is a great relief to learn that I am thought of only as "radical" and though I know that is not meant to be a compliment it seems quite the happiest way out and so I try to keep that aspect of my past in the public mind on the theory that nice people demand only one transgression and if they find a suitable sin they won't go snooping around for more. Perhaps I have overplayed it a little, become too dogmatic and angry. (Extremes of any sort embarrass small-town people. They are dead set against overexertion and for that reason even opera singers and violinists make them uncomfortable because it seems a pity the notes won't come forth without all that fuss and foolishness.)

Even I was taken in by my act and it did seem to me that when I lived here I thought only of politics. One afternoon, overwhelmed by nostalgia and yearning for the hopeful, innocent days in which we used to talk about the "vanguard of the future," I went to the old courthouse. Here our radical group, some six or seven snoring people on a good night, used to meet. I found the courthouse unchanged; it is still the same hideous ruin with the familiar dirt and odor of perspiring petitioners and badgered drunks who have filed in and out for a hundred years, the big spittoons, the sagging staircase. When I left I heard the beautiful bells ringing to announce that it was five o'clock and I went home in a lyrical mood, admitting that I had spent many happy, ridiculous days in this town.

For some reason I could not wait to reach the garage next to our house where my father keeps his fishing equipment. I saw there the smooth poles painted in red and green stripes and I intended to rush into the house, throw my arms around my father's neck, and tell him how many times in New York I had thought of him bent over his workbench, and that I despised myself for criticizing him for going fishing instead of trying to make money.

But just as I stepped upon the back porch I stopped and pretended to be admiring an old fat hen which the neighbors had intended to kill long ago but hadn't found the heart to do so because the hen has a human aspect and keeps looking at them gaily and as an equal. I was not thinking about the hen; I was wondering, of course, why my family hadn't mentioned that my friend was living on the street. We had spent many hours talking about new tenants, deaths and births, who had become alcoholic or been sent to the asylum. It wasn't like my mother, a talented gossip, to forget such an arrival, and I concluded sorrowfully that she remembered all my lies and tricks and thought me guilty of the one, unforgivable wrong. Yet when I finally entered the house my family was in such a good mood I hadn't the nerve to mention my suspicions. Perhaps they want to forget me, I thought. Silly, proud people who must see the broad face of the boy on the street and recoil, thinking, "Oh, my sweet daughter! What dreadful horrors she was born with. . . . Some genes from an old Tennessee reprobate who cropped up in the family, passed on, and now wants to live again in her."

I will force nothing, I decided. It will all come out and then I shall leave forever, vanish, change my name, and begin over again in Canada.

Several nights later I went to visit a friend in the neighborhood, a girl who weighs over two hundred pounds and who is so fearful of becoming a heavy, cheerful clown that she is, instead, a mean-spirited monster. And yet her malice, which is of a metropolitan order, is often quite entertaining, and I might have stayed longer if I had not begun to imagine the inspired tales she could tell on me. Her small eyes seemed to contain all my secrets and I could see her plump, luxurious mouth forming the syllables of misdeeds even I could not name. At nine o'clock I went home where I found the house dark and supposed my family had gone out for a few minutes, perhaps to the drugstore or across town to the ice-cream factory. This was the moment at last. I felt it acutely.

There he was, sitting on the steps, smoking a cigarette. I realized it was he the moment I saw the figure, the wide, slumping shoulders, the head turned somewhat to the side. Even in the dark I felt his slow, calm, somnolent gaze on me.

"Is that you?" he asked in a low, untroubled voice that is unlike any I have ever heard before. It seems to come at you from a great distance, rolling like a wave.

"Yes, it is," I answered lightly and in exactly the opposite way I had planned. But after I had spoken so hospitably I began to worry about my family. They might return at any moment, and I couldn't bear them to find him here, couldn't endure their curious glances, questions, and recollections of the past.

"Don't bother me!" I said rapidly. "I don't want to see you. What are you doing living around here anyway? It isn't fair for me to come home to this. . . . I'm different now."

I could see his face quite well now and apparently he too had changed because he actually registered an emotion. He looked at me with disgust, his mouth opening slowly and curiously, his lazy eyes blinking at me reproachfully.

"Bother you?" he said. "What do you mean? Come back to what?"

I began to tremble with impatience. "Don't you see?" I whispered desperately. "I don't want them to know I've seen you again. It would just start up the old argument."

He put his hand on my arm to steady me and I looked angrily into his wide, immobile face. It was not frightening, but simply infuriating for it had a kind of prehistoric, dumb strength, so that he looked like some Neanderthal ruler, superb and forceful in a savage way, and quite eternal. My ghastly darling.

"Never mind. Dear God, it's too late now," I said, because I saw the car driving up in front of the house and in a fit of weakness I sat down beside him on the steps and buried my face in my hands.

I did not look up when I heard my parents saying something dryly and politely, saying nothing much because they sounded tired and sleepy. The perspiration on my forehead dampened my hands, but somehow I was able to stand up and bid my old friend good night. I smiled at him and he returned this last gesture shyly, and turning away his eyes seemed in the evening light a soft, violet color.

As I went into the hall I stopped before the mirror and saw that my cheeks were burning and that there was something shady and subtly disreputable in my face. My mother was taking the hairpins out of her hair. The great mysterious drama had passed, but I knew that I could not stay at home any longer.

The next day I prepared to leave and I noted with astonishment that I had been at home nineteen days. We packed my bags, and my mother said she thought the trip had done me good.

"You're not quite as nervous as when you arrived," she observed.

"Not as nervous!" I said. "I'm a wreck!"

"Well, go on back to New York if it makes you feel better," she said wearily.

"I don't feel exactly wonderful there—"

"There's only one answer to that," my mother said, slamming the door as she walked out of the room. "There must be something wrong with *you!*"

I ran to the door and opened it so that she would be certain to hear me. "If there is something wrong with me it's your fault," I said triumphantly.

"Mine!" she called back. "What madness!"

For some reason this altercation put me in a good humor. Now that I was leaving my feelings shifted every five seconds from self-pity to the gushiest love and affection. I even began to think how nice it was at home, how placid. My father came in and I could tell from the serious expression on his face that he was thinking of important matters. I'm sure he meant to make me very happy but he had a way of expressing himself that was often misleading and so, with the most tender look in his eyes, he informed me that *in spite of everything* they all liked me very much. I graciously let that pass because I was, in my thoughts, already wondering whether once I was away, home would again assume its convenient sinister shape.

There was only one thing left to do in Kentucky, a little ritual which I always liked to put off until the end. My mother mistakenly believes that I mourn my dead brother and tomorrow morning there will still be time before the train leaves to drive out to the cemetery where he lies. The pink and white dogwood will be flowering and the graves will be surrounded by tulips and lilacs. At this time of the year the cemetery is magnificent, and my mother will not let me miss the beauty. When we get there she will point to the family lot and say, "Sister, I hate to think of you alone in New York, away from your family. But you'll come back to us. There's a space for you next to Brother. . . . In the nicest part. . . . So shady and cool."

And so it is, as they say, comforting to have these roots.

Anthem of the Locusts

DEAN CADLE

Dean Cadle was born in 1920 in a coal mining camp near Middlesboro, Kentucky. After serving in the U.S. Air Force in World War II, including a stint as a military photographer, he studied at Berea College, Stanford University, Columbia University, and the University of Iowa. Early in his career he taught English at Union College, the University of Kentucky, and the Detroit Institute of Technology. In 1959, after completing a master's in library science at the University of Kentucky, he began a distinguished career as a librarian, serving at UK, Southeast Community College, and the University of North Carolina at Asheville. After his retirement in 1983, he worked in the Mars Hill College Library. He died in 1998.

Cadle is known especially for his photographs of Kentucky writers and his critical work on James Still. His 1968 article "Man on Troublesome," which appeared in the *Yale Review*, is one of the touchstone studies of Still. Although Cadle's work has not been collected into book form, he was a prolific writer of essays, poems, reviews, and short stories. One of his early stories, "We Have Returned," won *Tomorrow* magazine's national award for best story in 1947. While at Stanford, Cadle studied under Wallace Stegner and in 1949 published "Anthem of the Locusts" and another story in the prestigious *Stanford Short Stories*. Numerous subsequent stories appeared in *The Carolina Quarterly*, *Southwest Review*, *Appalachian Heritage*, *Deep Summer*, and *Short Fiction International*. William S. Ward in *A Literary History of Kentucky* notes that Cadle's work often focuses on "people who must struggle against forces that would hold them down as they seek security and a mastery of their lives in an atmosphere that is hostile toward such strivings." Centering on a struggle whose source seems ancient and shrouded, "Anthem of the Locusts" gains its power from poetic imagery and the dark atmosphere of mystery and ambiguity.

◆

Logan Roberts laid his .22 rifle beside him on top of the flat sandstone rock and lit a cigarette, wondering why people in the camp disliked the sound of the locusts so much. Some of the people said their whirring was like a million rattlesnakes going at once, while others complained that they drowned the singing of the birds and that you couldn't hear your own voice.

It was true they did make a lot of noise, but their being there had not bothered Logan, and he supposed that was because they were something different. As he sat listening to their shrilling, unvaried rhythm swelling round him like some dizzying new music come to the mountains, he wondered if they did anything besides sing. He had not thought about that before. He knew little about them except that they were there, somehow coming quite magically, that they lived for a while and sang and then died, and that in a few days, after they had sung themselves to death, the rocks on the hillsides and the mountain paths would be strewn with their bodies lying by the thousands in the hot sun like strange seed blown from the trees.

"Hello, Logan."

He turned. Emily Fletcher was standing a few yards from him, beside a patch of stickweeds.

"Hello, Emily. What are you doing up here?"

"To hear the locusts."

"You can hear them in the camp."

"Better up here. I like to hear them."

She came over and leaned against the other side of the rock and, with her head lowered, looked up at him. She looked at everybody that way.

"Sounds like singing in the trees up here."

Logan guessed that the way she looked at people meant little to another woman. She always held her head bent slightly forward, even while walking, and when she looked at a person she did not raise her head but rolled her dark eyes up.

A few times he had felt like going up to her and placing an arm around her shoulders and with his other hand brushing the tangled mass of bangs off her forehead and looking into her disturbed eyes and saying, "Emily, honey, never, never look at a man that way unless you are ready to go through with everything." But most of the time he hurt from wanting to go through with everything.

"Are you resting?" she asked.

"For a few minutes."

"Can I rest with you?"

"If you'll be very good."

After a moment she giggled. Logan turned and looked at her. She had her back to him and was looking down the mountainside.

"What have you been doing, Emily?"

"Having fun."

"Doing what?"

"Oh—just having fun."

She was barefooted and wore a faded black dress that was too tight. Logan had never seen her wear a new dress, and the fullness that two years in the camp had given her body made all the dresses she wore too tight above the waist.

Logan moved over beside her on the rock, and raising his hand almost placed it on her shoulder to pull her toward him. Then he checked the impulse and dropped his hand back to the rock. With her back to him, she was still gazing down the hillside that fell away from them in the afternoon shade of the trees. Then she stood up and walked over to the path of stickweeds, and pulling off several of the leaves dropped them and watched them flutter to the ground

"Would you like to go walking with me sometime, Emily?"

"Oh yes, Logan. I would like to go walking with you. We could pick flowers and watch the birds. And now we could hear the locusts. I pray that I can, Logan. Can I?"

"If you won't tell anybody about it."

She had stopped dropping the leaves and stood looking at the ground, and Logan saw that a piece of a smile was playing on her mouth.

"You never ask me to go walking with you," she said. "Lots of men in the camp ask me to go walking, and some of them are married. Ma has to run them off from the house at night. But I don't go, Logan. They want me to be bad, and I don't want to be bad. But I would like to go with you. Only you never ask me."

"Well, let's go now, Emily. We can go back up the mountain."

"Got to wash my feet and get ready for church now. Will we go while the locusts are singing?"

"As soon as you want to go."

"Like singing in the trees. Will you come to church tonight, Logan?"

"I guess so. There's nothing else to do."

"I'm going to pray for you at the revival, Logan."

"Now don't start that, Emily."

"Everybody needs somebody to pray for them, Logan, and I'm going to pray for you."

"No, Emily, don't. I won't be your friend if you do."

"I'm your friend. And I'm a Christian, Logan, and a Christian has to do what the Lord tells him to do. Slate might fall on you some day and you would go to hell. I would pray for you then, but the Lord would say, 'You've waited too long, Emily. It's too late now. You oughta been praying for Logan while he was alive.' That's why I have to pray for you, Logan."

"But I don't want you to. Besides, if the people hear you praying for me in church and then see you taking a walk with me, they'll begin saying things about us. We don't want them talking about us."

"Oh, I would like for them to talk about me and you. People always talk about me. I know they do. But I don't give it any mind. I just pray for them. That's the only right thing to do. And it'd be wrong for me if I didn't pray for you, Logan."

"I said no, Emily. Don't do it." Then he added: "If you do, I won't go walking with you."

She stood gazing down the mountain and was silent. Then she said, "All right, Logan. It's a sin for you to be that way. But I got to pray for you. I'll pray for you to myself so nobody'll hear me. Then will you let me go walking with you?"

"Yes. But be sure you don't mention my name when you're praying."

"All right, Logan. Will we listen to the locusts?"

"If you want to."

"Good-bye, Logan. I'm going to wash my feet for church. I won't say your name."

He sat on the rock until she had had time to reach the camp; then he took up his rifle and went off the mountain.

While his mother was washing the supper dishes Logan sat on the porch and watched the people come down the alley and cross the footbridge on their way to the white weatherboard church on the hillside under the beech trees. There was a steady flow of people down the alley and across the bridge; they climbed the hill path under the interlaced branches that formed a green archway in the purple twilight.

A group of women and young girls in starched print dresses went across. Blue Jim Thomas, carrying his fiddle in a flour sack under his arm, crossed over; two men in overalls followed; then came Glen Herren with his guitar and his wife, Nell. Logan saw Emily leave the cabin on the other side of the pasture; hurrying along, she skirted the camp and came down the creek path to the bridge. Then Brother Miller, carrying his Bible clasped in his hand and with the prayer bags in the knees of his blue serge pants giving him a bowlegged walk, came down the alley to the bridge.

Logan sat on the porch listening to the singing long after the service had begun. The singing always sounded better in the camp than it did inside the church. The voices rose clear and musical, with the rising and falling rhythm of a stream tumbling over sandstone boulders in its swift descent down a mountain hollow, and flooded out over the camp like the golden voices of angels drifting through the nighttime; with the voices came the crying of the fiddle, and far down underneath, as though rising out of the dark earth of the camp, strode the unrelenting beat of a tambourine, not in time, not out of time, but setting a pace of its own that was a music to keep beat with the summertime pulse of one's blood.

After the singing had stopped Logan crossed the bridge and went up the dark hill to the church. There were no empty seats and the aisle was filled. He went in and stood behind Curt Simmons and his brother Roy.

Brother Miller was standing beside the mourners' bench and his voice was like thunder in the crowded room.

"Children, how can you be deaf to the plea of the Lord? How can you ignore the promise of glory that's been given you? At an unnamed speed you're bound for the bottomless pits of fire prepared for the unbelievers and the ungodly. You're headed for the land called hell, my friends, and darkness'll be your home. There'll be weepin' and wailin' and a gnashin' of teeth down there and your cries of pain'll be heard from border to border of the flamin' pit of destruction. You'll no longer know the voices of your friends, for they'll be turned to shrieks of pain. Your eyes'll no longer know the beauty of these here hillsides and the coolness of their clear streams, for you'll be wrapped in the flames of the lake of fire and brimstone that's hell. There'll be no comfort, there'll be no end to this damnation, for you're in hell, my friends, and hell is eternal."

Brother Miller beat the air with his unfurled hands and pounded his palms with his fists. His face was flushed and his breath came fast. He cupped his palm over his right jaw and preached on.

Moths, green and yellow and fuzzy-winged, and bugs with black armored backs, flew in and out the raised windows and buzzed around in the glow of the light bulbs. Lightning bugs spotted the shadowy rhythm of the darker recesses of the room with their golden flashes.

Brother Miller joined the Christians who were on their knees around the mourners' bench. The heads of the Christians were turned upward and their eyes were closed. Their prayerful cries and exclamations rose loud and plaintive on the warm air of the summer evening.

Emily knelt at one end of the bench. Martha Courtney was on her knees in the center of the floor and rocked back and forth. Wisps of dark hair had slipped from the knot low on her neck and waved like sunburned corn tassels in a summer breeze. Her arms were in the air above her head and her worn fingers flexed nervously. She screamed her prayers, her voice falling then rising unintelligibly above all the others.

". . . . skimo, my God! Sweet Jesus! Oshmo umli . . . ."

Brother Miller stood up and began preaching above the prayers of the Christians and the sinners.

"It's time, my children, you're kneelin' in the dust of the alleyways and under the trees of the mountainsides. Come pray for your salvation, my children, for the Lord has said, 'Believe in Me and you'll have everlastin' life.' Talk of your rich men in the streets of the big cities; talk of your palaces 'cross the sea, but give me Christ and everlastin' life, give me Christ of Calvary, the man with the scarred hands, give me Christ and glory. Amen, children! Amen!"

"Amen!" Deacon Abe Turner said.

"Amen!" Curt Simmons said at Logan's shoulder.

"Quiet, d-damn it," his brother Roy told him. "They'll run you out."

The Christians were still on their knees around the mourners' bench. The rest of the people were standing. They stood close against each other, their bodies touching and their breath warm on each other's neck. They stood and sang loudly and in time to the strumming of the guitar and to the throbbing beat of the tambourine that pulsed through the hot air and beat on and on down under the voices and the flow of song-words like the pumping of a giant heart.

All eyes were focused on the small arena where the sinners and Christians were kneeling. Brother Miller stood to one side of the group with one hand clasped about his jaw and with the other hand pointing upward; his mouth was open in talk but the words were lost. The Christians and sinners prayed on, and the minutes of the evening swept by in cadence to the insistent, undertone palm-beat of the tambourine.

A thin, immature scream split through the tumult as a young girl leaped to her feet from the mourners' bench. She flung her skinny arms into the air, and her mouth, strained wide in her small red face shouting the praises of God, was like the mouth of a new-hatched bird.

"The power of God's amongst us!" Brother Miller yelled. "Sinners, come before it's too late. Come taste the sweet power of Jesus."

There was another scream, piercing and joyful in its spontaneity, and all eyes turned on Emily, who was leaping up and down at the end of the mourners' bench.

"Look at that!" Curt Simmons said, nudging his brother.

"She's sh-sh-shimmying right, ain't she?"

"Up and down, up and down."

"Ba-ba-balling the jack, ain't she?"

Emily shouted in the same spot, flinging her arms wildly and disjointedly about her. Then gradually her leaping decreased, and finally she stood flat on the floor, her body shaking all over. Her dark head was thrown back and her eyes were closed in her white face, spotlighted in all its twisted, ecstatic emotion. Her lips trembled, forming words that fell unheard on waves of noise.

Her entire body was now seized by movements of frenzied agitation. She stood with her feet spread and her knees slightly bent. There were spasmodic jerks in her shoulders, straining them far back and stretching tighter the front of her black dress. She rolled on the balls of her feet, giving a swaying motion to her entire body; her hips moved in a circular pattern, back and forth and from side to side. And the repeated jerkings of her shoulders gave a rigidity to her arms, forcing them to bend at the elbows, and created tremors that seemed to flow downward through all the muscles of her body, quivering through her hips under the black cotton.

"Ch-Ch-rist!" Roy Simmons said.

"Don't call on Him," Curt said. "He can't help you."

"Amen!" Brother Miller screamed.

He had preached through all the shouting. He was perspiring and his shirt stuck to his body. He had rolled the sleeves above his elbows and put his tie in his pocket. He wiped his face with his handkerchief and wrung out the water on the floor. He clutched the wet cloth in his hand and preached on.

"My Christ is comin' to earth again, my friends. Comin' on a cloud of glory. Uh, ah yes! Comin' with a host of the holy angels, and I'm goin' home. There'll be weepin' on that mornin.' There'll be prayin,' friends, and there'll be wailin' 'cross the face of this old earth. And on that mornin,' my sinner friends, there'll be glory never known to man. Uh, ah yes! There'll be singin' in the elements and this old earth is a-goinna open up, this old dirt is a-goinna fold back and the saved in Christ are a-goinna rise up and join the heavenly host."

A song was begun and several Christians began pushing their way through the crowd to talk with sinners they would like to lead to the mourners' bench. Logan saw Emily's white face coming boldly between the shoulders of the men in the aisle. She came up to him and locked her hands around his arm above the elbow and pressed his arm against her breasts; with her head lying on his shoulder she began crying and talking. The music and the tambourine and the song-words were going again and there was so much noise Logan could barely hear her words.

". . . . I would die for you, Logan. God loves you too, Logan . . . . Oh, I feel so good tonight. If you was saved I'd never stop shouting . . . ."

Logan kept shaking his head, but Emily had her eyes closed. With his arm against her he could feel the tremors that continued to sweep through her flesh, and he could feel the heat and the perspiration on his bare skin below the roll of his sleeve.

When she kept on talking he raised his head and looked at her. In one corner of her mouth there was blood, and it had run in a thin line across her chin. Logan took out his handkerchief and wiped the blood from her chin and touched the cloth to the corner of her mouth. Emily opened her eyes and moved them over his face the way hands may be moved caressingly over the face of another. Liveliness shone through the tears that filled her dark eyes and she looked at him calmly and unwaveringly. She smiled at him then, and her lips with the smile on them were no longer the weak lips that had always said so many little things and always smiled late.

"I'm not going, Emily. Go on back."

When she released his arm he went outside and leaned against a beech tree in the dark and smoked. He could still hear the voice of Brother Miller.

"I'm a-goinna be among that heavenly number, friends. I'm a-goinna sing at God's right hand and I'm a-goinna walk them streets of gold. I'm a-goinna say, Good-bye, old earth, good-bye, I'm goin' home. Uh, ah yes! Up there I'll know my friends, and I'm a-goinna shake the hand of Paul. I'm a-goinna shout by the river of God and I'm a-goinna say, Amen, I'm home, I'm home. Uh, ah yes!"

Logan lit another cigarette and went off the hill and walked through the alley to the edge of the pasture. The night was dark and quiet; even the frogs were not croaking and there was not one cricket zizz. He sat down on the warm grass and waited until he heard footsteps in the path.

"Emily?"

There was no answer. He got up and walked to the path and put his arm around her. She did not speak, and so he began walking with her toward the dark line of trees where the pasture began a gradual climb into the black wall of the entangled mountain.

He paused under the elm tree near the cabin and placed his other arm around her. The moist dress was now cool to the touch of his arms and the strong perspiration smell of her body filled his nostrils. Emily leaned heavily against him and her head lay on his chest. He whispered her name but she did not speak. He raised her head and kissed her but she did not kiss him. Her lips were dry and firm. She dropped her head back to his chest.

"It's quiet, Logan."

Holding her more closely, he raised her head and kissed her again.

"I wish they'd sing at night."

Again he searched for her lips, but she was moving in his arms, straining his embrace, and then she slipped loose. He reached out his hands for her, but she turned and moved toward the cabin, leaving him standing under the elm in the silence of the dark pasture.

Lost Land of Youth

JESSE STUART

One of Kentucky's most prolific and cherished writers, Jesse Stuart was born in 1906 in Greenup County. He was educated at Greenup County High School and taught there after earning a college degree at Lincoln Memorial University in Tennessee. In the following years Stuart also served as high school principal and county school superintendent, experiences that formed the basis of one of his most well-known books, *The Thread that Runs So True* (1949). Stuart's first book, a collection of poems titled *Man With a Bull Tongue Plow,* was published in 1934 and was followed two years later by his first collection of short stories, *Head o' W-Hollow.* His early autobiography, *Beyond Dark Hills,* appeared in 1938, and his first novel, *Trees of Heaven,* in 1940. Once Stuart began to succeed financially as a writer, he devoted himself full time to writing, though he intermittently returned to teaching in the following two decades and served as a guest lecturer at various colleges and universities. He completed his final book, *The Kingdom Within: A Spiritual Autobiography,* in 1979 following a stroke that left him virtually bedridden. He died in 1984.

A natural storyteller, Stuart published more than four hundred stories and nearly sixty books of poetry, fiction, and nonfiction, many of which are kept in print by the Jesse Stuart Foundation in Ashland, Kentucky. His contribution to the popularity and growth of the American short story at mid-century is immense. In recent times, though, the critical attention to his short fiction has waned, but readers throughout the country remain drawn to his subjects and themes, especially his portrayal of rural values and love of the natural world. The majority of his most popular stories appeared in the 1930s and mid 1940s. "Lost Land of Youth," though a later story and seldom reprinted, is a good example of his work in the genre. First published in 1950, the story portrays an individual's return home and the unsettling encounter with the heritage he has foresaken.

◆

Bert mused on his own fate as he drove along, looking at the old tobacco barns filled with bright burley. He observed the tobacco stubble on the rugged slopes and the little creek bottoms. These were the same places tobacco grew when he was a boy. But the valley had changed. The giant timber was replaced by second growth on the rugged slopes not suited for tobacco. He could remember, and he could see it from the photographs of memory, the long trains of mule teams going down the old Lost Creek road with two and three hogsheads of tobacco on each jolt wagon, pulled by two husky mule teams, on its way to the Hopewell railway station, where it was shipped on this branch-line railroad to warehouses. Now, the railroad was gone. This had happened, as so many other things, in his lifetime. He had seen giant virgin yellow-poplars, sixty feet long, pulled down the Lost Creek road with twelve yoke of oxen. Now, the second-growth logs were trucked away to the mills as the tobacco was trucked away to the warehouses.

Bert remembered in his youth that Lost Creek was a little world of its own. There were two churches and two schools. There was one big store. It was a general merchandise store that kept a little bit of everything: hardware, groceries, seeds, feeds and clothes. It kept everything the Lost Creek people had to have. It was a closed-in world too, due to the roads. It took a man one day to get to Blakesburg by train and one day to return. If he rode horseback it took him four days. Now, Bert had driven in his new automobile from Blakesburg to Lost Creek in thirty minutes. Lost Creek was no longer the little closed-in world he had known in his youth. It was as open as an autumn leaf in the wind to the outside world. A man could even live on Lost Creek now and have his business in Blakesburg.

As Bert drove along observing the wind-ruffling shimmer of golden leaf-clouds slanting upward from the valley toward the bright October skies, he remembered how he had planned to marry Mollie. He had picked out a little farm with more creek bottoms than any other farm on Lost Creek. He had planned to grow more and better burley than any Lost Creek farmer. He was driving past the farm he had chosen now. From the road on the rugged slope above, he could look down at the little creek bottoms. This seemed to him like a long lost dream of his youth. He wondered what would have happened if he had bought these creek bottoms and he had married Mollie. What if he had lived on in this rugged valley of the midday sun? Would he have loved the coming and going of the seasons when he tilled the land? Would he have loved the little joys and sorrows of his people in this little closed-in world? Would he have been happier? Would life have been better this way?

For Bert Hoskins was thinking of his own life and his own happiness. The farther he drove up Lost Creek, the more the world of his youth and his lost dreams returned to him. He remembered how he had loved Mollie, how he had worn out shoe-leather, walking the paths with her going to church, to weddings, corn-huskings, apple-peelings, bean-stringings, candy-pullings, funerals, parties and square-dances. Then he thought of the one little thing that changed his whole life. It was that little something, like the shape of a hand or the curve of a lip that makes a man love a woman. It was that little something like the quivering of a leaf in the soft wind that makes a man decide whether he loves a hill or a valley. This was the little something that caused Bert Hoskins' course of life and love to be changed.

He applied for a position clerking in the Lost Creek General Store. He was one of the up-and-coming young Lost Creek tobacco growers when it happened.

When the vacancy occurred, all the eligible young men on Lost Creek applied for the position. When Baylor Landon, a resident of Blakesburg, and the owner of the Lost Creek General Store which was a branch of his large Blakesburg General Store, interviewed his applicants personally, Bert Hoskins got the position. And this changed his whole life.

Baylor Landon, one of Greenwood County's best business men, knew something about men as well as merchandise. Bert Hoskins was such a good worker, so alert to all selling possibilities and so obliging to his customers that when they came to buy at the Lost Creek General Store, they asked for Bert to serve them. He was one of the most popular and efficient clerks Baylor Landon had in either store. He transferred Bert Hoskins after only six months in the Lost Creek General Store to the large store in Blakesburg. While in Blakesburg, Bert was invited to the Landon home where he met Nettie Landon, the wealthy merchant's only daughter. Bert Hoskins didn't return to Lost Creek. He didn't return to his little world of the midday sun. He left the land of his people not to return for reasons of his own. For he married Nettie Landon.

He left behind him Mollie Didway. He left behind him five generations of his people sleeping on the high Lost Creek hill. He left behind him people who talked of his marrying the Boss' daughter and his "getting above" his own people and his world of Lost Creek. Now, Bert was returning for the first time to the world of his youth. He was returning to the old familiar scenes of his first love with Mollie Didway. The Upper Lost Creek Church was in sight. He could see the tall sycamores whose autumn leaves were a cloud of rippling gold in the early afternoon sun. He could see the crowd gathered there like in the days of his youth. The yard was filled with men and boys. He knew the house couldn't hold them all when Lost Creek people turned out to a funeral.

He parked his car at the far end of a long line of cars. Then he walked back to the church. For a minute he stopped and looked at the church. It was much the same as it had always been except it needed a new coat of paint. The grove of sycamores had grown many feet taller. They towered far, far above the church steeple now. They seemed to be struggling to reach as high as the rugged cliffs on either side of the valley to get the first slanting rays of morning sun and the last afternoon rays when the sun went over the wall. When Bert, now a handsome well-dressed business man of fifty, walked up where men and boys were sitting on the brown autumn grass, or standing in little groups talking, he spoke to the first group. They greeted him but eyed him as Lost Creek men had always eyed a stranger when he walked into their midst. Not one of the old men or boys knew him. Bert overheard one fellow asking who he was. He heard the man say the stranger looked familiar. He heard him whisper he had seen his picture in the *Blakesburg News* once.

Bert Hoskins walked up to the church door and looked inside. The house was packed with women, girls, children and a few men. Nearly all of the men and a few women were standing in the aisles. Bert estimated five hundred people had come to Lonnie Didway's funeral. Bert watched for a brief time the young couples making love. He heard the older women talking about their housework and their children and Lonnie Didway, a fine and respected citizen, who had passed away. He heard them admit several times Lonnie had lived more than the Bible's number of years allotted to man. They agreed it wasn't too bad after all. Not as bad as if he had been snatched in the prime of his youth, or his middle age when the responsibility of his children would have been thrust upon his wife. So many such funerals Bert had remembered from his youth. Funerals he had attended with Mollie Didway by his side. They had sat in this same church and had made love as the young couples he was watching now.

A strange feeling swept over Bert when he heard the uneven tenor of the country voices singing a hymn to the mournful organ music. He walked away from the door. He hadn't seen Mollie Didway inside the church. He had looked over most of the house. Of course, he couldn't look in many places for the people stand-ing in the aisles had blocked his view. Now, he walked across the dying-brown autumn grass. He walked over and sat down on the gnarled brace roots of the largest sycamore, a place where he and Mollie had sat many times in their young days before this tree was as tall as the church steeple.

And, while the people sang inside the church, while the preacher prayed and preached, Bert Hoskins sat waiting and thinking. He had inherited Baylor Landon's business and his fortune. His only son, Landon Hoskins, now married to one of Blakesburg's most beautiful women, Ellen Sparks, had taken over the business. Bert spent but little time with the business where he had given the productive years of his life. Not all the productive years. For Bert Hoskins was still an active man. He spent his autumns in Michigan and the Dakotas hunting pheasants and his winters in the Florida sunshine deep-sea fishing. But he wasn't a happy man. Something of his early youth kept coming back. He had loved his wife, Nettie Landon. They had gotten along well enough together. They had never quarreled like he had quarreled and "made up" with Mollie Didway. Life in Blakesburg with Nettie had been a pattern and routine life. In material things he had had everything he'd wanted. He had inherited a fine home. He had driven expensive automobiles. He had worn the most expensive tailored suits. Had ordered them from Chicago and New York. He and Nettie had been the best dressed couple of Blakesburg. And, at her death, his son and daughter-in-law had come to live with him in the "old Landon home." He loved his daughter-in-law. She had tried to make him happy.

Two years after Nettie's death, Mollie Didway's husband, Bill Didway, passed away. It was then Bert started speaking more often of Mollie than he did of Nettie to Landon and Ellen. He reminisced over his old courtships on Lost Creek. He told how many pairs of shoes each year he had worn out climbing the rock-bound paths with Mollie. He seldom mentioned Nettie's name. He didn't mention her name enough to suit Landon. Landon had suggested he go to Florida early this year. He had gone to Florida but he didn't stay more than a week. He gave his reason for coming home, deep-sea fishing for the first time in his life had made him deathly sick.

When he returned, he started telling of his youthful romance with Mollie. He described her beauty to Ellen and Landon. He went back to an old album and took her picture to carry in his billfold. He told Ellen and Landon he believed she was the most beautiful girl in the world. He told them about her long black hair, her brown eyes and long black eye lashes. He spoke about her slender body and how she could dance all night with him, how she could climb the steep slopes and work in the tobacco field. His son and his daughter-in-law didn't understand. But they understood on this day when he had heard that Lonnie Didway would be buried. He told them he was going to the funeral. They knew it was his first time back to Lost Creek. They understood, too, the death of Lonnie Didway was not the reason he was going back.

Bert sat thinking about how everything had changed while the seemingly endless sermon went on. He was thinking about how lonely he was at his home in Blakesburg. It wasn't the same as it had been since his son had taken over. It wasn't the same and it would never be the same. And he thought about how strangely Landon had acted when he knew that he was going to the funeral. Bert knew his son would not tell him what to do. Life was still before him and he had good years ahead. He knew if Mollie felt the way he did, they might be able to share the late summer and early autumn of their lives together since they had missed the springtime and the early summer. His son wouldn't have anything to say about it. He would not ask him to return the business. He didn't need it. And if he did anything at all, it would be something else anyway. He might return, he thought, to Lost Creek now that there was a good road. Lost Creek was the lost world of his youth but he would return to it. He would pick up where he had left off thirty years ago. These thoughts came to him while he sat waiting. He knew what he wanted. He was going after it.

The golden sycamore leaves swept down beside him. They spilled on the dying-brown autumn grass with every little gust of October wind. He sat on the roots of the tree and he occasionally looked up to watch a leaf zigzag to the ground. For no one knew him here. There was no one to talk to unless he let it be known who he was and that he had once lived here. That he had left here thirty years ago. Besides, he didn't want to tell anybody he had been away thirty years for reasons of his own. He didn't want them to know he was here for a motive other than the funeral either. He thought it was better to sit quietly and watch the leaves, flying in the bright October wind like flocks of south-going birds. Better to watch the larger leaves zigzag slowly to the ground. For it had been a long time since he had sat down under a tree and contented himself watching the leaves come down like big drops of yellow rain. The only reason he was doing this was to see the face of one whom deep in his heart he had loved throughout the years.

Bert grew impatient waiting for the sermon to end. The time seemed endless. And he was a man of action. He had worked fast all his life. He had covered ground hunting and he had covered ground in business too. He had driven his car fast. If his car couldn't "deliver the goods" he gave it "a trade-in" on a new one that would.

He couldn't sit contented watching the leaves any longer while he waited for the one face on earth he knew he loved. He arose from his uncomfortable seat on the sycamore root and walked over to the church door. The sermon ended just as he reached the door. He didn't have much longer to wait. Just another prayer and another hymn.

Then, Bert watched the pallbearers walk up the aisle carrying the coffin laden with wild autumn flowers. He watched the people file into a double column behind the pallbearers. Bert stood close enough to the door so he wouldn't miss a face. He looked each one over as she came through the door. Many passed and he had not yet seen Mollie. He knew that the years had changed her some. But he had in mind now how she would look. He knew that he would know her. He thought that she would know him. Minutes he stood there, while they kept coming, looking at the faces of the Lost Creek people. But Mollie's face was not among them. He waited beside the door and looked searchingly until the last old man, with a long white beard, walked from the church by the aid of his cane. Mollie was not among them. Then he went inside the church to see if she was inside. The house was empty. Flower petals and clumps of yellow mud from the brogan shoes were scattered over the floor. A strange feeling came over him. He hurried outside the church.

He looked at the procession of Lost Creek people and people from the valleys and hills beyond Lost Creek as they streamed across the valley toward the mountains. The men and boys had left the church yard now and had fallen into the line of march. The church yard was lonely and empty and the dying-brown grass was flattened everyplace where men and boys had sat. He wondered if Mollie had been inside the church.

Then he hurried to join the procession of slow-moving people. When he reached the rear of this great exodus, he walked up beside the old man with the long white beard and the cane. He asked the old man if he had seen Mollie Didway at the funeral. He told Bert that she was inside the church for he was standing at the door when she entered. He told Bert, he knew she was inside the church for he was so close to her that he could have touched the hem of her dress when she walked up the steps. He said Mollie Didway was now somewhere in the line of march. Bert wondered how he could have missed her. He thought she could have been behind someone when she came from the church and that was why he had failed to see her or she had failed to see him.

Bert followed the procession to the foot of the mountain. There the great movement of marching feet came to a halt while a fresh set of pallbearers took over for the first part of the hill. Then the procession started moving again. When the rear of the great exodus reached the base of the mountain, Bert stopped. Not one of the older men or women stopped. They kept moving on. Bert Hoskins was the only one not to climb the mountain. He stood looking for a minute up the steep slope at the great procession of people from the world he once knew, as they climbed slowly in a seemingly never ending line toward the tryst of the blue October sky and brilliant shimmer of leaf-gold clouds.

He knew that he would not climb this mountain he and Mollie used to climb together every time there was a funeral. There wasn't any use. He wasn't interested in the funeral. It meant nothing to him. He thought for a moment, as he stood watching fresh pallbearers take over high upon the mountain, that he would go back to the car. He would drive back to Blakesburg and forget his returning to the land of his youth and his search for the one woman on this earth he knew he loved. But he knew he couldn't forget.

Then, another thought came to his mind. He would wait at the foot of the mountain for this was the only way for them to return. He would wait until everything was over on the mountain top. He would wait until they returned. This would be better. He thought it was possible he had not yet seen Mollie's face. He could have the old man with the cane point her out to him, if he failed again to recognize her.

While he waited the October wind whipped the dead leaves from the black oaks, tough-butted white oaks, maples, beeches and poplars on the mountain slopes. The heavier oak leaves zigzagged to the leaf-strewn ground like slow drops of red rain. And the broad feathery poplar leaves floated over the valley like flocks of golden birds. This was the first time Bert Hoskins had paid much attention to autumn. This gave him a feeling of sadness. He felt like a stranger in a strange land. It made him feel that the whole world was a mass of dying leaves and that he was definitely a part of this dying world. He could see bright death all around him, in the vegetation on the earth and in the people he knew in his youth when they were all younger and knew each other by name. Now, Lost Creek was a lost world and a dying world. The dreams of his youth were lost and dying dreams. Even the song of the autumn wind was as melancholy to him now as the organ had been when it played hymns in the church. He was a stranger in the lost world of his youth. He didn't know anybody. Not one person had recognized him.

He knew it was a dead and dying world unless he recognized Mollie. He knew, too, he would not ask the old man with the white beard and the cane or any person to point her out to him. He had to find her. He had to know her. She had to recognize him. It had to be that way. And while the mournful autumn wind chanted a dirge for his Lost Creek world he waited. He looked toward the tryst of gold and blue for he heard their voices. He heard the laughter and the shouts of the young children as they were the first to come over the skyline. He could see them against a backdrop of blue and above a shimmer of gold. Then he heard the jovial laughing of men and women now that everything was over and it was time for get-togethers, laughter and fun. That was the way it had been here thirty years ago.

The boys and girls passed him, first shouting and laughing, as they ran into the Lost Creek Valley. They paid no attention to the waiting stranger. They didn't wonder why he hadn't climbed the mountain. That wasn't anything to them. They were having fun. And beyond this autumn was spring for them. Take the good bright days in full stride under the sun. Take them while they were good. Take them while they could. Then came the older people and Bert stood where the path came down the mountain. He stood where he could observe each face. He waited as if he were looking for someone he knew would come down from the mountain. He searched each face. And he searched and searched until the young loving couples came down with arms around each other. Bert Hoskins understood this kind of love. That's the way he and Mollie had come down this mountain together. The lovers passed and behind them were a few old men and women. The old man with the white beard and the cane was the last again. Bert looked up the mountain to be sure Mollie was not walking down alone. She was not there.

Mollie, why didn't I know you, he thought, as he followed the wild procession toward the church, with your indelible photograph stamped in my memory? Where was this beautiful dream of lost youth he had so often contrasted to Nettie? Where was she, his beautiful Mollie, whom he could always fall back upon from his world of reality? Now, the autumn wind, he knew, was chanting a more melancholy dirge than could ever be played on the Upper Lost Creek Church organ. Why had he destroyed this dream? Why had he returned? The answer was simple. He had to return.

Fur in the Hickory

BILLY C. CLARK

Born in Catlettsburg, Kentucky, in 1928, Billy C. Clark grew up hunting and trapping in the foothills along the Big Sandy River. He put himself through high school while serving as his own guardian and living in a vacant building that offered year-round access to the school. Following his graduation, Clark served in the military for four years and then returned to Kentucky, where he studied English with Hollis Summers and others at the University of Kentucky. To date, he has published seven novels: *Song of the River* (1957), *Riverboy* (1958), *The Mooneyed Hound* (1958), *The Trail of the Hunter's Horn* (1958), *Useless Dog* (1961), *Goodbye Kate* (1964), and *The Champion of Sourwood Mountain* (1966). His widely acclaimed memoir chronicling his childhood and adolescence, *A Long Row to Hoe*, was published in 1960, and his collection of short stories, *Sourwood Tales,* appeared in 1968. The Jesse Stuart Foundation in Ashland, Kentucky, has recently published new editions of many of his books. Clark's most recent work is *By Way of the Forked Stick* (2000), a collection of four intertwined stories.

Clark's work, thoroughly grounded in Appalachian culture, reflects the pervasive oral storytelling tradition both in tone and delivery. His stories are reminiscent of those of storytellers gathered around the stove of a country store, but they are also modern in their blend of directness and unwritten portent of something greater than the "what happened next" of oral narration. First published in 1953, "Fur in the Hickory" portrays respect for elders and reflects the optimistic vision of a happy union of tradition and technology that was so prevalent in post–WWII America.

"You can talk about that new repeating rifle of yours all you want," the old man said to the boy as they made their way up the slope of the hill toward the ridge where the shagbark hickories grew. "It's your gun and only natural that you ought to have some feeling for it. But me? When I go for squirrel I aim to put meat on the table. You don't see me carrying a repeating rifle, either. I take my old musket. Been with me a long time. Went through the war together. Brought a brag once from General Morgan himself." The old man stroked the barrel of the musket and jerked it into firing position. "Yep, when I lay an eye down the sights, I want to know there's fur under the hickory. It's the eye, too, Jacob. Remember that. The eye is one of the reasons you see so many fellows carrying them repeating rifles now days. Afraid one shot won't do it. Don't trust their eye or their gun. So they go to repeaters to cut down the odds."

The weeds along the path were wet from a light rain, and the old man, walking in front, took up some of the rain with his britches legs and the pants made a low whistling noise. Daylight was beginning to break over the ridge, and no wind was stirring. The trees were taking shape. Birds were stirring in the tree limbs along the path and as they moved in the wet branches the boy cocked his ears, thinking that the noise might be a squirrel jumping through the trees, traveling to the hickories on the ridge. It was a good way to locate squirrels, listening for the sprays of water made by squirrels hitting the limbs. The old man had taught him this.

On the ridge the old man stepped ever so lightly. He stopped under a shagbark hickory. Daylight was shifting fast now through the limbs of the trees. The old man stopped and picked up a half-chewed nut. He held it close to his face.

"Sampling," he said, pushing the nut into a pocket. "Too low on the ridge yet." And he looked off to where the ridge peaked. He glanced again at the new repeating rifle the boy carried.

"Times have changed," he said, walking stoop-shouldered. "When I was a boy your age I'd have been laughed out of the mountains for carrying a gun like that. If you had to shoot more than once at the same target you went back to practicing. And squirrels! If you hit a squirrel with a bullet, you didn't dare take him home. Bark 'em, that's what we did. Hit the tree right under the squirrel's chin and knocked the wind from 'im. Not a scratch on the squirrel. Everyone carried a musket and no one hit a squirrel." The old man leaned against the side of a black oak and took a deep breath. "Wasn't that we couldn't get a repeater, either. City fellows came around all the time trying to sell guns like the one you tote. But when you made a brag then in the hills, you had to prove it. And no man ever came that could match his gun against a musket. I ain't wanting to brag, but I never got beat."

The old man picked out a black oak on the ridge and sat down at its foot. Less than fifty feet away stood a large shagbark. The boy sat down beside him and stared at the leafless limbs of the hickory.

"If I'd a had to use a repeating rifle, I probably would've quit long ago," the old man said, placing the musket across his lap and stroking the long barrel. "They didn't call me Barkem Tilson for nothing, you know. But you got too many Sunday hunters now. Highfalutin outfits, and just move in and blow the tops out of the trees. But not me. When I shoot, there's just one ball. When I look down the barrel, there's business coming out the other end."

The light broke now and shone on the old man's long gray hair and beard. Sweat caused by the long walk up the mountain ran down the wrinkles of his face. He took a piece of homemade twist from his pocket, balled it in his hands and stuck it in his jaw.

"Can't rightly expect a fellow to do much shooting today, though, I reckon," he said. "The world's moving too fast for them. And they don't have to depend on their guns like we did. Not even in wars like they have today. I mean they get back miles away and bang away at one another. Never see the man that fired the gun. But with General Morgan you had to look the enemy in the eye. Just bring them repeating guns in here today and blow a squirrel beyond recognition. Most times don't even bother to skin it out. Just hang it on a fence somewhere and let the crows have it. Just wanted to kill it, not eat it. Want to take the spite of the whole world out on as little a thing as a squirrel. We never done that. What we killed we ate. What we couldn't eat we let grow until we got hungry again. Not many of the fellows today would carry a gun heavy as a musket. You just ask your ma. She can tell you I always kept meat on the table when she was growing up. You got to get close to your gun, Jacob. Treat it like a woman. But you're a little young yet to know about that."

The boy placed the repeating rifle across his knee, in the same position that the old man had placed the musket.

"Listen!" the old man said, just above a whisper. A light spray of rain fell and made a noise hitting the brown, autumn leaves on the ground. The spray was too even to have been caused by the wind and too heavy to have been caused by a bird. The boy looked toward the shagbark. He saw the bushy, gray tail of the squirrel blowing in the morning wind that had begun to work in the tops of the trees. The old man had the musket to his shoulder. His hands were unsteady as he tried to level the long barrel of the musket. He squinted his eye, opened it, and looked once more down the long barrel. Then the sound of the gun echoed through the woods, and a few birds took wing.

The boy watched the gray squirrel slide behind a limb and disappear. The old man lowered the musket, rubbed his eyes, and wiped the sweat from his face.

"Knocked the wind from that gray," he said. "Thought your old grandpa was just blowing to the wind, didn't you? Too old to be traipsing the mountains, your ma said. Shaw. I saw that ball nip the bark right under his chin. Go pick him up, Jacob. I'll reload. Be careful you don't scratch the barrel of that new repeating rifle of yours against one of them saplings on the way. You'd best waited for the musket to be yours." And the old man chuckled so hard that the boy saw his teeth.

The boy walked under the hickory. He stirred the dead leaves. He didn't know what he should do. He couldn't tell the old man that he had seen the squirrel slide behind a limb and then cross out. He watched the old man as he slid the rod down the musket barrel. The old man was still grinning. Finally, the boy walked back to the oak and stood in front of the old man.

"Didn't find a mark on the squirrel, did you?" the old man said, looking up and grinning.

"I couldn't find the squirrel," the boy said. "Maybe he crawled under the dead leaves on the ground and hid. Those leaves are heavy and a squirrel will do that."

"Don't I know that!" the old man said. "I taught it to you. But it didn't happen that way with this squirrel. Now if you can't see a squirrel stretched out on the ground how do you ever expect to see one in a tree? You got to use your eyes, boy."

The old man got to his feet, frown on his face. He walked over under the shagbark, the musket swinging limp in his hand. He kicked at the leaves, scattering them over the ground in heaps. Then he put his hand on a young sapling and shook it. The boy knew that the old man was testing to see if the squirrel was still in the shagbark. If the squirrel was there the movement and noise from the sapling would cause him to move and be detected. But the boy knew no squirrel would move. The squirrel was gone. The old man had missed.

"I think I'll go on out the ridge and sit a spell," the boy said.

The old man didn't answer. He was staring into the shagbark.

The boy walked along the ridge, picked a good spot and sat down. And he thought of the old man. How sad he had looked. How he had kept his eyes off him while he looked for the squirrel. And he remembered his mother telling that he should watch after the old man. He was pretty feeble. Shouldn't be going so high on the mountain at his age. But that he would keep right on going so long as there was breath to him. The boy worried. He got up and sneaked back out the ridge to check on the old man.

He saw that the old man was back sitting beneath the oak. The musket was across his lap and his head was bent on his chest. He was asleep.

On his way back out the ridge the boy heard a spray of water hit the ground. He froze and turned his head slowly. The big gray squirrel ran along the limb of an oak and stopped in the fork of the tree. The boy raised his rifle slowly. He took a deep breath and tried to remember all that the old man had told him. He aimed under the squirrel's chin. He squeezed the trigger and the squirrel fell. The boy picked him up and looked quickly for signs of a mark. But there was no mark on the squirrel. The boy had barked his first squirrel and he felt proud and happy. He tucked the squirrel under his belt.

The old man was still under the oak with his head dropped. The boy sneaked under the shagbark and placed the squirrel in open sight. Then he sneaked away and hid behind a tree. He bent, picked up a rock and threw it under the shagbark. The old man jumped at the noise. He looked around. And then his eyes rested on the shagbark and he rose to his feet. He saw the squirrel before he was under the tree. He grinned, looked around, picked the squirrel up and examined it. Then he tucked it under his belt and walked back to the oak and sat down.

The boy waited a while longer before he walked to the oak.

"I heard a shot," the old man said. "Did you get him?"

"I thought I had him, Grandpa," the boy said. "But I must have shot just as he jumped."

The old man rose again to his feet. The bushy tail of the big gray stuck from his belt. The boy looked at the squirrel.

"I didn't hear you shoot again, Grandpa," he said.

"Didn't shoot again," the old man said, grinning.

"Then you found the squirrel under the shagbark!" the boy said.

"Found him?" the old man said. "Never was lost. Right there under the tree all the time. Just wanted to see if you had learned to use your eyes. Well, don't worry. You got a long way to go, but you'll make a hunter."

The old man scanned the tops of the trees. The wind was heavy now. The woods were noisy.

"Wind's too strong to hunt more now," the old man said. "Maybe I'll give you the chance to try that repeating gun of yours again in the morning. Or maybe you'll be wanting to borrow my musket."

The old man laughed as he walked down the ridge and the musket swung back and forth in his arms.

"I'd like that, Grandpa," the boy said.

The Gift

JANICE HOLT GILES

Janice Holt Giles was born in Altus, Arkansas, in 1905 and at age four moved with her parents to Kinta, Oklahoma. When she was twelve, her schoolteacher parents moved to Fort Smith, Arkansas, and she subsequently studied at Little Rock Junior College and took extension courses from the University of Arkansas. After divorcing her husband of sixteen years, Otto J. Moore, she accepted a position in 1939 as director of religious education at First Christian Church in Frankfort, Kentucky. She moved to Louisville in 1941 to work for the dean of the Presbyterian Theological Seminary. Two years later, on a bus trip to visit her aunt in Texas, she met Henry Earl Giles, a soldier bound for Camp Swift, near Austin. They began to correspond regularly and were married on the day of his return from active duty in 1945. Four years later they moved to a farm near her husband's boyhood home in Adair County, Kentucky, where she completed her first novel, *The Enduring Hills* (1950). She lived in Adair County until her death in 1979.

Giles published two dozen books, including three that she co-authored with her husband. Most of her writing is in the form of novels set in the West and in Kentucky. Among her Kentucky novels are *Miss Willie* (1951), *Tara's Healing* (1951), *The Kentuckians* (1953), *Hill Man* (1954), *Hanna Fowler* (1956), *The Believers* (1957), and *Run Me a River* (1964). Her nonfiction includes *40 Acres and No Mule* (1952), *A Little Better than Plumb* (1963), and *The Damned Engineers* (1970). Her short stories, many of which display Giles's love of local dialect, have not been collected in book form, but a few of them, including "The Gift," appear with nonfiction pieces about the West and Kentucky in *Wellspring* (1975). Set on the prairie and originally published in 1957, "The Gift" is one of Giles's most beloved short stories, a universal tale of a young girl's impossible but very real love.

◆

Nearly every day she went out to the big gate and waited for him to come swinging home across the prairie. She climbed to the post and sat there patiently, her hands folded in her lap.

She was a round, apple-cheeked little girl, not very tall for eight. But when she waited for Jeff to come home, she felt slender and tall and fair like a princess. She waited like a princess, quietly and decorously, in her tower atop the gatepost.

If he had been to the lower range, he would come into sight on the rim of the prairie straight out of the west, the sun behind him like a golden chariot wheel, both he and his piebald pony gilded with its fire.

If he had been to the upper range, he would come from the north, out of the foothills of the Winding Stair Mountains. She would not see him as quickly then, for the darkness of the mountains would hide him until he came out of their shadows.

She could never decide which direction she would rather he came from, and she never knew which to expect, for he left home long before she was awake in the morning. If he came from the west, she saw him sooner, but it took longer for him to reach home. It sometimes seemed like an eternity before he grew from a speck on the horizon to a man on a horse. If he came from the north, he emerged suddenly from the shadows into full view, and it was no time at all until he was riding up to the gate, smiling at her, lifting her solemnly from her perch to the saddle in front of him.

She liked the suspense of not knowing. She liked sitting there waiting, facing the west but turning to the north from time to time, trying to guess where he would come from. Sometimes, when she thought she had seen him, she slitted her eyes to make him small and almost invisible again, to prolong the suspense a little longer, to fool herself that it wasn't he. Those were the days when she was aware of the shortness of time, when she knew, profoundly, that the time of waiting was really the best, that once he had reached the gate and lifted her onto his horse, all too soon they would reach the corral and the moment for which she had waited would be over.

He never waved to her from the prairie, and she never waved to him from the gatepost. She simply waited, and he rode toward her. When he reached the gate, he would smile at her. She knew, truly, that that was the perfect moment, for her love would swell inside her until she felt big with its swelling. She sometimes could not bear to see his lean, dark face lifted toward her, the smile parting his lips until his teeth showed white. She sometimes could not lift her eyes higher than his thin hands holding the reins for fear the swelling love inside her would burst. She felt strangely aquiver then, achey and shivery.

He would smile and say, "Hello, Sallie."

She would reply, returning his smile, "Hello, Jeff."

He would open the gate, ride through, close it, and then he would sidle his horse up close to the post and lift her down. He never asked her if she had been waiting long, if she were hot, what she had been doing all day, if she had been a good girl. He never talked foolishly to her at all. Instead he walked the horse slowly to the corral, sometimes never saying a word, sometimes telling her the most beautiful things. "I saw the big brown trout in Beaver Creek today."

"Was he in the big pool?"

"Yes. He was lazy and sleepy today, just lying there in the water, down close to the bottom, hardly moving at all. I watched him for an hour, and he didn't move more than a few inches in all that time."

She knew, then, he had eaten his lunch on the bank of the creek, in the shade of the cottonwood tree, and that he had lain on the grassy bank and watched the trout in the clear, shallow waters of the big pool.

Another time he would tell her the beavers had finished their dam, and she would know he had been working the ravine where the creek flowed small and narrow and fast between the sides of the mountain, and while he talked she could see the beavers, their brown sides glistening with water and sun, their broad tails slapping, their slim, flat heads nosing twigs and branches and mud into place.

Once in the mountains he had seen an eagle. "He was a golden eagle, as gold as the sun, and he sailed down the canyon not more than six feet away from me where I stood. Not a feather on his wings moved, he sailed so stilly, and the sun glinted off his head like a mirror."

If he had been to the lower ranch, far out on the level prairie, he might tell her, "There was a lizard on a rock today, just sitting there, sunning himself, and a fly came by, and quicker than you can tell it, the lizard's tongue flicked out and the fly was gone."

She could see it, the lizard blue-flamed in the sun, the rock gray beneath him, waiting motionlessly until the fly flew past. She could see the incredibly rapid flick of the stiletto tongue, and the settling back, then, into immobility, of the lizard. "Did he go away then?"

"No, he waited for another fly."

And she knew that Jeff had eaten his lunch in the shade of the rock, and that he had sat, shoulders propped against the granite surface, watching the lizard catch flies.

He never told her that he had been branding calves, that he had been rounding up cattle, that he had been mending fences. She knew that. He was hired to do that, and it was unnecessary for him to tell her. He told her instead what he had seen—a big brown trout, beavers at work, an eagle sailing down the canyon, a lizard catching flies. And when they reached the corral, he slid out of the saddle and lifted her onto the ground. Politely, then, knowing he must take care of his horse, she thanked him and told him good night.

Sometimes she did not have to wait for him. When he worked about the place, he was there all day, and she followed him around, her pink sunbonnet shading her face, her yellow braids swinging beneath it, her short, sturdy legs tireless behind him. She held the staples for him while he nailed wire fencing in place. She held a piece of lumber while he sawed it in half. She held the oilcan while he worked on an old motor. Her father would say, "Jeff, don't let Sallie get in your way."

And Jeff would slant his eyes at her under the brim of his hat and smile and say, "She never gets in the way."

Her father would laugh and pull one of Sallie's braids. "You like Jeff a lot, don't you, baby?"

And she would be ashamed of him, for his foolishness and his childishness.

She did not like Jeff. She liked dozens of people, but what she felt for Jeff was so different it was as if she herself were a different person with him. She loved Jeff, dearly, wholly, utterly.

Depending upon her mood, he was sometimes a prince, sometimes a knight, sometimes quite satisfactorily just the foreman of her father's ranch. She never told him or anyone that she planned to marry him when she was grown, or that she planned to grow up very fast to make it possible. She never told anyone that when she waited on the gatepost so patiently, or followed at his heels about the place, she was in training to be his wife.

When her aunt had been planning to be married, she had overheard her mother tell her, "In this country a wife has to do a lot of waiting for her husband—a lot of waiting while he's off seeing to things, and she has to be a help to him. Remember that, Susan, and don't be impatient with Jim."

Sallie remembered it, and she set herself to learn to wait patiently, to hold staples and oilcans and pieces of lumber helpfully. She meant to be a good wife to Jeff when the time came, and it was inconceivable to her that it should not come.

But she never told him so.

There came a day, in the early fall, when she had to say to him, "I am going away to school next week."

"I know," he said. "Your father told me. You're going to stay in town with your aunt and go to school."

He was cleaning his rifle, and she was holding the gun grease for him. "I expect," he said seriously, "you will do well in school. You have got a good mind, Sallie."

She was pleased that he thought so. "I expect I will," she said. He rubbed thoughtfully on the gun barrel with an old cloth. "Books are a fine thing to know."

She nodded. "My father says so."

"I never got to know enough about books, myself. I've always wished I had."

"Why didn't you?"

"I had to go to work."

"But you know a lot of things that aren't in books."

"Yes, but it would help me, though, to know more that's in the books. I'd be a better man, I expect."

Although she did not know in what way Jeff could be better than he was, she did not argue about it. If he said so, it must be true. "I intend to study real hard," she told him. Since he thought so highly of books, she must apply herself to them.

"You do that. Not everyone has the chance for an education. You must make the most of it."

As the last days went by, she was conscious of restlessness in herself, not being able to settle happily to any play or task. The impending change hung over her, making her wander about. She came to each familiar chore and thing with the knowledge it was going to be left behind, and she stored up its familiarity to take with her into this new world.

She came finally to the last day and to her goodbye to Jeff. They rode into the corral, and he lifted her off the horse. "I am going tomorrow," she said.

"Yes." He did not tell her to be a good girl; he did not remind her again of her duty to the books. He held out his hand, as if she were another man. "I will miss you," he said.

She took his hand, felt its hard, calloused palm, and for the first time felt tearful and afraid. A lump choked her throat, and she had to swallow twice, very hard. "I will miss you, too," she told him.

He squatted beside her then, and she looked directly into his eyes, which were now on a level with hers. Wonderingly, she noticed there were little gold flecks in them and that there were fine, weathered wrinkles at the corners. Then he smiled at her, and she wanted terribly to fling her arms about his neck, hang on to him, and let the stinging tears she was holding back have their way. Instead, she continued to search his eyes. "You will be here when I come back?"

"I will be here."

She sighed. In nine months she would be back home, and he would be here. But then *he* would be waiting, and *she* would be riding toward him. From the corner of her eye she saw her father coming. Hurriedly she murmured, "Goodbye now," and went away into the house.

If he said goodbye, she did not hear him. Her ears were stopped by the beating of her heart.

The nine months were long, but she did not pine or dream overly much. She had always the confidence of her knowledge. They would pass and she would be going home and Jeff would be there. She studied dutifully. She made friends with the other schoolchildren, and played their games with them at recesses and during the noon hour. She helped her aunt with the housework and minded the new baby for her.

But with her whole being she knew that she was faced toward home. She moved through the day and the months with the inner knowledge that she made progress by walking backward. She moved with time, but with her face turned away.

She did not expect to see Jeff during that long time, but twice he came to town. He came in October, when he was taking a shipment of cattle to market in Kansas City, and again at Christmas.

When he came in October, he seemed strange to her at first, dressed as he was in a dark suit and with shirt and tie such as her father and uncle wore. He sat across the room from her on the small sofa by the fire and talked to her uncle about the cattle market, about the hurried ways of the city, about trains coming and going. Gradually, as he talked, the strangeness wore off, and when he spoke directly to her, and smiled at her, he became himself again. "The leaves are beginning to turn," he told her, "in the mountains. The old cottonwood by the big pool on Beaver Creek is yellow already, and so many leaves have fallen on the water that the whole top of the pool looks like a thick yellow carpet. You'd think you could almost walk on them, there are so many."

He asked her if she wanted any special thing from the city. "I don't know," he told her seriously, "how good I'd be at picking out something for you, but I could try."

Feeling unaccountably shy before her uncle and aunt, she refused to name anything, but her aunt spoke up. "She's been wanting some red slippers. There's a pair in the mail-order catalogue she's been wishing for. I'll show you."

She brought the catalogue, and Jeff studied the picture. Then he nodded and had her stand on a piece of brown paper while he drew the outline of her feet. "So I'll be sure and get the right size," he told her.

She did not know when he came back from the city, for he must have gone directly home to the ranch without stopping in town, and nothing at all was said of the red slippers. Sadly, she thought he had forgotten, but without effort she forgave him. He'd been very busy, she told herself.

At Christmas, though, he came with a message and gifts from her parents. The message said they were sorry they could not come to spend the holidays in town with her as planned, but her mother was ill. The gifts were loving and thoughtful ones—a beautiful new doll (for they did not know she was too old for dolls), a plaid taffeta dress and a soft, silky fur muff and cap. Jeff gave them to her, and when he had admired them with her, he handed her another package, which he had laid on the table when he came in. "Mine looks kind of skimpy alongside your folks' presents, but I thought you might like it."

He had wrapped it clumsily, in red paper. Slowly she took off the wrappings, her heart beating suffocatingly up into her throat. It was a small chest he had made her from cedarwood, just big enough for ribbons and handkerchiefs, and he had carved her name, "Sallie," in the top. She put her nose down to smell the sweet, fresh smell of the wood, and rubbed her hand over its satiny top. She could see him working on the chest, evenings maybe, in the bunkhouse, choosing the pieces of cedar, careful to select those with both red and yellow in them, whittling out each piece, fitting it to the next one, sanding them down to this soft smoothness, and then finally, with his knife, perhaps, cutting her name in the top. She could see his hands, thin, brown, holding the knife. The chest made every other gift seem small and insignificant. She touched it gently, as she felt she always must.

"Aren't you going to open it?" he asked her then.

Surprised, she looked up at him. "Is there something inside?"

He nodded, and when she lifted the lid, there were the red slippers, a little crowded, but he had managed to wedge them in. It was too much that he should have made her a cedarwood chest. The tears almost came, but she blinked them back. He came to her rescue. "Try your slippers and see if they fit."

He busied himself to give her time, drawing up a chair and settling a cushion for her to rest her feet on. The slippers fitted exactly, and as she swung them, eyeing their twinkling toes, her mood shifted, and she felt as bubbly and light as the slippers. Jeff looked at them, his head cocked on one side. "Looks to me," he said, "as if those were dancing shoes. I don't know if they'd stand up to trudging around the ranch much."

"They're for Sunday best," she told him. "I only mean to wear them on very special occasions."

He nodded. "That's what I thought they were for."

Then he swung up his hat and put it on rakishly. "I've got Christmas business of my own," he confided. He looked at her, his flecked eyes larky and happy. "Merry Christmas, Sallie."

She could not at all find the words to tell him thank you. All she could say was, "Merry Christmas, Jeff."

At the door he turned and spoke again. "I saw wild turkeys in the canyon yesterday. A whole flock of them. I almost didn't see them, they were so near the color of the leaves, brown and speckled. But the old tom gobbled and gave himself away."

Thus he added one more gift to her merry Christmas.

Those were the two times that broke the long winter. In May her father came for her, and when they headed home for the ranch, her turnabout feeling left her, and she felt as if for the first time since she had left it she was faced in the right direction.

She asked questions eagerly, about her mother, about the house, about the cows and horses. She circled all around the subject she most wanted to hear about, knowing she did not really want to hear about it until she could hear it from Jeff himself. Several times she came near the edge of a question concerning him. "Has the herd at the lower ranch wintered well?"

"Fine. There'll be a good shipment this year."

"Has there been enough rain this spring to bring out the pastures on the upper range?"

"Plenty. Beaver Creek has been running full all spring."

Once her father started to say something of his own accord. "Jeff has—"he began, but she forestalled him. "Oh, look, there's a prairie dog."

She did not want to hear. It was her old game of suspense, not knowing, waiting a little longer for the perfect moment. He would be there, waiting. Not on the gatepost as she had waited, but there, somewhere about the place, and she would soon see him, and he would smile at her and say, "Hello, Sallie." She smoothed the folds of her plaid taffeta dress and bent forward to see the tips of her red slippers. He would know, when he saw them, that this was a very special occasion.

He was there at the gate, waiting, to open it for them. And he smiled at her, and at the sight of the smile on his dark face her love swelled up, as always, making her heart feel tight and ready to burst. He said, "Hello, Sallie," and he helped her out of the buggy. He saw the red slippers, too. She saw his eyes drop to them, and when he looked back up at her, his smile widened.

He did not say anything before her father, though, as if he knew he must not. The red slippers were just between themselves. Instead, he went to help her father with her trunk, and she stood, waiting, looking about at the familiar buildings, glad and happy to be at home again. At the back of the orchard, then, she saw a new building, a small frame house, painted white. "What is that?" she asked.

"That's Jeff's new house. He's going to get married next week. Couldn't have him bringing a bride home to the bunkhouse."

In the short years of her life, nine of them, she had known what it was to be cold, for on the prairie the wind and snow blew icy cold straight out of the north, unimpeded. But never before had she felt the kind of cold that froze into her bones at that moment. It was as if the cold started in the marrow of her bones and spread slowly into her flesh, congealing it and turning it hard as stone.

She could not move, and so she stood, frozen, and waited as her father and Jeff, laughing together now, carried her trunk into the house. She saw the rough bark of the locust tree under which she stood, and she heard the bees humming among the blooms. She smelled the heady sweetness of the blooms, and she felt the bulk of the house behind her. She saw the sun lying blindingly bright on the grass beyond the shade of the tree, and she saw the fences and felt an ant crawling on her ankle. But she really saw only the small frame house in the orchard, and she really felt only the coldness between her shoulders.

She heard the screen door slam, and in a moment Jeff was standing beside her again. She found that she could move, then, and she squared around to face him. "You said you would be here when I came back," she accused.

"I am here," he said quietly.

"No," she told him.

"But I am," he insisted.

"No," she repeated.

He squatted beside her as he had done when she told him goodbye. He put his hands on her shoulders, and she could not bear them. She twisted away. "Sallie, what is wrong? Have I done something? Aren't we friends anymore?"

She looked at him strangely. "We weren't friends. We weren't ever friends."

"I thought we were. I thought we were good friends."

His eyes still had the small golden flecks in them, and with anguish she thought of this woman he was going to marry, who would all her life look into them, and at whom he would smile, and whom he would tell about the brown trout and the eagle and the lizard. "Why are you going to be married?" she burst out angrily at him. "How could you be? I loved you! I was going to marry you!"

His face sobered suddenly, and he looked away from her, one knee going down to the ground to brace himself. He did not say anything for a long, long time, and, waiting, she tried to regain her composure. It shocked her that she had burst out at him and confided those hopes to him. She had never meant him to know until the time came, but she had blurted them out, in her pain, and it outraged her to be so betrayed by her own feelings. She waited, not knowing what he would say, or if he would say anything, not knowing why she waited, except, perhaps, from habit of waiting.

When he spoke finally, he did not remind her that she was only a little girl, that she did not know the meaning of love, that someday she would grow up and meet a fine boy her own age and marry him and be happy forever after. He did not tell her she would learn to love his wife, that she must visit them in the new house. He did not say to her, laughingly, that she would forget all this, or that if she did remember it, in time, she would laugh at the memory. He said none of these expected and wholly untrue things to her. Instead he said, "I love you, too, Sallie, and if things were different, I would feel very honored to have you marry me. I love you so much, Sallie, that even though I am going to marry someone else, I will never love her in quite the same way. All my life you will be my dearest love, my unobtainable love."

He turned to face her then and gathered her very close in his arms. She felt the hard strength of them tight about her, and the roughness of his cheek against hers. She cried, then, not stormily as a child cries, but quietly, as a woman cries, and he allowed her tears for a long time. Then he spoke again. "You see, Sallie, you are a princess, and a princess can never marry a commoner. A princess can only marry a prince."

"You are a prince to me."

"That's only because you love me. I am the commonest sort of commoner."

His analogy was just reasonable enough to be nearly believable. Dimly she understood that because she was her father's daughter and would someday inherit all these vast lands and herds, and because he was a cowhand, rough and unlettered, there was a likeness to the princess in the storybooks. He loved her, but he could never marry her. She clutched him tighter, wanting to believe. "But you do love me? You always have and you always will?"

"I do love you. I always have and I always will."

"The most?" She whispered it.

"The most."

Gently, tenderly, and even proudly he denied his deepest love and presented the denial as his finest gift to restore a small girl's sense of dignity, to heal a small girl's sense of treachery.

She wiped her eyes on his shirt sleeve and drew away from his arms. She looked at him, the dark, sober face, the flecked, troubled eyes. And she recognized the denial for what it was. Sadly she knew she had compelled it. He loved this woman he was going to marry, for he would not be marrying her otherwise. She guessed that his Christmas business, which had made him so gay, had been with her.

But instinctively she recognized also the splendor and the kindness of his denial. And since she had willed it from him and her pride was restored by it, she must not now, she saw, do him the dishonor of refusing it. She must not shame him by unbelief. Gently, then, tenderly and bravely, she received it. With pain still shining in her eyes, with coldness still chill between her shoulders, she took his face between her hands and kissed him sweetly on the forehead. "We will always love each other," she told him, "but we must always hide our broken hearts."

He closed his eyes at the touch of the cool, soft young lips, and when he opened them she was walking away, the red slippers, forgotten, twinkling in the sun. With a strange sense of loss he watched her, feeling oddly that at that moment, for him as well as for her, it was very nearly true.

The Fourth at Getup

A.B. Guthrie Jr.

Alfred Bertram Guthrie Jr. was born in Bedford, Indiana, in 1901 and moved with his family to Montana at the age of six months. He attended the University of Montana, moved to Lexington, Kentucky, at the age of twenty-five, and was hired as a cub reporter by the *Lexington Leader*. He eventually rose to the position of executive editor but left the paper in 1947 to pursue fiction writing and to teach creative writing at the University of Kentucky. In 1953 he returned to Montana and lived there until his death in 1991.

Guthrie's first novel, *Murders at Moondance,* was published in 1943. His novels *The Big Sky* (1947), *The Way West* (which won the 1949 Pulitzer Prize), and *These Thousand Hills* (1956) were adapted to film. He published five other novels, as well as *The Blue Hen's Chick*—a memoir in part about his experiences in Kentucky—and *A Field Guide to Writing.* He also wrote two screenplays, *Shane* (1953) and *The Kentuckian* (1955); a children's book; one volume of poetry; and a collection of environmental essays. His sole collection of short stories, *The Big It*, appeared in 1960.

In his novels Guthrie wrote about the West, which embodied egalitarian frontier society well into the twentieth century; he is held in high esteem among authors and readers of westerns. According to Guthrie biographer Thomas Ford, Guthrie was profoundly affected by his Kentucky experience, particularly with the Kentucky social hierarchy that was so sharply divisive in comparison to the more democratic and informal society found in the West. Guthrie addresses precisely this issue in the "Fourth at Getup," which, though set in Montana, concerns itself with contrasting the informal, democratic society of Getup with the class-conscious and tradition-bound society of Kentucky, represented here by a group of traveling women from the upper crust of Bluegrass society.

◆

It was the Fourth of July there in Getup, Montana, and we had just had a parade that everyone said was pretty good even if a little long on ranch machinery and saddle stock and short on fancy works.

The rodeo would come later. Now people were just milling around, shouting hello and having some horseplay the way they do when they are feeling free and easy. Everyone in the county was there—ranchers and ranch hands, dude wranglers, bronc stompers, townspeople, men, women and children. They crowded the sidewalks and spilled out into the street and laughed and yelled and dodged the firecrackers that the small fry were popping in spite of the marshal. Overhead, pennants and bunting were flapping patriotically to a breeze that kept sifting the dust around.

I had put my horse down in the stockyards corral after the parade and was pushing up the street, stopping every once in a while to shake hands with locals I hadn't seen in nine or ten months, my winter quarters then being in Kentucky, when a lady I recognized as a tourist even without the slacks appeared out of the crowd and called my name, putting Mister ahead of it. While she took in my outfit of cowboy boots, red shirt and broad-brimmed hat, it came to me that she was a passing acquaintance from the Bluegrass State. She had three lady friends in tow, whom she identified as fellow residents. I would have known they weren't Montanans anyway. Here wind and weather put their brand on face and hair, and girls too big for slacks, if they wear them at all, manage to wear them without the appearance of defiance in front and apology behind.

"We were just passing through on the way to Glacier Park," my acquaintance said, "and we ran into the parade and, of all things, spied you riding in it. We're going to stay for the rodeo. We've never seen one."

"I've never been west before," another of the ladies said. "Is it—" she made a helpless little sweeping gesture with one hand while she tried for the right words— "is it all like this?"

To the east the bare hills, tan as panther hide, climbed from the valley and leveled into benchlands that ran treeless out of sight. South, a couple of bald buttes nosed for the sky. To the west, twenty miles beyond a vacant lot grown up with gumweed, the main range of the Rockies reared, blue and purple with distance, stone and persevering pine. One of the cottonwoods that flanked Main Street had decked the lady's hair with a wisp of down.

"All the same," I answered—but I knew she was thinking of cozy confines, of soft verdure, of bluegrass lately bloomed, of oak and maple and sweet gum and maybe of a colt by Bull Lea frisking in a paneled pasture.

"Look," I went on to them all, "my wife will want to see you. She's around somewhere." I didn't tell them she would be either at the drugstore or the bar, the odds being in favor of the bar. There were just those places to look. Everything else was buttoned up.

I bunched the four ladies and got them going and, just on the chance, stuck my head in the drugstore, but, barring a thousand kids, there wasn't anyone inside except people who were celebrating by pulling on chocolate malts.

I hazed my four ladies up the street toward the bar. I wished it was designated by "Lounge" or "Cocktails," but it wasn't. In Montana we went as far as we could go when we changed saloons into bars.

It was noisy outside, from noises inside and out, and the ladies looked at one another and then at me, asking was it really all right.

I pushed them on in.

The place was thick—men and a few women crowded along the bar itself, men and women at the tables on the other side, men and women standing in the middle, all jawing and laughing and sometimes clapping one another on the back. One of the women had a baby in her arms. When we passed her, she was trying to get the baby to call the bartender Jelly Belly.

The lady who had asked if the West was all alike turned back with some flutter and said to me, "I never!"

I told her it was all right, but even as I squinted around for my wife I was back in Kentucky with the lady, sitting on a columned porch, and colored boys with white jackets and soft voices were serving mint juleps made by Irvin Cobb's recipe, and the talk was of ancestors and landholders and James Lane Allen, of old and established and perished yet imperishable things, of the antecedents that made a region and, making it, made it comfortable. Not caste-bound but correct and comfortable, you all know.

While I was scanning the faces, a friend who was only part Indian but might have had his face on a nickel came up and threw his arm across my shoulders and told me, as he had many a time before, that his dad was one of the best friends Charlie Russell, the painter, ever had, and I could ask Charlie if it wasn't so except Charlie was dead. And don't think he was drunk, either, or anyhow not drunk enough to be telling lies.

I had to reassure the ladies again.

My wife was in the back room, which was closed off from the front by an open doorway eight feet wide. With her were six or eight others, including her mother and her father, who was known to everyone as Tom and who was the last of the rugged individualists except for Hoover. They were seated at the round table used for pinochle on duller days. The ladies were sipping on beers and the men were drinking highballs or shots. The men all had their hats on. In rural Montana you don't uncover except in the presence of the flag or the dead and not always then.

My wife recognized the acquaintance from Kentucky and greeted her and got introduced to the other ladies and started presenting them to the gang at the table.

One of the crowd was a man named Tippy who had had quite a few considering the time was not yet noon. When it came his turn to meet the ladies, he pushed back his chair and got up, saying by George he had never kissed a girl from Kentucky. He managed to grab the nearest lady's hand. He pulled her to him and smacked her on the cheek. Her partners edged back out of range.

We pulled up more chairs, and Tom motioned to the bartender, who came up and said, "What'll it be, ladies and gents?" In Getup most people, men at any rate, drink ditches, which is short for ditchwaters, which is short for ditchwater highballs, which means bar whisky with tap water.

While they were ordering a man came in and stood quiet. He began to glower while I tried to remember him. I got up and went over and shook hands.

"I'm sorry," I said. "I remember you, but not your name."

"The holy hell you don't! You used to!"

I could see that the visiting ladies heard him.

"It'll come to me," I said. "What you been doin'?"

"Same as usual." He considered "same as usual" for a while. "I've done more'n my share of hard work. I'm through with it. Writin' must be nice." He stood there with some hard resentment in him, with all the noise and whirl around him, and looked at the hard work he had done, stacking hay, feeding cattle, building fence, helping with the lambing and the calving. He couldn't have done much of anything else, not from his looks.

A lame-armed old man in old coveralls got me out of that hole. He broke in on us, telling me one arm was still gimpy all right, but the other was good. He gave my wrist a hard twist.

The bartender brought the drinks, and I saw that each of our visitors had her little piece of money on the table in front of her. I guess they had been traveling dutch. At about that time Tom saw the money, too, and said, "Naw! Naw!" to this outlandishness. Guests buying drinks, and women guests to boot! He thrust a bill on the bartender, and the ladies, murmuring protests, put their change back in their pocketbooks.

Soft stuff, they had ordered. The bottles at the sides of their glasses showed as much. Soft stuff! Soft stuff on the Fourth of July! So maybe they didn't sit on shaded porches and sip mint juleps and exclaim at Bull Lea's son. Maybe they belonged to the opposition, to the fundamentalist church and the missionary society and to the book club I'd heard about whose members in a moment of doubtful grace tried to identify the bad word in *Strange Fruit,* tried to identify it, since they were good ladies all, by means of secret, write-in nominations of which none hit the mark.

Of such was Kentucky, too. Or of such was the Bluegrass, along with whisky and horses and history. And they made one. Divided we stand, the saved and the damned united and all saved by dedication to custom and origin. Right now my wife and two of the ladies were talking, talking the polite, endless small talk, the on-and-on personality-talk that was part of the custom, the voices of the visitors sounding singularly soft and light and lovely after the flat harshnesses of the West.

Out in front a man yelled above the rest, calling someone a goddam son of a bitch. Except for the ladies, who tried not to, we didn't pay any attention. From the tone you could tell it was nothing to get excited about.

Now Tom saw what the visitors had ordered. To his protest they answered that they wanted to be themselves so that they could really enjoy the rodeo.

Tom lit a cigar and waved it at them. "Whisky don't hurt you here," he told them. "Country's so high and dry you burn it up quick. You breathe it right out. Not like in them southern states where I shipped a carload of broncs once. You take three or four drinks in that climate, and they pile up on you, and first thing you know you're loco." He added, as if admitting a personal infirmity, "Beer's different anywhere. Beer bloats me."

This last might have been lost on them, for Del Crockett had ambled up. Del was a good guy who looked like something dredged up from the sea. He had, and still has, great, shiny eyes and a broad face and two outsize stomachs divided by his belt and a hand that looked as if it had just come out of the guts of a tractor. On his head was a hat that had peered up at many a crankcase and blown around a lot of corrals.

Right after he had been introduced, Del excused himself and sidled around the man who still stood glowering now and then at me. His object was the gents' room. Before he went in he took off his hat and hung it on a hook outside, as if this was a ceremony to uncover for.

Tippy was two drinks drunker. He saw Del's hat on the hook and got up, fairly steady, and ran over and plucked it off.

The man I didn't remember didn't move.

Tippy pranced back with the hat and insisted that one of the ladies take it. "It'll be a keepsake. Somep'n to recollect Getup by."

She took the edge of the brim between the tips of her thumb and forefinger and held the hat away from her. With a new sweatband it would have looked better inside.

The bartender came over.

"A little drink'll make you feel better," Tom said to the guests.

"Thank you, suh," one of them answered quickly, "but we feel mighty fine."

Del came out of the toilet and looked for his hat and didn't see it until he focused his gargoyle eyes on us. A big smile split his face then, and he came and took his hat from the lady and put it on his head.

"She wanted it for a keepsake," Tippy said. "Let her have it for a keepsake."

"Y'ever see the like of this?" Del asked the lady.

She shook her head.

"Just one big family," he said, and started patting her on the back with that big, thick, friendly crankcase hand.

A colored man walked through the open doorway from the front, bound for the gents' room. His name was Cowboy Lee, and not without reason. He could stick a bad horse with a loose-jointed grace that made the feat look simple. I spoke to him, and he answered easily, calling me by my first name.

Again my eye fell on the man who stood in moody silence, and all at once it came to me. I went to him. "Willie!" I said. "Willie Geggler! How long since we worked together on the old 5T?"

Willie's face softened, and a flicker of a smile came on it. "Been a long time, all right," he answered, and nodded and trailed into the other room.

Questions were swimming in the eyes of two of the ladies when I sat down. "Old friend," I said. "Willie Geggler." I didn't add that he had always been a little loco; all of us in Montana had the seeds of his insistence in us.

My two questioners looked around and then back at me, still questioning. I made a gesture to take in the place and all the people and all they had observed, and it was in me to explain with some high phrase like frontier democracy and to enlarge on it. "We're young here," I said and let it go at that and was at once glad and regretful that we were.

"You'll need to take it easy for a while after riding all them rodeo broncs," Tom told the visitors. It took them an instant to understand how he meant it. "Why don't you come by the house afterwards and see how home folks live?"

My mother-in-law seconded him.

"Thank you all so much," one of the ladies answered for the rest, "but I don't guess we'll have the time."

The ladies got up and, one by one, the men. The ladies said they had had a wonderful, a sure-enough wonderful time. Everyone shook hands with them. Tippy said he never had kissed a Kentucky girl goodbye, either, not anyhow until then.

I took the visitors to the door. They were easier to get out than in.

Back in the back room the old man had to show me again how good his good arm was. My mother-in-law said it was time to think about lunch. Tippy told my wife the visitors were nice. Tom took the cigar from his mouth and looked at it and shook his head and said, "Sure takes all kinds of people all right." Then he ordered another round, whisky not hurting you in that high, dry climate.

1960–1980

You will see their secret faces, hear their silent voices, and taste the truth they bit from the blood-red apple. But no Garden of Eden for those [Gideon's] children, or for us, either. It is never easy to enter other people's lives; it is harder to try to understand them. What *does* make them simple, complicated, superorganized or completely unstructured? Like Lucifer falling, we feel at a loss to understand How, or When, or Why. . . .

JANE STUART, INTRODUCTION TO *GIDEON'S CHILDREN*

The universal hero story that Joseph Campbell describes to us is about the youth who is summoned by natural forces to leave home. . . . You leave home and you cross a threshold, which is a jumping off place, and you find yourself in an exotic land, like the U.S. Army, or California in the 1960s, or college in any era. . . . As writers and artists and scholars, we write down our experiences and our thoughts, and thus they are visible. But most people don't do that; their experience remains private. But even so, every person's experience is in some way universal.

GURNEY NORMAN, INTERVIEW IN *THE IRON MOUNTAIN REVIEW*

The Vireo's Nest

HOLLIS SUMMERS

Hollis Spurgeon Summers Jr. was born in Eminence, Kentucky, in 1916 and grew up in a series of locales across the state. The son of a Baptist minister, Summers earned an A.B. degree from Georgetown College, an M.A. from Middlebury College, and a Ph.D. from the University of Iowa. Beginning his teaching career as a high-school English teacher, he taught English at Georgetown College (1944–49), the University of Kentucky (1949–59), and Ohio University in Athens (1959–86). He died in 1987.

In addition to a long and distinguished career as a teacher, Summers was a prolific writer and an influential short story theorist. His first four publications were novels: *City Limit* (1948), *Brighten the Corner* (1952), *Teach You a Lesson* (1956), and *The Weather of February* (1957). He published much poetry in journals and magazines and produced four volumes of poetry in an eleven-year period following his fourth novel. He also edited two influential anthologies, *Kentucky Story: A Collection of Short Stories* (1954) and *Discussions in the Short Story* (1963).

Summers published two collections of stories: *How They Chose the Dead* (1973) and *Standing Room* (1984). Many of the stories in *Standing Room*, such as "A Hundred Paths" (which appeared in *O. Henry Prize Stories* in 1977), reflect the pragmatic and vaguely superficial nature of the aspiring middle-class of the late 1970s and early 1980s. Also included in this collection are some of his earlier stories, among them "The Vireo's Nest." Originally published in *Prairie Schooner* in 1960, this antic-filled story plays off of Kentucky's Garden myth while revealing a woman's loneliness and personal triumph with a blend of humor and subtle pathos.

◆

The rustic slab at the entrance to the camp said Artist's Colony of Kentucky. On either side of the word *Kentucky* stood a stylized mountain. The sign had been painted in neat thin letters by a girl who, ten years later, was given a show at the Mexican-American Cultural Institute as well as the Sharonville Public Library. That is why Dr. Thornton, the founder and director of the colony, kept the sign. Even though the artists were all writers now, they didn't mind being called artists. They frequently talked about the girl who had painted the sign, although few could recall her name.

As usual the prospectus and the actuality of the colony were several degrees apart. Bill Moore, the instructor in short story and poetry, said the promise and the reality were light years apart. But Bill Moore was twenty-four and fresh out of the University of Kentucky with a Master's degree and a privately published volume of verse. Dr. Thornton's A.C.K. bulletin, *Mountain Breeze,* had quieted considerably through the years. In 1940 when the colony was founded, he had announced Ernest Hemingway as a faculty member, merely because Ernest Hemingway had been invited.

This year his instructional staff of three were all present: Dr. Eloise Delgado, a professor of biology from Louisville, returning for her seventh summer; Dr. Thornton himself, who conducted the essay workshop in addition to his other duties; and young Bill Moore.

Dr. Delgado was in charge of the nature walks as well as the craft hour. She was a tall woman with beautiful snow-white hair. Janice Watts and Bill Moore kept telling each other that she was a dead ringer for a snowy crested crane. Neither Janice nor Bill was an authority on bird life; they were not even sure that the snowy crested crane existed, but they enjoyed their joke and giggled together at dinner every time Mrs. Titelbaum, of Philadelphia, announced her discovery of another rare specimen. Mrs. Titelbaum was always seeing exotic birds previously unknown to the mountains of Kentucky. Miss Delgado was very patient with her.

"Snowy crested crane?" Janice whispered to Bill. Janice was from Knoxville, and only eighteen. Her parents were doing Europe.

"No private jokes," Dr. Thornton said from the head of the table whenever Janice and Bill took a giggling fit.

But the twenty ladies of the colony were sympathetic with the young people. "Leave them alone," someone would say, and Mrs. Titelbaum always remarked that you were only young once, take it from her, Grandma Moses. Mrs. Titelbaum liked to refer to herself as the Grandma Moses of literature. She was working on a history of Philadelphia.

Even Mary Scott defended the young people in her own quiet way. "It's good to laugh," she said the fourth evening she was at the colony. It was an interesting thing for her to say, because nobody had seen her laugh, up to and including that moment. She smiled, yes, but she was a strange one. She had been a week late for the June session. She was Mrs. Scott and she came clear from Texas; she had no children. She said she had read Dr. Thornton's announcement in a writers' magazine, but she didn't volunteer the story of her life the way everybody else did. Mrs. Titelbaum was offended by Mary Scott at first, which was unfortunate since Mary's cabin was right next door in Circle One. But when Mrs. Titelbaum discovered, after careful questioning, that Mary's husband had died only a month ago, she took it upon herself to protect the young widow. Mrs. Titelbaum felt terribly bad over Mary's loss. She had lost three husbands herself, but not by death.

The evening Mary Scott said, "It's good to laugh," Bill and Janice took their usual walk along Meditation Path, from the lodge to beyond Circle One. In the midst of their customary and spirited kissing in the shadows, Bill told Janice he couldn't endure the colony if it weren't for their little walks together. Already the bell for Inspiration sounded. Bill said, "God damn," again and again into Janice's ear. The words tasted like food. He wished he dared to shout "God damn," at the meeting. "God damn Thornton," Bill said.

"Please, please, honey." Janice rubbed her hand up and down Bill's neck. In her right hand she held her flashlight. Everybody carried a flashlight after sunset, but Janice's was the only one decorated with jewels. "Honey." Bill's hair was coarse, and she was head over heels in love with him. She knew it positively.

"Him and his spiritual emphasis," Bill said brokenly. Dr. Thornton thought positively in all directions. Dr. Thornton boasted that the Artist's Colony was the only non-alcoholic writers' center in the world. Dr. Thornton said the mountain air was more intoxicating than any beverage.

"Honey, honey, sweet." Janice dropped her flashlight, but, fortunately, it was uninjured. "Write a poem about it. Write a poem and get it out of your system. Sweet, sweet." She thought of herself as Elizabeth Barrett to Robert.

It was a fine moment for the two of them.

But walking back to the lodge, hand in hand, their breathing almost normal again, Bill said, "That Mary Scott, I like her looks."

"All right, I guess." Janice shrugged her plump shoulders.

"She's smooth. And she's the only woman here under ninety—except you, of course."

"She hasn't bought your book yet," Janice said. She thought of letting go of Bill's hand, but decided against it. Every other member of the colony had purchased Bill's volume the day the session opened. Several had even sent to Louisville for copies of Dylan Thomas and Walter Benton on Bill's recommendation.

"What's buying a book? What's money?" Frequently Bill spoke against money, although he knew that Janice was an honest to goodness heiress.

"You be careful, or I'll get jealous." She yanked her hand away, scraping her large diamond dinner ring against the flesh of Bill's hand. She hoped she had hurt him.

"Baby, baby," Bill said, realizing that the conversation was clear out of hand, and realizing anew how much the Meditation Walks meant to him. "She's forty if she's a day. Look at me, sweetheart."

Mary Scott was not forty. She was only thirty-four.

Janice and Bill embraced again, dangerously near Circle Five and Pegasus—the lodge which was the heart of A.C.K.: dining room, classroom, conference room, and quarters for Dr. Thornton. "Hmmmm," Janice said, and Bill said, "Once more," as the last gong for Inspiration beat wildly against their ears. They strained against each other and it was Janice who muttered, "God damn."

But they were not the last to arrive at Pegasus. Dr. Thornton tapped a pencil on the table. "Where's Mrs. Titelbaum?" he asked crossly, and then, more gently, "We don't want anybody to miss anything." Dr. Thornton looked hard through his little pig eyes at Bill Moore. In spite of himself Bill offered to run up to Mrs. Titelbaum's cabin.

"Never mind. We'll wait three more minutes." Dr. Thornton turned his head slowly to smile at each individual member of the colony, including Bill. A thousand times Dr. Thornton had been told his smile was captivating. "Hypnotic, even," one woman said three seasons ago.

The Inspiration was composed of music and readings. Dr. Thornton owned a very fine record player and a collection of the complete works of Tchaikovsky as well as other favorites. If the members of the colony failed to bring original work, the records were played. Dr. Thornton was fond of saying that truly great music forced language from the soul. "Listen tonight and you'll have reams of original work for tomorrow night," Dr. Thornton said, even if nobody had brought any original work for three days.

"Do we all have something to read tonight?" Dr. Thornton asked when the three minutes were up. It was really four minutes and ten seconds. Mrs. Titelbaum had still not appeared.

Bill had brought a poem—an old poem he'd written in Lexington, but he didn't dare appear without something. "I have a new little piece," he said, and three of the ladies applauded.

"I have another chapter of my Benny the Bug," the woman from Horse Cave said.

One lady had at last finished her personal experience paragraph which was due in Dr. Thornton's class a week ago.

Dr. Thornton leaned back in his chair. "This is more like it," he said, smiling until his eyes actually disappeared.

But the original work was destined to be postponed for another evening. Mrs. Titelbaum began calling before she reached the porch. "Everybody! Everybody, quick!"

Dr. Thornton tried very hard to be a patient executive. Many people often spoke of his patience. He had never allowed anything to disrupt the Inspirations— they were the proof of the pudding, he often said so. But he had never had Mrs. Titelbaum as a colony member before.

"I've found a vireo's nest," Mrs. Titelbaum shouted, waving her unlit railroad lantern back and forth. Mrs. Titelbaum owned the largest light in the colony. "I've really found a vireo's nest."

Miss Delgado lifted her long white neck. "Really? I've been searching for one all summer."

"Really and truly. In Circle One. In our cluster of cabins." She looked accusingly at Miss Delgado, and then she looked accusingly at Bill Moore.

Janice Watts turned her head. Janice lived in Circle Four with her aunt—she was positive that Dr. Thornton had placed her as far as possible from Bill on purpose. Janice did not want Mrs. Titelbaum to look accusingly at her. She was sorry, for a moment, that she had laughed every time Mrs. Titelbaum had announced a new bird.

"If you don't believe it, come see."

Miss Delgado was rising, and so was Mary Scott.

"A vireo's nest," Mary Scott said quietly. She liked the sound of the words. "If we don't go now, there won't be enough light," Miss Delgado said. "We will not use our torches on the nest." She spoke with authority. Janice removed her finger from the pearl button of her flashlight.

Dr. Thornton started to tell them to keep their seats. But five more ladies rose, and then three. Dr. Thornton had to raise his voice to announce: "Our Inspiration this evening will be devoted to a lecture on the vireo from Dr. Delgado." There was nothing else he could say. "Remember—tomorrow night—everybody—everybody with a manuscript."

Dr. Thornton took two little skipping steps to get to the front of the group. He was angry. Anybody would have been angry. But he was a patient man. And it was important for the colony members to realize that he was, likewise, a man of flexibility.

There really was a bird's nest in the maple tree which stood smack dab in the center of Circle One. Janice would have to admit it was a vireo's nest, a red-eyed vireo. Miss Delgado said so, and Miss Delgado knew everything. You could almost see the little greenish grayish thing sitting there; you could almost see its red eye. Everybody stood very quietly in front of Bill's cabin, and learned everything there was to know about the vireo—its sex life, and everything. Bill stood very close behind Janice. She wished she had found the nest as a present for Bill. It was really a darling nest: it was shaped like an egg itself, and it hung there, not six feet from the ground, light in the fork of some little tiny twigs.

Janice could have found the nest if she hadn't been so excited over that Bill Moore. She'd waited in front of his cabin a dozen times while he went in to get something. She didn't know why she couldn't get up the nerve to go in the cabin herself. Sometimes she just couldn't figure herself out.

Janice Watts leaned hard against Bill. And the rascal was moving his hands against her back. He was really kneading her back. Miss Delgado kept talking in her sweet voice which wouldn't scare a bird. Miss Delgado would say just anything. She was saying something about "crotch" now; she was saying, "the crotch of the tree."

Miss Delgado gave a rather long lecture, for she was an authority on the vireo, at least the twelve vireos of the United States. She mentioned the tropical vireos only in passing. "They feed chiefly on insects. They devour worms, insects, and their larvae," she said in the same voice in which she had spoken of mating habits. "Like the flycatcher, they are capable of snatching insects on the wing." Miss Delgado was not sure, but she thought the author of Benny the Bug winced.

She spoke until there was no more daylight. Again she cautioned the colony members against throwing the beams of their lights into the nest. Dr. Thornton announced that from now on they would start their nature walks at the nest of the red-eyed vireo. "Operation Vireo," Dr. Thornton said, and they were dismissed to go to their cabins and write, write, write.

Benny the Bug asked Bill for a manuscript conference up at Pegasus. There was nothing Bill could do but go with her. There was nothing for Janice Watts to do but go to her cabin and write, write, write. She wished to hell her parents had let her come to the conference alone. Her great-aunt Anna Jane wore wool socks to bed and walked with a cane. Janice didn't speak to Aunt Anna Jane any more than absolutely necessary, so she managed a good bit of rewriting on the first chapter of her novel about the Knoxville Country Club set. The book was going to be something like *Bonjour Tristesse,* only Tennessee.

Mary Scott took comfort from the vireos. Even though the rains started the morning after Mrs. Titelbaum's discovery, Mary visited the nest at least a dozen times a day. She stood like a tree in the rain and watched. It was good to think about the vireos, male and female, who resemble each other. It was good to anticipate their young—Miss Delgado had promised that the young would be "diminutive adults." Mary Scott did not brood over childlessness, but she liked to think about the vireo family. The four white eggs, speckled with brown and black, looked the way eggs should look. Mary Scott tried to smile in the rain. Then she went back to her cabin to write letters.

She did not try to write anything but letters. Mary Scott had given up her little poems a long time ago—when Thomas first got sick. She had come to Kentucky to get away from the house where Thomas had breathed painfully for so long. She thought about Thomas almost all the time, but she did not talk about him except on rare occasions to Mrs. Titelbaum, poor soul, who needed confidences.

Everyone was kind in the colony. They all assured Mary Scott that the rain was very unusual. Mary Scott tried not to mind the rain. Still, her underclothes were clammy, her towels stayed damp, and the mushrooms sprouted scarlet and orange around her cabin. After the third day of the deluge, she had the ridiculous feeling that the mushrooms were stationary and she was dwindling, like Alice in Wonderland. On occasion, the scarlet eye of the vireo itself loomed monstrous. Mary included the *Alice* notion in all of her letters. She wrote her friends at home, and she wrote Thomas' family in the east. The dampness made the shift key on her typewriter sluggish, creating capital letters where none were intended. "I'M NOt angry," she wrote her mother in Houston. "IT'S Only this machine." She was taken with the idea of a typewriter with a mind of its own, and carefully included the sentences in a number of letters.

After a week the sun came out. Mary Scott knew the sun was out before she opened her eyes.

"Good morning, good morning, good morning," Mrs. Titelbaum called at the door. "Time to visit our babies."

Mary Scott had overslept. She could not remember when she had overslept before. For a moment she felt guilty. For a moment she wondered if Thomas had needed her.

"A minute. Just a couple of minutes."

Thomas had not needed her, of course. Thomas was dead. Mary Scott had waited on her husband for a year and a half. Then she had given him the extra tablets. Thomas said, "Thank you, Mary." Thomas said, "I love you, Mary."

Mary Scott looked at her eyes in the bubbled mirror over the washstand. For a moment she remembered the vireo's eyes.

Mrs. Titelbaum accompanied her to the bathhouse. She talked about the birds while Mary bathed her face in cold water. Mrs. Titelbaum began to remember birds in Philadelphia as Mary took her damp towel from the rod with her name over it. Dr. Thornton had done the lettering himself. Everything at A.C.K. was as carefully arranged as a kindergarten. "You're a dear," Mary told Mrs. Titelbaum, and the last breakfast bell began to ring.

Mrs. Titelbaum had been a little hurt when Miss Delgado said the red-eyed vireo was the commonest vireo in North America. She did not like to think of her birds as common. But now, now that the vireos were out, actually out . . . Well! She couldn't have been more delighted if she had laid and hatched them herself. Bill told her she was nothing but a mother vireo. Mrs. Titelbaum laughed as loudly as any of the group standing at a respectful distance from the maple tree. "Just look at them. God love their souls," Mrs. Titelbaum said, and Bill said, "See, I told you."

At dinner Dr. Thornton said that Mother Nature herself was concerned with the entertainment of the colony members. Janice said she still wished she had found the nest. Miss Delgado said, "Why, Janice!" Miss Delgado took the birth of the babies in her stride, but you could tell she was as pleased as anyone. "It's just you're used to Nature," Mrs. Titelbaum told her. Miss Delgado smiled serenely. The author of Benny the Bug asked the group what they thought of the idea of changing her title to Benny the Vireo. Mrs. Titelbaum was so excited over the idea that her eyes were moist.

Then—it was on a Friday, after lunch—one of the vireo babies got off the nest. It was the baby which Mrs. Titelbaum had named after herself—she was positive it was the same one. Janice found the little thing hopping through the brush by Bill's cabin. She had slipped up the back way to Circle One, determined this time to walk right up to Bill's door, to reach out her hand, to turn the knob—nobody ever locked a door at the Artist's Colony of Kentucky—and walk in. She hadn't planned exactly what she would do after she walked in.

But when she saw the vireo, she shouted. Mrs. Titelbaum, whose subconscious was keeping twenty-four-hour vigil over the nest, was at her cabin door in a flash. "I knew when I heard Janice Watts scream that something was wrong with the babies," Mrs. Titelbaum told each person who arrived at the scene. It was amazing how many colony members congregated. Even Janice's Aunt Anna Jane was there, cane and all. But Aunt Anna Jane had been on her way for some time. She had sensed that Janice was headed for Bill's cabin although she wouldn't have admitted it, not to a living soul.

Mary Scott stood behind the chattering group, feeling as detached as if she were a cloud. She had been writing to Thomas' father. Inadvertently she had written W.C. for Writers' Conference. She laughed aloud as she took the paper from the typewriter. You didn't write W.C. in a letter to Thomas' father, even if you meant Writers' Conference.

Dr. Thornton didn't appear at all because he was conducting his essay workshop up at Pegasus. His enrollment was down to three. Bill Moore slept through the whole confusion.

Mrs. Titelbaum was trying to scoop the baby into her rebosa when Miss Delgado sailed through the trees. For all her quiet ways, Miss Delgado's voice carried well. "Back. Back, everybody," she said, and everybody moved back. "The bird is to be left alone."

"I'm only trying to *put* him back," Mrs. Titelbaum said, and Janice identified the spot where she had first seen the baby; Benny's author said, "But he's so little," and Mrs. Titelbaum said, "I knew when I heard Janice Watts scream. . . ."

"The fledglings are almost ready to fly," Miss Delgado said more quietly than ever. "The parents will attend to their own young."

"What if something happens to him?" Mrs. Titelbaum was already defeated, but she felt it her duty to argue.

"He will very likely grow to adulthood," Miss Delgado was almost whispering. "If, by chance, a snake or some other enemy. . . ."

"Snake! My God!" Janice said.

"Janice Watts," Aunt Anna Jane said.

"But a snake!"

"Really, Miss Delgado." Mrs. Titelbaum placed her hand over her heart.

"I said he would very likely grow to adulthood." Miss Delgado stood taller than ever. "One accepts the pattern of Nature." Her voice came close to being emotional.

"A snake," Mary Scott said, but not aloud. She felt she should be sharing the horror on Mrs. Titelbaum's face, but *snake* was only a word like *death*. It was only a word on a typewriter.

"I know you all have work awaiting you," Miss Delgado said. Mrs. Titelbaum jerked her rebosa angrily around her shoulders. There was nothing to do but leave— not when Miss Delgado was determined to stand sentinel at the circle.

"They are without dignity," Miss Delgado said to herself as the women straggled away in their colored shoes, muttering to each other. She had seen a handsome black snake behind her cabin the day before yesterday and again this morning. She had frightened the snake away, of course. She had rapped her hairbrush against the screen. She had said, "Shoo," softly, so Mrs. Titelbaum next door would not hear. Almost every season there was a snake scare. Miss Delgado wondered, fleetingly, if she should have killed the animal and had it done with. But it had moved so beautifully. There was no movement more beautiful.

Miss Delgado was still standing at the edge of the circle when Bill opened his door. Bill Moore looked up at the sky, and yawned, and scratched his stomach with both hands. Then he saw Miss Delgado. She was not poised on one foot, but she gave that impression—it was the camouflage of sun through leaves.

"The parents were just coming," Miss Delgado said. She sounded sad rather than angry. Bill was sure she sounded sad. She explained about the little vireo. She said, "Hysterical women." Bill was sure he had heard her correctly. Then she shrugged her thin shoulders and crossed the clearing to her cabin. She did not even pause to look at the vireo's nest.

The parents did not get the baby. Dr. Thornton had great difficulty in settling the group for Inspiration. There were no manuscripts—he had anticipated that there would be no manuscripts: the camp was out of tune. He liked to think of himself as harpist, the members of the colony as strings. But the blasted vireo had nested in the mechanics of his instrument.

Dr. Thornton had chosen "Swan Lake" music and a Fritz Kreisler album for the evening. It was unfortunate indeed that both albums were 78 revolutions, rather than 33. With the changing of each record someone—Mrs. Titelbaum or some-one—would further untune the harp. "I just can't rest easy," Mrs. Titelbaum said, and "The poor little thing. The poor little baby."

Finally, after the last of the Kreisler numbers, he turned to Miss Delgado. He was going to ask her if something couldn't be done about the baby. Miss Delgado was really a very sensitive person. She seemed to anticipate his question. She turned her head slowly. Like a white flower on its stem, Dr. Thornton thought. He was suddenly struck by Miss Delgado's beauty. After seven sessions he was suddenly struck. "Remember, tomorrow night, manuscripts everybody," Dr. Thornton said, shattered by his own imagery.

None of the camp members ever saw the little vireo again. In fact, nobody except Mary Scott remembered him until the next morning after breakfast. Mary mentioned him to Mrs. Titelbaum, and Mrs. Titelbaum stopped at several cabins to discuss the poor little fellow. But by then it was too late for real mourning. All of their grief had been given to his three brothers, and the manuscript of Benny Vireo was already back to its original title. The author from Horse Cave had made the changes before the first breakfast bell.

Mrs. Titelbaum discovered the snake in the maple tree. She would always consider it the strangest thing in her entire life that it was she who discovered both the nest and the snake. She was returning from the bathhouse at ten o'clock. She was sure it was ten o'clock, because she had looked at her wrist watch in the dim light—you would have thought Dr. Thornton could have provided brighter bulbs for the bathhouse, at least. It was ten o'clock—she had thought it was nearer eleven.

As she headed across Circle One she turned her lantern into the tree. She did it deliberately. She even told Miss Delgado she had done it deliberately. And there was the snake. Its ugly face was right at the crotch of the birds' branch. He was stretching himself along the limb toward the nest. "Slowly, slowly, slowly," Mrs. Titelbaum said. She held her light on the snake—she'd never know why she didn't drop the lantern—and she screamed at the top of her voice. She screamed and screamed until almost everybody in the colony was there. She couldn't stop screaming.

Bill Moore and Janice Watts were the first ones. Mrs. Titelbaum was never so glad to see anybody in her life as she was Bill Moore. Janice had Anna Jane's cane, which was a lucky thing, though what the child was doing with a cane nobody ever thought to ask. "Kill him. Kill the son of a bitch," Mrs. Titelbaum shouted at Bill.

The movement of the snake was almost hypnotic. There was a moon, and then there were the flashlights rushing against the darkness and flooding the trees. Bill Moore had never seen a snake in a tree before. He had almost never seen a snake except in the Cincinnati Zoo. For a moment he wished that all of this were happening an hour ago. It would have been splendidly ironic if Mrs. Titelbaum had screamed just as Janice came into his cabin. Janice had been giggling. "Aunt Anna Jane won't follow me tonight," she said before Bill reached up to unscrew the center bulb.

"Do! Do something! Do something!" Mrs. Titelbaum's voice was ragged with fear.

"Rocks. Get rocks," Benny's author chanted. "Rocks."

"We must surround him," Bill said.

"Not yet. Wait. Wait." Dr. Thornton was breathing so heavily that it was painful to form words, but he had to speak. "Let him get to the nest before you strike." He filled his lungs with air. "We'll have a better chance if he gets to the nest."

Janice Watts began to cry. Her jeweled flashlight shook with her sobs.

"No," Miss Delgado said quietly. She wore a dark quilted bathrobe; her beautiful white hair hung loose over her shoulders. She moved past the semicircle of watchers into the glare of lights. She lifted her hand to the branch. The snake stopped.

"It stopped and looked at her, I'll swear it did," Mrs. Titelbaum was to say every time she told the story in Philadelphia. "She told us never to touch the tree even, and there she was reaching up for the nest."

"It's empty," Miss Delgado said. "I was afraid it would be." "Then she touched the snake's head with her long thin fingers," Mrs. Titelbaum would say. And no matter how many times she told the story, she shivered every time she came to the part about Miss Delgado's touching the snake's head.

Mary Scott had seen snakes before. Once on her father's ranch in Texas a rattler had killed a horse. And once, running through a wheat field, with some psychic knowledge she had jumped clear of a coiled rattler. But this was no rattler. He made no sound as he moved smoothly back along the branch, retreating from the cool fingers of a white-haired woman in a quilted robe. He was only a black snake, and there was no sound from anything. Mary remembered herself as a child, running with the wind. She had not thought of herself as a child for a long long time.

Someone threw a stone, barely missing Miss Delgado's head.

Mary remembered the other vireo, lost now, she was sure. "The red eye of vireo," she said to herself without fear.

Janice Watts hiccoughed, and the spell of quiet was broken. Miss Delgado turned away from the tree. "If we only had a gun," Bill Moore said. "Everyone be very careful, very careful," Dr. Thornton's breath was as loud as his words. "The nasty thing," Janice sobbed.

Mary Scott placed her flashlight on the ground. She moved to Janice Watts's side. She took the cane from Janice's limp hand. She counted the steps it took her to reach the tree. One, two, three, four, five. Then she swung at the snake's head. She felt the head give. She was conscious that her mouth moved with each stroke, almost as if she were still counting. She swung again and again. She swung, finally, with such force that she herself fell, scraping her arm against the stones of the path,

Mrs. Titelbaum began to applaud, and someone shouted, "Hurrah," and then they were around her, pulling at her. "Leave me alone," she said against her hands. "Please leave me alone."

Miss Delgado picked up the cane from the path. Almost as if in ritual, she lifted the snake's glistening body onto the cane. "It was a beauty," Miss Delgado said to anyone who was listening. "It is easily five feet long."

"Seven. It's seven feet," someone said.

"I'm all right. I'm all right, I tell you," Mary Scott said.

Miss Delgado placed the snake under the tree. "Stones," she said efficiently, and several of the women brought stones, stretching their arms to hand them to Miss Delgado. Efficiently she began to place a little pile on the pulp which had been the snake's head.

Mrs. Titelbaum got Mary Scott to her feet. "Poor baby," she said. "Poor courageous baby."

Mary Scott tried to laugh. But when she saw Miss Delgado, the laugh broke. She leaned against the rough bark of Miss Delgado's cabin. She pressed her hands behind her, hard against the rough bark. She was all right. She was really all right. She could talk about the snake. She could already talk about the snake. "When I was a child, the Mexicans used to take a stick and gouge the head into the ground," she told Mrs. Titelbaum who clucked behind her. "I couldn't do that."

"Of course you couldn't." Mrs. Titelbaum bravely held back her tears. "Of course not." Never would anybody hear the songs of her red-eyed vireos singing through the hot days of August. "Of course, of course."

"We could slit his stomach open maybe and save the poor little birds," Janice Watts said, approaching Miss Delgado. Bill Moore held Janice's elbow, standing a little behind her. He wanted to say something, but he couldn't think of anything to say.

"Nonsense," Miss Delgado said, beginning a pile of stones on the tail.

Bill turned his head away. Mary Scott was watching him. She was either watching him or staring into space. For a moment he thought about dancing with Mary Scott. It was only the sudden turning of his head which made him think of dancing. He was sorry he was so mixed up with Janice. It would have been fine, really fine, if Mary Scott were his friend. If he and Mary Scott went to bed together . . .

Bill lowered his eyes. He couldn't look at Mary Scott. It was funnier than hell how he felt, here, now, squeezing Janice's elbow. He would speak to Mary Scott, of course. He and Mary Scott would talk together up at Pegasus. But that would be all. It was a god damned shame. It was god damned ridiculous. It was god damned ridiculous to feel this way, as if Mary Scott were the god damned sun and you couldn't look at her but for a second.

"It's moving. It's moving," Janice screamed.

Bill thought so too. He held Janice's elbow tighter than ever.

"Muscular reaction," Miss Delgado said, adding another stone.

Dr. Thornton clapped his hands together. "We're going to have coffee up at Pegasus," he shouted. "We'll wake the cook and have coffee and doughnuts. How does that sound?"

"It sounds just wonderful," Janice said, turning her round wet face up to Bill. "We'll go get Aunt Anna Jane."

They were all delighted over the thought of coffee and doughnuts. They squealed, but only for a moment. Already they were quieting. They linked arms. Already some of them were moving away from the Circle. Already their voices were as relaxed as if they were leaving church, or an evening of television.

"First, we'll sterilize the cane," Bill said. He spoke more loudly than he had intended, but it didn't matter. Several of the ladies said it was a very good idea.

"Our heroine should lead the way," Dr. Thornton said, "Where's our heroine?"

"Here she is. Right here," Mrs. Titelbaum said proudly.

Mary did not lean against the cabin. She stood very straight.

"Not tonight," Mary said. She smiled, almost shyly. It was god damned ridiculous to have thought of her face as the sun. "I don't think so tonight."

"She should get to bed, poor dear. Of course she should." Mrs. Titelbaum scowled at Dr. Thornton. She put her arm around Mary's waist.

Janice's foolish face was scowling, too. "What if there should be more snakes? Oh, Bill what if there are more?"

Mary Scott cleared her throat. "There probably won't be any more, Janice," she said.

"Exactly." Miss Delgado rose from her twin monuments.

"They aren't very dangerous," Mary Scott said, looking straight at Miss Delgado. "They have no hands for protection—only a small mouth."

"That is very true, Mrs. Scott," Miss Delgado said.

For a moment Mary was afraid she was going to cry.

Later, after Mrs. Titelbaum had tiptoed out of Mary's cabin to join the coffee and doughnut party, Mary slipped a pair of slacks and a sweater over her pajamas. The snake was barely visible in the light of the clouded moon. It lay like the shadow of a maple limb between Miss Delgado's little rock piles.

Mary Scott walked over the whole camp, clear down to the highway and back again. She used her flashlight only a few times. It was surprising how well she had learned the camp, and anyhow, there was the moon. At the entrance she did flash her light for a glance at the sign with the stylized mountains. She tried to recall the name of the artist, but the name wouldn't come.

"Thomas," she said once, but only once.

The Little-Known Bird of the Inner Eye

ED MCCLANAHAN

Born in Brooksville, Kentucky, Ed McClanahan moved at age sixteen with his family to Maysville. After earning a B.A. in English at Ohio's Miami University, he briefly attended graduate school at Stanford University in California before returning to Kentucky, where he earned an M.A. in English from the University of Kentucky in 1958. He then taught at Oregon State College until 1962, when he was awarded a Wallace Stegner Fellowship in Creative Writing from Stanford. McClanahan remained at Stanford until 1972, taught at the University of Montana until 1976, and later at the University of Kentucky and Northern Kentucky University. Since the 1960s his short stories and essays have appeared in popular magazines such as *Playboy, Esquire,* and *Rolling Stone.* In addition to his first and widely acclaimed novel, *The Natural Man* (1983), McClanahan has published one other work of fiction in book form, *A Congress of Wonders* (1996); a memoir, *Famous People I Have Known* (1985); and a collection of interviews, articles, essays, and stories, *My Vita, If You Will* (1998).

McClanahan's literary efforts span four decades and reflect the increasingly rapid social changes of the late twentieth century. While *The Natural Man* draws heavily upon the author's Kentucky childhood and adolescence, as does much of his later work, the earlier story "The Little-Known Bird of the Inner Eye" (1961) is faithful to the tone of its time. In the 1960s many Americans, focusing on the present and future, were reinventing themselves while deliberately disassociating themselves from their personal heritage. Set in the Pacific Northwest, McClanahan's story is a succinct display of this trend; at the same time, it illustrates the experimentation and exaggerations of the creative literature of the period.

◆

He does not know that I exist. Or if he does, he must see me the way a wild canary sees a bird-watcher, through the big end of the field glasses, a tiny thing a million miles away, while the canary becomes, to the watcher, enormous, framed in a double-vision circle bigger than the earth.

But once he did. For three whole days he knew me, and we even almost talked once.

I am again on that street for the first time. It is one of those warm, gray Northwest fall days that bear with them a feeling of rain, even though it will not rain for several weeks yet. The town assails me with decay. Vacant houses, empty shop windows, the stinking corpse of a dog wheelmarked in a gutter, fat flies at its eyeballs, the blind eyes of people on the streets, faces rotten with worry, despair. And behind the low roofs the looming barrenness of the gray hills, stump-pocked, pressing their dead weight against the town. Fruit cannot drop through this thick air. . . .

Yet I had come for beauty to this place where there were hardly even shadows (for lack of trees to cast them). Had carefully in Kansas made my choice of places (1927 *World Atlas:* ". . . heartland of the great Pacific Northwest timber country . . . abounds with lush forests . . ."), had driven truck and fed a starving cement mixer, saved money, fought my father ("I don't see why the goddamn hell you can't be an artist right here in . . ." "I'll go back to college next year. What you can't see is this is something I have got to do. It's my own goddamn money . . .").

And got here, too, smelling of buses, riding the last of those only yesterday into this vast dead orchard haunted by the ghosts of long-gone trees. I had stood and watched the bus roar off and leave me in this place far worse than Kansas, and said to myself I'd by God stay till spring no matter what.

In my suitcase, sharing space with my clothes, were traveler's checks, and chisels, sketch pads, brushes, and one fine new welding torch. My pride in those things got me through the day, though their weight to carry made me take the first room I could find, a long, dusty loft above a garage, with rafters, a greasy sink, and one small window. But by afternoon it also had a hot plate, some plastic dishes, whitewashed walls, a chair and table (with my torch a centerpiece), a used mattress (soon to make some logger's lusty daughter happy?), and a rented acetylene tank with needled eyes that followed me about the room. At night I tried some sketches, gave it up, and slept off two days of buses, dreaming of blond-breasted girls who loved me for the beard already started. But now today, and this street, as warm and moist as the gut of the dead dog. I seek an open door, and find one, beneath quivering neon: Orville's Eye-Deal.

The room is long, narrow, dark, lighted only by a second neon sign, red, Heidelberg Beer, above the big mirror behind the bar. There, a fat man in a white shirt reads a newspaper. His white shirt becomes, in the mirror, red from the neon. He does not look up until he hears the bar stool scrape on the bare floor as I sit down.

"Heidelberg," I tell him. In the dark coolness of the room my sweat turns cold, and I can smell its cooling.

As he hands me the beer I see the word *Orville* stitched in careful script above the pocket of his shirt. He looks pleasant in his fatness, and when he grins he shows bad teeth.

"You ain't been in before," he tells me.

"No. I just got in town yesterday. From Kansas."

"Well, if you're smart you'll get right back out again. Kansas? I wish I had me

Kansas and this place had a feather up its ass. Then we'd both be tickled. You ain't here to look for work?"

"No." I hesitate, wondering how to say it so it will sound as if I said it often. Then, "I'm an artist. A sculptor."

(Too much pride there: I should have practiced saying it. But Orville only laughs.) "Hell of a place for an artist to come to. When I come here twelve years ago it was a pretty place. But now there ain't no trees. Or hardly any. They was seven thousand people here in this town then, and now there ain't but two thousand, and they ain't here for long. It takes trees to run a lumber town."

"Well, I hope it lasts till spring. Because that's as long as I'll be here."

Orville grins. "I expect it will. But don't bet on it. I'm goin' to the can. You holler if anybody comes in. Holler Orville." He disappears through a door at the far end of the bar. I study my image in the mirror. The glass glows translucent red from the beer sign, and the reflection of my face absorbs the redness and is absorbed by it. I study it more closely, squinting, suddenly aware of something else there in the red, a movement, something alive. And then I see them, just above the image of my right shoulder, a pair of tiny yellow eyes, bright with fear, a triangle of a face too small to be a face, chinless, straggled gray goat-beard beneath a slit of mouth, nose that is a beak and not a nose at all, the eyes, the eyes that glisten yellow-white in the shadow of the old hat pulled down to cover as much as possible, and all the rest is redly glowing. He is not really there behind me at all but here inside my head, looking out through my own eyeballs at my reflection in the glass.

I turn on my stool—slowly, slowly—to face him, and he *is* really there, near the wall, a creature so small within the great mackinaw coat and heavy logger's boots that it does not seem possible he could even carry them, let alone wear them. As I look at him his eyes glisten even brighter, and I see a slight movement somewhere within the enormous coat, as if the frail body is not wearing it but hiding in it.

"Hello!" I say, in a voice so gentle that I can hardly believe it is my own. "Would you like a beer?"

The eyes turn pure gold, and the mouth twitches once, twice, and there is a sound not human but almost visible, like a musical note hanging there gleaming in the dark silence, a coo, a trill, filled with fear as the song of the emperor's nightingale, and I suddenly stare blankly at the bare wall where he had stood. He is gone, almost without my realizing his going, the great boots taking him strangely soundless through the open door and gone, the boots filled not with human feet but spindly-fingered things that clutch electric wires all night, head tucked under wing, the sandpiper feet that flee the giant waves on the hard sand.

A voice behind me. Orville, returning silent from the can. "Bet you never seen one like him before," laughing.

"No," I tell him, turning back to my beer. "Who is he?"

"Name is Freddy, I don't know what else. Been around here ever since I can remember, all his life, I guess. They say he comes from a family all normal sized, he's the only one of the bunch that's like that."

"What's he do for a living?"

"He's got a little place out towards the coast, where the loggers ain't got to yet, just a little old shack made out of logs and mud, with pasture for two, three cows and a little garden space. He's got an old pickup truck, too, and he comes to town pretty near every afternoon. He most always comes in here, but it's a funny thing, he don't never drink anything, a beer or anything. Just stands around, off back in the corner where he don't get stepped on by the loggers when they're in here after they get off work. They are a pretty rough bunch, but they don't seem to bother him any, they let him alone, and so it's kind of like he wants to be where they're at even if they are so big and it scares him. Would you have another beer?"

I did. I had another beer, and then another, and several more, and the loggers came to fill the long room with noises and hard hats, and in the men's room a heavy-muscled logger showed me where his buddy with the clap had pulled the water pipes loose from the wall above the urinal, and Freddy did not come back that day. I walked home in the gray twilight, the dead hills smoked with hot fog, and no bird sang. That night I made red sketches, dozens of them, yet even as I made them I knew he was not there, that when he left he took himself along, left nothing behind to copy down with crayons.

But the next afternoon I was back in Orville's, and so was Freddy, crouching furtive and fearful amid the muscles and hard hats, handful of trembling terror caressed gently by the rough noises of loggers drinking, loggers saying soft as they came in "Hello Freddy" in which was unsaid, *I helped cut down the tree your nest was maybe in today, and damn I'm sorry,* and then they drank and laughed and did not look at him again. And they teased him only once, when a giant all shoulders and beard and belly said through foam, "Aaaah, c'mon, Freddy, have a beer!" I watched the golden glitter, the tiny twitch, the sudden absence—too quick to call it disappearance—of him from the room. "Now see what you done, big sunnabitch. You run him off now. You know he don't never." The last another logger, or two, or three, all edge-voiced angry at their friend, who said, "Well, sheeit," but looked sorry and said no more. So I went home too.

The next day, then. Just me and Orville, for a while. Orville saying (wiping glasses), "It's a funny thing how they are about him. They don't like for one another to tease him. I see them get in fights over it sometimes. It's just how they are about him."

Soon after Orville said that, Freddy was there, just there, coming not through the door but emerging, tiny red triangle face, in the mirror, like always, a fist of face on wrist of neck, watching as I watched. A movement in the little throat, and I waited, Great Bird-Watcher in the Sky, Cosmological Ornithologist, to catch the song that's caught by hearing, to trap the prey that's trapped by seeing. It came finally, the word-notes hanging fragile and quivering in the dark air: "*I . . . I don't drink no beer.*" And he was gone again.

I had him. And having caught him, in the moment of catching lost him. This, then, was mine: to see the bird, to hear the song, to possess only the hearing and seeing, no more, no pinch of salt would help me. Yet still I hoped, and hoping brought me back to Orville's the next day, the fourth.

A woman. A woman at the bar, alone except for Orville, talking loud to him, like a logger. I came in in the middle of a sentence.

". . . so he threw me out. After I had rode all the way from Seattle with him in that goddamn truck, and I treated him good all the way, and the son of a bitch threw me out. When he could of took me clear to Fresno. So now I got to hitchhike all that way."

She did not notice me until she heard my quarter hit the bar. Then she turned. "Why hello, honey. Why don't you buy me a beer too?"

I looked at her, suddenly aware of perspectives that the darkness of the room had at first obscured. She was a giantess, huge, not fat, great muscular body bound tight in shiny black velvet pants and vest, hard thighs bursting, massive breasts heavy yet held high and full, and as she spoke she leaned toward me, flashing white teeth in lips like blood, then slid to the next stool nearer me, moving somehow graceful, a cormorant that is too big to fly yet can and does it with that heavy flowing grace when hunting little things. Close to my face now the mass of wild black hair, and I could smell its warm electric. One hard breast touched my arm. My hand trembled as I dropped another quarter on the bar.

Orville reached for a second beer. "All right. You can have this one. But if you drink any more you got to buy it yourself. I don't mind for a man to buy a lady a beer, but you can't come in here to bum."

"Christ," she said. "I bought one already, didn't I? What the hell is it to you who pays for me a beer?" She turned back to me. "Here I come all this way, and they all treat me like this. Clear from Ketchikan I come, and then this bastard throws me out of his goddamn truck, way out on the highway so I have to walk clear into town, and now *this* bastard don't want to sell me beer. What a goddamn hole."

"Ketchikan?" I said.

"You know, Alaska. All that way." She raised her bottle to drink, and as she did I felt her hand on my leg, rubbing, saw the hand there, thick-fingered, strong, nails long and polished whitesilver, hand taloned to tear open small soft bellies with, and I wished it had not touched me.

"What did you leave for?" (The hand I wanted gone still there.)

"Winter," she said. "Too goddamn cold up there. I'm going to Fresno till it gets warmer. I can't stand . . ." The fingers tightened suddenly on my thigh, the talons in my flesh, and she was staring at the mirror, seeing there the little face, flecks of gold that glistened already not for me and loggers ever again, but for her, for midair mating with the eagle swooping screaming openclawed upon him.

Freddy.

She whirled on her stool to face him. "Well Lord God," she said, her voice for once not loud, yet still it broke the silence like a shriek.

"You let him alone," Orville said from behind the bar. "He ain't botherin' you none."

"Hell's fire," she said, louder, "I ain't goin' to hurt him." Freddy stood against the wall, and I thought I saw a flutter of his heart, a tiny tremor in the mackinaw. "If you ain't the littlest son of a bitch I ever saw." She motioned to him. "Come over here."

He came to her, boots soundless on the wood floor, and her with claw distended, talons sinking light in mackinaw, gone, she picked up beer and them gone, guiding him to the far end of the bar, them too far from me, one-two-six stools off, her talking quiet to him, and all I heard was "You sure a little son of a bitch." And over tiny shoulder I saw the last of glitter, the end of twitch.

Then loggers. Standing strangely off, almost silent—"Hey, Arch, have a beer," but quiet, no hello Freddy, no *I cut down*—listening, her talking soft so none could hear. And finally pointed silver on brown bottle upturned, she standing massive bending for small square bag on floor, and they (claws making deep dents in the mackinaw) moved through the door, he looking not at us but her, to the sidewalk and gone.

Orville came from behind the bar and followed them, the room quiet with breath-holding, Orville through the door standing motionless on the sidewalk, looking after them. A long time passed that way. And then Orville came back, shrugging fat shoulders. "They went to the Timely Hotel. Went right in, by God."

"Went right in," Orville said not much later, the loggers gone, the room soft in dark silence. And I went home to my room, the walls all red from sketches pinned, the products of three nights' restless crayon, pulled them down and carefully ripped them into small neat squares. Because I knew then that no craft could make of him a work of art that one could touch: too delicate; the slightest breath would crush it. But in the night I awoke with sweat and trembling, all tangled in the clammy sheet, and made another sketch, this time not red but dead charcoal on white, a black thing winged and huge with cruel beak and claws that dripped black blood.

The next day there was no Freddy. But Orville said, "He's done been in today. And you know what he done, he bought hisself a case of beer—didn't even know what kind he wanted, so I gave him Heidelberg—and he carried it off, but it was like it weighed a ton, and I guess it did, to him. So I went out to the street and watched him, and he hauled it down there to the Timely Hotel. So I reckon she's still there."

"Well," I said, "I guess what he does is his own business."

"No it ain't," Orville said. "I could of stopped it. I could of threw her out before he came in yesterday. But hell, I didn't know." He looked down, his fat face sagged with sadness.

That night in the studio, the sketch before me, I made my own red glow, black iron that turned to solid fire in the soft roar of heat from the welding torch, and a thing took slow shape as I worked. When I could work no more, I stood and looked at its just-started form, and saw the bigness of it, as big as there was iron to make it, then saw not it but her, her body crushing his beneath it in the rumpled Timely bed, him not on top but under, his soft plucked belly scoured bloody by the coarse hair rubbing, the great breasts staring blind into the golden eyes, the claws scraping bright ribbons in the taut opalescent skin of his palmwide back. Black velvet flung to drape limp and shapeless across a chair, battered hat jaunty on the bedpost, mackinaw, pants, boots on the floor by the bed, and there the image ends, but what strange loves have those walls seen?

Then weeks of work, nights of watching iron dead and cold take life from heat and grow until at last I could perceive in it the vision, could almost hear the beating of the iron wings and the roaring rush of sky-thinned air in the spinning plunge from the clouded sun, cold talons tensed to seize the small warm body heedless hovering far below. And sometimes, as I twisted sweating steel to fashion those cruel claws, I felt them clutch and tear the flesh of my own back, and knew a little of what Freddy knew.

To Orville's only once in all that time. I fled the beaked black angel with its ponderous looming grace, fled through cold dry rain (dry because it had no life to water) to Orville's warmth and beer, and he said:

"You ain't been in lately."

"I had a lot of work to do."

"Freddy still comes in to get the case. Every day," he said.

"She . . . ?"

"Still there," Orville said. "I got the whole thing from the night clerk at the Timely. Now you ain't goin' to believe this."

"What?" I said.

"The bridal suite, by God. You wouldn't think they had one at the Timely, but they do, and them two took it. About a week after they first went up there, and been there ever since. It costs three-fifty a day, and when they went there is when he sold his pickup truck. At first he just stayed up there during the day, and then went home of an evening. But they say now he don't never leave town."

"The bridal suite?" I said.

"Yes by God," Orville said. "And there ain't nobody seen her since that first day she come in here. She don't never leave the room, just sends him out to run for hamburgers about six times a day. They say last week he took out a loan from the bank on his place, too. He couldn't of got much, though, nobody wants it. It ain't worth nothing to nobody but him. So I reckon it won't be long, now."

The door behind me rattled, and I turned to see for the first time the entrance of Freddy, who came no more by way of mirrors (had he ever?). Saw the clenched gray face, eyes sunk goldless in the gray, drained, their gold sucked out to pay for beer bought by the case, for hamburgers, for bridal suite.

"Case Of Heidel . . . berg," he said, voice tiny, weak, its music suffocated by the struggle to say the words. His hand disappeared somewhere within the mackinaw, searching, emerged with crumpled dollars as Orville brought the beer. I saw the buckling of the little legs as he lifted the heavy case, heard him moan faintly, helpless watched him stagger as he moved through the door held open by a logger coming in. The logger filled the doorway as he watched Freddy and his burden go.

"Ain't a goddamn thing a man can do to help him," Orville said. "I want to tell him ever time he comes. But hell, I can't. I don't know what I'd say, even if I could tell him."

That night I embedded in the hot soft iron of a taloned palm a small red feather, a secret hidden there that none but I would ever know.

And went no more for weeks to Orville's, but worked and saw completion of the black birdangel, anchored now by a heavy concrete base, and wondered that my floor could hold it up. Wondered too how I could get it home to Kansas in the spring, devised fantastic plans for making shipment money, even though I knew that I was wasting dreams, that she would roost there till she pulled the building down upon herself, an eagle's aerie fallen to the town's dead dust. For I had neither door nor window big enough to free her from my loft, and she was trapped for good.

Yet when at night I lay on my mattress and watched her swooping motionless in the corner of my room, I was glad for the safety of that concrete anchor, because sometimes in my sleep I heard the heavy beating wings and felt myself carried up toward the fog-hazed moon, claws loosening in my flesh, plunging, whirling, my body jerking awake as it broke the highest branches of the tallest trees. Those times, I stayed awake to think of little birds, new-hatched, lying blue-bellied in puddles on spring sidewalks after storms.

"She's gone. Been gone oh about two months, I guess it is. She left just like she come here, all of a sudden, and nobody seen her leave. Except the night man at the Timely, said she left way late at night, dressed the same as when she come, with them black pants and all. But he said she had on a red coat, looked like it was brand-new."

"Coat?" I said. "She didn't have a coat that first day."

"That's what I said, too. So I asked around, and I found out he bought it for her. Freddy, I mean. They claim he walked right in the Bon Ton Shop, they say he had a bag of hamburgers with him, and told them what he wanted, and what size, and they showed one to him and he paid cash for it and walked right out. Didn't even have them wrap it up. Just carried it off, with the hamburger bag stuck out to keep from gettin' grease on it."

"What happened to him when she left?"

"They say he stayed up there in that room, that bridal suite, for three whole days. All by hisself, and never come out to eat or nothing. So finally they got worried down at the Timely, and they went up and banged on the door, and after they had banged for a long while the door opened and he come out. Never said a word, just walked right past them and on down the stairs and stood at the desk till somebody come and told him how much he owed. And then he pulled out a handful of money, the night man said they had to count it for him, and they give him back two dollars of it, and he went on out."

"Was two dollars all that he had left?"

"I reckon. The bank took over his place some while back and sold it to the lumber company. They claim they're goin' to log off his trees and start up a new mill out there. I've bought me a piece of ground near where it's at, and I guess I'll build me a new place when they start up. But I reckon you want to know what's become of him."

"Yes."

"Well, if you stay here awhile today you'll find out. He goes around behind the stores to pick up bottles and newspapers they've throwed out. He brings the bottles here to sell to me. Don't nobody know where he sleeps, and they say he eats mostly just scraps out of the garbage, but whenever he gets enough bottle money saved up he goes down to the White Castle restaurant and buys hisself a hamburger. You wait around awhile, you'll see him, he'll be in."

But I didn't. I didn't wait to see a treeless Freddy, earthbound for lack of branches. I went instead back to my room and through my window watched a sparrow in wet misery huddle on a telephone wire. Then slow darkness, and through the sparrow's feet curled tight about the wire hummed currents somewhere felt by Freddy's feet, his boots collecting raindrops at the bottom of the pole.

A streetlight soon came on, and my iron bird cast a great black shadow on the wall, with my own shadow cowering under it. I reached out to touch her steel claw, clasped it tightly, saw my white fingers take those cold black talons, and felt a feathery tickle in my palm.

Such tickles are but the rub of love, and feeling it I saw that room again, this time not Freddy's but my own breath smothered in the hot flesh of her breasts, my own thighs pounded by those driving hips, and I could smell warm hair again, and sweat and love, all smells that Freddy knows. I had then become Freddy, and Freddy had become my own desire, had saved for her what I had kept for paler doves to pluck from me. I was to have no great black bird, except my iron one, whose cold steel claw my hand was making moist.

The sparrow on the wire waited in the rain for the heavy wings of some night-flying predator to swoop and carry him to clouded heights his own small wings could never reach. I saw the sparrow twitch with cold and fear and joy, and my feet ached to curl and feel the message Freddy sent him through the wire. I clutched the steel claw tighter. And longed for spring to come and free me from this place.

Bare Bones

SALLIE BINGHAM

Born in 1937 in Louisville, Kentucky, Sallie Bingham is a novelist, short story writer, playwright, and noted patron of the arts. She attended The Collegiate School for Girls and Ballard High School in Louisville, and then moved to Massachusetts in 1954 to study at Radcliffe College. After earning a degree in English in 1958, she married Whitney Ellsworth, later a cofounder of *The New York Review of Books*, and lived in Boston and New York. She divorced and remarried in the 1960s, a decade that produced many of her short stories. Following a second divorce, Bingham returned to Louisville in 1977 and remarried in the early 1980s. There she served as book editor for *The Courier-Journal* and taught creative writing at the University of Louisville. In 1986 she established the Kentucky Foundation for Women and launched its quarterly journal, *The American Voice*. Bingham has lived in Santa Fe, New Mexico, since 1991.

Among her nine books to date are *After Such Knowledge* (1960), *Passion and Prejudice: A Family Memoir* (1989), *Small Victories* (1992), and *Straight Man: A Novel* (1996). Her plays include *Milk of Paradise* (1980) and *Paducah* (1985). She has published two short story collections, *The Touching Hand* (1967) and *The Way It Is Now* (1972). James R. Frakes, writing in *The New York Times Book Review*, has noted that Bingham's power, like that of Katherine Mansfield and Eudora Welty, comes from her "unblinking gaze." Her stories have appeared in *The Atlantic Monthly*, *Mademoiselle*, *Redbook*, *The Georgia Review*, and elsewhere and have been reprinted in *O. Henry Prize Stories* and *Best American Short Stories*. The final story in *The Touching Hand*, "Bare Bones" first appeared in *Redbook* in 1965 and was honored the following year in *O. Henry Prize Stories*. It is a gripping portrayal of loneliness, obsession, and private revelation.

◆

Lilly Morrison had been divorced for almost a year. In the beginning she had wanted it, impatient of delays, as though the divorce were her reward for three years of marriage. But when the reward fell due and she was finally alone, she almost regretted it. Not him—she seldom thought of him, her gentle, dark husband. Him she did not even miss. But for a long time she felt lost without the life he had provided for her. There was suddenly so much space around her, there were such lengths of time, and her efforts to do something about it—to buy curtains or take her child to the zoo or invite friends to dinner—sank into the void without leaving a trace. She cried while she washed the dishes from her little parties, for none of it seemed substantial, none of it took up any space; and the people who had been so kind to her at dinner disappeared into their own lives as soon as the door was closed. She began to feel that she herself was disappearing, as though she had existed only as a fixed bright image in her husband's nearsighted brown eyes.

She began to be curious about him, as though he had taken away a part of herself, a secret quality on which her vitality depended. Of course she was not curious about him, but rather about what he had taken away. She could not remember ever having been curious about Jay Morrison. He had followed her too closely for that. She had never caught sight of him across that space which separated her from men who did not want her. Jay had always been so close.

Only now, alone, in the waste of her life, she began to wonder about him, and even to be angry. It seemed unfair that he had drawn off so much of her strength. How could she have known he had that power? He had never shown it before; only in leaving had he stripped her to the bone. She kept hearing from sly friends that he was going out with this woman or that, that he was giving parties. And she grew more curious about him, and more angry, as though he were living on her happiness.

It had been part of the agreement that Jay would see their little boy Willy every Saturday. Lilly felt the arrangement was for Jay's sake, rather than for Willy's. The child was mercifully vague about his father—fond of him, but lightly attached. He had scarcely known him before the break. Jay, however, seemed to feel that his self-respect depended on his connection with the little boy. So every Saturday morning the maid dressed Willy in the clothes his mother had laid out and took him to the park, where she handed him over to his father. Lilly, of course, never went; there was a certain decorum in all their arrangements which had to be maintained. Yet for some reason she was always in the living room when the maid came back, and the scrape of the key in the lock depressed and frightened her.

"All right, Lenora?" she would call anxiously, and, "Yes, he's fine; he's with his daddy now," the maid would inevitably reply. There was nothing more to be said; the mission had been accomplished, the child had been handed over. Yet it was not the child that Lilly was missing.

Her Saturdays were so idle. She tried to believe that it was all right to be doing nothing, feeling nothing, to let time slide by. But she wasn't old enough or stale enough to be satisfied with that. She had no illusions about her life, but she did expect to be busy. During the week she had a whole range of appointments, errands, commitments; her desk calendar swarmed with tiny, precise notations. But on the weekends she had nothing. Everyone else went to the country or shrank into their families; she had only a sense of expectation. So one Saturday when she was laying out Willy's blue suit she said to the maid, quite abruptly, "I think I'll take him to the park myself, Lenora."

The maid did not answer at once. She was polishing the little boy's red shoes. "Certainly, Mrs. Morrison," she said finally.

"What do you mean, certainly? Do you think I ought not to go?"

The maid studied one of the red shoes, then spoke. "That's up to you, Mrs. Morrison."

The cheek of her! Lilly thought. She was always hinting, and then shrinking back into her official position. Lilly couldn't get a straight word out of her. At that moment Willy dashed in and hurled himself against Lenora's knees. She put her arm around him. "Time to get dressed, big boy." While Lilly waited, a little to one side, the maid lifted the boy onto the table and took off his overalls. She soothed him with little chuckling endearments as she undressed him, and the child seemed to grow limp as he listened. Lilly felt obliterated. There was something terrible about the boy's limpness; he stood there in his white training pants as though Lenora could do anything with him. Lilly elbowed her way in finally with the little blue suit pants. The boy looked at her vaguely and smiled.

"I'm taking you to the park today," Lilly told him. Then she picked up his foot and dropped it through the leg of the blue pants. Her shoulder brushed Lenora, and the maid stepped back.

"You want to finish him?" she asked.

"Yes." Lilly lifted the little boy's other foot into the leg of the pants. Lenora still hovered uncertainly. "I'll manage," Lilly said sharply, and the maid went out of the room with a tiny rustle of protest in her nylon uniform.

"See Da-Da?" the child asked, leaning against Lilly.

"Yes. I'm going to take you to meet him." She got him into his white shirt awkwardly—he was so pliable—and then she took his hand and led him to the elevator.

Halfway down, she realized that she did not know where she was supposed to take him. A meeting place in the park had been decided on, but she couldn't remember where it was—the arrangement had been made almost a year before. She hesitated in the lobby, holding the child by the hand. It would be too humiliating to go back up and ask Lenora; what a triumph for the girl! So she sent the elevator man up for the information.

He was grinning when he came back down. "She says by the boat pond, by the statue on the far side," he told her slyly.

Lilly started off down Seventy-second Street, leading the little boy. He dawdled, dragging his feet, his whole weight hanging from her hand. "Carry me, carry me," he said after awhile, and she picked him up and carried him until she was tired and then put him down. "Walk, Willy—you're a big boy." But he hung from her hand, whining. They turned into the park. It was a damp, warm day, with high clouds, and hot sunlight breaking through from time to time. In that gaseous light the new leaves in the park looked poisonous. The grass too was wet, and very green. The child splashed through a puddle and Lilly shouted at him. Her voice sounded brittle and strange. She wished that she had worn her white gloves, or even a hat. She did not want to look forlorn.

From the top of the hill she looked down on the boat pond, the promenade, the wet trees. It was all deserted. On the far side the statue of the storyteller sat hunched in a small, paved square. Lilly started down the hill, pulling her son. Across the way, on the other side of the pond, she saw someone else picking his way down.

She could not tell whether or not it was Jay, and she watched intently as the dark figure came down the hillside. He did not seem to be in any particular hurry, and without thinking, she slowed her own steps; it would not do to get there before him. He dawdled along the edge of the pond, paused, kicked at something. Surely Jay would have been in more of a hurry.

Lilly stopped. Suddenly she felt uneasy. If the man was not Jay, who would he be? She was sure that whoever he was, he was coming to meet her; there could be no other reason for his appearance. But if it was not Jay, who would it be? She was not particularly timid, and it did not occur to her that the stranger might do her some harm. But he was definitely meant for her; he was practically aimed in her direction. She hesitated on the path, holding Willy, who was crying.

The man approached around the curve of the pond. She could see his over-coat and his hat. Jay never wore a hat. At that she felt a terrible sinking, as though her resistance, her physical vitality, were sinking down. She did not have the strength to move. The boy, pulling at her hand, seemed remote and powerful. Then the stranger walked slowly to the statue and stopped, looking up at it.

So Jay had taken to wearing a hat. Jauntily Lilly went on down the path. She wondered which of his lady friends had suggested that. She herself would never have dreamed of it; his thick dark hair was one of his few definite characteristics, and if it was hidden, his face would look entirely neutral. She went on, hurrying now, pulling Willy. She would hand the boy over, chat a moment and then go off about her business. She was glad that she had worn her new suit, and for a moment she saw herself as he would see her, striding down the hill, her skirt swinging, her legs shining. . . . The sun broke through the clouds.

The man turned around, and she saw that it was not Jay. She stopped and waited. He glanced at her, glanced past her and turned away. She felt her hands grow damp and she started forward as though to call him back. Incredulously she watched him saunter off. It was almost as though he had not seen her; he had looked straight through her. Looked straight through her! At that she picked the child up, as though to prove her presence. The man was already on the other side of the pond.

The child clung to her, and she began to stroke him mechanically. "Da-Da, Da-Da," he wailed. Tears ran down his cheeks. Lilly sat down on a bench to comfort him. At the sight of his tears, she sobbed dryly. "He'll come, Baby, he'll come." Tears ran at last down her cheeks and dropped on the child's head. She felt utterly alone, obliterated.

Looking up, she saw Jay hurrying toward her. He was not wearing a hat.

"Where have you been?" she cried. "There was a man here."

He sat down beside her. The child's sobs and her tears alarmed him. "What happened, Lilly? Did some———"

"Oh, nothing like that!" She was outraged by the crudeness of his supposition. She began to jounce the child on her knee to silence him.

"Well, then, what happened?" Jay asked, amazed. "I'm only four minutes late," he added.

She thrust the child at him. "I'll expect him back at five. Be sure to let him have his nap." She turned away, feeling naked without the child.

Jay seemed to call after her, or to make some gesture in her direction. But she hurried off, in a fury.

For a few hours she kept herself busy, spurred on by her indignation. She took a lamp to be mended and argued with the electrician; suddenly on the verge of tears, she stormed out of the shop. To become the kind of woman who raged at electricians! She knew he was jeering at her behind her back. Her handsome suit, her jewelry, her prettiness, which she had never doubted, were suddenly no protection. She felt as though she were walking the street naked, in hideous want, shamelessly holding her hand out. Every man who passed eyed her knowingly, humorously, with interest. She hurried along with her eyes down.

By four o'clock she had run through her alternatives. The living room, closed all day, was hot and stale; she did not want to be lurking there when Jay brought the boy home. In desperation she telephoned all her friends. Most of them were out—after all, it was Saturday. But even when someone answered, Lilly talked vaguely, about nothing, bored at the prospect of seeing anyone. It didn't seem worth the effort after all. She left them confused; there was a rasp in her voice that contradicted her vagueness. They could not tell what she wanted.

At last, at five o'clock, she brushed her hair and powdered her nose, and on the spur of the moment pinned a flower on her suit.

Jay smiled when he saw her. "You're looking better," he said.

"Did I look so terrible before?"

"You looked scared to death," he said, handing her the child, who was asleep.

"I wasn't scared," she said with dignity. "Why didn't you let him have his nap?" And she turned away, letting Jay go.

The child did not wake up, and she put him to bed regretfully after holding him for a few minutes in her arms. She did not think it was right to intrude on his sleep. Then she had nothing to do, and it was Saturday night. She pretended it didn't matter. Her weekend, after all, was no different from her week; she slept every day until ten or eleven o'clock and stayed out as late as she pleased. Yet it bothered her to be alone on Saturday night.

She took a bath to console herself and afterward stood naked in front of the mirror. She was still slight, almost girlish, with her pale blonde hair and her slight, limp body. Her hips and thighs were as slender as a young girl's. But there were lines around her throat, and her arms looked dry and thin. She knew suddenly that she would never have another child. Her body seemed hateful in its uselessness, and she pulled a nightgown over her head.

Then she could not sleep, and she tossed in a kind of fury. Her life had been snatched away from her. It did not seem any more that she herself had thrown it aside; it had been snatched, snatched because of her innocence. How could she have known what it would mean to be alone? Her marriage had disappointed her, and so she had decided to try something else. She had been taught to expect a great deal, and it was not her fault if she was constantly disappointed. The world was simply not equal to her expectations. In the closets and drawers of her parents' house her little dresses, her colored slippers, preserved in tissue paper, attested to her destiny. The tiny shoes were to be filled with champagne, the tiny dresses to be dismantled with kisses, and if life proved churlish, it was not the fault of her equipment. She had always asked for more and expected more, quite fearlessly. But now there was no one to give.

She got up and crept into her child's room. He was asleep, lying curled in on himself. She did not dare to kiss him, he looked so solid and self-contained. His peacefulness seemed to have nothing to do with her; he would thrive on her ruin. She went out and closed the door softly, frightened by her anger.

In the bedroom she turned on the light to look at the clock. It was not even midnight. The whole night lay in front of her, unpredictable, threatening, each of its hours strange. She lay down on the bed and looked at the round spot of light the lamp cast onto the ceiling. After a while she raised her hands and looked at them, holding them quite close to her eyes. They were slender, capable, unaffected by her age or condition. She admired them as though they belonged to someone else. She had never bothered to take off her wedding ring—it was a convenience, like her married name, to be used when she needed it—and now she looked at the thin gold band with delight. At least she still had that claim on the past. She slipped it off and looked for the initials engraved inside. They were worn almost entirely away. The karat stamp, now, was much clearer.

Superstitiously she slid the ring on again. But the thought of the lost initials, worn away already after less than three years, began to afflict her. She wondered how much else had been lost. Her memories of her marriage seemed faint, abstract, commemorative: Jay's face when the baby was born, her birthday parties. It was all disconnected, changed. She turned over on her face. Was the rest of her life—was this moment, even—to be lost, worn off by time? The intensity of her feeling seemed no proof against the evaporation of her life. She wondered if Jay had kept more of their marriage—surely he would have, since he had valued it more. Suddenly determined, she dialed his number.

The telephone rang and rang. She hung up after a while. Where would he be at midnight on a Saturday? Once she had known every detail of his life—had known, with a sense of suffocation, exactly where he was every minute of the time. Now she couldn't even guess. She remembered the gossip, the kindly hints of her friends. She had been glad then that he had found someone, condescendingly glad. Now the thought made her frantic—not with jealousy, but with the horror of her isolation. He could not cast her off as though they had never been married, as though she no longer existed. She dialed his number again.

After that she had no way of stopping. She felt as though she were keeping a vigil over her own life. She timed herself carefully; a half-hour had to pass between calls. Waiting, she lay in a trance, staring up at the spot of light on the ceiling. Around two o'clock she remembered the name that had been mentioned casually now and then: Celia Clark. She knew her—a blonde girl, exactly her own height and size. They even shared schools. That was like Jay—to fly to a second edition. She was outraged by the neatness of it. It was necessary to dial Information to get the girl's number.

The telephone rang five or six times before it was answered. There was a long pause, and then the girl said, "Yes?" She had been asleep, and her voice was hoarse. Lilly opened her mouth to say something, to question, accuse. "Yes? Yes?" the girl demanded, reviving to anger. Lilly hung up without speaking.

It was two thirty. She telephoned Jay again. This time he answered.

"It's me," she said.

"Is Willy all right?"

"Of course! I've been thinking about you," she explained.

There was a pause. She heard the tinkle of ice in a glass.

"Where've you been?" she asked, almost gaily.

"Look, Lilly, it's too late for this."

"All right. I'll call you tomorrow."

"That's not what I mean."

"Then what . . . I'm lonely, Jay—I'm all alone." Her voice broke, and she poured her tears into the receiver.

It's too late, Lilly," he repeated across her sobs. She heard the familiar tremor in his voice, but it no longer affected his words. They had become automatic. "You should have thought of this a year ago. I knew something was up when I saw you in the park." That was to himself, with satisfaction.

"I need you," she said, blindly seizing on something.

"It's not me you need."

"I can't get on any longer by myself."

"Look," he said gently, "you'll be all right in the morning. You'll sleep late and get up and put on your pink robe and have your English muffins. Tomorrow's Sunday," he reminded her.

"I hate Sunday!" she cried. "I can't stand for tomorrow to be Sunday!" It was a cry out of the old time.

"Good night, Lilly." After a moment she heard a click. He had hung up.

She sat dazed, the dead receiver in her hand. She could hardly believe that he had turned her down. She could hardly believe, even, that she had made an offer. Yet there was the receiver in her hand, to prove that she had been turned down. He had taken something away from her and he did not intend to return it. He had stripped her to the bone. She lay on her face and sobbed and bit the pillow until the groveling sounds frightened her, and she lay still.

After a while a few words formed in the roaring void of her mind. I am twenty-six, she thought, and I am divorced, and I have a child. She had never added it up before, and the words seemed cumbersome and strange. I am twenty-six, and I am divorced, and I have a child. Is that all? she cried in anguish. And the answer came back pedantically, You are twenty-six, and you are divorced, and you have a child. It was so strange, so small and hopeless—a revelation, yet small and hopeless. She turned the three facts over and over, like three pebbles in her hand. They were cool and solid and round, and she did not know what she would find to do with them. But they were—they existed; and suddenly she felt the weight of her life, of herself, laid upon her bare bones.

White Anglo-Saxon Protestant

ROBERT HAZEL

Robert Hazel was born near Bloomington, Indiana, in 1921. After earning an A.B. from George Washington University and an M.A. from Johns Hopkins, he taught creative writing at several universities throughout the country. In 1953 Hazel published his first novel, *Lost Year*, which drew upon his previous and current experiences of living in Louisville. *A Field Full of People,* his second novel published the following year, mined his background of growing up in rural Indiana, an experience that is also elemental to much of his short fiction and poetry. Hazel's third and final novel, *Early Spring*, appeared in 1971. He was a prolific poet as well, publishing five collections between 1961 and 1993, the year of his death. Early in his career, following the success of his first two novels, Hazel moved to Lexington in 1956 and taught at the University of Kentucky until 1961. It was here that Hazel was teacher and mentor to several budding Kentucky authors, among them Ed McClanahan, Gurney Norman, Wendell Berry, and Bobbie Ann Mason.

Hazel published only a few short stories, all in the late 1960s and 1970s, but each is remarkably good. "White Anglo-Saxon Protestant" appeared in *The Hudson Review* in the winter of 1966–67 and was reprinted in *Best American Short Stories*. His short fiction clearly mirrors the timbre of the times. Whereas many of the stories published in America between 1945 and 1960 explore personal identity as the result of regional influence, in the 1960s and 70s, communications and personal mobility began to compete with heritage: Americans were suddenly able to assume membership in and a sense of identity with pockets of society previously alien to them. In Hazel's stories, these identities form an uneasy coexistence, represented here as antebellum sensibilities collide with contemporary urban issues.

◆

Here comes Hampden now, on his way to kill me. He staggers past Minetta's Tavern, the long red and white banner of the Gaslight Cafe, the green oval sign of the Kettle of Fish. Now Rienzi's Coffee House with its disarrayed chessboards and miscegenous couples drooped in the scummed windows, and the Funky Antique Shop. And now the Folklore Center where a crowd of students have collected, filling the steps and eddying out to the old granite curb of MacDougal Street: young partisans of Joan Baez and mourners of Medgar Evers, with their guitars, wearing jeans, boots and checkered flannel shirts, Negro boys and girls with a certain gravity, and self-conscious Jewish kids hugging banjos—all ready to go down to Cambridge, Maryland, to protest segregation on the Eastern Shore. They appear sixty percent excited and scared, thirty-nine percent honest, and one percent crazy out of their young heads, all reminding me of myself as an undergraduate when I told my professors I was of the religion of Socrates, Jesus and Gandhi, and wrote a petition to the British Crown to free India. How young I was, how young they are!

Yesterday Nathan came to me, his professor, a Kentuckian with an accent, and Nathan wanted to know about going to Maryland. I said, "Yes, I know. They will hate you in particular, Nathan, because you're a New York Jew Communist and the Klan is looking for you." Nathan grinned, looking noble and frightened and curious. I said, "Nathan, those people have a strange religion. The morality is all King James *Old Testament,* but the conscious ethic is all *New Testament.* It's their way of embracing the Chosen People and denying this pack of Jews in the same breath. In the South, Moses doesn't even cut any ice because he was an Egyptian nigger. It's all New Dispensation, all Jesus. And in the South, Jesus is a German. Have you seen those calendar pictures of Christ that hang on the walls of parlors and bedrooms all over the South? No? Well, Billy Graham looks like all of them in composite. There's a real case of life imitating art. Jesus is a real Luftwaffe Ace, as in Dali's insane painting of the Last Supper. It was actually hung in the National Gallery of Art in Washington, you know." I paused and stared at Nathan. "And, Nathan, don't go down there with any illusions about Southern cowardice. The Southerners aren't any more afraid of you than you are of them. They believe their cause is just, too. They really believe that Negroes are inferior creatures, an inferior species—the way you and I don't keep dogs on leashes because we're afraid of dogs. We just want the power to compel obedience from an inferior creature, and the leash secures that power for us." I waited a moment, then said, "Nathan, there's a bitter thing to dispose of, by action and imagination. When I was your age the enemies were Harry Bennett's company police clubbing the workers, and then fascism. Good luck. Watch yourself. And when you get back, bring Rama up for coffee."

Nathan is standing down there near the red door of the Folklore Center. I watch his tall, courageous, excited and false posture: false by a small fraction only because he is in love, as only a nineteen-year-old boy can be, with the daugther of a famous Negro expatriate. Rama is a startlingly pretty girl and Nathan is very handsome. They are too beautiful for tear gas, fire hoses, and dogs.

And here comes Hampden, reeling past the Folklore Center. He is near enough now for me to see his skewed tie, the coffee-blotted shirt, the jacket and slacks that don't match, pulled on in a drunk hurry, the slacks with a dark river down the left leg where Hampden has pissed himself; see the thin, neat hair, the expensive pipe jutting from a frayed pocket; even see the creases of distaste near his Mississippi-Puritan mouth as he walks in brisk spurts, in confused surges, past the line of Negro and white students. Hampden shoulders some of them, not accidentally, on his way to the Golden Pizza parlor directly across the street. Hampden, my old friend, an editor with Aegean House, a stolid pipe-smoker, a spouter of conservative publishing maxims in what he considers a crooked and opportunistic publishing house, calmly affirming the freedom of authors, the wisdom of scholars, deploring the recent "tawdry" under-the-table deals between reprinters and hard-cover firms which turned traditional publishing upside-down; Hampden the rational-seeming proper man who is also consumed by Rimbaud, Wolfe and Dylan Thomas, an editor who believes in the Maxwell Perkins myth of Creative Editorship, a man with an attractive and intelligent wife, a ten-year-old son who batted .580 in the Little League in Merrick, an energetic Deep South hunter and fisherman who takes five-mile walks in a tweed jacket rough as a Kentucky cob, with the gait of an Englishman, toe before heel, who swallows a hundred bottles of assorted vitamins and proteins, whose belts are of the thickest English leather, who does thirty pushups before breakfast and who is not convinced that Westbrook Pegler doesn't still have "something of the old verve."

And here he comes down the swingingest block in the Village, down MacDougal between Minetta's Tavern and the San Remo, jostling "the cheap integrationist bastards" in front of the Folklore Center. Hampden puts shoulder to shoulder, cagily scuffing ever so little, as if feeling out his enemy, as he jars past. Both Negroes and whites that he brushes wheel involuntarily, change faces quickly, but do not follow to trample the drunk white man. Nathan's face is alert, almost hostile, but open to doubt, because Hampden has jostled cannily, as a drunk man will who is shot through with hatreds too strong to become obvious until he wants to turn back, at some moment, and scream them. Hampden is on his way from Merrick, hungry beyond recall of eating, weakened, sick, stumbling toward the Golden Pizza to spend twenty cents for a slice of dough, tomato and rubbery cheese, trying to remember, I guess, why he feels he has to come up here to kill me. It is because he thinks I made a pass at his mistress.

Hampden had, by intelligence and judgment, worked up to a good spot on a man's magazine, then jumped to Aegean House, without even three hours of college credits. Then his wife spent four years getting a Columbia Ph.D., with an excellent dissertation on Alexander Pope. Hampden had spent his boyhood pleading for pennies from a sluttish mother in the town of Bucksnort, Mississippi. Then his wife tried to give him dollars from fairly well-to-do parents on Long Island. My girl and I were constant guests at Hampden and Regina's place, an apartment sticky and sterile as antlers with Danish modern furniture, given them by her parents. We saw the struggle begin.

From a confident, pipe-smoking, hi-fi-playing man who enjoyed his skill at chess, at carving a duck for his friends, Hampden became a wife-slayer who made laconic disparagements of Regina in our presence, in small asides which she was sure to overhear. After all, Pope was a hunchback, and any woman who would choose to do research on a hunchback—the inferences were clear. If Regina went out of her way to try, with all pathetic concentration, to bake Southern cornbread, Hampden mentioned in a too-quiet tone, that, of course, if one doesn't have water-ground meal, the bread is not to be compared with the original Mississippi Choctaw bread in food value and flavor. If Regina put records of folksingers on the hi-fi, Hampden rejected the disks with a mechanical click that could be heard all over the room, a hard silence, a punctuation mark for his wary and quiet speech about young Communist folk-singers, and that anyone knew if the words Lincoln or People were mentioned in song titles, the songs were Red, "the latest Bronx Renaissance." Puffing vigorously on his straight-grained Algerian briar, Hampden looked deeply at his wife, a Yankee, and at Fauna, who lives with me, and remarked as if musing to himself, "Funny how all my Liberal friends are putting their kids into private schools. They won't say it's because there are too many goddam stupid lawless niggers in the public schools. No. They talk about better math instruction and 'development opportunities.'"

Fauna set down her after-dinner brandy with a loud clatter, a feminine disagreement with Hampden. But Hampden had a sure Southern weapon against Fauna: he considered her much too beautiful to talk seriously to. Hampden could express his hatred of Fauna by shutting her mouth with a chocolate mint and assuming, with slyly gentle gestures, that she was much too feminine *ever* to disagree with him. With Fauna it was not so much a matter of taking Regina's side as it was simply loathing this man Hampden, who sat there drawing on his pipe in patriarchal grandeur, too much like her own unbending Spanish father, too perfectly encased in his own defenses, too unreachable.

When Regina began her research on Pope, Hampden began to cultivate a young woman author who, as it turned out, was a fine translator of German, one of the best in America. Hampden edited two of her books. She is Margery Parsons, and she is the reason why Hampden is coming up here to kill me. Last night after Hampden left his "other apartment" here in Manhattan where he shacks with Margery, I dialed his home number out in Merrick. Regina answered. She told me she was moving out and taking their son to her parents' house at the far tip of the island. I had to phone Margery Parsons then because I knew if Hampden wasn't back up there, with her, he would be down on the East Side, drunk and challenging the retired fighters in Lulu's Bar on Second Avenue, and the old fighters not even glancing up when Hampden gave the trite, bellowed challenge, "I can lick any man here!" and the heads of the fighters not even moving, bored, and Hampden diminished to nothing, standing there crazily drunk and wishing: wishing for cut eyes and a dislocated jaw, a masochist in heat like a bitch for assault by other men. I knew they wouldn't even accord him a nod of manhood, wouldn't knock him into a coma but would grin at him, if anything, with the curious kind of pity that men who have been hit give to men who want to be hit. And there he would be in Lulu's Bar, stifled absolutely, or with his translator of Rilke, his sex relations with her only a stab at his recognizably intellectual wife—and how could a high school boy from Mississippi try to kill the spirit of a wife who had a Ph.D. except to lay a lady-scholar whose translations and essays were "definitive"?

Going there in the winking cold lights of the Golden Pizza, Hampden holds all the darks and lights of honesty and deceit, tenderness and murder on his shoulders. If one of his friends was ill, Hampden would phone eight times a day. He would bring medicines, food, books. I could not begin to catalogue his spontaneous gifts to Fauna and me, ranging from Turnbull's *Letters of Fitzgerald* to a smoked fish. Fauna was suspicious of potato salad and fish. She said, "He just wants to patronize me because I'm Jewish. He just wants to get me out of the way so he can lay you, Richard." I said, "Darling, could you just try to believe, for five seconds, that he simply thought you might like the food?"

Often at night I hear Italian sausages frying there in the Golden Pizza, turned lazily and expertly by a flat-bellied boy who serves a greasy sausage and a smear of fried onions and peppers on a soft roll. He makes small talk, New York illiterate small talk with all the unescorted girls who come in: "Eh, ya dun remember me, eh? Out to da beach, yeh, Joneses Beach last summa, yeh. Ya hadda straw hat on." At night I often wake up, hearing the hiss of frying sausages in my own kitchen. It is just an echo off the tenement wall.

But to see an old friend who is drunkenly burning his mouth on a slice of pizza just to get the energy to come up here and kill me—and all because I had to phone his mistress to try, at least, to find out where he was so I could keep him out of Lulu's Bar and the nut ward at Bellevue? Margery made the mistake of telling Hampden that I had phoned. When he got in touch with her from a phone booth at 14th and 2nd Avenue, she had cooed, "Richard is *so* concerned. Are you *drinking* again?" Then Margery had to report to me that Hampden said the *awfulest* things, like I'll kill the treacherous bastard! And Hampden had taken my call to Margery as an attempt to cut his balls and throw them out into the winter snow, as he and I had cut pigs in our Southern boyhood. He would have been flattered, Fauna said, if I had made a pass at Regina. He could have swept such a pass away with a good-humored, superior, buddy-buddy gesture, as a way to caress him, too, through Regina's body. I said to Fauna, "Or maybe in an even more destructive way, with this wife and mistress bit, like the way a farmer will allow you to kick a mare he already owns, but not one he is going to buy."

Hampden seldom drank during the years of his increasing success as an editor. Instead, he read hungrily—as a matter of fact, he is better read than either Regina or me—and he exercised strenuously to stave off a potbelly. He teased me constantly about putting on weight, and when I pointed to his flab he sucked in his breath and declared, "But my muscles have *definition* underneath." Quickly he became a food faddist. He chewed lean sirloin, swallowed the blood and spat out the pulp. He claimed that was the way Marciano had dieted on the eve of a fight. He became exaggeratedly concerned about his appearance. Once when he visited his mother in Mississippi, he brought back a mysterious bottle of clear liquid that he doused on his hair; and, incredibly, the whisk of white on his temples was black again. A Chickasaw formula. He spent more money than he could afford on tailored clothing. His record collection was large, but not so impressive as it was meant to impress us. I thought he had a lot of middling-to-poor stuff, but when I told him so, he didn't take it well, but very seriously declared that my academic taste, my formal education with its stultifying degrees had destroyed my ability to sense and feel genuine music. His pipes, expensive, handsome, varied in size and design, glowed in their walnut rack on his hi-fi-stereo cabinet. Hampden teased me about sticking to my boyhood tastes for fried pork, hot bread and pies, and for my habit of downing double bourbons, "a poison which attacks the cells of the brain directly." He kept a generous bar, but there was a twinge of superiority in his gestures as he poured for Regina, Fauna and me. Once when I lost a train of thought after six drinks, Hampden remarked that he was glad he didn't require an alcoholic coma for a sense of well-being, that he preferred to keep his wits about him. And suddenly, as I lolled my head in amazement, Hampden dived to the floor, did a dozen fast pushups, stood erect, inhaled deeply and announced, "I won five hundred dollars on the first Schmeling-Louis fight. Any well-conditioned German can take a nigger." The fact that Hampden was about six years old when that fight took place didn't appear to faze him at all. After that, he sat popping chocolate-flavored protein pills into his mouth, chewing slowly and pontificating about the low condition of education. Columbia had gone downhill fast. Everybody knew that New York University was a joke. How could I teach there? Didn't I recall Wolfe's disgust with The Factory and its little Jews? Hampden could ask me this even in Fauna's presence, knowing she is Jewish but genuinely forgetting it because, to him, Fauna was a good Jew because I loved her, so automatically she was removed from his disparagement. When I said, "Goddam it, Hampden, will you cut out this shit?" he was only momentarily rebuked. He seized the word and spun into a long digression about how everybody knew that academic degrees were a lot of shit. Didn't we know that Ph.D. meant piled higher and deeper? Regina was embarrassed. Quickly she served coffee and cake. Hampden, without realizing it, ate two huge wedges of chocolate cake with fudge icing, while delivering me a lecture on my "perverse consumption of pork gravy and bourbon, with all those calories and saturated fats."

Hampden drank once a year. Yearly he went to his doctor for a checkup. After the data on lungs, heart, blood pressure, etc., were out of the way, the doctor asked Hampden how much he smoked. "I smoke a pipe." "Oh, that's nothing." "How much do you drink?" "A quart per year." "Oh, that's nothing to worry about." "But I drink it in twenty minutes." Hampden could not resist the thrust. He wanted to see the doctor swallow painfully. What the doctor didn't know was that once a year Hampden not just got bombed out of his mind but prowled the streets, provoking fights, got badly beaten and was scraped up by the police from some walk or doorway in a dark part of town, and wound up in Bellevue Hospital, ill and penitent under Regina's solicitous gaze. He needed her mutely accusing, tear-filled eyes that he resented and loved. His allergy to alcohol was so severe that even on two beers he became belligerent. Walking out of a bar, he would say, "Dick buddy, I think I could take you." I'd say, "Hell, you don't want to take me. You're tough and hard, and I'm out of shape." "Yeh, yeh," Hampden would say happily, until his tension built again in another fifteen seconds and he would say, "I think I could take you, Dick buddy." When I assured him again of the mismatch—though I could have tilted him into the gutter with a finger—Hampden only sustained his frustrations which ran across his brain in little jerky ups and downs like the scrawl of a seismograph recording earth tremors.

Until Hampden fell off the wagon twice, nearly losing his life the second time, I didn't realize what a corked-up bottle of unflowing violence he was 364 days of the year. His resolves, disciplines, defenses of a rural Southern combat infantry-man in Normandy were the cork in the bottle whose label read: I am the whitest, strongest, most intelligent, industrious and virile man in a city of polyglot, weak-willed, lazy, tax-supported parasites in history. And inside the opaque bottle lay the preserved foetus of a Mississippi waitress who had left her brutal husband for a horse trainer. And the alcoholic father wandering in a kind of dazed, incomprehending sorrow from the ragged pine flats of Mississippi to the sour 50–cent beds in Manhattan's Mills Hotels for transients, and from those wire-mesh cages to his cobblestone death-bed under the cold iron lattice of the 3rd Avenue El near a Chinatown mission.

A faint smile on his smooth face with its large forehead under slickly combed hair, Hampden carved our Thanksgiving turkey. He praised Regina's stuffing—just the proper amounts of salt, pepper and sage, particularly the sage, which he said was the true test of a stuffing. It was a good beginning. Regina was flushed from the kitchen, her nicely done hair coming loose a little bit, attractively, her generous smile warming the room. Fauna had sipped three martinis and her thin face glowed gold-brown with little beads of sweat and oil and her flecked brown eyes had gone fiercely soft like those of a puma. Fauna had let her hair fall down her back "to revive an old lover," she teased. "And besides, besides, Richard, I'm too old for a ponytail, and besides, I'm tired of being the picture of a healthy animal. I want to be a sick intellectual like you!" She pounced down onto my knees. Her small dancer's body felt tight and expansive at the same time. I asked, "Why is it that most dancers get knotty muscles but you stay fluid like a swimmer?" Fauna put her nose against mine and stared, comically cross-eyed. "Because my body *sings,* you funny man." Regina teased, "Well! Do you two want to go upstairs before dinner?" I had had four drinks and loved Regina and Hampden and Fauna, loved myself even. But I became aware that Hampden had begun a sort of dreamy soliloquy, talking to himself again, but demanding that we hear it, just loud enough to register over the Montavani record on the player.

Hampden kept up a sardonic commentary on the writers, painters, lawyers he knew, and books he was editing. I didn't have to listen very closely to notice, actu-ally to hear the pressured vapors of hate escaping thinly past the cork in the bottle: Mailer's tragedy was to have discovered sex at the age of 36. Woodstock didn't paint; he masturbated on canvas. Wealthy teenagers had torn up a Back Bay mansion. They ought, all of them, to be lined up naked and have their cocks sliced off by their homosexual Scoutmasters, and their loss bewailed by a chorus of seven-year-old nigger virgins—at eight, of course, nigger wenches wouldn't be virgins. Eisenhower should have gone into Cuba and swatted Castro like any other dirty fly, not play dead like that drunken Irish boy in the White House, *which reminds me* that history has a curious way of making events turn out for the worse. Hitler, a man of clean habits, of great personal purity, who could have unified Europe and made Napoleon's dream come true, who could have unified Europe against the Communist threat, was defeated by a semi-literate American paralytic and an alcoholic British Tory.

Oiling the bowl of his pipe by rubbing it against the wing of his nose, rapidly chewing another protein pill, Hampden described what, to him, was the final ludicrous breakdown of a soft, liberal society. It involved a current newspaper campaign for safe driving to save the lives of children, and it had been touched off by the deaths of two children who were run down by cars in Jackson Heights. Hampden spoke with slow gravity. "That's the soft society for you. It tampers with survival of the fittest. Remember, Dick, when you and I were kids and our parents told us to stay off the street, we obeyed. We were intelligent enough to stay out of the path of cars. Any kid who is too stupid to stay out of the street isn't worthy to survive." And Hampden appealed to me for confirmation, as one old country boy to another, which was embarrassing in the immediate chatter of protest from Regina and Fauna. Then Hampden drove another nail. "Remember your friend Marty. Marty was a cheap little fag nut who had to drown himself in his own bathtub because he was a Liberal and Liberals have no reason to survive."

Fauna bristled. She had loved our friend Marty, whose tumultuous life and early suicide had echoed her own sense of brevity and terror. Regina rebelled because her husband was guilty of "a stupid generalization." Fauna cried, "That's cruel of you, Hampden. You know that Marty wasn't killed by any creed. He was killed because he couldn't find out who he was. He was the Little Prince. And there's no world for little princes." And Hampden grunted, "I distrust books by French writers who write delicately about wind, sand and stars. I'll take an American like Jim Farrell who belches, farts and screws women."

That evening turned out badly, worse than usual. When Fauna made a retort, Hampden let his resentment of her come into the open. He called her a pseudo-intellectual slob who read Max Lerner and worshipped Eleanor Roosevelt and *dabbled* in faggy dances produced by Charles Weidman from an Ohio humorist whose fables "reeked of homosexuality." When Fauna determinedly told him that art is no respecter of persons, that talent has no sex, that any number of persons with talent, be they male, female or neuter can build something beautiful, Hampden still could not back down without trying to construct another platform. Regina had turned on a television documentary about the Hungarian Uprising. Events had reached the stage where a Catholic priest was gunned down by Heydrich's elite troopers because the priest had hidden a few rebels in the basement of his church. At this point Hampden said briskly, "He ought to have been disrobed first, or unfrocked, or his *dress* taken off, or whatever those corrupt bastards in the Church call it. He was unfit to be a priest. He knew the Laws of the Occupation. The trouble is these gypsy Hungarians have no respect for law. Just like the Jews and niggers. Always breaking the law, then yelling when they are justly punished, *which reminds me* of a lousy book I had a hand in publishing. It was called *Rosaries and Rice,* or something. Lousy book about how when the Red Chinese took over a village where there was this nunnery, they made a rule that the nuns were not to play their radios for a certain period of time. A simple rule. So the nuns played their radios. So the local commander politely reminded them of the rule and requested that the good sisters comply. So, naturally, the nuns, taking orders only from Jesus Himself, turned on their radios again. So the commander quite properly confiscated all the radios. But this nun, this Mother Superior, this Chief *Dyke* or whatever she's called, yelled bloody murder just as if an atrocity had been committed, just as if she hadn't known the law. No civilized man," Hampden said, "could help sympathizing with that poor commander, confronted, as he was, by a plague of locusts on cultural loan from Rome!"

Hampden turned off the TV and put a record on the hi-fi. Regina sort of bubbled with her outraged lips. Fauna started to make a speech. Her father is Catholic, and though she hated him, she had made a kind of hazardous compromise with his faith by getting involved with Dorothy Day's brand of Catholic action. But Fauna was too upset to cope with Hampden. His unrelieved needling had reduced her to a stutter of nerves. She was sweating and short of breath. All she could do was gasp, "Vicious—hateful—vicious!" and try to knife Hampden with her eyes. I said, "Come off it, Hampden. Tell us something you *love,* for a change." Hampden tamped his pipe. He muttered around the stem, "I love truth. I love justice. I was just trying to state certain facts, *which reminds me* of what Pound said about—" and he was preparing to take off on another trap-play up the broken middle of logic when I shot him a glance and said, "Yes, I know what Pound said about Confucius, Roosevelt and the Virgin. What else you got?" Hampden grew silent, morose, and went to change the Montavani record for one by Nelson Riddle.

Fauna and I had lived together for about a year and a half. We weren't what anyone would call happy: either we were ecstatic or in agony, too high or too low, eating apples in bed and whispering or throwing them and yelling accusations. I'm older than Fauna and have sort of run out of hope, lost enthusiasm for many things that excite her, like sitting up all night in a cafeteria on Sixth Avenue, reading the Sunday *Times,* talking with our friends about "the nature of creativity"—all these futile things that the very bright and the very young delight in doing, these beautiful creatures of twenty who haven't yet discovered they will die. And the constant strain of having to try to make everything I said sound like an insight—I was Fauna's hero as well as lover—had got to me, especially since I ran out of money from the novel I had published and had to take this teaching job. I was teaching all day and writing half the night, and Fauna was bringing me coffee or bourbon, whichever, but growing restless about being nothing but a "dutiful beast of burden," as she called herself. When I was working, I would reach out as she passed my table and touch her thigh, not really paying her the attention she craved, and say, "You're such a perfect sensualist, perfectly oriented around food and physical movements." Fauna would retort, "All we have is passion. I'm so utensible! Is that a word, Richard?" Fauna would cuff my jaw and demand a kiss.

Before I took this job, I reacted completely to her spontaneity. We would be munching knishes on Houston Street and Fauna would say, "Richard, let's go ride the Staten Island Ferry. I want to see all that dirty water turn white!" It might be five degrees above zero, but off we'd go, blue in the face, I in a sheepskin and Navy watch cap, Fauna in her latest garb imitative of the wool garments of Peruvian women, and a long shawl. When the wind slapped the wool against her face, and she was about half-shot on Scotch and Drambuie, Fauna said irritably, "Shawls can get *very* mad for having wind blow them in people's faces!" Brushing the tassels away like flies, Fauna looked comic, very young, very dear. She liked to make up malapropisms that imitated her mood exactly. Squinting her eyes against the cold white foam in the boat's wake, Fauna cried, "I must go to an optimist and get some glasses." I laughed, "You want an eclectic skillet, too?" And coming back, half-frozen through the rough, dirty four o'clock morning streets of lower Manhattan, she murmured desolately, "I can't face it, Richard. This place perjures me."

But after I began to teach I didn't have many ways to indulge Fauna's whims and random motions. I couldn't go to bed at four and teach at nine very many weeks in a row. We had built up some tension, anyhow, about a year ago when she slept with a guy, a painter I knew. She had brought home a camera he gave her, and wanted to take my picture with his camera on Christmas morning. I needed fidelity from her, so I kicked her out. She went to San Francisco with her dance group and several weeks later, when she got back to the city, I felt guilty about booting her out—and besides, Fauna and I love each other more than either of us can care for anyone else, by far—so I found out she was working in her spare time for Dorothy Day's projects, like the *Catholic Worker* and the charity farm on Staten Island. I found Fauna and took her back.

Hampden had had to spend several weeks on the West Coast, trying to make big promotional deals, tie-ins between his publishing house and a movie studio—something he detested; he was certain that the Hollywood hucksters and the rich, ignorant Texans were soon going to own New York publishing and dictate policy—and he had Hooded me with picture postcards, usually scenes of swank hotel swimming pools garlanded with "starlets," which, he explained, meant beauty contest winners from Missouri and Nebraska who have to blow moguls. I wrote back, "Dear Hampden, I have read *The Deer Park*." A day or two later, a short letter came. Hampden was at a manic peak:

Hey, Dick!

According to my mythical lady, a Vogelweide is literally a bird-meadow, and vogeln, in the vernacular, is "the bird," or as we would say, "to employ one's bird," possibly in a meadow. Now a small bird such as yours makes a very small impression in a meadow; however, an enormous bird with magnificent plumage such as mine makes every blossom quiver with its flight.

Ho!
Goethe

Hampden's glee about his mistress's publication was not simply boresome. He had called Margery Parsons his "mythical lady." He had become fixed on a little boy's pride in the size of his genitals. I began to worry, and decided to write him a long ramble, more or less just to keep company while he was out there in Los Angeles, but also to tell him about how Fauna and I came together again.

Dear Hampden,

I went to one of these absurd cocktail parties that publishers give to launch new books by writers who sell exceptionally well. This party was for Golding, and the fad is still on, all out of proportion to his accomplishment. Golding takes a thin slice of Conrad's decay theme and exploits it artificially. But I guess the Ivy League sophomores who have made Golding a best-seller haven't got around to Conrad. Before Golding it was Salinger, then Roth, and now it's Updike whose balloon floats over the city. Calder Willingham is going to puncture that one.

At any rate, I went to the party, and there was the standard young promotion whore who does publicity, etc., holding a martini out to me, with a professional smile. Did I want to meet Francis Brown of the *New York Times?* Did I wish to meet Mr. Golding? Would I like another drink? Oh, *yes* Aegean published your novel. It was a very big success, wasn't it, yes. I *knew* I had heard of you, though I haven't read your book yet, something to look forward to.

As you know, I was with Golding at the Queenstown Arts Festival last fall, and he was very English-charming, and his wife, too. But it's difficult to try to talk with someone whose work you don't admire. And I had no reason to want to meet Sir Francis Brown of the worst-best middlebrow review we have. (But I'd still rather read the old ladies' bookclub *Times* crap than the pretentious *New York Review of Books,* with its Robert Lowell orientation, for Christ's sake.) But after a third martini—it was about 4:30 P.M. by then—I had only one thought: to go back downtown to the Village and get my beautiful faithless Fauna back.

I don't really care, Hampden, if you feel it was good riddance when she left. I understand what you mean. But you must realize that you have a damn cruddy antagonism toward Fauna because she fights back when you attack her, just as your Regina does. But you don't have to carry your battles with Regina into Fauna's house. Fauna is an energetic kid of 20 who has to do three things at the same time. She has to love me, has to dance, has to pick up stray poetic con artists like a kid who never had a puppy or a kitten. She has to distribute the *Catholic Worker,* has to boycott schools if Le-Roi Jones says so. There's a starved quality to Fauna, and I've run short of food. But there are many good hours, days, months even, left for Fauna and me, and I'm going to take them because I want her more than any other woman I've ever known. When she becomes restless again, and goes, she will yell and hiss and spit and grab a steak knife, which I'll take away from her, and that will be her way of saying, I love you, Goddam you! Hell, I can see it all, but I want it and I walked straight into it again last night.

Before I got Fauna back last night, I had no way to see, to feel, no way to think and feel the same way at the same time. Too much university and strangeness of new situation with trivial details to absorb like cotton taking up blood, my blood. I need her to feel alive, to know myself. As we used to say in the country, I need her like grass needs horseshit. So there you are. Anyhow, I left that stupid party and went down to the corner of 6th Avenue and 8th Street where she was hawking the *Catholic Worker*. Years ago I met Dorothy Day, who runs the publication and the Worker farm where she tries to rehabilitate rummies, etc., you know, Save the Unemployed Union Men, Save the Negro from Slavery, Save the World from War; she's a fine and beautiful-souled woman right out of Bernard Shaw. And the only flaws in her greatness are (1) that she has a religion, and (2) she is optimistic about people who have to destroy themselves; so she has a priest bless the food passed out to these poor guys who have dedicated themselves, beyond recall, to their own deaths.

It was Friday, about 5:00 P.M., and snowing, and the *Catholic Worker* was out—a very good issue which has some excellent reviews of books on the Montessori method of letting children grow up freely (My God, how you and I could have used some of *that!* As children we never heard of freedom, much less felt it); it's about the Italian *casa del bambini* experiments by Dr. Maria Montessori; and there's also a good article by Thomas Merton in this issue. Anyhow, there on the corner in the snow, looking like a Dreiser waif, was Fauna, without makeup, looking thin, but cheerfully freezing her ass to peddle papers for one cent, one penny, because she believes in what she's doing. Fauna held out a paper. I stood to one side, out of her direct view. She was looking straight ahead, passing out papers, taking in pennies, aware of the presence of somebody, but not wanting propositions from strangers, only to distribute the *Worker*.

Only one cent?
Yes, one cent, sir.
This is a pacifist paper, isn't it?
Well, uh, we promote peace.
I teach in a university. Suppose I get caught reading this?

Well, uh—

(I felt her disgust with an academic square.)

Give me a paper, please, miss.

She gave me a copy and I paid the one cent.

Are you a pacifist, miss?

Yes, sir.

To what lengths would you go to pacify me, miss?

(I saw her shudder slightly and was afraid she had recognized my voice, or my corny humor, or both.)

Her voice was shy.

Why don't you come to one of our meetings, sir? We have meetings every Friday evening on Chrystie Street.

The address?

It's in the paper, sir.

You're a pacifist, miss. You admire Lord Russell. Tell me, do you personally disarm?

What, sir?

If I were to assault you, would you unilaterally disarm and smother me with loving peace?

You really should come to one of our meetings, sir.

I will, if I can buy you a unilateral espresso afterwards.

(She smiled in confusion and irritation at a square, a hick, a simple con man, a recognized antagonist, a mocker.)

I stepped in front of her.

Honey, all you need is a red cap and a little iron pot.

Fauna clutched the papers to her stomach. You? You? Oh. God!

With one thin arm she pointed at my face and began to laugh.

I started laughing, too. We stood there, laughing uncontrollably. People passing by gave quick curious glances, as if watching two lunatics convulsed and about to collapse in the snow.

You! she cried.

No, *you!*

Richard? My own Richard?

She had stopped laughing.

Come on home, Fauna.

Take me home, Richard. Oh, God, take me home!

And that's how we got together again. And, Hampden, if she has to leave her "cruel Richard" I hope it won't be soon. I love her. When will you return from the fleshpots of California so you and Regina and Fauna and I can resume some good habits, like going down to Mott Street for Chinese food?

> Ever,
> Dick

I read over the letter to Hampden. It didn't sound good, at all. I had pleaded my weaknesses. I had pleaded for understanding. I saw myself as a very tired man, excusing my failures in advance. I had identified myself with certain of Hampden's attitudes toward Fauna. But this was not really quite true. It was too pat, too facile to be the whole truth. I know I love Fauna. I know I love Hampden. I know I love Regina. I know I love my student Nathan, who is going to Maryland to protest segregation. I know I love his girlfriend Rama, too. I know I am a loving and desperate man.

Since Fauna came back we have had a lot of good talk, good food, good music—like Horace Silver at the Village Gate, Cecil Taylor at the Five Spot, and Coltrane uptown. Evenings when I have to mark student papers, Fauna reads, waters the plants I bring home to her, dreams of living in the country. She wants to get pregnant and go to Kentucky, and me grow vegetables and her cook them, wants to "know the soil." I realize it's only her new kick. She says, "Give me pleasure. Give me pleasure and babies, Richard. They'll have my skin and your brain."

Watching, listening, I can't keep from loving her. Her hair swirling on a pillow while she reads, her hands trying inexpertly to cook Spanish dishes, her unique creation of a mystifying chaos: a loaf of bread on the flush tank in the bathroom, the sink sponge and her panties stashed in the refrigerator along with frozen shrimp and ice cubes veined with vodka, her clothing in a trail from bathroom to bed as if she were a pioneer woman captured by Indians and leaving bits of cloth for me to follow to rescue her, her eyes sulky and refractory, her face expectant when I come home, her rushing out into the hall to meet me, springing into my arms, locking her legs around my waist, kissing, saying, "Play horsey with me, Richard. I have a good seat, or a good saddle—how do Kentucky girls say it?" I play with her. We horse around, eat at 11:30, play chess until 1:00, play blackjack for dimes until 3:00. By that time I have drunk enough not to care if I have to teach early because Fauna has become magic and her dreams almost believable. If I could believe Fauna, we will have children and eat wild berries and buds and roots and dandelions and live on a mountainside where thrushes sing at dusk, and eat groundhogs and rabbits. Christ, I can see her face if I ever brought her a rabbit I shot, the head pulled off against my boot, the raw carcass skinned and filmed with blood. The poor girl would wet her pants, then puke. But, hell, I'll let her live in an unreal world for as long as she can. I love her too much not to try to keep her happy.

But within a month Fauna began to complain about being the body-servant for a "Goddam professor" who demanded coffee every half hour. "You don't talk to me anymore," she said. "You don't take long walks with me anymore. Why did you take this stupid teaching job, Richard?"

She pushed my papers aside and sat on my lap. "I can give you a year off right now, with my dancing bit, a whole *year*, Richard. We've got the money."

"I can't just resign, honey. I can't just up and quit this job after a few weeks. You know that."

"Job!" Fauna said. She clenched her hands. "All I know is you're killing yourself with this job. You don't write well anymore. You don't talk anymore. You come home dead. Listen. Listen, Richard. You remember what Behan said Dylan said to a cat who told him he had a good job. He said there's no such thing as a good job. A job is death without dignity."

"That's true, I guess. Don't you think I have cursed my poor white ancestors in their Goddam cheap pinebox coffins a million times?"

"Richard. Richard, let's get out of here. You don't need this teaching bit. We've got money enough for a whole year in Kentucky."

"But, honey, what then? It's not just this job. If I walk out of here now, I'll never be able to get another teaching job in any college. And what other kind of work can I do that gives me summers off? The summers are what I have to live for. Then I'll come back to life, and work."

"No, Richard. No, you can't die nine months a year just to live the other three! Listen, Richard. You *said* we could get by in Kentucky, in the mountains, in a little farmhouse on fifteen hundred dollars a year. For both of us, and a baby, too, you said. Listen—"

"But, honey, we don't have money saved up ahead. We can't just go out there for a year and at the end of the year stare up at the sky and pray for manna."

"Listen. Listen, Richard. We have over eighteen hundred dollars in my savings account. Here. Here, I'll show you!"

Fauna leaped from my knees and danced to her dresser and took out a small blue book. She studied it fiercely.

"Honey," I said quietly, "we spend that much a year on Heaven Hill and Liquid Prell shampoo."

"Don't be sarcastic, Richard. We have the money. See? See? Right here." Her fingernail dented the last figure in a column. "Please, oh, please, Richard!"

I said, "You have the money. I have a job."

Her face turned gray as lead.

Communication dwindled rapidly after that. Fauna kept a cheerful mask on her face. I tried, too. Each morning I got up, showered, shaved, and before I left to walk across Washington Square Park to the university, I put my lips on her sleeping face and kissed and pressed gradually until she was half awake, just conscious enough to know who it was kissing her face. I didn't wake her completely—her dance rehearsals were at 4:00 P.M.—but just made her aware of my love before she lapsed again into deep sleep. She would phone me at the university and ask, "Richard, did you kiss me this morning? I think so, but I *have* to know. Richard, did you take your sandwich I made you? I put fresh Italian bread with the left-over steak and lettuce and mashed potatoes and some cottage cheese, just the way—"

"Mashed potatoes and cottage cheese in a sandwich?"

"But, but, Richard, I know how you love them!"

"Honey, please put the tomato juice in the refrigerator instead of the toilet paper, will you, next time?"

"But, Richard, I *like* cold toilet tissues. And in summer I put my panties in the refrig. It's so cool and reassuring."

"Honey, go back to sleep, will you?"

"Do you love me a little?"

"Yes."

"You evil man! You're supposed to say a *lot!*"

"Yes, honey."

"I love you, Richard. When can you come home? I can't wait to talk with you and fuck with you. When you kiss me I get all these crazy things going. I'm Pavlov's bitch. When you ring your bell, I'm ready to go."

"Fauna, my darling."

That was the way it went. I'd get up and find notes stuck on the refrigerator door, the stove, the bathroom mirror—stuck with Scotch tape or masking tape.

Richard,

When you get home I will be at the A & P (a big sale) for some steaks and artichokes. Should be home about 7:00 latest.

Richard's Fauna

P.S. Had some day at Carnegie. Kicked some creep in the balls. He was lying on the floor in the wrong position.

and

Mah dahling Sugah,

Where did I get that from, I wonder!

I'll be at the laundry, the FUCK IT YOURSELF kind. Back about 7:00. I stole a bill from you. Your change is on the table.

I love you so very much today, all day—you'll never know, unless you touch me and talk to me.

"Titty-Boo ME," Lil Old, ah mean.

and

Dearest,

Even if we could not communicate last night, I still would like you to know there is coffee in the refrig, and that I love you. Why don't you wake me up, so we can talk???

Fauna Lawrence

I was getting up slowly in the mornings, dreading the spiritless winter days of lecturing huge groups of students—sometimes 140 at once—in a dingy old theater, a microphone hung on a string around my neck. William Butler Yeats and William Carlos Williams? I had begun to hear myself repeating things into the scratchy microphone. I had no communication with the students, either. And the bundles of papers, wound with rubber bands, were heavy under my arm. Home through the snow to find Fauna curled on the couch, fresh-looking, her hair washed and brushed, bringing me a drink, Fauna, hopeful of the kind of talk and nuance and careful warm touch that we had had months ago. It was pathetic, futile. I could not bring spring to her blood. She could not wait for my summer. I was learning the value of silence. She was beginning to learn the mysteries of speech.

One morning there was no note. I wondered about the last one, signed Fauna Lawrence. She had added my last name. I looked at her pillowed head, her Botticelli face. I walked over and knelt beside the bed and listened to her breath. For one moment I was about to raise the window, throw all the student papers down into MacDougal Street, make a phone call to the university that I had tuberculosis and was going to Arizona, and undress, and crawl back into bed again, and cradle her in my arms, and say, when she sighed and fed me into her, Love me now. And when you wake up, my darling, you can pack a bag for Kentucky. I kissed her nose, got up, went to the closet for a necktie, combed my hair, dropped three sets of keys into my pocket. I had been shown the cities and riches of the Earth, and I was dressed and tonsured for death. Sick, I walked to the table to pick up books and papers for a nine o'clock class. On the coffee table I saw a packet of cards, imitative of IBM cards, with staggered perforations. Fauna had gone into the garish little booth recently set up two doors north by some Times Square con men, and had her "scientific character analysis" clicked off on cards by a computer.

GRAPHOMETER

FAUNA LAWRENCE

Address	Nowhere	
Street	*City*	*State*
Occupation	Nothing	No. 032850

I flipped the packet of cards. They read:

> OFTEN YOU WANT TO BE CENTER OF ATTRACTION
> EXPRESSIVE WITH A VERY ACTIVE IMAGINATION
> YOU ENJOY HIGH STANDING IN SOCIAL GROUP
> YOU SELDOM REFUSE A CHALLENGE
> YOU ENJOY THE COMPANY OF THE OPPOSITE SEX
> YOU PREFER A CAREFREE UNHURRIED EXISTENCE

And beside this crazy packet of little cards was a notice of the school boycott, scheduled for today, February 3. It was published in mimeograph by the Greenwich Village, Chelsea Branch of the NAACP.

The first name I saw was Rex Tolliver. Fauna and I had met him, admired him, talked with him in Queenstown a few months back. We had all his records. We felt Rex was the best of all the horn men going, better even than Miles. There had been a bad scene. All of us were boozed up and I thought Rex had made a pass at Fauna, or they had made passes at each other, or whatever, and I had taken Rex's trumpet away from him and hit him with it. Fauna thought I had slugged Rex because he was a Negro. I guess Rex thought so, too. Trouble, trouble. Naturally I hadn't heard from Rex.

And now he was at the Village Gate again. I buttoned my collar. It was too tight. I went to the university and hung the little black cord of the microphone about my neck.

It was three days before Fauna came back. She marched into the apartment, not even buzzing but using her key. She said, "Hello, Strom Thurmond, how are you today? How's lil old you, Sugah? Still killing time with the college kiddies?"

She was happily, belligerently drunk.

"No doubt you have been celebrating the defeat of the Yankee Germans, Irish, Italians and Swedes in the Civil War—excuse me, I mean the War Between the States. Where are the pigs-feet, Baby? I expected a real barbecue with white whiskey. Or have you been celebrating your great SINS by washing your socks? That's the way the mansion molders, Baby!"

Fauna went to the cabinet and poured me a double Heaven Hill.

"Here, Richard Bilbo Thurmond Byrd, son of Mighty William Faulkner, have a touch. Does that *scan* like 'Hiawatha'? Poet. Poet, my ass. You're dead and you know it!"

She examined her flowers on the windowsill.

I asked, "How's Rex?"

"Rex? Oh, he's great. You should catch him at the Gate before he splits. You should water my plants. Why haven't you watered my cactus—I mean my cacti, Richard?"

Fauna poured herself a thick drink on the rocks and gave me another. I had not eaten all day, and the booze became an angry electricity in my head and stomach.

I said, "You cheap shit, you cheap little whore, I can see you going helter-skelter for three days and nights!"

"Oh, Me!"

"Yes, you, you with your whore's habit of walking insolently before strangers, letting your whore's eyes linger. You, you'd crow over any bastard's cock any morning. I can see you!"

"Oh, can you now?"

"Can I ask honesty from you? No. You always imagine you're on stage. I can see you, you with your simple whore's pride, you can climb on the merry-go-round and hold on to a wooden horse's mane with chipped paint, with your own chipped and peeling soul. You think this is *excitement,* you with your whore's dream of the brass ring, with your childish fist full of candy you never had before. So wear paper money in your hair. Tape it to your breasts. Go ahead. Be Queen of the Carnival in a white dress, you in your flimsy parachute drop at Coney Island, you with your hi-fi mind in your plastic skull!"

"You—" Fauna began contemptuously.

I interrupted, "You don't tell me nothing, for Christ's sake. I can see you."

She brought me another bourbon, and I went back to work on some student's paper on Yeat's Crazy Jane poems.

"Can I stay here tonight, Richard?"

"Stay any place you like. Stay with Cardinal Spellman. Stay with Rex Tolliver. Anywhere you want."

Fauna went into the bathroom. I heard a bottle drop, and a short cry. When I went in, she had two rubber bands looped around her elbow, burrowing into the flesh, making the veins strut. She held a spoon with some white powder and a few drops of water in it. She was trying to warm the white solution in the spoon with a match. I threw the spoon into the sink and broke the rubber bands from her arm. I shook her.

"Who turned you on this junk? Who the hell gave you this junk?"

She held herself against me, sweating, cooing, with hungering mouth and thighs. I imagined her, for the past three days, going from man to man, the half-baked poets, the sleazy painters, the far-out jazzmen.

Fauna murmured, "Yours, yours, Richard, forever and ever."

"Yes, until tomorrow," I said.

Fauna jerked her head back. Her hair fell out in dark rays. Her mouth was dry and blue.

Fauna shrieked, "You Goddam tight-assed bastard! You're just like Hampden! You *are* Hampden!"

She ran to the kitchen and drew my hunting knife out of its leather sheath. She whirled and ran at me with the blade. I turned her arm, the knife fell, her thin body crashed into the window. I took her in my arms. All at once she grew quiet. A half-moon of glass had fallen from the pane. Like two sleepwalkers we picked up the shattered glass and laid the pieces in a saucer. I led Fauna to the bathroom and washed her wrist with white soap, toweled it dry and stretched a Band-Aid across a small cut. I kissed her wrist, fingers, forehead, eyes. I took Fauna to bed and pulled her long hair smooth on the pillow as I entered and felt her ankles come to rest, crossed on my back. After she had come, whispering, "God! God! Oh, Richard! Oh, God!" she fell asleep. I got up quietly, poured a cup of black coffee, and gazed back at her, her mouth still except for small puffs of breath, her high clear forehead where black hair flowed like tar, the sharp little triangle of pubic hair, musky and curled, and her ankles that I could reach around with thumb and finger—all fragile, ill, her head full of father and me, father-Richard, and full of Thomas and Cummings and Ginsberg and Jones, all mouth and vagina, all ingestion and puking, all garlic and whiskey, terror and love. I had never loved and hated anyone so much.

I woke up about 4:00 A.M. A cold wind was driving snow through the broken window. I took a grocery bag and stuck it to the pane with masking tape, dressed quickly and wrote Fauna a brief note to leave her key on my worktable. Then I went out and rode the subway uptown and downtown between the 4th

Street and 125th Street stations, back and forth, until it was time to go to the office.

When I got home in the evening, there were Fauna's keys, as I had asked, and a fresh pot of coffee—her good-bye gift. Fauna left a letter under her keys on my table.

My Richard,

What is your day like? Mine is rejection like it was going out of style. But I know that we're good, if we just could be. *Some* contact is better than none, even if we just touch the same piece of paper. No one can touch, I mean muss up the place in me where the real words ·go and leave their placenta(s?). Fuck/hate/love. Do you know what I mean, my Richard? Because if you don't, nobody else can or will, and I will be too alone, I mean really *loneless.* Is that a word, Richard?

I went in your wool robe downstairs to the candy store and bought a green balloon. I swung the balloon across the street, but nobody saw it. It went up and up, and you were not here to catch it. Is this a terrifying play of/or life?

You keep me more than I can say or stay, but I *want* to stay. You are the only man I always wanted to present me to, like a gift. You are where I can keep from being a shit.

You have your bourbon to come home to, and your old cardboard box of photographs of your poor white parents. But I don't have any of this like you do. All I have is my Richard. I mean all I have is I am more than *sometimes.* Grass implies greenly soon, even under this snow we pile on each other. I mean I want us to be happening/happy.

Please water my plants. Please listen to our Trane albums. Please buy me a thermometer I can stick up my ass so we'll know when our beautiful fucking will make a son for you. Please phone me at OR 4–7200.

Fauna

P.S. William Carlos Williams died today. I don't think he cares.

I made a note to phone her late this evening. Then I went to the closet for a coat, to go downstairs and wrestle Hampden out of the Golden Pizza, drag him up here and drench him with coffee. If he had a weapon to kill me with, I'd have to pin his arms and yell for a cop to help me handle him. I went back to close the window against the snow. I saw Hampden come out of the pizza shop and take off, in a stumbling trot, after a Negro boy.

The Negro boy, about nineteen or twenty, was drooling drunk, and he was following a white girl, pleading with her to talk with him. Twice the girl turned and threw off his awkwardly pawing hand. The third time she stopped stiff-legged and cursed him, her head thrust out like that of a furious goose, hissing at his pained and dejected face. The pity was that I could see he wanted only to talk with her, to be recognized as a human being, a man, a person worth talking to. That was when Hampden caught up with him. Hands clinched, arms stiff at his ribs, body rocking forward, Hampden began to shout.

"You black sonofabitch, where do you come off? You Harlem bastard, just because you're in the North, where do you come off? Do you think you can proposition a white girl on the *streets?* You Goddam black-assed CORE hero! Just because you can knife white subway riders and get away with it, do you think you can get away with grabbing at a white girl on the Goddam street? Where do you come off? Haven't you ever heard of Emmett Till!"

When Hampden attacked the young man, the crowd from the Folklore Center, and a dozen passersby, surrounded them. By the time I ran downstairs and pushed through the crowd, Hampden lay by himself on the walk near the curb. His shirt was soaked with blood, and he was bleeding from the mouth. I took off my coat and folded it under his head. I heard the hooves of a mare that a mounted policeman rode.

"Hampden?"

"Dick? Dick buddy? Dick, they had all these basketballs. They kept dribbling all these balls between my legs and yelling junior Globetrotters! Dick—"

When I realized Hampden was dead, I felt around for the wounds. He had been stabbed several times. But the young Negro boy hadn't done it. He was sitting on the curb, head in hands, in a pool of his own vomit. The policeman dismounted, came over and helped me carry Hampden's body under the awning of a liquor store. I gave the cop Regina's parents' phone number. I told him that I would take charge of the funeral arrangements in the morning. In about three minutes MacDougal Street was flooded red by the circulating lights of police cars and a police ambulance. A dozen policemen dispersed the crowd. On the walk Hampden's weapon lay, a small bone-handled penknife that he used to scour the bowls of his pipes. That was what he had fought his enemies with, and that was what he was going to kill me with, too.

I stood up, looked up. My students Nathan and Rama were staring at me. Nathan, with his anxious white face, Rama, in her subtle passive darkness, her octoroon shadow lightening and darkening as the lights swept across her face.

Nathan asked, incredulous, "Professor?"

I said, "Forgive him, Nathan. And forgive whoever killed him."

Their faces were tight, cold, unanswering.

I asked, "Will you have coffee with me? It's another forty minutes before your bus leaves for Cambridge."

Nathan said, "No thank you, sir."

The sir sounded underlined.

"We were old friends," I said. "At least you could try to respect that."

I took a call from Regina. Between sobs she told me she had phoned a Veteran's Administration official at his home in Queens. The VA were going to fire rifles over Hampden's grave because he was a combat infantryman. I phoned Margery Parsons. She did not intend to go the funeral, but was full of excusing words: "My husband and I have been terribly concerned about Hampden." I phoned the Department secretary at her home that I would not be in for the next two days and arranged for graduate assistants to take my classes.

It was after dark already. I put on my black suit and went downstairs again and sat in front of the *No Loitering* sign on the stoop, waiting. I took out Hampden's penknife and pared my nails.

It is impossible to know what is going on here. Certainly no one person knows. Probably it cannot even be found in the experience of all the people here. There is too much that nobody ever wanted or wished for, but somehow happened.

Some drunk Ivy League brat in a cashmere coat is burning up a beautiful TR 3 across the street. A weekend bohemian on the way uptown to pick up his girlfriend at the Plaza. A car moves through MacDougal Street: Chrysler convertible, New Jersey cream-colored tags; six lesbians coast on a pathetic-lively weekend excursion, phys-ed teachers from some small New Jersey college (anyone for tennis?); a tough baby at the power-steering wheel, a bob-haired, full-fledged AFL-CIO dyke, leading a little colony through the hog-sausage and 20–cent pizza alley of MacDougal Street. God is their eunuch. God is their radiator ornament, a smooth chromed bird without a cock. Among Bronx guitar players, those callow descendants of Nashville and Hazard, the Chrysler glides, stops, moves, stops—you can't get through here on the tourist weekends—among the fat white girls on the arms of Negro folksingers, the lean Negroes and the enormous-thighed white girls from the Bronx and Nebraska with their ribby-proud Negro men who want to be white, in their dirty jeans, the sullen Negro guys who play guitars badly and moan interminable imitations of Belafonte and Ray Charles. And the bob-haired bull-dyke in the cream-colored Chrysler nervously gooses the accelerator, rocking through MacDougal Street. She tries to park for hog-sausage sandwiches with stale fried onions and peppers heaped on buns. She cannot even get close to the curb until the neighborhood boys with spotless leather jackets and tapered black trousers clear the way. The dyke makes a poor stab at parking. One of the Italian boys leans ominously, grinning hugely, and gives directions: Cut, cut, atta baby, cut. When the rattled dyke brings the Chrysler lurching in, all the Italian boys clap hands like rifle fire, and cheer loudly. The lesbians are aware that they are being ridiculed; they grab sausages and pizzas and hasten away, edging the long car out into traffic again, led by the eunuch God on the flood, back, by the Holland Tunnel, to Jersey. The outing has been pointless, the tension created is the juicy necessity to get back to the campus housing project where they can fight to exhaustion over the prettiest field hockey girls, the sleekest tumblers, the swimmers in the Olympics Trials, the flat-chested breast-stroke babies of sixteen, smelling of chlorine and one-piece wool-crotch swim suits.

MacDougal Street has begun to fill up for the weekend. More out-of-town kids drift in: white boys with delicate bangs, tight jeans and sandals; girls with dirty hair, great wallowing buttocks and hanging breasts—they tumble out of old Nashes and Plymouths, sit on the dented fenders and tune their guitars. They sing loudly and off-key: "Ain' gonna study war no more . . . gonna bury that atom bomb right on the White House lawn. . . ."

Two fairies weave through the crowd. The older, brasher fag puts his arm around the younger fellow's neck, sneaks his hand down and pinches a nipple. The young fag, with a huge mass of carefully sculptured curls above a petulant face, chirps, "Don't be so indis*creet* in public. Now *sthop* it!" He leaps away from his lover, curtsies a few paces ahead, waves a white handkerchief daintily. "Well, come on, come on," he calls. He continues, though, to walk about four paces ahead, waving the kerchief. As he passes the candy store, the neighborhood boys cheer loudly. "Yay! Yay!"

As blond and bland as a calendar Christ, a long-haired and bearded boy in black turtleneck sweater beneath his denim shirt, and wearing faded jeans and rawhide boots, saunters self-consciously up and back through the block. He knows he is pretty as a picture and is more than willing to be looked at, his fair medallion profile and pale skin luminescent in the cold wind: Jesus, by Salvador Dali.

A little girl, directly in front of me, calls in a forlorn voice, "Glo-ree-uh! Glo-ree-uh!" There is a pause, then the tousled head of a middle-aged woman appears five flights up, beside her a delicate little girl about eight, her face wearing city-pallor, dying into death early, the little hands and scrawny hair. "Can Glo-ree-ah come down?" The woman's city-voice bellows, "Haf an howah!" The little girl disappears. A boy about six appears beside his mother. The woman takes him into her flabby arms, presses him to her rotund face. She sucks the little boy's ears, mouth, eyes, neck. He struggles but cannot escape. In a moment two girls of eight are turning a dirty rope, one end tied to the No Parking sign. Tourists and natives, indulgent, walk in the gutter among precise coils of dogshit so the little girls can keep the rope turning: "Step on a crack. Break ya mothah's back": girl-chants, city-rhymes for rope skipping, the thin stiff legs awkward, missing the beat, the rope slapping against dirty-fresh girl flesh, skinny, white, dirty.

A beautiful Negro girl idles by, eating a caramel sucker half the size of a paperbook. The Negro driver of a laundry truck slows the machine to a crawl, leans out and calls softly, "You gonna give me a bite?" The girl, obviously flattered, affects contempt. "I give you a bite on you ass!" He grins, asks, "You wanna pull my pud?" She puts him down. "You ain' got 'nough for me to pull on!" She returns the caramel sucker to her mouth. The driver laughs quietly and nudges his accelerator.

A Jewish boy and a Negro boy in their early twenties stop near the stoop where I sit and gesticulate frantically, arguing:

"Become a Marxist or you'll never get your freedom!"

"I don't want your help. You're passive. You can be appeased by the capitalists you pretend to hate. They will give you money, but they won't give me my civil liberties. They buy you off so you keep kicking *me* for *them!*"

"Okay. If you don't want my help, try to do it yourself. You'll see. You won't get your freedom until you come to socialism."

"Socialism! Huh! You're doubly passive. You're a Jew and a socialist. You won't help me!"

They move on, still gesturing, toward the San Remo.

Two Negro men, middle-aged, poorly dressed and carrying a jug of red wine, pass. One says, "I hate 'em all. I hate all the bastards!" The other says, "No, man. I'm a good nigger. I'm a friend of the white man."

In a repainted, salmon-colored Cadillac, two young white couples, the men with open shirts, the girls with gaudy scarves tied over orange-dyed hair full of curlers, brake to a cushiony stop. The driver hits the horn. Above the two-tone horns, a rock-and-roll singer on the full-blasted radio yells:

Let's get drunk and rock all night!
All right, sweet daddy, all right!
Let's get drunk and rock all day!
Okay, sweet daddy, okay!

The neighborhood boys have closed in on the candy store. When a pretty girl who is walking alone approaches, they form a line across the walk, blocking her way. If she moves toward the curb, they move in front of her. They touch her hair, her breasts, her buttocks. Apparently the girls know the rules of this game. If they give the guys a free feel, the line sags, an opening appears, and they can go through. If they fight, they are in trouble. There are several dark doorways near the candy store. Some of the staircases lead to the tarpaper roofs. The girls know this, and they simply turn and twist and slap lightly and make remarks, but they don't make the mistake of becoming too obviously angry.

After a girl is felt and let pass, the Italian boys seize a little kid, a boy about twelve. They practice mass attack. One guy pinions the little boy's arms while another fakes punches to his head and stomach, and kicks to his groin. There is no quaint idea of "honor" here, of one-against-one. They are in the real jungle where a pride of lions will attack a lone zebra. The little boys learn quickly. In front of the candy store the leather-jacketed, slim-pants guys fake punches, wheel, fake, grab, feint—and laugh.

A Negro boy about sixteen pedals up on his delivery bike. It is a three-wheeled contraption, a big metal box on springs, with a bicycle frame and seat behind. Two of the neighborhood boys casually walk out to the curb and stand on the springs of the delivery cart. Jumping up and down, they break the springs, which fall on the left front wheel. Another boy goes up to the seat and crowds the Negro boy away. The Negro boy is paralyzed, afraid to say a word. He knows what he would get. The Italian boy wants to "see how the seat fits." He "fixes" the seat. Meanwhile two other guys in the gang break the right axle of the grocery cart. Without a word, the Negro boy climbs on his wobbling bicycle seat. The cart limps off like a crippled duck, scraping iron and rubber. The jeering calls follow him: "Dun it work bettah dis way? Da wheels is *even* dis way. Din I tell ya it works bettah dis way?"

I got up and crossed the street to the Golden Pizza. I needed cigarettes. The big-gutted boy in charge makes small talk with unescorted girls who come in. He has a tic which makes his head jerk sideways every three seconds. He jerks his head, makes wisecracks, scratches his head, scratches his crotch, scratches his ass, then slices an Italian sausage. He says, "Da guy had five stab wounds. Yeh. Yeh. Right in fronta da Folklore Centah!" In unhurried moments he counts a box of Trojans under the counter.

On the lamp pole in front of Minetta's Tavern, somebody has pasted a crudely drawn cartoon: two Amos and Andy-type Negroes are kissing the cheeks of a white girl between them. The caption is: *New York Post* Legislates Morals. Under the caption somebody else has chalked: Fascist Bastards! On the glass wall of the telephone booth outside the drugstore there is a huge advertisement for the latest wide-screen spectacular. And written across the heroine's exposed breasts is the legend: She Sells More Damn Pussy the Bitch.

In a doorway two small boys are exploding red rolls of caps with pieces of brick. As each one explodes they shout an accompanying "Pow!" Seeing me, they spring up and point six-gun fingers and scream, "You die! You die!" Their pale faces glisten with excitement. I sense the unreleased torture, anguish, murder in their young bodies. In their dark prison of bricks and criminal insanity, I walk past the wet smirch on the cement where Hampden's body lay a few minutes ago. New life has closed around that spot, its cancerous cell that will grow again, rapidly.

Nobody knows what is going on here. No man can make any sense of even his own life for the past week, let alone anyone else's. Less than a week ago Fauna and I sat, holding hands, in the Loeb Student Center of New York University where Erich Fromm gave a lecture, during which he said: ". . . violence is the experience of human impotence to change things and persons by means of reason, love and example . . . violence is the reaction of those who feel incapable of using their constructive human powers. . . ." I know that within three blocks of the lecture hall, while Fromm was speaking, somebody was being assaulted, right then, any then, in any moment as it transforms itself from now to then and is lost; it is lost in violence. In their vivid, hypnotic glee, the little boys shout, "You die! You die!"

I was raised in rough country. I've been shot at. The first time was when I ran up on a guy who was stealing muskrats out of my traps. I was sixteen then. Three days a week, I hang a microphone around my neck and lecture about poetry. I am thirty now. I come home in the evening, drink, dream. Every time I dream, I think I am alive. Every time I remember a dream, I think I have lived. But then I wonder. The disaster of life. Is it beautiful, as I had hoped?

My secretary at the office has a boyfriend who slugged her, blacked her eye, then threw her on the floor and kicked her ribs. That was less than a day ago. I saw her bruised face under the carefully applied makeup. Assault and murder are common forms of love. I think of the young woman crying for help, being kicked by her lover. I think of the poor Negro boy who simply wanted a white girl to talk with him. I think of Hampden, skidding away in the police ambulance, already dead. I think of a young man with a knife that went in five times, running from the police, who will catch him, or not.

I am tired of violence, and that means I am tired of people. People hide under the shadow of the word *inhuman*. But all acts are human. To knife a man is as human as to kiss a child. I am growing tired of people, and that means I am fed up with myself, with my own criminal impulses. I am tired of the horror of everyone and myself. I am full of the horror of people. We are too beautiful and too horrible. Once, in Kentucky, I had a gamecock that won five straight fights in the toughest pits. I retired him to the run. He was a magnificent bird, simple, clean, brilliant of feather. He was life clearly put. His internal principle, his purpose, was to kill and procreate. After that comes the vacuum of politics and psychology. Governments and doctors fail. I fail. Fauna fails. Hampden fails. The yet uncaught man who killed Hampden fails. Everywhere the failure spreads like waves from a single rock dropped into a pool. Love, the very ridiculous idea of love, fails. I do not think people will learn, not love, but the very least kindness to each other in my lifetime. I do not think I will talk about poetry again.

I bought two packs of Pall Malls at the Golden Pizza and came back up here to the apartment.

I lean on the sill in illusory light. In a random pattern other heads darken the old buildings. The snow is falling harder. About eight feet above the rusted cornices of the tenements a three-quarter moon looks motionless and scarred, not yet shining. In the street below there are many blurred shouts and cries. Across the street an old Italian couple live in their only window. The old man wears a white stocking cap indoors. Man and wife trim each other's nails, laboriously, attaching importance to the act, as the old do. I feel surgically removed. I try to inhale the odor of life, feeling a brief sense of being alive when Fauna gives me that dark-eyed unfathomable glance of the chronic New York waif with thin face, herself cold, frightened, her long hair and brown eyes gold-flecked, flaring, diminishing like lights in a theater.

At 10:00 P.M. there are insistent bongos, guitars, shouts, falling bottles. The long sadness of Catholic bells begins. The old couple pause in their single window and cross themselves. Bells from Father Demo Square. Night in a place far from Italy. Without their prayers, without their grief, the God of Peter would become sad as they.

The street boys in their black tapered pants, their black loafers, their white shirts open at the throat, begin to catch huge wet snow-flakes. They begin to catch the snowflakes on their tongues. They field them as if the flakes were baseballs, pivoting with comic grace to catch a flake that burns out in one cold spot on the tongue, for a fraction of a second. They watch way up, to follow a flake as it enters the downdraft of the brick canyon, and trace it all the way down to a car top or the pizza parlor awning. If it falls free, they take it on their tongues and laugh in crazy innocence below the huge snowflakes they take as sacraments on their tongues.

One boy breaks from the gang and begins to dance in the snow. The others set the beat, very fast, with clapping hands. It is not like anything you ever saw at City Center, or in the phony *West Side Story* acrobatics. His dance is alive, real, final.

Somehow, maybe with lookouts, they know when a cop is coming. All the neighborhood boys disappear into the candy store, into the doorways. When the cop walks by, juggling his stick artistically, nobody is there.

The two Negro men, ignored by the thinning lines of people carrying limp slices of pizza, black guitar cases, umbrellas, are setting up their strange instruments under my window. One has a homemade drum, the head secured by strips of rubber cut from an old inner tube. The other has a heavy string tacked to a pine slat and fastened to the middle of a galvanized washtub. Bass and drum. They get all set up, then nod to each other. They play and sing "Route 66" and "Come On to My House" and a few other upjump things. Then they get serious, pause, as if they were in a club or concert hall, to consult about the next number. Slowly, bluely, they begin to play "Sunday Kind of Love."

Nobody pays any attention to them, or to the coffee can they placed on the sidewalk for coins. They play the song in the snowy street without coats or hats, just as if everybody were hearing, or if only they are hearing. It doesn't matter. Their music rises to my window. Their sadness is slow, quiet, sure. They are dead before they start. They know that. We are all dead in this place: white, Negro: dead.

I try to imagine a time of love and goodness. I try to imagine God, or at least imagine a time when God may have lived. There is always a feeling that a human being ought to be more than a brick with an obscene word scraped into its face in an old wall. That a man ought not be in despair, alone, to die in the street, as Hampden did, or die standing up, listening to music, as I do now.

Play Like I'm Sheriff

JACK CADY

Jack Cady was born in Columbus, Ohio, in 1932 and grew up in Ohio, Indiana, and northern Kentucky. Following a stint in the Coast Guard from 1952 to 1956, he returned to Kentucky, received a B.S. from the the University of Louisville, and worked for a time as an auctioneer. This eclectic series of occupations continued as Cady subsequently worked as a Social Security claims representative in Corbin, Kentucky; a truck driver in the Southeast; a tree high-climber in Massachusetts; a landscape foreman in San Francisco; an assistant professor of English at the University of Washington, Seattle; and a visiting writer at Knox College in Illinois, Clarion State College in Pennsylvania, Sitka Community College in Alaska, and Pacific Lutheran University in Tacoma, Washington. He currently lives in Port Townsend, Oregon.

Cady's first book, *The Burning and Other Stories,* was published in 1972 and received the Iowa School of Letters Award for Short Fiction. Set in Northern Kentucky, the title story appeared in *The Atlantic Monthly* in 1965 and was reprinted in *Best American Short Stories 1966.* Three other pieces from *The Burning and Other Stories* were reprinted in *Best American Short Stories* over the next five years. Cady's other work to date includes seven novels, among them *The Off Season* (1996); three additional short story collections, the latest of which is *The Night We Buried Road Dog* (1998); and a work of criticism, *The American Writer: Shaping a Nation's Mind* (1999).

The Burning and Other Stories, which includes "Play Like I'm Sheriff," reveals Cady's ability to portray individuals caught up in invisible, herculean struggles as they face life and attempt to connect. Set in a migratory city, "Play Like I'm Sheriff" first appeared in 1968 in Pikeville College's *Twigs* and was reprinted the following year in *Best American Short Stories.* The story is similar in tone and style to that of Anton Chekhov, Ernest Hemingway, and Raymond Carver in that the dialogue, details, and the unsaid signal an immense undercurrent of meaning.

◆

Sunset lay behind the tall buildings like red and yellow smoke. The cloud cover was high. Shadows of the buildings fell across the circle that was the business center of downtown Indianapolis. The towering monument to war dead was bizarre against the darkening horizon. On it figures writhed in frozen agony, except when they caught the corner of his eye. Then they seemed to move, reflecting his own pain.

About the circle a thousand people hurried. The winter cold was nondirectional as the circle enclosed the wind and channeled it here and there. The temperature was nearly freezing. Lights in store windows began to glow with attraction and importance. Everywhere there was movement.

He stood before a store window, a young man of slight build with uncut black hair, looking at coats. There was tension about his eyes. Occasionally his mouth moved. Muttering. Then his face would tense under a surge of mental pressure.

The mannequins in the window smiled; tiny female smiles dubbed on faces above plaster breasts and too-narrow legs. Some of the coats were gaily colored. Others were black with fur collars. Some were fur. The wind hailed against his thin work jacket but he was not cold. He was accustomed to weather much harder than the kind blowing.

There was no question in his mind that he was a little insane. He sobbed. Not because he was insane, but because his wife had not ever had a nice coat. Only a few times had she had really nice dresses. He felt a deep and very personal shame. She had come so far with him. He sobbed, trying to divert his thoughts and remembering that he had read that madness was never admitted. He wondered if anyone else had ever admitted it to themselves. He thought of the man who would be his wife's new husband and wondered if he would buy her fine clothes.

Farther down the street he believed there might be another store. He walked slowly, looking. Unhappiness depressed his body so that he walked with a slight stoop. Before he found another store a girl idled along beside him, walking slowly, just fast enough.

"Hello," she said, and smiled a little cleaver of a smile. He was taken by the look of her, but in his mind there was no inventory. He was conscious only of a female image. It was very general. Light and dark hair mixed. A slim girl with a pretty face. He was fooled at first, vaguely wondering if she were lost and wanted direction. The word direction sang in his head and caused him to smile.

"Hello," he told her. He walked at the same pace. She fell in beside him. It seemed almost as if they were going somewhere. As if there was a place to go and something that must be done when they arrived.

She was silent for a little while. "Do you know," she said finally, "I've come from home with practically no money. I could stand a drink. Or a sandwich." Her voice had started softly. It ended strained.

He looked at her. "Come on. It's cold here."

In the half light of the bar she seemed younger and more unhappy. He took time to look, surveying her across the table while he felt in his pocket for the fifteen dollars that must buy restaurant food and bus fare to work for the next four days. He found himself wanting to go home, reacting familiarly with despair as he realized for some thousandth time that it was impossible.

As always with women he was shy. Now he did not know how to tell her. He did not want to miscall her and edged around it.

"I'm pretty broke, myself," he told her. "Will be all this week."

She did not leave. She did not seem disturbed about the money.

"I'll pay for the drinks. The money part wasn't true. I have some."

"I don't understand."

She suddenly seemed smaller. Almost like a child. "Talk," she said. Her voice was also smaller. She looked at him as if she were lost. "Talking to. There's lonesome in the wind. I walked to the bus station, and there was lonesome in the crowd. Like something evil hovering . . . I haven't talked to anyone for more than a week."

Her voice, as much as what she said, told him. He looked directly at her. "You're crazy, too. You've found a good ear. A good voice."

"Yes, crazy. I just want to know that someone cares. Cares just something. Want you to know. Want me to know." She hesitated. "You are so unhappy. Look so unhappy. I wouldn't have been able to speak otherwise."

"Maybe no one does care. You said it. There's lonesome all over."

She watched him. Her coat hanging beside the booth was new.

"Norma," he said. "Norma Marie."

"It isn't, but I know what you mean."

A crowd of couples came through the doorway. They were laughing. He watched them then looked at her. "What do they know?" he asked.

"How to pretend," she said. "I don't really like to drink. Let's go."

They walked a long way off the circle to a parking lot. The wind pressed at the back of his legs. The girl wore no hat. Her hair was blowing.

The car was good but not new. She drove it for a long time out of the center of town. He wondered if he was supposed to make love to her, then wondered if he could. Instead of touching her he lit a cigarette and passed it. His hand was trembling.

"No," she said, taking the cigarette. "I don't think so. At least not now." She smiled at him and he felt ashamed, felt himself withdrawing into recollections of another time which held more shame. "I'll do better," he told his wife under his breath. The girl touched his hand.

"Talk," she told him. "Talk away at the lonesome first. Maybe that's all it will be."

"Do you tell me or do I tell you?"

"I don't know." She drove slowly for several minutes. He watched the streets and then the sky where the clouds seemed to be lowering. There was no light except along the streets.

She turned a corner. He realized suddenly that she was also nervous, more than she had been. "My house is down this block," she told him. "I have a whole house."

"You don't even know my name."

"I think it's Johnnie. If it isn't, lie to me."

"You guessed right," he lied. "But I haven't been called that in years." He thought it sounded authentic.

"You lie good," she told him.

"Only to myself."

The house was a tall white frame. The driveway and porch were dark. She parked the car at the back of the drive.

"My grandmother's house," she told him. "Then mother's. Then mine. Any sound will be grandma trying to get out of the attic." She laughed faintly.

"You mean haunted?" He watched her, wondering at her nervousness and at himself. The pressure of his hurt, the tension in his mind, was not relaxed but was relaxing. He quickly pulled the hurt to him because it was his and familiar. "Haunted?" He wondered if she were not worse than himself.

"Sure. Ghosts get as lonesome as people." She tried to smile and it did not work. "At least, I think they must." She stared through the windshield at the sky. "I think it will snow."

She turned to him, the tension seeming to break a little with controlled excitement. "I pretend a lot. Since I was little . . . . Well, for a while I didn't pretend. Yes, I did. But now I pretend a lot. Like when you were little you know, and you said 'Let's play like I'm the sheriff and you don't know I'm here and you come around that corner.' . . ."

"I remember."

"All right. Now, I'll play like Norma and you play like Johnnie and we'll go into our house and I'll fix dinner. And while I fix dinner you can sit in the kitchen and talk. And be friendly. And good, and tell me how well I'm doing, because . . . ." She turned to him. Her eyes held tears that she would not allow to come. "Because he never did, you know."

"But, you pretended." He could not help interest.

"Of course. Didn't you?"

The question alarmed him. He sat watching the sky through the windshield and was quiet for a long time. Finally he turned toward her. "Yes, but I called it lying to myself."

"It is. Do you like the real way better?"

"No." The longing for something that could not be came back hard. He felt it, then fought it, surprising himself. "All right. Pretend." He opened the door on his side and she watched him. He got out, walked in front of the car and around to open the door for her. When she got out it was with a smile that he believed, and not a muscular gesture. "You never did that before," she whispered.

"I will now," he told her. "I will show you more care now, but I'm sorry for before."

"Don't be sorry." She took his hand and they walked around the old house. "People should use their front doors," she told him, "it makes them more important."

The house looked like a museum. The furniture was of mixed periods. He recognized some as old and valuable. There was antique glassware sitting about. The rooms were ordered and neat.

"We are the fourth generation in this house," she said. "It's always good to think that."

"I don't know much about my family," he said truthfully.

"I know," she told him, "but that's not important. As long as we're proud of us."

He took her coat, holding it and looking about.

"Thank you," she said. "The closet under the front stairway will do." She moved from him, through a series of rooms to the back of the house. He hung the coat and his jacket in the closet, which was empty except for an old trench coat. He looked at the coat, thinking it long enough to fit him but made for a heavier man. Then he walked through the rooms where she had gone. He found her working at the counter in the kitchen. The kitchen was modern, contradicting the rest of the house. He stood, not quite knowing what was expected of him. "Can I help you?"

"No," she smiled. "Just sit with me." Her movements at the counter seemed natural and nearly familiar. She looked at him seriously, then hesitated. "I'm glad to have you home." Her voice was faint, but it seemed clearly determined.

He was surprised, then remembered. "I'm glad to be home."

There was a different kind of worry on her face. "I was afraid. Well, you like Charlotte too well. I wish she were married."

He looked at her. "Not that well. A friend."

"Too well, and she's awfully crude."

"Yes," he said. "I wish she would move. Tough. Very hard."

"She's been gone since you left, and I thought."

"Of course. But, here I am."

"Sometimes. Oh, I'm sorry. Sometimes you're hard and I don't understand."

He was startled and then defensive about being charged with something he could never be. "I'll not be that, not anymore. I'm different now, you know. I've stopped losing my temper." He wondered if he were saying it right. The girl had her back turned, working rapidly. Then she turned to face him. Her face held shame.

"I'm sorry about something, too. I was going to kill myself if I didn't find you tonight. You'd been gone so long."

He was startled. "How long has it been?"

"Nearly five months. Your mother called last night and said you were on the coast. She wanted the rings back. She wasn't kind." She turned back to work. "How did you get home so soon?"

"I flew." He did not understand his action, but he rose and walked to her. He touched her shoulder.

"Sometimes," she said, "you used to touch me here." She placed his hand in her hair. "It'd be all right if you muss it." He touched gently under and about her hair.

"Thank you," she said, then turned to him with a pretended smile because the hurt was deep in her eyes. "Now go," she told him, "or go hungry."

"I'd rather go hungry."

Her hands shook over the bowl. "Thank you again," she said. He returned to his chair. "Kill yourself?" He wondered, thinking that she was even more troubled than himself. Then he denied it out of an obscure loyalty to his own trouble. He wondered if there were not more complications than he could handle, and he wondered that he cared.

"My grandmother was so happy," she said. "This fine house, fine husband and nice children. But my mother was not. So I locked her in the attic."

"Your mother?"

"No. You know when we buried her. But grandma died when I was little. I helped carry her things to the attic. They told me . . . . I don't know. Whatever you tell children. But she has lived in the attic ever since. But I locked the door. Against losing her, you know."

"But, kill yourself?"

"By going to sleep. In a special way. Someday, and that day was tonight, I think, it would have come on so very lonesome. With you gone. With you gone. And only people to talk to who wanted to buzz at you. Friends, you know." Her back was still turned. He watched her tense, then clench her hands and he heard the bitterness in her voice. Then her hands relaxed a bit. Her voice was low and strained. Worse, he thought, than it had been.

"When no one cares. What to do?"

"What were you going to do?" He was surprised at the softness of his voice.

"Get the key and unlock the door. Then I was going up the steps. Very narrow. Very straight. And I'd go quietly and catch her asleep. And I'd say 'Grandma, grandma,' and she would come, like when I was little . . . . I had a dog once, remember I told you, but he died. That dog loved me. I played with him when I was a little girl. And grandma loved me—and, she'd touch me and hold me and make me like a little girl again, because, because . . . ." Her speech stumbled and the tensions moved to tears and heavy weeping. "Because I'm so damn lousy—at being a woman."

He moved to her quickly around the counter and held her while she wept. She was tense in his arms. Her body seemed slim nearly to thinness. He was confused. Wondering who. Wondering what was her name.

"Norma," he said, and held her closer.

She raised her head to look at him while still weeping. "Do you want me? Will you want me? I'll do so very badly." She lowered her head. "But I'll try. Because I'm crazy now. I'll be lots better crazy."

"Wait," he told her. "Come now, calm down." He felt nearly afraid. "Come, sit down." He moved to try to lead her to a chair.

"No," she told him. "It's all right. It will be all right." She moved back toward him. He smoothed her hair as he held her. They stood for several minutes until her weeping subsided. Then she turned and left, to come back with a handkerchief. She was trying to smile.

"I took my vacation to find you. The whole two weeks."

The continued pretense made him angry. He reacted in a way familiar to him and became very quiet. It occurred to him that she needed him more than he needed her. It was a strange and warm feeling to be needed. Then it occurred to him that he might be lying to himself again.

"I changed jobs." He paused. "The other wasn't that good anyway." A rush of misgiving overcame him. He had surprised himself by having been taken by the pretense. "I wanted to do better."

"Better?"

"Not right away." He heard shame in his voice. "In a little while you get raised."

"Don't worry about money. Oh, please, not now. Don't worry." She turned to the window then turned back with a tiny laugh.

"See," she told him, "I was right. It's snowing."

He stood and went to the window. The snow was light and carried by the wind. "A light fall," he said.

"It will get heavier." She was placing silver and dishes on the table. "I just have wine." Her voice was apologetic.

"Just a little," he told her. She looked up quickly.

"The table looks so pretty," he said.

"Thank you."

"And the house looks nice."

"I kept it for when you came. Now we'll eat before it's cold."

The meal went well. They ate quickly. She seemed more at ease to him. Once or twice the unfamiliarity of his surroundings surprised him. Or he looked at the girl and recoiled at the pretense. When that happened memories of his wife and memories of his loss and aimlessness came back. His mind would try to recede each time into the trouble. Instead, he would speak.

"When I was little," he told her, "we'd watch a snow like this. Kid hungry, you know. If it were early in the year, like tonight, Dad would watch for a while. If it got heavy he'd get the sleds out of the barn. We'd polish the runners."

"Great Grandfather died on a night like this," she told him. "When I was very little. I mostly remembered the snow. I've always loved it. Like a fresh beginning in the morning."

"You've always lived here?"

"Always here." She looked at him reproachfully, maintaining the pretense. "I didn't know you ever lived on a farm. You should have known about Great Grandfather."

"Yes."

She smiled, then stood to clear the table. "But I'll tell you something the cousins never told you. He didn't come to Indiana because of the oil wells. He left Philadelphia in front of a shotgun."

"Girl?"

"The family skeleton. No, that's not kind to say. Because the girl died soon after. I don't know how."

He helped to clear the table while she placed dishes in the sink. "He was an old rip, I guess. But I've always loved the snow."

While she ran water in the sink he moved to help her. She turned, surprised, but said nothing. They worked together quietly.

He stacked the dry dishes on the counter. When the work was done she began putting them away.

"Do you know," she said, "I'm so tired. I seem to get tired quicker, lately."

He watched her. Unsure. "I figured it out because I'm the same way. Every minute you're awake you're tensed up, burning energy. I sleep a lot."

"Good," she said. "Come with me." She took his hand and they walked slowly through the house to ascend the front stairway. At the top of the stairs she hesitated. He stood beside her, moving away a short distance. He did not hold her hand.

"No," she said. "That way is the door to the attic." There was some quality of determination in her voice. She took his hand and led him down a hall to the front bedroom. The room was very dark until she pulled the shades at the front window. Tall trees stood bare before the house, partially obstructing a streetlight. The snowfall was getting heavier. It was still being pushed by the wind.

"Please stand here," she said and squeezed his hand. He stood, watching through the window and listening to her movement about the room.

When she spoke her voice was faint. "You used to like to watch me but I was shy. I still am but not so much."

He stood watching the snow. The onetime familiar feeling of excitement filled him as the snow swirled about the streetlight. When she stepped beside him she was naked to the waist.

"I love you," she said, "I was so stupid to doubt." Her breasts were lighted by the faintness of the snow-shrouded streetlight. They were shadowed underneath. The light fell across her face and hair so that he saw that she was beautiful with the prettiness. Her face seemed even more sensitive than before. Then across her face there seemed a small realization of fear.

"We stood this way once," she murmured.

He nodded, saying nothing, but knowing that with the fear and the pretense he could not make love to her.

"Would you like to sleep now?" he asked.

"Yes." She smiled. The fear vanished as she saw his understanding. "But, first. Hold me, please." He put his arm about her waist then moved to touch her.

"Thank you," he said, and he did not know why.

"Come." She led him to the bed which was on a darkened side of the room. She lay down and he removed his shoes then lay beside her. He did not touch her. They were quiet. He listened to her breathing. It seemed to him that the darkened room was filled with questions and the questions were mostly about himself.

"Norma?"

"Yes."

"Are you still pretending?"

"I'm not sure. In parts, I think."

He paused. "I always blamed myself, you know. Never figured anyone was wrong but me."

He touched her hand. It was relaxed and did not respond. Her breathing was quiet. For a moment he felt badly. "Maybe I was right," he said. "Nobody does care. Maybe nobody cares for anybody."

"Don't," she said. "You're feeling wrong. Not for you they don't care that way. Maybe they don't care. Not for me. But each cares that no one cares for the other."

"That isn't enough, is it?"

"No. That isn't enough. But it's enough to keep yourself from dying. And, thank you."

"My mind gets so full of the other . . . ." He realized what she had said. He tried to draw back a small feeling of pride.

"And mine," she told him. "But can you pretend a thing until it's real?"

"I think it's what we haven't learned." He touched her hand again. This time she held his. "In the morning when we get up I'll say hello to you. I'll say, 'I love you, Norma' and you'll say . . ."

"I'll say, 'I love you, Johnnie.'"

"And I'll go to work."

"If the streets aren't impossible I'll drive you. Then I'll go back to work. And when work is over . . . ." She stopped. He wanted badly to tell her that at least he was really wondering about tomorrow.

"You don't know," he told her instead.

"That's the truth. Yes. That's the truth. I don't. Maybe it's how hard you pretend, Johnnie." She turned to him and whispered her shyness. "Before we sleep, will you pretend something if it doesn't hurt? Will you kiss me and say good night and call me Catherine? Not Cathy, but Catherine. Then I'll pretend for you and call you . . . ."

He held her and kissed her. He was surprised at her response in the short kiss. Her body against his seemed in some way familiar. He did not know if it was the familiarity of the form of Norma who was not there or the familiarity of the stranger who was. There was a rush of pressure in his mind. He had lived with it for so long. Now he fought it back.

"Thank you, Catherine," he told her. "And, something that just occurred. Maybe you have to love yourself a little first, Catherine."

She touched his hair. His hand felt necessary to him against her back. He wondered what his hand meant to her.

"Pretend, Catherine," he whispered gently. "Good night, Catherine," he said.

The Taste of Ironwater

Jim Wayne Miller

Jim Wayne Miller was born in 1936 in Leicester, North Carolina. He earned a B.A. in English at Berea College and a Ph.D. in German at Vanderbilt University. In a distinguished career as a teacher and writer, Miller taught as a professor of German and creative writing at Western Kentucky University from 1963 until his death in 1996. He also served as poet-in-residence at Centre College (1984); as a visiting professor in Berea College's Appalachian Studies Workshop (1973–1980); and as a long-time staff member of the Hindman Settlement School Writers Workshop.

Known primarily as a poet, Miller published seven volumes of poetry: *Copperhead Cane* (1964), *The More Things Change, the More They Stay the Same* (1971), *Dialogue With a Dead Man* (1974), *The Mountains Have Come Closer* (1980), *Vein of Words* (1984), *Nostalgia for 70* (1986), and *Brier: His Book* (1988). He edited nine other volumes of anthologized poetry and criticism and published two novels, *Newfound* (1989) and *His First, Best Country* (1993).

Although Miller's short stories have not been collected, he produced throughout his career an impressive number of stories since the appearance of "The Lily" in 1958. On the whole Miller's short fiction addresses the ongoing conflict between the traditional and the modern worlds and often explores the defining characteristics of one's cultural heritage. "The Taste of Ironwater," which originally appeared in *Mountain Life and Work* in 1969, explores this theme with a poet's eye and the ability to examine the greater whole through one person's struggle with the symptoms of a greater malaise, separation.

◆

"Remember the time old Haskill Bayes made that wagon with bicycle wheels?" L.C. said. "Run us off Stringtown Hill through that bob-war fence, like to killed us? I don't believe kids down home has fun like that anymore. Shoot! there ain't hardly any kids in Wolf Pen anymore, you know, Buddy?"

"That's right," Buddy said without looking up from the interlocking wet rings he was making on the bar with his glass. He had been sitting there when somebody behind him had hollered "Buddy!" and slapped him on the back so hard he'd wanted to turn around and coldcock whoever did it. But there'd stood L.C. Buck, old boy he'd gone to school with down home, big-mouthed and pop-eyed as ever, sort of frog-faced. Buddy reckoned there wasn't a bar in Columbus he could go into without running into somebody from down home.

"Them was the good times we had down home, you know, Buddy?"

"That's right."

"We didn't know how good we was havin' it, you know?"

"I guess not."

"It's different, you know, livin' off up here, workin,' practically ever'body a rank stranger. Like Imogene and me, we been livin' in this trailer park goin' on two year and we still don't know hardly anybody, not like people down home knows one another. And you take, lots of folks from Wolf Pen's up here workin,' but just gettin' up, goin' to work, comin' home, you hardly ever see anybody."

Buddy stared into his beer. What was he supposed to say to L.C.? He liked it just that way—not seeing anybody. Buddy's Dad had a room over on Oak, was a night watchman at Detrex, but Buddy hadn't seen him in two-three weeks. Didn't want to—him or anybody else. That way people weren't all the time nosing into your business. Maybe L.C. hardly ever saw anybody from down home, but . . .

"Somebody said you was drivin' a truck down in Ashland after you got out of the Air Force," L.C. said.

"I been quit that."

"Where you at up here, Buddy?"

"I'm over at—I'm with Ohio Rubber."

"Shippin' that foam?"

"Yeah, and fan belts, radiator hoses."

"Never figured on you gettin' hitched, though, Buddy. Little time off from the ball and chain, like me, huh?"

Buddy would sure-God like to know where L.C. picked up all his news! "Man, I got two weeks off. Evie's visitin' her folks—out in New Mexico."

"Yeah, somebody said you was stationed out there. What's she look like, Buddy? You got a picture of her?"

Buddy shrugged. "She's blond. That's about it."

"Built?"

"You better believe it."

"You all got a house or apartment?"

God! folks from down home must be the nosiest people in the world. "Right now I'm batchin,' L. C. Lookin' for a place. When Evie gets back— What ever happened to Haskill?" Buddy figured L. C. would know. He knew everything else.

"You know, that scutter went to college. They opened up that college over at Flat—when?—three or four years ago. It's just one building but they say it's college, said old Haskill was on the doorstep waitin' for them to open for business. He was in the Army a couple a years, then he worked here on construction off and on a while. Mostly off—you know how it is. But they say he done real well in his books. I believe he's workin' for the state now and gettin' more school. It's just a two-year thing down there at Flat. I knowed Haskill wasn't nobody's fool, but I never thought he was smart enough to go to college."

"Hell, anybody's smart enough to," Buddy said. "I know guys from the Air Force—"

"You, maybe, Buddy, but not me. I can just look at a book and go right to sleep. Now, I might like the kind of school Ronald Gene Crowder took over in Ashland. You remember him, made a tool maker. If I was a single man, I might sorter like to go into something like that."

"What did Haskill study to make?" Buddy said.

"Don't know exactly. I never got the straight of it—Hear about Odell Kilgore? Made a preacher! Yeah, here in Columbus. Used to be the biggest hell-raiser around, didn't he? Remember the time Mr. Farley had you down in the office for smokin', looked out the window and there went old Odell down on all fours, along that rock wall, sneakin' off to the pool hall? Like tryin' to keep a dog out of a slopbucket, keepin' Odell outta that pool hall! Yeah, he got the call. He's assistant pastor over at the Pilgrim Holiness on Spring. Don't think it pays anything. He works for Lowes Construction. Lotta people from down around home goes over there. You'd think you was down home, the way they sing and shout and carry on. I went over there a time or two—they had a supper. Odell preached a real good piece, full of the spirit."

"Son-of-a-gun," Buddy said. He finished his beer.

"You know, Buddy, if I had my druthers, there ain't a better place to live than down home. People don't put on the dog or nothin'. Imogene and me, we go down home ever' weekend just about, unless I have to work over. Only you can't make a livin' down home, not anymore."

Buddy got up to leave.

"Listen, Buddy, maybe we can get together sometime."

"Yeah, L. C. I'd like to. Soon as I get squared away . . . Evie gets back and all."

Everywhere he went, it was somebody. Maybe it was because he hung out in a lot of beer joints, but ever-where he went in Columbus he ran into somebody from down home, and Buddy Ratliff didn't want to see anybody. He was taking a long vacation. Every morning he lay a long time hearing cars passing, horns blowing, doors slamming, then—

fell out of the sack about noon and put on drinking clothes—Wranglers, a maroon form-fitting, long-sleeved shirt with his initials embroidered on the pocket, and black engineer boots he always polished before he turned in, a habit from Air Force basic,

stood at the dresser in the sour room that smelled of dirty socks and dead air, always with the same wish that his chin and nose weren't so sharp, his lips so thin, his ears so big—like a sad-faced hound-pup,

combed his silky black hair until it glistened and rippled into a DA in back, giving him, when he flexed the muscles in his jaws and narrowed his eyes to slits, the needed dash,

thundered down the steps of the rooming house and hit the light squinting.

He had a '56 Ford but the way it sucked gas Buddy just could make it from one filling station to the next. At least, it seemed that way. So unless he wanted to pawn something else (last week his camera, this week his pistol), he just walked. Sat all afternoon in a tavern, maybe ate chili in a White Castle, then hit another joint and just sat,

nursing one beer for hours,

thinking about Evie, folks down home, and now about Haskill Bayes,

losing himself in the smoky half-light, the noise of a football game on TV, guys sitting and standing, hollering, making bets on plays, or crowded around pinball machines where players hunched the machines and banged the sides with the heel of their hand while the machines rattled and clacked,

filling ashtrays with shredded bits of matchbooks,

listening to the jukebox somebody played,

staring, not really seeing the oily-smooth, red, yellow, blue, green changing of its colors,

just letting his mind idle,

shaking salt into his glass of draft, watching the streaming white tail of beads rise slowly through the gold back to the foamy head.

Day after day.

Funny how you'd mention somebody, or get word of them, the way L. C. told him about Odell Kilgore, then first thing you knew you'd run into them. That Sunday night, around ten-thirty, when Buddy was lying on the bed in the dark listening to the radio, Odell Kilgore came by—Odell in a blue suit, his crisp black hair receding, black eyes staring right through Buddy. And hands—the hardest, roughest hand Buddy ever shook. Buddy was wary of Odell, a preacher now, putting -ings on his words, and Buddy didn't believe Odell had just dropped by on his way from church. How did Odell know where he was staying, anyway?

Yes, Odell was preaching now; he invited Buddy to worship services.

Buddy shrugged. "You know me. Never was much for goin'. Always ruther be out somewheres else, up to some foolishness."

Odell sat in a chair with one foot up on a rung, cracking his knuckles. "You know, Buddy, lots of folks leaves down home and they come off up here to Columbus or some place else, Detroit or somewhere, and they're lost—like they've wandered off the path. You know, Buddy, when we were growin' up down in Wolf Pen, we didn't have the problems we run into later on in life. I come off up here to work and I suffered—suffered spiritually. I didn't know what it was at first; I just knew I was hurting. I was drinking, gambling, submitting to the temptations of the flesh— you name it, brother, I was doing it. Buddy, I was down to the point where my hands just shook all the time."

Buddy dropped his head like a sinner on the back row at a revival. He reckoned Odell was going to give him that treatment.

"I woke up one morning, Buddy, and before I opened my eyes, I knew I was at the parting of the ways. I knew I was going to have to make a change. The Lord spoke to me that morning. He flat out told me I was living against His will. I give in to Him. I said, 'Lord, I'm going to give myself unto you, do whatever you want to with me, not my will but Thine be done, and I'm going to stick with you if it takes the kitchen sink.' And he hasn't let me down, Buddy, not once. You know, Buddy, the Bible says, 'Draw near unto the Lord and He will draw near unto you.'"

Buddy glanced up and Odell laid his hand on Buddy's shoulder. "Are you in trouble, Buddy?"

Buddy shrugged. "Trouble? Shoot, no! Heck, I'm fine, Odell. Got a good job, gettin' in overtime."

"Buddy, I wouldn't be anything but flat honest with you. Your Mom—you know I always thought the world of her—she's worried about you, Hoss. She told me right out in front of the church-house down in Wolf Pen last night, said she thought you's in trouble."

So it was Mom who'd sent Odell. "Mom's a worrywart, always was."

"Buddy, lookit me. You're lyin' t'me. You're out of a job and you know it. Your Dad wrote home, said he didn't think you was working, said you's laid off or quit, he didn't know which, a while back, and he didn't think you ever went back, couldn't get anything out of you, hardly ever seen you anymore. All I know is what your Mom told me, Buddy—about you and your wife separating and all."

Buddy's face flashed hot.

"Your Mom give me your address, Buddy, asked me to come by and see you. Said to tell you she sends her love. You'll be in my prayers, Buddy, and our door stands open, our welcome mat is out."

After Odell left, Buddy cut off the light and lay on the bed where the sign from the auto-parts store across the street blinked red and green on the covers, lay thinking: *They know, they know down home.* Evie never had liked it around home, hadn't liked his folks either. She'd just gone off into a world of her own, got fat, and never had any passion. When she went back to New Mexico to visit her folks, Buddy had known even before he got the letter that she was long gone. Thinking: *They know.* He was going to bawl. His body drew into a knot and he sobbed twice, hoarse, croupy—but he didn't bawl. He lay there with the sign blinking red and green . . . and thought of home.

It was November, and Wolf Pen would be gray and muddy, but he always remembered it the way it was in spring and early summer: the two rows of once-yellow, one-time company houses, the alley in between, not a house square anymore, they'd all been built onto, all leaning, lurching, sinking, porches sloping to one end, tin roofs rusty, rumpled, curled, or tarpapered with black splotches of patching. Catbirds called in willows by the branch; hummingbirds sometimes darted into the yard, blue-green and gold, hovered over flowers growing inside whitewashed tire bodies, in discarded blue enameled buckets, then zoomed off again. And above the rows of tin and tarpaper roofs, almost hidden from view by shade trees—Graveyard Hill, green and neat, even in winter, the only thing in Wolf Pen really kept up (the church did it), with its trimmed hedge, rows of stones and mason jars, with plastic flowers.

He could see them at home: Mom sitting by the coal stove with her Sunday-school lesson in her lap, following the lines with her finger, her lips silently forming the words; his sister Gladys in the green chair by the what-not stand, writing a letter to Jason Thornberry, off working on a drilling rig in Pennsylvania; his brother Frank stomping his feet on the porch, shaking the whole house, coming in from loafing at the store, rubbing his hands over the stove, telling Mom to lay him some supper.

Buddy could see it as clear as the grains of sand on the bottom of a spring. And lying there, thinking of home, hating it, loving it, he was so homesick for that place he could taste it, like lying on his stomach at a spring down home, drinking the ironwater with its rusty taste—water that stained coffee cups, dippers and waterbuckets.

All he had to do was get in the Ford and head out. It was getting on toward midnight. If he left now, he could be home by daylight. He might as well go home, for a few days, anyway. Maybe he could go down and stay until Dad came home Thanksgiving, or if Dad worked then, until Christmas. Then he could go back up with Dad and start all over—looking for another job.

No. He'd been doing some hard thinking the past few days, and he'd decided he couldn't start that shuttling back and forth between down home and a job some-where else—working, getting laid off, or quitting, going home in a junk car and laying around, knowing pretty soon he'd be taking off again, the way his Dad and most men from down home had been doing for years now, since the mines closed. If he went home this time, it wouldn't be just a layover.

He wouldn't have to say a word about Evie. They already knew . . . Mom sent her love.

Buddy didn't mess around when he got a wild hair. By midnight he was out of the room (drawers standing open, key in the door—he would have had to leave in a couple of weeks, anyway, when the rent ran out). In Circleville he filled up the tank on a credit card and rolled on . . . through Circleville . . . Portsmouth . . . over the bridge into Kentucky (Goodby, Ohio, Buddy thought) and down that road snaking through the hills—thinking about a thousand things, but no matter what he started out thinking of, he always ended up thinking about Haskill Bayes and Ronald Gene Crowder, how they did so well in school and got good jobs right there around home. Buddy had thought and thought about it and he honestly couldn't believe old Haskill was any smarter than he was.

By three in the morning he was just a skip and a jump from Redmon. He rolled over the railroad tracks, over the first bridge, boards slapping under the tires. He was warm and awake and whistling like a teakettle, for now every hollow tree, power pole, every cluster of mailboxes, every road sign riddled with bullet holes was familiar; every swimming hole under every rickety bridge held some memory. "Hello, home!" Buddy said, turned up the radio and started singing along.

He skidded up to the two-way stop and sat idling a moment looking at the road signs. It was twelve miles over to Flat. The tank was still better than a quarter full. He decided to drive over to Flat and take a look at that college.

No, sir, there was something about being home—you were surer of yourself. Off up yonder, like L.C. said, even when you had work, you weren't satisfied, because you knew you weren't home. You didn't live there because you wanted to, but just because that's where the job was, so you worked just so you could come home every once in a while. Folks from down home who worked off in the same town might never see one another until they came home on a weekend or holiday, like Thanksgiving or Christmas. Maybe the ones from around home who went to the church where Odell preached, maybe they saw each other more, but . . . It was practically all about death and not enough about living to suit Buddy. Take Graveyard Hill, so pretty and green, so well-tended, like a golf course, practically, but down at the foot, where everybody lived, all the houses about to fall in, the alley in between them black with cinders, everywhere piles of junk with weeds growing out of them, so many people living off commodities, just waiting to die and be carried up on the hill where it was pretty and green.

Buddy's headlights picked up the sign: Flat Community College. He turned down the radio. Off to the right he could see the bluish ring of mercury lights around the college. He coasted into the parking lot and cruised around the brick building, which was entirely surrounded by the parking lot. Well, there she was. He thought colleges had dormitories where the students lived, but he reckoned this one didn't; the students just came during the day and lived at home. That would suit him better if living in a dormitory was like living in a barracks. He rolled back out onto the road.

On the straight stretch he wound the old Ford up and headed home. Way down the road his headlights picked up a possum, its eyes glowing like agates. He whipped around it and started making up a silly song. He was so giddy he embarrassed himself. But he was on home ground now, over the last bridge, his headlights sweeping white-barked sycamores standing by the creek, and he was so excited his legs started trembling. His foot danced on the gas pedal; the Ford went jumping along. Now on past the churchhouse (Hello, churchhouse!), past the store (How do, store?), its front pasted with a hundred tattered snuff, cigarette and soft-drink signs. There was the cut-off.

The road home was worse than ever. Looked like Frank would throw some rocks into the worst holes. He tried to keep out of the ruts, but when he started over the only rise, the rear wheels slipped in and started spinning. Maybe he could spin her right on over the top. He backed up, took a run, showering down on the gas. Didn't make it. Dad-dammit!

He shut off the Ford and sat a minute thinking: The first thing he had to do come morning was get some rocks into those ruts, get Frank to trim his hair, Mom to press his clothes, clean up and drive over to Flat and talk to somebody. Find out how he stood with the GI Bill. He got out of the Ford and started walking in a windy night with high clouds blowing. Dead weeds hissed around him. A dog barked down at Thornberry's. Maybe he'd just come home to loaf like Frank, to haul old folks into town Saturdays to pick up commodities they lived off of while they were waiting to be carried up on Graveyard Hill. But he was sure of one thing: He was not going to be leaving in a few weeks to work a while and then snap back home, like a doll on a rubber band. He was home. If Haskill Bayes could do it, he believed he could. Maybe if he found out what books he had to read and studied up before he started in school. . . .

Graveyard Hill thrust up still and black to his left; beyond it the dark ridge lay like a bearded man asleep. But the sky was lightening behind it, and Buddy could hardly wait for day to come.

The World's One Breathing

DAVID MADDEN

Born in Knoxville, Tennessee, in 1933, David Madden attended Iowa State Teacher's College, the University of Tennessee, San Francisco State College, and Yale Drama School. His distinguished teaching career has included Appalachian State Teacher's College, Centre College, the University of Louisville, Kenyon College—where he was assistant editor of the *Kenyon Review*—Ohio University in Athens, University of North Carolina at Chapel Hill, and Louisiana State University, where he was writer-in-residence and is now the Founding Director of the United States Civil War Center. Madden has published eight novels, among them *The Beautiful Greed* (1961), *Brothers in Confidence* (1972), *The Suicide's Wife* (1978), *Pleasure-Dome* (1979), *On the Big Wind* (1980), *Cassandra Singing* (1969; reissued 1999), and *Sharpshooter: A Novel of the Civil War* (1996), which was nominated for the Pulitzer Prize. He has also published ten plays, several critical and historical studies, and many textbook anthologies, including *The World of Fiction* and *Studies in the Short Story*.

His short story collections are *The Shadow Knows* (1970) and *The New Orleans of Possibilities* (1982). Both showcase Madden's gift for subplot development and his command of dialogue, earning him inclusions in *The Pushcart Prize* and *Best American Short Stories*. Displaying these gifts as well as Madden's intimacy with the culture of rural Eastern Kentucky, "The World's One Breathing" depicts a very modern tension between the callings of the world and the callings of home.

McLain wakes. The motor is idling, the bus is shuddering, and he is startled to see old men rising from seats in the front. "Could have wiped out every one of them," says the driver, "in a single swipe." Three seats behind him, McLain rises to look through the front window. "They must be *living* right."

"Where's *this*, driver?"

"Almost to Truckston."

"Why are we stopping?"

"Ask whoever's driving that rolling whorehouse."

McLain sees now that the bus has stopped alongside an outmoded mauve Cadillac that straddles the double yellow line, the wipers still flapping, the headlights dimming out. Five men stand around it, getting into position to push. An overloaded coal truck, a pickup, and two other cars are parked east and west along the road.

Most of the old men are out of their seats, clustered around the driver, trying to get a good view. McLain glances at them. When he fell asleep, the bus had been empty. The sudden presence of ten or eleven old men surrounding him makes him nervous.

The five men begin to push the Cadillac backward to the side of the highway behind the coal truck.

The bus jolts, the old men reach for their seats, bumping into each other.

"Hey, Rans, stop this slop bucket," says an old man, his voice so deep McLain imagines an injured throat. "Let a body see what the hell's going on."

When Rans stops the bus again, McLain walks to the front. "Listen, I've got to get to Black Damp soon as possible. . . . My mother's dying."

"You don't *sound* like you're from around here, mister," says Rans, looking up at McLain as if he doesn't believe him.

"I've been away. Up North."

"I figured . . ."

"My brother lives around here, though, in Harmon. . . . I'd appreciate your not stopping unless you have to. . . ."

"Okay, mister, leave it to me, you're in good hands when you travel with Rans. Ain't that right, Mr. Satterfield? "

"That's right, Rans," said one of the old men behind McLain.

"Now, these old fellers here got all the time in the world," says Rans. "We dropping 'em off at Harmon for a little reunion of the disaster of nineteen and twenty-one."

"That was before my time," says McLain, trying to be friendly.

Returning to his seat, McLain looks at his watch. Five o'clock. The mountains, like Manhattan skyscrapers, make darkness come early.

"Truckston!" announces Rans. "Here she *comes* . . . There she *goes!*"

In the reek of bodies on the bus, McLain imagines his mother, her breath coming in tiny explosions, lying in the iron bed where his six brothers and five sisters were born—four dying in infancy or early childhood of diseases—where he was the last to be born, a few months after his father had suffocated a mile underground. After her funeral, he will sleep as he must have slept the first day of his life, and wake to gaze through veils of half-sleep upon the company town—as strange to him now as it must have been then.

"Somebody's playing with that snow-machine up yonder. Keeps shutting off and on." The old men think Rans is a card. McLain does not.

In the gray light, a coal truck passes, overloaded, a light skin of snow over the chunks of coal. Hairpin curves, smoke from cigars and rancid pipes, the old men's voices, fits of snow on the windows—McLain dozes.

Fall asleep, I might freeze to death. "Say driver, I wonder if you'd mind turning your heater on?"

"Elmo, is he making fun of me?"

"Can't never *tell* about a Yankee," a one-armed old man replies, goodnaturedly.

McLain wishes he could see the mountains the bus is crossing. He has gone back only in dreams and nightmares. The contrast—being physically in the mountains after eleven years—is a shock, producing nausea, inducing sleep. He slept flying across the continent from San Francisco. In fits of wakefulness between naps on the plane, he felt a drowsy eagerness to see again the mountain landscape that has haunted his dreams. He hates the way these people live, but he cannot reject the mountains that helped to set their style. In his travels for ABC, he was always aware that whenever he moved toward or into mountains, or could simply *see* them from a distance, he began to unwind. But in the lowlands, in the cities, remembering the life he had escaped disgusted him. He had talked himself out of the assignment to cover the explosion of Consolidation Coal Company's Number 9 in Farmington, West Virginia, in December last year, not expecting that the coverage would continue for days, giving him the exposure he needed to make CBS aware of him.

"'Let's remember Pearl Harbor. . . .'" A hunchbacked old man startles his seat partner.

"Who's that singing?" asks the deep voice.

"It's a two-headed anniversary. 'And go on to vic-tor-ry. . . .'"

"But ours comes first. Twenty years ever before I give thought *one* to a jap."

"Besides," says another old man, "it's December twenty-first, not seventh."

And three men are on their way to the moon. McLain shakes his head at the willful ignorance of a busload of old men.

The old men reminisce about the mine explosion in Harmon in 1921. McLain tries to remember hearing about it when he was growing up, but he has forgotten. Their voices are weaker than Rans's. Over the rattle and rumble of the bus, McLain catches fragments. The picture that takes shape is of ten old men, some crippled, some one-legged, some crook-backed, some blind, some afflicted with black lung, journeying to a reunion with other survivors of one of the earliest catastrophes in Appalachian coal-mining. McLain catches the names of those who perished: Grayden, Garland, Buck, Morgan, Frank, Woodrow, Kennis, Hop, Lonzie, Toney. These survivors had moved on to other minefields, perhaps a few to Black Oak before it became notorious for methane gas poisoning and its name was changed to Black Damp.

McLain wants to ask if they remember Tavilas Grybus, but he doesn't want to get drawn into the group. If the rest of the world had forgotten an event it once thought unforgettable, these old men would not have forgotten. Had his father survived the Black Oak explosion of 1931, perhaps he would be sitting among these old codgers, and McLain, living under his father's, not his mother's name, would be. . . . Where *would* he be? Working in the mines? McLain doesn't want to listen, yet he *does* want to listen, but he doesn't want to get drawn *in*.

"Now, I don't remember that feller there."

"I been trying to place him, but for the *life* of me. . . ."

The two old men in front of McLain are silent a while. Then the one-armed man leans across the aisle, holding to the seat in front of him with his only hand, and says, "Hey, mister!" A hunched old man turns around. "We been studying. What's *your* name?"

"Fred Stooksbury."

"Said 'Fred Stooksbury,'" says the one-armed man to his partner. "Well, I don't recall . . . ," he says to the hunched man.

"Don't you remember me? I'm the feller used to always go—" he does a rusty imitation of an old-time locomotive—"and we'd be way underground, and I'd yell, 'Watch it, boys, here comes the Cincinnati *express*!' and every time, some new feller'd forget and jump back, and we'd all laugh. Remember?"

"That's a good 'un. Bet *that* give us all a good laugh."

"Oh, yeah, it was a killer."

"You remember what he's talking about?" the one-armed man asks his friend.

"Seems like I ort to, but for the *life* of me . . . ."

'*For the world's one breathing. . . .*' The words bewilder McLain until he remembers the dream and grasps for the rest. '. . . . *may attain at last true time.*' No, '*may attain at* first *true time.*' "First" seemed so strange last night that now he had quite naturally said "last." After the party, celebrating the end of his first continued report over CBS television, the San Francisco State College riots, McLain tossed and turned until four A.M. Then, out of a half-waking dream came: "For the world's one breathing may attain at first true time." Deliberately, so he could remember the words, he forced himself awake. Then he slept until the telephone rang at seven, and his brother said, "Kenneth? This is Carl. You better come down here, Momma's almost gone." Like the old mountain folk, like his own mother—knowing, when the baby kicked violently in her belly, that its father was trapped in the mine— McLain had dreamed a premonition.

"Buckrock!" announces Rans. "Here she *comes*. . . . There she goes. . . ."

A short way along the valley, TRUCKS CROSSING shows up in the bus lights. The bus slows. Seeing gigantic logs, McLain remembers the days of the logging boom during the war. Bright lights flooding the bus through the front windows make him squint. Looking between the old men's heads across the aisle through the windows, McLain sees an official car parked on the wrong side of the highway, its lights on bright.

A smaller light bounces up to the driver's side of the bus. Rans slides back his window, letting in a spume of snow that curls like a scarf around his neck and fizzles out gently over the heads of the old men.

"That you, Rans?"

"What you doing with your badge on, Hutch?"

"You see anybody afoot?"

"Yeah. Several."

"One of them was probably Harl Abshire."

"Now, *I'll* tell one!"

"He was *spotted*. Stold a Cadillac off somebody. Gas run dry on him in the middle of the highway, and he struck out a-walking it. Reverend Weaver recognized him, offered him a ride, and he lit out running, off into the trees."

"Man that busted out nine years ago, I can't feature him running still."

"We hoped he'd be on this bus."

"Well, if he was, it'd be for free, 'cause I ain't forgot."

"You talk just like the *rest* of 'em."

"And proud *of* it. Mind if I move on? I'm carrying a man that needs to be in Black Damp."

As the bus begins to roll, it occurs to McLain that they might this instant be injecting into his mother's veins the artificial blood of the corpse.

McLain touches a hole in the upholstery of his seat. His numb fingers feel the sharp point of paper tucked there. A love-note, intricately folded, such as he had passed in the white frame schoolhouse. "Dear Lamar, Where *were* you? Love, Tama." McLain refolds it, replaces it, and imagines Lamar reading it.

This morning, Ann and her two kids were among the thousands who watched the Apollo 8 blastoff. He had not had a chance to tell her not to come. Tonight, while the kids go to a movie, she will come to his motel. When the doorbell rings, David Stein will answer. McLain feels that missing his most important coverage for CBS is a disaster, but he suspects that missing his first rendezvous with Ann is, as his mother would say, "a blessing in disguise," for one day she will obtain her divorce, and McLain doesn't want to marry her kids.

"Ain't a jail built by man can hold Harl Abshire." With his cane, the old man whacks the seat in front to stress his point.

"Let the other Abshires get word of this," said the deep-voiced man, "and won't all the deputies in these mountains be able to hold him."

"If they catch him," said a blind man.

You said it, brother, thinks McLain. *The word made flesh. Bigger than words, bigger than life. Even bigger than TV. The drowsy lid, the slack jaw, the snuff-streaked cracked lips, hands limp in lap, reason slack, the pores of the mind closed to foreign matter, wide open to fables. And why not? A hunger the tongue can taste and tell. The compulsion to tell it. Veils of tobacco smoke drifting inside, veils of snow drifting outside.* Beginning to *see* the fugitive now, via the telstar of his imagination, McLain sneers, for he has never heard of Harl Abshire and doesn't like to believe that new legends are born out of such sterile soil. He tries deliberately to see the astronauts, the earth receding at their backs, the moon looming larger, but he cannot get them in focus. When McLain wakes up in Black Damp, they will wake up circling the moon.

"This cold dropped sudden," says Rans. "They was *working* on this highway when I come through here this morning."

As the bus moves across the mountains at a hiker's pace toward Black Damp, McLain thinks of his mother as a skinny old hawk, moldering in her nest. She has never been beyond Harmon, twelve miles from Black Damp, nor wished to see beyond her view of slate dumps, collapsed coal tipples, and dirt slides from strip mining on the surrounding hills. McLain's constant motion and his parents' stasis are relative in time, he realizes, for his great-great-grandfather McLain, an indentured servant, fled a Virginia plantation and lived with an Indian woman in a cave in these mountains—a fugitive for seventy years. The blood of the exterminated Indians still flows in McLain's dying mother. His father had spent half his life dreaming of escaping his native land, a country so small and obscure, McLain once spent an hour looking for it on the schoolhouse map. When he was twenty, his father fled Lithuania, following rumors of the American Dream, and, in a region the nation now rewarded as a nightmare, found the quiet bliss of hard work some men call slavery. And the second half of his life, his father had burrowed deeper and deeper into black gold. Had Tavilas Grybus stayed in Lithuania, McLain would be living now in a country Russia had swallowed. The idea of trying to persuade his mother to see these speculative ironies makes him smile. For his mother called his own escape from Black Damp an unforgivable crime against her and his father. Though he doesn't believe in the crime any more, he is still trying to shake off the guilt. But the force that draws his thoughts if not his body back, no matter how many miles of land and culture he puts between Black Damp and himself, is not just guilt. It is a nostalgia that mocks all his achievements and ambitions, for he feels no nostalgia for the scenes of his gradual escape and ascent—Lexington, Huntington, Pittsburgh.

The bus slides into a curve. The snow is packing and freezing.

"Rans, stop and ask that man does he know anything about Harl."

"You ain't no curiouser than *I* am, but I got a man on here trying to get to his dyin' mother. Schedule has to be met—that's all!"

Turning his head, pressing his cheek against the cold pane, McLain glimpses a man bent over against the snow, trudging up the mountain.

"She was a Hobbs before she married old Abshire," says the man with the injured voice, and most of the others, catching the name, turn around, or lean across the aisle. "Drug him off that hillside rock farm to breathe coaldust. Them days you worked by candlelight till midnight . . . you drug in and fell like a tree cut down on the bed—barely miss your ten-year-old boy as he got up to take your place." The sudden realization that the old man is performing for *his* benefit, startles McLain and he feels shy. "Well, one day Harl says to Mr. Keathley, 'Today, I've turned fourteen and I reckon hit's bout time I *retired*.' After that he never went *inside* a mine, 'cept to plant that dynamite they hired him to set off in May of nineteen and fifty-nine. Took the money them union boys gave 'im and bought coal that he dumped on every unemployed porch in town. That year when the snow was worse than it is now."

"Didn't folks claim it was the worst snow of the century?"

A while later, McLain hears a car pass at high speed, sees it take a steep curve in front of the bus as Rans mashes on his horn with a flourish. "That's okay, neighbor, we'll be along to pick up the pieces d'reckly."

"Shoot," says the blind man, "I bet my ass that was Harl—stold him another Cadillac."

McLain tries to stay awake, straining to listen to the old men. Though they talk of different things their voices meld in a harmonious drone.

"My boy just come back from *De*troit. Not a lick of work *no*where."

"Wick Thompson brung his whole family back from Chicago last week. Come a strike, he said he'd rather starve around home."

McLain remembers the riots in Cleveland last August, the strange sight of looters moving slowly down the sidewalk, as if attracted by a magnet, to a store directly in front of Albert's TV cameras, McLain cautiously moving closer, holding the mike to pick up the voices and the noises of merchandise being wrenched from neat displays.

Suddenly, the sound of a locomotive. Everybody turns and looks at the old man. He croaks: "Watch it, boys, here comes the Cincinnati *e*xpress!" But nobody responds with recognition to the old horseplay routine.

Embarrassed, McLain gazes out the window. Snow, tons of it, falling. Still, as two centuries ago when white man and red man huddled together in the caves one can still see, alongside the auger holes.

"Get ready to cuss, mister, when we hit Hightown," says Rans, his voice sounding different when he speaks to McLain.

"How come?" McLain feels silly, yelling conversationally over the heads of the old men as some turn to look at him.

"Strike. Streets full of folks milling around. Move? Hell, they wouldn't move for a coal truck coming a hundred miles an hour. Poke along from curb to curb like they got forever."

The bus enters Hightown just as a train's caboose clears a crossing.

"Look at that!" says Rans. A plastic Santa Claus hangs from a street light over the main intersection. "Thanksgiving dishes still in the sink and here it is Christmas!" Looped from pole to pole, other decorations hang along the street.

"Well, they got him!" says Rans. McLain recognizes the mountain tone of satisfaction that the inevitable has come to pass.

The old men rise to peer through the glass the wipers have smeared. McLain sees groups of people up ahead—two bunches along the right curb, another strung out from them like an arm, reaching toward the railroad track that crosses the busiest street in the middle of town.

At the edge of the crowd by the curb, Rans stops the bus. "I reckon I damn well have to get out and look, too, mister."

"Listen, I've paid my fare to get to Black Damp."

"Hell," says Rans, getting out, "I'm from around here myself."

Standing in the doorway of the empty bus, reluctant to intrude, hoping Rans will remain aware of him and feel impelled to resume the journey shortly, McLain looks down upon the three separate groups, people in each distracted by activities in the others.

Nearest the bus, people hover around a wounded policeman. Others squat in two ragged rows, examining a trail of blood that leads to the railroad crossing. The policeman's cap lies crown down in the gutter, snow rising in the bowl of it as slush drips from the soles of his shoes.

A larger crowd huddles around a pregnant woman who stands on the curb hugging her son's face against her belly. Around her feet in the gutter lie dented cans, labels smeared, a squashed loaf of bread, liver in plastic wrap. An old man wearing a miner's helmet holds a can of pork and beans, and a young woman keeps brushing snow off a bag of corn meal. The pregnant woman's son holds a carton of eggs, the yolk of a broken one dribbling onto the toe of his shoe. The rest of her groceries, too mangled to pick up, lie around her feet.

". . . coming out of the A & P," she is saying, catching her breath after each word to suppress hysteria, "when he come right at me and kissed me smack in the mouth."

"I *saw* it," says the old man in the miner's helmet. "He stepped right up to her, and her with a bag of groceries in one arm, holding the boy's hand with the other, and he looked to me he had tears in his eyes before he kissed her all of a sudden."

"I never knowed a Abshire to shed tear." McLain can't see who spoke.

"*Then* what?" a girl asks the pregnant woman.

"I dropped my groceries and he bent to pick 'em up, then Sherman come over and said something to him, and Harl shot him and commenced to run in the street and Sheriff Clevenger come out of the cafe shooting at him and hit him and he kept staggering toward the tracks and jumped on the caboose of the train."

A tubercular-looking man muscles into the inner circle of the crowd and looks at the woman, the boy, and the groceries. "What happened here?"

"I saw it happen," said the old man, holding the can of beans in both hands, peering from under the helmet as if from under a rock.

"Let *her* tell it."

"I was just coming out of the A & P and he comes right up to me and kisses me on the mouth."

"And it was Harl Abshire?"

"Sure as the world *was.*"

"Then what?"

"Well, I drop my groceries on the sidewalk."

"He hurt you?"

"No, it was just that it *floored* the fool out of me."

"What did he say?"

"Nothing. Tried to catch my groceries before the poke burst and it all spilled out, him clutching that broken poke against his belly, half-squatted."

"And then what?"

"And then Sherman come up to us and he says, 'Harl, they alooking for you.' Stooped over to him, you know, with his hands on his knees—me in the middle."

The boy twists his face, red from the cold and his mother's grasping affection, and looks up at her.

"What'd Harl *say?*" asks the tubercular man.

"Not a word, he just let the poke slip and reaches over like reaching across the table for a biscuit and takes Sherman's pistol out of his holster and shoots him."

Powder burns had blackened her hands that press the boy's shoulder toward the cradle of her hips. *When her hands thaw,* thinks McLain, *they'll hurt.*

"Maybe he didn't hear what it was Sherman said."

"Likely he didn't." McLain loves the way her mouth moves.

"How come him to kiss you, lady?"

"If they catch him, I'd like to ask him that one myself. And why he let you damned men hire him to blow up that tipple in fifty-nine and get his ass throwed in Harmon jail—and where he's been since he busted out nine years ago."

"You knowed him before?"

"Before he kissed me?"

"Hell, man," says a grocery clerk who has run out into the cold coatless, "her and Harl was sweethearts back yonder."

"You looking for trouble?" She doesn't even look at the man. McLain shivers.

"Don't ever' man along Red Bird Creek know it?"

"Yeah, and now ever' man in Hightown'll know it—my husband to boot."

"*Then* what did Harl do?" asks the tubercular man.

"Say, who the hell *are* you, anyway? Some deputy?"

"No, ma'am. I'm from just up the pike a ways."

"Well, he jumps that freight that was passing through."

Coal gondolas. Blood and snow and slag and the smell of gunpowder and the taste of a woman's mouth. McLain wants to kiss her himself, go home with her, make love to her, inhaling the fumes of coal burning in the grate.

Her eyes rove erratically over the faces around her, but though McLain is elevated in the stairwell of the bus, they don't fall on *his* face. *All that's missing,* he thinks, *is a television camera.* He knows that if he were in possession of a mike, he would be in possession of the scene, and thus of her. And he would not be invisible to her as he was now, but the realest person in Hightown.

Hoping to persuade Rans to move on, McLain steps down, into a vacant place left by a man the sheriff has sent away on an errand. As the sheriff turns back to the wounded policeman, McLain bends over and watches the victim's eyes open.

"I just said to him, 'Harl, they alooking for you," says Sherman. "We used to deer hunt together when we's boys. But I reckon he didn't see my face for my cap. I didn't mean him no harm in this world, Sheriff."

Momentarily, Sheriff Clevenger's shoulder eclipses Sherman's face, then moves again, revealing Sherman's eyes where the light glows faintly, then goes out.

The Sheriff staggers backward as he gets up, scuffing blood into the snow. Looking into McLain's eyes, he says, "Well, maybe *this*'ll satisfy 'em awhile." The intimacy in his voice makes McLain blink, awkwardly. "Who are *you,* mister?"

"Kenneth McLain, trying to get to Black Damp."

"To who?" The Sheriff's knees are wet.

"My mother may be dead by now."

Sheriff Clevenger looks at McLain blankly, then turns away.

Three men stare at McLain. Their eyes glance down, then up, then stare. Looking down, he steps backward out of the blood.

"*Then* what happened?" someone asks the woman.

McLain moves closer to the curb.

"He kissed me. Leaned over my grocery bag and kissed me right on the lips."

"Drunk, I bet."

"Tasted like Pabst Blue Ribbon." The pregnant woman smiles for the first time.

Rans is climbing back into the bus. Men, women, and children crowd on behind him with such violent and common impulse that he is lifted up the last step and hurled into his seat. The door shuts McLain out. He scuttles around the front of the slowly moving bus to the driver's window, using his cold knuckles to knock on the glass.

Rans looks down at McLain. "One man's got to get off!"

The doors open, a boy steps down, and McLain shoves himself up into the stairwell, crams himself between two young men in miner's clothes. The single lamp on their helmets and the grime on their faces subdue their eyes as they look into his.

The bus jolts over the railroad tracks. Through nearly opaque panes in the door, McLain sees the woman on the curb, hugging her child, telling it again. Her lips signify, "I was coming out of the A & P . . . ," but McLain can't hear her voice.

"He'll jump off in the woods before the next crossing." As much certainty vibrated in Rans's voice going out the west side of town as when he had said, "Well, they got him," coming in on the east side.

The bus is packed now with people who want to catch up with Harl Abshire, but who don't want the Sheriff to capture him. They have given seats to the crippled among the old men, and the blind man sits in the front seat above where McLain stands in the stairwell.

"If he was ever going with her, *I* never heard tell of it."

"Fact I never heard of her at all." This old man leans forward from the seat behind the blind man. "Some Damrons up Red Bird Creek, but no Rhetha *I* know of."

"Well, *now* you do," said a man in overalls, who was not in the group going to Harmon for the reunion of the survivors of the 1921 explosion.

"A boy half-grown and another simmering on the back of the stove."

"Reckon who's the father of the first—the one that looks to be *nine* years old?" A woman in a coat the style of the Thirties, probably donated through the Red Cross after last spring's flood, draws the attention of the men seated near her and others standing over her, and she is pleased.

Though the incident was simple enough in naked outline, no tongue, not even his mother's, could tell lucidly enough what the boy's blue eyes had seen.

The bus is a packed hive of talk, heat, smoke, stale breath. Dizzy, swaying on his feet, unable to doze. McLain picks out phrases and snatches of talk.

"More traffic than normal, and the weather worse than usual."

"Roaming around, hoping to get a glimpse of The Fugitive. Hey, that one still on TV?"

"Not if you live in the valley, but up on Pine Mountain, my sister gets it."

"After nine years, ain't nobody can tell it the way it happened."

"Well, say you had the facts? What would you do with them?"

"File 'em away, I reckon."

"Give me a good story *any* day."

Reflected on the windshield, Rans's face glows green and red, his eyes catching sparks of light from the dash panel. As the bus moves up and down mountainsides, the wipers flicker like a camera shutter, and the road winds up on the spool of the wheels like television tape, developed differently by each person on the bus, all of them feeling the same rhythm coming up through the rubber of the tires into the soles of their feet as they stand, through the cushions into their butts where they sit. Harl's eyes are the lens of a TV camera, thinks McLain, recording at high speed, mindlessly, as he runs, scenes McLain and other witnesses reach moments later.

"Harl sent the money in secret some way and they had the monument put up for his momma and daddy."

"Harl was a feller always liked a body to be remembered."

"*Was*? Shut up that *was*. Let Sheriff Abshire—I mean, Clevenger—say *was*, if he can."

"Say, mister," asks one of the old men, looking down into the stairwell, "ain't I seen you somewheres before?"

"Maybe."

"You might not *sound* like you're from around here, but your face ain't a stranger."

Imagining the old man sitting in front of his television, saying to his wife, "I like that young feller's face," delights McLain. But the old man's eyes will dim out one evening soon, as McLain stands in hot sunlight in Jerusalem in front of a cafe a terrorist's bomb has blown to splinters and sand.

When he became an announcer for the television station in Huntington, he imagined his mother sitting alone in the house, her only neighbors the other two widows allowed to live in the defunct company town, watching him on the news. When he went on to Pittsburgh as a newscaster and later to New York City on a local station, knowing that she couldn't pick him up always depressed him. But when he had finally got a position with ABC last February, he imagined his mother watching all the news shows, hoping to catch a glimpse of him, proud of her son when he reported about Murf the Surf from Miami, Robert Kennedy's campaign from California, the race riot from Cleveland, the eruption of a dead volcano from Costa Rica, the murder of Ramon Navarro from Hollywood, Jackie's wedding from Greece, the peace talks from Paris. And as she watched man circle the moon, he had hoped to explain it all to her from Cape Kennedy. But this morning Carl had told him on the telephone that for the past year his mother had lived alone in Black

Damp, and, the other two widows having died, the electricity from Harmon had been cut off.

There is a chance the bus will get him to Black Damp before she dies, and that chance now seems as important to him as the one her dying has denied him. For a man has to get exposure. Look at Dan Rather. He happened to be in Dallas when Kennedy was shot. For days, the nation saw and heard his reports. A few months later, he was reporting from the White House lawn. McLain has been fighting a long time for a chance like that. Following McCarthy and then Kennedy, he watched the sustained coverage of Martin Luther King's assassination, of the student riots at the Sorbonne, of the assassination of Robert Kennedy, of the launching of Apollo 7 with the feeling of having missed some great opportunities for exposure. His feature on the girl who shot Warhol was never used, although the one he did on wall paintings in Harlem streets was shown. His sustained reports from Resurrection City in Washington resulted in an offer from CBS. For weeks he had been covering the student riots at San Francisco State—he looks at his watch—and right at this moment, David Stein is taking his place at Cape Kennedy. It is six o'clock, and he hears a voice, clearly: "This is the CBS Evening News, with Harry Reasoner in New York . . . Dan Rather in Washington . . . Roger Mudd in San Francisco . . . Mike Wallace in Paris . . . Eric Sevareid in New York . . . Kenneth McLain at Cape Kennedy . . . and Walter Cronkite at Cape Kennedy." Now at this "great moment in history"— he hears the voice of Walter Cronkite—McLain's mother is dying and David Stein takes his place. He hates himself for blaming his mother. But her forgiveness for the past and her blessing for the future will be almost enough to make up for the loss.

The bus stops again. The shuddering idle of the old World War II military bus makes McLain feel simultaneously his mother's and Harl's labored breathing, and his own becomes fitful. Dreading another delay, McLain looks between two heads out the front window. The bus lights make the back of a car stand out vividly, though the snow is an undulating curtain. The Sheriff's car, leading the caravan, is parked in the road up the hill, its lights shining on coal gondolas that block the highway at a crossing. They are searching the train and the surrounding woods. As McLain stares, trying to get the total picture and make sense of it, the snow stops.

"I'm getting off here, Rans. See my cousin's Chevy."

"Damned if it ain't Deer Creek crossing! Believe I'll walk it from here. He just might cut up 78 to Raby. I know that holler like I know my own shoes."

When Rans opens the door, a wall of cold air presses against McLain's back and seeps in among the packed bodies, dissipating the hot vapor of breath and body heat that has made him sweat.

"Or he might take a notion to cut south to Breezy," says an old woman wearing an army overcoat. "Come on, Cecil." A fat man in his late thirties takes her hand, stumbles off the bus behind her, drooling, "Snow's stop, snow's stop. . . ."

As others follow, McLain flings himself into one of the empty seats by a window. Car lights come toward the bus. McLain stands again and sees through the front window that the coal train has moved on. The bus begins to roll. Near the crossing, McLain sees cars in front turn off, north and south onto 78, into black wilderness.

"More highway patrol boys toward Harmon," says an old man, sizing up the situation.

A few cars continue west toward Harmon and Black Damp. At the crossing, more people get off the bus. Now, only McLain and the maimed old men and a few others remain. He returns to his original seat. His small suitcase has served as a footstool for muddy shoes.

McLain notices one old man who has not yet spoken, and when others speak to him, he just sits there, like a tongue-tied child. But, somehow his silence gives force and authority to what the others say. With a fellow-feeling for the old man, because McLain himself is silent, McLain glances at him now and then, wanting to hear, if he *does* speak.

Out there, beyond the frosted glass, are the woods. Puny woods since the logging days and after the fires each year. McLain sees only snowbanks that seem to foam against the bus. Above them, darkness. But he imagines trees, ground, pits under the snow that can wrench an ankle as suddenly as a sneeze stops the heart. And Harl is running, gun in hand, steely air rasping his throat, his heart shuddering through his stomach, his legs, his pounding feet, packing down snow. Blood has congealed around the wound, the brass bullet stinging like a wasp. Or has he fallen against the dull-blade edge of a cold rock? Sheriff Clevenger would be glad to see glistening blood.

Watching the headlights of oncoming cars—many one-eyed—approach from far up the highway and pass the bus makes McLain sleepy.

Waking, he feels a hip against his own. "Harl? That you?"

"You all hear that?" The high voice sounds electronically augmented, like a kid's in a rock band. The hip is sharp, an old man's. "Feller thinks I'm Harl Abshire." Cackles clatter in the dark, sharp air. For a moment, McLain thinks it is the silent man. "Got a cigar you'll turn loose of for a nickel?"

"Sorry, I don't smoke."

"I need me a good old Red Dot," he says, getting up. Rans shifts gears and the one-armed old man lunges back to his seat in front of the silent man.

Nine years since Harl broke out of Harmon jail, thinks McLain. *What's he been doing all that time? HONEST CITIZEN OF PLEASANTVILLE, OHIO UNMASKED AS FUGITIVE. The wife and kids will receive word of his flight. Disillusionment. But not hiding in the hills all that time, surely. Reel nine, butchered by forty years' mishandling in the nation's projection booths.* McLain turns to look out the window, sees only his own dull eyes on the pane against the dark. *Then suddenly out of nowhere (think of the millions of things that come out of nowhere—most overpopulated place known to man) an out-of-state mauve Cadillac, abandoned in the middle of Highway 80 outside Truckston, straddling the line, gas tank bone dry. Warm as toast inside, the wipers waving goodbye to Harl, hello to Rans and passengers, as the lights dim and blink and implode. Like the heart's last voltage, seen in the eyes. Survivor's reunion. Mythmaker's reunion. Rake their balls as they talk—radiant heat. Eat, smoke, wipe, spit, fart, rake balls, lift butt and shift, pat belly, belch—embellishments on the evolving figure of the fugitive that bestrides the snow-spread landscape like a figure on a cave wall. The darkness, the cigar, pipe, and cigarette smoke obscure the eyes. Blind old Homers. The ruby lights from the dash, the sweeping lights of passing cars, show only shadowed sockets. Some are eyeless, some lack eyeballs though not the inner light, but all are black hollows in the moving dark of the bus. Blind old Homers. Bards. . . . Rhetha's eyes as Harl kissed her. . . . And did my mother's eyes close forever in that moment? For the world's one breathing may attain at first true time.*

Snow again on the windshield, spitting, trying to stick, wind-whipped.

McLain sleeps in the bed where he used to sleep with three brothers and sisters and his mother, and wakes a few moments later, still on the Red Bird bus. "We to Harmon yet?"

"Not yet." Unable to tell who spoke, McLain wonders if it was the silent man.

"White Station!" announces Rans. "Here she *comes* . . . There she *goes!*"

McLain overhears the old man with the hunched back say to his seatmate, "Don't it seem like you ort to *know* that face?"

As the old man answers, "Well, it being so dark in here . . ." McLain imagines him leaning across the aisle, staring at his face.

"What you want to bet this turns out the worst snow of the century?" asks another old man.

Did something blossom in Harl Abshire, then fall to seed and fester, McLain wonders, *until he had to act? Impulse struck him. In his bed at night beside a respectable, ignorant wife . . . on the toilet in the morning . . . on the road to work in some factory— where? In Indianapolis, Chicago, Detroit, Baltimore? Or some small town? And he had stolen a Cadillac and simply driven in the general direction of his dreams, run out of gas, and started hiking it, as in the old days. Until he came to Hightown.* As strange to him now as Black Damp will be to McLain. He imagines Harl looking for Rhetha at her old house, finding sunken foundations and weeds, or a strange family, or a landslide from strip-mining higher up on the mountain. He searches. Suddenly, he sees her standing on a curb in front of the brutally new A & P, hugging groceries, holding her son's hand, about to step off against the traffic.

What did her boy see? Something to compete with events on television? A happening? A love-in? Who sponsored this Candid Camera setup, this comic situation that backfired? One day, the boy will go over the chronology of his life, and the possibility may occur to him that the man who kissed his mother, then shot a policeman with his own gun, and leapt onto a train passing through town, was his own father. To be given an opportunity to reinterpret radically all one's life up to a certain moment—an exhilarating sense of rebirth? Or the precipitation of a slow dying? *That boy. That boy.* To be envied or pitied?

McLain feels now the loss of his own children. He has lost touch with the girl he met and married in Lexington and who divorced him in Huntington. From the girl he married and divorced in Pittsburgh, he gets only a Christmas card each year, with a group picture of her and the boy and the girl McLain sometimes longs to see in the flesh. His father loved the mines. Well, McLain likes his freewheeling life in New York, always on the move.

In the dark bus, where he sees nothing inside or outside, McLain sees fields full of sunken, rusted machinery, trash dumps, slag heaps, auger holes, coal smoke pouring out of chimneys, wrecked cars in dry creek beds, swinging bridges, mineshafts, junk put to bizarre uses in yards, burnt hillsides, strip and pit mines. When it was still daylight, he saw below him, then lost it, then saw it again above him, a clearing for the expressway that Carl said would wipe out Black Damp by next summer and link the mountains with the U.S. highway.

Where Indians once scalped pioneers of his blood in the forgotten past, merchants in the near future will bloodlessly scalp the tourists who will come to see the driftmouth of the mine where Tavilas Grybus was trapped in 1931. The Chamber of Commerce in nearby Harmon will resurrect that story, which, even as far as Asia, had lived in the headlines for a week. In summer, the log cabins in the hills will be air-conditioned, in winter boarded up. This region that had overslept, yawning in the face of the twentieth century, will finally awaken from the Age of Coal and start to dress for the Age of Space. On the fringe, still, ghostlike denim figures blink at the strange transformation. But the denim too is in the final fadeout. The dead cliches will be resurrected in new shapes and fabrics, and CBS will present them live. Black Damp died five years before McLain fled from it, and now they will bury the decomposed corpse under a lava flow of asphalt. McLain knows that he has never made the break. Now tractors and bulldozers are doing *for* him what he has been unable to do for himself.

Harl hurls himself through the woods, leaving a ragged trail of blood on the snow. *Don't kill him, just catch him. Or let him flag the bus and ride out of Sheriff Clevenger's reach, but move—get me there, Rans.* . . . McLain realizes that the life of the legend will be briefer than his own life, because when these blind Homers die, the habit of nonutilitarian speech will vanish from the earth. So Harl may die tonight, and his story some day after tomorrow, but now, as he runs, he is free—in the lives, the racing imaginations of his witnesses—no past, no future, only the instant. McLain shuts his eyes wearily and hopes to sleep again.

He wakes to see the last of the old men step down in Harmon on a corner he doesn't recognize. They hobble blindly among coal tipples, a single yellow bulb dangling from each. He tries to make out the silent old man, but the dark figures coalesce into a stiff, almost immobile frieze, the silent, the blind, the one-armed, the one-legged, the hunchbacked, indistinguishable from each other.

"Black Damp coming *up!*" announces Rans.

His father's bones never saw the light of day. But McLain did. And he and his mother and brothers and sisters stayed in Black Damp. The owner permitted them to live on in the town, even after the last of her sons left the mines to go to the war or to the defense plants or to the hospital with "black damp," and the mines themselves were sealed. McLain, light and bones, will flee for the last time, and his mother, with his father, and some of his brothers and sisters, will remain.

McLain often sat on the porch with his mother, listening to her tell how much his father loved his life, though he saw daylight only on Sundays and then was "in a fit" to know what to do with himself. "He's buried right where he lived. He never complained when he was alive, and you can bet your stars he ain't complaining now." McLain would look up at the driftmouth, but his imagination could never corroborate her testimony. "The mines'll come back. Just you wait and see." Afraid they might, McLain had not waited to see, he had graduated from high school, knowing that that was the first step out of the mountains. As he grew up, he watched his brothers and sisters leave Black Damp, seldom returning, except for Carl, who taught science in Harmon High. And finally, when he was twenty, having been an announcer at the Harmon radio station for two years, McLain moved to Lexington and took his mother's family name. When he went back to see her at Christmas, she locked the door. But on her deathbed, the bed in which he was born, she will forgive him, release him.

He conjures up the three-room frame house with the small front porch, living room, bedroom, kitchen, the small back porch, the outhouse. Sitting in the television truck last summer during the Chicago police riots, he imagined her working in her garden of pole beans, tomatoes, cucumbers, morning glories climbing the front porch, the back porch, the outhouse, wearing an old-timey sunbonnet that was her mother's. Every spring, the Black Fork of the Pine River flooded the house, and after the water receded, she dragged all the furniture into the yard. Somehow the back streets of Saigon reminded him of the smell of the house in Black Damp, always rank with the odor of floods—one for each year of his past—the smell of fear for each year of his future. And in the fall, the suffocating, acrid smoke of brush fires mingled with the stench of floods and of smoldering slag heaps in the cracks and crevices of the house, in the mattresses dried in the sun, in his clothes, most of them donated after the flood of the year before. As he drifts into sleep again, McLain imagines the slag heaps among which he was born, and rains washing tons of mud down against his mother's white, soot-stained house, and rocks rolling down the denuded hills, hitting the roof. Like the people who lived on the slopes of active volcanoes, she felt at home, and all the places McLain had "covered" were alien.

Someone is pulling at him, he feels like a child, awakened in the night, shoved toward a cold doorway, who must run on numb feet, knees wobbly, to escape fire. Over his shoulder, he sees Rans, getting behind the steering wheel, revving the motor. Looking back into the cave of the bus, McLain sees that the seats are empty—except for the long one at the back, where a man sits, and as McLain stares at him, trying to see his face in the dark, the man slowly, very slowly, keels over. The man is Harl, and McLain decides that he is dreaming and can let himself fall the same way out of the stairwell of the bus into soft snow without hurting himself. He falls, it feels good to let go, he hits the ground, it hurts.

Snow melting in his mouth revives him. Exhaust fumes make him retch, sting his eyes. Veils of snowfall drift over red lights on the rear of the bus as they fade.

Pain, colors ringing in one eye, McLain stands. His eyes on the lamplight in the window of his mother's house, he walks over a white, uneven landscape. The barking of a dog becomes louder, faster, more vicious. As he walks toward the light, dragging his suitcase through the snow, his feet sinking almost to his knees, he is afraid, with each step, each labored breath, the lamp will go out.

White Rat

Gayl Jones

Gayl Jones was born in Lexington in 1949. Her mother was writer Lucille Jones, and her grandmother, Amanda Wilson, was active as a church and school playwright. No doubt influenced by the literary women in her family, as well as her acknowledged spiritual philosopher Don Steele, Jones received a scholarship to Connecticut College; she earned the prestigious Francis Steloff Award for Fiction for her short story "Roundhouse" in 1970 while still an undergraduate. In 1974 Jones published the play *Chile Woman*, and in 1975, after earning her D.A. in creative writing at Brown University, she taught at the University of Michigan, the same year as the publication of her first full-length novel, *Corregidora*. In 1976 Jones published her second novel, *Eva's Man*, and followed it in 1977 with *White Rat*, a collection of short stories. In addition, Jones has published two books of poetry, three other novels, and a critical study, *Liberating Voices: Oral Traditions in African American Literature* (1991). Among Jones's awards are a Breadloaf Writer's Conference scholarship, Shubert Foundation grant for playwriting, an Arthur Miller Award, a Yaddo Fellowship, and a citation as a finalist for the National Book Award. In addition to writing full time, Jones has in recent years taught briefly at Wellesley College in Massachusetts. She lives in Lexington.

"White Rat" is her most well-known and widely reprinted story. In it, as she does throughout her fiction and poetry, Jones explores issues of race, sexuality, and class conflict as central to the human condition. Her penetrating presentations of poverty and anger invite the reader to explore strata of society where he or she might otherwise never venture. The effect is an electrifying combination of repulsion, insight, understanding, and compassion.

◆

I learned where she was when Cousin Willie come down home and said Maggie sent for her but told her not to tell nobody where she was, especially me, but Cousin Willie come and told me anyway cause she said I was the lessen two evils and she didn't like to see Maggie stuck up in the room up there like she was. I asked her what she mean like she was. Willie said that she was pregnant by J.T. J.T. the man she run off with because she said I treat her like dirt. And now Willie say J.T. run off and left her after he got her knocked up. I asked Willie where she was. Willie said she was up in that room over Babe Lawson's. She told me not to be surprised when I saw her looking real bad. I said I wouldn't be least surprised. I asked Willie she think Maggie come back. Willie say she better.

The room was dirty and Maggie looked worser than Willie say she going to look. I knocked on the door but there weren't no answer so I just opened the door and went in and saw Maggie laying on the bed turned up against the wall. She turnt around when I come in but she didn't say nothing. I said Maggie we getting out a here. So I got the bag she brung when she run away and put all her loose things in it and just took her by the arm and brung her on home. You couldn't tell nothing was in her belly though.

I been taking care of little Henry since she been gone but he 3½ years old and ain't no trouble since he can play hisself and know what it mean when you hit him on the ass when he do something wrong.

Maggie don't say nothing when we get in the house. She just go over to little Henry. He sleeping in the front room on the couch. She go over to little Henry and bend down an kiss him on the cheek and then she ask me have I had supper and when I say Naw she go back in the kitchen and start fixing it. We sitting at the table and nobody saying nothing but I feel I got to say something.

"You can go head and have the baby," I say. "I give him my name."

I say it meaner than I want to. She just look up at me and don't say nothing. Then she say, "He ain't yours."

I say, "I know he ain't mine. But don't nobody else have to know. Even the baby. He don't even never have to know."

She just keep looking at me with her big eyes that don't say nothing, and then she say, "You know. I know."

She look down at her plate and go on eating. We don't say nothing no more and then when she get through she clear up the dishes and I just go round front and sit out on the front porch. She don't come out like she used to before she start saying I treat her like dirt, and then when I go on in the house to go to bed, she hunched up on her side, with her back to me, so I just take my clothes off and get on in the bed on my side.

Maggie a light yeller woman with chicken scratch hair. That what my mama used to call it chicken scratch hair cause she say there weren't enough hair for a chicken to scratch around in. If it weren't for her hair she look like she was a white woman, a light yeller white woman though. Anyway, when we was coming up somebody say, "Woman cover you hair if you ain't go'n' straightin' it. Look like chicken scratch." Sometime they say look like chicken shit, but they don't tell them to cover it no more, so they wear it like it is. Maggie wear hers like it is.

Me, I come from a family of white-looking niggers, some of 'em, my mama, my daddy musta been, my half daddy he weren't. Come down from the hills round Hazard, Kentucky, most of them and claimed nigger cause somebody grandmammy way back there was. First people I know ever claim nigger, 'cept my mama say my daddy hate hoogies (up North I hear they call em honkies) worser than anybody. She say cause he look like he one hisself and then she laugh. I laugh too but I didn't know why she laugh. She say when I come, I look just like a little white rat, so tha's why some a the people I hang aroun with call me "White Rat." When little Henry come he look just like a little white rabbit, but don't nobody call him "White Rabbit" they just call him little Henry. I guess the other jus' ain't took. I tried to get them to call him little White Rabbit, but Maggie say naw, cause she say when he grow up he develop a complex, what with the problem he got already. I say what you come at me for with this a complex and then she say, Nothin, jus' something I heard on the radio on one of them edgecation morning shows. And then I say Aw. And then she say Anyway by the time he get seven or eight he probably get the pigment and be dark, cause some of her family was. So I say where I heard somewhere where the chil'ren couldn't be no darker'n the darkest of the two parent and bout the best he could do would be high yeller like she was. And then she say how her sister Lucky got the pigment when she was bout seven and come out real dark. I tell her Well y'all's daddy was dark. And she say, "Yeah." Anyway, I guess well she still think little Henry gonna get the pigment when he get to be seven or eight, and told me about all these people come out lighter'n I was and got the pigment fore they growed up.

Like I told you my relatives come down out of the hills and claimed nigger, but only people that believe 'em is people that got to know 'em and people that know 'em, so I usually just stay around with people I know and go in some joint over to Versailles or up to Lexington or down over in Midway where they know me cause I don't like to walk in no place where they say, "What's that white man doing in here." They probably say "yap"—that the Kentucky word for honky. Or "What that yap doing in here with that nigger woman." So I jus' keep to the places where they know me. I member when I was young me and the other niggers used to ride around in these cars and when we go to some town where they don't know "White Rat" everybody look at me like I'm some hoogie, but I don't pay them no mind. 'Cept sometime it hard not to pay em no mind cause I hate the hoogie much as they do, much as my daddy did. I drove up to this filling station one time and these other niggers drove up at the same time, they mighta even drove up a little ahead a me, but this filling station man come up to me first and bent down and said, "I wait on you first, 'fore I wait on them niggers," and then he laugh. And then I laugh and say, "You can wait on them first. I'm a nigger too." He don't say nothing. He just look at me like he thought I was crazy. I don't remember who he wait on first. But I guess he be careful next time who he say nigger to, even somebody got blonde hair like me, most which done passed over anyhow. That, or the way things been go'n, go'n be trying to pass back. I member once all us was riding around one Saturday night, I must a been bout twenty-five then, close to forty now, but we was driving around, all us drunk cause it was Saturday, and Shotgun, he was driving and probably drunker'n a skunk and drunken the rest of us hit up on this police car and the police got out and by that time Shotgun done stop, and the police come over and told all us to get out the car, and he looked us over, he didn't have to do much looking because he probably smell it before he got there but he looked us all over and say he gonna haul us all in for being drunk and disord'ly. He say, "I'm gone haul all y'all in." And I say, "Haul y'all all." Everybody laugh, but he don't hear me cause he over to his car ringing up the police station to have them send the wagon out. He turn his back to us cause he know we wasn goin nowhere. Didn't have to call but one man cause the only people in the whole Midway police station is Fat Dick and Skinny Dick, Buster Crab and Mr. Willie. Sometime we call Buster, Crab Face too, and Mr. Willie is John Willie, but everybody call him Mr. Willie cause the name just took. So Skinny Dick come out with the wagon and hauled us all in. So they didn't know me well as I knew them. Thought I was some hoogie jus' run around with the niggers instead of be one of them. So they put my cousin Covington, cause he dark, in the cell with Shotgun and the other niggers and they put me in the cell with the white men. So I'm drunkern a skunk and I'm yellin' let me outa here I'm a nigger too. And Crab Face say, "If you a nigger I'm a Chinee." And I keep rattling the bars and saying "Cov,' they got me in here with the white men. Tell 'em I'm a nigger too," and Cov' yell back, "He a nigger too," and then they all laugh, all the niggers laugh, the hoogies they laugh too, but for a different reason and Cov' say, "Tha's what you get for being drunk and orderly." And I say, "Put me in there with the niggers too, I'm a nigger too." And then one of the white men, he's sitting over in his corner say, "I ain't never heard of a white man want to be a nigger. 'Cept maybe for the nigger women." So I look around at him and haul off cause I'm goin hit him and then some man grab me and say, "He keep a blade," but that don't make me no difrent and I say, "A spade don't need a blade." But then he get his friend to help hole me and then he call Crab Face to come get me out a the cage. So Crab Face come and get me out a the cage and put me in a cage by myself and say, "When you get out a here you can run around with the niggers all you want, but while you in here you ain't getting no niggers." By now I'm more sober so I jus' say, "My cousin's a nigger." And he say, "My cousin a monkey's uncle."

By that time Grandy come. Cause Cov' took his free call but didn't nobody else. Grandy's Cov's grandmama. She my grandmama too on my stepdaddy's side. Anyway, Grandy come and she say, "I want my *two* sons." And he take her over to the nigger cage and say, "Which two?" and she say, "There one of them," and points to Cov'ton. "But I don't see t'other one." And Crab Face say, "Well, if you don't see him I don't see him." Cov'ton just standing there grinning, and don't say nothing. I don't say nothing. I'm just waiting. Grandy ask, "Cov, where Rat?" Sometime she just call me Rat and leave the "White" off. Cov' say, "They put him in the cage with the white men." Crab Face standing there looking funny now. His back to me, but I figure he looking funny now. Grandy says, "Take me to my other boy, I want to see my other boy." I don't think Crab Face want her to know he thought I was white so he don't say nothing. She just standing there looking up at him cause he tall and fat and she short and fat. Crab Face finally say, "I put him in a cell by hisself cause he started a rucus." He point over to me, and she turn and see me and frown. I'm just sitting there. She look back at Crab Face and say, "I want them both out." "That be about five dollars a piece for the both of them for disturbing the peace." That what Crab Face say. I'm sitting there thinking he a poet and don't know it. He a bad poet and don't know it. Grandy say she pay it if it take all her money, which it probably did. So the police let Cov' and me out. And Shotgun waving. Some of the others already settled. Didn't care if they got out the next day. I wouldn't a cared neither, but Grandy say she didn't like to see nobody in a cage, specially her own. I say I pay her back. Cov' say he pay her back too. She say we can both pay her back if we just stay out a trouble. So we got together and pay her next week's grocery bill.

Well, that was one 'sperience. I had others, but like I said, now I jus' about keep to the people I know and that know me. The only other big sperience was when me and Maggie tried to get married. We went down to the courthouse and fore I even said a word, the man behind the glass cage look up at us and say, "Round here nigger don't marry white." I don't say nothing just standing up there looking at him and he looking like a white toad, and I'm wondering if they call him "white toad" more likely "white turd." But I just keep looking at him. Then he the one get tired a looking first and he say, "Next." I'm thinking I want to reach in that little winder and pull him right out of that little glass cage. But I don't. He say again, "Around here nigger don't marry white." I say, "I'm a nigger. Nigger marry nigger, don't they?" He just look at me like he think I'm crazy. I say, "I got rel'tives blacker'n your shit. Ain't you never heard a niggers what look like they white." He just look at me like I'm a nigger too, and tell me where to sign.

Then we get married and I bring her over here to live in this house in Huntertown ain't got but three rooms and a outhouse that's where we always lived, seems like to me, all us Hawks, cept the ones come down from the mountains way back yonder, cept they don't count no more anyway. I keep telling Maggie it get harder and harder to be a white nigger now specially since it don't count no more how much white blood you got in you, in fact, it make you worser for it. I said nowadays sted a walking around like you something special people look at you, after they find out what you are if you like me, like you some kind a bad news that you had something to do with. I tell em I aint had nothing to do with the way I come out. They ack like they like you better if you go on ahead and try to pass, cause, least then they know how to feel about you. Cept nowadays everybody want to be a nigger, or it getting that way. I tell Maggie she got it made, cause at least she got that chicken shit hair, but all she answer is, "That why you treat me like chicken shit." But tha's only since we been having our troubles.

Little Henry the cause a our troubles. I tell Maggie I ain't changed since he was borned, but she say I have. I always say I been a hard man, kind of quick-tempered. A hard man to crack like one of them walnuts. She say all it take to crack a walnut is your teeth. She say she put a walnut between her teeth and it crack not even need a hammer. So I say I'm a nigger toe nut then. I ask her if she ever seen one of them nigger toe nuts they the toughest nuts to crack. She say, "A nigger toe nut is black. A white nigger toe nut be easy to crack." Then I don't say nothing and she keep saying I changed cause I took to drink. I tell her I drink before I married her. She say then I start up again. She say she don't like it when I drink cause I'm quicker tempered than when I ain't drunk. She say I come home drunk and say things and then go sleep and then the next morning forget what I say. She won't tell me what I say. I say, "You a woman scart of words. Won't do nothing." She say she ain't scart of words. She say one of these times I might not jus' say something. I might *do* something. Short time after she say that was when she run off with J.T.

Reason I took to drink again was because little Henry was borned club-footed. I tell the truth in the beginning I blamed Maggie, cause I herited all those hill man's superstitions and nigger superstitions too, and I said she didn't do something right when she was carrying him or she did something she shouldn't oughta did or looked at something she shouldn't oughta looked at like some cows fucking or something. I'm serious. I blamed her. Little Henry come out looking like a little club-footed rabbit. Or some rabbits being birthed or something. I said there weren't never nothing like that in my family ever since we been living on this earth. And they must have come from her side. And then I said cause she had more of whatever it was in her than I had in me. And then she said that brought it all out. All that stuff I been hiding up inside me cause she said I didn't hated them hoogies like my daddy did and I just been feeling I had to live up to something he set and the onliest reason I married her was because she was the lightest and brightest nigger woman I could get and still be nigger. Once that nigger start to lay it on me she jus' kept it up till I didn't feel nothing but start to feeling what she say, and then I even told her I was leaving and she say, "What about little Henry?" And I say, "He's your nigger." And then it was like I didn't know no other word but nigger when I was going out that door.

I found some joint and went in it and just start pouring the stuff down. It weren't no nigger joint neither, it was a hoogie joint. First time in my life I ever been in a hoogie joint too, and I kept thinking a nigger woman did it. I wasn't drunk enough *not* to know what I was saying neither. I was sitting up to the bar talking to the tender. He just standing up there, wasn nothing special to him, he probably weren't even lisen cept but with one ear. I say, "I know this nigger. You know I know the niggers. (He just nod but don't say nothing.) Know them close. You know what I mean. Know them like they was my own. Know them where you s'pose to know them." I grinned at him like he was s'pose to know them too. "You know my family came down out of the hills, like they was some kind of rain gods, you know, miss'ology. What they teached you bout the Juicifer. Anyway, I knew this nigger what made hisself a priest, you know turned his white color I mean turned his white collar backwards and dressed up in a monkey suit—you get it?" He didn't get it. "Well, he made hisself a priest, but after a while he didn't want to be no priest, so he pronounced hisself." The bartender said, "Renounced." "So he 'nounced hisself and took off his turned back collar and went back to just being a plain old every day chi'lins and downhome and hamhocks and corn pone nigger. And you know what else he did? He got married. Yeah the nigger what once was a priest got married. Once took all them vows of cel'bacy come and got married. Got married so he could come." I laugh. He don't. I got evil. "Well, he come awright. He come and she come too. She come and had a baby. And you know what else? The baby come too. Ha. No ha? The baby come out club-footed. So you know what he did? He didn't blame his wife He blamed hisself. The nigger blamed hisself cause he said the God put a curse on him for goin' agin his vows. He said the God put a curse on him cause he took his vows of cel'bacy, which mean no fuckin,' cept everybody know what *they* do, and went agin his vows of celibacy and married a nigger woman so he could do what every ord'narry onery person was doing and the Lord didn't just put a curse on him. He said he could a stood that. But the Lord carried the curse clear over to the next generation and put a curse on his little baby boy who didn do nothing in his whole life . . . cept come." I laugh and laugh. Then when I quit laughing I drink some more, and then when I quit drinking I talk some more. "And you know something else?" I say. This time he say, "No." I say, "I knew another priest what took the vows, only this priest was white. You wanta know what happen to him. He broke his vows same as the nigger and got married same as the nigger. And they had a baby too. Want to know what happen to him?" "What?" "He come out a nigger."

Then I get so drunk I can't go no place but home. I'm thinking it's the Hawk's house, not hers. If anybody get throwed out it's her. She the nigger. I'm goin' fool her. Throw her right *out* the bed if she in it. But then when I get home I'm the one that's fool. Cause she gone *and* little Henry gone. So I guess I just badmouthed the walls like the devil till I jus' layed down and went to sleep. The next morning little Henry come back with a neighbor woman but Maggie don't come. The woman hand over little Henry, and I ask her, "Where Maggie?" She looked at me like she think I'm the devil and say, "I don't know, but she lef' me this note to give to you." So she jus' give me the note and went. I open the note and read. She write like a chicken too, I'm thinking, chicken scratch. I read: "I run off with J.T. cause he been wanting me to run off with him and I ain't been wanting to tell now. I'm send litle Henry back cause I just took him away last night cause I didn't want you to be doing nothing you regrit in the morning." So I figured she figured I got to stay sober if I got to take care of myself and little Henry. Little Henry didn't say nothing and I didn't say nothing. I just put him on in the house and let him play with hisself.

That was two months ago. I ain't take a drop since. But last night Cousin Willie come and say where Maggie was and now she moving around in the kitchen and feeding little Henry and I guess when I get up she feed me. I get up and get dressed and go in the kitchen. She say when the new baby come we see whose fault it was. J.T. blacker'n a lump of coal. Maggie keep saying "When the baby come we see who fault it was." It's two more months now that I been look at her, but I still don't see no belly change.

The Affair with Rachel Ware

Jane Stuart

Born Jessica Jane Stuart in Ashland, Kentucky, in 1942, Stuart is the only child of the writer Jesse Stuart and his wife, Naomi. Her first published work, *A Year's Harvest*, appeared in 1957 while she was still in high school. She subsequently attended Stuart Hall, a preparatory school in Staunton, Virginia, and Western Reserve University (now Case Western) in Cleveland, Ohio, where in 1964 she received her A.B. with majors in Greek and Latin. Following her undergraduate degree, Stuart attended Indiana University in Bloomington, where she received master's degrees in classical languages and literature and a Ph.D. in Latin. She has taught and lectured at several colleges and universities, mostly in Florida. Her published work includes eight collections of poetry, among them *Eyes of the Mole* (1967); *Transparencies* (1986), which also includes some prose; *The Wren and Other Poems* (1993); *Passage into Time* (1994); *Cherokee Lullaby* (1995); and *Journeys* (1998). Her novels include *Yellowhawk* (1973), *Passerman's Hollow* (1974), and *Land of the Fox* (1976). To date she has published one collection of short stories, *Gideon's Children* (1976).

Like her father's work, Jane Stuart's poetry and novels concern themselves primarily with the Kentucky experience. Her short fiction, however, displays the urgency and immediacy so critical to the success of a modern short story. The stories in *Gideon's Children* are glimpses of the human condition and seem to depend upon a certain sense of familiarity and the reader's recognition of circumstances and attitudes. "The Affair With Rachel Ware" offers the reader familiar suburban circumstances and a self-absorbed protagonist whose attitude is consistent with the era. Like so many modern short stories, this story reflects timeless questions concerning motive and the human capacity to connect with each other.

◆

The problems all began with the woman next door, and they shouldn't have. That is, there shouldn't have been any problems, because life was just like that. Men and women, birds and bees. Springtime and the fancies of a first love always passed. After that came the summer, and, when people loved then, you just didn't talk about it. You assumed that they were old enough to know what they were doing and you left them alone. You didn't point your finger at the woman next door, and snicker. You didn't wink knowingly at that woman's neighbor, either, implying that you knew he was getting it. You left them alone. You let them lie in their bed of summer roses, and if you knew, really knew what was going on, you kept your mouth shut. All that talking just showed that you were jealous, anyhow.

Jealous, or impotent maybe, Harry thought with a shrug. Oh well, people were people. Everywhere the same. If there weren't any problems, they'd find some. They'd dig them up from the past or make them up from right now. Life was, it seemed, intended to be one continuous soap opera. Sponsored by Brillo-pad minds and syrupy sweet whispers. Hush-hush words croaked out during the brief intermissions of what-was-going-on-next-door.

Shit, Harry thought. What a mess he had made of his simple life. Or rather, what a mess *they* had made of it. Tried to make of it. Made of it.

And all because of Rachel Ware.

Maybe it didn't really matter, though, Harry thought, now that it was all over.

What was over, though? What could ever really *be over?* What had happened had happened, and there was no way of erasing it now. It would be a part of him forever, his first stigma in small-town life, small Southern town university life. A cross to bear that they would assign to him forever.

So that was Christianity, bearing a cross forever? Never being able to forget, never being forgotten? Whenever some new couple moved into the community and asked about the house next door, they'd be told, *Oh, yes, the Wares used to live there. . . . They moved, of course. She was having an affair with Harry Thomas. . . . He still lives here.* And then when he met the new people, the Jacobses or the Izaras or the Steins or whoever they would be, he would be pointed out as Harry, the one who had had the affair with Rachel Ware.

Rachel. Had that really been her name? And had she really ever lived there? And *had* he been involved with her?

He shook his head and smiled bleakly at his own rationalizing. Of course she had lived there. For six years she had lived there with her dull husband George Ware and her two model children, Tracy and Little George. And of course he had had the affair with her, if that's what it had to be called. (Calm down, that's just the way it is, he said to himself. Everything has to be labeled these days.)

So what was wrong with it all, anyway? What was he supposed to do, just sit inside his house all day and write children's stories and pretend that he didn't know about her, pretend that she didn't exist, pretend that she wasn't lonely and bored and looking for someone to talk to, someone to love and someone to love her?

Hadn't he, a Jew, done the Christian thing after all? Hadn't he given her a little love, a little understanding, a little companionship? Hadn't he made her life a little bit happier, in those few weeks when dull George had been gone to Europe and they had met first in the yard to talk about who was going to cut her grass and his grass and then she had come over to ask him if he would mind helping her change a fuse because all her bedroom lights were out—her bedroom lights, would you believe that?—and she couldn't see to read at night and write letters to her husband before she fell asleep. She probably cried herself to sleep, too, only she never told him about that. She never talked much about herself and she never complained about George. But how could she? She wouldn't have known where to start.

Rachel Ware had been a pretty woman. *Had been.* Jesus, there he was already thinking of her in the past tense, as if she were dead and buried instead of being packed up like a box of groceries and moved away to California where she could get her master's degree in basket weaving, look after the two children who didn't really need her attention, and cater to dull George's every whim. And really she was still alive, out there trying to live a new life and forget—or make her husband forget—that she had once transgressed against his virility, his devotion, his charity to an orphaned girl who needed love and a family. Had transgressed against George, who was always hot to take on a new cause and obtain another possession in the bargain . . . at a bargain.

The trouble with people like Rachel was that they were too trusting. And they traded themselves too easily. Why should Rachel have married just because she was eighteen and had no family to take care of her? That was the ripe time of life. She should have flown off on her own fragile wings and seen the world for what it was. Instead she opted for some false sense of security that a stable New Englander could give her: a home, a family. But first a husband—my God, what a husband.

And it had been that way with him, too, Harry realized. She had come flying into his arms without realizing what she was doing. The yard needed cutting, the fuse needed changing. And there was Harry Thomas, just moved in to the neighborhood and living all by himself. Of course, she didn't know that he lived alone. She didn't know that at the last minute he hadn't brought his wife there with him because his wife had said the hell she would move to Florida without Abby, and Harry had told her the hell she would bring Abby along. So his wife had walked off with her neighbor—Abby, a nice young divorcee who'd taught Gail a thing or two in the two years they had lived in New York. And Harry had uncorked a bottle of champagne and privately celebrated getting rid of Gail so neatly with no divorce, no settlement, no alimony. If Gail wanted to go with the girls, let her go. After all, it was a free world, wasn't it? Long live the Melody Club and Women's True Liberation Movement. . . .

Harry had moved on to Florida by himself and taken the very good job of associate professor of English at the university. He liked the department with its assortment of would-be writers, professional critics, and pseudocasual grad students. All on the make, of course, but clever enough to try to hide it. Lots of beer drinking late into the night at some girl's pad, poetry reading there behind the pot plants, crossed bare legs, cut-offs, halter tops, frizzy hair. Disguises to hide their earnestness, because they really did want to make it. It wasn't at all like the North, where you knew you were O.K. because you were Jewish and couldn't fail. Because you had contacts who promoted you and friends who told you how great you were. Because your mother loved you, after all, and so did your father, and your brothers and sisters who bought all your books and even gave them as bar mitzvah presents . . . and to hell with your screwed-up wife who didn't understand how great you really were!

So Harry had liked Florida. Enough to make the big splurge and buy himself a small house in a nice quiet neighborhood—a neighborhood full of children! That way he could observe them to his heart's content and write anything that came to mind. No more searching out children, no more spending his Saturdays in the New York slums, his Sundays in the park, his evenings at youth centers and roller rinks and square dances. Here were real, live children who played honest-to-God children's games and lived the way children should live when they are young and free. They hit and kicked each other, they screamed and called each other names, they taught each other the facts of life—all wrong, of course, but then that left something for their parents to teach them right.

These children woke him up firing their water pistols at his windows and beating their sticks against his curb to sharpen them into swords. And once they realized that he didn't mind, once he had passed the test and become their friend, they obliged him by climbing his trees, digging up his yard, overturning his garbage cans as they rummaged for good finds. And then bringing him beer from their parents' outdoor iceboxes, mislaid golf balls, minnows from the creek for his aquarium. All as peace offerings. He returned their hospitality by keeping his freezer full of popsicles and his back door unlocked. And he read his stories to them when they wanted to listen, joined them in their games—sometimes—when they asked, and listened to them when they came to him with the kind of problem that couldn't wait until their parents got home from work, whoring, or whatever they did that took up their time and kept them away from home eight hours a day.

He also borrowed from them, stole from them, and raped their little minds incessantly for ideas. After all, he was a writer, *an author,* and children's books were his specialty. He wanted to write real books, and here was reality. . . . So he opened up his heart and his head and he looked and listened and loved every minute of it.

The neighbors thought he was strange at first and were careful about letting their children go around him. After all, he might be a pervert, mightn't he? After all, who really liked children, anyway? But then, they learned—he let it slip—that he had just ended a very unhappy marriage (he didn't say how), and they understood that he was lonely and missing the children he either had or didn't have. Or couldn't have. Yes, Harry Thomas was a ripe apple to gossip about, and little Southern towns always need a new subject to slander.

I don't give a shit, Harry told himself, and he really didn't. He was a self-possessed person, a complete man. Now that he had gotten rid of Gail, moved away from New York, and come to a place where he could be himself and develop his talents, he could afford to amuse the neighbors. He didn't have to pull the rags of decency and self-respect about his thin, frail (frail? he weighed 175 and stood at least 6'2") body. At last he could let himself go.

Maybe that's what had made Rachel Ware so attractive to him. He was at last a free man. And she was still a bird in a cage, a pretty yellow canary who had never learned to sing and never learned to fly.

"Oh, fly with me, Rachel," he had wanted to say to her that day when she came across to see about the yard. But he hadn't. He had only agreed that he would share the expenses of a lawn man since their property lay side by side (an omen?) and it wouldn't have looked right if hers had been neat and his not, or vice versa, now would it?

No, certainly not, he had agreed, smoking his pipe and watching her carefully. A good-looking woman. Long brown hair, blue eyes, and a decent figure. She must swim or play tennis to keep in shape. Not too young, not too old. A ripe age, probably about thirty-five or thirty-six. Two children, a house, and a husband, though. Too bad.

Then that about the fuses. "I blew a fuse," she giggled, and Harry couldn't believe that.

He'd fixed the fuses and she'd given him a glass of wine—warm and sweet— and he'd stayed long enough to drink it and tell her about the book he was writing. Her children, Tracy and Little George, had been there, of course—she wouldn't have let him in, otherwise—and they'd listened wide-eyed and never given away that they knew all about the book because, after all, they were in it.

After that, things had just happened naturally. Big George came and went, one business trip after the other, each one longer than the one before. And Rachel stayed at home to run the house, raise the children (with Harry's help, of course— she must have realized that), and go to school. She was studying art at last. Her life-long ambition had been to go back to school and get the education she'd never had because her parents had died, then she'd married, then the children had come (she said-but do children really *come*?), and they'd never had the money or the time for her to go to school. Now she was free. Wistful but free. Lonely but free. The yellow canary that didn't know how to sing, didn't know how to fly.

Harry often met George and Rachel at dinners and cocktail parties given by different social-climbing neighbors. And always he watched them and wondered why Rachel said her ambition was just to go to school, to "get an education." Wasn't it really to escape? Didn't she want to get away from home, husband, family? Didn't she want a life of her own, a trade, a talent? Well, why didn't she admit it, for Christ's sake? Why did she keep calling that an education? No college degree was going to give her those things . . . college was just a front. And someday, when she was an educated woman with a degree and a lot of useless knowledge, she'd realize that she was twice as lonely—and completely alone and naked.

Then George Ware left on another business trip. Three weeks in England, two weeks in Spain. All company work, of course, all business. No way for Rachel to come along. No way for her to join him for a spring vacation. George had to *work*, he had to *travel*, he had to buy out Europe by starving himself and cheating on his per diem so he could bring home more beautiful things to adorn his already beautiful home—clothes for his wife, toys for his children. . . . Prints, pottery, carpets. Things. Possessions. Exquisite obsessions.

And Rachel had stayed at home, and Harry had remained next door. Rachel had gone to school and Harry had worked on his books when he wasn't going through the motions of teaching a class or attending a faculty meeting or flirting with someone's ugly wife at a party he'd had to attend or risk losing his job. Or at least his front as an available and acquiescent bachelor.

Then Tracy had broken her arm and it had been Harry who rushed Rachel (crying), Tracy (scared), and Little George (impressed and disappointed—why hadn't it happened to him?) to the hospital. After that, Little George had his share of the glory. He came down with the measles and Tracy caught them from him. It had been Harry who did their grocery shopping and went to the post office to mail more letters to George and, when he had finished the errands, bring home a bottle of wine and some flowers to cheer up Rachel who had finally had to drop out of school for the quarter but would make it up, yes, she was sure.

Hadn't it been the natural thing for him to do, then, to stay for supper more than once when he had shopped for the food and paid for most of it, bought the wine, arranged the flowers, and cheered up the children—and Rachel? And when his air-conditioning went on the blink, hadn't it been the right thing for Rachel to do to offer him George's study so he could finish his book? And how could he have refused? His office at the university was not air-conditioned and he could not work in a hot house. Besides . . . he sort of wanted to be near her, he guessed. Maybe he *was* lonely . . . he knew that she was. And then, she might need him. The children might need him.

Then one evening, when the children were asleep and the dinner dishes cleared up, when he was tired of writing and she was tired of looking through her art books and magazines, one evening when there was nothing on television and they had talked about everything they had in common and everything they hadn't, they just found themselves in bed together. It seemed the natural thing to do. And once they had done it, not doing it again would have been unnatural.

In bed they were beautiful people. Harry was a happy adult who didn't think about children, what they were doing, what they were thinking, what they would think up next that would leave him a step behind. Rachel didn't worry about being uneducated and an orphan, a Hausfrau and a failure. They needed each other; they wanted each other. They fulfilled each other, and, yes, they almost loved each other.

Harry slept in his own house at night, unless he forgot, to keep the neighbors from talking. And Rachel kept up her long letters to George, letters telling him that she was fine, the children were fine, everything was fine, not to hurry and come home but to stay on and enjoy himself once he was there. The children didn't question them, and if they knew what they were doing—and children always seemed to know what Harry was doing—they didn't object. After all, children were happy when the adults around them were happy, weren't they?

But there were neighbors, and the neighbors did talk, maybe even write letters. For George did decide to come home. Rachel didn't cry when she told Harry, as they lay for the last time in George's bed and she was kissing his face and holding him to her very quietly, that she *dreaded* seeing him again.

"Seeing who?" Harry had asked.

"Him," Rachel whispered. "My husband."

"Oh," Harry said, impressed. He had almost forgotten about George.

How did George ever find out about it? Harry wondered. Did some neighbor tell him, after all? A coded letter to eastern Europe? A telegram to Oslo? A call in the night to Madrid? Or did he suspect them all along, was his fine nose trained to ferret out trouble? Was he a bloodhound at heart?

Or maybe Rachel broke down and confessed, kneeling at his side on his first night back. She was the type that would do that. She was the type of woman who was strong with a good man and weak with a bad one. Her way of fighting back at George was by dealing out underhanded blows that would take him off guard and really let him have it. She wasn't the type of woman who could just live with him, put up with him, and do her own thing. She had almost learned to fly, but she wasn't the kind of bird who could trust her own wings. No moral judgment implied, Harry hastened to add as he watched the children playing in the big climbing tree in his back yard. That's just the way she was.

Was. She was gone, after all. George Ware had put up the house for sale, sent the children to his parents for two weeks, and taken Rachel off to Mexico on a second honeymoon. Jesus Christ, how tacky could you get? Did he think he could make her love him just by sleeping with her for a week or two?

But by the time they came back, hand in hand, the house was sold and George announced that he had taken a better job in California. He called it a promotion; said that his firm was transferring him.

All done in a matter of two weeks, or maybe three.

Everyone smiled knowingly and said that George Ware had been wanting to move for a long time and that this was just an excuse . . . "this" meaning his wife's affair with the writer Harry Thomas. And George evidently *had* lucked into a better job in California, a job with more money and more travel. Now he could stay on the road forever and leave Rachel in her new little California house with the two children to play in their cinderblock yard after school when Rachel was trying to study and make up the credits she had lost by transferring.

Harry also heard that George had almost put his foot down on Rachel's going back to school, but in the end she'd won out and now she was back with her nose to the grindstone, working hard to get an education so she could see what life was all about. She'd probably had to promise him she wouldn't have any more affairs, Harry said to himself as he took notes of the new game the children had devised. They were filling up plastic milk containers with water, carrying them high up into the climbing tree, and dropping them to the ground with a flourish. "Bombs away!" they'd scream. "Get the Germans!"

"Why the Germans?" Harry said to himself. "Why is it always the Germans who get bombed? Why not the Japanese? Or the French? Or the English? Why the hell the Germans?" Because that's what their parents teach them, he answered himself. Love and Hate. Black and White. Yes and No. Facts were facts, clear cut, well defined, and . . . well, *factual*. There to be memorized—the computer mind—tick tick tick. There were no theories to life, no probabilities, no maybes. There was no middle ground, and imagination was a foreign word to men like George and women like Rachel Ware.

And their children? Heaven help them. Thank God he wasn't a parent, Harry thought. Other people's children were all right . . . but thank God he and Gail had not reproduced. Could you imagine a little Harry Thomas and a little Gail Webber Thomas? No. But what he could imagine was a little George Ware, grown out of his beautiful long-haired childhood and turned into another Dull George, wanting only money, prestige, and possessions. And he could see little Tracy on her first prom night, her long brown hair pulled up and clipped under a flower, her blue eyes covered with mascara. Another Rachel. Another empty woman living out an empty life and never knowing what it was all about, even when she held it in her hands and felt its heartbeat.

Maxine

GURNEY NORMAN

Born in Grundy, Virginia, in 1937 and raised in Hazard, Kentucky, Gurney Norman has inspired generations of young writers, teachers, and critics and has become a mainstay of Kentucky letters and Appalachian studies. His mother was a teacher; his father was a coal miner and World War II veteran. He was raised primarily by both sets of grandparents in rural homes. In the late 1950s Norman attended the University of Kentucky, where he published several short stories in the university's literary journal, *Stylus,* and in 1960 earned a bachelor's degree in journalism and English. He then attended Stanford University in California, where as a Wallace Stegner Fellow he studied creative writing with, among others, the Irish short story writer Frank O'Connor. Following Stanford, and after a two-year stint in the U.S. Army, he returned to his hometown to work for two years as a writer and photographer for *The Hazard Herald*. In 1967 he returned to California and subsequently served as an editor of *The Last Whole Earth Catalog*, in whose margins in 1971 his serialized novel *Divine Right's Trip: A Folk Tale* premiered with illustrations. He has written and narrated three television documentaries on Kentucky history for PBS and has helped compile and edit several scholarly works, among them *Confronting Appalachian Stereotype*s (1999). His current work includes the novel-in-progress *Crazy Quilt*.

Norman's acclaimed short story cycle, *Kinfolks: The Wilgus Stor*ies, was published in 1977 by Kentucky's Gnomon Press. The collection later appeared as part of the Southern Authors Series published by Avon Books. Beloved throughout the region and widely used in classrooms, *Kinfolks* has become a classic and one of Kentucky's grassroots literary successes. Three of the stories have been adapted to film: "Fat Monroe," starring Kentucky-born Hollywood actor Ned Beatty; "Night Ride"; and "Maxine." The penultimate story in *Kinfolks*, "Maxine" is a poignant story of loss, separation, escape, and compassion.

◆

Maxine had ridden the bus eleven hours, from Detroit to Blaine, Kentucky, and by the time her cousin Wilgus met her at the station she was exhausted. She was a little hysterical too after the week she'd just spent with her daughter Cindy, so at the edge of town Wilgus went in a liquor store and bought Maxine a bottle of Mogen David to drink as he drove her home.

"Cindy was living in the dingiest goddamn hotel I ever seen," said Maxine. "No windows, no bathroom, no nothing. Damn baby due. Had three dollars when I got there. And that sorry Billy nowhere in sight."

She sipped the wine and handed the bottle to Wilgus. Wilgus didn't feel like drinking, particularly Mogen David, but he took a sip to be companionable and handed the bottle back to Maxine.

"Cindy knew where the little son of a bitch was at, but she didn't want to tell me," Maxine went on. "I reckon she's afraid I'd kill him. Said she'd changed her mind about Billy. Said they'd made up, was going to work things out together. Calls and gets me to come all the way to Detroit, then when I get there, tries to act like it ain't none of my business. Like the thing for me to do is just get back on the bus and go home. Her sitting there with that little round belly, face all lean, I swear Wilgus, she looked like some kind of war orphan."

Maxine sipped her wine.

"So where was Billy?" asked Wilgus.

"This other hotel, three blocks away. I went and found him, I told him if he didn't get Cindy out of that hotel to a better place, and get hisself a job, and generally treat my youngun better, I'd stick him in jail 'til he never got out. I told him if he run off from Cindy anymore I'd hunt him down and cut his goddamn guts out. I's so mad, I could of killed him right there."

Maxine took another drink of wine, then lit a cigarette. But after three puffs she put it out and went on talking.

"So anyway, it took us all week, but I reckon they're finally settled. It ain't much of an apartment but at least it's got a bathroom in it. Billy went to work for Manpower. I reckon he'll stick at it a month or two."

"I thought Billy was going to turn out better than that," said Wilgus.

"Shit," Maxine snorted. "If Cindy was looking for something worthless to take up with, she sure found it."

Maxine sipped the wine and handed the bottle to Wilgus and this time he took a good long drink.

They were driving along the Rock Creek road, headed east toward Bonnet Creek where Maxine lived, twenty-five miles from Blaine. The road through the Rock Creek valley was paved but it was so narrow there was barely room for two cars to pass. Every few miles Wilgus had to ease the car half off the road to let a coal truck pass, twenty-ton empties, most of them, the drivers headed home after their last run to the loading ramps at Champion. Except for the trucks there was very little traffic on the road. And by the time they got to Whitaker Crossroads, half way between Blaine and the mouth of Bonnet Creek, there weren't very many people outside either. The first few miles out of town they had seen people working in their gardens or sitting on their porches, raising their hands in greeting as they passed by. But it was nearly dark now. The valley was filling with the shadows of the hills that rose on either side of Rock Creek. A mile beyond the Crossroads, Wilgus turned his headlights on. Then he reached over and put his arm around his cousin and drew her to him.

To help Maxine get her mind off her troubles, Wilgus started talking about the trip he was going to take to California later in the month. Wilgus had graduated from the University a few weeks before. He planned to go back in the fall to graduate school. Before settling in for another round of study he wanted to change his pattern for awhile, get away from books, away from Kentucky, have an adventure off someplace he'd never been before. To set forth in his car and head west with no precise plan or destination was unlike anything Wilgus had ever done before, and the prospect of the journey had filled his mind ever since school was out.

"Yeah," said Maxine when Wilgus had outlined his scheme. "I know what you're going to do. You're going to get out there to California and forget to come back. Homefolks'll never see you again."

Maxine made her remark jokingly but Wilgus was serious when he answered. "No," he said. "I'm coming back."

Maxine sipped her wine. "Well," she said. "I wouldn't blame you if you never come back to this place. If I could go with you I sure as hell wouldn't come back."

"Now there's an idea," said Wilgus. "Why don't you come along? We'd have a fine old time."

"Maybe I could find me a cowboy out there to marry," Maxine laughed. She sipped her wine. "Ay, Lord," she muttered, "I pity any cowboy that'd take up with the likes of me."

"He'd be a lucky cowboy," said Wilgus.

Maxine grunted, and drank more wine. "No," she said. "I don't want no cowboy. But I would like to go out there and see the sights someday."

"What I want to see is the Grand Canyon," said Wilgus.

"Lord, honey, don't take me to no canyons," said Maxine. "If I's at a canyon I'd dive off head first into the damn thing and be done with it."

"No, now," said Wilgus. "I wouldn't let you do that. What we'd do is walk down in it. Go exploring. We could ride those burros they've got. . . ."

"Lord God!" Maxine laughed, sitting up suddenly. "Don't put me on donkeys! I look foolish enough as it is. I'll soon be a *grandma,* Wilgus."

"The Lone Grandma," Wilgus teased. "Get you a mask, a white burro. . . ."

"*Hush!*"

But Maxine couldn't help laughing at the image and Wilgus laughed with her. They both took a drink of wine.

"Maybe that's what I ought to do," said Maxine after a while. "Get me a gun and a mask and go around killing my enemies. Anybody that pissed me off, I'd shoot 'em down."

"And justice would be done," said Wilgus. "You'd feel *good* about it."

"I'd shoot Billy Dixon's ass plum off," said Maxine. "And then there's one or two on Bonnet Creek I'd like to kill. Kill me a couple of strip miners. Few sons of

bitches over at the courthouse. When it was over I'd shoot myself. Blow my brains
out with a big ol' .44."

"No, now Maxine. You don't want to do that."

Maxine sipped her wine. "Don't bet on it," she said.

When they left the county pike and headed up the unpaved road that ran
beside Bonnet Creek, they fell silent for awhile. Wilgus drove in first gear as he
maneuvered the car around the larger rocks and deeper ruts of the narrow lane. In
the old days, when Maxine was a child on Bonnet Creek, the highway department
had maintained their road as well as any in the county. But after the ridges above the
valley were strip-mined and the creek began to lose its population, the people who
remained were lucky if the county graded their road every other year. In the winter
only vehicles with four-wheel drive could make it as far as Maxine's house. Wilgus's
Ford was making it now only because it was July and the road had been baked hard
by the sun. Every half mile or so the road crossed the creek and in places ran in the
creekbed several yards before rising on the other side. In the dark it took them half
an hour to drive the four miles from the highway to Maxine's house near the head of
the hollow. Neither spoke until Wilgus pulled up in front of the house and said,
"Well, here we are."

I reckon so, said Maxine.

At least she thought she said it. She was so weary and disoriented after her
long day's journey she wasn't sure if she had spoken out loud or merely thought the
words.

"Everything looks all right," said Wilgus. "At least nobody burned your house
down while you were gone."

I wouldn't care if they had, Maxine thought.

"Did I say that?" she asked.

"What?" asked Wilgus.

Maxine didn't answer immediately. After staring out the window at the dark,
familiar shape of her house she said, "This place feels like the end of the world to
me."

"It's the same old Bonnet Creek," said Wilgus.

Not the same, Maxine thought.

"Did I say that?" she asked.

"About the end of the world?" asked Wilgus.

"Something."

Maxine was too tired to go on with the thought. She was so tired she couldn't
even tell if she was crying or not. It felt as if she was. But somehow she didn't seem
to be making any sound, and there weren't any tears in her eyes. But her shoulders
were shaking and when Wilgus noticed that they were, he slid across the seat and
put his arms around her, a full hug this time. Maxine leaned into his side without
restraint and felt her tears begin. For a long time she cried in Wilgus's arms like a
baby. As she cried she pictured Cindy as a baby, crying in her arms. Briefly Maxine
dreamed she *was* Cindy, come home with Wilgus to Bonnet Creek again.

But as Wilgus helped her out of the car, it was only her same old self who was home.

"It's just me, folks," she sang out in the dark as Wilgus led her across the yard. "Just old stupid Maxine."

"You're a wonderful Maxine," Wilgus whispered.

A left-over piece of shit is all I am, Maxine thought.

"I didn't mean that," she said out loud.

"Shhh," said Wilgus. "It's okay."

Wilgus helped her up the steps and across the porch to the front door. Then, his arm around her waist, her head upon his shoulder, they entered the dark and airless house and made their way along the hall to the back bedroom. Fumbling in the dark, they found the bed and sat down on the edge.

"If I was Cindy and we all loved me," Maxine sang as Wilgus took off her shoes.

"Shhh," said Wilgus. "Be quiet, now."

"What all have I said?"

"Nothing, honey. Hold still now."

Maxine felt her cousin's hands unbutton her blouse and slip it off her arms. She felt him lay her on the bed and unzip her slacks, then slip them off her legs. She felt his good warm hands upon her legs and arms and shoulders as he pushed her into the center of the bed. Then she felt him lie down on the bed beside her and take her in his arms.

Oh lover, Maxine thought.

"I didn't mean," she said, startled, drawing away.

"Shhh," said Wilgus. "Just be still. It's all okay."

Maxine hugged her cousin's arm against her breasts. "I love you," she said out loud.

"And I love you," she heard him say. "You sleep now."

And dream.

Maxine dreamed Wilgus kissed her on the mouth. She dreamed he touched her breast, then stroked her face with his hand. Then she dreamed she heard his car start up outside. As she listened to its sound grow fainter down the hollow, Maxine dreamed that she was with him, that she was Cindy, riding away with Wilgus, headed west, somewhere.

Rent Control

WALTER TEVIS

Born in California in 1928, Walter Tevis moved with his family to Lexington, Kentucky, when he was ten. After graduating from Model Lab School in Richmond, Tevis served one term in the U.S. Naval Reserve. He returned to Kentucky and earned an A.B. in English from the University of Kentucky and subsequently taught high-school English for six years, while also teaching part-time at the University of Kentucky. Recognition for some of his fiction, especially *The Hustler* (1959), prompted him to pursue and complete an M.A. at U.K. and an M.F.A. at the University of Iowa. In 1978, after having taught creative writing for thirteen years at Ohio University, Tevis left teaching and moved to New York City. As he explained later, this tension between teaching and writing resulted in personal problems that he eventually conquered and ultimately led him to full-time writing. This tension, or some variation, is central in Tevis's work: the man or woman alone to fail or prevail—as is the case in *The Hustler* and *Queen's Gambit* (1983)—or the alien soul in some real or fabricated exile, such as in *The Man who Fell to Earth* (1963) and many of the stories included in *Far From Home* (1981). Tevis is probably best known for his three novels adapted to the screen, the last of which was *The Color of Money* (1984). Some of his other works include the science-fiction novels *Mockingbird* (1980) and *The Steps of the Sun* (1983). He died in 1984.

"Rent Control" is one of several magical realism stories in *Far From Home*, which includes the award-winning title story about a janitor who encounters the miracle of a vibrant whale in an indoor swimming pool in Arizona. Set in New York City within layers of enclosures, "Rent Control" pushes to the extreme the themes of isolation and rootlessness so characteristic of the fiction of the 1960s and 70s. The two characters in the story do manage to find happiness, but their private and other-worldly felicity is hidden from the outside world—and it has its price.

◆

"My God," Edith said, "that was the most *real* experience of my life." She put her arms around him, put her cheek against his naked chest, and pulled him tightly to her. She was crying.

He was crying too. "Me too, darling," he said, and held his arms around her.

They were in the loft bed of her studio apartment on the East Side. They had just had orgasms together. Now they were sweaty, relaxed, blissful. It had been a perfect day.

Their orgasms had been foreshadowed by their therapy. That evening, after supper, they had gone to Harry's group as always on Wednesdays and somehow everything had focused for them. He had at last shouted the heartfelt anger he bore against his incompetent parents; she had screamed her hatred of her sadistic mother, her gutless father. And their relief had come together there on the floor of a New York psychiatrist's office. After the screaming and pounding of fists, after the real and potent old rage in both of them was spent, their smiles at one another had been radiant. They had gone afterward to her apartment, where they had lived together half a year, climbed up the ladder into her bed, and begun to make love slowly, carefully. Then frenetically. They had been picked up bodily by it and carried to a place they had never been before.

Now, afterward, they were settling down in that place, huddled together. They lay silently for a long time. Idly she looked toward the ledge by the mattress where she kept cigarettes, a mason jar with miniature roses, a Japanese ashtray, and an alarm clock.

"The clock must have stopped," she said.

He mumbled something inarticulate. His eyes were closed.

"It says nine twenty," she said, "and we left Harry's at nine."

"Hmmm," he said, without interest.

She was silent for a while, musing. Then she said, "Terry? What time does your watch say?"

"Time, time," he said. "Watch, watch." He shifted his and looked. "Nine twenty," he said.

"Is the second hand moving?" she said. His watch was an Accutron, not given to being wrong or stopping.

He looked again. "Nope. Not moving." He let his hand fall on her naked behind, now cool to his touch. Then he said, "That *is* funny. Both stopping at once." He leaned over her body toward the window, pried open a space in her Levelor blinds, looked out. It was dark out, with an odd shimmer to the air. Nothing was moving. There was a pile of plastic garbage bags on the sidewalk opposite. "It can't be eleven yet. They haven't taken the garbage from the Toreador." The Toreador was a Spanish restaurant across the street; they kept promising they would eat there sometime but never had.

"It's probably about ten thirty," she said. "Why don't you make us an omelet and turn the TV on?"

"Sure, honey," he said. He slipped on his bikini shorts and eased himself down the ladder. Barefoot and undressed, he went to the tiny Sony by the fireplace, turned it on, and padded over to the stove and sink at the other end of the room. He heard the TV come on while finding the omelet pan that he had bought her, under the sink, nestling between the Bon Ami and the Windex. He got eggs out, cracked one, looked at his watch. It was running. It said nine twenty-six. "Hey, honey," he called out. "My watch is running."

After a pause she said, her voice slightly hushed, "So is the clock up here."

He shrugged and put butter in the pan and finished cracking the eggs, throwing the shells into the sink. He whipped them with a fork, then turned on the fire under the pan and walked back to the TV for a moment. A voice was saying, ". . . nine thirty." He looked at his watch. Nine thirty. *"Jesus Christ!"* he said.

But he had forgotten about it by the time he cooked the omelets. His omelets had been from the beginning one of the things that made them close. He had learned to cook them before leaving his wife and it meant independence to him. He made omelets beautifully—tender and moist—and Edith was impressed. They had fallen in love over omelets. He cooked lamb chops too, and bought things like frozen capelletti from expensive shops; but omelets were central.

They were both thirty-five years old, both youthful, good-looking, smart. They were both Pisces, with birthdays three days apart. Both had good complexions, healthy dark hair, clear eyes. They both bought clothes at Bergdorf-Goodman and Bonwit's and Bloomingdale's; they both spoke fair French, watched *Nova* on TV, read *The Stories of John Cheever* and the Sunday *Times*. He was a magazine illustrator, she a lawyer; they could have afforded a bigger place, but hers was rent-controlled and at a terrific midtown address. It was too much of a bargain to give up. *"Nobody* ever leaves a rent-controlled apartment," she told him. So they lived in one and a half rooms together and money piled up in their bank accounts.

They were terribly nervous lovers at first, too unsure of everything to enjoy it, full of explanations and self-recriminations. He had trouble staying hard; she would not lubricate. She was afraid of him and made love dutifully, often with resentment. He was embarrassed at his unreliable member, sensed her withdrawal from his ardor, was afraid to tell her so. Often they were miserable.

But she had the good sense to take him to her therapist and he had the good sense to go. Finally, after six months of private sessions and of group, it had worked. They had the perfect orgasm, the perfect release from tension, the perfect intimacy.

Now they ate their omelets in bed from Spode plates, using his mother's silver forks. Sea salt and Java pepper. Their legs were twined as they ate.

They lay silent for a while afterward. He looked out the window. The garbage was still there; there was no movement in the street; no one was on the sidewalk. There was a flatness to the way the light shone on the buildings across from them, as though they were painted—some kind of a backdrop.

He looked at his watch. It said nine forty-one. The second hand wasn't moving. "Shit!" he said, puzzled.

"What's that, honey?" Edith said. "Did I do something wrong?"

"No, sweetie," he said. "You're the best thing that ever happened. I'm crazy about you." He patted her ass with one hand, gave her his empty plate with the other.

She set the two plates on the ledge, which was barely wide enough for them. She glanced at the clock. "Jesus," she said. "That sure is strange. . . ."

"Let's go to sleep," he said. "I'll explain the Theory of Relativity in the morning."

But when he woke up it wasn't morning. He felt refreshed, thoroughly rested; he had the sense of a long and absolutely silent sleep, with no noises intruding from the world outside, no dreams, no complications. He had never felt better.

But when he looked out the window the light from the streetlamp was the same and the garbage bags were still piled in front of the Toreador and—he saw now—what appeared to be the same taxi was motionless in front of the same green station wagon in the middle of Fifty-first Street. He looked at his watch. It said nine forty-one.

Edith was still asleep, on her stomach, with her arm across his waist, her hip against his. Not waking her, he pulled away and started to climb down from the bed. On an impulse he looked again at his watch. It was nine forty-one still, but now the second hand was moving.

He reached out and turned the electric clock on the ledge to where he could see its face. It said nine forty-one also, and when he held it to his ear he could hear its gears turning quietly inside. His heart began to beat more strongly, and he found himself catching his breath.

He climbed down and went to the television set, turned it on again. The same face appeared as before he had slept, wearing the same oversized glasses, the same bland smile.

Terry turned the sound up, seated himself on the sofa, lit a cigarette, and waited.

It seemed a long time before the news program ended and a voice said, "It's ten o'clock."

He looked at his watch. It said ten o'clock. He looked out the window; it was dark-evening. There was no way it could be ten in the morning. But he knew he had slept a whole night. He knew it. His hand holding the second cigarette was trembling.

Slowly and carefully he put out his cigarette, climbed back up the ladder to the loft bed. Edith was still asleep. Somehow he knew what to do. He laid his hand on her leg and looked at his watch. As he touched her the second hand stopped. For a long moment he did not breathe.

Still holding her leg, he looked out the window. This time there were a group of people outside; they had just left the restaurant. None of them moved. The taxi had gone and with it the station wagon; but the garbage was still there. One of the people from the Toreador was in the process of putting on his raincoat. One arm was in a sleeve and the other wasn't. There was a frown on his face visible from the third-story apartment where Terry lay looking at him. Everything was frozen. The light was peculiar, unreal. The man's frown did not change.

Terry let go of Edith and the man finished putting on his coat. Two cars drove by in the street. The light became normal.

Terry touched Edith again, this time laying his hand gently on her bare back. Outside the window everything stopped, as when a switch is thrown on a projector to arrest the movement. Terry let out his breath audibly. Then he said, "Wake up, Edith. I've got something to show you."

They never understood it, and they told nobody. It was relativity, they decided. They had found, indeed, a perfect place together, where subjective time raced and the world did not.

It did not work anywhere but in her loft bed and only when they touched. They could stay together there for hours or days, although there was no way they could tell how long the "time" had really been; they could make love, sleep, read, talk, and no time passed whatever.

They discovered, after a while, that only if they quarreled did it fail and the clock and watch would run even though they were touching. It required intimacy—even of a slight kind, the intimacy of casual touching—for it to work.

They adapted their lives to it quickly and at first it extended their sense of life's possibilities enormously. It bathed them in a perfection of the lovers' sense of being apart from the rest of the world and better than it.

Their careers improved; they had more time for work and for play than anyone else. If one of them was ever under serious pressure—of job competition, of the need to make a quick decision—they could get in bed together and have all the time necessary to decide, to think up the speech, to plan the magazine cover or the case in court.

Sometimes they took what they called "weekends," buying and cooking enough food for five or six meals, and just staying in the loft bed, touching, while reading and meditating and making love and working. He had his art supplies in shelves over the bed now, and she had reference books and note pads on the ledge. He had put mirrors on two of the walls and on the ceiling, partly for sex, partly to make the small place seem bigger, less confining.

The food was always hot, unspoiled; no time had passed for it between their meals. They could not watch television or listen to records while in suspended time; no machinery worked while they touched.

Sometimes for fun they would watch people out the window and stop and start them up again comically; but that soon grew tiresome.

They both got richer and richer, with promotions and higher pay and the low rent. And of course there was now truly no question of leaving the apartment; there was no other bed in which they could stop time, no other place. Besides, this one was rent-controlled.

For a year or so they would always stay later at parties than anyone else, would taunt acquaintances and colleagues when they were too tired to accompany them to all-night places for scrambled eggs or a final drink. Sometimes they annoyed colleagues by showing up bright-eyed and rested in the morning, no matter how late the party had gone on, no matter how many drinks had been drunk, no matter how loud and fatiguing the revelry. They were always buoyant, healthy, awake, and just a bit smug.

But after the first year they tired of partying, grew bored with friends, and went out less. Somehow they had come to a place where they were never bored with, as Edith called it, "our little loft bed." The center of their lives had become a king-sized foam mattress with a foot-wide ledge and a few inches of head and foot room at each end. They were never bored when in that small space.

What they had to learn was not to quarrel, not to lose the modicum of intimacy that their relativity phenomenon required. But that came easily too; without discussing it each learned to give only a small part of himself to intimacy with the other, to cultivate a state of mind remote enough to be safe from conflict, yet with a controlled closeness. They did yoga for body and spirit and Transcendental Meditation. Neither told the other his mantra. Often they found themselves staring at different mirrors. Now they seldom looked out the window.

It was Edith who made the second major intuition. One day when he was in the bathroom shaving, and his watch was running, he heard her shout to him, in a kind of cool playfulness, "Quit dawdling in there, Terry. I'm getting older for nothing." There was some kind of urgency in her voice, and he caught it. He rinsed his face off in a hurry, dried, walked to the bedroom and looked up at her. "What do you mean?" he said.

She didn't look at him. "Get on up here, Dum-dum," she said, still in that controlled-playful voice. "I want you to touch me."

He climbed up, laid a hand on her shoulder. Outside the window a walking man froze in mid-stride and the sunlight darkened as though a shutter had been placed over it.

"What do you mean, 'older for nothing'?" he said.

She looked at him thoughtfully. "It's been about five years now, in the real world," she said. "The real world" for them meant the time lived by other people. "But we must have spent five years in suspended time here in bed. More than that. And we haven't been aged by it."

He looked at her. "How could . . . ?"

"I don't know," she said. "But I know we're not any older than anybody else."

He turned toward the mirror at her feet, stared at himself in it. He was still youthful, firm, clear complexioned. Suddenly he smiled at himself. "Jesus," he said. "Maybe I can fix it so I can shave in bed."

Their "weekends" became longer. Although they could not measure their special time, the number of times they slept and the times they made love could be counted; and both those numbers increased once they realized the time in bed together was "free"—that they did not age while touching, in the loft bed, while the world outside was motionless and the sun neither rose nor set.

Sometimes they would pick a time of day and a quality of light they both liked and stop their time there. At twilight, with empty streets and a soft ambience of light, they would allow for the slight darkening effect, and then touch and stay touching for eight or ten sleeping periods, six or eight orgasms, fifteen meals.

They had stopped the omelets because of the real time it took to prepare them. Now they bought pizzas and prepared chickens and ready-made desserts and quarts of milk and coffee and bottles of good wine and cartons of cigarettes and cases of Perrier water and filled shelves at each side of the window with them. The hot food would never cool as long as Edith and Terry were touching each other in the controlled intimacy they now had learned as second nature. Each could look at himself in his own mirror and not even think about the other in a conscious way, but if their fingertips were so much as touching and if the remote sense of the other was unruffled by anger or anxiety then the pizzas on the shelf would remain hot, the Perrier cold, the cars in the street motionless, and the sky and weather without change forever. No love was needed now, no feeling whatever—only the lack of unpleasantness and the slightest of physical contact.

The world outside became less interesting for them. They both had large bank accounts and both had good yet undemanding jobs; her legal briefs were prepared by assistants; three young men in his studio made the illustrations that he designed, on drawing pads, in the loft bed. Often the nights were a terrible bore to them when they had to let go of each other if they wanted morning to come, just so they could go to work, have a change of pace.

But less and less did either of them want the pace to change. Each had learned to spend "hours" motionless, staring at the mirror or out the window, preserving his youth against the ravages of real time and real movement. Each became obsessed, without sharing the obsession, with a single idea: immortality. They could live forever, young and healthy and fully awake, in this loft bed. There was no question of interestingness or of boredom; they had moved, deeply in their separate souls, far beyond that distinction, that rhythm of life. Deep in themselves they had become a Pharaoh's dream of endless time; they had found the pyramid that kept the flow of the world away.

On one autumn morning that had been like two weeks for them he looked at her, after waking, and said, "I don't want to leave this place. I don't want to get old."

She looked at him before she spoke. Then she said, "There's nothing I want to do outside."

He looked away from her, smiling. "We'll need a lot of food," he said.

They had already had the apartment filled with shelves and a bathroom was installed beneath the bed. Using the bathroom was the only concession to real time; to make the water flow it was necessary for them not to touch.

They filled the shelves, that autumn afternoon, with hundreds of pounds of food—cheeses and hot chickens and sausage and milk and butter and big loaves of bread and precooked steaks and pork chops and hams and bowls of cooked vegetables, all prepared and delivered by a wondering caterer and five assistants. They had cases of wine and beer and cigarettes. It was like an efficient, miniature warehouse.

When they got into bed and touched she said, "What if we quarrel? The food will all spoil."

"I know," he said. And then, taking a deep breath, "What if we just don't talk?"

She looked at him for a long moment. Then she said, "I've been thinking that too."

So they stopped talking. And each turned toward his own mirror and thought of living forever.

They were back to back, touching.

No friend found them, for they had no friends. But when the landlord came in through the empty shelves on what was for him the next day he found them in the loft bed, back to back, each staring into a different mirror. They were perfectly beautiful, with healthy, clear complexions, youthful figures, dark and glistening hair; but they had no minds at all. They were not even like beautiful children; there was nothing there but prettiness.

The landlord was shocked at what he saw. But he recognized soon afterward that they would be sent somewhere and that he would be able to charge a profitable rent, at last, with someone new.

1980–2000

My work seems to have struck a chord with a number of readers who have left home and maybe who have rejected it, and I think it startles them because they thought they were rid of it. I left that kind of world, too, but never could quite get rid of it, and it haunted me.

BOBBIE ANN MASON, INTERVIEW IN *CRAZYHORSE,* 1985

I had a hard time breaking free of the hills. A real hard time, actually. I was very curious about the outside world, but it just didn't do me much good out there. . . . I always thought I was looking for something, something intangible. I didn't really know what I was looking for, but I felt that I was. My brother, one time, told me that he didn't think I was looking for anything. He thought I was running away.

CHRIS OFFUTT, INTERVIEW IN *CONVERSATIONS WITH KENTUCKY WRITERS*

Residents and Transients

BOBBIE ANN MASON

Born in 1940, Bobbie Ann Mason grew up on a dairy farm in Mayfield, Kentucky. At age fourteen, she served as national fan-club president of The Hilltoppers, a popular musical group founded at Western Kentucky State College in Bowling Green. After earning her bachelor's in English from the University of Kentucky in 1962, she moved to New York City, where she wrote for television and movie celebrity magazines. The following year she entered the State University of New York at Binghamton, where she earned a master's in English. In 1966 she entered the doctoral program at the University of Connecticut, eventually earning her Ph.D. in literature with a dissertation on Vladimir Nabokov's novel *Ada*. She then taught at what is now Mansfield University in Pennsylvania until 1979, when she left the teaching profession to devote full time to writing fiction. She and her husband, Roger Rawlings, have lived in Kentucky since 1990.

Mason's "Shiloh," which appeared in the *New Yorker* in 1980, is one of the most frequently anthologized stories of the last two decades. Her collections include *Shiloh and Other Stories* (1982), which won the PEN/Hemingway Award for best first book of fiction and was a finalist for the National Book Critics Circle Award, the American Book Award, and the PEN/Faulkner Award; *Love Life* (1989); and *Midnight Magic: Selected Stories* (1998). Her other books to date include two literary/cultural studies, *Nabokov's Garden* (1974) and *The Girl Sleuth* (1975); three novels, *In Country* (1985), *Spence + Lila* (1988), and *Feather Crowns* (1993); and a Pulitzer-nominated memoir, *Clear Springs: A Family Story* (1999).

The central story in *Shiloh and Other Stories*, "Residents and Transients" portrays a woman's reinvigorated love of her heritage and the complexity and ambiguity of that love.

◆

Since my husband went away to work in Louisville, I have, to my surprise, taken a lover. Stephen went ahead to start his new job and find us a suitable house. I'm to follow later. He works for one of those companies that require frequent transfers, and I agreed to that arrangement in the beginning, but now I do not want to go to Louisville. I do not want to go anywhere.

Larry is our dentist. When I saw him in the post office earlier in the summer, I didn't recognize him at first, without his smock and drills. But then we exchanged words—"Hot enough for you?" or something like that—and afterward I started to notice his blue Ford Ranger XII passing on the road beyond the fields. We are about the same age, and he grew up in this area, just as I did, but I was away for eight years, pursuing higher learning. I came back to Kentucky three years ago because my parents were in poor health. Now they have moved to Florida, but I have stayed here, wondering why I ever went away.

Soon after I returned, I met Stephen, and we were married within a year. He is one of those Yankees who are moving into this region with increasing frequency, a fact which disturbs the native residents. I would not have called Stephen a Yankee. I'm very much an outsider myself, though I've tried to fit in since I've been back. I only say this because I overhear the skeptical and desperate remarks, as though the town were being invaded. The schoolchildren are saying "you guys" now and smoking dope. I can imagine a classroom of bashful country hicks, listening to some new kid blithely talking in a Northern brogue about his year in Europe. Such influences are making people jittery. Most people around here would rather die than leave town, but there are a few here who think Churchill Downs in Louisville would be the grandest place in the world to be. They are dreamers, I could tell them.

"I can't imagine living on a *street* again," I said to my husband. I complained for weeks about living with *houses* within view. I need cornfields. When my parents left for Florida, Stephen and I moved into their old farmhouse, to take care of it for them. I love its stateliness, the way it rises up from the fields like a patch of mutant jimsonweeds. I'm fond of the old white wood siding, the sagging outbuildings. But the house will be sold this winter, after the corn is picked, and by then I will have to go to Louisville. I promised my parents I would handle the household auction because I knew my mother could not bear to be involved. She told me many times about a widow who had sold off her belongings and afterward stayed alone in the empty house until she had to be dragged away. Within a year, she died of cancer. Mother said to me, "Heartbreak brings on cancer." She went away to Florida, leaving everything the way it was, as though she had only gone shopping.

The cats came with the farm. When Stephen and I appeared, the cats gradually moved from the barn to the house. They seem to be my responsibility, like some sins I have committed, like illegitimate children. The cats are Pete, Donald, Roger, Mike, Judy, Brenda, Ellen, and Patsy. Reciting their names for Larry, my lover of three weeks, I feel foolish. Larry had asked, "Can you remember all their names?"

"What kind of question is that?" I ask, reminded of my husband's new job. Stephen travels to cities throughout the South, demonstrating word-processing machines, fancy typewriters that cost thousands of dollars and can remember what you type. It doesn't take a brain like that to remember eight cats.

"No two are alike," I say to Larry helplessly.

We are in the canning kitchen, an airy back porch which I use for the cats. It has a sink where I wash their bowls and cabinets where I keep their food. The canning kitchen was my mother's pride. There, she processed her green beans twenty minutes in a pressure canner, and her tomato juice fifteen minutes in a water bath. Now my mother lives in a mobile home. In her letters she tells me all the prices of the foods she buys.

From the canning kitchen, Larry and I have a good view of the cornfields. A cross-breeze makes this the coolest and most pleasant place to be. The house is in the center of the cornfields, and a dirt lane leads out to the road, about half a mile away. The cats wander down the fence rows, patroling the borders. I feed them Friskies and vacuum their pillows. I ignore the rabbits they bring me. Larry strokes a cat with one hand and my hair with the other. He says he has never known anyone like me. He calls me Mary Sue instead of Mary. No one has called me Mary Sue since I was a kid.

Larry started coming out to the house soon after I had a six-month checkup. I can't remember what signals passed between us, but it was suddenly appropriate that he drop by. When I saw his truck out on the road that day, I knew it would turn up my lane. The truck has a chrome streak on it that makes it look like a rocket, and on the doors it has flames painted.

"I brought you some ice cream," he said.

"I didn't know dentists made house calls. What kind of ice cream is it?"

"I thought you'd like choc-o-mint."

"You're right."

"I know you have a sweet tooth."

"You're just trying to give me cavities, so you can charge me thirty dollars a tooth."

I opened the screen door to get dishes. One cat went in and another went out. The changing of the guard. Larry and I sat on the porch and ate ice cream and watched crows in the corn. The corn had shot up after a recent rain.

"You shouldn't go to Louisville," said Larry. "This part of Kentucky is the prettiest. I wouldn't trade it for anything."

"I never used to think that. Boy, I couldn't wait to get out!" The ice cream was thrillingly cold. I wondered if Larry envied me. Compared to him, I was a world traveler. I had lived in a commune in Aspen, backpacked through the Rockies, and worked on the National Limited as one of the first female porters. When Larry was in high school, he was known as a hell-raiser, so the whole town was amazed when he became a dentist, married, and settled down. Now he was divorced.

Larry and I sat on the porch for an interminable time on that sultry day, each waiting for some external sign—a sudden shift in the weather, a sound, an event of some kind—to bring our bodies together. Finally, it was something I said about my new filling. He leaped up to look in my mouth.

"You should have let me take x-rays," he said.

"I told you I don't believe in all that radiation."

"The amount is teensy," said Larry, holding my jaw. A mouth is a word processor, I thought suddenly, as I tried to speak

"Besides," he said, "I always use the lead apron to catch any fragmentation."

"What are you talking about?" I cried, jerking loose. I imagined splintering x-rays zinging around the room. Larry patted me on the knee.

"I should put on some music," I said. He followed me inside.

Stephen is on the phone. It is 3:00 P.M. and I am eating supper—pork and beans, cottage cheese and dill pickles. My routines are cockeyed since he left.

"I found us a house!" he says excitedly. His voice is so familiar I can almost see him, and I realize that I miss him. "I want you to come up here this weekend and take a look at it," he says.

"Do I have to?" My mouth is full of pork and beans.

"I can't buy it unless you see it first."

"I don't care what it looks like."

"Sure you do. But you'll like it. It's a three-bedroom brick with a two-car garage, finished basement, dining alcove, patio—"

"Does it have a canning kitchen?" I want to know.

Stephen laughs. "No, but it has a rec room."

I quake at the thought of a rec room. I tell Stephen, "I know this is crazy, but I think we'll have to set up a kennel in back for the cats, to keep them out of traffic."

I tell Stephen about the New Jersey veterinarian I saw on a talk show who keeps an African lioness, an ocelot, and three margays in his yard in the suburbs. They all have the run of his house. "Cats aren't that hard to get along with," the vet said.

"Aren't you carrying this a little far?" Stephen asks, sounding worried. He doesn't suspect how far I might be carrying things. I have managed to swallow the last trace of the food, as if it were guilt.

"What do *you* think?" I ask abruptly.

"I don't know what to think," he says.

I fall silent. I am holding Ellen, the cat who had a vaginal infection not long ago. The vet x-rayed her and found she was pregnant. She lost the kittens, because of the x-ray, but the miscarriage was incomplete, and she developed a rare infection called pyometra and had to be spayed. I wrote every detail of this to my parents, thinking they would care, but they did not mention it in their letters. Their minds are on the condominium they are planning to buy when this farm is sold. Now Stephen is talking about our investments and telling me things to do at the bank. When we buy a house, we will have to get a complicated mortgage.

"The thing about owning real estate outright," he says, "is that one's assets aren't liquid."

"Daddy always taught me to avoid debt."

"That's not the way it works anymore."

"He's going to pay cash for his condo."

"That's ridiculous."

Not long ago, Stephen and I sat before an investment counselor, who told us, without cracking a smile, "You want to select an investment posture that will maximize your potential." I had him confused with a marriage counselor, some kind of weird sex therapist. Now I think of water streaming in the dentist's bowl. When I was a child, the water in a dentist's bowl ran continuously. Larry's bowl has a shut-off button to save water. Stephen is talking about flexibility and fluid assets. It occurs to me that wordprocessing, all one word, is also a runny sound. How many billion words a day could one of Stephen's machines process without forgetting? How many pecks of pickled peppers can Peter Piper pick? You don't *pick* pickled peppers, I want to say to Stephen defiantly, as if he has asked this question. Peppers can't be pickled till *after* they're picked, I want to say, as if I have a point to make.

Larry is here almost daily. He comes over after he finishes overhauling mouths for the day. I tease him about this peculiarity of his profession. Sometimes I pretend to be afraid of him. I won't let him near my mouth. I clamp my teeth shut and grin widely, fighting off imaginary drills. Larry is gap-toothed. He should have had braces, I say. Too late now, he says. Cats march up and down the bed purring while we are in it. Larry does not seem to notice. I'm accustomed to the cats. Cats, I'm aware, like to be involved in anything that's going on. Pete has a hobby of chasing butterflies. When he loses sight of one, he searches the air, wailing pathetically, as though abandoned. Brenda plays with paper clips. She likes the way she can hook a paper clip so simply with one claw. She attacks spiders in the same way. Their legs draw up and she drops them.

I see Larry watching the cats, but he rarely comments on them. Today he notices Brenda's odd eyes. One is blue and one is yellow. I show him her paper clip trick. We are in the canning kitchen and the daylight is fading.

"Do you want another drink?" asks Larry.

"No."

"You're getting one anyway."

We are drinking Bloody Marys, made with my mother's canned tomato juice. There are rows of jars in the basement. She would be mortified to know what I am doing, in her house, with her tomato juice.

Larry brings me a drink and a soggy grilled cheese sandwich.

"You'd think a dentist would make something dainty and precise," I say. "Jello molds, maybe, the way you make false teeth."

We laugh. He thinks I am being funny.

The other day he took me up in a single-engine Cessna. We circled west Kentucky, looking at the land, and when we flew over the farm I felt I was in creaky hay wagon, skimming just above the fields. I thought of the Dylan Thomas poem with the dream about the birds flying along with the stacks of hay. I could see eighty acres of corn and pasture, neat green squares. I am nearly thirty years old. I have two men, eight cats, no cavities. One day I was counting the cats and I absent-mindedly counted myself.

Larry and I are playing Monopoly in the parlor, which is full of doilies and trinkets on whatnots. Every day I notice something that I must save for my mother. I'm sure Larry wishes we were at his house, a modern brick home in a good section of town, five doors down from a U.S. congressman. Larry gets up from the card table and mixes another Bloody Mary for me. I've been buying hotels left and right, against the advice of my investment counselor. I own all the utilities. I shuffle my paper money and it feels like dried corn shucks. I wonder if there is a new board game involving money market funds.

"When my grandmother was alive, my father used to bury her savings in the yard, in order to avoid inheritance taxes," I say as Larry hands me the drink.

He laughs. He always laughs, whatever I say. His lips are like parentheses, enclosing compliments.

"In the last ten years of her life she saved ten thousand dollars from her social security checks."

"That's incredible." He looks doubtful, as though I have made up a story to amuse him. "Maybe there's still money buried in your yard."

"Maybe. My grandmother was very frugal. She wouldn't let go of *anything*."

"Some people are like that."

Larry wears a cloudy expression of love. Everything about me that I find dreary, he finds intriguing. He moves his silvery token (a flatiron) around the board so carefully, like a child learning to cross the street. Outside, a cat is yowling. I do not recognize it as one of mine. There is nothing so mournful as the yowling of a homeless cat. When a stray appears, the cats sit around, fascinated, while it eats, and then later, just when it starts to feel secure, they gang up on it and chase it away.

"This place is full of junk that no one could throw away," I say distractedly. I have just been sent to jail. I'm thinking of the boxes in the attic, the rusted tools in the barn. In a cabinet in the canning kitchen I found some Bag Balm, antiseptic salve to soften cows' udders. Once I used teat extenders to feed a sick kitten. The cows are gone, but I feel their presence like ghosts. "I've been reading up on cats," I say suddenly. The vodka is making me plunge into something I know I cannot explain. "I don't want you to think I'm this crazy cat freak with a mattress full of money."

"Of course I don't." Larry lands on Virginia Avenue and proceeds to negotiate a complicated transaction.

"In the wild, there are two kinds of cat populations," I tell him when he finishes his move. "Residents and transients. Some stay put in their fixed home ranges, and others are on the move. They don't have real homes. Everybody always thought that the ones who establish the territories are the most successful—like the capitalists who get ahold of Park Place." (I'm eyeing my opportunities on the board.) "They are the strongest while the transients are the bums, the losers."

"Is that right? I didn't know that." Larry looks genuinely surprised. I think he is surprised at how far the subject itself extends. He is such a specialist. Teeth.

I continue bravely. "The thing is—this is what the scientists are wondering about now—it may be that the transients are the superior ones after all, with the greatest curiosity and most intelligence. They can't decide."

"That's interesting." The Bloody Marys are making Larry seem very satisfied. He is the most relaxed man I've ever known. "None of that is true of domestic cats," Larry is saying. "They're all screwed up."

"I bet somewhere there are some who are footloose and fancy free," I say, not believing it. I buy two hotels on Park Place and almost go broke. I think of living in Louisville. Stephen said the house he wants to buy is not far from Iroquois Park. I'm reminded of Indians. When certain Indians got tired of living in a place—when they used up the soil, or the garbage pile got too high—they moved on to the next place.

It is a hot summer night, and Larry and I are driving back from Paducah. We went out to eat and then we saw a movie. We are rather careless about being seen together in public. Before we left the house, I brushed my teeth twice and used dental floss. On the way, Larry told me of a patient who was a hemophiliac and couldn't floss. Working on his teeth was very risky.

We ate at a place where you choose your food from pictures on a wall, then wait at a numbered table for the food to appear. On another wall was a framed arrangement of farm tools against red felt. Other objects—saw handles, scythes, pulleys—were mounted on wood like fish trophies. I could hardly eat for looking at the tools. I was wondering what my father's old tit-cups and dehorning shears would look like on the wall of a restaurant. Larry was unusually quiet during the meal. His reticence exaggerated his customary gentleness. He even ate french fries cautiously.

On the way home, the air is rushing through the truck. My elbow is propped in the window, feeling the cooling air like water. I think of the pickup truck as a train, swishing through the night.

Larry says then, "Do you want me to stop coming out to see you?"

"What makes you ask that?"

"I don't have to be an Einstein to tell that you're bored with me."

"I don't know. I still don't want to go to Louisville, though."

"I don't want you to go. I wish you would just stay here and we would be together."

"I wish it could be that way," I say, trembling slightly. "I wish that was right."

We round a curve. The night is black. The yellow line in the road is faded. In the other lane I suddenly see a rabbit move. It is hopping in place, the way runners will run in place. Its forelegs are frantically working, but its rear end has been smashed and it cannot get out of the road.

By the time we reach home I have become hysterical. Larry has his arms around me, trying to soothe me, but I cannot speak intelligibly and I push him away. In my mind, the rabbit is a tape loop that crowds out everything else.

Inside the house, the phone rings and Larry answers. I can tell from his expression that it is Stephen calling. It was crazy to let Larry answer the phone. I was not thinking. I will have to swear on a stack of cats that nothing is going on. When Larry hands me the phone I am incoherent. Stephen is saying something nonchalant, with a sly question in his voice. Sitting on the floor, I'm rubbing my feet vigorously. "Listen," I say in a tone of great urgency. "I'm coming to Louisville—to see that house. There's this guy here who'll give me a ride in his truck—"

Stephen is annoyed with me. He seems not to have heard what I said, for he is launching into a speech about my anxiety.

"Those attachments to a place are so provincial," he says.

"People live all their lives in one place," I argue frantically. "What's wrong with that?"

"You've got to be flexible," he says breezily. "That kind of romantic emotion is just like flag-waving. It leads to nationalism, fascism—you name it; the very worst kinds of instincts. Listen, Mary, you've got to be more open to the way things are."

Stephen is processing words. He makes me think of liquidity, investment postures. I see him floppy as a Raggedy Andy, loose as a goose. I see what I am shredding in my hand as I listen. It is Monopoly money.

After I hang up, I rush outside. Larry is discreetly staying behind. Standing in the porch light, I listen to katydids announce the harvest. It is the kind of night, mellow and languid, when you can hear corn growing. I see a cat's flaming eyes coming up the lane to the house. One eye is green and one is red, like a traffic light. It is Brenda, my odd-eyed cat. Her blue eye shines red and her yellow eye shines green. In a moment I realize that I am waiting for the light to change.

Yours

JOE ASHBY PORTER

Born in 1942, Joe Ashby Porter grew up in Madisonville, Kentucky. He earned an A.B. from Harvard, studied at Cambridge University as a Fullbright Fellow, and received both his M.A. and Ph. D. at the University of California at Berkeley. He is currently a professor of English at Duke University. His works include the novel *Eelgrass* (1977); a scholarly study, *The Drama of Speech Acts: Shakespeare's Lancastrian Tetralogy* (1979); and two collections of short stories, *The Kentucky Stories* (1983) and *Lithuania* (1990).

Porter's short stories are possibility-laden exposures of the human condition. He suggests the nature of many of his Kentucky stories in the foreword to *The Kentucky Stories*: "I did spend childhood and adolescence in Kentucky, and set foot outside the state only four times I can remember, so that Kentucky was once reality itself, almost. But then during the following years, when circumstances kept me away except for the briefest visits, Kentucky became what it is in these stories, a state of mind. It is a state of listening for the grave and reedy voice that comes out of nowhere and with complete assurance begins its inexplicable tale. . . ." In the episto-lary story "Yours," the protagonist finds himself in heritage-rich Bardstown, Kentucky. It features an observant and witty narrator making connections with people he happens to encounter, and the reader is left to speculate on the meaningfulness of his gestures. Much of the meaning and power of this story rests on the balance between estrangement and membership.

◆

You remember we used to talk about traveling in Kentucky and seeing my father's birthplace. I was in the mountains and I've been here in Bardstown for a week. The hotel is 130 years old and parts of the town are beautiful.

Today for breakfast I walked to a café in the business district: worn linoleum, a juke box, "Vera" and "Connie" according to their badges, the establishment's first dollar framed between an inspection certificate and "If you're so Smart/Why aren't you *Rich?*" in faded Day-Glow green. Feisty little Vera gave me an inquisitive smile. I'm off newspapers for the moment and to fill the breakfast time this morning I plotted a graph of my life on a napkin. The eight or nine other customers had pegged me for a tourist. A plumber and a shopkeeper were arguing placidly about cars. The day was beginning.

I spent some time in the local bookstore, alone except for the proprietress. There was a good supply of biography and children's but otherwise the supply was freakish. I finally bought a paperback Agatha Christie I didn't think I'd read, a heavy and expensive *Architectural Heritage of Kentucky* and our favorite film star's autobiography. Then I walked. Spring comes more deliberately here and the streets are almost deserted. I carried my books in a shopping bag with handles.

Gravitating toward houses that were old but not renovated, I walked through poorer and poorer neighborhoods into a black district at one edge of town. Older women taking the sun on their porches watched me with curiosity. In the doorway of a grocery stood a short stocky fellow around thirty. As I came near he asked me how I was doing. He said, "You're not from here, are you?" He had been married but his wife had died, he lived in a pair of rooms behind the store. "What kind of living do you make?" I said. "Do you want to get married again?" He said it was the onliest thing he looked forward to. I said, "Listen, I'd like you to have one of these books here." He chose the one with pictures of mansions. "Good luck," I said. He said, "The very same to you."

In five minutes I was in rolling pastureland with occasional ponds and clumps of trees. I just kept walking away from town, climbing fences and giving wide berth to the grazing cattle, happy not to see anyone for a couple of hours until I came to the navel of the universe, the Platonic idea of the farmhouse with dust and a yellow dog, thoughtful hens under the hydrangea, wads of cotton stuck in the screen door to discourage flies. "Hoo-oo," I called. The breeze had risen, white clouds were piled high in the blue sky, wash flapped on the line.

"My, who's that?" Peering and smiling the mistress of the house appeared, tall as I am and heavier, around sixty and laughing at my city clothes and sunburn. "Are you lost?" She had a twinkling direct smile like a nun's. I asked for a drink of water. "Yes, yes, come in. Do you have time?" Inside it was cool and smelled of lavender. "I'm Katie Sisk, everybody calls me Katie," she said. I sat in the small dining room and she brought a pitcher of ice water and then potato salad and ham sandwiches and lemon meringue pie. I told Katie what I'd left, where I'd been, how when I'd begun wandering or fleeing I'd seemed to be reborn. She said, "Well goodness gracious," smiling and shaking her head without a hint of approval or disapproval. After a while we worked into an odd sort of a conversation: she was crocheting, I was sipping coffee, I would ask almost any question that popped into my head, she'd reply and then there would be silence until I thought of something else to ask.

"Did you always live around here, Katie?"

"I was born in this house."

"Did you ever have a serious illness?"

"I go to bed soon after dark and I'm up before sunrise. Now and again I might have a touch of the rheumatism."

"Ever been to a quilting bee?"

"More than I can remember. I'm surprised you know what they are."

"What do you think of me, Katie?"

"What kind of a question is that? Heavens."

"Are you ever gloomy?"

"Goodness!"

"Katie, I have two books here in my shopping bag. I'd like you to have one."

"No, there wouldn't be any point. My eyes aren't so keen as they used to be, and then I never did do much reading. I'll give you a ride back to town though, if that's where you're going. I have some shopping to do."

I rode beside her in her pickup truck and when she let me off she said, "Stay out of trouble."

It was 3:30 and I was tired enough for a nap and yet something inclined me to prolong the afternoon. In the window of a place called "Curios and Antiques" some depression glass table settings of a sort I remembered from childhood caught my eye. Inside the store even I could tell that the merchandise was mostly worthless gimcrackery. That and the clutter pleased me, and the fact that I had to scan the place several times before I saw the owner sitting in the rear, an etiolated Mark Twain gussied up with fly-away hair and string tie but thin and wan, immobile as a turtle on a log, watching me.

He smiled and nodded. At first he left me to wander on my own but soon he began, still sitting where he was, to comment on whatever I happened to be looking at. I was noncommital but I must have seemed an easy mark because he warmed to his task, feeling me out by quoting prices—at first reasonably unreasonable ones and then, when I showed no dismay, more and more outrageous ones, fluttering his eyelids and caressing the junk. His energy and cunning entranced me. "Wasn't there something," he asked, "something in the window you were noticing from the street?"

"Yes," I said. "The green glass tableware."

"I should have guessed. Ravishing, isn't it?"

"Yes," I said, "it is."

"Yes, Yes, Czechoslovak, you know. Eighteenth century. Very rare."

I felt giddy. "They're well preserved."

"Aren't they. The family that . . . but I'm not at liberty to disclose the story."

"I see. And about the price?"

He spoke in an undertone behind his hand. "I had them appraised last month and he said two five for the set. But you obviously appreciate them, so I could arrange a discount. I'd hate them to go to someone who. . . ."

"I wonder if I could sleep on it," I said. "I don't like to ask you to hold them, though."

"Not at all."

"I'll try to stop in tomorrow then. Oh, and by the way, I bought some books this morning and then discovered I won't have time to read them. I'd like you to have one."

He pounced on the autobiography. "I've literally been dying to read this. Could

I? Just to borrow?" As I left he laid his hand on my arm. "I hope you won't let yourself be put off by . . . by these people." He gestured toward the world outside his shop. "They do have their little points."

Returning to the hotel I almost danced. I slept, showered, and went down to dine in the hotel restaurant. Sometimes I think differences in restaurants' bills of fare shrink to insignificance compared to differences in ambience. Food's food but place is all there is. This one still has up its Christmas decorations and there's a mural of the region's history beginning with Indians and culminating in this hotel. A candle floated in a brandy snifter on my table. There were no conversations near enough for eavesdropping, and so I cogitated.

It was then that I thought about you and wondered why I shouldn't love your small-mindedness after all. Surprised? I often have surprising revelations lately. In fact it was they that first made me suspect I had suffered rebirth—the revelations that showered over me in the little train chugging down through the crazy towns, as with every mile more of you and the rest of my life was torn from my mind. Dining slowly I remembered that train ride only three months ago through the snowy night, the various stations at any of which I might have alighted, and finally the next day the station from which I telephoned to say I was off to seek my fortune and would not be back.

After a mint julep pie and coffee I took another walk, up back streets, across a gas station parking lot under a full moon with dogs barking, new leaves moving on the trees and the stars I remember from childhood shining down through the clear air. It seemed that only our treading would keep the earth turning. A policeman in his patrol car asked, "What'cha up to, friend?" There were a few fireflies even this early in the spring. The public library was closing as I passed.

It was 9:30 and I came back to the hotel. Quiet laughter and music drew me to the bar where I settled back into a red Naugahyde booth with a cognac in the dark. Eight or nine other people were there and as I watched them and heard scraps of their conversation it occurred to me that this was a cast party celebrating a run that had lasted fifty years for some of them already.

An attractive dark-haired girl came in alone. I invited her to join me and to my surprise she did. She was Alice, in her early twenties with white skin, large eyes and a wide unsmiling mouth, living in the hotel until she found an apartment. She'd come from Mississippi to be assistant buyer in a clothing store. I sketched my history and recent travels and she asked where I planned to go next. I said I hadn't thought about it. Half closing her eyes she said she'd have gone to New York except that her father didn't want her to be so far away. Her father is called Beau because he was so handsome. Alice's favorite color is orange, but violet looks better on her. She said she eats onion sandwiches, "Just bread and mayonnaise and lots of onion. They give me headaches but I eat them anyway." And then unexpectedly she said, "I have to go now," laying her white hand on mine.

"Alice," I protested.

"Really, I can't."

The Agatha Christie was in my pocket and so I took it out and gave it to her. "I bought it this morning but I don't think I'll get around to reading it."

She smiled for the first time and then bent down and kissed me on the cheek. Yes, I was disappointed, but if I stay on here something more might happen tomorrow or the next day.

After Alice had gone I sat in the bar for an hour longer remembering the day. The black grocer, Katie the farm woman, the antique dealer and Alice from Mississippi all in one day, a pretty good average. Toying with that fact must have prompted a fantasy of an old and intricate lodge somewhere in wooded mountains where they and I could all be together for weeks at a time, all each other's disciples as we wandered the long hallways or gathered at night around the fire. Why isn't there such a place anyway? when clearly there ought to be. There are fewer things in heaven and earth than are dreamt of in my philosophy.

It was after eleven when I came up to my room. I remembered you again, and decided to write this letter. Not that I suppose I owe it: it's a gift. And so I've sat down at my desk and filled up these pages, saying quite a bit less about you than I'd expected to. I'm sorry. I'll be gone from here by the time this reaches you. I doubt that we'll ever see one another again. If we do, we won't be recognizable. Still and all I remain, with love, sincerely yours.

A Fellow Making Himself Up

Leon V. Driskell

Leon V. Driskell was born in 1932 in Georgia. After earning his B.A. and M.A. at the University of Georgia and his Ph. D. at the University of Texas, he taught at Birmingham Southern College and the University of Cincinnati before coming in 1964 to the University of Louisville. His books are *The Eternal Crossroads: The Art of Flannery O'Connor* (co-authored with Joan Brittain, 1972), *Passing Through: A Fiction* (1983), and *Turnabout* (co-authored with Sue Driskell, 1995). His stories have appeared in, among other journals, *Prairie Schooner, Carolina Review, Georgia Review*, and *Wind Literary Journal*. One of his stories, "Martha Jean," was reprinted in *New Stories from the South: The Year's Best* in 1986, and several others were named "Distinguished Stories of the Year" in *Best American Short Stories*. Founder of the former journal *Adena* and a long-time reviewer for *The Courier-Journal*, Driskell died in 1995.

In an interview with L. Elisabeth Beattie, Driskell discussed his cycle of short stories, *Passing Through*, which includes "A Fellow Making Himself Up": "The Buddhist term for what we do on the circle in the cycle of experience, from conception and birth through the joy, pain, sorrow, loss, and all the rest, to death and reincarnation, is translated frequently as 'passing through.' It's what it's all about. And, of course, there is no place to be except where you've been before. . . . I am discovering myself in the process of becoming myself." First published in *Wind Literary Journal* in 1982 and named a "Distinguished Story of the Year" in *Best American Short Stories*, "A Fellow Making Himself Up" is a comic tale of a man's chance development of an identity and his subsequent contentment with home.

◆

What uncle Lester liked most about Rosco was that he had named himself, and Lester thought he had picked the perfect name. He did not look like a Ralph, or Robert, or Rupert, but exactly like a Rosco. Audrey said she did not think it was so great to be named Rosco, for she could not think of a single movie star, or even TV personality, with *that* name. Uncle Lester admitted that Rosco had not exactly named himself all the way, for he had started out with what his parents had decided to call him, which was R.P. White.

To Lester what uncle Rosco had done was better than any story in a book, even the ones about the frog who turned into a prince or the poor boy who became Lord Mayor of London. Lester made Rosco tell him all the details many times, and even when he was a baby, or practically one, he would make Rosco go back and tell it again if he left out any part of it.

Lester mostly called Rosco, Rosco—without any uncle before it—and you could tell he liked the sound of it. He had looked in the Owenton phone book to see if he could find any other Roscoes. It took him a whole afternoon to read all the first names. He found four of them, but he felt better when he called up and learned that one of them was deceased and another had moved off to Henry County.

How it happened that Rosco got the name R.P. White was that he was the eighth baby, and, by the time he came along, his parents had run out of names along with practically everything else. They had used up some perfectly good names on babies who had died, and Rosco said he guessed they felt funny about using the same names twice, especially since the dead children were buried a hundred yards from the front porch.

Their names and dates were painted on slate stones, and they were also listed in the family Bible, which uncle Rosco said he would give a pretty to have so he could show it to Lester.

Sallie Garland White/Jan 9 1902–Feb 2 1902
(At Rest Now)

Han. Leonidus White/June 11 1903–Oct 7 1903
(God's Own)

Eben. Ulysses White/Oct 30 1904
(Precious Moment)

Rosco knew what all was on the stones, and he said Han. stood for Hannibal which was too long to fit on the slate, and that Eben. stood for Ebenezer. Uncle Lester was glad that Rosco did not get either of those names, but he did not say so. He had seen an Ebenezer (and an Ichabod) on TV.

Rosco was stingy with nothing but words, and, with Lester, he was not even stingy with them. His hands hung a mile out of his sleeves, as Ichabod's did, but his shoulders were broad as a barn door, and Lester could not imagine him running from a headless horseman or anything else. Lester wasn't sure how he felt about the name Ulysses, for he knew that Ulysses was a hero and had traveled far as Rosco had, but he also knew that Ulysses was Greek—and the Greek who owned the cafe had been partly to blame for Lurline's going to the Women's Detention Center. Lester thought that since it was his name Lurline signed to a check he should have had some say about things, and not some Greek who wasn't even kin to Lurline.

Rosco said his Daddy had once worked at a textile mill in Walhalla, S.C., for a man named R.P. Swift, so when Rosco's Mama said *What can we name this one?* he came out with R.P.

"R.P.?" said Rosco's Mama. "What kind of name is that?"

They ended up writing it down in the family Bible anyhow—R.P. White, Dec. 6, 1917. That was how they named the children back then, at least in Walhalla. They wrote the name down in the Bible. None of them ever had a birth certificate, and uncle Rosco said that had caused him a world and all of trouble, though, as he said, you would think anybody with a grain of sense who saw him standing there would take it on faith that he had to have been born, even if he didn't have papers to show for it.

Until Rosco decided to name himself, lots of people said to him what his Mama had said to his Daddy.

"R.P.?" they would say. "What kind of name is that?"

His teachers would always tell him that he had to have more name than that. "You go home tonight," they told him, "and ask your Mama what those letters stand for so I can write it down." Uncle Rosco said he could never understand why certain people put so much stock in knowing things just so they could write them down.

One teacher told him that if he did not tell her his *real* name, she was going to call him Rastus—and how would he like answering to a nigger name? She called him that a time or two until he told her his Mama said 'Rastus was short for Erastus and could not be what the *R*. stood for in his name—and besides, his Mama said *Erastus* was a lovely name. The teacher said she wondered who Mrs. White thought *she* was, but she stopped calling R.P. *Rastus* and took to calling him Robert, but he would answer to nothing but R.P.

Uncle Lester figured it was lucky that Rosco did not stay in school very long, for that teacher would have ended up naming him herself before he had a chance. Rosco said that he was never much for sitting indoors, and when his Daddy began to need him around the place, he just quit going to school though he did sometimes borrow books to read at night when the work was done.

By then, it was the Depression, though Rosco told Lester that the only difference he could see between the Depression and what come before was that the Federal Government began to notice that folks were poor. One of Rosco's brothers went off and joined the CCC. Rosco could not remember what the letters stood for, so Lester looked it up in the World Book and found out it was the Civilian Conservation Corps, and uncle Rosco said that was right. He said there was a CCC camp just below Franklin, N.C., and he had been there, once. He said the boys there learned to plant trees and cut them down and how to build stone steps and walls on the National Park grounds. They had uniforms to wear and learned how to drive trucks and string electrical wires without hardly ever electrocuting themselves.

Another brother lied about his age so he could join the Navy and see the world, and what came of that was that he was at Pearl Harbor when the Japs made their sneak attack and he like to have been killed.

Rosco's sister, Rose Cameron White, took up with an older man and headed west not to be heard of for years. When Lester asked what happened to her, uncle Rosco shook his head. It seemed that Rose Cameron had prospered and now owned a large wheat ranch and had run through two more men. Another sister got herself married right off as soon as she was fifteen, though as Rosco's Daddy always said, she would have done better to head west too.

After a while Rosco's Mama died trying to have another baby. Rosco said she had already had eleven or twelve, had lost count, and was too old to have any more but didn't know what to do. His Daddy got married again soon so he would have somebody to look after the younger chaps.

"Chaps?" interrupted Lester.

"Chaps," uncle Rosco confirmed. "That's what Mama always called us children. Chaps, don't ask me why."

Rosco said he decided it was time for him to leave, and when Lester asked if his Daddy's new wife was a wicked stepmother, he said she was a good lady but that he did not feel at home with her. She was not much older than he was, and he felt funny every time he saw his Daddy hug and kiss her. He would think of his Mama and how old and tired seeming she had always been, and that made it hard for him to get used to a new, pretty Mama.

He did not get far the first time he ran away. Somebody in a buggy (he thought maybe it was the doctor) picked him up and brought him home before anybody even knew he was gone. They did not know he had run away until he told them, and he had time to help with the chores before he got his licking.

The next time he tried, he made it. He was fifteen and big for his age, and it was easy for him to find work even when all he got in exchange was his food and a pallet to sleep on. After a year or two, he took to sending an occasional postcard home, and once at Christmas he had sent a money order, but it was a long time before he saw any of his people again.

Mostly he bummed around, but he told Lester that he always kept himself neat and clean so nobody would think he was a hobo. He looked for work, and he sometimes settled in at a place for three or four months and then he would move on. He got all the way to California, and, though he liked the climate, he did not care for the people. None of the ones he met seemed to be where they ought to be, and most of them were trying to pretend they were not from where they came from. They were from all over, from North Dakota and Arkansas and Tennessee, but they all told him that California was God's country and they hoped they never had to go back to where they came from.

"Me," said Rosco, "I didn't think their Hoovervilles beat the mountain shacks I knew back home, and back there we at least didn't have guards walking around the fruit groves like they did in God's country. Every other person you'd meet would ask if you was an Oakie, and I said I didn't know that I was but I would answer to that name as soon as I would to 'cracker,' which is what they called people from Georgia."

Rosco was in Norfolk, Virginia, when the war broke out, so he just stayed there and worked in the shipyards. After a spell, he went from unskilled to skilled and joined the union and almost got himself married. If he had done that, he would never have come to Kentucky and met Mama Pearl, or any of them. He named himself there, in Norfolk, Virginia, at the place where his girlfriend worked.

The woman Rosco nearly married was named Irma and was a waitress at what Rosco called a greasy-spoon and pick-up joint. One night in 1942, Rosco was sitting at the counter in the eating half of the Gypsy Bar and Grill. "The *gyppy* bar and grill?" interrupted Lester.

"No," said uncle Rosco. "Though the words *gyp* and *gypsy* are probably kin, I have known a good many gypsies in my time and I have not found that they are any more likely to try and cheat you than other folks. Where Irma worked was called the Gypsy Bar and Grill because they had these round glass globes, like crystal balls, on the tables, and all the girls wore headrags and big loop earrings."

"Was Irma a gypsy?" uncle Lester wanted to know.

"I guess not," said Rosco. "I never noticed any of them was able to see much into the future, least of all Irma."

That night in 1942, uncle Rosco was feeling blue. The war was not looking good—Things Looked Bad for Democracy. He did not know if or when he would be drafted, and he did not know how he felt about killing people even if he did know that God was on our side. He was waiting for Irma to get off work at midnight, and he hoped they would have a few laughs together and he would start to feeling better. Business slowed down in the cafe, and Irma began horsing around, first with one fellow and then another. Then she began razzing Rosco about his name.

She introduced him to a fellow she said was Angelo ("But don't let *that* fool you," she said winking at Angelo), and then she said, "Angelo, this here is R.P. White. Just don't ask me what that R.P. stands for, or I may tell you."

The men at the counter all laughed, and some of them started making up things that R.P. could stand for, and, though he tried, Rosco could not make himself laugh, and he said he felt his face going redder and redder. Pretty soon what they were saying got bad enough that it bothered even Irma, so she broke in and told them what she had read in the *Reader's Digest* while she waited to get her hair fixed.

"It was in this part they call 'Humor in Uniform,'" she told them. "This hick from somewhere down South got drafted, and the sergeant told him to write down his full name—"

"It's a wonder he could write," Angelo said.

"He could write," Irma said, "but he didn't know what to do, because all he had was initials before his last name, which was Jones."

"What's wrong with that?" Rosco wanted to know, but nobody paid him any attention.

"Sooo," Irma concluded. "He wrote down R (only), P (only) Jones, and the next morning at roll-call, they called him Ronly Ponly Jones."

Everybody but Rosco screamed with laughter, Irma louder than anyone else. Then somebody called Rosco Ronly Ponly and they all laughed some more.

Rosco stood up then, and looked hard at Irma until she stopped laughing.

"My name is not Ronly Ponly or any of those other things you have been saying," he told them. He was going to say his name was R.P. White and what is wrong with that? but one of the men said, "If your name is not Ronly Ponly, then what is it?"

"Rosco," he said with sudden inspiration. "Rosco P. White."

He walked out of the Gypsy Bar and Grill then, and he never saw Irma again.

The next morning he signed on with the merchant marines and spent the next two years at sea. When the man in charge at the merchant marines gave him a form to fill out and told him to print his name in full, Rosco thought again of Private Ronly Ponly Jones. He stared at the sheet of paper for a minute, and the man said, "Go ahead. Put your full name right there on the page. Last name first, no initials."

Uncle Rosco said that he printed WHITE, ROSCO—and since he had never thought about what the *P.* could stand for, he wrote down PAGE. He was so pleased with his new name that he had his social security card changed, and, after he got out of the merchant marines, he went looking for Irma. He said he wanted to let her know who he was.

The short-order cook at the Gypsy Bar and Grill said he thought Irma had married somebody named Angelo, but somebody else said they didn't think so. And somebody else said the man Irma was living with might or might not be her husband, but she knew for certain that he was no angel—and, from the looks of Irma, she had found that out, too. The short-order cook said he had never noticed that Irma was what you could call perfect.

Uncle Rosco said, "What's in a name anyhow?"

At this point in the story, Lester would always scowl and say under his breath "Plenty. There's plenty in a name."

One day Lester said it out loud. "There's plenty in a name," he told Rosco.

"If you had stayed R (only), P (only) White, Irma would have called you *that* all your life, and you would probably still be hanging around waiting for her to get off work and you would never have come to Kentucky and fallen in love with Mama Pearl, and we would never have known you or anything and we would not be a family."

Uncle Rosco thought hard about what Lester had said.

"Well," he said finally, "I just made up those names as I went along, but for a fellow making himself up, I guess I didn't do half bad, did I?"

He looked down over the barn and out to where the tobacco was yellowing in the field.

"Not half bad," he answered himself. "Let's go split some wood, so maybe we can have hot biscuits for supper."

Winter Facts

MARY ANN TAYLOR-HALL

Born in Chicago and raised in Florida, Mary Ann Taylor-Hall has lived in Kentucky for more than twenty years. She has taught creative writing at the University of Kentucky and has participated in various writers workshops. Her books include the novel *Come and Go, Molly Snow* (1995) and the short story collection *How She Knows What She Knows About Yo-Yos* (1999). Her short stories have appeared in *The Kenyon Review*, *The Paris Review*, *Shenandoah*, and *Ploughshares*, as well as *Best American Short Stories*. A winner of the PEN/Syndicated Fiction Award, she has received grants from the National Endowment for the Arts and the Kentucky Arts Council. She and her husband, James Baker Hall, live near Sadieville, Kentucky.

As *Publishers Weekly* has noted in a review of *How She Knows What She Knows About Yo-Yos,* Taylor-Hall's women protagonists "know what they want from the world and are grappling with how to get it." Bart Schneider of *The New York Times Book Review* has said that most of Taylor-Hall's women characters "have woven a shroud of solitude around themselves. What they yearn for stands outside the traditional roles prescribed for them. . . . But behind the ample surface charms here, it's always clear that these women are striving for a quiet dignity." Published originally in 1983 and featured in *The Available Press/PEN Short Story Collection* two years later, "Winter Facts" is a story of separation and rejuvenation, of a woman struggling to put down new roots and the ensuing spiritual revival.

◆

She had come in August. Now it was November. She had started a wall with rocks that she dug out of the garden plot. As she got more serious about it, she had her friends bring them to her by the wagonload—rocks were one thing everybody had plenty of out here. Now the wall was maybe forty feet long, two feet high, solid, regular, sloping as the land sloped, between the back lawn and the vegetable garden.

She called it the vegetable garden, though she hadn't planted anything in it yet, and had serious doubts that anything could grow there—the soil, besides being heavy clay, was packed down hard, from years of being the feed lot for the Dunn's ponies. But she was digging in compost from the old falling-down sheep barn across the road. Sometimes now, she saw earthworms in the turned-up shovelfuls of clay.

She took pains to avoid cutting into them. They labored along, slippery and private, leaving intricate, promising channels in their wake. Asleep, sometimes she dreamed of tilth, of dark, fertile soil crumbling in her hands. Once, nodding off late at night over a book, she'd had a clear vision of a row of small, round, evenly-spaced heads of Bibb lettuce. She counted them off by their round green names, *love, love, love*.

She didn't always dream of gardens, of course. A couple of nights before, she had dreamt she was on a pogo stick, bouncing up and down in the same place, in a rage. She was using the pogo stick like a jackhammer, trying to break through the surface that supported her. Her hair fell in her face, tears streamed from her eyes. She hammered and hammered with the pogo stick, getting nowhere.

But in the light of day, it seemed to her that she was getting somewhere. She thought of herself as a person with ambitions, plans for the future—to make her garden, to extend the wall all the way to the wire fence, to establish a perennial border in front of it.

This evening she was planting iris rhizomes which she had dug up from around an abandoned cistern and separated into forked pieces. She arranged them in groups in front of the wall. For a while, as she worked, the evening hung still above her, a perfect deep electric-blue dome fractured by the bare black branches of the locust trees that ringed the garden. Each time she lifted her leg to push the shovel down, she felt the letter in the front pocket of her jeans, bending stiffly against her thigh. Sturdy expensive bond from the law firm in the far-off city where her husband was working part-time these days in the mail room, to make enough money to buy his painting supplies.

Her shovel struck rock. She traded the shovel for the pick and probed along, learning where the rock went by the sound of metal against stone—there and there and there, until finally the pick drove silently down. She played it then, it caught, she pitted her weight against the weight of the rock. It lifted. She moved the blade of the pick further under, changed sides, braced and pulled back as hard as she could. The heavy earth buckled up, the shape of the rock disclosed itself. She shoveled soil away, knelt and got her hand under the jagged edge. She bent into the deep mossy smell of the earth at night, worked the whale-shaped rock around to stand on end, pivoted it out of the crater formed by the absence of itself. The heavy soil kept the shape of the rock that had lain against it for, what, centuries? Eons. She tried the word aloud, hoping to imagine what it meant. Where she stood had once been the bottom of the ocean, she knew that much.

She struggled, lifting the rock, and muscled it up the bank, scraped the moist clay off it, to examine what she had unearthed. Intact scallop fossils were embedded in the rough side, a large, definite, three-branched fragment of coral. She rolled the rock end over end and lodged it in her wall, fossil side up.

The last light drained from the sky all at once. It was the time when for a while you thought you could still see but you couldn't. The next ridge over, the Dunn's lights were on, looking lonely. The stars came out, clear, hard, all of a sudden. When she had first come here from the city, she had felt frightened, at a loss, under the huge, uninterrupted fact of the heavens. Now she had grown accustomed, knew where to look for the constellations.

The wall shone white in the light from the porch. She knelt and planted the last iris roots in the dark, broke up the soil with her hands and patted it over them, then headed toward the house. She kicked off her boots on the back porch, turned on the light in the kitchen. The fire in the wood stove was going out. She raked the live coals to the front and reloaded it, then filled the kettle and put it on the stove.

She fished the letter out of her pocket, held it carefully with the sides of her hands—she found she didn't want to get it dirty. Her name—Kate Gallagher—and address were arranged handsomely, generously, across the envelope. The black ink drove boldly into the paper. His handwriting was all he had to offer her now, and she had come to feel it was a fraud. She couldn't see any reason to open the envelope. Inside would be just more black ink, more handwriting, telling her what she already knew. She hadn't heard from him in over a month. "You sound very far away," she'd said on the phone, experimentally. "It's a bad connection," he'd quickly explained. The last communication she'd had from him was a report of a movie about the Spanish Civil War that he'd seen at the Bleeker Street Cinema. It seemed he'd liked it a lot. She responded on a picture post card—two grinning farmers waist-high in tobacco plants. On the back she wrote, "Tell the truth now if you know it, Jack." And he had. Every day from then till now, she would wait for the blue Scout truck to pull away, then go down the stone path to look in the mailbox. The only mail she got was addressed "Boxholder."

She looked at the bright, primitive little room, taking note of the sweat pants on the back of the chair, the ashes under the stove, the night black and unpeopled outside the window. She realized she was seeing it through his eyes. Feeling his dismay.

There was no reason for dismay. This was her winter home, hung with quilts against the storms to come. She had a rocking chair, a cot, even a yellow kitten, asleep now under the stove, a foundling from the Dempster Dumpster. She was thinking of getting a dog. She had two jars of wild plum jelly and a basket of black walnuts. There were persimmons in a bowl, with which she planned to make a pie from a recipe she'd found in *Stalking the Wild Asparagus*. Because of the uncertainty of her situation, she had been till now mainly a forager. In the coming spring, she would evolve into a planter. She had gardens on the brain. She thumbed grandly through catalogues, making lists, sat up late drinking hot toddies and reading last year's issues of *Organic Gardening*.

Or sometimes James Joyce. She had recently felt moved to copy this sentence out of *Ulysses*. "Time has branded them and fettered they are lodged in the room of the infinite possibilities they have ousted." She looked at the comforts she had gathered together in this room in which she was lodged: bowls and boards, a jar of chick peas and one of brown rice. Potatoes in a sack. A postcard of the Durer owl pinned to the wall. A bottle of J.W. Dant, a tin of jasmine tea, a hot water bottle. A few books, a radio, a small television. Worldly goods laid by against hunger, cold, loneliness. She had abandoned the other rooms of this house one by one as the season changed—there was no way to warm them. She had moved the cot into the kitchen. She made her home here now. She took sponge baths in front of the stove, brushed her teeth in the kitchen sink. She turned on the radio sometimes and danced between the table and stove, in the room of the infinite possibilities she had ousted. She was also reading Thomas Merton. What he said was, "Nothing one chooses is unbearable."

When she arrived here, it was full summer, and she wandered at night barefoot from room to room in the dark, feeling the smooth pine boards beneath her feet, looking out one open window, then another. There was a sweet warm smell in the house, like old books—perhaps it came from the walls, covered with layers of peeling wallpaper. She arranged wildflowers in jars, watched the shadows of leaves moving in the wind on the many-colored walls. That was euphoria, innocence. Now she was settled in with the winter facts of her situation.

From the kitchen window she could see the road winding through bare oak trees, then up toward Mr. Dunn's old barn, with six pieces of machinery rusting around it. Nearer to the house were the redbud thickets, the doomed elms, the peach tree and the ash. Through October, as the truth caught up with her, she woke sometimes in the night, crying. Her tears flowed down, drenching the pillow, the front of her nightgown. She would get up and stand by the window, the sobs still shaking her. "This is excessive," she would think, amazed and frightened by the number of tears she seemed to have in her, the pain she felt, the anger. Sometimes she actually screamed out, as though a blunt knife had been stuck in her gut.

The haze sat on the hills, but no rain came. The flies banged against the windows, the locusts raised their dry, electronic clamor, until the frost put an end to it. Then she began to be cold and moved into the kitchen, and lay still and straight on her cot at night, near the stove, feeling sometimes that her life had a definite shape, a weight.

She remembered the last thing she'd said to him, at Pennsylvania Station, when he'd gotten her settled, lifted her suitcase onto the overhead rack. She'd whispered, hoping that she meant it, "I'll miss you a lot."

He had looked at her, his green eyes far back in his head and formal, and said nothing.

She was going away for a vacation, a little time to be alone. He would come down later and ride back with her on the train along the river. That was the way they'd left it.

Through all of drought-struck October, she had waited for the mail and listened to the wasps singing inside the walls of this tarpaper tenant house. Her friends Sam and Cora had by then offered to let her have the house in perpetuity—"Whatever that means," Sam said. The house had been empty for three years, until Sam and Cora acquired it and invited her to stay in it for a while. There were empty birds' nests in the chimney, squirrels in the attic.

Mr. Dunn had grown up in this house. She discovered in the back of the linen cupboard a sentence written on the bare plaster wall in black ink. *C.D. Plus P.W. I love Pearl W. and I am going to get her too. Chester Dunn, March 10, 1940.* It was a precise large up-and-down handwriting, nothing hasty or surreptitious about it. It was as if he had laid his cards on the table, daring fate to come along and make a liar out of him. She didn't know whether it had or not. She didn't know Mrs. Dunn's first name. Neither did Sam and Cora. She hoped it was Pearl.

The headlights of a car slipped by the kitchen window going down the hill. The old refrigerator throbbed in the silence. She dropped the envelope on the table. His own hand had touched it three or four days before. She was impatient with herself for thinking such a thing, but went on, turning the idea over laboriously. Right now, in a room as real as this one, he was alive, his brain was still working, flashing splendid images across his eyes. She could find him. He was still on the earth, breathing in and breathing out, he wasn't dead. But it made no difference, gone was gone, dead or alive. That part was over. She had a wall to build.

She turned on the television. The blond weatherman was her current erotic interest. He knew what was in store for her—he had her highs and lows in his radar eyes, he knew what was coming, unseasonable snow from the Great Lakes.

She filled the blue plastic basin with warm water from the kettle. She turned her hands slowly in it, examining them as the garden dirt rolled off. They were raw and red and scraped, a burn on her wrist, calluses at the base of each finger, uneven nails embedded with clay. A wasp sting swelled one knuckle. "Well, that's what happens," she thought. She washed her hands gently, carefully, paying special attention to the blue insides of her wrists. She was thinking of the thing that had happened to Mr. Dunn a few weeks before, the terrible story that had flown up and down the pike, as if the shock couldn't contain itself—how he'd gotten his hand caught in the corn shucker, couldn't reach the ignition to shut the thing off, how he pulled against it for a long time, to keep from feeding more of himself into the mechanism, hoping all the time somebody'd come along, until finally, feeling himself weakening, he'd taken out his knife and cut his hand off. She wondered how he'd gotten through the bone. It wouldn't have been one clean stroke, not with a pocket knife. Once he'd started, he couldn't back out. The blood pumping right out of his body. The strong pulse.

Afterward, he'd made a tourniquet with his belt and managed to crawl to the road, where Richard Lemmons found him and got him to the hospital—just in time, too, they said.

She glanced at herself briefly in the mirror she had propped on the window sill. She was a red-headed woman. Her hair was caught back on her head in an unkempt washerwoman's knot and today was her thirty-fifth birthday. Her sharp naked face was all bone now, three points, cheek, cheek, chin. It was clear what kind of old woman she would make, the wiry kind. But the girl she'd once been was also there, big-eyed, startled. At thirty-five, her face held her whole history, past and future.

That's why she'd heard from him today. It wouldn't have seemed decent to let her birthday go by without resolving the thing. He had his standards.

She went back to the table, opened the letter and read it hastily. "Divorce is not a pleasant word," it said. She found herself nastily mimicking this ridiculous sentence out loud. Something about telephone poles spinning past and a sentence beginning, "Would that—"

She dropped the letter on the table and went to wash the dishes. Her cracked green teacup told her fortune.

Jack was the one who liked to know what his fortune was. They had shuffled the Tarot pack—seriously, thoroughly, concentrating on the question. They had thrown out the coins for the *I Ching*. Jack wasn't ever particularly interested in the oracle's description of his present state. He wanted to know what the lines changed to. What came next. He said he believed in process, flux, but what he really believed was that the present moment, stripped of future possibilities, was intolerable. He hoped that time would carry him somewhere else. Somewhere better.

What she wanted, she thought, was to stand still, with time moving through her, for the rest of her life. He would call this being embalmed before you were dead. The idea of stasis horrified him. She didn't think of standing still as stasis anymore.

In the summer, when she first came here, riding to town with Cora and Sam on occasional evenings, she would pass the Dunns' house and they would be sitting on the porch, one on each side of the door, in their matching red metal lawn chairs. Sitting there motionless and silent, faces forward, looking out over the shady lawn that fell steeply toward the road, with its old dense beds of iris and vinca, birdbaths and stepping stone paths. *C.D. plus P.W.* Fifty years since passion and determination had made him write that on the cupboard wall. How had they liked it? Was it enough for them? Was it plus or minus?

Whichever, their pony was outside her window again. She heard the intimate steady crunch, the snorts and sighs. She was sorry about Mr. Dunn but she wished he'd fix his sorry fence. She hated that pony. Two nights ago, he'd eaten some little dogwood trees and an apple tree she had set out. She usually just yelled at him and ran him off, but he always came back, it was hopeless. Maybe she could find out where he was getting through and patch the fence herself. She put some popcorn kernels in a pan and went outside.

She stood a little way from him. He was a squat, comical little pony, with a lackadaisical sassy sway and a long mane he liked to toss. She shook the kernels in the pan and he looked up at her, figuring the percentages. She edged nearer; so did he. She got her hand on his rope halter and said, "Come on, you jerk." He came peacefully and ploddingly, without further ado. They walked along the curving road, in the dark. She let him lower his nose into the pan from time to time. When they got to the little white house she stopped on the road and called out, "Mr. Dunn!" She saw him looking out the window through the green drapes. It occurred to her that he might not have any idea who she was, though she always waved when he passed in his pickup truck. He came to the door, squinting through the porch light. "It's Kate Gallagher, from up the road? I've got your pony—you want me to put him in the barn?"

"Well," he allowed, in a thin, undecided way. He got his jacket down from a hook. She saw Mrs. Dunn behind him, trying to help him get into it. Maybe this wasn't the way they did things around here. She was probably bothering them. "He came to my yard again, so I thought I'd get him while I could," she called.

"He'll be right down, honey," Mrs. Dunn cried out. She was tall and square in her navy housedress. He put on his grey felt hat and came down the path, making little throat-clearing noises, long legs in grey wash pants, the white bandage at the end of his arm looming. When he got to the pony, who stood beside her snorting and trying to lower his head and graze, he took the halter in his left hand and, clearing his throat again, said, "I wonder what I'd get for this thing if I was to sell him by the pound."

She laughed. He stood there, smiling and nodding under his grey hat, his close-set eyes looking over her head. "I guess he's too smart for a pony," she said.

"Too blame hungry for one, I know that."

"You want me to help you get him in the barn?"

"Well. If I turn him out in the field, he'll just go right back to y'all's yard again." They walked together on the road toward the barn. "I'll see to the fence tomorrow. I hate how he's been bothering y'all."

"That's all right." She didn't know whether to tell him she lived there by herself. He ought to know by now. Maybe he couldn't believe it, or thought it was impolite to notice.

After a while, he explained, shyly, "I've had some trouble keeping up, what with my hand and all." His right arm hung by his side as if it had nothing to do with him.

She didn't let herself look at it. "You feeling all right now, Mr. Dunn?"

"Feeling pretty good," he said, bowing his head politely toward the barn ahead of them.

"I'm glad to hear it."

They walked on under the bright stars, the pony plodding between them. She thought they were a stately crew. After a few steps he held up the bandaged stump with tentative merriment. "They're going to fit me out with a hook directly. Just in time for strippin' season." He glanced at her, grinning a little cautious grin.

"Maybe you'll revolutionize the whole tobacco industry," she ventured.

He opened his thin lips in an appreciative soundless laugh. "That's right. 'Fore long, ever'body in this county is going to be wanting them a hook."

She glanced at the stump then, she couldn't help herself. The club of bandage, and then nothing. He brought it down to his side self-consciously. "I sure do admire you," she said. "Being able to—to do that. What you did."

"Didn't have but one other choice." He nodded, a bright fixed look on his face under the rim of his hat. He turned then to spit politely off to the other side. "I was just glad I had my knife."

They walked together into the dark, leaning barn, tier on tier of tobacco rising up. There was a stall down at the end. He and the pony went ahead, ducking under the cured leaves, sidestepping bales of straw and mowers and tubs. "It's kindly tied with baling twine," he said, apologetically.

He and the pony waited while she picked out the knot and opened the stall door. He led the pony in and then came out and rummaged around in the dark till he found a water bucket. He turned on the pump and filled it, lifted it with difficulty with his left hand. She didn't think she should offer to help. She held the door open and he carried the bucket into the stall. But he couldn't hoist it onto the hook on the wall with one hand. He set it down and bent to it quickly with his other hand, then remembered it wasn't there. He grabbed the handle again with his left hand and stuck the handless arm under, too. He managed to raise it that way. She stepped forward quickly to help—her hands, his hand, and the stump all lifting the heavy bucket onto the hook. "Thanks," he said, nodding in a dignified way, then turned to the pony. "Now I ain't *givin'* you nothin' to eat, so you'd just as well not to ask. You done already grazed down their whole yard."

She tied the string back. "Who's going to untie this tomorrow?" she asked.

"I'll let that sucker stay there for a day or two. Till I get the fence mended."

They walked back out to the road in silence. He thanked her again. "I'll help you with the fence tomorrow, if you want me to," she offered.

"Naw, she'll help me. She's a pretty good helper."

She thought Mrs. Dunn's name had to be Pearl. If it wasn't, she didn't want to know.

She walked back up the road, saw the lights from her kitchen window shining through the trees. She wasn't sure what *in perpetuity* meant, either. There was the little house, with its fallen-off front porch and rotted window frames, its patchy lawn full of burdock and plantain, its leaning outhouse. When she looked at it, she looked at it with love and domestic determination. *Eventually* was a prayer—eventually, full of grace. She saw stone fences, perennial borders, an orchard down the north-facing slope. She saw a porch swing, a storm door. She looked at the house not as a person camping in it with two saucepans and a cot while her marriage fell apart, but as a person who meant to stay.

She went in the house and fixed herself a drink. She looked at the letter on the table and without malice picked it up and threw it in the stove. She'd get in touch with a lawyer in the morning. She was thirty-five now. What she was still hoping for was sweet human constancy, fixity. She watched the end of the news—Arab women squatted with their heads in their long hands, swaying, grieving.

When the news was over, she fixed herself some potatoes with cheese grated on top and a sliced tomato. After she'd eaten, she turned on the radio. It was George Harrison. *Little darlin', seems like years since it's been here*—She danced. She saw her reflection moving against the window pane. She danced in the kitchen in her muddy jeans with the knees bagged out. It was her birthday. She was quite alone tonight, but she was not at all unhappy. *It's all right,* sang George. She danced and danced, not knowing that the state was headed for the longest, coldest winter on record, that the wind coming through the cracks would blow the dish towel off the nail, that the snow would fall to the window sills and stay for months. Underneath it the thick layer of mulch she had laid on top of the garden would gradually break down and make a little topsoil. She didn't know that she would get a yellow dog who would one day, meaning no harm, lick the yellow kitten to death in the snow. She didn't know that she would finish her wall and that one July evening, on the broad, smooth, shallow, fossil-filled slabs of limestone, she would stretch out full-length with the heat of the sun still warm in the stones, that she would look up through the leaves of the peach tree at the pearly evening sky, Mozart coming out through the kitchen window on the breeze, the Dunns' little black pony even then on his way up the hill toward her garden—cantaloupe, beans, tomatoes, corn, all in their twilit rows, wheeling through their season on the earth.

The Fugitive

RICHARD CORTEZ DAY

Richard Cortez Day was born in Covington, Kentucky, in 1926. He grew up in Michigan and attended the University of Michigan, where he received a B.S. in mathematics and chemistry and an M.A. in English. After serving four years in the United States Navy, he attended the University of Iowa, where he earned a Ph.D. in literature. He was a professor of English at Humbolt State University in Arcata, California, until his recent retirement. Day has come later to the literary front than have many of his contemporaries, but his work displays a sophistication and timeliness that suggest his mastery of the craft of fiction. *When In Florence* (1986), his first and to date only published collection, features fifteen interrelated stories and sketches. These stories portray the depth of sensitivity to the human condition that characterizes all of his work. His short fiction has appeared in *New Mexico Quarterly*, *Massachusetts Review*, *Kenyon Review*, *Redbook*, *Quarterly West*, *Carolina Quarterly*, *New England Review*, *Proza Americana* (Romania), *Damernas Varld* (Sweden), *Stories for the Sixties*, *Imagining Worlds*, and *The Pushcart Prize*.

First published in 1984, "The Fugitive" is representative of a cultural period that finds individuals frustrated both by their compulsion to identify with their own cultural history and with the difficulties they experience in complying with this need. Having escaped or been exiled from his ancestral self, Day's protagonist is confounded by his instinctive response to an interloper with whom he shares common roots; his resulting inner conflict advances this story beyond the scope of a simple narrative into a fine example of the modern short story.

◆

Matthew Furman wore the look of a man whose house has been taken over by skunks. He sat in his pickup, glaring through the rain at the cabin. His neck hurt. Thirst pinched his throat. "Dammit," he said, and started the engine. He backed around in the clearing, pointed the truck toward town, and said, "Dammit to hell." He raised his head and looked at himself in the mirror. In the matted hair, the cheeks caved in and bristly with three days' stubble—in the eyes red-rimmed and with a network of veins in the whites—he saw the face of a man who had outsmarted himself. "Goddammit," he said and, thirsty though he was for whiskey, drove forward and stopped over the same dry spot. The dice swung back and forth from the mirror.

It wasn't skunks in the cabin. Her name was Annie Reardon. In town last Saturday night, after a few drinks at Toby and Jack's, he had jumped into the truck for the short drive to El Rancho Remuda, where he planned to do some dancing, spread himself among the divorcees, then choose a mount. But he never got to the Remuda. Within two blocks he spotted this one parked at the curb, gripping the steering wheel and jerking back and forth like a child on a stuck trike. The green Ford had Kentucky plates. He swerved in ahead of it, got out, and ambled back. "What's wrong, sweetness? Won't she run?"

"It's out of gas," she said. "Would you fetch me a can?"

Her voice was pure music. For years he hadn't heard that sweet Kentucky speech from a woman's mouth. It reminded him of cool well water in a beechwood bucket, of the breeze in the willows by Troublesome Creek, back home in Hindman. She had wavy hair to her shoulders and eyes whose color he couldn't determine in that light, but shining like stones in a streambed.

"Don't be too sure," he said. "Just pop the hood—I'll have a look." He opened it, thumbed the fan belt, jiggled the distributor wires. He closed the lid and put on a woeful face. "It's the fuel pump," he said, "or maybe a plug in the gas line." He glanced around inside. She was loaded to the roof with suitcases, cardboard boxes, and pillowcases stuffed full.

"The gauge says empty," she said.

"Then it's the fuel pump. It ain't pumping gas to the gauge." He let out a sigh. "I reckon I could call a tow truck to haul you to the Exxon up the street. Then I could run you to a motel." In his experience, if you threw enough troubles in a woman's way, she was yours.

He watched her mouth firm up, her face tighten. She swallowed her fate and adjusted to the lump. He waited. With honey in his voice, then, he said, "Here, now, I hate to see a stranger all alone and helpless. If you'd consent to stay at my place, with me and my wife and children. . . ."

"I wouldn't want to put you out," she said.

"Put me out? Why, it's no trouble at all." He paused, smacked his forehead, and said, "I plumb forgot. I wonder if that old cable is still in the truck. My bumper's too high to push you, but with a cable. . . ."

"I'd be obliged," she said.

"I'm William T. Mason. I love the way you talk."

"Annie Reardon," she said.

He all but had her. When she learned there was no wife or children, he would flat-out fall on his knees, say he couldn't help himself, struck as he was by love and mindless from her beauty. No woman he'd ever met could resist a bold man on the floor, begging for mercy.

He backed the pickup to her, hooked the cable, and flashed a thumbs-up sign. He started the truck and, with a small jolt, pulled her into the traffic. He hummed a tune as he drove. At the cross street just before the station, he obeyed the stop sign. The blow knocked him back in the seat, shoved the truck forward. The cable twanged and she hit him again. "Aw," he said, and got out.

Her bumper had gone in under his. Both headlights looked sadly down as her radiator water ran off in the gutter. He shook his fist. "Can't you read? That sign says Stop."

"What was you going so fast for? How bad is it?"

"I hope you got insurance," he said. He towed her on into the station and unhooked the cable. "Hop out. There ain't a thing more to do with her tonight."

She opened her door and, by using both hands, lifted one leg out and set it down. Then she did the other leg. She hung a knitting bag on her shoulder. She brought out some aluminum crutches and fitted her forearms into the bands. When she tried standing, it looked as if someone had hold of her from behind. On the second try, she pulled free and jacked herself upright.

It wasn't even a whole woman. The shawl came down over the dress, and the dress fell to below the boot-tops. He couldn't say how much was alive, but it seemed as if the dead part might begin at about the waist. In the car were no footpedals, just levers on the steering column. She said, "It's special built. That's the brakes and thatere's the gas. It's automatic. I'll talk to the man while you load my things in your truck."

On the ten-mile drive along Creek Road, he thought of ways to be rid of her. He found only one. Where the blacktop ended and the lights shone on a No Trespassing sign, he said, "I took advantage of you in town there. I ain't got a wife and children. I ain't even got a dog. I did have one, but she took sick and I had to shoot her."

"What was you fixing to do with me, Mr. Mason?"

"My name ain't Mason, either. It's Matt Furman. Look, I'll run you back in, to a motel."

"No, Mr. Whatever-it-is, open the gate and get on, before it rains on my things. Is this your woods?"

"I wish it was. I'm just the watchdog of it."

He got out, opened the gate and drove through, then closed it. Two hundred yards up a rutted road, the cabin stood in a clearing. With the flashlight, he went around and helped her down. "It's the end of the world here," she said. "Is that noise a waterfall?"

"It's the creek, full of runoff. Watch your step."

He laid the beam on the ground in front of her. She set each crutch forward with the foot on the same side, rolling like a boat as she went. But she went fast. He hurried past her, opened the door, and switched on the overhead light. "What do you want carried in?" he said.

"All of it. I don't want it out in the wet or stolen."

"Now, I ain't unloading it all in the house. I'll put a tarp over it."

"Mr. Whatsit—who lured me out here? Who caused me to wreck my car? Tote it all in. I see only the one bed. Where am I to sleep?"

"In it. I'll sleep on the sofa."

He brought in load after load. When he dropped a carton an inch, she said, "I seen mules smarter'n to throw a box of dishes." He gave her a look but didn't lash back, poor cripple that she was. As he set down the last suitcase, she said, "Now find me some clean sheets, then step outside. This has been a trying day."

Only partly drunk to begin with, he had sobered to where there wasn't a wisp of pleasure in him. He gave her the sheets, then walked through the woods to the bluff above the creek. As he relieved himself down into it, a wind gusted in the trees and the rain came. He watched the cabin until the bedlamp went off.

Inside, stumbling over boxes in the dark, he took two blankets from the closet and, without undressing, stretched out as well as he could on the couch. His neck was on one arm of it, his ankles on the other. In between he sagged like a hammock. He said, "What part of Kentucky do you come from?"

"The town of Dwarf, not far from Hazard."

"Where was you heading when you ran out of gas?"

"To my sister's in Salem, Oregon. I thought you said my fuel pump went out."

"I could of been mistaken. I ain't a mechanic."

She waited a second, then said, "Mr. Whosit, you are a nasty man. You seem old for such tricks. Why ain't you married and settled?"

"I ain't that old yet."

"Your life is in the wrong place," she said. "If it was in your soul, instead of down there, you wouldn't find yourself in a mess all the time. I learned not to set store by the flesh. Flesh can be bent and broken, twisted and eaten up. But the soul stays firm. I spent six months in the hospital, then a year in a home, waking with pain and going to bed with it at night. But through it all, my soul was a rock in the stream of suffering. Not a day goes by but I thank the Lord for my strength."

"What happened to you?"

"I run into a coal train."

"Was you drunk?"

"I don't drink. No, I didn't see it till I hit it. The blinker signal wasn't working, so the railroad had to pay all my bills. They bought me that car you wrecked."

"Hold on, I didn't wreck it. You did. How old are you?"

"In my new life I'm five years old. I was twenty-one when the Lord sent me into the side of that train."

Furman snorted. "The Lord don't miss. Tonight, he rammed you into the back end of my truck. If I was you I wouldn't set foot in a car."

"Don't make fun, mister," she said. "Life is test after test. You seem smart enough, but you're ignorant. You ain't had the experience. Any fool can laugh before it happens. It's afterwards that I would like to see your face. Some prove out, but most fail. You, I think, would fail it."

To stay balanced on the sofa, he crossed his arms on his chest. On the roof the rain whispered and from below came the steady rush of the creek. The stove clicked as it cooled. He said, "Let's see if I got it straight—the Lord shut your eyes to that stop sign."

"Don't they ever sleep in California?"

"I want to be sure I got it right is all."

"Hush and let me rest. This here bed smells musty. You ought to air it out."

"It's a test," he said. "Is your nose strong enough to take it?"

"What my nose can't take," she said, "is drink. Your breath would peel paint. I'll thank you to abstain while I stay here."

If asked what California was like, Furman would have said, "About like Eastern Kentucky, only the trees are bigger and there ain't no coal." If asked about the ocean, he would have granted that there was one, that Outlaw Creek ran into it fifteen miles down the valley from where he lived. But he didn't often see it. When he did, when he happened to be high on a hill and glance out, he was surprised to find it there, a foreign, blue-gray curved plate, tilted skyward. It was a strange presence, the ocean. He'd gone to the beach once but hadn't enjoyed it. The weight of all that water, the malevolent hiss of the surf: the thing never stopped moving. It thumped and roared with a life of its own. It made him as jumpy as a cat in a brushfire.

He had come here from Kentucky twelve years before, on his way to Canada. Back in Hindman the draft was after him to go to Vietnam and be killed. To his mind the draft, like a net made of smart snakes, would snag him if he took the straight way north, so he slipped west to skirt it. When he got to Arcata, his car died. He left it by the freeway. After living for a time in the hotel, he found a seasonal job on a logging crew for Backrack Timber. Then he answered a newspaper ad for a caretaker, got that job too, and moved out to Nathaniel Barnes' timber tract, into a rent-free cabin.

He never went home to Hindman. Even when the draft ended he stayed in California, for it hadn't been only the draft he'd run from, but also Jean Rae Benson's father who'd claimed, by virtue of his daughter's condition, her right to marriage. A stringy hill-farmer with a red Adam's apple, he'd tried throwing a net over Furman one day at the Aramco station. He had him against the wall, with a knotty arm on each side of him, as he recounted in a slow voice what the Bible said about sowing and reaping. Furman watched the Adam's apple sliding up and down the long neck. Benson said, "Jean Rae is comin' on sixteen, and that's a poor life ahead, with a baby and all, if you was to get killt in the army."

"It ain't my baby," Furman said.

Benson drew his lips back and showed his chew-stained teeth. It was a kind of smile. "Ifn it ain't yourn," he said, "hit's a immaculate conception."

The baby could have been Furman's. It could have been three or four other men's too, or even God's. He didn't stay for the blood test. He threw some clothes into his old blue Dodge and cut out westward. Fifteen miles from Hindman, he passed for the last time through the town of Dwarf.

It rained Sunday, Monday, and Tuesday. Annie Reardon kept him out in it, running errands. She sent him to the garage for the estimate on her car, then to the insurance agent in town; she sent him to the grocery store, to the laundromat, and back to the garage to check on the repairs, while she expanded into the cabin. As if by magic, her possessions escaped from the bags and boxes, lodging in his bathroom, kitchen, drawers and closet. He never caught her at it, but would blink and another blouse was in with his workshirts.

She took over the cooking and washing up. She was more agile crippled than he was sound. She cooked on one crutch and washed dishes on none, propping her body against the sink. When she set the table she loaded up an arm like a waitress and, on a single crutch, heeled around the divider. She crocheted, sang hymns to herself, said grace over the food, and read the Bible before going to bed. She liked sitting in the tub for an hour. She knew right from wrong to the width of a fine hair, and didn't hesitate to let him know which side of the hair he stood on. She had a tongue like a wood-rasp. He thought he'd never hear the end of how his lust had cost her the 100–dollar deductible on her insurance.

Always before, he'd praised a woman's upper parts to gain access to the lower, but this one was a living contradiction—above the shoulders a beautiful Mona Lisa except for her tongue, but below the waist a dead tree, her lap a fork where two sticks met, with maybe an abandoned bird's nest in there out of sight.

By late Tuesday he couldn't stand it anymore; he had to have a drink. He splashed out to the truck, backed around in the clearing, cursed, drove forward again and, as the dice swung from the mirror, splashed back through the mud to the cabin. She hadn't moved. From the armchair by the stove she threw him a glance and went on crocheting. He sank onto the sofa, which let him down to where he had to view her from between his knees.

In her fingers the hooks flashed. She said, "A rule I follow is to never make a mess I'll have to clean up later. It's from passion we make messes. Then we must pay the price. Looket the prints you left on the linoleum. Was it worth it to stomp in with muddy boots?"

"I'll hire me somebody to clean it, a pretty girl in a short skirt. One that likes a friendly drink and don't preach." He watched her face. She didn't blink, and her fingers didn't miss a loop. He lifted his hands and said, "I wish the Lord would fix the TV."

"The TV? Here you got the garden spot of all the world, God's green woods all around and a sweet creek running down below, and you'd watch ads for soap? What I would do this evening, if I was you, is to take a bath. You smell like a animal."

"How I smell is my own business."

Her mouth tightened. "The Lord made humans and the Lord made beasts. Which one are you?" The hooks flashed in her fingers. The yellow work lay in folds on her lap. Her hands moved like spiders in a web.

"What are you making, a rug to preach on?"

"It's a baby blanket for my sister. She's due this month. But if I was to preach from it, you might profit by hearing."

He raised an arm and sniffed. It wasn't an animal smell at all. It was a little strong maybe, but human, his own human odor. He said, "What was it like to hit a train? Did it happen in slow motion, like drowning in the sea?"

"I never drowned in the sea. Nor I think did you."

In the woods he'd had some close calls. Sometimes a rogue log would jump downhill at him, and it always seemed like slow motion. Bits of bark sailed, dirt mushroomed up, and his body moved ponderously out of the way as if under a weight of water. "I mean, was it like a dream—all slow and spooky?"

"I don't recall it. All I know is, I woke up in the hospital in a new life, shed of the old one. I left a wrecked car on one side of that train and came out the other, in pain but all new." The spiders paused in the web. "It was a miracle," she said.

"Praise God. Are we going to eat tonight?"

"Warm the stew," she said. "Waste not, want not."

Dreaming of home, he woke up but fell back into it again, and there they were, the three children at breakfast, sitting on cane-bottom chairs—Mallie's hair already dark, Ben's still blond—as their mother ladled mush into the bowls. He saw the faded apron, printed with bluebells, and saw the round, muscular arm. He tried to see her face, but it was above him in a cloud of steam. He tried waving the steam away, but his arm had withered.

"Do you plan to sleep the day through?" she said, and he opened his eyes to find her looking down at him. "The weather has changed," she said. "I came far out of my way to see the shoreline. Today you can take me to it."

It was full daylight. She had already made the bed and put breakfast on, and that smell: he didn't have to look to know what it was. He'd always thought of it as a white smell, a weak smell. He got to his feet and saw, past the divider, steam seeping from around the pot lid on the stove. He went to the bathroom. When he returned she was ladling white mush. She put a lump of butter in each bowl, sprinkled brown sugar on, and poured in a layer of milk. He watched the butter melt out in yellow streaks. In the pot there was plenty left. He foresaw tonight's supper: corn-meal mush fried in bacon fat if there was money, in canned lard if there wasn't.

"Are you in a trance? Take the bowls to the table."

They sat down, and she dipped her head. "Father we thank You for this food, bless it to our use and us to Thy service, Amen." She picked up her spoon. "You have mice. One ran over the coverlet in the night."

Behind her, sunlight flamed in the treetops on the ridge across the creek. Against the light, her hair seemed to have caught fire. He began eating, and at the soft, grainy texture of the stuff he closed his eyes and saw a sunlit Troublesome Creek and Mallie and Ben, wearing only white underpants, playing in the shadow of the sycamore. They were throwing stones across the water. He must have said something, for they stopped and gazed up at him, the light pooling in their eyes.

"You're dribbling on your shirt," she said.

He pushed his bowl away. Except for his sister, they were all dead, his father killed in a mine cave-in just after Ben was born, Ben in a car wreck the night of high-school graduation. Mallie had sent him three postcards in twelve years. One said that their mother had died, though not from what; the second that she'd married; and the third, from Florida, that she lived there now and had named her baby Matthew, after him.

He carried the bowls to the kitchen. While she washed up, he went to the bluff and looked down on the brown moil of water. He threw a stick in and watched the current take it. He picked up a big rock and chunked it over: it splashed and was gone. From the branches overhead, water dripped on the leaf mold, and the morning sun slanted through the trees in moist beams.

She opened the door and came out crabwise.

On the drive she looked around at the March blooms: wild mustard, daisies, Queen Anne's lace. As they passed a cherry in flower, she said, "It's spring. I should of been in Oregon Sunday last, and look where I landed."

"You ain't landed," he said, turning north onto the freeway. "This here's the road you'll take tomorrow."

In the sunlight, red clover enlivened the embankments, and a few miles from town they saw a whole hillside of yellow broom. Where the freeway swerved close to the ocean, he pulled off onto a frontage road and drove until he found a trail she could manage, then parked with a dune between him and the water. "You go ahead. I seen the ocean already."

She fitted her arms to the crutches and set off, lurching through seagrass and yellow lupine. From beyond the low sandhills came the surf's thunder. He rolled the windows up but still could hear it. The sound affected his breathing; there didn't seem to be enough air in the cab. He opened the windows again, then the doors, and finally got out and walked back and forth on the road. The musky scent of lupine stuck in his nostrils. He opened his mouth for air.

A long hour passed before he saw her scuttling between two dunes, kicking at the seagrass with her crutches. He waited by the open door, then helped her in. "I thought a whale got you," he said. He started the engine and headed for the freeway.

She smelled of the salt wind, and her hair was blown to tangles. She had high color in her cheeks. Her eyes, like bits of the sea, were a bright blue-gray. "It's God's creation," she said. "If I lived here I would see it every day of my life."

"Don't it scare you?"

"The ocean? It ain't but water. Looket what I found."

From her dress pocket she brought out a double handful of seashells. "You ought to throw them dice out and string shells up."

"It goes clear to the sky," he said.

"What does?"

"The ocean. That sea out there."

"It does not. It goes over to China is all. It's round, like a eyeball, and Columbus sailed over it to the New World."

"That was the Atlantic," he said.

"It's the same. All the oceans are connected. The land is broken up, but the sea is one."

Furman didn't know if that was true or not, but he did know that if she thought the sea was only water she hadn't seen the full extent of it, the reach and weight, the unnatural skyward tilt. At the No Trespassing sign on the gate, he said, "I'm going to show you something."

This time he drove past the cabin and on up the logging road. She braced herself as the truck leaned. At a level spot he stopped and shifted to four-wheel drive. The old road, water riven and grown over with alder shoots, spiraled up the mountain. To the sides, trails branched off like veins in a leaf. She said, "Don't get us stuck." The cab rocked and she grabbed the door handle. "You're going to tip us over." She hung on as the dice did a full loop and rattled on the mirror.

Near the top they emerged from the trees into a meadow of wildflowers. "Bluebells!" she said. "Why, it's a painted lake. Stop and look at it."

He kept on going. Birds scattered ahead of them, and off to the right two does and a fork-horn swivelled their ears and watched. The fork-horn leaped first, then the does, and all three vanished into a stand of oak.

"Where are you taking me?"

He pushed on to the summit and stopped at a flat, layered rock. He went around the truck. "Come on, I'll lift you up there."

"I can do it," she said. "You keep your hands off me."

It was a chest-high step for her. She put the crutches up, then placed her hands on the stone and, by pure strength, heaved her body up and sat on the edge. Then she swung around, got one leg and a crutch under her, and pulled upright. He climbed up and handed her the other crutch. He steered her to a farther foot-high step, helped her up, and pointed to the east.

The valley opened out below, pure green, with a brown river snaking through it. Straight across, mountains rose up and, behind them, a higher range where the green turned blue with distance. Away to the north stood three snowy peaks. A hawk sailed over the valley, tilting its wings and curving. "There now," he said, "we're in the sky."

"It's earth," she said. "The sky's up yonder."

"Then turn around," he said. This was what he'd brought her for. She stood on the step above him. As she turned he watched her face, to note the shock.

She said, "Is that the town down there? Where's the Exxon?"

"Dammit, look straight out. That's the ocean. It's as high as we are, it slants to the sky—look at it."

"It don't," she said. "'God made the firmament, and divided the waters which were under the firmament from the waters which were above the firmament.' That's the Bible, mister." She gazed down on him and took pity. She pointed one crutch straight up. "Thatere's the sky," she explained. She thumped the other crutch on the rock. "This here's earth. If the two was to meet, it wouldn't make sense."

He looked out at the great, strange plate of ocean, the bluish presence curving up and around. In the middle distance three buzzards circled. He looked up at the sure face above him, at the windblown hair, at the steady eyes that took their color now from the green trees on the slope. Her hair moved in the breeze.

Then she stirred. She stepped down beside him. "Let's get on back. I got to pack my things."

He witnessed the reversal, in hurry-up time, of the magic by which her household had grown into his, and without elation he sat across from her over a supper of fried mush. She kept her thoughts to herself. He had no thoughts except that, for some reason, he didn't feel right. After supper he took a hot bath and shaved off his four-day beard. In the mirror he saw her blue bathrobe on a peg behind the door. Using her towel, he caught a whiff of violets.

He dressed in clean clothes, combed his hair, and presented himself for judgment. She glanced up from her fingerwork and said, "Did you scour the tub?" He went back and scoured it.

She took a full hour for her bath. He heard splashing and thumping in there; he heard a snatch of a hymn: "Nearer My God to Thee." She came out in the blue robe, hair bound in a towel, and flooded the air with violets. She sat in the armchair, laid the crutches on the floor, and her fingers went to work again at once.

Sunk in the sofa, he watched from between his knees. He raised one hand level, hiding all but her head. In the turban-like wrap, her face all shiny from the bath, she looked like an Arab queen. He put both hands up, thumbs together, and framed her in a square U. Her head was bowed toward the work in her lap, and her face, calm and composed, seemed fuller somehow, especially in the lips.

He brought the tips of his forefingers together, closed one eye, and observed her through the slit. She must have put lip balm on, for in the lamplight her mouth looked wet.

"Are you playing peeky-boo?" she said. "Go on outside and play it, so I can go to bed. Morning comes early."

It was as if a faith healer said, "Walk." He struggled up and went out. The sky had stayed clear. Puffs of cloud, scooting past the half-moon, whitened, then darkened. At the bluff he urinated in a silver arc toward the creek that, forever moving, shattered the moonlight to glitter. From below came the rushing watersound, and above, a soft wind ghosted through the trees.

When she turned off the bedlamp he went in, set the draft on the stove, and removed his shoes. He sagged onto the sofa. As his eyes adjusted he saw that, though the trees screened the moonlight, it wasn't entirely dark. Enough light leaked in to show him her shape in the bed and the boxes at the foot of it. He crossed his arms to hold the blankets on. "Goodnight," he said.

"Goodnight." She shifted beneath the covers.

He thought ahead to Monday when, if the wind held and no rain came, he'd be back in the woods after the winter layoff. Before then he had to buy new boots and bootsocks, work on his chainsaw, grease and change the oil in the pickup. He had to buy mink oil for the boots and lay in a week's food. Once work started he'd leave in the dark and get home in the dark, with no time to shop. She cooked with too much grease, Kentucky style, as his mother had done, who, like a bit of leaf in Troublesome Creek, had floated off to eternity.

His mind slewed like a sprint-car on a dirt oval. He wished a faith healer would say "Sleep," for he couldn't. He couldn't turn over on the couch. His neck felt dead. As the moon sank, more light entered, advancing to the bed. She slept on her back, maybe dreaming, her breath shallow and skittish. He couldn't see her face, but that dark patch on the pillow was her hair. He wondered what she looked like asleep.

Most men had wives to do for them. On his crew you could tell the married men by the lunches they brought. Even young ones just starting out had mothers to fix meals and do the wash. The divorced ones soon fell apart from drink and bad diet. Her face, he imagined, softened when she slept. The moonlight had crept to where he could almost see.

His thought-storm wouldn't stop, and no wonder: his bladder was full again. If he was to sleep at all, he'd have to make a trip. He pushed the blankets off, set his feet on the floor, and stood. He tiptoed forward.

The bedclothes convulsed. The lamp clicked on. She sat with her back to the wall, holding the covers to her chin. Her right hand held the butcher knife pointing straight at his belly.

"Try that," she said, "and I'll cut it off you."

"What in the hell?"

"Go on back over there."

"I reckon I can use my own damn toilet, can't I?"

"Use it," she said. "Then get back to your own side."

At the toilet he couldn't get started. To think that every night since Saturday she'd taken the knife to bed, waiting to kill him. It was past belief. "Gratitude!" he called out. He finally squeezed forth a tight stream.

He flushed the toilet and went out. "Trust," he said. "I bring you in and feed you, and all you can think is rape. I'd sooner rape a polecat. I'd sooner rape my truck."

"Suit yourself," she said. "Just don't try it on me."

She waited until he was on the couch again, then snapped off the light.

"What kind of a woman are you? Goddamn it to hell, I never raped anybody in my whole life."

She said nothing.

"What in hell brought you my way? Why didn't you go to Oregon by the straight road? You had no call to come through here."

She wouldn't speak. He ground his teeth and glared upward.

At last the sofa took vengeance. He woke up groaning, his vertebrae fused, his neck a solid bar. He heard her in the bathroom. He tied his shoes by feel; he couldn't tip his head forward. When he tried lifting the first box, he found he couldn't bend his back. An iron hand gripped him by the nape. He wobbled to the truck with the box. When he returned, she was stripping the bed. "Will you want breakfast?" she said.

"I ain't hungry."

"There's no call to pout, mister. When it comes to trust, I place it on high. I find it's wasted here below."

"Go live on high then." He hoisted the next box.

Her appetite didn't seem impaired. She made a full breakfast of bacon and eggs, while he came and went, and then she washed the dishes and cleaned the stove top and counter. When he finished he waited outside, watching the sun lean in on the cabin. Steam rose from the roof, from the wood sorrel where the sun fell. It wisped upward and vanished.

She came out finally, her knitting bag swinging from side to side, and he went in for the last suitcase. He tossed it in the pickup. He climbed into the cab and groaned. At work again on the baby blanket, she said, "What's wrong with you?"

"I got a sore neck."

"You look green," she said. "You ain't healthy."

He pushed her crutches off the gearshift and started the engine. "I'll be better directly," he said.

On the drive to town she worked at the blanket. She was still working when, at the Exxon station, he pulled in beside her car. "Good," he said. "She's fixed."

"Wait," she said. She hooked a few more loops, then wove an intricate knot at the corner. From the bag she took a pair of scissors, snipped the yarn, and said, "There now, it wasn't all time lost."

As she folded the blanket, he got out and began transferring her household. Then she got out and went inside. In a few minutes, she came back with the bill. "If you would raise the hood?" she said. He did it, and she leaned in. "Is that a new radiator? He charged me for a new one. Which is the water pump? Does it look new? Does it all look properly installed?"

"Ask on high," he said. "I ain't a mechanic."

"Mister," she said, "my innocence cost me four days and a hundred dollars. I don't want to break down on the road."

He sat in the car and started it. He watched the temperature gauge as the engine heated. Overriding the pain in his neck, then, he got on hands and knees and looked underneath for leaks. He tested the headlights. "She seems all right," he said. "When you buy gas, get the water checked."

He finished packing the car.

Her way of entering it was to back up to the seat, then drop. She stowed the crutches behind her. With her hands she lifted the legs in one at a time. She pulled the door shut.

"Well, mister," she said.

"My name is Furman, goddamn it. Matthew Furman."

"Whatever it is, I hope you'll mend your ways. A smart man don't need but one lesson. You ought to get a dog to replace the one you shot. It ain't good to live as you do, a beast alone."

"Preach on," he said. "Preach to the birds and bushes all the way to Oregon."

Looking straight ahead, she freed her hair from the shawl, turned the key, and shifted to Drive. She touched the gas lever and rolled to the street. Without a glance back, she eased into the stream of cars flowing north.

Now that he didn't have to be so nice, he urinated on a tree close beside the cabin, then went inside. She'd left nothing but invisible fingerprints and the weak smell of violets. The place was his own again, the day and night were his, and he was free to follow where desire might lead, with no one to whip him for it. He stood between the stove and bed and turned his whole body in a circle as he looked around.

He had the king of all stiff necks. The pain took root somewhere just above his hips and sent tendrils curling up inside his head. On top of that, because of no breakfast, there was a storm in his stomach. If he had eaten breakfast, he wouldn't be half sick. If she hadn't drawn that knife on him, he would've had breakfast. If she hadn't run out of gas or left Kentucky or hit that coal train, he wouldn't have slept four nights on the sofa and be cramped with a neck so sore it made his eyes water.

He backed to the bed, sat down, swung his feet up, and stretched out at full length for the first time since Saturday. If he could catch a nap, sleep backwards in time, then he would wake up as fresh and ready as if none of this had happened.

She'd left a trace of violets, her spoor, on the pillow. When he knocked it off the bed, his head rested on something foreign. He reached and found she'd hidden something for him, two of the little scallop shells she'd picked up on the beach. He turned them over in his hand, and then remembered. "Aw, it ain't," he said.

But he knew it was. He dragged himself from the bed and out the door, and well before he reached the truck he saw the absence at the mirror. He'd had those dice since he was old enough to drive; they'd dangled from the mirror of the old Dodge he fled west in. There was no telling how many times they'd saved his life on the road and in the woods, and now the strings hung empty. She'd by God clipped them off with those scissors of hers.

He went to the bluff and flung the shells over, but didn't see the splash. At high noon it was bright down there, the sun bearing on the water, and the shells just vanished in the glare. The light moved like liquid metal. It was a flood of light in motion, rising, filling the valley, golden when he first looked, but then unbearably clear and colorless. He shut his eyes and turned away, and at once a pattern sprang up inside his lids, a black river on a blinding field.

He thought he must have ruined his eyesight, for when he looked he saw a world gone green. Between him and the cabin, and somewhat off the ground, a green river writhed in air the color of trees' blood. On the veined backs of his hands the skin had a greenish cast, and in the woods he felt a peculiar agitation, like water stirring. The light seeped down through a green, weightless sea.

It wasn't even air. Holding his breath he lifted a leg, an arm, and began pumping in slow motion toward the truck. He caught the door handle, got inside, and got the motor going. He rocked in the ruts to the gate, leaped out, and vaulted over. He gulped and could breathe, rubbed his eyes and his sight snapped back.

He stood there panting, looking all around. It was the same old woods. There sat his truck on the other side of the gate, the engine still ticking over. He could hear the creek. That stirring in the trees, it was only the wind. The woods had their natural light and shade again. "What was it?" he said, and turned his head from side to side. The exertion seemed to have freed his neck some.

A step at a time, while looking all around, he opened the gate and drove the pickup through. He closed the gate and looked back in over it. There was nothing. It was the plain woods, just trees and bushes, floor growth, animals, birds, and bugs. He shook his head and said, "Don't that beat all?"

In the cab again, he saw the sunlight shimmering on the blacktop. In the mirror he saw words that made no sense:

ᴐИI225AꟼƧƎЯT OИ

Did she for one minute think he couldn't find other dice? She in her special Ford, a green dot shrinking away toward Oregon? Why, hell, the auto supply in town sold drilled dice in all colors, and at the same stop he could have steak and eggs at the Alibi, then invest in new boots at Canclini's. Shoot, he might just drop in at Toby and Jack's and pick up where he left off last Saturday, only this time make it all the way to El Rancho and get a whole woman.

But it wasn't the same. That damned Kentucky woman had ruined his way of thinking, had sucked all the pleasure from life. He felt not a tatter of desire to run to town.

He shut off the engine. The sound of the creek came up, full of uncertainties. Behind him the green woods stirred and whispered. The spring sunshine brightened everything around him. He sat where he was, absolutely still, at the end of a road that twisted through the vibrant light toward the town and beyond, toward the invisible ocean.

The Perfecting of the Chopin Valse No. 14 in E Minor

Sena Jeter Naslund

The daughter of a music teacher mother and a physician father, Sena Jeter Naslund was born in 1942 in Birmingham, Alabama. In high school she was a cellist with the Alabama Pops Orchestra. She is a graduate of Birmingham-Southern and the Iowa Writers' Workshop at the University of Iowa, where she earned both her M.A. and her Ph.D. in creative writing. Following her graduate work she taught for a year at the University of Montana, and since 1973 has taught at the University of Louisville. She is co-editor of the *Louisville Review* and the Fleur-de-Lis Press, housed at Spalding University. Her work includes three novels, *The Animal Way to Love* (1993), *Sherlock in Love* (1993), and *Ahab's Wife or, The Star-Gazer* (1999), which was a Book of the Month Club selection; and two short story collections, *Ice Skating at the North Pole* (1989) and *The Disobedience of Water* (1997). Her short stories have appeared in *The Georgia Review, The Iowa Review, Michigan Quarterly Review, The Paris Review, The Indiana Review, The Alaska Quarterly Review*, and elsewhere. She lives in Louisville with her husband, physicist John Morrison, and her daughter, Flora.

"The Perfecting of the Chopin *Valse No. 14 in E Minor*" first appeared in *The Georgia Review* in 1985 and was collected in *Ice Skating at the North Pole*. Naslund has said the story "suggests that art (music) and the beauty of the home flower garden provide a kind of consolation in the face of death." A magical realism tale set in Louisville, it portrays a woman and her pianist mother coming to terms with the prospect of the mother's aging and dying, journeying beyond.

◆

One day last summer when I was taking a shower, I heard my mother playing the Chopin *Valse No. 14 in E Minor* better than she ever had played it before. Thirty years ago in Birmingham, I had listened to her while I sat on dusty terra cotta tiles on the front porch. I was trying to pluck a thorn from my heel as I listened, and I remember looking up from my dirty foot to see the needle of a hummingbird entering one midget blossom after another, the blossoms hanging like froth on our butterfly bush. Probably she had first practiced the *Valse* thirty years or so before that, in Missouri, in a living room close enough to a dirt road to hear wagons passing, close enough for dust to sift over the piano keys. How was it that after knowing the piece for sixty years, my mother suddenly was playing it better than she ever had in her life?

I turned off the shower to make sure. It was true. There was a bounce and yet a delicacy in the repeated notes at the beginning of the phrase that she had never achieved before. And then the flight of the right hand up the keyboard was like the gesture of a dancer lifting her arm, unified and lilting. I waited for the double *forte*, which she never played loudly enough, and heard it roar out of the piano and up the furnace pipe to the bathroom. Perhaps that was it: the furnace pipe was acting like a natural amplifier, like a speaking tube. Dripping wet, I stepped over the tub and walked through the bathroom door to the landing at the top of the stairs. She was at the section with the alberti-like bass. Usually her left hand hung back, couldn't keep the established tempo here (and it had been getting worse in the last seven or so years), but the left hand cut loose with the most perfectly rolled over *arpeggio* I had ever heard. Rubinstein didn't do it any better.

I hurried down the steps; she was doing the repeated notes again as one of the recapitulations of the opening phrase came up. I tried to see if she had finally decided to use Joseffy's suggested fingering—2, 4, 3, 1—instead of her own 4, 3, 2, 1 on which she had always insisted. But I was just too late to see. She finished with a flourish.

"Bravo!" I shouted and clapped. The water flew out of my hands like a wet dog shaking his fur. She leaned over the piano protectively.

"You're getting the keys wet," she said, smiling.

"You played that so well!"

"Suppose the mailman comes while you're naked?"

"Didn't you think you played it well?"

"I'm improving. You always do, from time to time."

"This was SUPER."

"Thank you," she said and got up to make her second cup of coffee.

"Did you remember to take Hydropes?" I yelled. She's quite deaf, but refuses to wear her hearing aid while she practices. *You know how music sounds over the telephone*, she said to me once; that was what a hearing aid did to sounds.

"Did you take H?" I shouted a little louder.

She threw one of her white sweaters over the Walter Jackson Bate biography of Keats. "Don't read the last two chapters late at night," she said. "It makes you too sad."

I had taken to reading about romantic poets and their poetry, too, to relieve the glassy precision of my work at the pharmaceutical lab. I left the books around, and as she had done since I was a child, she read what I read—usually two hundred pages ahead of me. I put on her sweater, its wool sticking to my damp skim

"I took H early this morning," she continued. "Did you take A?"

Aldomet is my high blood pressure drug. She takes it, too, but not till afternoon. I take it three times a day.

"No," I said. "I've forgotten again."

And I forgot about the *Valse in E Minor*. Maybe that performance was a fluke. Maybe I was mistaken.

It was not long after this that a rock in the garden began to move. It was thigh high and pockmarked, and the pocks were rimmed with mica. The arcs of mica had the same curve as a fingernail clipping or the curve of a glittering eyelash.

Our garden was on a small scale by Louisville standards—about fifty by forty feet. We had landscaped it, though—rather expensively for us. A stucco wall hung between four brick columns across the back. Herringbone brick walks were flanked by clumps of iris, day lilies and chrysanthemums so that we had spots of spring, summer and fall bloom. There was a small statue of a girl looking up at the sky and spreading her stone apron to catch the rain. The apron was a birdbath. It was that sort of yard. Pretty, costly per square foot, designed to console us for our lack of scope. I had some dwarf fruit trees across the back, in front of the stucco wall.

The previous owner had had the mica boulder placed over a large chipmunk hole so no one would accidentally step in. The placement was imperfect aesthetically, and my mother said it ought to be moved, but I didn't want to go to the bother to hire somebody to do it. Sometimes I'd see her lean against the rock, her basket full of the spent heads of iris or day lilies, or windfall apples, or other garden debris. We were neat.

One bright night when the mica was arcing in the moonlight, I saw her going out there in her pajamas. She carried one of the rose satin sofa cushions, and its sides gleamed in the light. She put the cushion on top of the rock, climbed up, and sat on it. She looked like a bird sitting on a giant egg, a maharani riding an elephant, a child on a Galapagos tortoise.

I felt unreal, frightened, standing beside the bedroom curtain peering out. And stunned. I sat down on the bed, touched another satin cushion, smoothed it, soothed it. I held the cool satin against my cheeks. My tears made dark blotches on the fabric. I wanted to lie down, to deny her madness in the garden. And I did. I turned the cushion to the dry side, lay down on it and went to sleep.

In the morning the teakettle shrieked, she poured the water for her instant coffee, called "Good Morning" to me, and all was ordinary.

When I walked in the garden, I noticed the rock had shifted. Around the base was a crescent of damp stone where crumbs of still-moist earth clung. The boulder had rotated a little, as though Antarctica on a giant globe had slipped northward a hundred miles into the South Pacific. Perhaps the rock had been more precariously balanced than I had thought. Perhaps her weight had caused it to shift—a slow-motion version of a child sitting on a big beach ball.

But from that morning I began to see a change in her health. She was tired. She was less ready to smile, and her eyes took on a hurt quality. Each day she seemed to get up later. She asked to eat out, and she ate ravenously, at Italian restaurants. She ate like a runner—huge quantities of pasta.

But the food did no good. Each day she was weaker.

And each day the ugly earthy area on the rock rose higher and higher out of the ground. What had been a slight crescent of dirt became a huge black island covering several thousand miles in the Hawaii area.

She changed her diet from high carbohydrate to high protein. I wanted to speak to her about her eating, but it was as though there was a bandage across my mouth.

I tried once, in the kitchen, to say "Mama, why are you eating in this crazy way?" But all I could say was "Mmmm, Mmmm. . . ."

She glanced at me in that quick, hurt way, and I hushed.

Then the gag seemed to change its location. Instead of being across my mouth, it seemed to be tied on top of my head and to pass under my chin. It was the kind of bandage you see on the dead in nineteenth-century etchings—something to hold the jaw closed, something Jacob Marley might have been wearing when he first appeared to Scrooge. Again, I felt it in the kitchen. I tried to say "Mama, Mama, what are you doing to yourself? Why are you so tired?" But I couldn't even drop my jaw, couldn't get my mouth open for a murmur.

That night I stayed awake to watch the rock. At midnight, I knelt on my bed and peered out the window. There was no human form perched on the rock. Nevertheless I watched and watched. About 1:00, when I was quite drowsy, the rock suddenly glittered. It was as though the mica were catching light at a new angle. Sometimes this happens if a lamp is turned on in the house, or one is turned off. But there was no change in the lighting and yet this sudden sparkling, flashing out of light. My mouth tried to open in a silent and spontaneous *Oh!*, but it was as though the binding cloth were in place. I was not permitted this small gesture of surprise.

Then I saw her rise up from behind the rock. She moved very slowly. Her movement was the kind I make in dreams when I feel panic, panic and also a heaviness, an inertia that scarcely permits forward motion. Her shoulders stooping, her hands and arms hanging like weights, she slowly began to walk down the bricks toward the house. I wanted to leap to meet her, to tell her, to tell her *Nevermind. Nevermind you don't have to do it, I'll hire a crane, I'll hire the neighborhood boys, I'll hire a doctor day and night, Don't try this, here, here let me help.* But I was immobilized.

The cloths that had bound shut my jaw now bound my entire body. I could not flex my knees. I tried to heave myself off the bed; I would roll to her help. But my body was as rigid as a statue.

I was forced to remain kneeling on the coverlet, looking out the window, watching her toiling past the ruddy day lilies. At a certain point, she passed beyond my sight line. There were three small steps there; and my ears strained to tell me that she had negotiated them all right, that now she was opening the storm door, now she was coming in from the night, that she had not fallen at the last moment, that she was not lying hurt right at her own safe door, that she had not struck her head on the steps—but my hearing failed, too. All of my senses were suddenly gone, as though I had received a blow to the head.

I awoke in the early hours to a loud thunderclap. The weather was changing early. It was late summer, and the fall rains were coming. Our air seemed like the ice water you stand strips of carrots and celery in to crisp. Day lilies were drooping and the chrysanthemums straining upright, ready to grow and take over the garden. I checked the statue of the girl. Serrated yellow leaves from a neighboring elm had blown into her apron.

The boulder had rotated 180 degrees from its original position. The black cap rode at the north pole. Below it the rock was clean and traces of mica sparkled in the sunlight. But I fancied the darkness was spreading, an earthen glaciation coming down to nullify the brightness of human accomplishment.

I knew it was hopeless to attempt to ask her any questions. Even as I tried mentally to formulate an inquiry, my body stiffened. I resisted that stillness. I would not be frozen into stone in my own garden in late summer. I would not take on that terrible rigidity. I would not allow my body to imagine death.

Her health began to improve, but it gave me no joy. I knew that this improvement was temporary. That August, gesturing toward the garden, a friend who raised berries told me that death was part of life; she pointed at the seasonal changes. We stood on the patio talking while the Chopin *Valse No. 14* rolled out the windows.

I explained that each time my mother played it now, it was better. Sometimes it was improved only by the way a single note was played, but suddenly that note, once dead, leaped into life. And then the next time, the notes around it would be more vital, would be like flowers straining toward the light, inspired by one of their number who had risen above them. The whole surface of the music was becoming luminous.

I told my friend that the gulf between the seasonal lives of flowers and the lives of human beings was unbridgeable. The *forte* drowned out my voice, a *forte* big enough now to fill the garden.

Our garden was the perfect place for a garden party, but I had never had one there. I preferred to have one friend over at a time, or two. But two weeks after the weather change, I discovered that invitations had been issued to almost every person of my acquaintance to join me and the chrysanthemums for a gourmet dinner. *Gourmet!* To join me *and the chrysanthemums!* They weren't ready!

As usual, I had worked late at the laboratory. When I came out to the car, the pink glow of the sunset was reflected in the windshield. Amidst the wash of pink, a folded card had been placed under the wiper: an invitation for six o'clock. It was already half-past six. There wasn't a potato chip in the house, and we'd eaten our last TV entree; I was supposed to get more on the way home. While I stood there fingering the stiff paper, I realized how many people had smiled at me that day, had said *See you later* or *Looking forward to it* or *Thanks for asking*—all mysterious, muttered fragments scattered over the day, everybody being especially gracious to me, or worse, *encouraging.*

Could I run home, maybe cook flowers? I was a very poor cook; my mother was no cook. We had long benefitted from eating out and from TV dinners. They were the expensive TV dinners—pretty and tasty, even if always too salty.

As I sped home, I thought that at least my mother would be there to greet them. Like an illuminated billboard, the invitation flashed at me again. I recognized the handwriting. It was her writing. Large letters, angular, the capital A half-printed, looking like a star.

There were so many cars that I had to drive past the house looking for parking. Other latecomers—there was my supervisor—were sauntering down the sidewalks toward home. I parked almost two blocks away.

As I walked home as fast as I could, half a block away, I smelled the party. I gasped. Yes, my jaw *was* allowed to drop in amazement: *Oh!* heavenly aromas.

There was roast beef! No, not just roast beef—something richer, more savory. Beef Wellington. I could envision the pastry head of a steer decorating its flank. But the odor of bacon, too, why bacon? It couldn't be, but there was a choice of entrees, just like when we had two separate frozen Stouffers. Trout was broiling under strips of bacon. There! There was a waft of garlic butter, for escargot.

And desserts had been freshly baked. That was angel food cake in the air, and there was the sweet cinnamon of apple brown Betty, and there, the orange liqueur that goes *flambé* with crepes suzette. She had prepared three desserts. But you can't just have main courses and desserts! Where were the vegetables? She had forgotten the vegetables. Memory *was* becoming uncertain: I *had* heard her hesitate to enter the second theme of the *Valse*.

My supervisor was poised at the head of our walk, sniffing. I shouldered past him.

"Vegetables?" I exclaimed.

"Who cares?" He inhaled deeply.

I managed to make myself enter the house quietly. There was that civilized murmur in the room. The sound you hear in the finest restaurants, the bliss of conversation elevated by the artistry of food, of the tongue bending this way and that in ecstasy.

There she stood chatting, her hearing aid in place. She who had been reclusive, a devotee of music alone, for years. I noticed there was a dusting of flour on her hands and arms, up to her elbows. She seemed unaware of the flour, stood relaxed and comfortable as though she were wearing a pair of evening gloves.

"Mother," I said, "are you all right?"

She reached out and squeezed my elbow. Her grip was steadying. "Of course," she said. "I was just telling your friend we should have parties more often. I'm enjoying myself so much."

"All this food?" I said lamely.

"I can read a book, as you know. I got down James Beard, Irma Rombauer. I hadn't looked in Fanny for years."

"Are there any vegetables?"

"Sautéed celery, new peas in sherry sauce." She pointed at some covered dishes. "Here comes the mailman."

Other people began to arrive. People I had lost track of years before. How did she find them? I started to ask, but the hinge of my jaw began to resist; the familiar paralysis gently threatened. Questions had become out of order.

My salivary glands prompted me. Eat, *eat*. She had my plate ready for me—flamboyant and multi-colored. It held something of everything. When I inhaled, I seemed to levitate six or seven inches—or float, that feeling you get walking neck deep in a swimming pool on your big toes. Glancing down, I saw my food had been arranged on a new plate, the tobacco-leaf pattern that I had admired in the Metropolitan Museum catalogue. Seventy-nine dollars *per*. And each guest had one. I was rich.

One guest held no tobacco-leaf plate. Indeed, he wasn't eating. I didn't know him, had never known him, I was quite sure. He was standing beside the piano talking with mother. He was grossly fat, with reddish hair, what was left of it; he was mostly bald. Only his nose seemed familiar. It was a large and romantic proboscis, lean and humped—no, arched. They were discussing fingering. Mother was drumming the air—4, 3, 2, 1—and he was responding 4, 2, 3, 1. But then on one, he gave the rug a quick jab with this foot. Ah, he was suggesting the last of the repeated notes be quickly pedalled. What an idea! Joseffy certainly never hints at such an effect.

Mother looked delighted. She too jabbed the rug with her foot. No, he shook his head, *not quite fast enough*. He actually reached over and grasped her right leg above the knee, grasped the quadricep muscle and forced a quick tap of the imaginary sostenuto pedal. Now he was savoring the unheard sound. With his face tilted up in the lamplight, I suddenly recognized him. At least I recognized a part of him. It was the nose of Frederick Chopin.

My mouth fell open. It was to gasp, I thought. But instead these words fell out, double *forte*, "Let's all go into the garden now." And I rotated—gracefully I could tell—to lead the way through the French doors. But why, when the chrysanthemums weren't ready?

The garden was ablaze in torchlight. Real torches, like the Statue of Liberty holds up, but with long handles planted in the ground, or jutting out from the back wall, torches like you see in some paintings of the garden of Gethsemane with that rich Dutch light flickering everywhere. And the chrysanthemums had been multiplied.

No longer just my neat mounds of red cushion mums. There was rank on rank of mums of all colors and forms. Spider mums in oranges and yellows. Giant football mums in purples, lavenders and whites, star-burst mums, fireballs and a thousand tiny button mums massed against the stucco wall. All the guests were gasping with delight. They hurried to stand among them, cupped individual blossoms like the chins of favored children; long index fingers pointed through the flickering light at flowers just beyond. When the guests knelt to study whole clumps, their bodies disappeared among the rows of flowers and their heads floated among them, heads themselves like large flowers or cabbages. Above us smiled the crescent moon.

I wanted to turn, to say *Mother, come look, come join us, they are so beautiful, thank you, thank you, they have never been so beautiful*, and of course I could not turn back. My body gasped with grief. The dreadful *rigor* seized me. Then all that was replaced with the turbulence and then the gaiety of the Chopin *Valse No. 14 in E Minor*.

Could I hold my breath throughout? Could I thus make the moment permanent? Could I make the air hold that music forever, vivid as a painting, more permanent than stone, sound becoming statuary of the air? And would the performance be perfect at last? Who played? Was it *he* or *she?*

I held my breath on and on as each passage of loveliness, the lightest, most gay of sounds, swept past. But where was the pedal touch on the fourth of the repeated notes? Of course it was withheld, withheld till the phrase was introduced for the last time, and then the pedal, a suggestion of poignant prolonging, a soupcon of romantic rubato, a wobble in rhythm, the human touch in the final offering of art. Then it ended.

Then, only then, the air rushed from my lungs. "BRAVO!" I shouted. Unbound, my jaw seemed to be permitted to open all the way to my heart. "HOORAY! HOORAY!" I shouted, raising my fist and punching the air over my head. All the guests shouted "BRAVO!" their fists aloft. And dozens of Roman candles, skyrockets, pinwheels shot up into the air, burst gloriously high above our heads, bloomed like flowers forced by a movie camera. I felt her standing behind me, her hand a warm squeeze on my elbow.

The next morning I found her note saying that she wanted to vacation in England. She had taken a morning flight. England because they spoke her language there. I walked into the bright garden. Of course, she had hired a clean-up crew to take away the spent torches and the mess. The gauzy crescent moon, the ghost of a thorn, hung in the blue.

I visited the rock. It had been rolled six feet west, to the artistically correct place. The dark continent had returned to the bottom of the world, no longer visible at the juncture of rock and grass. The rock was right side up and mica glittered over its dome. Where it had stood gaped the chipmunk hole, wide enough for a human thigh. A dark, pleasant hole.

Ah, there was the chipmunk already, poising at the rim of damp earth, blinking in the sunlight.

Diary of a Union Soldier

PAT CARR

Born in an oil camp in Grass Creek, Wyoming, in 1932, Pat Carr earned a B.A. and an M.A. at Rice University and a Ph.D. at Tulane. She has taught at Rice University, Texas Southern University, Dillard University, the University of New Orleans, the University of Texas at El Paso, and, from 1988 until the mid-1990s, Western Kentucky University. Her books include a critical study, *Bernard Shaw* (1976); an archeological study of ancient Native American poetry, *Mimbres Mythology* (1979); a collection of Civil War letters, *In Fine Spirits* (1986); a collection of myth-tales, *Sonahchi* (1988); a cycle of Civil War stories and poems, *Our Brother's War* (with Maureen Morehead, 1993); and four short story collections, *Beneath the Hill of the Three Crosses* (1970), *The Grass Creek Chronicle* (1976), *The Women in the Mirror* (which won the Iowa Short Fiction Award in 1977), and *Night of the Luminarias* (1986). Her stories have appeared, among many other places, in *Kansas Quarterly*, *Yale Review*, and *Georgetown Review*, as well as *Best American Short Stories*. She and her husband, Duane Carr, who also taught at Western Kentucky University, live in Arkansas.

As Leonard Michaels has noted, Carr's stories portray with subtlety "the most delicate and exquisite psychological situations." Like Chekhov, Carr strives to render a character's mood and emotion through precise detail. "Diary of a Union Soldier," which first appeared in 1985 in *The Southern Review* and later in *Our Brother's War*, is a compelling and haunting tale of compassion and veiled love.

◆

Dead branches were scraping so resolutely across the roof that it was only when the wind slackened that the thud of the cannons echoed up from the grove. But even as she heard the muted guns, she didn't associate them with an actual engagement, and when she saw him at the steps, not having heard him crash through the woods, just seeing him appear in silence at the porch, she didn't realize that he'd come from a battle.

He put out a hand toward the post for support, and she could tell he was hurt, and perhaps that was why she wasn't afraid of him, why she opened the door as he staggered onto the porch.

"I'd appreciate a drink of water, ma'am," he said with soft politeness. "I noticed your well, and I wouldn't bother you, but it'll take considerably more strength than I've got right now to raise the bucket by myself."

He wasn't wearing a cap, and his eye sockets were ashen with exhaustion. She couldn't see any blood on him, but she thought he might collapse along the porch boards any second.

"You look like you could use a chair as well as some water," she said.

"Yes, ma'am."

She opened the door wider, moved her skirt aside, and he lurched by her, angled across the room until his knees cracked into the bed rim and he dropped face down on the coverlet.

The hand he had tucked in his pocket fell loose, and then she saw the blood, trickling down the back of his hand, separating at the knuckles, dripping off the fingers.

She stepped inside and closed out the wind.

"You'll bleed to death unless you staunch that."

"Yes, ma'am," he said as politely, in a voice slightly muffled by the bed quilt.

She walked over and looked down at him. He was a tall man, possibly Sy's age, muscular and fit, but the side of his face turned toward her had begun to gray.

"And I guess you can't do that by yourself either."

"No, ma'am."

She stood a second longer, but the puddle of blood on the floor beneath his hand was widening.

"Well, you'll have to shift a bit for me to get off your jacket."

She felt herself raising her voice before his closed eyes as if somehow his wound had deafened him as well.

"Yes, ma'am."

He gingerly twisted his torso.

"Ah-h-h."

Droplets of sweat beaded his forehead.

"That's enough. I can work the buttons through," she said, speaking in that same tone to protect his feelings, to cover the cry she knew had been involuntary.

The brass belt buckle and the buttons were cold, but the dark wool itself was sweaty and warm to her touch. She hadn't seen a Yankee uniform before, and she was impressed at how sturdy and new the jacket was.

"I don't have anything against you Union soldiers," she began, to keep talking in case he moaned again and would be shamed at her overhearing. She worked the buttons through the stiff buttonholes.

"Sy voted to stay with the Union, but when the state decided to go Confederate, he joined up with the rest. Everyone around here pretty much went along. Is it your arm?"

"And I'd guess my back," he said, through clenched teeth.

He opened his eyes directly into hers and she saw that they were a green so brilliant that it was nearly chartreuse. She wondered why she hadn't noted them the first thing.

"Crabb fell right beside one, and when I stooped to help him up, some Secesh got me from the brush," he said in a single breath, his jaw still rigid.

She had the jacket unbuttoned and was starting to ease it off the gray ticking undershirt.

"Crabb was dead," he said in the same clamped voice as if his friend Crabb were someone she knew and had asked about. "Go ahead, ma'am. It's no use to keep stopping. Just pull off the sleeve all at once if you can. Ah-h-h."

She realized that she was clenching her own jaw as she tugged the sleeve away from his bloodied hand.

The gray undershirt had become so soaked that the cloth itself seemed to have dissolved into blood. A slaughtering smell filled the room, and she swallowed her breath against it.

"You'll have to raise up and help me get off your shirt. I can't bandage you with it on."

He closed his eyes, gave what she took as a nod.

"M-m-m-m-m," came through his lips, so tightly shut they'd almost disappeared, but he balanced himself on the elbow still encased in the jacket sleeve, then swayed up enough to be upright.

She quickly pulled the jacket off his good arm and tossed its heavy bulk to the floor. She undid the two buttons of the undershirt and peeled it back from his arm, his head, then down again away from the wound. It reminded her of the bloody skin of a frying rabbit as she flung it after the jacket.

Fresh blood instantly coursed down his arm. She forced herself to lean over and peer at his shoulder. The blood was welling up around the torn flesh and shredded muscle and running down his bare back.

She shivered slightly, tried to control the shaking of her hands as she hurried to the chest at the foot of the bed. Sy always killed the rabbits and chickens for her, and she averted her eyes from the blood already caking on her fingers.

"The ball is probably still in your back."

She tried to sound calm as she opened the trunk, but she could hear the quaver.

"As soon as you get back to your own side, a doctor can pick out the fragments for you. I'm just going to stop the bleeding."

The extra sheet was on top, fortunately, and she didn't have to bloody any of her other things looking for it. She lifted it out, closed the curved lid, and bit through one corner of her hemstitching. The muslin had been washed to the consistency of soft baby linens, and it tore in easy strips.

She stood up again to lay each fraying ribbon of cloth on the bed, continued biting, tearing until she had ripped up the complete rectangle of the sheet. The rushed activity had replaced her inner shaking, and when she told him not to move, her voice was calm again.

He had sagged aside as if unaware that he wasn't sitting erect, and he didn't try to straighten as she held one end of the makeshift bandage at his collar bone and began to wind the cotton strips as tightly as she could around the bleeding shoulder and back. She concentrated on the new white cloth that twined around and around, tried to ignore the sight of the first patch of cotton that had soaked scarlet in an instant. She bound the arm against his side, wrapped the widths of cotton around, anchored the end of each strip with another winding.

Then she was reaching for the final strip, twisting it over the others, holding it too while she awkwardly plucked a pin from the cushion on the washstand.

When the end was secure, she checked the thick layer of white bandaging and was certain that only a doctor could have done any better. She took a deep breath.

But the man had his eyes closed as if he'd fallen asleep sitting up, and she couldn't think how to congratulate her own doctoring or what to say to get his attention. His skin was dark beside the white of her ruined sheet, and black hair grew on his chest, tangled in the hollow between the muscles. Sy's chest was as devoid of hair as Scofield's, the slave Sy hired from Doc Tibbens at harvest time, the two of them haying side by side, their bare chests glistening in the sun. The Yankee's chest hair was almost as thick as that tumbling over his forehead, and she was suddenly embarrassed by his semi-nudity.

"You lie back while I get you that water," she said quickly.

His good arm was aimed toward the foot of the bed, and she grabbed the pillow to change it for him, but almost before she'd plumped it into position, he leaned onto it and relaxed with a barely audible sigh. He hadn't opened his eyes.

She scooped up the pitcher and went outside. The sunlight was thin through the leafless trees, but the wind had softened, warmed to something more like spring than December, and she heard the distant cannons as she began to lower the bucket.

Sy had been good about bringing in the water, too, and she was awkward with the rope even though he'd been gone half a year. It seemed to take her even longer than usual, but at last she struggled the bucket onto the stone rim and tilted it to fill the pitcher and rinse her hands. The steady firing in the grove continued as she returned to the house.

The man was deep asleep. His lips had opened slightly with his steady breathing, showing his crooked white, white teeth.

She stood holding the pitcher of water and looked down at him. Any woman would call him a good looking man with all those black curls and the startling green eyes that were beneath the closed lids. His black eyelashes were long, and his parted lips seemed too soft to belong to a man. Sy was shorter, stockier, his face round with an Irish pug rather than a fine straight nose like this man's, and Sy's hair had retreated, making him resemble a plump, aging baby when he was sunk into a pillow asleep.

But even a strong, fit man asleep with a bare chest could take cold in a December cabin when the sun went down. She put the pitcher on the table and returned to the oak chest for her company quilt.

As she gently tucked the quilt around him and straightened up again, she saw his jacket and the bloodied undershirt wadded together, staining her floor.

She could just kick them outside, push them off the porch with her shoe, but even as she thought about doing it, she knew that really wasn't an option. She, of course, had to rinse them out for him and let them dry before the fire. Any woman would do the same. Despite his being a Yankee, even Melissa Pruitt would do that much.

She stacked an armload of juniper onto the already burning logs, filled the kettle with water and hung it over the fire. As she was bringing in the round metal tub from the porch, she noticed that the sun was disappearing behind the hills, leaving the sky a murky lavender. She couldn't hear the guns any longer.

She set up the washtub, gingerly lifted the undershirt and jacket one at a time with forefinger and thumb. The jacket was heavy in her hand, and just as she tipped it over the edge of the tub, a small book fell from the pocket, flopped like a dead white bird on the floor.

She let the jacket fall and reached down for the book.

In the growing dusk of the room she could see rows of handwriting, dates that separated the paragraphs of tiny script. It was a diary.

The cover was missing, but the spine had been sturdily sewn, and most of the little book seemed intact. She put it on the table and felt in the other pockets of the jacket, but there was nothing more.

She glanced at him.

The quilt covered him from chin to boot tops, but she could picture the hand that had grasped the newel post as he'd climbed the steps. It was a lean hand with long slender fingers well able to hold a pen and write those neat straight lines of script.

Steam from the tea kettle claimed her attention, and she lifted the handle with a swatch of her skirt, poured the boiling water over the jacket and shirt. Blue dye and blood instantly blackened the water.

She sloshed his clothes down in the water with her broom, pressed them against the metal tub side, but she could see that to wash out the blood would take more water, a scrub board, some strong lye soap, and after a few minutes she leaned the broom against the fireplace again, wrung out the jacket and shirt, and draped them over a chair before the fire. She emptied the dark water off the edge of the porch, not sure when she went back in if the blood stench had lessened or if she'd merely become used to it.

She added more logs to the fire and sat down at the table. There would have to be a good blaze going all night since she'd be sitting up. When she lit the candle, the flame immediately glittered on the spirals of ink in the diary as if the words had been freshly inscribed. Her eye registered a date before she looked away.

September 5th, 1862.

She glanced at the bed once more. The quilt was rising and lowering slowly with his breathing. He'd never know.

She straightened her back against the laddered slats of the chair, but knew how she would feel if someone read a diary that she'd written.

September 5th, 1862.

That day she would have sawed wood, hauled water, foraged a basket of wind-fall apples to pare and dry. But there'd be no cause to keep a diary unless she intended to record more than that, unless she planned to write the truth in it. And yet what good would the truth do anyone? She was already a party to that truth, not needing to write it to know it, and the words would only wound Sy if he chanced to read them.

But then, the Union soldier's diary probably wasn't personal.

No man she'd ever met would have written personal thoughts in a book that could be read by anyone and could give away what he actually felt. None of her brothers, nor Sy, nor even her sober, honest father, would have put to paper any close personal thing. Perhaps no man did that. Perhaps no man could risk letting a woman know what he really thought. Perhaps every man believed he had to guard himself, to disguise, to try to be something he wasn't for a woman's benefit.

The soldier was probably like that as well.

Good-looking men like him were even more careful to maintain the myths about themselves they thought women wanted. He'd have been careful not to write anything that would reveal to his wife more than he wanted. And he was certain to be married. He was far too comely a man for a woman to have turned him down if he'd asked, and naturally someone his age would have asked. Possibly he was even on a second wife like Sy. But, unlike Sy, he'd have married some younger woman who would adore him and want to give him a new brood of children.

His little book with its fine script wouldn't be personal, and she would never have such an opportunity to learn about the war, never another chance to know first-hand the reality of a battle with its gunsmoke and mangled bodies and all the horrors of battlefield deaths whose details she could only partially imagine.

Yet even as she told herself the diary would be the only way she could glimpse the masculine event of war, that was no justification.

The candlelight danced in the loops of his words and she held her shoulders erect for another moment.

But then why should she have any qualms about reading his diary. He was the enemy.

She pulled her chair closer to the table, placed the diary directly in the candlelight.

September 5th, 1862

We arrived at St. Louis at 10:00 a.m. It was an exceedingly hot day, and many of us unaccustomed to being bundled up in the amount of woolen goods we had on and the 50 pounds of load we had to carry, found to our satisfaction that there was no fun in soldiering.

As she read on in the tiny inked script, it was as if she could hear his voice speaking the words.

All hands are in line fully equipped with 40 pounds of cartridges in our boxes and our knapsacks on our shoulders. We remained in ranks holding up our loads until we got tired and were then marched off by companies to rest ourselves and to ponder on what might be the reason for not being on the move. We forgot that great armies led by great men must accustom themselves to various things and that those things must be learned gradually or the soldier would not rightly appreciate them.

Back home he was perhaps a newspaper man or maybe a teacher like her father; he obviously wasn't just a farmer who had become a common soldier.

October 9th, 1862

Rain-rain-rain. Rain in showers, rain in almost torrents, rain in pretty little showers, rain with all its changes, with every variation to render it interesting. Cooking in the rain, eating in the rain, almost sleeping in the rain, for gentle brooks are gurgling all round us. When the rain had saturated us to the skin, it ran in little rivulets down our backs and those poor fellows who had no holes in their boots to let it out were compelled to carry double rations of water.

She looked up. Her eyes adjusted to the orange firelight that illuminated his profile, and she studied him.

What a wonder and a pleasure it would have been to have a man like that around. Someone lean, chiseled, and noticing. The kind of man who actually saw the world and was amused by it, not the kind who merely plodded through the days not knowing, merely doing what everyone else did. The Yankee with his bright chartreuse eyes was certainly the kind of man she'd have chosen if she'd had any say in the matter.

She tried to visualize his wife as she looked at him. He'd have had his pick of any of the women in his town, she was sure of that, and he could have swept off the very prettiest, a Yankee Melissa Pruitt. But, no, despite her pale beauty, Melissa Pruitt had no understanding, and a man with his penetrating glance would never have married someone like that. Melissa had sent off her Nathaniel with tearful and patriotic bravery, assuring him, and everyone else in the town square, that she was willing to sacrifice him for his sacred duty. The Yankee's wife would never have said that. Nathaniel Pruitt with his flat gold eyes that might have been cut from gourd rinds was one thing, but this Union man was something different. No woman on either side would have willingly allowed him to die on the battlefield, whether to preserve the Union or to save Southern liberty.

And she abruptly recognized a feeling of great sympathy for the wife from whom he was absent. The absence of Sy or Nathaniel Pruitt was an inconvenience to her and to Melissa, but to be apart from such a man as this was more than that.

She watched his sleeping face, watched the quilt border his breathing for a few more seconds, then she pulled her stare back from him and looked down again at the diary.

Our camp is in a field of rag-weed so high and rank that you cannot distin-guish a man from a horse. A stagnant pond close by, containing the half-decayed carcasses of mules, horses, and hogs is the water we must use. I saw many a poor fellow with swollen tongue and parched lips quench his thirst at this mire-hole. Others would fall back in dismay, sick at heart at the loathsome sight. This to a soldier is our first lesson in satiating our thirst from stagnant stinking sink holes.

The room had begun to chill, and she got up quietly to put another armload of wood on the fire. She didn't know if her fingers were shaking from cold or from the stimulant of the scenes he was describing. She took her cloak from its hook and wrapped it around her as she sat back down.

I don't know but I must think Iowa soldiers have been brought a long way to do a very small business.

He was from Iowa.

The wife back in Iowa who wept for his departure would be watching for his return from a window much like hers. The woman in the day would be doing what she did, in the evening would be knitting him a pair of woolen socks. But of course she would have his children to attend to as well, for he was a man who would have fathered children.

She turned the little diary over to mark its place, and took up the candle, carried it toward the bed. The candle flame showed him in a golden glow, the plane of his jaw, the laugh creases at the corners of his sleeping eyelids and his lips, the straight clean line of his nose.

As she stood gazing down at him she remembered an etching in one of her father's books, a scene of Psyche, candle in hand, bending over the graceful profile of a sleeping Cupid. She'd studied that page for hours as a child, memorizing the dark etched curls, the petal-curved eyelids, the delicate nostrils of the handsome Cupid.

She reached down and laid her hand on the man's forehead.

As her fingers stretched across his flesh, she quickly told herself that she was determining whether or not he had a fever.

His skin was vibrant, warm, yet not too warm. He didn't flinch back from her palm, but took a relaxed sleeper's breath as if he were accustomed to being touched in the night.

She felt her own face grow hot at the pattern of her thoughts, and she looked away from him. She crept back to the table and set the candle down as silently as possible. The candle flame wavered and flickered above the nobbed and melting wax.

She sat down, still flustered, turned the little book over, and found her place. She had to read the next passage twice before her nervousness abated enough for the words to focus again.

I am penning these lines on the battlefield of Wilson Creek in the rain. A pit in which our dead were placed has been uncovered by the beating rain, and human bones and skulls lay exposed to our view. I wish a burial sufficiently deep to protect me from such exposure.

She read about the lack of food, the snow and the river crossings that froze the men's feet as they were herded on, and she saw that the war he wrote about wasn't the glorious and heroic affair Melissa Pruitt wanted it to be.

Yet, among the bitter scenes, she felt a jolt of pleasure whenever she read the names of her own towns in his handwriting, Prairie Grove, Fayetteville, spelled out in his neat lines, and it was as if somehow they were sharing those places.

I have noticed many fine farm and orchards enclosed by stone fences and on which have been fine residences, but which have been burned and the fences broken down and the farm orchards laid waste.

What a shame it all was. Trees like her apple orchard so carefully nurtured on its slope. Fingers picking off the tiny withered apple leaves, watering the roots through the summer drought with buckets from the well, and then an army marching, kicking aside the stone fences, chopping down the trees and burning them in the sight of the woman who had cherished them. And a handsome Yankee wounded, his shoulder so mangled that he might well lose the use of his arm. How sad and useless the waste of it all.

Her eyes began to burn, but she read on with a sense of urgency. He'd be leaving in the morning, and she'd have no further chance to absorb his words, to know him.

December 7th, 1862

Since 12 o'clock the battle has raged with fury. The artillery opened from either side and the infantry poured forth its incessant volleys in quick succession. The 19th, 20th, and 94th were put in battle array. Our company, acting as skirmishers, took position in a corn and stubble field directly opposite one of the enemy's batteries. We lay low, for bullets flew thick around us, and we seemed to be fair targets for their sharpshooters. But we returned their fire with an energy and determination that must have convinced them we were at least soldiers. We had advanced nearer to the foe than we should have and were in danger of being cut off from the main body of our army by rebel cavalry, and the 20th Iowa was ordered . . .

The back pages had been ripped off with the cover, and the diary stopped in the middle of a sentence.

It was eerie that he'd written about the cannon she'd heard beyond the ridge. He'd documented the same gunfire she'd heard from the porch. Like a reawakening that was happening exactly as it had in a dream. He was describing what she had been noticing while they were miles apart. They were countries apart, and yet they had been aware of the same things at the same time.

Then he and his company had been ordered to advance or to retreat, and he may have written of that on one of the missing pages before he'd been wounded by the Confederate bullet.

She closed the little diary and held its coverless pages between her palms. It slightly warmed her hands and it was almost as if she were touching his forehead again. Holding his words was somehow like holding his face, pressing the eyes that had seen the events and had thought those words to write. She closed her eyes and felt that she was on the brink of a discovery, a tentative philosophical knowledge about herself. If a woman didn't know a man's thoughts, how could she love him? Unless she knew what he actually had inside, she was merely accepting what everyone else said she was supposed to honor—the appearance of goodness or decency, the appearance of strength. And to make up her own mind and get beyond the surface, a woman had to know the depth of a man, had to know the true strength that grew from understanding, not bull heft or muscle.

She sat with the little book and her hands on the table.

But how was a woman ever to know that interior of a man? How could she see the heart, the soul, without the words? And if the Yankee were a well man, would he be a talking man? She was able to know about his bemused view of life, his almost detached view of the war because he'd happened upon her cabin with his diary in his pocket and she'd looked inside it. She'd read what he'd written, and she held the clue to what was actually within him. But had his wife ever gotten that chance?

She looked up from the table.

Gray light had filled the window square, and the fire had burned to embers without her noticing. It was already dawn.

How lucky his wife would be to have that little diary to read when he got home.

She sat totally still another few seconds, listening, but there was no sound of cannons. Only the moan of the wind clung to the dawn air.

She carefully lifted the quilt from his chest the gentle way she'd tucked it around him. The bandage of torn sheeting was still in place, as pristine white as when she'd bound it. But he must have been bleeding internally. Even as she tried to save him and make him comfortable on her bed, awaiting the morning to send him back to his Union doctor, he had been bleeding to death.

As she sat throughout the night, she had never entertained the thought that he might die.

And yet he had.

She gazed down at the mask his face had become and realized how much she had wanted him to live.

When the daylight reached her pasture, she would walk toward the grove of battle sounds. She'd find a Union or Confederate troop that would know how to deliver his body to his Iowa company. Whoever she found would know how to claim his things and get them to his folks.

His wife must have the little book.

A woman could read, re-read it, and thus fall in love continuously with the man who had written the observations. That Iowa wife who could have been the sister she'd never had, who could have been herself actually, would appreciate the gift of eternity. If she had been married to such a man, how dearly she would treasure his diary and how grateful she would be to the unknown woman on the opposing side who had saved and returned it to her.

The handsome Yankee soldier, who still had so much left to say, had stopped writing the day before—no, two days earlier—and he'd never be able to fill other pages of a diary for the weeks or months that the war might last.

She stood in her cloak beside the bed and the room lightened. The December sun became pale yellow on the frozen windowsill, but no color touched his silent profile.

It was no use building a fire before she left.

Someone in the Union company would know his name. His wife would probably want the other things in his haversack as well as the precious diary.

She didn't try to be quiet any longer, and her heels cracked loudly on the pine boards as she walked away from the bed, took her bonnet from its peg, and tied the ribbons at her neck with iced fingers.

She had only heard him ask for a drink of water, murmur a few words as she bandaged his fatal wound, and yet she knew him better than she'd ever known any man.

She reached across the table and picked up the tiny book once more.

Then, before she realized she was going to move, she was bending down, opening the cedar chest. She held the lid with one hand while she reached below the layers of cloth, secreted the diary between the folds of her wedding dress.

She stood up again, carefully shut the trunk. She gazed at the profile of the man on the bed, and took a jagged breath that in the cold air of the room sounded like a branch against glass. Then she opened the door to the gray yellow morning and went outside.

That Distant Land

WENDELL BERRY

Wendell Berry was born in Henry County, Kentucky, in 1934. After graduating from Millersburg Military Institute in 1952, Berry attended the University of Kentucky, where he co-edited the university literary magazine, *Stylus*, and in 1955 won the Dantzler Award for his short story "The Brothers." Graduating with a B.A. in English in 1956, Berry completed his master's degree the following year, while winning the Farquhar Award for Poetry and publishing two more short stories. Earning a Wallace Stegner Fellowship in 1958, Berry studied and taught at Stanford University in California until 1960, when his first novel, *Nathan Coulter*, appeared. After traveling in France and Italy on a Guggenheim Fellowship and teaching at New York University in the Bronx, Berry came home to Kentucky in 1964 to stay. Periodically teaching English at the University of Kentucky and elsewhere, while continually working his farm with his wife, Tanya, Berry has published more than forty books. Among his many poetry collections are *The Wheel* (1982), *Entries* (1994), *A Timbered Choir* (1998), and *Selected Poems* (1998). Among his books of nonfiction are *The Hidden Wound* (1970), *A Continuous Harmony* (1974), *The Unsettling of America* (1977), *Standing by Words* (1983), *What are People For?* (1990), *Another Turn of the Crank* (1995), and *Life is a Miracle* (2000). His novels, in addition to *Nathan Coulter*, include *A Place on Earth* (1967; revised 1985), *The Memory of Old Jack* (1974; revised 1999), *Remembering* (1988), *A World Lost* (1996), and *Jayber Crow* (2000). His short story collections are *The Wild Birds* (1986), *Fidelity* (1992), and *Watch With Me* (1994). He has earned numerous awards, among them the T.S. Eliot Award for Creative Writing and inclusion in *Best American Short Stories* and *New Stories from the South*.

Appearing originally in *The Wild Birds*, "That Distant Land" is a story of rural homecoming. It reflects many of Berry's themes, including the wheel of life, fidelity to home, the weblike connections between people and land, and memory as an abiding and sustaining part of community.

◆

For several days after the onset of his decline, my grandfather's mind seemed to leave him to go wandering, lost, in some foreign place. It was a dream he was in, we thought, that he could not escape. He was looking for the way home, and he could not find anyone who knew how to get there.

"No," he would say. "Port William. Port William is the name of the place."

Or he would ask, "Would you happen to know a nice lady by the name of Margaret Feltner? She lives in Port William. Now, which way would I take to get there?"

But it was not us he was asking. He was not looking at us and mistaking us for other people. He was not looking at us at all. He was talking to people he was meeting in his dream. From the way he spoke to them, they seemed to be nice people. They treated him politely and were kind, but they did not know any of the things that he knew, and they could not help him.

When his mind returned, it did so quietly. It had never been a mind that made a lot of commotion around itself. One morning when my grandmother went in to wake him and he opened his eyes, they were looking again. He looked at my grandmother and said, "Margaret, I'll declare." He looked around him at the bright room and out the window at the ridges and the woods, and said, "You got a nice place here, ma'am."

My grandmother, as joyful as if he had indeed been gone far away and had come home, said, "Oh, Mat, are you all right?"

And he said, "I seem to be a man who has been all right before, and I'm all right now."

That was the middle of June, and having come back from wherever it had been, his mind stayed with him and with us, a peaceable, pleasant guest, until he died.

He did not get out of bed again. What troubled us, and then grieved us, and finally consoled us, was that he made no effort to get up. It appeared to us that he felt his time of struggle to be past, and that he agreed to its end. He who had lived by ceaseless effort now lived simply as his life was given to him, day by day. During the time his mind had wandered he ate little or nothing, and though his mind returned his appetite did not. He ate to please my grandmother, but he could not eat much. She would offer the food, he would eat the few bites that were enough, and she would take the plate away. None of us had the heart to go beyond her gentle offering. No one insisted. No one begged. He asked almost nothing of us, only to be there with us, and we asked only to be with him.

He lay in a room on the east side of the house, so that from the window he could look out across the ridges toward the river valley. And he did often lie there looking out. Now that he felt his own claims removed from it, the place seemed to have become more than ever interesting to him, and he watched it as the dark lifted from it and the sun rose and moved above it and set and the dark returned. Now and then he would speak of what he saw—the valley brimming with fog in the early morning, a hawk circling high over the ridges, somebody at work in one of the fields—and we would know that he watched with understanding and affection. But the character of his watching had changed. We all felt it. We had known him as a man who watched, but then his watching had been purposeful. He had watched as a man preparing for what he knew he must do, and what he wanted to do. Now it had become the watching, almost, of one who was absent.

The room was bright in the mornings, and in the afternoons dim and cool. It was always clean and orderly. My grandfather, who had no wants, made no clutter around him, and any clutter that the rest of us made did not last long. His room became the center of the house, where we came to rest. He would welcome us, raising his hand to us as we came in, listening to all that was said, now and again saying something himself.

Because, wherever we were, we kept him in our minds, he kept us together in the world as we knew he kept us in his mind. Until the night of his death we were never all in the house at the same time, yet no day passed that he did not see most of us. In the morning, my mother, his only surviving child, or Hannah Coulter, who had been his daughter-in-law and was, in all but blood, his daughter, or Flora, my wife, or Sara, my brother Henry's wife, would come in to spend the day with my grandmother to keep her company and help with the work. And at evening my father, or Henry, or I, or Nathan Coulter, who now farmed my grandfather's farm and was, in all but blood, his son, would come, turn about, to spend the night, to give whatever help would be needed.

And others who were not family came: Burley Coulter, Burley's brother Jarrat, Elton and Mary Penn, Arthur and Martin Rowanberry. They would happen by for a few minutes in the daytime, or come after supper and sit and talk an hour or two. We were a membership. We belonged together, and my grandfather's illness made us feel it.

But "illness," now that I have said it, seems the wrong word. It was not like other illnesses that I had seen—it was quieter and more peaceable. It was, it would be truer to say, a great weariness that had come upon him, like the lesser weariness that comes with the day's end—a weariness that had been earned, and was therefore accepted.

I had lived away, working in the city, for several years, and had returned home only that spring. I was thirty-one years old, I had a wife and children, and my return had given a sudden sharp clarity to my understanding of my home country. Every fold of the land, every grass blade and leaf of it gave me joy, for I saw how my own place in it had been prepared, along with its failures and its losses. Though I knew that I had returned to difficulties—not the least of which were the deaths that I could see coming—I was joyful.

The nights I spent, taking my turn, on the cot in a corner of my grandfather's room gave me a strong, sweet pleasure. At first, usually, visitors would be there, neighbors or family stopping by. Toward bedtime, they would go. I would sit on a while with my grandmother and grandfather, and we would talk. Or rather, if I could arrange it so, they would talk and I would listen. I loved to start them talking about old times—my mother's girlhood, their own young years, stories told them by their parents and grandparents, memories of memories. In their talk the history of Port William went back and back along one of its lineages until it ended in silence and conjecture, for Port William was older than its memories. That it had begun we knew because it had continued, but we did not know when or how it had begun.

It was usually easy enough to get them started, for they enjoyed the remembering, and they knew that I liked to hear. "Grandad," I would say, "who was George Washington Coulter's mother?" Or: "Granny, tell about Aunt Maude Wheeler hailing the steamboat." And they would enter the endlessly varying pattern of remembering. A name would remind them of a story; one story would remind them of another. Sometimes my grandmother would get out a box of old photographs and we would sit close to the bed so that my grandfather could see them too, and then the memories and names moved and hovered over the transfixed old sights. The picture that most moved and troubled me was the only consciously photographed "scene": a look down the one street of Port William at the time of my grandparents' childhood—1890 or thereabouts. What so impressed me about it was that the town had then been both more prosperous and more the center of its own attention than I had ever known it to be. The business buildings all had upper stories, the church had a steeple, there was a row of trees, planted at regular intervals, along either side of the road. Now the steeple and most of the upper stories were gone—by wind or fire or decay—and many of the trees were gone. For a long time, in Port William, what had gone had not been replaced. Its own attention had turned away from itself toward what it could not be. And I understood how, in his dream, my grandfather had suffered his absence from the town; through much of his life it had grown increasingly absent from itself.

After a while, my grandmother would leave us. She would go to my grandfather's side and take his hand. "Mat, is there anything you want before I go?"

"Ma'am," he would say, "I've got everything I want." He would be teasing her a little, as he was always apt to do.

She would hesitate, wishing, I think, that he did want something. "Well, good night. I'll see you in the morning."

And he would pat her hand and say very agreeably, as if he were altogether willing for that to happen, if it should happen, "All right."

She would go and we would hear her stirring about in her room, preparing for bed. I would do everything necessary to make my grandfather comfortable for the night, help him to relieve himself, help him to turn onto his side, straighten the bedclothes, see that the flashlight was in reach in case he wanted to look at the clock, which he sometimes did. I was moved by his willingness to let me help him. We had always been collaborators. When I was little, he had been the one in the family who would help me with whatever I was trying to make. And now he accepted help as cheerfully as he had given it. We were partners yet.

I was still a young man, with a young man's prejudice in favor of young bodies. I would have been sorry but I would not have been surprised if I had found it unpleasant to have to handle him as I did—his old flesh slackened and dwindling on the bones—but I did not find it so. I touched him gratefully. I would put one knee on the bed and gather him in my arms and move him toward me and turn him. I liked to do it. The comfort I gave him I felt. He would say, "Thanks, son."

When he was settled, I would turn on the dim little bedlamp by the cot and go to bed myself.

"Sleep tight," I would tell him.

"Well," he would say, amused, "I will part of the time."

I would read a while, letting the remembered dear stillness of the old house come around me, and then I would sleep.

My grandfather did only sleep part of the time. Mostly, when he was awake, he lay quietly with his thoughts, but sometimes he would have to call me, and I would get up to bring him a drink (he would want only two or three swallows), or help him to use the bedpan, or help him to turn over.

Once he woke me to recite me the Twenty-third Psalm. "Andy," he said. "Andy. Listen." He said the psalm to me. I lay listening to his old, slow voice coming through the dark to me, saying that he walked through the valley of the shadow of death and that he feared no evil. It stood my hair up. I had known that psalm all my life. I had heard it and said it a thousand times. But until then I had always felt that it came from a long way off, some place I had not lived. Now, hearing him speak it, it seemed to me for the first time to utter itself in our tongue and to wear our dust. My grandfather slept again after that, but I did not.

Another night, again, I heard him call me. "Andy. Listen." His voice exultant then, at having recovered the words, he recited:

There entertain him all the saints above,
In solemn troops and sweet societies
That sing, and singing in their glory move,
And wipe the tears forever from his eyes.

After he spoke them, the words stood above us in the dark and the quiet, sounding and luminous. And then they faded.

After a while I said, "Who taught you that?"

"My mother. She was a great hand to improve your mind."

And after a while, again, I asked, "Do you know who wrote it?"

"No," he said. "But wasn't he a fine one!"

As the summer went along, he weakened, but so slowly we could hardly see it happening. There was never any sudden change. He remained quiet, mainly comfortable, and alert. We stayed in our routine of caring for him; it had become the ordinary way of things.

In the latter part of August we started into the tobacco cutting. For us, that is the great divider of the year. It ends the summer, and makes safe the season's growth. After it, our minds are lightened, and we look ahead to winter and the coming year. It is a sort of ritual of remembrance, too, when we speak of other years and remember our younger selves and the absent and the dead—all those we have, as we say, "gone down the row with."

We had a big crew that year—eight men working every day: Jarrat and Burley and Nathan Coulter, Arthur and Martin Rowanberry, Elton Penn, Danny Branch, and me. Hannah Coulter and Mary Penn and Lyda Branch kept us fed and helped with the hauling and housing. And Nathan and Hannah's boy, Mattie, and the Penns' children, Elsie and Jack, were with us until school started, and then they worked after school and on Saturdays. We worked back and forth among the various farms as the successive plantings became ready for harvest.

"What every tobacco cutting needs," Art Rowanberry said, "is a bunch of eighteen-year-old boys wanting to show how fast they are."

He was right, but we did not have them. We were not living in a time that was going to furnish many such boys for such work. Except for Mattie and Jack, who were fourteen and eleven, and would have liked to show how fast they were, if they had been fast, we were all old enough to be resigned to the speed we could stand. And so, when we cut, we would be strung out along the field in a pattern that never varied from the first day to the last. First would be Elton and Nathan and Danny, all working along together. Elton, I think, would have proved the fastest if anybody had challenged him, but nobody did. Then came Mart Rowanberry, who was always ahead of me, though he was nearly twice my age, and then, some distance behind me, would come Art Rowanberry, and then Burley Coulter, and then, far back, Burley's brother Jarrat, whose judgment and justification of himself were unswerving: "I'm old and wore out and not worth a damn. But every row I cut is a cut row."

In my grandfather's absence Jarrat was the oldest of us, a long-enduring, solitary, mostly silent man, slowed by age and much hard work. His brushy eyes could stare upon you as if you had no more ability to stare back than a post. When he had something to say, his way was simply to begin to say it, no matter who else was talking or what else was happening, his slow, hard-edged voice boring in upon us like his stare—and the result, invariably, was that whatever was happening stopped, and whoever was talking listened.

I never caught up with Elton and Nathan and Danny, or came anywhere near it, but at least when the rows were straight I always had them in sight, and I loved to watch them. Though they kept an even, steady pace, it was not a slow one. They drove into the work, maintaining the same pressing rhythm from one end of the row to the other, and yet they worked well, as smoothly and precisely as dancers. To see them moving side by side against the standing crop, leaving it fallen, the field changed, behind them, was maybe like watching Homeric soldiers going into battle. It was momentous and beautiful, and touchingly, touchingly mortal. They were spending themselves as they worked, giving up their time; they would not return by the way they went.

The good crew men among us were Burley and Elton. When the sun was hot and the going hard, it would put heart into us to hear Burley singing out down the row some scrap of human sorrow that his flat, exuberant voice both expressed and mocked:

Allll our sins and griefs to *bear*-oh!

—that much only, raised abruptly out of the silence like the howl of some solitary dog. Or he would sing with a lovelorn quaver in his voice:

Darlin', fool yourself and love me one more time.

And when we were unloading the wagons in the barn, he would start his interminable tale about his life as a circus teamster. It was not meant to be believed, and yet in our misery we listened to his extravagant wonderful lies as if he had been Marco Polo returned from Cathay.

Elton had as much gab as Burley, when he wanted to, but he served us as the teller of the tale of our own work. He told and retold everything that happened that was funny. That we already knew what he was telling, that he was telling us what we ourselves had done, did not matter. He told it well, he told it the way we would tell it when we told it, and every time he told it he told it better. He told us, also, how much of our work we had got done, and how much we had left to do, and how we might form the tasks still ahead in order to do them. His head, of course, was not the only one involved, and not the only good one, but his was indeed a good one, and his use of it pleased him and comforted us. Though we had a lot of work still to do, we were going to be able to do it, and these were the ways we could get it done. The whole of it stayed in his mind. He shaped it for us and gave it a comeliness greater than its difficulty.

That we were together now kept us reminded of my grandfather, who had always been with us before. We often spoke of him, because we missed him, or because he belonged to our stories, and we could not tell them without speaking of him.

One morning, perhaps to acknowledge to herself that he would not wear them again, my grandmother gave me a pair of my grandfather's shoes.

It was a gift not easy to accept. I said, "Thanks, Granny," and put them under my arm.

"No," she said. "Put them on. See if they fit."

They fit, and I started, embarrassedly, to take them off.

"No," she said. "Wear them."

And so I wore them to the field.

"New shoes!" Burley said, recognizing them, and I saw tears start to his eyes.

"Yes," I said.

Burley studied them, and then me. And then he smiled and put his arm around me, making the truth plain and bearable to us both: "You can wear 'em, honey. But you can't fill 'em."

It got to be September, and the fall feeling came into the air. The days would get as hot as ever, but now when the sun got low the chill would come. It was not going to frost for a while yet, but we could feel it coming. It was the time of year, Elton said, when a man begins to remember his long underwear.

We were cutting a patch at Elton's place where the rows were longer than any we had cut before, bending around the shoulder of a ridge and rising a little over it. They were rows to break a man's heart, for, shaped as they were, you could not see the end, and those of us who were strung out behind the leaders could not see each other. All that we could see ahead of us would be the cloudless blue sky. Each row was a long, lonely journey that, somewhere in the middle, in our weariness, we believed would never end.

Once when I had cut my row and was walking back to start another, Art Rowanberry wiped the sweat from his nose on the cuff of his sleeve and called out cheerfully to me, "Well, have you been across? Have you seen the other side?"

That became the ceremony of that day and the next. When one of us younger ones finished a row and came walking back, Art would ask us, "Have you seen the other side?"

Burley would take it up then, mourning and mocking: "Have you reached the other shore, dear brother? Have you seen that distant land?" And he would sing,

Oh, pilgrim, have you seen that distant land?

On the evening of the second day we had the field nearly cut. There was just enough of the crop left standing to make an easy job of finishing up—something to look forward to. We had finished cutting for the day and were sitting in the rich, still light under a walnut tree at the edge of the field, resting a little, before loading the wagons. We would load them the last thing every evening, to unload the next morning while the dew was on.

We saw my father's car easing back along the fencerow, rocking a little over the rough spots in the ground. It was a gray car, all dusty, and scratched along the sides where he had driven it through the weeds and briars. He still had on his suit and tie.

"Ah, here he comes," Burley said, for we were used to seeing him at that time of day, when he would leave his office at Hargrave and drive up to help us a little or to see how we had got along.

He drove up beside us and stopped, and killed the engine. But he did not look at us. He looked straight ahead as if he had not quit driving, his hands still on the wheel.

"Boys," he said, "Mr. Feltner died this afternoon. About an hour ago."

And then, after he seemed to have finished, he said as though to himself, "And now that's over."

I heard Burley clear his throat, but nobody said anything. We sat in the cooling light in my grandfather's new silence, letting it come upon us.

And then the silence shifted and became our own. Nobody spoke. Nobody yet knew what to say. We did not know what we were going to do. We were, I finally realized, waiting on Jarrat. It was Elton's farm, but Jarrat was now the oldest man, and we were waiting on him.

He must have felt it too, for he stood, and stood still, looking at us, and then turned away from us toward the wagons.

"Let's load 'em up."

If You Can't Win

JAMES BAKER HALL

James Baker Hall was born in 1935 in Lexington, where he lived throughout his childhood, primarily in the home of his paternal grandparents. After graduating from Henry Clay High School, Hall went on to earn a B.A. from the University of Kentucky and an M.A. in literature from Stanford, using what later became his first novel, *Yates Paul: His Grand Flight, His Tootings* (1963), as his master's thesis. Since then he has published five volumes of poetry, among them *Stopping on the Edge to Wave* (1988) and *The Mother on the Other Side of the World* (1999); two novels; a book of photographs, *Orphan in the Attic* (1995); and numerous articles and reviews on photography. His short stories, as yet uncollected, have appeared in numerous periodicals. He has taught and lectured at Stanford University, New York University, MIT, University of Connecticut, Cummington Community of the Arts, and since 1973 has taught creative writing at the University of Kentucky. He and his wife, Mary Ann Taylor-Hall, live near Sadieville, Kentucky.

Like the fiction of Eudora Welty, Hall's short stories reflect his photographic eye. The essential details are selected and framed so that the reader's subconscious will compose the entire picture. Hall is adept at this skill, and his relaxed narrative style often conceals the painstaking selection of details. "If You Can't Win" is rural in setting, world-wise in tone, and tragicomic in vision. A story of compatible contradictions, it addresses the negative effects experienced by the narrator as she attempts to perform an act of kindness and generosity. "People think that an open heart means joyousness or happiness, and that seems to me foolish," Hall has said in an interview with L. Elisabeth Beattie. "I mean an open heart is a suffering soul. Joy and beauty and an embrace of life is the end of it if you keep it open, it seems to me. But right up and through that is a great anguish and pain."

◆

"You oughtn't to feed Old Blue candy bars," my husband has told Peggy, a hundred times, showing her how to hold an ear of corn in one hand and work the kernels off into the other. "See? How easy it is?" Over and over he went through each step, showing her how to hold the kernels out in the palm of her hand, just so. "He won't bite. It feels real good. Try it. Old Blue won't bite."

I know something is up when I stop by the station a little after noon and find it locked, his TEMPORARILY CLOSED EMERGENCY sign propped in the window (the last three letters of EMERGENCY squeezed in); and I see what it is when I make the turn and start up the hill. There on the roof of our house, riding the spine like a runaway sawhorse, sits Peggy in all her splendor, two hundred and thirty-seven pounds in a white night gown, looking like a Picasso weathervane.

I've been up all night at the hospital, most of it in ER, and Peggy, bless her troubled soul, I'm fed up with Peggy, I don't care who she is or how she got into this—real fed up. I would have said that nothing Peggy could do would surprise me any more—in fact did, a few nights ago, to Billy, lying there back to back in the dark, fully clothed on our own bed so as not to excite our guest Peggy there on the other side of the wall, whispered it, my sweet nothings 1980s style—but there she is, holding onto the antenna pole for dear life, like an umbrella in a high wind. The same Peggy who wouldn't climb up on a chair to mount the horse she had come over a thousand miles to have and to hold and presumably to ride, wouldn't even discuss it, her life-long fantasy—that we had disjointed our lives to make real for her, Billy and I. Whenever we try to mess around, which has never been all that frequent or showy, God knows, she goes to rattling her candy wrappers in the next room, whenever we try to talk even. She's been here only a little more than two months, and already I understand exactly, in my nerve endings, what her mother Eve meant when she said that, given Peggy, it was more trouble to have a man around than not—even a saint (certainly compared to my first husband Lord the Big D Byron) who gets up at four a.m. to work in the tobacco and comes home fourteen hours later smelling like a gas station and gets wasted and goes to sleep on the floor, more or less immediately. Although the other night in response Billy whispered back that he wasn't going to close the station any more, Peggy was on her own, the neighbors and all their pets too, it was everybody for himself now, still I'm not surprised, given where Peggy has got herself this time, to see him there with her, shoulder high to the gutter atop the ladder, pleading—bless his tired, patient, dependable soul. There's a kind of poetry in Billy too, just as there was in my other husband, only a different kind: the first two or three times he had to close the station to go extricate Peggy from messes she got into walking to Squiresville and back after candy three or four times a week—after we had forbid it, the trip, the candy, all of it—he was so sweet I wanted to cry. One husband running around with his poems in one hand and his cock in the other is enough.

And to complete this curious little picture, there as I turn in the drive is Old Blue, who when I was last here was as far as anybody could tell in good health, or what for him any more passes for good health, collapsed right in the middle of the yard, as though he had seen what I just saw.

Maybe he thought that Peggy was going to jump off on him, another of our schemes to get her up on his back.

Or maybe all that candy finally caught up with him.

What I'm thinking is, the only thing sacred any more is a sense of humor, and that's overrated—you know what I mean? I mean sure Peggy is ludicrous, and Lord Byron the Big Dude, and me myself, Ms. Upstream of Harrison County (I should have been a nurse, there would have been no problem then), elbow deep in one farting overweight human being after another, scrambling all the time to pay for a car and an office full of equipment so that I can scramble all the time to pay for the farm I barely have time to sleep on and for a membership in a country club so I'll have a place to take a break from all the scrambling where I can find more (lucrative) scrambling to do. And Billy too, though I hate worst of all in his case to admit it, the man-shaped 10W-40 spot on the livingroom rug next to which sits the alarm clock, where his loving wife always puts it before going to bed—his and hers alarm clocks, romance of the '80s—and his father too—Christ, Billy's father is the most ludicrous of us all. But there isn't anything funny about Peggy, not even when she's straddling the center beam, not to me, not any more, not really. I'm thinking how sad she is, and Eve is, and now Billy and I, how sad we all are, and there Old Blue is, dead in the front yard—he knew. One of the most remarkable things about Eve— I'm realizing this for the first time now, as I park far enough away from the dead horse to get the flatbed in—is how completely lacking in self-pity she is, for after only nine weeks of taking care of Peggy I'm full of it, there's nothing else to me. With little more than a wave of the hand to Billy (who if the truth be known has been a temporarily-closed emergency ever since I met him, just like I have) I hustle inside to call for help. The last thing the woman cardiologist-cum-GP needs is something dead in the yard to add to the Goodyear legend. That's what the lowlife down in Squiresville call Peggy, the Goodyear. The first time Billy had to rescue her she had been followed all the way down there by a pack of dogs, like she was in heat (which is one way to describe the way Peggy walks when she's fresh, head back, sniffing the air like it was perfume and she had money in her purse). Only one of the dogs got mean, or so it seemed to her, and she coldcocked it with a limb as big around as her arm, a half chow that belonged to the one old lady between our house and Squiresville you didn't want anything to do with. I could get along without seeing Billy's father today, or ever again for that matter, but he has the only hoist around, so he's the first person I call. I get him on the CB, he's only a few miles away. Then Eve.

I have a friend old enough to be my mother, that's Eve, who has a daughter my age, thirty-three, that's Peggy—who's never had a boyfriend and has lived with her mother all her life, lying around the house watching TV and wanting a horse. Peggy is simple-minded, but you can't tell it right off, and nobody talks about it. Eve feels sorry for her, and does everything she can for her, and I feel sorry for Eve. She saw me through my first marriage; if it hadn't been for Eve I would probably still be up there dropping out of med school every semester to wait tables in Ithaca so I could live in the woods with Lord Byron. He was a hunk, the Big One was (no more than Billy though), but he was too busy always messing around with other women to hold a job. Eve knew what it was like to live with a monster (though neither of us would ever have called Peggy that), and she told me, numerous times. "I love him!"

I kept saying. I believed (and probably still do, underneath it all) that pretty much whatever is suffered in the name of love (true love, now) is beyond reproach because inescapable, one has no choice really, and that those who don't understand that don't know what love is. "Oh dear," Eve would say whenever I started talking about love.

Where I came from (and have, it seems, ended up), Harrison County, Kentucky, sophistication was what went on in certain of the shopping malls in Lexington, and art too. Before I walked into Eve's house the only paintings I ever saw were in the basement of the Ben Franklin's, and the model rooms at Sears. Eve had been all over the world, had lived in Hawaii, in Japan, in places I had never heard of, literally (Sri Lanka for one), and in Paris, where she went to the Sorbonne and graduated from the Cordon Bleu. Somewhere along the way, which included two marriages, one to a banker, and the other to a career diplomat, she had picked up—in addition to Peggy—a real spread, over two hundred acres in upstate New York, most of it in woods. The Big One and I lived in what used to be the groundskeeper's house rent-free in exchange for work, Peggy-sitting and plant-watering mostly, virtually all of which I did.

This was 1967 to 1972, 180 miles from Woodstock, and the Big Dude was in his time, a continuous drug-blast of friends and vans coming and going, music and poetry to read, and Eve, the perfect mother none of us had, who in her completely dignified way thought that Mick Jagger was the greatest thing to happen culturally since FDR—someone was always strung out on something, and she was always there, a place to stay, a knowing ear, even money when it was needed—Eve loved it all. It wasn't just my first marriage she saw me through, it was my first civil disobedience, my first arrest, posting bail for me, and she saw me through my parents' reaction too. She would make Peggy turn down the TV, and then after the lord's poetry reading, serve some desserts I couldn't remember the names of and show us first editions. I didn't know what a first edition was. I didn't know what a lot of things were until I met Eve, my husband foremost among them. "I love him!" I kept saying, and Eve would say, "But, Kitty, we all *love* him." I'm married to him, I insisted, for better or worse! Finally Eve just quit saying anything, by way of getting me to hear what I was saying.

Right from the start I knew that Eve was my liberator, I just didn't know which prison I was in. On the couch under the long tapestry telling the lives of the saints I used to lie, tears in my eyes at times, listening to classical music and promising myself an education, a real one, and travel. She was a lady, that was my take on her, and still is, a lady through and through, as well as a saint. As part of her ongoing effort to keep Peggy out of the hospital or cemetery and from in front of the TV, Eve took her for a walk every day the weather permitted, and sometimes when it didn't, long walks, a more unlikely couple you've never seen. In addition to being round, Peggy is tall, nearly a foot taller than her mother, who even now has a body of a woman in her twenties, an absolutely flat stomach, wonderfully thin ankles and wrists, and a posture to go with it, a real presence—a thoroughbred out working with a Belgian, a familiar sight to all of us who drove those roads. For the first mile or two Peggy walked with her face tipped up, as though she was balancing pleasure on the tip of her nose, looking at everything there was to look at, at her head loose as a ball-bearing in its socket, the great lumbering gait of her size, as though she was going down hill always, in a straight line, nothing in the way, a great smile on her face, usually, waving at every car that passed, stooping down to do it even when there was no reason.

"Toot-toot," she says sometimes when I'm out walking with her around here, and giggles, never missing a stride, but halfway into the walk, especially in warm weather, she wilts, dramatically, which is the way she does everything, from the rooftop as it were. The only time Peggy ever got up on Old Blue he just stood there for a minute switching his tail, and then knelt down, front legs first. "Hoa!" Billy shouted. "Hoa you sonofabitch! Stand up! What the crazy hell you doing!" I can still hear him, but it was obvious we had to have a fall-back plan, trying to keep her healthy and honest with chores, which turned out to be, almost immediately, considerably more trouble than it was worth. I got so I could hardly stand the sight of her. Wanted to strangle her with the bridle or the bedsheet the next time I heard another candy wrapper.

That was some of the time. There were other times when I wanted to cry. Big women around here have a chance if not an outright advantage: the men are used to them, don't have a whole lot of choice, and for most, the fact that she is a little simple doesn't create a problem, a lot of them don't even seem to notice—but not quite as big as Peggy, the margin being, for a start anyway, all that candy. What I mean is, we've been (as they say) tireless in our efforts, but to no avail. If anything she's gained. Day after day I come home exhausted, smelling of the day's accumulation of diseases and frustrations, and praying for some help, with which I can get to the club nine miles away before dark to swim my laps and without which I can't, having left absolutely clear and simple instruction, and there Peggy is, lying in front of the TV, surrounded by candy wrappers, crying at *Gilligan's Island* or *Hee-Haw* and imitating commercials (which she has a real genius for doing), having forgotten, always, whatever it is I asked her to do.

This isn't the first time I've decided to send her home, but it's the first time I've gone so far as to call Eve; I'm planning to tell her that Peggy will be on the next plane, that very afternoon if we can put it together. But while I'm sitting here at my desk waiting for the connection to be made, staring at the roof and listening to Billy, who's up there now trying to convince her that it's not her fault Old Blue keeled over, you can't founder a horse on candy—what a sweetheart he is, really, the Big D had absolutely no patience with her at all—it begins to dawn on me for the first time, bright lady that I am, just how dangerous the situation is. Peggy is terrified, too frightened to utter a word. And with good reason—she's not really agile enough. I gather from what I hear that when Old Blue went down, Peggy went up, the next thing she knew she was on the roof, which makes about as much sense as she usually makes, and she's stuck there now.

I'm getting ready to postpone talking to Eve until Peggy is safe, when somebody answers—only it isn't her, it's the Lord Dude, who supposedly owns the cabin now, no more plants to water, no more Peggy to sit, not for the last nine weeks at least. I was never jealous of Eve because, one, she was out of the Big One's league and he knew it; two, she was a saint; and three, Peggy, she was never without Peggy even when Peggy was elsewhere, not for long enough anyway. Which is why Peggy is down here, to give her a break, one that she can do something with. So I figure I've dialed the wrong number, which I've done before, and quickly make up my mind whether I want to talk to him or not, which I don't, no way. But instead of hanging up, which even as it doesn't happen I think I'm doing—I mean I decide, clearly, to hang up—I'm saying "You sonofabitch!" and off we go into another of our long distance harangues. I've long since quit hating him for running around on me, mostly anyway, but the one thing I can't seem to get over is, he made me take my maiden name back before he would give me a divorce. It cost me one hundred and twenty-five dollars, for the lawyer (and a woman at that, which added to my indignation) to walk a piece of paper across the street—and all because he whose brain is rotted from chemicals doesn't want my license in his name for fear I'll deal scripts, or could, which to this day makes me livid. I'm not only a responsible adult citizen, I'm proud of it, something he'll never understand, I've worked my bohunkus off at it, upstream all the way, and I'm not putting up with any more zuluing from old brain-rot about selling out to the country club, who thinks he's changed because he's macrobiotic, but hasn't.

When Billy hears me screaming he knows exactly what is going on and starts banging on the roof with his flat hand, not because he is jealous or fed up as it turns out, which is what I think, for he has every reason to be (maybe not jealous, surely fed up)—but because his father is here with the hoist. "How's your sex life?" my father-in-law asks me.

You would think that Billy has been talking to him, except that Billy (who is, I must say it again, a hunk too, every bit as pretty as the Big One and infinitely preferable) doesn't think there is anything the matter with it, not as far as I can tell. After the Big D, I didn't either, not for a while anyway. Even if Billy did think that, he would never say anything to his creepy father about it, if for no other reason because they don't talk. At the dinner table the Captain as he calls himself passes messages to the boy as he calls Billy through me, he always has, and I cooperate, don't ask me why—but Billy is too cooled out nowadays to answer. His father was an officer in the army during the Korean war, did two tours of combat, and Billy was among the first to burn his draft card during Vietnam—which pretty much contains the logic of everything that has ever happened between them. My father-in-law told me once that he thought I was too much for Billy, meaning a filling station attendant oughtn't to be married to a doctor. Every time I think I know just how creepy he is, he ups the ante. "You want to know how creepy he is?!" I'm always asking Billy, as if he didn't know at least as well as I do.

When the Captain gets out of the truck, he acts as though he doesn't even notice that Peggy is up on the roof, and, when he does notice because I won't let him not, finds nothing especially strange about it—or Billy up on the ladder proposing to her, about what you'd expect from Billy. If Billy isn't asleep whenever his father comes around, he soon is, for the messages are all about how much better a man his father is, as evinced whenever all else fails by the fact that he owns the station, still, and the boy had better not forget it. Here he comes this minute, the Captain, sliding up to me as he always does, going for the Camels in his breast pocket, a particular little smile on his face, his woman smile, and he keeps sliding. He has this way, as soon as you align yourself to talk, of twisting you around, as though the sun is in his eyes everywhere except at your elbow—where he can sneak a better look at you than you can at him. He hasn't even said anything yet—how's your sex life comes later—and already we've gone around in one complete circle. That's how creepy he is. I would kick him in the groin, except that it's against my principles to acknowledge that he has one. If I were Billy I would be asleep all the time too, for sure. On the second circle, we talk business, the airport and the dog factory, and then out of nowhere comes the sleazy question.

"How's your sex life?"

I pretend not to hear.

At the first exit, I get off, trading places with Billy so he can help with the horse—which is the undoing of all my plans. In order to talk Peggy down I have to get next to her fear, and the minute I get there she starts crying. "You're all right," I keep telling her, "we're going to make it." Not just next to it, inside it—we're on the pitch, sitting down and inching, I'm out in front, showing her how. When she . . . I don't know what she does, slips somehow, I hear her start to slip, bare feet on shingles—and then, just as mysteriously, stop. She's locked up now, her whole body, she can't even talk—and the hard part, getting her turned around so she can back down the ladder, is yet to come. "You're all right," I keep telling her, even though she knows better than I do that she isn't—until finally Martha Ray comes to the rescue. "Take it from a big mouth," I say, imitating her imitation of her favorite commercial—"Take it from a big mouth!" she says back, showing me why she doesn't need the tranquilizer Billy has fetched from my bag, and says it again after each rung, bravo, bravo, Billy and I cheering the big mouth. There's no way, once she's down, that I'm going to jam her onto the next plane home. In fact we end up for the rest of the day bragging a whole lot on her for going up and down the ladder, and meaning more than half of it too. Precisely how much longer I intend to subsidize Lady Slime's affair with my ex is yet to be determined, but for a while longer, that much for sure—I'm telling her how close I came to sending her home, she's crossing her heart and hoping to die if she eats any more candy.

When it comes time for me to call Eve and tell her not to go to the airport and the Big D answers again, Peggy is stretched out on the sofa in front of the TV watching the Special Olympics and Billy is asleep on the floor—I'm pretty much free to deal with it straight on. My first reaction is, to say nothing, dead silence. "Hello," the sonofabitch says again, and I say "OK sonofabitch, I've got one question to ask you." It's his turn to go silent now. "Are you ready," I ask him, watching Billy to make sure he's asleep, it wouldn't do for him to overhear this, wouldn't be worth it, and the Big One, reaching deep, the creep, says, "I'm always ready," and I say, "Are you balling Eve?" and he says, "What business is that of yours," and I say, "Don't you give me any shit," and he says, "Don't give me any shit," and I say, "How long?" and he says, "Do you want to speak to Eve or what?" and I say, "For as long as Peggy's down here, right?" and he says, "Answer my question," and I say, "Answer mine!" and he says, "I'm putting Eve on," and I say, "Don't you dare!" and he says, "Why not?" and I say, "Peggy's not coming," and he says, "Good," and I say, "Fuck off, will you," and he says, "How are you otherwise?" and I say, "How am I supposed to know?" and he says, "Not so good, huh?" and I say, "Not so good," and he says, "Things are real good up here," and I say, "I gather," and he says, "Did you and Peggy make up?" and I say, "Sort of, I guess."

When I get off the phone I go sit next to her, on the floor in front of the couch. On the TV screen a seventy-one-year-old retarded woman comes in fifth in the fifty-yard run, is girlishly shy at the microphone—and Peggy and I are both crying. I'm far from being over the idea that slimy Eve had the Big One in mind for herself right from the start, and that for the last nine weeks I've been Dr. Chump herself, but the fact is: anguish that ten years ago would have taken weeks to work through, months, years, I whip through now in a matter of minutes, and with half a mind really, less: I'm at least as interested in the Special Olympics. On the TV one muscular dystrophy patient, with the help of side walkers, takes to horseback, I could cry again, and another to the parallel bars. Peggy is down on the floor with me now, in my arms, the weight of her, the flesh of her, wet with tears, even her great arms wet, bless her, she weeps the whole time. Beside us on the floor, Billy wakes up from under a blanket of tissues long enough to take her hand. Somewhere in the right background of my thoughts Crosby, Stills, and Nash are still singing *Suite: Judy Blue Eyes* and the Moody Blues are still looking for someone to change their life, and I am, as usual, practicing disdain and/or outrage for the day's glib conde-scension to the late sixties, whereas in the left I'm defending myself, as always, as earnestly as ever, against the accusation of selling out. Maybe I'm as out of it as Peggy, but from what I know it's still important that I'm working for myself and not Dow Chemical or Humana or IBM, that I have (please excuse the expression) made something of myself, that I love my work (mostly), that I love my husband and am true to him—when how many others from those days can say as much? I even by god defend when necessary the scramble—is it any wonder people's lives shift as they grow older from sex (sex, all you can hear any more is sex!) to money? With money at least you can tell how much you've got, some of the time anyway. At one point in the program they show a sign that one of the participants made, the letters tortured and jumbled up and painfully beautiful: *I hope I win but if I don't I hope my effort is courageous*—when I see that I say amen.

Bypass

LISA KOGER

Born in Ohio in 1953 and raised in West Virginia, Lisa Koger earned a B.S.W. (bachelor in social work) at West Virginia University, a master's in journalism at the University of Tennessee, and an M.F.A. at the Iowa Writers' Workshop. She has taught creative writing at the University of Iowa, the Graduate Studies Center in Rock Island, Illinois, and Mississippi State University, and has participated in workshops at Hindman Settlement School, Simmons College, and Duke University. She is the author of *Farlanburg Stories* (1990), one of the few debut short story collections to be published by W. W. Norton. Her stories have appeared in *Seventeen*, *Ploughshares*, *The American Voice*, *Kennesaw Review*, *Kentucky Voices*, and many other venues. Koger lives with her family in Pulaski County, Kentucky, near Monticello where her husband, Jerry, grew up.

Of *Farlanburg Stories*, Anne Rivers Siddons has noted that Koger "explores the country of the Southern heart with the comic intensity of Florence King and the antic darkness of Eudora Welty." Koger comments on her sense of place in her essay in *Bloodroot*: "I want to know where people live. I want to feel that a character's personality, his behavior, and the choices he makes are, to some extent, the result of where he finds himself geographically and of where he has been. . . . It doesn't matter whether that place is as large as Philadelphia or as small as Scooba, Mississippi. It's the size of the feeling that counts." Published in *Kennesaw Review* in 1987 and in *The American Voice* later that year, "Bypass" is the opening story in *Farlanburg Stories*. Filled with Koger's humor and wit, it portrays an individual's instinctual quest for something genuine, no matter how trivial, something that will begin to reroute him toward home and meaning.

◆

Friday night and Earl has a taste for chicken. The craving slipped up on him, fox-like, sometime late in the afternoon. Tonight, he doesn't want Ruth's Crispy or Wanda's Golden Fried or chicken from any of the other joints in town. He doesn't want chain-food chicken from one of those bright new places on the bypass, either. It scares him to eat at places where there are signs that tell him billions have eaten the same thing. There's more than safety in numbers, he knows.

What he really has a taste for is home-fried chicken. The kind his mother made. Earl's mother has been dead almost twenty years. She wasn't an outstanding cook or an especially clean one. She dripped sweat on the plates and scratched her legs with her butcher knives. But she knew the importance of feeding a man.

"You're a helluva good woman," Earl wishes he'd said to her just once, but he didn't. Appreciation is a bonus given to the dead. Now that Earl's approaching middle age himself, he'd settle for half what's coming to him if he could only have it early.

At the stoplight on Main Street in downtown Farlanburg, he signals left and heads north on Route 19 out of town. School's just let out, and the streets are filled with yellow buses beginning their routes. Earl recognizes most of the faces behind the bus windows because he teaches those faces for a living. In Farlanburg, a man can farm if he has one, teach if he doesn't, or drive a truck for Hallawell Chemical Company and get cancer by the time he's fifty. All three jobs will kill him. It's a matter of how long he wants to linger.

He stops at the Bi-Lo and gets some chicken—a family pack, bulging with breasts, legs, and thighs. He plans to drop by the ceramic shop where his wife, Brenda, works and see if he can talk her into coming home and frying it up for him. Chicken is not the only thing he'd like to talk her into, but given the state of things between them, he figures chicken is as good a place as any to start.

Something is wrong with Earl's marriage but not with Brenda's. When he tries to talk to her about it, she looks at him as if he's just told her his athlete's foot has come back. This is a personal problem, her look says. Why are you discussing this with me?

Brenda doesn't discuss personal problems. She prefers to keep busy instead. During the past three years, she and Earl have enclosed the carport, knocked out a side wall to enlarge the living room, replaced the kitchen cabinets, and built a deck that wraps around three sides of their three-bedroom house. They did most of the work themselves, and it looks it. On weekends, when Earl runs down to the hardware store for more paneling or nails, Lonnie, who works in home repairs, slaps him on the back and tells him he's the busiest man he knows. Earl agrees, but he doesn't know *why* he's so busy. He saw nothing wrong with the house in the first place.

"Maybe not," says Brenda, "but it doesn't pay to have too much time to sit around and think."

Earl will be forty come September, and he *wants* to think. He knows he's not the man he was at eighteen, but there's nothing wrong with his ears. He hears something eating away at his happiness just as surely as he hears mice gnawing inside Brenda's kitchen cabinets at night.

Mice aren't the only things gnawing away at Earl's house. There are Kivetts. The Kivetts are Brenda's people. Strange rangers, the Kivetts. They come to Earl's house, eat his steak, and treat him like he's not at home.

"They're just quiet," Brenda says. "You tell me what you want them to say, and I'll make sure they do."

Earl isn't sure what he wants from the Kivetts, including Brenda. Whatever he wants, it seems to be too much.

Tonight is steak and Kivett night at Earl's house. Every Friday night is steak and Kivett night at Earl's house. It's been that way for most of the last fifteen years. Earl can afford steak if he's careful, but it's still a luxury to him. He hates putting something as special as steak into the mouths of people as unspecial as the Kivetts.

Usually, it's the mister and missus. Sometimes Brenda's sister, Mary, comes, too. Mary is forty-one and has been brain-damaged since birth. She wears pigtails, has blue eyes, and lets her mama dress her in a different shade of anklets every day of the week. The real giveaway is Mary's disposition. She's *so* happy. More so, Earl thinks, than any normal adult could possibly be.

Earl is jealous of Mary's happiness, but he likes her. Sometimes he thinks there's nothing really wrong with her at all—that she's playing some sly, accommodating sort of game. Other times, he's sure she's a prophet with a message she's waiting to deliver.

At any rate, Mary fills Earl with hope. He never knows when she's going to do something that will help him remember how to laugh or say something that says more than she means. He long ago gave up expecting such things, from Brenda or the mister and missus.

"I don't know what you want from me," Brenda says whenever Earl complains. She looks at him and blinks. Her face is a closed door. "Do Not Disturb," the sign says.

Earl has learned to keep quiet, but inside his head, a steady drip tells him life is not supposed to be like this.

Earl stops at the shop to see if Brenda will knock off early and come home with him. The place is hot and packed. Women are jammed shoulder to shoulder around the tables, smoking, scraping and sanding frogs and miniature Christmas trees. It's eight months until Christmas.

Brenda is timing a load of ginger jars in her "oven" and painting eyes on a unicorn for a friend. She works with the intensity of a woman who's just discovered what she does best. "Don't forget to glaze the bottom of your salt and pepper shakers, Kimberly Jean," she says to a woman across the table. "Loved that decal you used on your chamber pot."

Brenda's been in the ceramics business almost three years. At first, she got ticked off when Earl called her kiln an oven. "It's a kiln, Earl honey," she said. "How do you expect people to take me serious if you go around calling my kiln an oven?" She doesn't get ticked off anymore. She doesn't call Earl "honey," either. To get ticked off at someone or call him "honey," you have to have feelings for him, and Brenda seems to have lost all hers for Earl. Her mouth hasn't said the words. Her body does the talking. "You leave me cold as a snake," it says. Earl isn't sure what he's done wrong, but judging by the way Mrs. Kivett treats the mister, he must've done the same thing.

"What're you doing here?" Brenda says when Earl walks in. "I thought you were gonna get the steaks and come pick me up at five." She glances at her watch. "It ain't anywheres near five." Brenda wears her blonde hair short and curly like a poodle's. She's still a good-looking woman, but at thirty-eight, she's beginning to get that look that says, "I bite."

Earl looks at his watch like the time is news to him.

"What you got in that sack, Earl?" Melanie Woodford asks. "He's so sweet," she says to the others. "He's brought her something."

"What you got, Earl?" a couple of women chime in.

Earl drifts toward Brenda's table. "Nothing. Just a chicken." He shrugs and lays it on a window sill.

"He's brought her a chicken." Someone laughs.

"I told you it was nothing," Earl says to Brenda, who is not laughing.

The women return to their scraping, and Earl pulls up a chair behind Brenda. "How much longer do you think you'll be here?" he whispers.

"Hard to tell," she replies in a voice that, to Earl, is unnecessarily loud.

He scoots his chair closer, crowding against some greenware shelves. "How about quitting early this evening and coming home with me? We'll fry chicken together and talk. Just look at this," he says, reaching for the sack. He pulls the chicken out and whistles with approval. "What a bird! We'll have fun. Just the two of us. We'll fix a nice supper and have it ready by the time the girls get home."

Brenda touches up one eye of her unicorn. "Mama and Daddy are coming by at six for steaks. You know that."

"Call 'em. Tell 'em we can't do it this evening," Earl says quietly. "We'll fix this chicken. Just you and me. Like it used to be."

Brenda looks up. "Don't lean against those shelves thataway, Earl. You bust up any of my greenware, and the girls'll ride you outa here on a rail. Ain't that right, Edna?" she says to the woman on her left. Edna is a big woman with red knuckles and little eyes. She looks like she does ceramics only when she can't find a fight.

Earl nods. He puts the chicken in the sack, then scoots his chair away from the shelves. He clasps and unclasps his hands and looks at the floor like a benched player watching his team lose the game. "Tell you what," he finally says, resting his elbows on his knees. He's aware that every ear in the room is listening. "I'll go in there to the phone right now and call 'em. OK? What good's a phone if you can't use it at a time like this." He looks at the women and laughs, but it sounds like a bark. "I'm gonna go in there, ring 'em up, and say, real nice, that it's nothing against 'em, but that my wife and I want to be alone and fix chicken by ourselves tonight. They'll understand. Most people would understand that. What do you say?"

Brenda tilts her head to the side as though she is considering the matter. "Edna honey," she finally says. "Your soup bowl has seams up the sides that are gonna need sanding. Hand me a piece of that green scour pad, why don't you, and I'll show you how to rub it down real good."

The speed limit on the bypass is fifty-five. Earl's doing forty. He could do twice that and get away with it because the Farlanburg police don't come out here.

People in Farlanburg didn't want the bypass, but you couldn't go so far as to say they were against it. Those who had something to sell were the exceptions. They were afraid the bypass would hurt their business. They were right. Hardest hit were the Tumblin girls in tight polyester pants who did business from the rock wall at the north end of town. They counted on the caravans of trucks that passed through.

Others, who sold something more legitimate, have spent too much on advertising to postpone the inevitable. Their gaudy signs have sprung up overnight. "Sleep cheap! Kids eat free! Mom too!"

Earl didn't want the bypass, and he has nothing to sell. He's suspicious of people who spend millions of dollars to take him around something when he can see more by passing through.

He grew up in this section of the county in a white frame house that isn't white anymore. It's bright yellow and, thanks to the bypass, sits about three hundred feet from where it used to. Earl's sister still lives there. This evening, he feels the need to drive out to see her. He's not going to see her as much as he is to see himself, he knows, the way he used to be. He wants to sit in the paneled living room, sip a Coke, and look at pictures of himself when he was young and sure that the best was still ahead.

He remembers when there was nothing out here but fields, farmhouses, and a barn every now and then. He used to cut through those fields on rainy Sunday afternoons just to lie in the hayloft of the barn with "See Rock City" painted on its side. "See Rock Cit-y, See Rock Cit-y," the rain said as the drops hit the roof, ran down the tin, and dug holes in the manure below. He would lie in the hay, eat ham and mustard sandwiches, and plan his life the way he wanted it to be: college (out of state, of course), a stint in the army where he'd prove himself in Ranger school or in the Special Forces. He'd sign on as a mercenary after that. Spend a couple of years in the jungles of some foreign country. Then back to the U.S. of A. and someplace like Houston or San Francisco, a good job, good wife, and a couple of kids.

When he was sixteen, he and a friend, Bucky Eads, pooled their money and bought a car. A '61 Dodge with no muffler and rusted tail fins. They drove to Chattanooga one weekend to see Rock City.

"Somebody lied. It wasn't half what it's cracked up to be," Earl kept saying as they drove home that night, headlights flashing across his face.

"Doesn't matter," Bucky said.

But to Earl it did. He wouldn't be sixteen forever, he told himself. He'd have a job. Money to travel. He'd see places that'd make Rock City look sick.

He stayed in town to go to college. Figured he'd save money by going to Farlanburg State. He planned to clear out the day after graduation.

During his junior year, he started dating Brenda. He'd known her since high school when she was Wayne Sayer's girl and so good-looking she wouldn't give him the time of day. By this time, she was Wayne Sayer's ex with two kids to raise, and she was willing to give Earl anything he wanted. She gave it so willingly and so well that Earl forgot his plans. He graduated, married Brenda, and decided that the rest could wait.

Kim and Kerry, Brenda's girls, are seventeen and eighteen. They have red hair like their daddy, linebacker faces, and give no indication they'll ever leave home. They giggle and poke each other whenever Earl is in the same room. He has never been a religious man, but he's a grateful one. He gives thanks every night that those girls have never asked to call him "Daddy."

So Earl is back at Farlanburg High with the feeling he never really left. He teaches history and American government to kids who don't want to know about either. They want to smoke behind the lunchroom, jump up and down at pep rallies, and rub against each other in front of the lockers. Some days, Earl is tempted to tell them things he didn't learn in college. He'd start by saying he's older than he ever planned to be.

Home has never felt the same to Earl since the house was moved. Without concrete walks or flowers around the porch, it looks like it just fell out of the sky and landed in the field one night.

Earl's sister, Trudy, drives the bookmobile for the library, and she doesn't have time for flowers like her mother used to. She doesn't understand the need for them, either. "Imagine getting all worked up over a marigold!" she often says, wrinkling her nose and curling her upper lip like a horse.

Trudy has never been married, but she'd like to be. Part of the reason she hasn't is that she'd *very* much like to be. When she was in high school, she was president of the Future Homemakers of America, and she and her girlfriends used to spend Saturday afternoons looking at engagement rings in Hurt's jewelry store window. They had visions of tree-lined streets, Hotpoint stoves, and everlasting marital bliss.

Most of Trudy's friends got married. On the rare occasions when she sees them in town on Saturday mornings, they dash from their cars to the grocery store, then to Murphy's to pick up something for their kids. They remind her of locust shells, she once told Earl—brittle, empty versions of the people they used to be. Sometimes, she thinks they avoid her because she isn't married. Other times, she could swear they are signaling to her to stay away, trying to warn her about something with their weary, sunken eyes.

Earl parks his car in the yard, which is nothing more than a small square of orchard grass that Trudy's been mowing. He picks up the chicken. It's bled through the sack and onto the seat. He stares at the spot, rubs it, then gets out.

Birds swoop from the roof to the power line as he walks toward the porch. Peepers sing from the ditch behind the house. Earl knocks loudly, waits, then knocks again. "Anybody home?" he yells, opening the door and stepping inside. The house is quiet. He puts the chicken in the kitchen sink.

"Trudy?" He hears a stirring in one of the back rooms as though something has just come to life, then the ssstt, ssstt, ssstt, ssstt of slippers on the hallway linoleum.

"Earl?"

"It's me."

Trudy pokes her head through the curtains at the entrance to the hallway and looks suspiciously around the room.

"I'm alone. Brenda had to work late," Earl says.

"Law, that woman of yours goes after it, don't she?" Trudy steps from behind the curtains. "It's just as well this evening. I don't want anybody seeing me looking like this." Her hands move self-consciously over her stomach and thighs. "I'm bloated. Must have been something I ate."

"Maybe you're pregnant."

Trudy snorts and waves her hand, but she continues to watch Earl's face to see if he's going to laugh at the idea. She has put on a lot of weight since high school and might easily be mistaken for a woman in her second trimester. Her bobbed hair sticks up in the back, and a pillow or cover has left a red tatoo on the side of her face. She has the dream-swollen look of a woman who sleeps too much.

"I woke you up," Earl says.

"No, you didn't. I was just resting my eyes."

Despite the fact that it's mid-April and warm enough for wasps and bees, Trudy's gas heater is going full blast. Parched plants sit on a table near the window, their yellow, leafless stems skewed toward the light. The world outside looks fuzzy and unfocused because the plastic on the windows hasn't been taken down.

Trudy scoots a footstool toward the heater and motions Earl to the couch. She rubs her forehead, then fiddles with her hair. "I don't know what's got into me," she says. "I come home from work, and I'm so tired. Today I was just gonna rest my feet and legs for a spell, and the next thing I know, I look up, and it's two hours later, and I hear someone banging around the house. I have to slap myself to wake up. 'Trudy, girl,' I say. 'You better watch out or the same thing's gonna happen to you that happened to Gladys Farnsworth last week.' Someone broke in and stole her TV and electric blanket and Lord knows what all. Like to have cleaned her out and her asleep in her bed the whole time. It's hard to say what would've happened if she'd been younger and better looking. I don't know what I'd do if I was to wake up and find a man in the house with me." She pauses to catch her breath. "How long can you stay?"

"Not long," Earl tells her. "I was just out this way and thought I'd stop in a minute."

"You can stay longer than that. I know you can. You haven't been out here for at least three weeks. I got some frozen dinners. I'll put a couple in the oven, and we can talk."

"I bought a chicken. We could fix it. Have mashed potatoes and the works just like Mom used to."

"I got some good spaghetti dinners. With lots of meatballs," Trudy says, heading toward the kitchen.

Earl follows and sits on a stool beside the stove. The kitchen hasn't changed much since he was a boy except that it's cleaner and less busy. The only thing new is a microwave on the counter.

"A present," Trudy says. "From me to me." She winks. "You live alone long enough, you learn to treat yourself. The man at Big Lots says these things are safe. He bought one last Christmas for his son. Lucy at the library told me she read where microwaves can give you cancer up to twenty feet." Trudy shrugs. "Who knows what to believe. We've all got to go sometime. I'd a whole lot rather be killed by a microwave as by a man in my house." She takes a package from the freezer while holding back an avalanche of TV dinners with her other hand. "Have some spaghetti with me."

Earl shakes his head. In all the years he lived here, he never saw his mother fix a meal that wasn't made from scratch.

"Come here a minute," Trudy says. "I want you to see how this thing works." She opens the microwave door, pops her dinner in the tiny oven, and punches some buttons. "That's all there is to it. Isn't it one of the cleverest gadgets you ever saw?" She peeks through the microwave window and smiles.

"It's Friday night," Earl says. "You ought to be out doing something."

Trudy looks at him with genuine surprise. "I am doing something. I'm fixing supper and talking to you." She bends her knees and moves her face a little closer to the window. "I'd just give anything to know what goes on in there, but I'm afraid to get too close to the thing after what Lucy said."

"I want to talk," says Earl.

"Good," says Trudy. "Let's talk." She moves her hand around the outside of the microwave like a magician showing an audience there are no trick wires. She shakes her head. "You'd think there'd at least be some heat."

Earl shifts his weight from one leg to the other and looks around the kitchen. "I think there's something wrong with me," he says.

Trudy looks alarmed. "Where?"

Earl shakes his head. "Not like that. I mean wrong like I'm missing something. You know? Then other times I think I'm the only one who's not."

Trudy relaxes. She chews on a fingernail, then holds her hand out to inspect the damage.

"And then there are times when I think no one's missing a damn thing. Maybe there just isn't any more," Earl says.

The buzzer goes off. Trudy sets her dinner on the table. "Are you sure you won't eat with me?"

"I'm sure," Earl says.

She begins to cut up meatballs. "I know what you mean. I miss being married. People say you don't miss what you've never had." She shakes her fork at Earl. "That's a bunch of baloney. You remember that man who came here once with Uncle Rymer?

The one who had lost some fingers?" She takes a bite and signals for Earl to wait a minute while she chews. "Doesn't matter. You were little. Anyway, this man had lost his fingers. Lawn mower, I think. I remember him sitting here in the kitchen one night telling Mom and me how much he missed those fingers. He said he could still feel them even though they weren't there anymore. We thought he was the biggest liar we'd ever heard. Now I'm not so sure. I think a person can miss a part of himself even if it's *never* been there." Trudy frowns as though she has confused herself.

"Being married isn't everything," Earl says.

"It is if you've never been married." Trudy stares at Earl a moment, then leans across the table. "I want to tell you something. The strangest thing," she says, whispering. "I was at the library the other day, and I saw this book. The title just jumped out and grabbed me like a hand around my throat. *How to Make a Man Fall in Love with You.* That's what it said. I'll admit I was tempted, and I stood there a good long while. I knew if I stood there long enough, I'd pick that book up, so I just left. 'Trudy, girl,' I said, 'there's not a thing in this world wrong with you. You're fine just the way you are, and it's not your fault men can't see that.'"

Earl reaches for Trudy's hand, but she moves it.

"I believe in marriage," she says fiercely. "I got to believe in something."

Earl nods.

"Listen to me," she says. "You're not missing a thing. You've got it all, and you've got it good. And whatever you've got that's less than good is a whole lot better than nothing. Take it from one who knows."

Trudy finishes her spaghetti and carries her pan to the sink. She wipes her eyes on a dishtowel. "Law!" she exclaims brightly. She holds up the chicken and looks at Earl. "Who put this thing in here? You shoulda said something about this, Earl, honey. Has it been laying out the whole time you were here? It'll rot on you if you aren't careful." She gives the chicken to Earl.

As Trudy walks Earl to the car, she talks about the weather. "Cheer up," she says. "It's spring. And don't stay away so long next time. It gets pretty lonesome out here."

"Come over," Earl says. He gets into the car.

"What's that?" She points to the red spot on the seat.

"Chicken blood."

Trudy curls her lip and laughs. "Looks like it died there."

"It did," Earl says and drives away.

On his way home, he stops at the Chicken Coop, home of Ruth's famous Crispy Fried. A group of high school kids lounge on the hoods of their souped-up cars in the parking lot. "TGIF" they have written on the sides and dusty rear windows. Hearing their laughter, Earl suddenly feels like he's in a foreign country and cannot speak the language. He knows what the letters mean. What he's forgotten is the feeling that made him want to write them in the first place.

Inside, a dark-haired woman with oily skin stands behind the counter. She looks like she's eaten livers and gizzards every day of her life.

While Earl waits in line, he rattles the change in his pockets and looks around the room. Men, his age and older, all without their wives, seem to be waiting for something, too. They look like they're not sure whether it's something that hasn't happened or something that already has and somehow passed them by. Chuckie Wright, Neal Page, Alan Donovan—all graduates of Farlanburg High. They have more in common tonight than diplomas and chicken, Earl knows.

Near the door, Louie Taylor sits by himself, smoking and staring out the window. He graduated the same year as Earl; he was captain of the basketball team. He has the face of a man who's only recently begun to appreciate what he has lost. Now he drives for Hallawell and jokes around town that if hauling chemicals doesn't kill him, living with his wife, Connie, will.

Earl rattles the change in his pockets so loudly now that a couple of men in line in front of him turn to look. Suddenly, he's very hungry and mad about having to wait. He heads for the door. Louie flashes a big-toothed grin and grabs him by the arm.

"How's it going, Earl ole buddy?" he says. "Doing the town tonight?"

Earl forces a smile. "On my way home," he says. He looks at the pile of bones on Louie's tray.

"I'm going to quit eating here because of these deformed chickens," Louie says. "Damned things don't have no legs or thighs. Nothing but backs and wings." He laughs loudly and rubs his balding head.

"My mother made a helluva fried chicken," Earl says.

"No kidding," says Louie. "Mine, too. When you figure out how they did it, let me know, will you? Seems either one of us could do a sight better than this."

At home, Earl pulls in the driveway, shuts off the motor, and leans his head back against the seat. The curtains in the house are closed, but he has a clear picture of what's waiting for him inside.

He opens the car door, picks up the chicken, and gets out. The smell of steak is everywhere. Inside, he walks down the hallway, leaving a trail of blood behind him on the rug. The mister is sacked out in the recliner in the living room, his hand loosely holding the remote-control box for the TV. His mouth is open, ready to receive any leftovers that might come his way while he sleeps.

Mary's lying on the couch, eyes closed, hands together under her cheek. It's hard to tell whether she's sleeping or praying.

Earl can hear Kim and Kerry giggling in their room. Brenda and the missus do dishes. Glasses, plates, forks, and spoons. Brenda methodically washes and plunges them into the water to rinse. She holds her lips together tightly as if she's afraid something inside her might rupture if she spoke.

Mrs. Kivett dries. When she sees Earl standing in the doorway, she opens her mouth but doesn't say anything. She's spent a lifetime not saying anything, and she's proud of it. She can't stand the sight of the mister, but she can honestly say they've never had a fight.

Brenda looks up. She spies the pool of blood from the chicken forming on the linoleum. "What are you doing?" she shrieks.

The missus looks at the paper towels but doesn't move. Her hand flutters nervously about her throat.

Earl throws the chicken on the kitchen table and starts toward his and Brenda's room. As he passes through the living room again, he glances at Mary, who has opened her eyes and is watching him. Her jaw drops for what he thinks will be a yawn, then ever so slowly she closes and reopens one eye. Mary smiles her secret smile. Today, she is wearing green anklets. She knows what it takes to be happy.

Earl stares at her for a moment, then looks at the floor. He returns to the kitchen, takes a bottle of oil from the refrigerator, then opens the bottom drawer of the stove.

Brenda starts to say something, but she shuts up as Earl turns around with a cast-iron skillet in his hand. He raises the skillet in the air. The missus whimpers.

"We have a problem," he says, as he turns the skillet over and dumps rat droppings onto the floor. He sets the skillet on the stove. To fry good chicken you have to boil your bird before you ever put it in the frying pan, his mother used to say. Earl doesn't have a recipe for chicken, and his chicken won't be as good as his mother's. But he smiles as he goes about his work. Frying chicken is not the only thing he'll have to talk himself into, he knows, but he figures it's as good a place as any to start.

Homeland

BARBARA KINGSOLVER

Born in 1955 in Annapolis, Maryland, Barbara Kingsolver grew up in the midst of alfalfa fields in Carlisle, Kentucky. At age seventeen she attended summer classes at the University of Kentucky and subsequently earned a degree in biology and English at Depauw University. After earning a master's in animal behavior at the University of Arizona in 1981, she launched her writing career at the Arid Lands Institute as a science writer, publishing pieces in venues including *The New York Times*, *The Virginia Quarterly Review,* and *The New Mexico Quarterly Review*. Kingsolver's success as a scientific writer led her to a career in nonfiction and fiction. In 1985 she became a freelance journalist and in 1987 a full-time writer. Her first book, *The Bean Trees* (a novel), appeared in 1988 and was followed the next year by *Holding the Line: Women in the Great Arizona Mine Strike of 1983*, which earned her a citation of accomplishment from the United Nations Council of Women. Kingsolver's second novel, *Animal Dreams*, appeared in 1990 and earned the PEN fiction prize and the Edward Abbey Ecofiction Award. Among her other books are *Homeland and Other Stories* (1989), *Another America* (poetry, 1991), *Pigs in Heaven* (1993), *High Tide in Tucson* (1995), *The Poisonwood Bible* (1998), and *Prodigal Summer* (2000).

In an essay in *High Tide in Tucson*, Kingsolver writes of the difficulties of returning home: "I have been gone from Kentucky a long time. Twenty years have done to my hill accent what the washing machine does to my jeans: taken out the color and starch, so gradually I never marked the loss. Something like that has happened to my memories, too, particularly of the places and people I can't go back and visit because they are gone. . . . Now that I live in a western city where shopping malls and swimming pools congest the landscape like cedar blight, I think back fondly on my hometown. But the people who live there now might rather smile about the quaintness of a *smaller* town, like nearby Morning Glory or Barefoot." The opening and title story in her collection, "Homeland" explores the nature of home, raising questions about what home truly is, and depicts the cycle of life and lore.

◆

I

My great-grandmother belonged to the Bird Clan. Hers was one of the fugitive bands of Cherokee who resisted capture in the year that General Winfield Scott was in charge of prodding the forest people from their beds and removing them westward. Those few who escaped his notice moved like wildcat families through the Carolina mountains, leaving the ferns unbroken where they passed, eating wild grapes and chestnuts, drinking when they found streams. The ones who could not travel, the aged and the infirm and the very young, were hidden in deep cane thickets where they would remain undiscovered until they were bones. When the people's hearts could not bear any more, they laid their deerskin packs on the ground and settled again.

General Scott had moved on to other endeavors by this time, and he allowed them to thrive or perish as they would. They built clay houses with thin, bent poles for spines, and in autumn they went down to the streams where the sycamore trees had let their year's work fall, the water steeped brown as leaf tea, and the people cleansed themselves of the sins of the scattered-bone time. They called their refugee years The Time When We Were Not, and they were forgiven, because they had carried the truth of themselves in a sheltered place inside the flesh, exactly the way a fruit that has gone soft still carries inside itself the clean, hard stone of its future.

II

My name is Gloria St. Clair, but like most people I've been called many things. My maiden name was Murray. My grown children have at one time or another hailed me by nearly anything pronounceable. When I was a child myself, my great-grandmother called me by the odd name of Waterbug. I asked her many times why this was, until she said once, to quiet me, "I'll tell you that story."

We were on the front-porch swing, in summer, in darkness. I waited while she drew tobacco smoke in and out of her mouth, but she said nothing. "Well," I said.

Moonlight caught the fronts of her steel-framed spectacles and she looked at me from her invisible place in the dark. "I said I'd tell you that story. I didn't say I would tell it right now."

We lived in Morning Glory, a coal town hacked with sharp blades out of a forest that threatened always to take it back. The hickories encroached on the town, springing up unbidden in the middle of dog pens and front yards and the cemetery. The creeping vines for which the town was named drew themselves along wire fences and up the sides of houses with the persistence of the displaced. I have heard it said that if a man stood still in Morning Glory, he would be tied down by vines and not found until first frost. Even the earth underneath us sometimes moved to repossess its losses: the long, deep shafts that men opened to rob the coal veins would close themselves up again, as quietly as flesh wounds.

My great-grandmother lived with us for her last two years. When she came to us we were instructed to call her Great Grandmother, but that proved impossible and so we called her Great Mam. My knowledge of her life follows an oddly obscured pattern, like a mountain road where much of the scenery is blocked by high laurel bushes, not because they were planted there, but because no one thought to cut them down.

I know that her maternal lineage was distinguished. Her mother's mother's father was said to have gone to England, where he dined with King George and contracted smallpox. When he returned home his family plunged him into an icy stream, which was the curative custom, and he died. Also, her mother was one of the Bird Clan's Beloved Women. When I asked what made her a Beloved Woman, Great Mam said that it was because she kept track of things.

But of Great Mam's own life, before she came to us, I know only a little. She rarely spoke of personal things, favoring instead the legendary and the historic, and so what I did discover came from my mother, who exercised over all matters a form of reverse censorship. She spoke loudly and often of events of which she disapproved, and rarely of those that might have been ordinary or redemptive. She told us, for instance, that Great-Grandfather Murray brought Great Mam from her tribal home in the Hiwassee Valley to live in Kentucky, without Christian sanction, as his common-law wife. According to Mother, he accomplished all of this on a stolen horse. From that time forward Great Mam went by the name of Ruth.

It was my mother's opinion that Great-Grandfather Murray was unfit for respectable work. He died after taking up the honest vocation of coal mining, which also killed their four sons, all on the same day, in a collapsed shaft. Their daughter perished of fever after producing a single illegitimate boy, who turned out to be my father, John Murray. Great Mam was thus returned to refugee ways, raising her grandson alone in hard circumstances, moving from place to place where she could find the odd bit of work. She was quite remarkably old when she came to us.

I know, also, that her true name was Green Leaf, although there is no earthly record of this. The gravesite is marked Ruth. Mother felt we ought to bury her under her Christian name in the hope that God in His infinite mercy would forget about the heathen marriage and stolen horses and call her home. It is likely, however, that He might have passed over the headstone altogether in his search for her, since virtually all the information written there is counterfeit. We even had to invent a date and year of birth for her since these things were unknown. This, especially, was unthinkable to my brothers and me. But we were children, of course, and believed our own birthdays began and ended the calendar.

To look at her, you would not have thought her an Indian. She wore blue and lavender flowered dresses with hand-tatted collars, and brown lace-up shoes with sturdy high heels, and she smoked a regular pipe. She was tall, with bowed calves and a faintly bent-forward posture, spine straight and elbows out and palms forward, giving the impression that she was at any moment prepared to stoop and lift a burden of great bulk or weight. She spoke with a soft hill accent, and spoke properly. My great-grandfather had been an educated man, more prone in his lifetime to errors of judgment than errors of grammar.

Great Mam smoked her pipe mainly in the evenings, and always on the front porch. For a time I believed this was because my mother so vigorously objected to the smell, but Great Mam told me otherwise. A pipe had to be smoked outdoors, she said, where the smoke could return to the Beloved Old Father who gave us tobacco. When I asked her what she meant, she said she meant nothing special at all. It was just the simplest thing, like a bread-and-butter note you send to an aunt after she has fed you a meal.

I often sat with Great Mam in the evenings on our porch swing, which was suspended by four thin, painted chains that squeaked. The air at night smelled of oil and dust, and faintly of livestock, for the man at the end of our lane kept hogs. Great Mam would strike a match and suck the flame into her pipe, lighting her creased face in brief orange bursts.

"The small people are not very bright tonight," she would say, meaning the stars. She held surprising convictions, such as that in the daytime the small people walked among us. I could not begin to picture it.

"You mean down here in the world, or do you mean right here in Morning Glory?" I asked repeatedly. "Would they walk along with Jack and Nathan and me to school?"

She nodded. "They would."

"But why would they come *here*?" I asked.

"Well, why wouldn't they?" she said.

I thought about this for a while, entirely unconvinced.

"You don't ever have to be lonesome," she said. "That's one thing you never need be."

"But mightn't I step on one of them, if it got in my way and I didn't see it?"

Great Mam said, "No. They aren't that small."

She had particular names for many things, including the months. February she called "Hungry Month." She spoke of certain animals as if they were relatives our parents had neglected to tell us about. The cowering white dog that begged at our kitchen door she called "the sad little cousin." If she felt like it, on these evenings, she would tell me stories about the animals, their personalities and kindnesses and trickery, and the permanent physical markings they invariably earned by doing something they ought not to have done. "Remember that story," she often commanded at the end, and I would be stunned with guilt because my mind had wandered onto crickets and pencil erasers and Black Beauty.

"I might not remember," I told her. "It's too hard."

Great Mam allowed that I might *think* I had forgotten. "But you haven't. You'll keep it stored away," she said. "If it's important, your heart remembers."

I had known that hearts could break and sometimes even be attacked, with disastrous result, but I had not heard of hearts remembering. I was eleven years old. I did not trust any of my internal parts with the capacity of memory.

When the seasons changed, it never occurred to us to think to ourselves, "This will be Great Mam's last spring. Her last June apples. Her last fresh roasting ears from the garden." She was like an old pine, whose accumulated years cause one to ponder how long it has stood, not how soon it will fall. Of all of us, I think Papa was the only one who believed she could die. He planned the trip to Tennessee. We children simply thought it was a great lark.

This was in June, following a bad spring during which the whole southern spine of the Appalachians had broken out in a rash of wildcat strikes. Papa was back to work at last, no longer home taking up kitchen-table space, but still Mother complained of having to make soups of neckbones and cut our school shoes open to bare our too-long toes to summer's dust, for the whole darn town to see. Papa pointed out that the whole darn town had been on the picket lines, and wouldn't pass judgment on the Murray kids if they ran their bare bottoms down Main Street. And what's more, he said, it wasn't his fault if John L. Lewis had sold him down the river.

My brothers and I thrilled to imagine ourselves racing naked past the Post Office and the women shopping at Herman Ritchie's Market, but we did not laugh out loud. We didn't know exactly who Mr. John L. Lewis was, or what river Papa meant, but we knew not to expect much. The last thing we expected was a trip.

My brother Jack, because of his nature and superior age, was suspicious from the outset. While Papa explained his plan, Jack made a point of pushing lima beans around his plate in single file to illustrate his boredom. It was 1955. Patti Page and Elvis were on the radio and high school boys were fighting their mothers over ducktails. Jack had a year to go before high school, but already the future was plainly evident.

He asked where in Tennessee we would be going, if we did go. The three of us had not seen the far side of a county line.

"The Hiwassee Valley, where Great Mam was born," Papa said.

My brother Nathan grew interested when Jack laid down his fork. Nathan was only eight, but he watched grownups. If there were no men around, he watched Jack.

"Eat your beans, Jack," Mother said. "I didn't put up these limas last fall so you could torment them."

Jack stated, "I'm not eating no beans with guts in them."

Mother took a swat at Jack's arm. "Young man, you watch your mouth. That's the insides of a hog, and a hog's a perfectly respectable animal to eat." Nathan was making noises with his throat. I tried not to make any face one way or the other.

Great Mam told Mother it would have been enough just to have the limas, without the meat. "A person can live on green corn and beans, Florence Ann," she said. "There's no shame in vegetables."

We knew what would happen next, and watched with interest. "If I have to go out myself and throw a rock at a songbird," Mother said, having deepened to the color of beetroot, "nobody is going to say this family goes without meat!"

Mother was a tiny woman who wore stockings and shirt-waists even to hoe the garden. She had yellow hair pinned in a tight bun, with curly bangs in front. We waited with our chins cupped in our palms for Papa's opinion of her plan to make a soup of Robin Redbreast, but he got up from the table and rummaged in the bureau drawer for the gas-station map. Great Mam ate her beans in a careful way, as though each one had its own private importance.

"Are we going to see Injuns?" Nathan asked, but no one answered. Mother began making a great deal of noise clearing up the dishes. We could hear her out in the kitchen, scrubbing.

Papa unfolded the Texaco map on the table and found where Tennessee and North Carolina and Georgia came together in three different pastel colors. Great Mam looked down at the colored lines and squinted, holding the sides of her glasses. "Is this the Hiwassee River?" she wanted to know.

"No, now those lines are highways," he said. "Red is interstate. Blue is river."

"Well, what's this?"

He looked. "That's the state line."

"Now why would they put that on the map? You can't see it."

Papa flattened the creases of the map with his broad hands, which were criss-crossed with fine black lines of coal dust, like a map themselves, no matter how clean. "The Hiwassee Valley's got a town in it now, it says 'Cherokee.' Right here."

"Well, those lines make my eyes smart," Great Mam said. "I'm not going to look anymore."

The boys started to snicker, but Papa gave us a look that said he meant business and sent us off to bed before it went any farther.

"Great Mam's blind as a post hole," Jack said once we were in bed. "She don't know a road from a river."

"She don't know beans from taters," said Nathan.

"You boys hush up, I'm tired," I said. Jack and Nathan slept lengthwise in the bed, and I slept across the top with my own blanket.

"Here's Great Mam," Nathan said. He sucked in his cheeks and crossed his eyes and keeled over backward, bouncing us all on the bedsprings. Jack punched him in the ribs, and Nathan started to cry louder than he had to. I got up and sat by the bedroom door hugging my knees, listening to Papa and Mother. I could hear them in the kitchen.

"As if I hadn't put up with enough, John. It's not enough that Murrays have populated God's earth without the benefit of marriage," Mother said. This was her usual starting point. She was legally married to my father in a Baptist Church, a fact she could work into any conversation.

"Well, I don't see why," she said, "if we never had the money to take the kids anyplace before."

Papa's voice was quieter, and I couldn't hear his answers.

"Was this her idea, John, or yours?"

When Nathan and Jack were asleep I went to the window and slipped over the sill. My feet landed where they always did, in the cool mud of Mother's gladiolus patch alongside the house. Great Mam did not believe in flower patches. Why take a hoe and kill all the growing things in a piece of ground, and then plant others that have been uprooted from somewhere else? This was what she asked me. She thought Mother spent a fearful amount of time moving things needlessly from one place to another.

"I see you, Waterbug," said Great Mam in the darkness, though what she probably meant was that she heard me. All I could see was the glow of her pipe bowl moving above the porch swing.

"Tell me the waterbug story tonight," I said, settling onto the swing. The fireflies were blinking on and off in the black air above the front yard.

"No, I won't," she said. The orange glow moved to her lap, and faded from bright to dim. "I'll tell you another time."

The swing squeaked its sad song, and I thought about Tennessee. It had never occurred to me that the place where Great Mam had been a child was still on this earth. "Why'd you go away from home?" I asked her.

"You have to marry outside your clan," she said. "That's law. And all the people we knew were Bird Clan. All the others were gone. So when Stewart Murray came and made baby eyes at me, I had to go with him." She laughed. "I liked his horse."

I imagined the two of them on a frisking, strong horse, crossing the mountains to Kentucky. Great Mam with black hair. "Weren't you afraid to go?" I asked.

"Oh, yes I was. The canebrakes were high as a house. I was afraid we'd get lost."

We were to leave on Saturday after Papa got off work. He worked days then, after many graveyard-shift years during which we rarely saw him except asleep, snoring and waking throughout the afternoon, with Mother forever forced to shush us; it was too easy to forget someone was trying to sleep in daylight. My father was a soft-spoken man who sometimes drank but was never mean. He had thick black hair, no beard stubble at all nor hair on his chest, and a nose he called his Cherokee nose. Mother said she thanked the Lord that at least He had seen fit not to put that nose on her children. She also claimed he wore his hair long to flout her, although it wasn't truly long, in our opinion. His nickname in the mine was "Indian John."

There wasn't much to get ready for the trip. All we had to do in the morning was wait for afternoon. Mother was in the house scrubbing so it would be clean when we came back. The primary business of Mother's life was scrubbing things, and she herself looked scrubbed. Her skin was the color of a clean boiled potato. We didn't get in her way.

My brothers were playing a ferocious game of cowboys and Indians in the backyard, but I soon defected to my own amusements along the yard's weedy borders, picking morning glories, pretending to be a June bride. I grew tired of trying to weave the flowers into my coarse hair and decided to give them to Great Mam. I went around to the front and came up the three porch steps in one jump, just exactly the way Mother said a lady wouldn't do.

"Surprise," I announced. "These are for you." The flowers were already wilting in my hand.

"You shouldn't have picked those," she said.

"They were a present." I sat down, feeling stung.

"Those are not mine to have and not yours to pick," she said, looking at me, not with anger but with intensity. Her brown pupils were as dark as two pits in the earth. "A flower is alive, just as much as you are. A flower is your cousin. Didn't you know that?"

I said, No ma'am, that I didn't.

"Well, I'm telling you now, so you will know. Sometimes a person has got to take a life, like a chicken's or a hog's when you need it. If you're hungry, then they're happy to give their flesh up to you because they're your relatives. But nobody is so hungry they need to kill a flower."

I said nothing.

"They ought to be left where they stand, Waterbug. You need to leave them for the small people to see. When they die they'll fall where they are, and make a seed for next year."

"Nobody cared about these," I contended. "They weren't but just weeds."

"It doesn't matter what they were or were not. It's a bad thing to take for yourself something beautiful that belongs to everybody. Do you understand? To take it is a sin."

I didn't, and I did. I could sense something of wasted life in the sticky leaves, translucent with death, and the purple flowers turning wrinkled and limp. I'd once brought home a balloon from a Ritchie child's birthday party, and it had shriveled and shrunk with just such a slow blue agony.

"I'm sorry," I said.

"It's all right." She patted my hands. "Just throw them over the porch rail there, give them back to the ground. The small people will come and take them back."

I threw the flowers over the railing in a clump, and came back, trying to rub the purple and green juices off my hands onto my dress. In my mother's eyes, this would have been the first sin of my afternoon. I understood the difference between Great Mam's rules and the Sunday-school variety, and that you could read Mother's Bible forward and backward and never find where it said it's a sin to pick flowers because they are our cousins.

"I'll try to remember," I said.

"I want you to," said Great Mam. "I want you to tell your children."

"I'm not going to have any children," I said. "No boy's going to marry me. I'm too tall. I've got knob knees."

"Don't ever say you hate what you are." She tucked a loose sheaf of black hair behind my ear. "It's an unkindness to those that made you. That's like a red flower saying it's too red, do you see what I mean?"

"I guess," I said.

"You will have children. And you'll remember about the flowers," she said, and I felt the weight of these promises fall like a deerskin pack between my shoulder blades.

By four o'clock we were waiting so hard we heard the truck crackle up the gravel road. Papa's truck was a rust-colored Ford with complicated cracks hanging like spiderwebs in the corners of the windshield. He jumped out with his long, blue-jean strides and patted the round front fender.

"Old Paint's had her oats," he said. "She's raring to go." This was a game he played with Great Mam. Sometimes she would say, "John Murray, you couldn't ride a mule with a saddle on it," and she'd laugh, and we would for a moment see the woman who raised Papa. Her bewilderment and pleasure, to have ended up with this broad-shouldered boy.

Today she said nothing, and Papa went in for Mother. There was only room for three in the cab, so Jack and Nathan and I climbed into the back with the old quilt Mother gave us and a tarpaulin in case of rain.

"What's she waiting for, her own funeral?" Jack asked me.

I looked at Great Mam, sitting still on the porch like a funny old doll. The whole house was crooked, the stoop sagged almost to the ground, and there sat Great Mam as straight as a schoolteacher's ruler. Seeing her there, I fiercely wished to defend my feeling that I knew her better than others did.

"She doesn't want to go," I said. I knew as soon as I'd spoken that it was the absolute truth.

"That's stupid. She's the whole reason we're going. Why wouldn't she want to go see her people?"

"I don't know, Jack," I said.

Papa and Mother eventually came out of the house, Papa in a clean shirt already darkening under the arms, and Mother with her Sunday purse, the scuff marks freshly covered with white shoe polish. She came down the front steps in the bent-over way she walked when she wore high heels. Papa put his hand under Great Mam's elbow and she silently climbed into the cab.

When he came around to the other side I asked him, "Are you sure Great Mam wants to go?"

"Sure she does," he said. "She wants to see the place where she grew up. Like what Morning Glory is to you."

"When I grow up I'm not never coming back to Morning Glory," Jack said.

"Me neither." Nathan spat over the side of the truck, the way he'd seen men do.

"Don't spit, Nathan," Papa said.

"Shut up," Nathan said, after Papa had gotten in the truck and shut the door.

The houses we passed had peeled paint and slumped porches like our own, and they all wore coats of morning-glory vines, deliciously textured and fat as fur coats. We pointed out to each other the company men's houses, which had bright white paint and were known to have indoor bathrooms. The deep ditches along the road, filled with blackberry brambles and early goldenrod, ran past us like rivers. On our walks to school we put these ditches to daily use practicing Duck and Cover, which was what our teachers felt we ought to do when the Communists dropped the H-bomb.

"We'll see Indians in Tennessee," Jack said. I knew we would. Great Mam had told me how it was.

"Great Mam don't look like an Indian," Nathan said.

"Shut up, Nathan," Jack said. "How do you know what an Indian looks like? You ever seen one?"

"She does so look like an Indian," I informed my brothers. "She is one."

According to Papa we all looked like little Indians, I especially. Mother hounded me continually to stay out of the sun, but by each summer's end I was so dark-skinned my schoolmates teased me, saying I ought to be sent over to the Negro school.

"Are we going to be Indians when we grow up?" Nathan asked.

"No, stupid," said Jack. "We'll just be the same as we are now."

We soon ran out of anything productive to do. We played White Horse Zit many times over, until Nathan won, and we tried to play Alphabet but there weren't enough signs. The only public evidence of literacy in that part of the country was the Beech Nut Tobacco signs on barn roofs, and every so often, nailed to a tree trunk, a clapboard on which someone had painted "PREPARE TO MEET GOD."

Papa's old truck didn't go as fast as other cars. Jack and Nathan slapped the fenders like jockeys as we were passed on the uphill slopes, but their coaxing amounted to nought. By the time we went over Jellico Mountain, it was dark.

An enormous amount of sky glittered down at us on the mountain pass, and even though it was June we were cold. Nathan had taken the quilt for himself and gone to sleep. Jack said he ought to punch him one to teach him to be nice, but truthfully, nothing in this world could have taught Nathan to share. Jack and I huddled together under the tarp, which stank of coal oil, and sat against the back of the cab where the engine rendered up through the truck's metal body a faint warmth.

"Jack?" I said.

"What."

"Do you reckon Great Mam's asleep?"

He turned around and cupped his hands to see into the cab. "Nope," he said. "She's sitting up there in between 'em, stiff as a broom handle."

"I'm worried about her," I said.

"Why? If we were home she'd be sitting up just the same, only out front on the porch."

"I know."

"Glorie, you know what?" he asked me.

"What?"

A trailer truck loomed up behind us, decked with rows of red and amber lights like a Christmas tree. We could see the driver inside the cab. A faint blue light on his face made him seem ghostly and entirely alone. He passed us by, staring ahead, as though only he were real on this cold night and we were among all the many things that were not. I shivered, and felt an identical chill run across Jack's shoulders.

"What?" I asked again.

"What, what?"

"You were going to tell me something."

"Oh. I forgot what it was."

"Great Mam says the way to remember something you forgot is to turn your back on it. Say, 'The small people came dancing. They ran through the woods today.' Talk about what they did, and then whatever it was you forgot, they'll bring it back to you."

"That's dumb," Jack said. "That's Great Mam's hobbledy-gobbledy."

For a while we played See Who Can Go to Sleep First, which we knew to be a game that can't consciously be won. He never remembered what he'd meant to say.

When Papa woke us the next morning we were at a truck stop in Knoxville. He took a nap in the truck with his boots sticking out the door while the rest of us went in for breakfast. Inside the restaurant was a long glass counter containing packs of Kools and Mars Bars lined up on cotton batting, objects of great value to be protected from dust and children. The waitress who brought us our eggs had a red wig perched like a bird on her head, and red eyebrows painted on over the real ones.

When it was time to get back in the truck we dragged and pulled on Mother's tired, bread-dough arms, like little babies, asking her how much farther.

"Oh, it's not far. I expect we'll be in Cherokee by lunchtime," she said, but her mouth was set and we knew she was as tired of this trip as any of us.

It was high noon before we saw a sign that indicated we were approaching Cherokee. Jack pummeled the cab window with his fists to make sure they all saw it, but Papa and Mother were absorbed in some kind of argument. There were more signs after that, with pictures of cartoon Indian boys urging us to buy souvenirs or stay in so-and-so's motor lodge. The signs were shaped like log cabins and teepees. Then we saw a real teepee. It was made of aluminum and taller than a house. Inside, it was a souvenir store.

We drove around the streets of Cherokee and saw that the town was all the same, as single-minded in its offerings as a corn patch or an orchard, so that it made no difference where we stopped. We parked in front of Sitting Bull's Genuine Indian Made Souvenirs, and Mother crossed the street to get groceries for our lunch. I had a sense of something gone badly wrong, like a lie told in my past and then forgotten, and now about to catch up with me.

A man in a feather war bonnet danced across from us in the parking lot. His outfit was bright orange, with white fringe trembling along the seams of the pants and sleeves, and a woman in the same clothes sat cross-legged on the pavement playing a tom-tom while he danced. People with cameras gathered and side-stepped around one another to snap their shots. The woman told them that she and her husband Chief Many Feathers were genuine Cherokees, and that this was their welcoming dance. Papa sat with his hands frozen on the steering wheel for a very long time. Then suddenly, without saying anything, he got out of the truck and took Jack and Nathan and me into Sitting Bull's. Nathan wanted a tomahawk.

The store was full of items crowded on shelves, so bright-colored it hurt my eyes to look at them all. I lagged behind the boys. There were some Indian dolls with real feathers on them, red and green, and I would like to have stroked the soft feathers but the dolls were wrapped in cellophane. Among all those bright things, I grew fearfully uncertain about what I ought to want. I went back out to the truck and found Great Mam still sitting in the cab.

"Don't you want to got out?" I asked.

The man in the parking lot was dancing again, and she was watching. "I don't know what they think they're doing. Cherokee don't wear feather bonnets like that," she said.

They looked like Indians to me. I couldn't imagine Indians without feathers. I climbed up onto the seat and closed the door and we sat for a while. I felt a great sadness and embarrassment, as though it were I who had forced her to come here, and I tried to cover it up by pretending to be foolishly cheerful.

"Where's the pole houses, where everybody lives, I wonder," I said. "Do you think maybe they're out of town a ways?"

She didn't answer. Chief Many Feathers hopped around his circle, forward on one leg and backward on the other. Then the dance was over. The woman beating the tom-tom turned it upside down and passed it around for money.

"I guess things have changed pretty much since you moved away, huh, Great Mam?" I asked.

She said, "I've never been here before."

Mother made bologna sandwiches and we ate lunch in a place called Cherokee Park. It was a shaded spot along the river, where the dry banks were worn bald of their grass. Sycamore trees grew at the water's edge, with colorful, waterlogged trash floating in circles in the eddies around their roots. The park's principal attraction was an old buffalo in a pen, identified by a sign as the Last Remaining Buffalo East of the Mississippi. I pitied the beast, thinking it must be lonely without a buffalo wife or buffalo husband, whichever it needed. One of its eyes was put out.

I tried to feed it some dead grass through the cage, while Nathan pelted it with gravel. He said he wanted to see it get mad and charge the fence down, but naturally it did not do that. It simply stood and stared and blinked with its one good eye, and flicked its tail. There were flies all over it, and shiny bald patches on its back, which Papa said were caused by the mange. Mother said we'd better get away from it or we would have the mange too. Great Mam sat at the picnic table with her shoes together, and looked at her sandwich.

We had to go back that same night. It seemed an impossible thing, to come such a distance only to turn right around, but Mother reminded us all that Papa had laid off from work without pay. Where money was concerned we did not argue. The trip home was quiet except for Nathan, who pretended at great length to scalp me with his tomahawk, until the rubber head came loose from its painted stick and fell with a clunk.

III

Before there was a world, there was only the sea, and the high, bright sky arched above it like an overturned bowl.

For as many years as anyone can imagine, the people in the stars looked down at the ocean's glittering face without giving a thought to what it was, or what might lie beneath it. They had their own concerns. But as more time passed, as is natural, they began to grow curious. Eventually it was the waterbug who volunteered to go exploring. She flew down and landed on top of the water, which was beautiful, but not firm as it had appeared. She skated in every direction but could not find a place to stop and rest, so she dived underneath.

She was gone for days and the star people thought she must have drowned, but she hadn't. When she joyfully broke the surface again she had the answer: on the bottom of the sea, there was mud. She had brought a piece of it back with her, and she held up her sodden bit of proof to the bright light.

There, before the crowd of skeptical star eyes, the ball of mud began to grow, and dry up, and grow some more, and out of it came all the voices and life that now dwell on this island that is the earth. The star people fastened it to the sky with four long grape vines so it wouldn't be lost again.

"In school," I told Great Mam, "they said the world's round."

"I didn't say it wasn't round," she said. "It's whatever shape they say it is. But that's how it started. Remember that."

These last words terrified me, always, with their impossible weight. I have had dreams of trying to hold a mountain of water in my arms. "What if I forget?" I asked.

"We already talked about that. I told you how to remember."

"Well, all right," I said. "But if that's how the world started, then what about Adam and Eve?"

She thought about that. "They were the waterbug's children," she said. "Adam and Eve, and the others."

"But they started all the trouble," I pointed out. "Adam and Eve started sin."

"Sometimes that happens. Children can be your heartache. But that doesn't matter, you have to go on and have them," she said. "It works out."

IV

Morning Glory looked no different after we had seen the world and returned to it. Summer settled in, with heat in the air and coal dust thick on the vines. Nearly every night I slipped out and sat with Great Mam where there was the tangible hope of a cool breeze. I felt pleased to be up while my brothers breathed and tossed without consciousness on the hot mattress. During those secret hours, Great Mam and I lived in our own place, a world apart from the arguments and the tired, yellowish light bulbs burning away inside, seeping faintly out the windows, getting used up. Mother's voice in the kitchen was as distant as heat lightning, and as unthreatening. But we could make out words, and I realized once, with a shock, that they were discussing Great Mam's burial.

"Well, it surely can't do her any harm once she's dead and gone, John, for heaven's sakes," Mother said.

Papa spoke more softly and we could never make out his answer.

Great Mam seemed untroubled. "In the old days," she said, "whoever spoke the quietest would win the argument."

She died in October, the Harvest Month. It was my mother who organized the burial and the Bible verses and had her say even about the name that went on the gravestone, but Great Mam secretly prevailed in the question of flowers. Very few would ever have their beauty wasted upon her grave. Only one time for the burial service, and never again after that, did Mother trouble herself to bring up flowers. It was half a dozen white gladioli cut hastily from her garden with a bread knife, and she carried them from home in a jar of water, attempting to trick them into believing they were still alive.

My father's shoes were restless in the grass and hickory saplings at the edge of the cemetery. Mother knelt down in her navy dress and nylon stockings and with her white-gloved hands thumped the flower stems impatiently against the jar bottom to get them to stand up straight. Already the petals were shriveling from thirst.

As soon as we turned our backs, the small people would come dancing and pick up the flowers. They would kick over the jar and run through the forest, swinging the hollow stems above their heads, scattering them like bones.

Dr. Livingston's Grotto

NORMANDI ELLIS

Normandi Ellis grew up in Frankfort, Kentucky. She earned a B.A. in journalism at the University of Kentucky in 1976 and an M.A. in English at the University of Colorado in 1981. After completing her graduate work she continued to live and write in Colorado, while sojourning throughout the U.S. and abroad. She later returned to Kentucky and now lives on a farm near where she grew up. "My return was a renewal," she has said in an interview. "At night I lie in bed listening to the creek flowing. I wake to vibrant hills of light. This place which I despised in my youth for its 'ordinary-ness' has become a refuge. My travels have taught me how to see the Garden of Eden exists here and now to those with eyes to see." She has published five books: *Awakening Osiris: A New Translation from the Egyptian Book of the Dead* (1988), *Sorrowful Mysteries and Other Stories* (1991), *Dream of Isis: A Woman's Spiritual Sojourn* (1995), *Voice Forms* (short-short fiction, 1998), and *Feasts of Light: Celebrations for the Seasons of Life Based on the Egyptian Goddess Festival Calendar* (1999). Her short stories have appeared in *The Southern Humanities Review*, *Westword*, *Appalachian Heritage*, *Chaffin Review*, *Agni Review*, *Wind Magazine*, *Word of Mouth 2: Short Stories by Women*, and other venues. She has also published numerous essays and created a six-part video series on Egypt titled *Ancient Light*.

First published in *The Southern Humanities Review* in 1989 and included in *Sorrowful Mysteries and Other Stories*, "Dr. Livingston's Grotto" is a twist- and pun-filled story of a man's accidental discovery of wholeness and genuine happiness while trapped in a most unlikely place.

◆

One day while Dr. Livingston's wife sat inside their air-conditioned, ranch style house and while Dr. Livingston clomped in muddied boots about the garden, staking his tomato plants with Mrs. Livingston's worn out panty hose, the ground in their back yard opened up, trembling a little, then yawned like a mouth, so that when Dr. Livingston turned toward the house, carrying his aluminum pie tin of ripe Better Boy tomatoes, he stepped unknowingly into the hole, and the earth surrounding it crumbled. He fell, slipping into the small, fresh cave, and disappeared without a sound.

It was a gentle fall, which surprised him. He landed on his rump, knees bent. The cave's entrance had been no larger than the average manhole cover; and once past the slippery, narrow shaft, the whole thing opened up into a large, limestone room lit only by the slanted sunlight streaming in from the hole above. All else in the cave was black.

Dr. Livingston stood, brushed himself off, determined nothing was broken, and tried to figure out how to raise himself back to the surface. After the harsh sunlight of the upper world, his eyes were not yet accustomed to the dark. Not knowing whether he stood near the edge of a precipice, he was afraid to move very far one way or the other. When he stretched out his arms on either side, he could barely see his hands. He stooped down and felt the ground where he stood. There was no ledge behind him that he could find, and so he sat down again to think.

He reached to the right and discovered one of his tomatoes; at least he thought it was a tomato by its weight and the roundness of it. It seemed still to hold the warmth of the sun. He put it to his mouth and bit. Juice and seed dribbled down his chin. He wiped the mess off himself with his shirt tail. Then he took out his pen-knife and cut the tender meat into wedges. He glanced longingly toward the cave entrance where the sunlight trickled in. *Oh*, he thought, *if I only had some salt.*

"Help!" he shouted. "This is Dr. Livingston. Help me!"

The words echoed, tumbled, and roared. Long after he stopped shouting he thought he could still hear himself in some distant reaches of the cave. *It must be an enormous place,* he thought. *If only I could see it.* He reached into his pocket and withdrew a book of matches, striking one after the other, but the matches fizzled because of the dampness. At last one took hold and gave off a feeble glow, just enough for him to see, before the match burnt out, a large stalagmite to his left, jutting up like an ancient tooth.

"Incredible," he whispered.

"Credible," the cave whispered back.

He tilted his chin up, trying to direct his voice toward the hole above him because he imagined the sound on the surface would be pitifully weak, drowned out by bird song, lawn mowers, sprinklers.

"Help. Help. Down here."

He had orchestra practice this evening and he had promised to mow the lawn. There were the loose bathroom tiles he'd promised Flora he would caulk. He thought of a thousand things as if thinking them could draw him back to the surface. Surely it wouldn't be long before someone heard him, or Flora called him to supper, or Ted Waterfield missed him at this evening's practice, or, barring any of the above, a neighbor heard his cry.

"Help. This is Dr. Livingston," he called again.

"Stun. Stun," the cave answered.

Inside Dr. Livingston's tightly sealed, air-conditioned house, Mrs. Livingston sat with three friends, equally as large as she, playing bridge and munching Lorna Doones held delicately between their thumbs and forefingers. Before each bid, she smoothed the skirt of her peach dress, fingered the pearls lying on her ample chest, and patted the bobbie pins back into her bun.

"Three hearts," she said.

Her partner, Mrs. Waterfield, raised her right eyebrow and cleared her throat. They were cheating, of course, passing signals back and forth like baseball players; but if the other two women knew it, they said nothing.

"Pass," said Mrs. King, biting her cookie.

Between bids all that could be heard was the low hum of the air conditioner. Usually, whenever Mrs. Livingston held a bridge party, her husband came in under the auspices of looking for something—a pan, a screwdriver, or some other excuse—just so that he could stand over her shoulder and peek at her cards. She thought it was nice that George had found something else to occupy himself this afternoon.

Dr. Livingston sat cross-legged amid the rubble that had fallen down with him. It was a wonder he hadn't been killed. He had heard of cows falling into such sinkholes. Of course, Bowling Green was riddled with caves, but he hadn't counted on having one open in his back yard. He wondered if his homeowner's insurance considered such things as acts of God.

His glow-in-the-dark watch read 2:47, the same time it read when last he checked it. He held it to his ear, shook it, and at last, pulled it from his wrist and flung it. The odd thing was that he did not hear it land, and he could hear everything in the cave, even his breath. It must have fallen into a hole and dropped a long way down. He wondered whether he was sitting on the edge of a huge precipice.

At first the cave had seemed thick with darkness, but as his eyes adjusted, he could see on the ceiling, just beneath where the sunlight angled in, a cluster of calcium carbonate deposits hanging like beads of pearls. It was beautiful, really; and it seemed odd to think that such a geologic wonder had been forming for centuries beneath his feet, that for all the gardens he had planted and lawns he had mowed, for all the farms tilled and bulldozers turning forest to subdivision, for all the highways and office buildings laid through the city that the earth had maintained its secret life, a life that went on deep within despite everything.

"Help! Flora!" he called. "Get me out!"

"Me out. Me out. Me out."

Finally he gave up calling and stretched out on the limestone floor. He would have to wait until someone came looking for him.

The afternoon drew itself out like a long sigh. The sun moved west, growing heavier, falling in a slow arc from its zenith. The light in the cave grew dimmer. Dr. Livingston got up on his hands and knees, crawling slowly across the slick limestone floor and, groping in the dark, managed to gather the rest of his tomatoes. He sat eating them one by one, calling for help in different voices between each bite.

"Help," he whispered, then "He-elp," he said in a low, rumbling voice. "Halp!" he squeaked.

He listened to the voices echoing back to him. It was only a game now, something to help pass the time. He wondered how long it would take Flora to miss him. Then he lay back silent, cradling his head in his hands, and stared up at the hole again. The blue in the sky deepened; the light began to fade. To his amazement he saw eight pale stars embedded in the afternoon sky, and it occurred to him that they had been at his back all the while he had been staking tomatoes in the garden.

"How clever is the world," he said, "to conceal its wonder."

"Wonder," the cave agreed.

Inside the cave it was quiet, really quiet, like a cathedral *(or a crypt,* he thought). He listened to his breath, his heart beat, the tomatoes churning in his stomach. He could hear the monotonous drip, drip, drip of water somewhere that sounded like a metronome. Dr. Livingston began to sing.

> In the mines, in the mines, in the Blue Diamond mines,
> I have worked my life away.
> In the mines, in the mines, in the Blue Diamond mines,
> Oh, fall on your knees and pray . . .

His baritone reverberated through the cave. It sounded quite good. He wished he had the whole orchestra down there. If he ever got to the surface again, he decided, he might invite Waterfield and a few of the others in. What a chorus that would make.

He began to wish he had some Rossini down there in the hole with him. He slapped his thighs beating out the time to *The Thieving Magpie.* "Ba-ba-ba bah ba bum!" It appeared he would miss orchestra practice this evening. He looked up toward the hole again. Yes, it was definitely getting darker.

"Help!" he called, but his heart wasn't quite in it. He was thinking about Rossini. "Ta-ta-ta-ta-ta-ta-ta-ta-ta-ta teedle-de-de," he sang.

The time passed. The sun set. It was black as coal inside the cave. In the seven hours since his fall, Dr. Livingston had played upon his now sore and burning thighs the music of Rossini, Vivaldi, and Beethoven, with a little John Philip Sousa thrown in for good measure.

"George? George?"

He paused in the midst of song. He thought he heard a voice somewhere. It seemed to come from miles away.

"George, where are you?"

He cupped his hands around his mouth, directing his voice upward. "Down here!" he shouted. "Flora, help me!"

"Where?"

"Here, this hole. Watch out."

But of course, she wouldn't fall in—Mrs. Livingston was too wide. He saw several flashes of light, then the beam appeared directly above him with Mrs. Livingston's face beside it.

"What are you doing down there?"

"Singing."

"Well, come on now. Your chicken's getting cold."

"I can't," he said. "I can't get back up. I fell into this hole. It's some sort of cave, part of the Mammoth Cave system, I'd venture to guess. Throw me down the flashlight and call someone for help."

She threw it down—it hit the stone floor with a clatter—and ran back toward the house. Dr. Livingston picked up the flashlight and bounced its beams on the walls around him. To his left, row upon row of stalagmites spiraled into the air, some of them reaching up and melding with the stalactites that dripped from above. He put out his hand and touched one. It was cool and slick and wet. There must have been iron deposits in the water, as the stone spires appeared rather orange and yellow in color.

He shined the light to his right, where a narrow passageway snaked off into the darkness. He followed, crawling on his belly, until it began to twist downward. He stopped where the tunnel dipped sharply and turned right over a mound of flowstone. Not wanting to lose himself in the dark, he inched himself backward. Without the sun, he would be hard-pressed to find the cave entrance again. He sat again in the cavernous room and waited for Flora.

"George! George!"

"Flora! Here!"

It took a while for them to locate each other in the dark. At last she appeared with a second flashlight.

"They say they can't come until morning."

"You mean I have to spend the night down here? Good God!"

Mrs. Livingston began to wail. He hated it when she cried. It was bad enough to have to listen to it; he was glad he couldn't see her eyes welling up with tears and her wet lower lip jutting out, trembling like a fat child's.

"Listen to me. Stop crying, for Pete's sake. It won't do any good. If I have to spend the night down here, could you at least bring me some dinner, a pillow, and a blanket?"

"And how am I supposed to get all that down?"

"Think, Flora. There's a long rope in the shed. Tie the stuff to the rope and lower it down."

She disappeared from the hole. He thought for a moment, then shouted, "Flora! Flora, wait!"

She came back.

"What?"

A smile crept over his lips. "Could you bring me my saxophone?"

The things he needed appeared one by one. First, Mrs. Livingston dropped down one of Dr. Livingston's old army blankets. It hit him on the head. Then the pillow appeared, followed by the rope which, inch by inch, lowered a bucket of Colonel Sanders' Kentucky Fried Chicken, complete with greasy biscuit and a little styrofoam cup of cold mashed potatoes and gravy.

"Sakes, Flora! I thought you made chicken," he said.

"I didn't have time. You know when you didn't come in after so long, we played another hand and then another."

"Well, who won?"

"I did," she said. "Just like always."

"You cheat."

There was a pause. "Yes," she said. "I have to defend my position."

She would never have admitted to such a thing if he hadn't been trapped in a cave. His situation must have seemed to her a matter of grave importance.

"You shouldn't cheat, Flora. It isn't nice," he said.

There came another silence. He could feel the bulk of her above his head, thinking. The tiny thoughts struggled up through the layers of Lorna Doones. He shivered. It frightened him to think of such a thing.

"Now, careful with my saxophone."

She tied the rope to the case handle and slowly, slowly it came down toward his outstretched hand, spinning a little on its length of rope. He untied it and gave a tug which signaled Mrs. Livingston to haul the rope back up.

He flung open the case, threw the strap around his neck and clipped his instrument onto it, then he wet his lips, sucked the reed, and gently began to blow. Closing his eyes he breathed out a long hollow note that sighed and hung in the air all around him, echoing clear to infinity. By God, he thought, in the bowels of the earth a man could really play the blues. He began again faster this time, higher; the sounds rolled one over the other. He played what was in his head—all those years the melodies he had strained to remember when he woke from a dream, the sounds he could never quite catch before through the din of afternoon traffic. He heard them now and played. It felt wonderful, as if he were flying in the dark.

He stopped to listen to the last note reverberating off the walls.

"You haven't heard a word I said," his wife complained. "You've been tooting that old thing the whole time. What I said was . . . I said to him, 'But you've got to come now and get him out. He can't stay in there all night.' Then he said, 'Lady, I work from nine to five. If you want him out, drive your car into the back yard, tie a rope to it and haul him out . . .'"

"Flora!" he cried. "Listen very carefully. I need your help. Go into the house and get my notebook and paper."

"What?"

"I said . . ."

"I know what you said. What on earth for?"

"Flora, please!"

Oh, why did she make him beg? She was like an irritable, petulant mother, whining after him all the time, making him repeat everything he said.

"And bring me a beer or two, will you? There's nothing down here to drink. Just bring the whole six-pack. I'll be sleeping down here by myself on rocks all night . . . It's the least you could do."

"Oh, all right!"

The flashlight went away and she with it. Dr. Livingston sat beneath the cave entrance looking up through the hole. It must have been a beautiful night above him. He saw his stars twinkling in the small patch of sky above. It was as if all the rest of the universe had gone away but for the stars that he could see. It reminded him of when he was a little boy and he used to camp out in his back yard at night. He put the saxophone to his lips and blew again.

In a moment his wife returned and lowered the beer, pencil, and paper, which she'd tied in a plastic grocery bag to the end of the rope.

"Now the rope," he said.

"What!"

"I said the rope."

"I know what you said. But that man said we could tie it to the car and pull you up. I mean we could try it . . ."

"It won't work," he said, thinking fast. "Use your head, woman. If I just stepped into this hole, then the top must be very thin. Why, the weight of the car could cave the whole thing in on me. The whole house might fall in tomorrow! You could fall in yourself any minute."

There was silence above him. He could tell she was thinking very hard about something, probably all the Lorna Doones she had eaten. She was trying to wish herself small.

"Now, throw me the rope."

She was reluctant to give it to him. It was the umbilicus that brought him food and drink; it was their only connection.

"There's a huge crevice here," he lied. "I'll have to tie myself to this ledge to sleep."

She dropped the rope to him.

"But, I'm not leaving you, George. If I have to sleep out in the grass with the crickets. I'm not . . ."

"Fine," he muttered.

He threw the light onto the cave walls, found the tunnel, then crawled through, pushing the saxophone and plastic bag ahead of him. When he reached the tunnel's end, he saw a huge yellow stalagmite beside the mound of flowstone. He tied one end of the rope to it and the other to his waist. With the saxophone and plastic bag in one hand and the flashlight in the other, he lowered himself over the flowstone and slid a long way on his rump until his feet touched solid stone beneath him. He walked a few feet and came, as they say, to the end of his rope where he saw that he was, in fact, on a rather small ledge no more than three feet wide. Within reach he saw a green florescent glow and thinking it a rock, he picked it up. It was his watch, and it still read 2:47. He flung it even farther.

Below him he heard a lyrical, hollow, gurgling sound and, flashing his electric beam, located a stream. He glanced about, realizing this second cavern was more enormous than the first. It was, he thought, like a mammoth concert hall with vaulted ceilings and numerous entrances and exits. He tossed the light about him and discovered that if he walked carefully along the edge to his left, there was a passage down to the bank beside the stream.

For a moment he stood hesitating, glancing at the tether that led back up, then he untied himself, letting the rope dangle. He walked sideways with his chest against the wall until he arrived at the edge of the stream.

Out of the corner of his eye, he caught several silver flashes and turned his light full upon them in the water. A school of small, thin fish, no bigger than his finger, darted about the stream. The light did not seem to bother them and upon closer inspection, when he hovered over the clear water for a better look, he saw that they were both albino and blind—not just blind, but eyeless. Where the flat discs of their eyes should have been was a slight indentation, nothing more, and through their pale, delicate skin, he perceived the fine, curved outline of their bones. He put his hand in the cold water and the fish darted away, as if somehow they felt his presence.

"Incredible," he whispered.

"Credible," the cave whispered back.

He opened the case, strapped the saxophone about his neck and turned off the flashlight. He wore the damp, cool darkness like a second skin. He felt not himself, rather he felt ultimate, as if the infinite melodies that might arise from his fingers and breath burned and twisted through him like dark fire. He closed his eyes and blew. In the darkness it seemed that he was creating worlds.

Time passed, but it was geologic time; he did not bother to measure it. At first, he had tried stopping after each song to catch the flow with pen and paper; eventually he gave that up. Invariably a new note rushed in to fill the empty space of the last. It was one song and he played it for all he was worth. After a while, he stopped playing altogether and simply sat drinking his beer and listening to the music in his head, until at last, he emptied himself out and all he could hear was the hollow gurgling of the stream and the metronome of the cave dripping.

He must have fallen asleep. Dr. Livingston stood and stretched himself. He wondered what time it was. Inside him there were more songs, but they were smothered by the rumbling in his stomach which meant that he was hungry. Flora's chicken dinner lay on the other side of the flowstone wall in the room upstairs. Mortal after all, he found his way back up the ledge to the rope hanging over the flowstone. It was more difficult this time—he was climbing uphill and had to keep both hands on the rope. He left the saxophone on the ledge and held the flashlight in his teeth.

Slowly, he inched his way up past the slick wall of mineral deposits and through the narrow tunnel until he came to the last turn. There, he noticed coming toward him a faint light, which surprised him. He switched off the flashlight and crawled toward it. When he entered the room, he saw with near-blinding clarity that it was day again and sunlight poured through the open pit, shining on the opposite wall.

Strangest of all, he spied upon his army blanket, a pinkish white, eyeless newt that lay basking in what must have seemed to it the sudden, in-flowing warmth. Its feathery red gills pumped fresh oxygen into its system as it held its skinny self up on spindly legs. It looked no more than a white pencil with appendages. Dr. Livingston watched its red gills flutter in the sunlight that it could not see, and it seemed a sad sight to him, this abrupt change in the cave's environment. Perhaps in several hundred years the newt and fish would grow eyes again. Perhaps they would come, as their ancestors must have done, to rely on sight, forgetting the world of vibration and sound. He wanted to shield it—it seemed so naive, so embryonic—to protect it from the ever encroaching outer world.

Dr. Livingston sat quietly in the far corner, watching the newt and eating his cold fried chicken. As soon as he was through, he would go back to his music and the stream. There seemed important work to do now. Very important. He might one day emerge himself, white-headed and blind, with a sheaf of music the likes of which no one else had ever heard. He would write what he could remember, and what he could not remember . . . well, he would have played it and that would have to be enough for any reasonable man.

He paused in mid-bite of his chicken thigh and stared again at the pale, slick creature on the blanket. It seemed to tremble visibly, then in a moment, it darted away into the dark recesses of the cave. He wondered what could have frightened it. In the next moment he felt it, too—a low rumbling that shook the ground, growing louder and louder, shaking him. The chicken wing slipped from his hand. Somewhere he heard rocks falling and thought of his beautiful orange stone icicles shattering on the cavern floor.

"No!" he shouted. "Go back!"

The truck roared through Dr. Livingston's back yard, across his tomato plants and stopped near the edge of the sinkhole. Mrs. Livingston spluttered and cried, waving her handkerchief. Four men leaped from the truck—a doctor with his black medical bag; two technicians in tan jumpsuits, who began removing ropes and lanterns and oxygen tanks from the truck; and an official-looking young man in a brown suit and tie. The green bullhorn tied to his belt loop swung like a pendulum as he flung his hand, snapping his fingers at the technicians, and pointing down the hole.

"All night I called to him," Mrs. Livingston wailed. "Talked to him, but he didn't answer. Oh God, do something! He's dead down there, suffocated or fallen or broken a leg or something."

The official young man spread his handkerchief over the grass to prevent a stain on his pants and, leaning over the edge of the precipice, shouted, "Dr. Livingston. This is Robert C. Cunningham, Jr. of the Commonwealth of Kentucky, Department of Parks and Recreation, Geological Investigation Division. Can you hear me, sir!"

"Yeah, I hear you," Dr. Livingston grumbled. "Your damn truck scared my newt."

He bit into his chicken thigh again, thinking hard. The bullhorn started in once more.

"Dr. Livingston. This is Robert C. Cunningham, Jr. of the Commonwealth's Department of Parks and Recreation. We're coming in for a rescue. Sir. Don't panic. I repeat, do not . . ."

"Hold it! Hold it!" Dr. Livingston shouted. "I'm right here and I can hear you fine. You don't need to blast my ears off with that thing. It echoes like crazy in here. What's the matter with you? Haven't you ever been in a cave before?"

There was a short pause and then it seemed as if the sun's light were cut away from him. He thought for a moment that they had sealed him in, then he realized it was only Mrs. Livingston leaning over the hole.

"Tarnation, George! Why didn't you answer me last night? You scared the pee out of me!"

"Dr. Livingston. This cave is the property of the Commonwealth of Kentucky and off-limits to the general populace . . ."

"What do you mean Commonwealth? This is my back yard. As far as you know this cave wasn't even here twenty-four hours ago. Who the devil do you think you are?"

"This is Robert C. Cunningham. I'm a speleologist with the Commonwealth of Kentucky, Department of . . ."

"All right. All right," he shouted.

"We've come to extricate you from the cave. Sir."

"Who needs it? Just throw me a couple of ropes over the edge . . ."

"You don't know what you're doing. You can fall, Dr. Livingston. Fall and die."

"So?"

"George, please. They're here to save you. Oh, what's the matter with him? Don't be stupid, George."

He muttered, gathering up his fried chicken box, his blanket and pillow, tidying the cave.

"We'll throw you a rope. Tie it around your waist. I repeat . . . Tie it around your waist. And we will haul you up."

"Well, wait just a minute," Dr. Livingston said. "I have to go back for my saxophone."

"His what?" the speleologist muttered to Mrs. Livingston.

"Saxophone. I don't know. He made me bring it to him."

Dr. Livingston tied his rope around his waist again and belly-crawled back through the tunnel toward the larger chamber below. This time he didn't need the flashlight. It was as if, twisting and turning, he could maneuver the narrow tunnel blind. *Good as the damn newt,* he told himself. He reached the flowstone and tied the rope to the stalagmite, then lowered himself down.

He reached out his hand slowly, feeling in the dark. A few feet away from him on the ledge, he located his saxophone. The case felt cool and eager for his touch. For a long time Dr. Livingston stood in the dark, listening to the stream, smelling the damp, earthy cave smell and tapping his foot tentatively to the monotonous drip drip drip of the cave.

"Bah-bum-pum-pum-pum," he sang softly.

"Bah-bum," the cave answered.

Dr. Livingston reached into his pocket, pulled out his penknife and cut the rope, then lowered himself into the main cavity. He clapped his hands in the darkness.

"Go now!" he urged the fish and his newt.

"Go now," the cave said.

He wished that he could crawl off with them down one of the unexplored tunnels. He thought of the wonders he would know, the music he could play; but he knew that sooner or later they would find him, and his heart cleaved like an ancient stone.

He sat by the stream, found a half-full beer, and finished it off; then he opened his case, slung the saxophone around his neck and wet his lips. He blew into it slowly. It was a sweet cry—a baleful, beautiful, resonant sound. He sat quietly a moment, listening to its echo. Music flowed through his veins like dark water, etching out secret caverns, filling him with wonder.

In this world, thought Dr. Livingston, there were just some things a man had to do. Then he licked his lips and breathed the song again.

Belinda's World Tour

GUY DAVENPORT

Born in Anderson, South Carolina, in 1927, Guy Davenport completed a B.A. at Duke University and a B.Litt. as a Rhodes Scholar at Oxford University. Following service in the Army, he taught English at Washington University in St. Louis. After completing his Ph.D. at Harvard in 1961, he taught for a while at Haverford College in Pennsylvania, and in 1963 began a long and distinguished teaching career at the University of Kentucky. In 1990 he won a MacArthur Fellowship and began writing full time. In addition to numerous translations and edited texts, his many books include the critical-essay collections, *The Geography of the Imagination* (1981), *Every Force Evolves a Form* (1987), and *The Hunter Gracchus* (1997); the poetry collection *Flowers and Leaves* (1966); and the short story collections, *Tatlin!* (1974), *Da Vinci's Bicycle* (1979), *The Jules Verne Steam Balloon* (1987), *A Table of Green Fields* (1993), *The Cardiff Team* (1996), and *12 Stories* (1997).

Davenport's short stories are experimental and learned, and they demand a great deal from the reader. He dispenses with much of the traditional conventions of fiction to create what he has described as "assemblages," a term borrowed from modern art. As Carl Singleton has noted, Davenport "fills his works with allusions from history, religion, art, and science—particularly classical ones—such that his scholarship is a bedrock of the fiction." First published in the *Santa Monica Review* in 1993 and included in *A Table of Green Fields*, "Belinda's World Tour" is an epistolary short story whose kernel was Max Brod's biographical reference to Kafka's writing postcards to a little girl. An example of metafiction, the story is as much about the little girl's encounter with the imagined marriage and world journey of her doll as it is about a reader's encounter with fiction. It reminds us of the power of story, of our own need to believe.

◆

A little girl, hustled into her pram by an officious nurse, discovered halfway home from the park that her doll Belinda had been left behind. The nurse had finished her gossip with the nurse who minced with one hand on her hip, and had had a good look at the grenadiers in creaking boots who strolled in the park to eye and give smiling nods to the nurses. She had posted a letter and sniffed at various people.

Lizaveta had tried to talk to a little boy who spoke only a soft gibberish, had kissed and been kissed by a large dog, and had helped another little girl fill her shoes with sand.

And Belinda had been left behind. They went back and looked for her in all the places they had been. The nurse was in a state. Lizaveta howled. Her father and mother were at a loss to comfort her, as this was the first tragedy of her life and she was indulging all its possibilities. Her grief was the more terrible in that they had a guest to tea, Herr Doktor Kafka of the Assicurazioni Generali, Prague office.

—Dear Lizaveta! Herr Kafka said. You are so very unhappy that I am going to tell you something that was going to be a surprise. Belinda did not have time to tell you herself. While you were not looking, she met a little boy her own age, perhaps a doll, perhaps a little boy, I couldn't quite tell, who invited her to go with him around the world. But he was leaving immediately. There was no time to dally. She had to make up her mind then and there. Such things happen. Dolls, you know, are born in department stores, and have a more advanced knowledge than those of us who are brought to houses by storks. We have such a limited knowledge of things. Belinda did, in her haste, ask me to tell you that she would write, daily, and that she would have told you of her sudden plans if she had been able to find you in time.

Lizaveta stared.

But the very next day there was a postcard for her in the mail. She had never had a postcard before. On its picture side was London Bridge, and on the other lots of writing which her mother read to her, and her father, again, when he came home for dinner.

*

Dear Lizaveta: We came to London by balloon. Oh, how exciting it is to float over mountains, rivers, and cities with my friend Rudolf, who had packed a lunch of cherries and jam. The English are very strange. Their clothes cover all of them, even their heads, where the buttons go right up into their hats, with button holes, so to speak, to look out of, and a kind of sleeve for their very large noses. They all carry umbrellas, as it rains constantly, and long poles to poke their way through the fog. They live on muffins and tea. I have seen the King in a carriage drawn by forty horses, stepping with precision to a drum. More later. Your loving doll, Belinda.

*

Dear Lizaveta: We came to Scotland by train. It went through a tunnel all the way from London to Edinburgh, so dark that all the passengers were issued lanterns to read *The Times* by. The Scots all wear kilts, and dance to the bagpipe, and eat porridge which they cook in kettles the size of our bathtub. Rudolf and I have had a picnic in a meadow full of sheep. There are bandits everywhere. Most of the people in Edinburgh are lawyers, and their families live in apartments around the courtrooms. More later. Your loving friend, Belinda.

*

Dear Lizaveta: From Scotland we have traveled by steam packet to the Faeroe Islands, in the North Sea. The people here are all fisherfolk and belong to a religion called The Plymouth Brothers, so that when they aren't out in boats hauling in nets full of herring, they are in church singing hymns. The whole island rings with music. Not a single tree grows here, and the houses have rocks on their roofs, to keep the wind from blowing them away. When we said we were from Prague, they had never heard of it, and asked if it were on the moon. Can you imagine! This card will be slow getting there, as the mail boat comes but once a month. Your loving companion, Belinda.

*

Dear Lizaveta: Here we are in Copenhagen, staying with a nice gentleman named Hans Christian Andersen. He lives next door to another nice gentleman named Søren Kierkegaard. They take Rudolf and me to a park that's wholly for children and dolls, called Tivoli. You can see what it looks like by turning over this card. Every afternoon at 4 little boys dressed in red (and they are all blond and have big blue eyes) march through Tivoli, and around and around it, beating drums and playing fifes. The harbor is the home of several mermaids. They are very shy and you have to be very patient and stand still a long time to see them. The Danes are melancholy and drink lots of coffee and read only serious books. I saw a book in a shop with the title *How To Be Sure As To What Is And What Isn't*. And *The Doll's Guide To Existentialism; If This, Then What?* and *You Are More Miserable Than You Think You Are*. In haste, Belinda.

*

Dear Lizaveta: The church bells here in St. Petersburg ring all day and all night long. Rudolf fears that our hearing will be affected. It snows all year round. There's a samovar in every streetcar. They read serious books here, too. Their favorite author is Count Tolstoy, who is one of his own peasants (they say this distresses his wife), and who eats only beets, though he adds an onion at Passover. We can't read a word of the shop signs. Some of the letters are backwards. The men have bushy beards and look like bears. The women keep their hands in muffs. Your shivering friend, Belinda.

*

Dear Lizaveta: We have crossed Siberia in a sled over the snow, and now we are on Sakhalin Island, staying with a very nice and gentle man whose name is Anton Chekhov. He lives in Moscow, but is here writing a book about this strange northern place where the mosquitoes are the size of parrots and all the people are in jail for disobeying their parents and taking things that didn't belong to them. The Russians are very strict. Mr. Chekhov pointed out to us a man who is serving a thousand years for not saying *Gesundheit* when the Czar sneezed in his hearing. It is all very sad. Mr. Chekhov is going to do something about it all, he says. He has a cat name of Pussinka who is anxious to return to Moscow and doesn't like Sakhalin Island at all, at all. Your loving friend, Belinda.

*

Dear Lizaveta: Japan! Oh, Japan! Rudolf and I have bought kimonos and roll about in a rickshaw, delighting in views of Fujiyama (a blue mountain with snow on top) through wisteria blossoms and cherry orchards and bridges that make a hump rather than lie flat. The Japanese drink tea in tiny cups. The women have tall hairdos in which they have stuck yellow sticks. Everybody stops what they are doing ten times a day to write a poem. These poems, which are very short, are about crickets and seeing Fujiyama through the wash on the line and about feeling lonely when the moon is full. We are very popular, as the Japanese like novelty. Excitedly, Belinda.

*

Dear Lizaveta: Here we are in China. That's the long wall on the other side of the card. The emperor is a little boy who wears a dress the color of paprika. He lives in a palace the size of Prague, with a thousand servants. To get from his nursery to his throne he has a chair between two poles, and is carried. Five doctors look at his poo-poo when he makes it. Sorry to be vulgar, but what's the point of travel if you don't learn how different people are outside Prague? Answer me that. The Chinese eat with two sticks and slurp their soup. Their hair is tied in pigtails. The whole country smells of ginger, and they say *plog* for Prague. All day long firecrackers, firecrackers, firecrackers! Your affectionate Belinda.

*

Dear Lizaveta: We have sailed to Tahiti in a clipper ship. This island is all pink and green, and the people are brown and lazy. The women are very beautiful, with long black hair and pretty black eyes. The children scamper up palm trees like monkeys and wear not a stitch of clothes. We have met a Frenchman name of Gauguin, who paints pictures of the Tahitians, and another Frenchman named Pierre Loti, who wears a fez and reads the European newspapers in the café all day and says that Tahiti is Romantic. What Rudolf and I say is that it's very hot and decidedly uncivilized. Have I said that Rudolf is of the royal family? He's a good sport, but he has his limits. There are no *streets* here! Romantically, Belinda.

*

Well! dear Lizaveta, San Francisco! Oh my! There are streets here, all uphill, and with gold prospectors and their donkeys on them. There are saloons with swinging doors, and Flora Dora girls dancing inside. Everybody plays *Oh Suzanna!* on their banjos (everybody has one) and everywhere you see Choctaws in blankets and cowboys with six-shooters and Chinese and Mexicans and Esquimaux and Mormons. All the houses are of wood, with fancy carved trimmings, and the gentry sit on their front porches and read political newspapers. Anybody in America can run for any public office whatever, so that the mayor of San Francisco is a Jewish tailor and his councilmen are a Red Indian, a Japanese gardener, a British earl, a Samoan cook, and a woman Presbyterian preacher. We have met a Scotsman name of Robert Louis Stevenson, who took us to see an Italian opera. Yours ever, Belinda.

*

Dear Lizaveta: I'm writing this in a stagecoach crossing the Wild West. We have seen many Indian villages of teepees, and thousands of buffalo. It took hours to get down one side of the Grand Canyon, across its floor (the river is shallow and we rolled right across, splashing) and up the other side. The Indians wear colorful blankets and have a feather stuck in their hair. Earlier today we saw the United States Cavalry riding along with the American flag. They were singing "Yankee Doodle Dandy" and were all very handsome. It will make me seasick to write more, as we're going as fast as a train. Dizzily, Belinda.

*

Dear Lizaveta: We have been to Chicago, which is on one of the Great Lakes, and crossed the Mississippi, which is so wide you can't see across it, only paddle-steamers in the middle, loaded with bales of cotton. We have seen utopias of Quakers and Shakers and Mennonites, who live just as they want to in this free country. There is no king, only a Congress which sits in Washington and couldn't care less what the people do. I have seen one of these Congressmen. He was fat (three chins, I assure you) and offered Rudolf and me a dollar each if we would vote for him. When we said we were from Prague, he said he hoped we'd start a war, as war is good for business. On to New York! In haste, your loving Belinda.

*

Dear Lizaveta: How things turn out! Rudolf and I are married! Oh yes, at Niagara Falls, where you stand in line, couple after couple, and get married by a Protestant minister, a rabbi, or a priest, take your choice. Then you get in a barrel (what fun!) and ride over the falls—you bounce and bounce at the bottom—and rent a honeymoon cabin, of which there are hundreds around the falls, each with a happy husband and wife billing and cooing. I know from your parents that my sister in the department store has come to live with you and be your doll. Rudolf and I are going to the Argentine. You must come visit our ranch. I will remember you forever. Mrs. Rudolph Hapsburg und Porzelan (your Belinda).

The Way It Felt to Be Falling

KIM EDWARDS

Kim Edwards grew up in Skaneateles, New York, and earned degrees from Colgate University and the University of Iowa. She taught for five years in Asia, including stints in Malaysia, Japan, and Cambodia. Her short stories have appeared in, among many other journals, *Ploughshares*, *Story*, *The Paris Review*, *Redbook*, and *Antaeus*. Many of them are collected in *The Secrets of a Fire King* and have earned awards, including a *Pushcart Prize*, a *Nelson Algren Award*, and inclusions in *Best American Short Stories*. Since 1996 she has lived in Lexington with her husband, Thomas Clayton.

In an interview with Kentucky Educational Television, Edwards commented on her connection with Kentucky: "I have noticed it in the teaching that I do, and the writings of other Kentucky writers that I have read—that there is an enormous sense of 'place' in their writing, this enormous love of the land, and deeply rooted sense of being in a place, and of a place, which I find interesting. I don't feel like I'm quite 'of this place' yet; but I'm hoping it will happen. I'm sure, after time, it will." Originally published in *The Three-Penny Review* and reprinted in *Pushcart Prize XIX* and *The Secrets of a A Fire King*, "The Way It Felt to Be Falling" was written while Edwards was an undergraduate at Colgate University. Her first serious attempt at short fiction, it was revised, she has said, seventy-five times before its publication in 1993. It is a story of risk and ascension, of a girl's need to climb out of a world that seems to be falling apart around her.

◆

The summer I turned nineteen I used to lie in the backyard and watch the planes fly overhead, leaving their clean plumes of jet-stream in a pattern against the sky. It was July, yet the grass had a brown fringe and leaves were already falling, borne on the wind like discarded paper wings. The only thing that flourished that summer was the recession; businesses, lured by lower tax rates, moved south in a steady progression. My father had left too, but in a more subtle and insidious way—after his consulting firm failed, he had simply retreated into some silent and inaccessible world. Now, when I went with my mother to the hospital, we found him sitting quietly in a chair by the window. His hands were limp against the armrests and his hair was long, a rough dark fringe across his ears. He was never glad to see us, or sorry. He just looked calmly around the room, at my mother's strained smile and my eyes, which skittered nervously away, and he did not give a single word of greeting or acknowledgment or farewell.

My mother had a job as a secretary and decorated cakes on the side. In the pressing heat she juggled bowls between the refrigerator and the counter, struggling to keep the frosting at the right consistency so she could make the delicate roses, chrysanthemums, and daisies that balanced against fields of sugary white. The worst ones were the wedding cakes, intricate and bulky. That summer, brides and their mothers called us on a regular basis, their voices laced with panic. My mother spoke to them as she worked, trailing the extension cord along the tiled floor, her voice soothing and efficient.

Usually my mother is a calm person, levelheaded in the face of stress, but one day the bottom layer of a finished cake collapsed and she wept, her face cradled in her hands as she sat at the kitchen table. I hadn't seen her cry since the day my father left, and I watched her from the kitchen door, a basket of laundry in my arms, uneasiness rising around me like slow, numbing light. After a few minutes she dried her eyes and salvaged the cake, removing the broken layer and dispensing with the plastic fountain which spouted champagne, and which was supposed to rest in a precarious arrangement between two cake layers held apart by plastic pillars.

"There." She stepped back to survey her work. The cake was smaller but still beautiful, delicate and precise.

"It looks better without that tacky fountain, anyway," she said. "Now let's get it out of here before something else goes wrong."

I helped her box it up and carry it to the car, where it rested on the floor, surrounded by bags of ice. My mother backed out of the driveway slowly, then paused and called to me.

"Katie," she said. "Try to get the dishes done before you go to work, okay? And please, don't spend all night with those dubious friends of yours. I'm too tired to worry."

"I won't," I said, waving. "I'm working late anyway."

By "dubious friends" my mother meant Stephen, who was, in fact, my only friend that summer. He had spirals of long red hair and a habit of shoplifting expensive gadgets: tools, jewelry, photographic equipment. My mother thought he was an unhealthy influence, which was generous; the rest of the town just thought he was crazy. He was the older brother of my best friend Emmy, who had fled, with her boyfriend and 350 tie-dyed T-shirts, to follow the Grateful Dead on tour. Come with us, she had urged, but I was working in a convenience store, saving my money for school, and it didn't seem like a good time to leave my mother. So I stayed in town and Emmy sent me postcards I memorized—a clean line of desert, a sky aching blue over the ocean, an airy waterfall in the inter-mountain West. I was fiercely envious, caught in that small town while the planes traced their daily paths to places I was losing hope of ever seeing. I lay in the backyard and watched them. The large jets moved in slow silver glints across the sky, while the smaller planes droned lower. Sometimes, on the clearest days, I caught a glimpse of sky divers. They started out as small black specks, plummeting, then blossomed against the horizon in a streak of silk and color. I stood up to watch as they grew steadily larger, then passed the tree line and disappeared.

When my mother was gone, I went back inside. The air was cool and shadowy, heavy with the sweet scent of flowers and frosting. I piled the broken cake on a plate and did the dishes, quickly, feeling the silence gather. That summer I couldn't stay alone in the house. I'd find myself standing in front of mirrors with my heart pounding, searching my eyes for a glimmer of madness, or touching the high arc of my cheekbone as if I didn't know my own face. I thought I knew about madness, the way it felt—the slow suspended turning as you gave yourself up to it. The doctors said my father was suffering from a stress-related condition. They said he would get better. But I had watched him in his slow retreat, distanced by his own expanding silence. On the day he stopped speaking altogether I had brought him a glass of water, stepping across the afternoon light that flickered on the wooden floors.

"Hey Dad," I had said, softly. His eyes were closed. His face and hands were soft and white and pale. When he opened his eyes they were clear brown, as blank and smooth as the glass in my hand.

"Dad?" I said. "Are you okay?" He did not speak, then or later, not even when the ambulance came and took him away. He did not sigh or protest. He had slid away from us with apparent ease. I had watched him go, and this was what I knew: madness was a graceless descent, the abyss beneath a careless step. *Take care* I said each time we left my father, stepping from his cool quiet room into the bright heat outside. And I listened to my own words; I took care, too. That summer, I was afraid of falling.

Stephen wasn't comfortable at my house and he lived at the edge of town, so we met every day at Mickey's Tavern, where it was cool and dark and filled with the chattering life of other people. I always stopped in on my way to or from work, but Stephen sometimes spent whole afternoons and evenings there, playing games of pool and making bets with the other people who formed the fringe of the town.

Some of them called themselves artists, and lived together in an abandoned farmhouse. They were young, most of them, but already disenfranchised, known to be odd or mildly crazy or even faintly dangerous. Stephen, who fell into the last two categories because he had smashed out an ex-lover's window one night, and had tried, twice, to kill himself, kept a certain distance from the others. Still, he was always at Mickey's, leaning over the pool table, a dark silhouette against the back window, only his hair illuminated in a fringe of red.

Before Emmy left, I had not liked Stephen. At twenty-seven he still lived at home, in a fixed-over apartment on the third floor of his parents' house. He slept all morning and spent his nights pacing his small rooms, listening to Beethoven or playing chess with a computer he'd bought. I had seen the dark scars that bisected both his wrists, and they frightened me. He collected a welfare check every month, took Valium every few hours, and lived in a state of precarious calm. Sometimes he was mean, teasing Emmy to the edge of tears. But he could be charming too, with an ease and grace the boys my own age didn't have. When he was feeling good he made things special, leaning over to whisper something, his fingers a lingering touch on my arm, on my knee. I knew it had to do with the danger, too, the reason he was so attractive at those times.

"Kate understands me," he said once. Emmy, the only person who was not afraid of him, laughed out loud and asked why I'd have any better insight into his warped mind than the rest of the world.

"Can't you tell?" he said. I wouldn't look at him so he put his fingers lightly on my arm. He was completely calm, but he must have felt me trembling. It was a week after my father had been taken to the hospital, and it seemed that Stephen knew some truth about me, something invisible that only he could sense.

"What do you mean?" I demanded. But he just laughed and left the porch, telling me to figure it out for myself.

"What did he mean?" I asked. "What did he mean by that?"

"He's in a crazy mode," Emmy said. She was methodically polishing her fingernails, and she tossed her long bright hair over her shoulder. "The best thing to do is pretend he doesn't exist."

But Emmy left and then there was only Stephen, charming, terrifying Stephen, who started to call me every day. He asked me to come over, to go for a ride, to fly kites with him behind a deserted barn he'd found. Finally I gave in, telling myself I was doing him a favor by keeping him company. But it was more than that. I knew that Stephen understood the suspended world between sanity and madness, that he lived his life inside it.

One night, past midnight, when we were sitting in the quiet darkness of his porch, he told me about cutting his wrists, the even pulse of warm running water, the sting of the razor dulled with Valium and whiskey.

"Am I shocking you?" he had asked after a while.

"No. Emmy told me about it." I paused, unsure how much to reveal. "She thinks you did it to get attention."

He laughed. "Well it worked," he said, "didn't it?"

I traced my finger around the pattern in the upholstery.

"Maybe," I said. "But now everyone thinks you're crazy."

He shrugged, and stretched, pushing his large thick hands up toward the ceiling. "So what?" he said. "If people think you're crazy, they leave you alone, that's all."

I thought of all the times I had stood in front of the mirror, of the times I woke at night, my heart a frantic movement, no escape.

"Don't you ever worry that it's true?"

Stephen reached over to the table and held up his blue plastic bottle of Valium.

It was a strong prescription. I knew, because I had tried it. I liked the way the blue pills slid down my throat, dissolving anxiety. I liked the way the edges of things grew undefined, so I was able to rise from my own body, calmly and with perfect grace.

Stephen shook a pill into his hand. His skin was pale and damp, his expression intent.

"No," he said. "I don't worry. Ever."

Still, on the day the cake collapsed, I could tell he *was* worried. When I got to the pool room he was squinting down one cue at a time, discarding each one as he discovered warps and flaws.

"Hey, Kate," he said, choosing one at last. "Care for a game?"

We ordered beer and plugged our quarters into the machine, waiting for the weighty, rolling thunk of balls. Stephen ran his hand through his red beard. He had green eyes and a long, finely shaped nose. I thought he was extremely handsome.

"How goes the tournament?" I asked. He'd been in the playoffs for days, and each time I came in the stakes were higher.

Stephen broke, and dropped two low balls. He stepped back and surveyed the table. "You'll love this," he said. "Loser goes skydiving."

"You know," I said, remembering the plummeting shapes, the silky streaks against the sky, "I've always wanted to do that."

"Well," Stephen said, "keep the loser company, then."

He missed his next shot and we stopped talking. I was good, steady, with some competitions behind me. The bar was filling up around us, and soon a row of quarters lined the wooden rim of the pool table. After a while Ted Johnson, one of the artists in the farmhouse, came in and leaned against the wall. Stephen tensed, and his next shot went wild.

"Too bad," Ted said, stepping forward. "Looks like you're on a regular losing streak."

"You could go fuck yourself," Stephen said, but his voice was even, as though he'd just offered Ted a beer.

"Thanks," Ted said. "But actually, I'd just as soon ask Kate a question, while she's here. I'd like to know what you think about honor, Kate. Specifically, I want to know if you think an honorable person must always keep a promise?"

I shot again. The cue ball hovered on the edge of a pocket, then steadied itself. There was a tension, a subtext that I couldn't read. I sent my last ball in and took aim at the eight. It went in smoothly, and I stepped back. There was a moment of silence, and we listened to it roll away into the hidden depths of the table.

"What's your point, Ted?" I asked, without turning to look at him.

"Stephen is going skydiving," he said. "That's my point."

"Stephen, you lost?" I felt, oddly enough, betrayed.

"It was a technicality," Stephen said, frowning. "Ridiculous! I'm the better player." He took a long swallow of beer.

"What bullshit," Ted answered, shaking his head. "You're absolutely graceless in defeat."

Stephen was quiet for a long time. Then he put his hand to his mouth, very casually, but I knew he was slipping one of his tiny blue Valiums. He tugged his hands through his thick hair and smiled.

"It's no big deal, skydiving. I called today and made the arrangements."

"All the same," Ted answered, "I can't wait to see it."

Stephen shook his head. "No," he said. "I'll go alone."

Ted was surprised. "Forget it, champ. You've got to have a witness."

"Then Kate will go," Stephen said. "She'll witness. She'll even jump, unless she's afraid."

I didn't know what to say. He already knew I wasn't working the next day. And it was something to think about, too, after a summer of skygazing, to finally be inside a plane.

"I've never even flown before," I told them.

"That's no problem," Ted answered. "That part is a piece of cake."

I finished off the beer and picked up my purse from where it was lying on a bar stool.

"Where are you going?" Stephen asked.

"Believe it or not, some of us work for a living," I said.

He smiled at me, a wide, charming grin, and walked across the room. He took both my hands in his. "Don't be mad, Kate," he said. "I really want you to jump with me."

"Well," I said, getting flustered. He didn't work, but his hands were calloused from playing so much pool. He had a classic face, a face you might see on a pale statue in a museum, with hair growing out of his scalp like flames and eyes that seemed to look out on some other, more compelling, world. Recklessness settled over me like a spell, and suddenly I couldn't imagine saying no.

"Good," he said, releasing my hands, winking quickly before he turned back to the bar. "That's great. I'll pick you up tomorrow, then. At eight."

When I got home that night my mother was in the kitchen. Sometimes the house was dark and quiet, with only her even breathing, her murmured response when I said I was home. But usually she was awake, working, the radio tuned to an easy-listening station, a book discarded on the sofa. She said that the concentration, the exactness required to form the fragile arcs of frosting, helped her relax.

"You're late," she said. She was stuffing frosting into one of the cloth pastry bags. "Were you at Stephen's?"

I shook my head. "I stayed late at work. Someone went home sick." I started licking one of the spoons. My mother never ate the frosting. She saw too much of it, she said; she hated even the thick sweet smell of it.

"What is it that you do over there?" she asked, perplexed.

"At work?"

My mother looked up. "You know what I mean," she said.

I pushed off my tennis shoes. "I don't know. We hang out. Talk about books and music and art and stuff."

"But he doesn't work, Kate. You come home and you have to get up in a few hours. Stephen, on the other hand, can sleep all day."

"I know. I don't want to talk about it."

My mother sighed. "He's not stable. Neither are his friends. I don't like you being involved with them."

"Well, I'm not unstable," I said. I spoke too loudly, to counter the fear that seemed to plummet through my flesh whenever I had that thought. "I am not crazy."

"No," said my mother. She had a tray full of sugary roses in front of her, in a bright spectrum of color. I watched her fingers, thin and strong and graceful, as she shaped the swirls of frosting into vibrant, perfect roses.

"Whatever happened to simple white?" she asked, pausing to stretch her fingers. This bride's colors were green and lavender, and my mother had dyed the frosting to match swatches from the dresses. Her own wedding pictures were in black and white, but I knew it had been simple, small and elegant, the bridesmaids wearing the palest shade of peach.

"I saw your father today," she said while I was rummaging in the refrigerator.

"How is he?" I asked.

"The same. Better. I don't know." She slid the tray of finished roses into the freezer. "Maybe a little better, today. The doctors seem quite hopeful."

"That's good," I said.

"I thought we could go see him tomorrow."

"Not tomorrow," I said. "Stephen and I have plans already."

"Katie, he'd like to see you."

"Oh really?" I said sarcastically. "Did he tell you that?"

My mother looked up from the sink. Her hands were wet, a pale shade of purple that shimmered in the harsh overhead light. I couldn't meet her eyes.

"I'm sorry," I said. "I'll go see him next week, okay?"

I started down the hall to my room.

"Kate," she called to me. I paused and turned around.

"Sometimes," she said, "you have no common sense at all."

Secretly I hoped for rain, but the next day was clear and blue. Stephen was even early for a change, the top of his convertible down when he glided up in front of the house. We drove through the clean white scent of clover and the first shimmers of heat. Along the way we stopped to gather dandelions, soft as moss, and waxy black-eyed Susans. Ted had given me his camera, with instructions to document the event, and I spent half the film on the countryside, on Stephen wearing flowers in his beard.

The hangar was a small concrete building sitting flatly amid acres of corn.

The first thing we saw when we entered was a pile of stretchers stacked neatly against the wall. It was hardly reassuring, and neither was the hand-lettered sign that warned CASH ONLY. Stephen and I wandered in the dim open room, looking at the pictures of sky divers in various formations, until two other women showed up, followed by a tall gruff man who collected $40 from each of us, and sent us out to the field.

The man, who had gray hair and a compact body, turned out to be Howard, our instructor. He lined us up beneath the hot sun and made us practice. For the first jump we would all be on static line, but we had to practice as if we were going to pull our own ripcords. It was a matter of timing, Howard said and he taught us a chant to measure our actions. Arch 1000, Look 1000, Reach 1000, Pull 1000, Arch 1000, Check 1000. We practiced endlessly, until sweat lifted from our skin and Howard, in his white clothes, seemed to shimmer. It was important, he said, that we start counting the minute we jumped. Otherwise, we'd lose track of time. Some people panicked and pulled their reserve chute even as the first one opened, tangling them both and falling to their deaths. Others were motionless in their fear and fell like stones, their reserves untouched. So we chanted, moving our arms and heads in rhythm, arching our backs until they ached. Finally, Howard decided we were ready, and took us into the hangar to learn emergency maneuvers.

We practiced these from a rigging suspended from the ceiling. With luck, Howard said, everything should work automatically. But in case anything went wrong, we had to know how to get rid of the first parachute and open our reserves. We took turns in the rigging, yanking the release straps and falling a few feet before the canvas harness caught us. When I tried it, the straps cut painfully into my thighs.

"In the air," Howard said, "it won't feel this bad." I got down, my palms sweaty and shaky, and Stephen climbed into the harness.

"Streamer!" Howard shouted, describing a parachute that opened but didn't inflate. Stephen's motions were fluid—he flipped open the metal buckles, slipped his thumbs through the protruding rings, and fell the few feet through the air.

Howard nodded vigorously. "Yes," he said. "Perfect. You do exactly the same for a Mae West—a parachute with a cord that's caught, bisecting it through the middle."

The other two women had jumped before but their training had expired, and it took them a few tries to relearn the movements. After we had each gone through the procedure three times without hesitation, Howard let us break for lunch. Stephen and I bought Cokes and sat in the shade of the building, looking at the row of planes shining in the sun.

"Have you noticed?" he asked. "Howard doesn't sweat."

I laughed. It was true, Howard's white clothes were as crisp now as when we had started.

"You know what else, Kate?" Stephen went on, breaking a sandwich and giving half to me. "I've never flown either."

"You're kidding?" I said. He was gazing out over the fields.

"No, I'm not." His hands were clasped calmly around his knees. "Do you think we'll make it?"

"Yes," I said, but even then I couldn't imagine myself taking that step into open space. "Of course," I added, "we don't have to do this."

"You don't," said Stephen, throwing his head back to drain his soda. He brushed crumbs out of his beard. "For me it's my personal integrity at stake, remember?"

"But you don't have to worry," I said. "You're so good at this. You did all the procedures perfectly, and you weren't even nervous."

"Hell," Stephen said. He shook his head. "What's to be nervous? The free fall is my natural state of mind." He tapped the shirt pocket where his Valium was hidden.

"Want one?" he asked. "For the flight?"

I shook my head. "No," I said. "Thanks."

He shrugged. "Up to you."

He pulled the bottle out of his pocket and flipped it open. There was only one pill left.

"Damn," he said. He took the cotton out and shook it again, then threw the empty bottle angrily into the field.

We finished eating in silence. I had made up my mind not to go through with it, but when Howard called us back to practice landing maneuvers, I stood up, brushing off the straw that clung to my legs. There seemed to be nothing else to do.

I was going to jump first, so I was crouched closest to the opening in the side of the plane. There was no door, just a wide gaping hole. All I could see was brittle grass, blurring then, growing fluid as we sped across the field and rose into the sky. The force of the ascent pushed me against the hot metal wall of the plane and I gripped a ring in the floor to keep my balance. I closed my eyes, took deep breaths, and tried not to envision myself suspended on a piece of metal in the midst of all that air. The jumpmaster tugged at my arm. The plane had leveled and he motioned to the doorway.

I crept forward and got into position. My legs hung out the opening and the wind pulled at my feet. The jumpmaster was tugging at my parachute and attaching the static line to the floor of the plane. I turned to watch, but the helmet blocked my view. I felt Stephen's light touch on my arm. Then the plane turned, straightened itself. The jumpmaster's hand pressed into my back.

"Go!" he said.

I couldn't move. The ground was tiny, an aerial map, rich in detail, and the wind tugged at my feet. What were the commands? *Arch*, I whispered. *Arch arch arch.* That was all I could remember. I stood up, gripping the side of the opening, my feet balanced on the metal bar beneath the doorway, resisting the steady rush of wind. The jumpmaster shouted again. I felt the pressure of his fingers. And then I was gone. I left the plane behind me and fell into the air.

I didn't shout. The commands flew from my mind, as distant as the faint drone of the receding plane. I knew I must be falling, but the earth stayed the same abstract distance away. I was suspended, caught in a slow turn as the air rushed around me. Three seconds yet? I couldn't tell. My parachute didn't open but the earth came no closer, and I kept my eyes wide open, too terrified to scream.

I felt the tug. It seemed too light after the heavy falls in the hanger, but when I looked up the parachute was unfolding above me, its army green mellowing beneath the sun. Far off I heard the plane as it banked again. Then it faded and the silence grew full, became complete. I leaned back in the straps and looked around. Four lakes curled around the horizon, jagged deep blue fingers. All summer I had felt myself slipping in the quick rush of the world, but here, in clear and steady descent, nothing seemed to move. It was knowledge to marvel at, and I tugged at the steering toggles, turning slowly in a circle. Cornfields unfolded, marked off by trees and fences. And still the silence; the only sound was the whisper of my parachute. I pulled the toggle again and saw someone on the ground, a tiny figure, trying to tell me something. All I could do was laugh, drifting, my voice clear and sharp in all that air. Gradually, the horizon settled into a time line a quarter of a mile away, and I was falling, I realized, falling fast. I tensed, then remembered and forced myself to relax, to fix my gaze on that row of trees. My left foot hit the ground and turned and then, it seemed a long time later, my right foot touched. Inch by inch I rolled onto the ground. The corn all around me tunneled my vision and the parachute dragged me slightly, then deflated. I lay there, smiling, gazing at the blue patch of sky.

After a long time I heard my name in the distance.

"Kate?" It was Stephen. "Kate, are you okay?"

"I'm over here." I sat up and took off my helmet.

"Where?" he said. "Don't be an idiot. I can't see anything in all this corn."

We found each other by calling and moving awkwardly through the coarse, rustling leaves. Stephen hugged me when he saw me.

"Wasn't it wonderful?" I said. "Wasn't it amazing?"

"Yeah," he said, helping me untangle the parachute and wad it up. "It was unbelievable."

"How did you get down before me?" I asked.

"Some of us landed on target," he said as we walked back to the hangar. "Others picked a cornfield." I laughed, giddy with the solidity of earth beneath my feet.

Stephen waited in the car while I went for my things. I hesitated in the cool, dim hangar, letting my eyes adjust. When I could see, I slipped off the jumpsuit and black boots, brushed off my clothes. Howard came out of the office.

"How did I do?" I asked.

"Not bad. You kind of flapped around out there, but not bad, for a first time. You earned this, anyway," he said, handing me a certificate with my name, and his, and the ink still drying.

"Which is more than your friend did," he added. He shook his head at my look of surprise. "I can't figure it out either. Best in the class, and he didn't even make it to the door."

I didn't say anything to Stephen when I got into the car. I didn't know what to say, and by then, anyway, my ankle was swelling, turning an odd, tarnished shade of green. We went to the hospital. They took me into a consulting room and I waited a long time for the x-ray results, which showed no breaks, and for the doctor, who lectured me on my foolishness as he bandaged my sprained ankle. When I came out, precarious on new crutches, Stephen was joking around with one of the nurses.

It wasn't until halfway home, when he was talking nonstop about this being the greatest high he'd ever had, that I finally spoke.

"Look," I said. "I know you didn't jump. Howard told me."

Stephen got quiet and tapped his fingers against the steering wheel. "I wanted to," he said. His nervous fingers worried me, and I didn't answer.

"I don't know what happened, Kate. I stood right in that doorway, and the only thing I could imagine was my chute in a streamer." His hands gripped the wheel tightly. "Crazy, huh?" he said. "I saw you falling, Kate. You disappeared so fast."

"Falling?" I repeated. It was the word he kept using, and it was the wrong one. I remembered the pull of the steering toggle, the slow turn in the air. I shook my head. "That's the funny thing," I told him. "There was no sense of descent. It was more like floating. You know, I was scared too, fiercely scared." I touched the place above the bandage where my ankle was swelling. "But I made it," I added softly, still full of wonder.

We drove through the rolling fields that smelled of dust and ripening leaves. After a minute, Stephen spoke. "Just don't tell anyone, okay Kate? Right? It's important."

"I'm not going to lie," I said, even though I could imagine his friends, who would be unmerciful when they found out. I closed my eyes. The adrenaline had worn off, my ankle ached, and all I wanted to do was sleep.

I knew the road, so when I felt the car swing left, I looked up. Stephen had turned off on a country lane and he was stepping hard on the gas, sending bands of dust up behind us.

"Stephen," I said. "What the hell are you doing?"

He looked at me, and that's when I got scared. A different fear than in the plane, because now I had no choice about what was going to happen. Stephen's eyes, green, were wild and glittering.

"Look," I said, less certainly. "Stephen. Let's just go home, okay?"

He held the wheel with one hand and yanked the camera out of my lap. We swerved around on the road as he pulled out the film. He unrolled it, a narrow brown banner in the wind, and threw it into a field. Then he pressed the accelerator again.

"Isn't it a shame," he said, "that you ruined all the film, Kate?"

The land blurred; then he slammed the brakes and pulled to the side of the deserted road. Dusk was settling into the cornfields like fine gray mist. The air was cooling on my skin, but the leather of the seat was warm and damp beneath my palms.

Stephen's breathing was loud against the rising sound of crickets. He looked at me, eyes glittering, and smiled his crazy smile. He reached over and rested his hand on my shoulder, close to my neck.

"I could do anything I wanted to you," he said. His thumb traced a line on my throat. His touch was almost gentle, but I could feel the tension in his flesh. I thought of running, then remembered the crutches and nearly laughed out loud from nerves and panic at the comic strip image I had, me hobbling across the uneven fields, Stephen in hot pursuit.

"What's so funny?" Stephen asked. His hand slid down and seized my shoulder, hard enough to fix bruises there, delicate, shaped like a fan.

"Nothing," I said, biting my lip. "I just want to go home."

"I could take you home," he said. "If you didn't tell."

"Just drive," I said. "I won't tell."

He stared at me. "You promise?"

"Yes," I said. "I promise."

He was quiet for a long time. Bit by bit his fingers relaxed against my skin. His breathing slowed, and some of his wild energy seemed to diffuse into the steadily descending night. Watching him I thought of my father, all his stubborn silence, all the uneasiness and pain. It made me angry suddenly, a sharp illumination that ended a summer's panic. The sound of crickets grew, and the trees stood black against the last dark shade of blue. Finally Stephen started the car.

When we reached my house he turned and touched me lightly on the shoulder. His fingers rested gently where the bruises were already surfacing, and he traced his finger around them. His voice was soft and calm.

"Look," he said. There was a gentle tone in his voice, and I knew it was as close to an apology as he would ever come. "I have a bad temper, Kate. You shouldn't provoke me, you know." And then, more quietly, even apprehensively, he asked if I'd come over that night.

I pulled my crutches out of the back seat, feeling oddly sad.

I was too angry to ever forgive him, and I was his only real friend.

"You can go to hell," I said. "And if you ever bother me again, I'll tell the entire town that you didn't jump out of that plane."

He leaned across the seat and gazed at me for a second. I didn't know what he would do, but it was my parents' driveway and I knew I was safe.

"Kate," he said then, breaking into the charming smile I knew so well. "You think I'm crazy, don't you?"

"No," I said. "I think you're afraid, just like everybody else."

I was quiet with the door, but my mother sat up right away from where she was dozing on the couch. Her long hair, which reached the middle of her back, was streaked with gray and silver. I had a story ready to tell her, about falling down a hill, but in the end it seemed easier to offer her the truth. I left out the part about Stephen. She followed me as I hobbled into the kitchen to get a glass of water.

I didn't expect her to be so angry. She stood by the counter, drumming her fingers against the Formica.

"I don't believe this," she said. "All I've got to contend with, and you throw yourself out of a plane." She gestured at the crutches. "How do you expect to work this week? How do you expect to pay for this?"

"Give me a break," I said, shaking my head. Stephen was home by now. I didn't think he would bother me, but I couldn't be sure.

"Working is the least of my problems," I said. "Compared to other things, the money aspect is a piece of cake."

And at that my eyes, and hers, fell on the counter, where the remains of yesterday's fiasco were still piled high, the thick dark chocolate edged with creamy frosting. My mother gazed at it for a minute. She picked up a hunk and held it out to me.

"Piece of cake?" she repeated, deadpan.

My mouth quivered. I started laughing, then she did. We were both hysterical with laughter, clutching our sides in pain. And then my mother was shaking me. She was still laughing, unable to speak, but there were tears running down her face too, and when she hugged me to her I got quiet.

"Kate," she said. "My God, Katie, you could have been killed."

I held her and patted awkwardly at her back.

"I'm sorry," I said. "Mom, it's okay. Next week, I'll be as good as new."

She stepped back, one hand on my shoulder, and brushed at her damp eyes with the other hand.

"I don't know what's with me," she said. She sat down in one of the chairs and leaned her forehead against her hand. "It's too much, I guess. All of this, and with your father. I just, I don't know what to do about it all."

"You're doing fine," I said, thinking about all her hours spent on wedding cakes, building confections as fragile and unsubstantial as the dreams that demanded them. My father sat, still and silent in his white room, and I was angry with him for asking so much from us. I wanted to tell my mother this, to explain how the anger had seared away the panic, to share the calmness that, even now, was growing up within me. Whatever had plunged my father into silence, and Stephen into violence, wouldn't find me. I had a bandaged ankle, but the rest of me was whole and strong.

My mother pulled her long hair away from her face, then let it fall.

"I'm going to take a bath," she said. "You're okay, then?"

"Yes," I said. "I'm fine."

I went to my room. The white curtains lifted, luminous in the darkness, and I heard the distant sound of running water from the bathroom. I took off all my clothes, very slowly, and let them lie where they fell on the floor. The stars outside were bright, the sky clear. The curtains unfolded, brushing against my skin in a swell of night air, and what I remembered, standing in the dark, was the way it felt to be falling.

The Idea of It

CHRIS HOLBROOK

Chris Holbrook grew up in Soft Shell in Knott County, Kentucky. He earned a B.A. at the University of Kentucky and an M.F.A. at the University of Iowa and has taught English at Alice Lloyd College since 1989. His stories have appeared in a variety of journals and magazines, including *Louisville Magazine* and *Now and Then*, as well as in the anthologies *Groundwater*, *A Gathering at the Forks*, and *Kentucky Voices*. His first collection of stories, *Hell and Ohio: Stories of Southern Appalachia*, appeared in 1997. He is the recipient of Morehead State University's Thomas and Lillie D. Chaffin Award for writing (1997) and has twice received an Al Smith Fellowship from the Kentucky Arts Council. He lives in Pippa Passes, Kentucky, with his wife, Mary Beth, and their daughter, Erin.

Robert Morgan has noted that Holbrook's stories are "elegies for land and lives disappearing under mudslides from strip mines and new trailer parks and highways. But they are also stories of humor and the mysteries that define us, of marriage in a time of change and ambiguities of allegiance, of the poetry of work." The recipient of *Louisville Magazine*'s 1995 fiction contest and the final story in *Hell and Ohio*, "The Idea of It" portrays an individual caught between present reality and nostalgic ideal, between the need to survive in the here and now and the longing to settle his family on his native ground.

◆

I tell my boy stories about growing up here. I ask him whether he wouldn't like a pony, like I had when I was his age. He says he'd rather have a motorcycle, one he could ride down to Florida. We're on the hillside above the cow pasture. The tin roof of the barn flashes sunlight at us whenever the cloud cover breaks.

"Florida is hot in August," I say.

"So is Kentucky," he replies.

We've cleared the brush around the house and barn lot, but the pasture is still thick with horse weeds, poison ivy, kudzu and sprouts of beech, sassafras, maple, and pine. I've considered buying goats for the sake of the kudzu and ivy.

"Making it okay?" I ask my boy.

Gabriel shrugs, pulls up some clumps of grass to toss at a ground squirrel that has popped up from the roots of a nearby oak tree. He's not used to this outside work. His face is red, and I'm afraid he's sick from being in the sun too much.

"How'd you like a cold drink of water?" I ask.

"We didn't bring any," he says.

"I mean some good spring water. Best water you ever drunk." I stand and motion for him to follow me up the hill. He sighs, as if I'm calling him to some hard task, and rises.

The spring I'm remembering ran from the last frost of winter to the first dry spell of summer, as cold as it was clean tasting. In springtime it roared, spewing white foam over rocks and logs. In summer it ran so quiet there was barely a sound to tell its whereabouts.

We used to come upon it in our play, call time-out from our pretend hunts and headlong chases to drink cowboy style from the wild water. We made dams from sticks and mud, boats from twigs and leaves, saw gemstones in water-smoothed pebbles, one game passing to the next in days that went with no in-between from the first of summer to the last.

It's likely dry now, but I'm betting the little bit of rain we've had this week will have left enough of a trickle to wet our throats. The only water Gabriel has ever drunk has been flavored by metal pipes and fluoride.

It's a hard climb over the ridge to the holler where I remember the spring running. Gabriel doesn't talk. He breathes hard, and I stop a few times to give him rest before he asks for it. I want to carry him because of how hard he's working, but then again I don't because of how old he's grown and because I want him to get the benefit of the climb.

"You'll get used to it," I tell him. "You'll be climbing these hills like a mountain goat!"

"I guess," he says.

The steep hill burns my thigh muscles. Near the top I have to angle sideways and dig the edges of my boots against the slope to keep upright. Gabriel slips a few times, and I have to reach my hand to help him, each time pulling him a little past where he'd lost his ground.

"Ain't nothing worthwhile comes easy," I say.

He doesn't answer, and in another minute we top the hill. We rest on one of the boulders that lie like the bones of a spine along the ridge tops. We look where the holler should be. What we see is bare ground, blasted rock, splintered trees, slate and low grade coal like black gore spilled from a wound. What we see is a pond filled with black water, runoff from a strip mine.

I've been told about the ten acres Grandpa leased for stripping. I've seen it before now, but I've not connected its location with the memory of my spring.

Gabriel wrinkles his nose at the rank water. "Are we going to drink that?" he asks.

"No" I say. "We're not going to drink that."

The best part of my childhood was spent on this farm here in eastern Kentucky. My dad worked in the mines then. Mom, Dad and me all lived here with Grandma and Grandpa. When I was ten Dad moved Mom and me to Dayton, Ohio. He got a job in a Frigidaire factory. He didn't stick with it though, or it didn't stick with him. After about a year we moved again, to Indianapolis, then the next year to Detroit, then to Pittsburgh, then to Cincinnati.

I'm not making out like those were bad years. We were not unhappy as a family, just unsettled like. I guess that being unsettled is what's kept with me most. Even after I married Cathy and we had our first kid, I couldn't be still. We've lived all over the midwest and even in California for a while, me taking whatever work I happened into, Cathy and little Gabriel dragging along behind. For a long while now, I've been scared of reliving my father's life.

The main thing I want is for my kids, Gabriel and the little one we have on the way, to know what it is to grow up in one place, to know one place as home.

Wherever we've lived, I've thought of the steep pasture behind the barn and Grandma's old milk cow standing under a shade tree still as a picture.

When Grandma died last year and left the farm to Dad, I scraped up all my savings and offered to buy him out. He said "no." It wasn't that he was going to come back and live here himself. Mom would've never left Cincinnati. But he didn't want to give up the idea of it.

"I know what you mean," I said. "How about I go live there and pay rent?"

He agreed to that. In a week we had packed all we cared for and made our move.

I've put in applications from here to Wayland. Whenever I go to look it's like I'm some kind of foreigner come in to take away somebody else's livelihood, somebody with more right to a living than me. When I speak these local boys roll their eyes at each other. They grunt and ask me where I'm from. I have to tell myself not to get mad. There's men who've lived here all their lives can't get any nearer a paycheck than me. There's talk of wage cuts and layoffs at the mines. Nobody's hiring.

I haven't worked in six weeks. I'm not likely to work in six more. When I first moved back, I gave myself to the end of summer to find a job. It's the middle of September now, and the days are cooling off. In another month the leaves will turn.

I was making fifteen dollars an hour hanging drywall in Cincinnati. Gabriel had gotten comfortable in his grade school. Cathy was training to be a nurse.

I think about these things we've given up. I think how Cathy didn't kick when I asked her to move, how she hasn't kicked yet.

A fellow I met at Garrett told me they were hiring at Silver Oak in Breathitt County. When I drove over the foreman told me he'd just laid off three men, but he'd heard that Allied was hiring in Harlan. When I drove to Harlan, I found some fellows in UMWA caps walking a picket line. I pulled up and said I'd heard they were hiring. One big miner with more beard than face leaned in my window. "Hiring scabs," he said and showed me the butt of a .44 stuck in his belt. I got out of there.

Some days I just drive around, see what all's changed in twenty years. There's one big strip site over on the Perry County end of Ball Branch that covers ten thousand acres, at least. One big knob of a mountain they're still honing down sticks up over Highway 80. It looks like one of those buttes you see out west.

I went camping one night just so I could sit on a ridge top and watch their dragline. The site is lit well enough that I could see it working from two miles off. The boom is as long as a football field. The bucket is big enough to park a Mack truck in. It runs off electricity, big generators inside a housing the size of a four story building. It runs day and night, raking up blasted rock and spill dirt, stripping down to the coal seams. God knows how many tons it's raked up. Just the sound of it is like some big monster come to eat up the world. I could run one if I got the chance.

There's rotten wood underneath the kitchen sink, loose stones in the chimney, and gas in the well water. Grandpa's chair, the couch, and some of the porch furniture has mold. I've stored it in the barn because I can't bear to put a match to any of it.

Cathy saw a black snake sunning itself on the rock border around her flower garden. She's had nightmares for three nights straight, seeing shadows and shapes on the bedroom walls. I tell her black snakes are good to have around. They eat mice and chase off the bad snakes. She wants me to kill it. I feel bad about the idea, but I sit on the porch with Grandpa's old twelve gauge, like I'm laying for it.

Cathy doesn't say she'd feel better suited elsewhere. I know it. She knows I know it. I'm not all the way used to this stuck-up-a-holler kind of life myself. Most times I love it, having a big garden to tend and miles of hills to hike and hunt in and a little creek for fishing and nobody around to bother me. Sometimes I'll step out on my porch in the middle of the night and let loose a big yell and feel like I've been set free from the world.

But there's times I wish my nearest neighbor wasn't a mile away, times I feel a little closed in by all the trees and mountains on every side. I'd like to go to the grocery without having to drive twenty miles. I'd like to get more than one channel on the TV without having to climb the mountain and reset the antenna every time the wind blows. I'd like not to have to truck my own garbage to the dump. I'd like to go to a baseball stadium and sit among the crowd. I worry about the only road in and out being so rocky and tore up I can barely drive it. I know I'll need a four-wheel drive this winter.

Sometimes I catch a whiff of cigarette smoke. It's a habit Cathy was supposed to quit when she got pregnant. I know it's only one or two once in a while, and I know it's just boredom and worry that makes her smoke. I hate to say anything.

Yesterday a neighbor brought us a peck of fresh picked green beans. Cathy cooked them with the strings still in. She didn't know. I didn't mean to criticize her, but I guess that's how it came out.

This morning I brought Grandma's quilting frames down from the attic and set them up in the living room. Cathy's been cutting out squares and studying pattern books for a week. When I came home, I found pieces of cloth scattered all over like they'd been caught in a tornado. Cathy was in bed. The room smelled of smoke.

"I have a headache," she said.

"How'd the quilting go?" I asked.

"I can't do it," she said.

Just before dark, I see the blacksnake crawling along the edge of the flower garden. There's enough light for me to see the white of his underside and to see him flick his tongue out. He lays on top of the rock border for a long time, poses there, like he's not alive but stuffed. When I shoot him in two, his severed halves leap up in a puff of dust and stone chips and flop among Cathy's marigolds.

Cathy comes outside when she hears the shot. When she puts her hand on my shoulder, her fingernail scrapes my neck a little, and I shiver. She goes back inside without speaking, and I know she thinks I'm mad at her for making me shoot the snake or for not being able to quilt or for not knowing to string green beans before she cooks them.

Jerry Everage is one of the few local boys who doesn't belong to the UMWA. I meet him one day in this little roadside tavern just beyond Wayland, and we get to be buddies over our beers.

"I don't believe in no unions," he says. "Them unions is just a gang of rogues, out for themselves. Time was they made sense, but no more. This day and time a man's got the right to work, whether he's union or not."

He's an all-right fellow, but I can see where his mouth might get him in trouble. When he clues me in on a chance to haul coal for Allied, I think first about that big miner with the .44. I think about being called a scab. Then I think, "Hell, a man does have the right to work if there is any." It feels good to tell Cathy I've found a job.

When I get in line to be loaded my first day in one of Allied's old Macks, a picket cracks my windshield with a piece of slate. There are off-duty county mounties and private guards hired to keep the union men back. They've cleared the barricade and made a way for us to drive through, but we still have to run a gauntlet of UMWA pickets. More than one rock bounces off my cab when I go out with my load.

It feels good to be driving a Mack truck, barreling down the highway, pulling my horn for any little boys that come out on the roadside to see me pass. The only times things get hot is around the mine, when I have to navigate through all those pickets. Some days their wives and kids come out with them and stand screaming obscenities, the worst I ever heard. Little kids and women. But then me and Jerry go drink beer after work, and he talks me into believing it's all right.

"Think about your own woman," he says, "your own kid."

I've set up empty oil cans on the rail fence between the pasture and hay bottom. Gabriel wants to shoot. The twelve gauge is going to kick more than he expects. I hunker down behind him as he takes aim, ready to brace him against the recoil. I sight over his shoulder, see the barrel waver, the gunsight dipping off the can. "Watch your aim," I say, and when I do he lowers the gun.

"I don't want to do it," he says.

"Why go ahead," I say. "There's nothing to it."

He hesitates but raises the gun again and aims. The barrel trembles as he tenses on the trigger. The sound of the shot rings my ears. The gunpowder burns my nose. Gabriel is moved back a step, but I haven't had to catch him. I see a puff of wood dust a little to the right of the oil can, then the can itself teeters and falls off the rail.

"How'd that feel?" I ask, taking the gun and breaching the barrel to pop out the shot casing. There's still a little cloud of gun smoke around us.

"What?" he asks. I realize his ears are ringing as much as mine, but he's smiling and rubbing his shoulder.

We walk over to the fence to find the can and count the shot holes.

"My ears are ringing," he shouts. He's still grinning.

"Mine are too," I say. "That gun kicks hard, don't it?"

He rubs his shoulder. "Not too bad," he says.

We count seven shot holes in the can. Gabriel is so happy he hit it that he wants to shoot again. He shoots better each time, and as we're walking home he wants to know if he can have his own gun and if we can go hunting sometime. I tell him squirrel season opens in a few weeks. He gets excited at the idea. I worry how Cathy will take to him hunting or even just shooting a gun. Guns mean something different to her than they do to me. That comes from her growing up in the city. I understand how she feels.

Supper is ready when we get home. We sit at the kitchen table and eat fried corn and boiled potatoes and green beans and yellow cornbread and sliced tomatoes and cucumbers. With all this good garden food, I don't even miss the meat we've not been having. My first paycheck caught us up on our bills a little, but there'll be no splurging for a while.

The evening cool enters the house through the open windows. Moths gather on the screens. Gabriel brags on his shooting while Cathy and I sneak grins at one other. I've not seen Cathy so cheerful since our move. It's like a light has come back on inside her. I know it's from having money again and feeling like we got some control in our lives. We talk about names for the baby and about what we still need to do to the house before it's born. She talks about finishing her nurse's training. She's already looked into a program she could drive to just over in Pikeville. We go onto the porch and sit listening to the night sounds—the crickets and frogs and night birds. Who knows what all? We watch bats flock into the sky, listen to them squeak as they hunt the swarms of gnats and mosquitoes.

I want to hug Cathy and Gabriel in my arms and say, "See what a good life we have here." Instead, I just rock real easy in Grandpa's rocking chair and don't make a sound for fear of breaking this spell we've come under.

After about an hour Cathy pushes herself up from her chair. I think how much she is starting to show from the baby. "It's time for bed," she says.

Gabriel and I say "okay" in the same breath, though I linger on the porch for a while, smoking one of Cathy's cigarettes for an excuse. When I finally go inside, I leave the door open, to air the house and keep it cool.

Teddy Sloane is about a third cousin on my daddy's side. I barely recognize him the day he comes to visit. He's bald and years older looking than his actual age, which is the same as mine. He wears a big beard that's like a dried-out bush hanging down his chest, his face framed by black horn-rimmed glasses.

"Don't you know me?" he asks, and I shake his hand like he's my long-lost brother, but there's truthfully not much in his face I remember from when we were little boys.

We visit for a while, then he asks me if I could help him tear down an old storage building on his place. I'm reluctant at first. It's Saturday, and I want to listen to a ball game on the radio with Gabriel, but I say all right. It's the best investment of time I've ever made. I salvage enough wood to fix our kitchen floor and get Teddy to come over the next weekend and help me carpenter.

I tell Cathy that Teddy is the best hand to work I've ever seen. He hardly ever speaks. Sometimes I'll forget he's even there and just got caught up in the job, and when I look over at him he'll be hammering away, never a letup. It's almost religious to watch him go at it.

The barn roof is our latest project. If I'm ever to have livestock or keep hay, I'll need to patch it enough to hold out the weather. I'm for just a quick fix, but Teddy wants it done right.

Gabriel will stand and hold our ladders or bring us nails or dropped hammers or drinks of water. I look up one day and he's standing on the top rung of the ladder with a roll of tin on his shoulder. I hold back telling him to get down. He's not the same boy I brought down here. I admire the change in him.

Some weekends Jerry Everage comes over to help, though most of what he does is drink beer and supervise. Sometimes he brings a little bag of dope that him and me smoke on when Gabriel's not around. He slows us down with all his talk, but what he takes away in work he makes up in entertainment value.

Jerry's an expert on whatever comes to mind. I'll argue back and forth just for the fun of it. Teddy mostly tries to ignore him. But sometimes I'll hear a big sigh or groan over something Jerry has said.

"Man's got the right to work." Jerry says. "It's un-American them unions trying to keep him from it." Same old speech.

Once in a while Teddy will try to dispute what Jerry is saying. I think more than anything he just gets tired of hearing Jerry run his mouth. "I kindly disagree," he'll say. Teddy is so soft-spoken it's hard to make him out, but Jerry will shut right up and listen hard. Then, when Teddy's had his say, Jerry will start back in right where he left off.

It's a relief when Cathy takes up with Teddy's wife. In some ways they're complete opposites. Lori's about as country as it gets. She's big boned and meaty and backwards talking, and she's not been out of eastern Kentucky her whole life, even to go to Lexington or Kingsport. In some ways they're a lot alike though. Lori has the busiest hands I've ever seen on a person. It's like if she can't keep them occupied they'll fly off like birds. That's how her and Cathy are alike. If Cathy's not occupied with something she gets so down on herself you can't live with her. Lori's been teaching Cathy to piece quilts and sew and make shucky beans. They'll sit together and talk and work at something a whole day.

The second weekend of October, we all go over to Teddy and Lori's place to pick apples. It's a sunny weekend. The fall leaves are at their peak colors—deep red and yellow and gold—and every time the wind blows a few more will fly into the air and swirl around.

Teddy and Lori have about a dozen trees of red and yellow Delicious. They've had a good year. The tree limbs are just about broke down with apples, and a bunch have already fallen off. We have to be careful of the yellow jackets swarming around the rotten ones.

Gabriel chases around the orchard with Teddy's two boys for a while, then we all pick apples. We pick twenty bushels from the limbs we can reach, then Teddy and I climb up in the tops of the trees and shake the branches. I almost fall out from laughing at everybody running from all those falling apples. Old Teddy is feeling so good, he stands up on a branch and squalls like a wild cat while he shakes it.

When we pick up what we've shook off, we have another ten bushels, and there's still more on the ground and in the trees. I catch Gabriel with his head turned and let him have it with a big mushy rotten apple. He's surprised at first, but it doesn't take him long to catch on. By the time we quit our battle, we're all covered in rotten apple mush. It's that kind of day.

It's almost another month before things turn sour. One day when I'm riding empty back to the tipple, I run into a state police roadblock. They motion me into the passing lane then escort me, one cruiser in front and one behind, all the way to Allied's. Just before the tipple, I see Jerry Everage's big red Mack sitting catty-cornered to the highway, like it'd been halfway wrecked. I try to slow down and take a look, but the cruiser behind me hits its siren to move me on. I make out that the windshield is busted, and I'm not so sure but what I don't see bullet holes in the driver's door. I get a little queasy in my stomach.

The UMWA men have backed off their pickets. They're mostly sitting on the hoods and tailgates of their pickups a ways off from the state police barricade. They're smoking, chewing, trading knives to put off their unease. I know that most of them are innocent, but they all look guilty.

The troopers lead me into the main office. The non-union mining crew that was on shift and most of the truckers are crowded in with the foremen and bosses. Everyone talks in soft voices, like at a funeral. We're told how somebody peppered

Jerry Everage's truck with an Uzi. An Uzi! How in the hell? Then he just run on off, whoever the hell it was.

We hear some more stuff like how this company doesn't give in to terrorism. How we're all a brave lot of men doing a difficult job. When I stand up and say, "I've done my military service," about a dozen fellows follow me out.

Jerry has already been discharged by the time I get to the hospital. He must not of been hurt much, if at all. He lit out for who knows where.

When I get home, I find Gabriel sitting on the porch with the twelve gauge in his lap. He's so serious looking, I almost grin. I never thought they'd hear the news before I got home. I never thought to call.

Cathy has cried till her eyes are red. She's pale, and I'm afraid she's about to pass out. I worry for the baby. We go round and round for a little while, but my heart's not in it. By the time Cathy's had her say, any thought I might have had of going back to Allied is out the window.

From where I sit on the pasture ridge, I can see just about the whole valley. The creek runs through the middle. The highway runs next to the creek. Houses are situated all along the road and the creek bank, like they've been washed up in a flood.

The sun is just coming up over the ridges. It makes a line as it moves down the mountains, like a border between night and day. The leaves have all turned their fall colors now, and with the sun shining like it is this morning, there's no prettier place on this earth. In another week all the trees will be bare, and when I climb up here, all I'll see is where the hills have been strip-mined.

Teddy says for me to sign up on welfare and draw food stamps. He says I qualify. Before I do that I'll pull up and head back north, stay with Mom and Dad until we're on our feet again. I could subcontract some drywall jobs or work construction. I know people still. I hate giving up on this place, though. I would like to tough it out. I would like to settle.

Sometimes I daydream about that pony I had when I was a little boy. I imagine I'm riding her fast across a bottom full of timothy. The timothy is almost ready for cutting and swishes against my legs as we gallop through. It's like we're flying, we go so fast. Sometimes I wonder if this is the same place I remember.

There's a dog barking somewhere. I hear the blast of a shotgun—some hunter up early or out late. I smell wood smoke, see it trailing out of a few chimneys. I think how a good store of firewood would cut down on my heating bills. I watch the sunlight make its way in a line down the mountains and think about the day we picked apples with Teddy and Lori and the day Gabriel shot his first gun. I think about the cold of winter to come.

Clouds

PAUL GRINER

Born in Boston and raised in upstate New York, Paul Griner has lived in Louisville, Kentucky, and taught writing at the University of Louisville since the mid 1990s. He earned a bachelor's degree in history at the University of New Hampshire, a master's in modern romance languages and literature at Harvard, and a master's in creative writing at Syracuse (where he won the Raymond Carver Prize for best short story by a graduate student). A former carpenter, painter, tour guide, and truck driver, as well as a Fulbright Scholar, he is the author of *Follow Me* (stories, 1996) and *Collectors* (a novel, 1999). His stories have appeared in various publications, including *Story*, *Playboy*, *Ploughshares*, *Zoetrope: All-Story*, *The Graywolf Annual Four*, and *Kentucky Voices*.

In a *Library Journal* review of *Follow Me*, Janet Ruth Heller notes that "Griner's protagonists—aloof fathers, exploitative artists, working-class rogues, and drifters—are usually obsessed with something (fingernails, grass, clouds, revenge) and have trouble connecting with other people. Often, they are older men looking back on their lives with new insight." Published originally in *Bomb* magazine in 1996 and collected in *Follow Me*, "Clouds" portrays an aging man coming to terms with his having been a distant father. It is a story of loss and consolation, of an individual's need to identify with a spot of ground and to find meaning in the ephemeral, whether it be the past or the clouds.

◆

I know all about clouds: cumulus, stratus, nimbostratus, cumulonimbus. It doesn't take much water to make most of them. A small summer cumulus a few hundred yards to a side holds no more than twenty-five or thirty gallons of water, not quite enough to fill a bathtub. Years ago, my wife miscarried. I still remember the bright triangle of blood on the back of her nightdress. Fourteen months later she delivered a boy at Rochester General, dead at birth. I never saw him, and we didn't give him a funeral. I never asked, but I believe stillborn babies are simply thrown away, or at least they were then. Afterward, we had two girls, five years apart, but never another boy. The dead one was recompense, I believe, for not wanting that first child.

Once a week I lie out in a farmer's field, beneath a copper beech high up on one of his hills, and classify all the passing clouds. I know what weather they'll bring, today and tomorrow, how they formed, and where. To do this undisturbed I pay the farmer thirty dollars a week, cash. I have for fifty-five years. My wife's name was Stan. She died fifteen years ago, and I had her cremated. I told my daughters that that was what their mother wanted, though it wasn't. I liked the idea of her smoke and ashes drifting up to the clouds.

Elise, my oldest, wonders about that thirty dollars, and wants to cut me off from spending it. I know this because I have heard her whispering to Gwen over the phone. My memory is going, Elise says, which is true in spots—sometimes I repeat myself—and she feels I must be losing the money or being fleeced because I have no real expenses, which is true, too, to a degree. But my hearing is just fine.

The farmer's name is Stillson, like the wrenches. He's about that skinny, too. He has a dozen years on me and the only real sign is his neck, which has deteriorated so badly talking with him is like talking with a turtle; his head always droops. Not that we talk much. We never have.

I wandered into his field after the miscarriage. I came home from the hospital and cleaned up the blood on the bathtub and the bathroom floor and went to bed, disoriented from two days without sleep and still afraid Stan might die. And I realized, for the first time, that our child—if that's what it was at five months—was gone. I couldn't say dead because I hadn't ever thought of him or her as alive, really, but nonetheless it was gone. This was a sharp knowledge. Learning it, I felt as if someone had peeled back my skin and muscle and ribs to grasp and bind my heart.

Lying on the bed, staring into the corner of the room, I knew I wouldn't sleep, so I got in the car and drove a while, turning right, left, whichever way I felt like or the road seemed to want to go or the car to follow. I went through the city and then beyond it, past miles of infrequent houses and barns and abandoned garages, and eventually ended up by this field, Stillson's, where I left the car and wandered up the hill and fell down exhausted beneath this copper beech, which was impressive even then.

Stillson woke me, prodding my shoulder with a muddy boot. I don't know what he thought—probably that I was drunk, because I was in his field and my car was half on the road, half against his fence, the driver's door open, the engine running. He seemed rather gruff. Coming to, I remembered that I'd watched the clouds for a long time and found them peaceful, found they filled some of the void that opened when I realized our child was gone, and had finally been able to sleep. I told Stillson I'd pay him thirty dollars a week from then on if he'd leave the small field exactly the way it was, and if I could come and lie there whenever I wanted to.

That was a lot of money back then. It still is, I suppose. Stillson, being the quiet type, never asked what it was for. He's taken his money and held up his end of the bargain, and I've just about never missed a week where I don't come and lie here for an hour or two in good weather, and sometimes in bad. Once a year, on the miscarriage's anniversary, I sprinkle a few more of Stan's ashes on the grass.

Perhaps it's the clouds' impermanence I find so comforting. Always changing, they can't hold grudges or bitter memories, and their shapes don't echo the ground they've covered. Even lenticular clouds, the dish-shaped cumulus over mountaintops that appear stationary for hours, are an illusion. Water molecules rise up one side of the mountain, blown by the wind, condense and enter the cloud, displacing other water, which blows down the far side and evaporates. The cloud is always moving, no more stationary than a river flowing through a lake.

I go to Stillson's field in all weathers: rain, heat, snow, fog. Fog, which is just clouds touching the ground, doesn't hold much water, either. Walking one hundred yards through fog, you'll only come in contact with half a glassful. I don't mind lying out in it. Winters I get stiff fast and have to leave, summers chiggers bite me, or ants or mosquitoes or flies. Just last week my doctor ran his fingers over a crescent of bites on my collarbone and told me I ought to have my bed linen changed more often. I got dressed and said I would, and let it go at that, but I maintained the memory of his fingers on my skin for hours, like a burn. No one has touched my chest since Stan died.

My daughter Elise wonders about the grass she finds on my collar from time to time. Stan never did. She may not have seen it, since we always had our laundry done. Elise says that's a waste of money, and she does mine herself, in fits and starts. If she hasn't done it for a month I send it out and when she sees the laundry tags she gets angry. She shows this by not talking to me while she cleans the house. Days I went to the field I told Stan I was golfing, as I did every other day of the week, and my friends lied for me. Of them, only Bitz is still alive, and he's not much good anymore. Last year he stopped me at the club. He'd bought a new hearing aid and said it had changed his life. He could hear things he couldn't when he was twenty. I steadied him by his elbow and looked right at him, a habit I'd acquired in the long years before the hearing aid, and said, "That's good, Bitz."

He checked his wrist and said, "It's three forty-five, since you asked."

With the few other old club members I see we don't talk so much as have an organ review: which ones work, which ones don't, whether we're going to get some replaced. Toward the end of Stan's life she used to check the obituaries every morning before going to play bridge, to see if her game was still on.

She got her name as a baby. Her brother wanted a brother, and thought she'd turn into a boy if he called her Stan. I started calling her that as a joke, and then somehow it became part of our intimate vocabulary, and then our public one. That happened with a few words or phrases over the years, *tinkle, toot,* others. It's funny how that works: you soak up the world like a cloud soaks up water, and you sprinkle little drops of yourself here and there. If someone collected them all, he might be able to tell what you were really like.

You can think of clouds as air movement made visible. On warm summer days, with the sky blue, pure white clouds widely spaced, each cloud represents small, scattered rising air currents. Today the clouds are round like coins. We always had a lot of money. Perhaps that was our downfall. We were used to traveling a lot, and when Stan first told me she was pregnant I thought it would be the end of the lives we'd led. I was selfish.

"What should we do?" she said, sitting across from me at dinner at the Algonquin, in New York, where we liked to travel weekends. A vast expanse of white linen, silver, and Limoges china, palm fronds in hammered brass urns, endless bottles of champagne, a jazz trio discreet and unobtrusive. I remember each of these details now, as if I studied them daily in a photograph. I looked at her, searched her serious face. Her eyes seemed to be pulling back; she seemed a long way from the life we'd lived, and I thought I knew what she wanted me to say. I don't think I wanted to say it, not really, but all these years later I can't tell if that's true or just wishful thinking. I turned over a fork and pressed my fingertip between the tines. "We could fix it," I said. Instantly, my stomach clenched. I wished I'd never spoken. Stan's eyes narrowed, the only sign of her disapproval, the only sign that she'd even heard me, for the band started up right after and we danced as we always had, as if the spotlight were on us and the world were watching. It seemed to be, then. Sometimes, recalling that dance, I think I already felt her distance as I held her, like she'd shrunk within her skin.

I remember that first day Stillson took my money without counting it—he never has, at least in my presence—and broke off a sprig of grass and chewed the sweet end for a minute while looking up at the sky.

"All right," he said. "But don't stay too long." He took the grass from his mouth and pointed it at some wispy cirrus above a range of hills. The sun shining through them made halos. "Those clouds over there mean rain."

That's what interested me, I guess. How he knew. I asked him, and he said, "It's the air's smell, partly, but mostly it's the clouds' shape. Feathery like that means a storm's coming."

It didn't look like it to me: they were only a few threads, miles up, and the rest of the sky was blue. I saw my first sun dogs, looking at them. But in two hours the sky was gray, the ground soaked from the rain.

So I started reading about clouds. I read Joshua Howard's works, the Englishman who first noted cloud differences and recognizable types, and every other book I could get my hands on. I read, I watched, I read some more. Soon I seemed to know as much as anybody about them. Those cirrus Stillson pointed out are always the first heralds of a coming storm, warm air pushing up over cold, expanding into clouds. Bitz and company, covering for me, thought I had a kept woman somewhere. They noticed my devotion. They kidded me about it—not often, but enough to show they were curious and wanted me to tell. I never did.

I have seen pink clouds and blue ones and orange ones, and—near a volcano—pure white clouds rimmed black with ash. I know about wind shear and tornadoes and waterspouts. I've traveled the world to see peculiar clouds: pink bubblelike ones over Borneo Bay, which occur only at the solstices; rainbow clouds above Victoria Falls; the towering thunderheads of Oklahoma. And once, a dark, perfectly round cloud over the sun, encircled by a rainbow. The sun shone through the cloud's center, like the light through an ophthalmologist's scope. This was right here in Stillson's field. But I've never seen anything someone else hasn't seen.

You'd think, as I'm forgetting things these days, I'd forget the money for Stillson, too, but I won't. That's from too long ago. Nearer things elude me, like my glasses. I went to the same optometrist two days in a row and picked out two pairs of glasses, the second so I wouldn't be in trouble if I lost the first, and the bastard sold me all four pairs. Halfway through paying for the third and fourth I remembered buying the first two, and I looked into the little fellow's eyes and saw that he knew, too, and had all along. I was too embarrassed to say anything. He cradled a Styrofoam coffee cup in both hands and he looked into it when he quoted me the price, as if he were reading it from the cup's bottom.

I wrote myself a note: "Next time you need glasses, get them at Optico, 621 East Ave," and pinned it to the wall by the front door. I may not remember why by then, but at least the little runt won't get any more of my money. Stillson's field I can't forget.

My daughters remember other things, especially Elise, who stops by often. Gwen lives out of town, and I see her no more than every few years. Once I told Elise how Stan and I wanted to play bridge at a friend's house when she was three months old. Both the cook and Blossom, our nursemaid, had the day off. We couldn't find a sitter, so we put Elise in a bureau drawer and shut it, leaving it open just a crack for air. She wouldn't have remembered, of course, but I told her anyway, to give her anger some focus.

A gift from a father who was not the best of one. We weren't taught to be, then. Servants brought up the children. Besides, the only person I ever fully loved was Stan. I have come close with Elise: I stopped drinking years ago because she asked me to, and when she vacations I find myself counting off days on my calendar, awaiting her return. She has been able to make me laugh, times when she's not too full of herself. Stan, I think, wanted a boy too. Maybe one she could raise to stand up to things in a way his father never did.

My father beat me every Saturday morning, and my mother died very young. She had vapors—she drank too much—and spent afternoons making long lists of European royalty and their favorite foods, as if they might stop by for supper. A gold-tipped fountain pen in cobalt-blue ink, that's what she wrote with, and I've never seen more graceful writing in all my life. I used to retrieve the crumpled lists from the trash bin and trace out the perfect curves and angles of her script, and writing letters now, I still sense her presence on my pages. Handwriting aside, hers was a hollow pursuit, to say the least, and I sometimes wonder if I'm not guilty of the same thing.

Losing Stan's presence was bad enough; losing our shared history was worse. Old jokes that no one else understood or thought funny; nicknames we'd given friends; places we'd eaten or made love. The first hotel we stayed in had a beaten copper pot for a sink. The smell of diesel bus fumes in the morning, or the perfume of oranges and apples set to bake on a woodstove, or the tang of gin and tonics on a sunny patio above the sea—all these had precise meanings for us, which lost their significance in this world when she died.

Before she went, I wanted to ask Stan if she remembered what I'd said at the Algonquin all those years before. She didn't bring it up after the miscarriage—all she cared about was getting pregnant again, which we did shortly—or after the stillbirth. At least not immediately. Then a year or two later, in the midst of a terrible fight, which began as a disagreement about new fabric for a wall covering, she said, "Well, if you don't like it, you can just 'fix it,' right?" she was standing across the room from me, furiously scratching the underside of one forearm, turning the skin a glowing red. I hadn't realized words could come out sounding so cold.

She pretended at first not to understand why I was upset. Later, after we had made up and made love, she said she'd done it to hurt me, which she had. She'd been wanting to get back at me for a long time, she explained, her head on my chest, her fingers knotted in my hair. I could smell the walnut oil from her shampoo. We were silent for a while—I saw the crescent moon enter and pass across our window—and when I asked if she would always feel that way she didn't answer: asleep, or feigning it. I listened to her breathing for hours.

I didn't have the courage to bring it up again before she died. What if she did remember, and that was what she would take of me to her grave, the memory of my failure at the one great test in my life? I preferred the illusion of the possibility of hope.

I almost envy Elise. Her husband had no money. She said she hated it, the crying, the yelling about bills, the kids underfoot. She could have used help, like we had. For three years she didn't read a book, and she felt like a telephone pole covered with creepers, the way the kids always grabbed her. She could never keep her floors clean. But every Tuesday she has dinner with her son, who lives a block away from her, fixes her car, brings her lilacs and tulips, calls her most nights after work. Her daughter writes twice a week from college. Neither of ours wrote us once in four years. Perhaps I'd feel differently about my children if I'd spent more time with them. I'm not indifferent to them, though that must be how it seems. Nor do I hold their coldness against me: they're paying me back in kind. It's just as well, I suppose. They don't follow me around, demanding that I account for my time. I don't want anyone else at Stillson's.

I still dream sometimes in French. Years ago, my father took me to France for summers, left me with a family in a small provincial town. No one there spoke any English, not even in the family I stayed with. Great pink camellias floated in glass bowls filled with water all through their house, cut from trees in their garden. I would stand looking up at the flowers' cupped shape through the water. I was five when we started this, nine when we stopped. The war. The Great One. I didn't know about clouds then. I wish I had. I might have noticed a difference between the air over France and my native sky. Saturday nights, the whole town went to the cinema. At intermission, everyone filed out into the village square, the men and boys on one side, the women and girls on the other. There was a small fountain in between, water splashing in the dark, the mossy bricks surrounding it damp and slippery, crickets calling from fragrant rows of wild mint. We would do our business against the wall, the women and girls watching, and then we'd all file back in and see the end of the movie.

Stan got involved in charity golf events. I thought once she was having an affair, the way Ray encircled her with his arms, showing her how to swing the club just so, the way she smiled up at him, leaned back into his chest. A sharp knowledge, but it didn't last. Ray was the club pro. I thought about it, thought about following her even, but realized she didn't have time for an affair. When she said she went to lunch with her friends, she had to go; they were always at the club. Bitz's wife was there, too. I would have heard. Nights she was with me. Movies, parties, the theater, sometimes the symphony. Twice a year we traveled. That's when I saw those different clouds.

I would read about them in a cloud atlas, study their forms—drawn, mostly, but photographed more recently—and decide which ones I wanted to see. I never chose, really, just let the knowledge come to me. I'd flip through the pages, not thinking, and something would strike me, a line, a certain cast of light, and I'd know: these were the clouds I wanted to see next. I'd look up where they were prevalent, and when, and get travel literature for the place, and convince Stan we should go. Most often that wasn't hard. Stan liked to travel. We'd visit museums, find good restaurants—duck, veal, skewered lamb rubbed with lemon and garlic and wrapped in bacon, all of which Stan loved—write letters to our friends. Stan, I'd say, I've always wanted to go to Borneo. She never remarked that I hadn't brought up this burning desire before. Sometimes I wondered if that indicated a lack of attention to what I said, because she didn't care; other times I hoped it meant she accepted my eccentricities, or loved the idea that she didn't know everything about me even after fifteen or twenty years of marriage.

Getting to see the thunderheads of Oklahoma I had to work on. I couldn't say I'd always wanted to go to Oklahoma, and once there, I had to beg her to go up in a plane with me, to fly right into them. The pilot was no problem. He doubled his fee. I was scared, secretly, that we wouldn't come back, and I wanted her with me, just in case. Not for comfort, but because years before, when we'd first started flying, we agreed we would always fly together, so that if something happened neither of us would be left behind. She didn't seem to remember that then, staring out the window at the swirling darkness, and I didn't bring it up. I wanted her to remember it on her own, and I didn't want her to disavow it. Perhaps it was another mooring line she'd cast adrift.

I remember scenes from all those years at odd times—reading the paper or checking the mail, I suddenly see myself walking past Lisbon bakeries in the heat of the day, or driving up the coastal highway under a violet dusk, a full moon rising over a stand of pines, or sitting dockside near some lake, water lapping, air crisp, a high wind blowing a few crimson leaves over the water. Sometimes light sets off the memories, sometimes smell. Our children appear in a few, not many. If I think hard I can often figure out the connections. Once, turning the soil in our garden, preparing it for bulbs, I remembered going into a dark, narrow shoe store in Autoire with Stan, where the cobbler measured her feet thirteen different ways. We spent an hour sorting through leather samples. She had six pairs made and mourned the passing of each one. The scene appeared as vivid as a movie in my mind, her fingers flipping through the leather, the smell of the tanned hides. After, I decided it was the light— a certain dull slant to it through the deep green leaves that meant it had to be an early fall afternoon. In spring, the same slanting light would be yellower. That night, after looking up the trip in one of my journals and discovering that we had indeed taken it during the fall, I mentioned the memory to Stan. She said that that afternoon, at about the time I'd been working in the garden, she remembered the same trip, though a different part. She'd found her pearl earrings on a windowsill. Picking them up, she saw herself buying them at L'Auberge, and wearing them that same night for a dinner in a small restaurant we saw starred in the Michelin guide a year later. I miss those odd coincidences. Perhaps there was nothing to them, but they seemed a sign of our love.

Mostly those years blur together. The country club, trips, the children in school and then in college, Stillson's field, books of clouds, Stan filling the house with flowers every week. She liked pink tulips on the polished black surface of the piano.

I don't have sharp memories of her physical presence now, and I can't hear her voice, consciously, though I do in my dreams, and unless I concentrate I can't make her move. All the movements she made, all the ones I watched her make for years: walking, skiing, arching above me, and I can't see any of them in my mind's eye. Only her lips move in the images I conjure up, though silently, and her face, turning away from me.

She was sick for five years at the end, and both of us knew what it meant. Sitting beside her in the last weeks I remembered that years before, one warm summer night soon after we'd moved out of the city, a place I thought had too many bad memories, we were lying in bed and Stan said, "I don't know where I'll go when I die." I said, "Nobody does," and jabbed her shoulder lightly.

"That's not what I mean." She pulled the curtain aside and looked out at the street. Crickets chirped, the pavement glowed yellow in the street light, the heat seemed to settle. Half her face was highlighted. "I mean I have no place to be buried. Everyone else in my family is together but there's no room anymore, and besides, I wouldn't want to be with them." She seemed inconsolable, and her words punctured me. I couldn't speak. We never talked about that toward the end. It's just as well, I suppose. It made cremation easier.

Stillson had a son. He was a quiet boy. I would often see them walking the fields together, Stillson pointing out to him airplanes or the way dust whirled before the wind. When they crossed the fields toward me, Stillson walked with his hand on the boy's shoulder. The boy would never come close. He stood by a fence post, watching, always the same one. There's a dent in it even now I swear his shoulder made. He died in the war. The week Stillson got the news was the only week he didn't come. We'd had six days of nimbostratus clouds that week, unusual for these parts, and I thought Stillson was worried about too much rain.

The next week, he wouldn't take the money from the week before.

The fence post is still there. From time to time I see Stillson rub it absently as he passes, as if it might bring him luck. I wonder if he even knows he's doing it.

Years may go by. I remember you too clearly. I wonder if Stan didn't, too. I lie back, feel the grass, springy beneath my shoulders, tickling my neck. There's not a cloud in the sky, just the blue heavens, arching and empty.

Barred Owl

CHRIS OFFUTT

Born in 1958 in Haldeman, Kentucky, a clay-mining town, Chris Offutt earned a B.A. in theater at Morehead State University and an M.F.A. at the University of Iowa. His books to date include a novel, *The Good Brother* (1997); a memoir, *The Same River Twice* (1993); and two short story collections, *Kentucky Straight* (1992) and *Out of the Woods* (1999). The recipient of a Guggenheim Fellowship, a James Michener Grant, an award from the American Academy of Arts and Letters, and one of *Granta*'s 20 Best Young American Fiction Writers, Offutt has published stories in *Esquire, GQ, DoubleTake, The Oxford American, Story,* and elsewhere. His story "Melungeons" was reprinted in *Best American Short Stories,* and several others have appeared in that annual's list of "Distinguished Stories of the Year." He has lived in New York, Massachusetts, Montana, New Mexico, and Paris, France. In 1998, he, his two sons, and his wife, Rita, moved to Rowan County, Kentucky, where he taught creative writing at Morehead State. They currently live in Iowa City, where he is a visiting faculty member at the Iowa Writers' Workshop and completing a third collection of stories.

In a review of *Out of the Woods*, Frederick Smock notes Offutt's central theme: "Throughout these stories there runs a tension—taut as a trip-wire—between staying and going. But it's also not that simple. More often it's a matter of getting thrown out and not having any place to go back to, or longing to go but not having the gumption." The stories, Smock continues, are "about our connection to the land, and what happens when that connection is stretched beyond what love or remembrance can bear." "Barred Owl" exemplifies this struggle. First published in *DoubleTake* in 1996 and included in *Out of the Woods*, the story portrays the long reach of home and some of the consequences of living out of its range or denying its call.

◆

Seven years ago I got divorced and left Kentucky, heading west. I made the Mississippi River in one day, and it just floored me how big it was. I watched the water until sundown. It didn't seem like a river, but a giant brown muscle instead. Two days later, my car threw a rod and I settled in Greeley, Colorado. Nobody in my family has lived this far off our home hill.

I took a job painting dorm rooms at the college here in town. The pay wasn't the best, but I could go to work hungover and nobody bugged me. I liked the quiet of working alone. I went into a room and made it a different color. The walls and the ceiling hadn't gone anywhere, but it was a new place. Only the view from the window stayed the same. What I did was never look out.

Every day after work I stopped by the Pig's Eye, a bar with cheap draft, a pool table, and a jukebox. It was the kind of place to get drunk in safely, because the law watched student bars downtown. The biggest jerk in the joint was the bartender. He liked to throw people out. You could smoke reefer in the Pig, gamble and fight, but if you drank too much, you were barred. That always struck me odd—like throwing someone out of a hospital for being sick.

Since my social life was tied to the Pig, I was surprised when a man came to the house one Saturday afternoon. That it was Tarvis surprised me even more. He's from eastern Kentucky, and people often mentioned him, but we'd never met. His hair was short and his beard was long. I invited him in.

"Thank ye, no," he said.

I understood that he knew I was just being polite, that he wouldn't enter my house until my welcome was genuine. I stepped outside, deliberately leaving the door open. What happened next was a ritual the likes of which I'd practically forgotten, but once it began, felt like going home with an old girlfriend you happened to meet in a bar.

We looked each other in the eyes for a spell.

Tarvis nodded slightly.

I nodded slightly.

He opened a pouch of Red Man and offered a chew.

I declined and began the slow process of lighting a cigarette while he dug a wad of tobacco from the pouch.

I flicked the match away, and we watched it land.

He worked his chew and spat, and we watched it hit in the grass. Our hands were free. We'd shown that our guard was down enough to watch something besides each other.

"Nice house," he said.

"I rent."

"Weather ain't too awful bad this spring."

"Always use rain."

"Keep dogs?" he said.

"Used to."

"Fish?"

"Every chance I get."

He glanced at me and quickly away. It was my turn now. If you don't hear an accent you lose it, and just being around him made me talk like home.

"Working hard?" I said.

"Loafing."

"Get home much?"

"Weddings and funerals."

"I got it down to funerals myself," I said.

"Only place I feel at home anymore is the graveyard."

He spat again, and I stubbed out my cigarette. A half moon had been hanging in the sky since late afternoon as if waiting for its chance to move.

"Hunt?" he asked.

I spat then, a tiny white dab near his darker pool, mine like a star, his an eclipse. I hadn't hunted since moving here. Hunters in the West used four-wheel-drive go-carts with a gunrack on the front and a cargo bin behind. They lived in canvas wall-tents that had woodstoves and cots. I'd seen them coming and going like small armies in the mountains. People at home hunted alone on foot. Tarvis looked every inch a hunter and I decided not to get into it with him.

"Not like I did," I said.

He nodded and looked at me straight on, which meant the reason for his visit was near.

"Skin them out yourself?" he said.

I nodded.

"Come by my place tomorrow, then."

He gave me directions and drove away, his arm hanging out the window. I figured he needed help dressing out a deer. I'm not big on poaching but with the deer already dead, refusing to help meant wasting the meat.

I headed for the bar, hoping to meet a woman. The problem with dating in a college town is that the young women are too young, and the older ones usually have kids. I've dated single mothers but it's hard to know if you like the woman or the whole package. A ready-made home can look awful good. Women with kids tell me it's just as tricky for them. Men figure they're either hunting a full-time daddy or some overnight action, with nothing in between.

This night was the usual Pig crowd, my friends of seven years. I drank straight shots and at last call ordered a couple of doubles. I'd started out drinking to feel good but by the end I was drinking not to feel anything. During the drive home I had to look away from the road to prevent the center stripe from splitting. I fixed that by straddling it. In the morning I woke fully dressed on my couch.

Four cigarettes and a cup of coffee later I felt alive enough to visit Tarvis. He lived below town on a dirt road beside the South Platte River. I veered around a dead raccoon with a tire trench cut through its guts. There were a couple of trailers and a few small houses. Some had outdoor toilets. At Tarvis's house I realized why the area seemed both strangely foreign and familiar. It was a little version of eastern Kentucky, complete with woodpiles, cardboard windows, and a lousy road. The only thing missing was hills.

I'd woke up still drunk and now that I was getting sober, the hangover was coming on. I wished I'd brought some beer. I got nervous that Tarvis had killed his deer in a hard place and needed help dragging it out of the brush. I didn't think I could take it. What I needed was to lie down for a while.

Tarvis came around the house from the rear.

"Hidy," he said. "Ain't too awful late, are ye?"

"Is it on the property?"

He led me behind the house to a line of cottonwoods overlooking the river's floodplain. A large bag lay on a work table. Tarvis reached inside and very gently, as if handling eggs, withdrew a bird. The feathers on its chest made a pattern of brown and white—a barred owl. Its wings spanned four feet. The head feathers formed a widow's peak between the giant eyes. It had a curved yellow beak and inch-long talons. Tarvis caressed its chest.

"Beaut, ain't it?" he said. "Not a mark to her."

"You kill it?"

"No. Found it on the interstate up by Fort Morgan. It hit a truck or something. Neck's broke."

The sun had risen above the trees, streaming heat and light against my face. Owls were protected by the government. Owning a single feather was illegal, let alone the whole bird.

"I want this pelt," Tarvis said.

"Never done a bird."

"You've skinned animals out. Can't be that big a difference."

"Why don't you do it yourself then?'

Tarvis backstepped as an expression close to guilt passed across his face.

"I never skinned nothing," he said. "Nobody taught me on account of I never pulled the trigger. I was raised to it, but I just wasn't able."

I looked away to protect his dignity. His words charged me with a responsibility I couldn't deny, the responsibility of Tarvis's shame. Leaving would betray a confidence that had taken a fair share of guts to tell.

I felt dizzy, but I rolled my sleeves up and began with the right leg. Surrounding the claws were feathers so dense and fine that they reminded me of fur. To prevent tearing the papery skin, I massaged it off the meat. Tarvis stood beside me. I held the owl's body and slowed turned it, working the skin free. My arms cooled from the breeze, and I could smell the liquor in my sweat. The hangover was beginning to lift. I snipped the cartilage and tendon surrounding the large wing bone, and carefully exposed the pink muscle. Feathers scraped the plywood like a broom. The owl was giving itself to me, giving its feathered pelt and its greatest gift, that which separated it from us—the wings. In return I'd give it a proper burial.

There is an intensity to skinning, a sense of immediacy. Once you start, you must continue. Many people work fast to get it over with, but I like to take it slow. I hadn't felt this way in a long time and hadn't known I'd missed it.

I eased the skin over the back of the skull. Its right side was caved in pretty bad. The pelt was inside out, connected to the body at the beak, as if the owl was kissing the shadow of its mate. I passed it to Tarvis. He held the slippery skull in one hand and gently tugged the skin free of the carcass.

"Get a shovel," I said.

Tarvis circled the house for a spade and dug a hole beneath a cottonwood. I examined the bird. Both legs, the skull, each wing, its neck and ribs—all were broken. It's head hung from several shattered vertebrae. I'd never seen a creature so clean on the outside and so tore up on the inside. It had died pretty hard.

I built a twig platform and placed the remains in the grave. Tarvis began to spade the dirt in. He tamped it down, mumbling to himself. I reversed the pelt so the feathers were facing out. The body cavity flattened to an empty skin, a pouch with wings that would never fly.

Hand-shaking is not customary among men in eastern Kentucky. We stood apart from one another and nodded, arms dangling, boots scuffing the dirt, as if our limbs were useless without work.

"Got any whiskey?" I said.

"Way I drank gave it a bad name. Quit when I left Kentucky."

"That's when I took it up. What makes you want that owl so bad?"

"It's pure built to hunt. Got three ear holes and it flies silent. It can open and close each pupil separate from the other one. They ain't a better hunter."

"Well," I said. "Reckon you know your owls."

I drove to the bar for a few shots and thought about eating, but didn't want to ruin a ten-dollar drunk with a five-dollar meal. I didn't meet a woman and didn't care. When the bar closed, a bunch of us bought six-packs and went to my house. I laid drunk through most of the week, thinking about Tarvis in the blurred space between hangover and the day's first drink. Though I'd shown him how to skin, I had the feeling he was guiding me into something I'd tried to leave behind.

A few weeks later I met a teacher who was considering a move to Kentucky because it was a place that could use her help. We spent a few nights together. I felt like a test for her, a way of gauging Kentucky's need. I guess I flunked because she moved to South Dakota for a job on the Sioux Reservation.

On Memorial Day I took a six-pack of dog hair to Tarvis's house, parked behind his truck, and opened a beer. At first I wanted to gag, but there's no better buzz than a drink on an empty stomach. I drank half and held it down. The heat spread through my body, activating last night's bourbon. I finished the beer and opened another.

Tarvis came out of the house, blinking against the sun. We went to the riverbank and sat in metal chairs. A great blue heron flew north, its neck curled like a snake ready to strike. The air was quiet. We could have been by the Blue Lick River back home. It felt right to sit with someone of the hills, even if we didn't have a lot to say.

I asked to see the owl and Tarvis reluctantly led me to the door. His eyes were shiny as new dimes. "Ain't nobody been inside in eight years."

The cabin was one room with a sink, range, toilet, and mattress. A woodstove stained from tobacco spit stood in the middle. The only furniture was a tattered couch. Shelves lined every wall, filled with things he'd found in the woods.

A dozen owl pellets lay beside a jumble of antlers. A variety of bird wings were pinned to the wall. One shelf held sun-bleached bones and another contained thirty or forty jaw bones. Skulls were jammed in—raccoon, fox, deer, a dozen groundhog. Hundreds of feathers poked into wall cracks and knotholes. There were so many feathers that I had the sense of being within the owl pelt turned inside out.

Tarvis pulled a board from the highest shelf. The owl lay on its back, wings stretched full to either side. The claws hung from strips of downy hide. Tarvis had smoothed the feathers into their proper pattern.

"You did a good job," I said.

"Had some help."

"Ever find Indian stuff?"

"All this came from hunting arrowheads," he said. "But I never found one. Maybe I don't know how to look."

"Maybe this is what finds you."

He handed me a stick from one of the shelves. It was eighteen inches long, sanded smooth and feathered at one end. He reached under the couch for a hand-made bow.

"That's osage orangewood," he said. "Same as the Indians used. I made them both. Soon's I find me a point I'll be setting pretty."

"You going to hunt with it?"

"No." He looked away. "I don't even kill mosquitoes. What I do is let the spiders go crazy in here. They keep the bugs down and snakes stop the mice. Hawks eat the snakes. Fox kills the duck. An owl hunts everything, but nothing hunts the owl. It's like man."

He put the owl on a shelf and opened the door. We went outside. The staccato of a woodpecker came across the river, each peck distinct as a bell.

"How come you don't hunt?" I said. He looked at me, then away, and back to me. His eyes were smoky.

"I don't know," he said. "Hear that woodpecker? Take and cut its beak off and it'll pound its face against a tree until it dies. Not hunting does me the same way. But I still can't do it."

The river shimmered in the wind, sunlight catching each tiny cresting wave. A breeze carried the scent of clover and mud. I slipped away to my car.

Work hit a slow spell. I was in a dorm I'd painted twice before and could do it blindfolded. The rooms repeated themselves, each one a mirror image of the last. I went in and out of the same room over and over. Sometimes I didn't know where I was, and leaving didn't help because the hallway was filled with identical doors.

The next time I visited Tarvis, I drank the neck and shoulders out of a fifth while he talked. He was from a family of twelve. His last name was Eldridge. He grew up on Eldridge Ridge, overlooking Eldridge Creek in Eldridge County. His people numbered so many that they got identified by hair color and their mother's maiden name. Nobody called him Tarvis. He was Ida Cumbow's fourth boy, a black-headed Eldridge. That's what finally made him leave. No one knew who he was.

Tarvis and I sat till the air was greyed by dusk. Night covered us over. We were like a pair of seashells a long way from the beach. If you held one of us to your ear, you'd hear Kentucky in the distance, but listening to both would put you flat in the woods.

An owl called from the river.

"There's your owl," I said.

"No, that's a great horned. A barred owl getting this far west ain't right."

"Maybe that's why it died."

Tarvis looked at me for a spell, his eyes gleaming in the darkness. He never spoke and I left for the Pig. The ease of Tarvis's company just drove in the fact that I didn't belong out here. Maybe that's why I drank so much that night. I woke up the next day filled with dread, craving water, and with no memory of what had happened at the bar. I used to think not remembering meant I'd had a great time. Now I know it for a bad sign, but a drink can cut that fear like a scythe.

I went back to see Tarvis at the height of summer. The river moved so slowly it seemed to be still, a flat pane of reflected light. Mosquitoes began to circle my head. Tarvis opened his door, squinting against the sun. He'd lost weight. His hands were crusted with dirt and he reminded me of the old men at home, weary from slant-farming hillsides that never yielded enough.

We nodded to each other, began the ritual of tobacco. His voice sounded rusty and cracked. He moved his lips before each word, forming the word itself.

"Found one," he said.

I knew immediately what he meant.

"Where?"

"Creek. Four mile downriver. Half mile in."

"Flint?"

His head moved in a slow shake.

"Chert," he said. "No flint in America."

"You make the arrow?"

He shivered. Mosquitoes rose from his body and we looked at each other a long time. He never blinked. I smacked a mosquito against my neck. He compressed his lips and went back inside, softly closing the door.

I spent the rest of the summer drinking and didn't think about Tarvis anymore. For a while I dated a woman, if you can call it that. We drank till the bar closed, then went to her house and tried not to pass out in the middle of everything. It eventually went to hell between us. Everybody said it would. She liked to laugh, though, and nothing else really mattered.

The day we split up, I got drunk at the Pig. Someone was in the men's room, and I went in the women's. It was commonly done. The uncommon part was falling through the window. The bartender didn't ask what happened or if I was hurt, just barred me on the spot. He thought I threw a garbage can through the window. He said that nothing human had broken it, and I wondered what he thought I was.

I took my drinking down the street, but it wasn't the same. I was homesick for the Pig.

A few months later a policeman arrived at my house and I got scared that I'd hit someone with my car. I was always finding fresh dents and scraped paint in the morning. The cop was neckless and blond, officially polite. He asked if I knew Tarvis Eldridge and I nodded. He asked if the deceased had displayed any behavior out of the ordinary and I told him no, wanting to side with Tarvis even dead.

"A will left his house to you," the cop said.

"Maybe he wasn't right when he wrote it."

"We don't think he was," the cop said. "But the house is yours."

He stood to leave, and I asked how Tarvis had died. In a slow, embarrassed fashion, he told me part of it. I went to the county coroner who filled in the gaps. It was his most unusual case, and he talked about it like a man who'd pulled in a ten-inch trout on a dime-store rod.

Tarvis had fastened one end of the bow to an iron plate and screwed the plate to the floor. Guy wires held the bow upright. He fitted an arrow with a chert point into the bow, drew it tight, and braced it. A strip of rawhide ran across the floor to the couch where they found him. All he had to do was pull the leather cord to release the arrow.

His body had been sent home for burial. As much as he'd tried to get out, the hills had claimed him.

I drove to Tarvis's house and gathered his personal stuff—a toothbrush and comb, his tobacco pouch, knife, and hat. I dug a hole beside the owl's grave and dropped it all in. It seemed fitting that he'd have two graves, one here and another in Kentucky. I filled the hole and smoothed the earth and didn't know what to say. Everything I came up with sounded stupid. It was such a small place in the ground. I wasn't burying him, I was covering over how I felt.

I left for town. My neighborhood was neat and clean, like dorm walls after a fresh coat. From the outside, my house looked like all the rest. The refrigerator held lunchmeat, eggs, and milk. The toilet ran unless you jiggled the handle. I didn't even go in. I bought a pint for later and drove to the Pig, forgetting that I'd been barred. I sat in the car outside. The windows of the tavern were brightly lit and I knew everyone in there. I'd not been to the Pig for three months and none of my friends had called me, not a one.

I drove back to Tarvis's road, pulled over, and cut the engine. I hadn't known how tore up the inside of the owl was, and I couldn't tell about Tarvis either. Both of them should have stayed in the woods. It made me wonder if I should have. I opened the whiskey. The smell was quick and strong, and I threw the full bottle out the car window. I don't know why. As soon as I did, I regretted it. The bottle didn't break and I heard the bourbon emptying into the ditch. I knew it wouldn't all run out.

I went down the road and parked in the shadow of Tarvis's house. The river was dark and flat. Long-eared owls were calling to each other, answering and calling. There was one female calling and three males hollering back, which reminded me of the Pig. Maybe Tarvis would still be living if he'd let himself take a drink to get through the hard parts. He'd gotten himself home, though, while I was still stuck out here in the world. I suddenly thought of something that drained me like a shell. I sat in the dark listening to the owls but there was no way for me to get around it. I missed Kentucky more than the Pig.

Deferment

DWIGHT ALLEN

Born and raised in Louisville, Kentucky, Dwight Allen earned a B.A. in English from Lawrence University and an M.F.A. in creative writing at the Iowa Writers' Workshop. A former *New Yorker* writer and staff member, Allen has published stories in various journals, including *American Short Fiction, The Southern Review, The Georgia Review, The Missouri Review, Shenandoah,* and *New England Review.* His work has appeared in *New Stories from the South,* and his story "Succor" was a finalist for the National Magazine Award in fiction. His debut collection of stories, *The Green Suit,* appeared in 2000. He and his wife, Nancy, and son, George, currently live in Madison, Wisconsin.

"Deferment" appeared originally in *The Southern Review* in 1998 and was later collected in *The Green Suit.* Set in Louisville in 1970, it is one of Allen's Peter Sackrider stories, which follow Peter, a would-be writer, as he searches for love and meaning in Kentucky, New York, Wisconsin, and the Northwest. With Peter embracing noncommitment, and with the Vietnam War looming large in the background, "Deferment" is rich in the implications of obsessive desire and attempts to subdue. The story is also rich in locality. Allen has said that it could have been set in no other place than Louisville and its suburbs: "The thick summer twilight that Lizzie runs through in her sundress, when her brother's dog is hit by a lady in a Falcon, is pure Kentucky air, less dense than the heavy honeysuckled air of literary places farther south, but rich and charged nonetheless. It smells of the Ohio River and it sometimes feels suffocating. . . . It signifies 'home' to me as much as anything."

◆

In the summer of 1970, I spent a lot of time trying to get a girl named Lizzie Burford to sleep with me. I had the idea that we would do it at the Goshen Motor Court, out on U.S. 42, near the county line. We'd lie in each other's arms and shiver as the air conditioner blew and the sweat on our skin dried. I was nineteen, a year older than Lizzie, and I thought about motels the way I later thought about churches: as places you could disappear into and lose yourself. I thought of the Goshen in particular because we sometimes drove past it on our way to or from doing nothing.

Once when we stopped at the filling station across the highway from it, I saw a woman smoking in a lawn chair in the grassy oval where the motel owner had planted zinnias around an old water pump. I asked Lizzie what she thought the woman was thinking about, and Lizzie said, "She's thinking she made a mistake. Or why is she sitting outdoors watching the traffic go by and he's in the room eating beer nuts or something?"

"Maybe she got cold in the air conditioning," I said.

"Maybe she wanted to hear the insects sing," Lizzie said, reaching for the can of beer between my legs. "And now she's thinking about walking across the highway so she can talk to *him*." She indicated the skinny boy washing bug spatters from the windshield.

"I like sleeping in motels," I said. This was more a statement of fact than a proposition.

"You're so romantic, Peter," Lizzie said, laughing, replacing the can of beer.

As I waited for the pump jockey to bring my change, the woman crossed the highway. She was barefooted. I wondered if the warmth of the pavement surprised her. Lizzie said, "Think of all the wrong boys you could end up with with breasts like hers."

I took Lizzie home and kissed her delicately on the mouth and then drove to the Frankfort Avenue White Castle and ate six of those silver-dollar-size burgers in about two minutes.

The next afternoon, on my way to work, I stopped by Lizzie's house. As far as I knew, I was the only boy in Jefferson County knocking on her door. This was so not only because she was flat-chested and had a lanky body in which the bones seemed to hang together in a complex, awkward way. It was so because she had a straight-A kind of brain and often carried herself in a manner that led some boys to imagine she was standoffish or prideful or touchy or all three. And then there was the matter of her being the daughter of an Episcopal preacher and of failing to behave like the hard-drinking, hell-raising offspring of Episcopal clergymen we all knew. She stole sips of beer from me and did not smoke.

When I entered the house, Miles, the Burfords' black Lab, sniffed me all over, then retired to the library. I followed Lizzie upstairs. We passed her parents' bedroom—the Reverend Burford was at St. Timothy's, Mrs. Burford was at the chiropractor's—and then we passed Lizzie's brother's room. Harry was in Vietnam. He'd been there for about two months.

Lizzie flopped down on her bed and resumed writing a letter to her brother. She wrote him almost daily, on stationery with psychedelic filigree which she'd bought at a head shop. I sat on the edge of the twin, watching her long, bare legs move back and forth, slowly, metronomically. I was aware of a dull ticking in my head. I took off my work boots and found a place beside her. I set my mouth within inches of a vaccination mark on her right arm. She was left-handed, the only left-handed girl in the universe, to my knowledge. Her handwriting was messy, difficult to discern.

"What are you telling Harry?" My breath came back at me off her freckled, summery skin.

"Just things. About my job." Lizzie worked in a Head Start program in the mornings. "How many times Daddy took his glasses off when he gave his sermon."

"How many?" I aimed the tip of my tongue at the pale center of her vaccination scar.

"Seventeen. It was a short sermon." She tucked stray hair behind her ear and then said, "You're cramping my style." I withdrew my tongue and rolled onto my back. I gazed at Lizzie's ear, the curve of it ending in that soft lobe with its tiny ring hole. I fingered the pack of Larks in the breast pocket of my shirt. Though I was nineteen, a sophomore-to-be at a college in Tennessee, I was by any definition except, perhaps, a technical one, a virgin. Once, during my freshman year, I'd gotten near-blind-drunk on grain-alcohol punch and found myself on top of a girl from Knoxville, who was also drunk and who kept saying, "Are you in? Are you in? I can't feel you."

I listened to the air conditioner rattle in the window frame. It was ninety-something outside. In an hour, I had to be at my job. I worked the four-to-midnight shift at a lumbermill off Dixie Highway, stacking boards that came off a planer. It was a summer job—the lowliest at the plant, next to sweeping sawdust. I'd chosen it over an offer to be a gofer boy for a firm of Republican lawyers.

I rolled off the bed and went to Lizzie's desk and picked up the photo cube that sat on a pile of books. There was a picture of Lizzie and Harry as children: Lizzie in a green, bell-shaped dress that made her look like a Christmas ornament, flashing slightly bucked teeth, and Harry in blazer and tie, his hand on his sister's shoulder. I rotated the cube to a picture of Lizzie in last year's prom gown, her teeth straightened, her shoulders so bare I felt I could touch them below the surface of the photo. I turned the cube again, to a snapshot of Harry in jungle pants and Army helmet, crouched beside a small black dog, sandbags in the background; Harry was squinting and he looked quizzical, the way dogs do when they tilt their heads to the side.

And then I studied the picture, taken that spring, of Lizzie as Mary the Maid in *The Bald Soprano*, her senior-class play. (She'd gone to a private girls' school that employed an ambitious drama teacher.) She wore a short black skirt with a frilly apron, and balanced uneasily on high heels. I thought she looked wonderful, even if she was dressed more like a cocktail waitress than a maid in a proper English home. The photograph was of the moment when she recited Mary's poem for the Fire Chief. Her hands were clutched together at her waist, and her head was tilted upward, heavenward, as if ecstasy had descended on her and left her mouth agape. This wasn't quite the first sign I'd had that she was capable of enrapturement, but it was the most explicit.

I opened the top drawer of Lizzie's desk in the hope of finding I knew not what exactly. The letters I'd written her from college that spring, letters all swollen with praise (some of it borrowed) for the parts of her I'd been allowed to kiss?

"What are you doing in my desk, Mr. Nosy?"

"*Rien.*" I crossed the hall to Harry's room. The blinds were pulled and the windows shut tight. The air felt ancient, as if it were being preserved for Harry to breathe when he came back. The two trophies on the bureau—both for swimming—gleamed faintly. A knotted necktie hung from a drawer knob. On the floor were two crates of LPs, mostly jazz, mostly musicians I knew only by name. Harry was deep, though not in an academic way, judging by his failure to hold on to his student deferment. He had fallen behind at college and then had dropped out and gone to Montreal, where he'd planned to spend the war. But when his draft notice arrived, he returned home. Lizzie said he'd felt guilty.

I put a record on Harry's portable Magnavox and sat in his wide-bottomed armchair and listened to Thelonious Monk play the piano. He played the melody in snatches and then nervously jumped away from it, like a man with a hundred worries. I closed my eyes. I thought of Harry crouching next to the little black dog in the Mekong Delta or wherever he was in that country of which my ignorance was extensive. (Once, when Lizzie read me one of Harry's letters in which there was a description of a sunset, I thought, *There are sunsets in Vietnam?*) Wasn't dog considered a delicacy in Asia? The dog and Harry vanished and I saw myself lying naked on crisp white sheets at the Goshen Motor Court, waiting for a woman to come out of the bathroom, where she was washing her feet.

"Do you like it?" Lizzie had slipped into her brother's room and was now sitting on my knees, her hands pinning mine to the armrests. She meant the music.

"Yeah," I said.

"More than Buffalo Springfield? More than Joni Mitchell in her big yellow taxi?"

"Yeah."

"Liar," Lizzie said. "Pants are on fire."

In Lizzie's eyes, soft black islands encircled by blue-gray irises casting changeable light, I saw that she couldn't say to herself that she found me undesirable, even if she could say I didn't impress her. In her mouth, in the ample fleshiness of it, I saw, or imagined I saw, her willingness to accept my devotions, at least until the end of the summer, when she went away to college. She was going to Chapel Hill on a scholarship.

I leaned forward to kiss Lizzie, but I was in an awkward position and she didn't meet me halfway and I couldn't reach that far—or that high, rather. And so I put my mouth on her more accessible breast, a small wonder beneath her ribbed jersey. I was permitted to let my lips rest there a moment, like a child being offered consolation, long enough that I felt her nipple rise in response. Oh, I was allowed certain liberties, to use a phrase that even then was old-fashioned, but Lizzie wouldn't let go of her virginity easily. She had discussed me in her letters to Harry, and he had told her that you had to be careful whom you entrusted your soul to. (I didn't say, *I don't want your soul, I just want your funny body. Temporarily. For the summer.*) At any rate, she wasn't prepared to surrender herself to me "just because you have a boner and I have a vagina it can go into." She laughed when she said that. Her frankness threw me, even made me blush.

When Lizzie pulled away and I lifted my head, I saw the Reverend Burford in the doorway. He was short and gray-haired. There was something molelike about his face, as if he didn't spend enough time in the sun. His forehead was marked with lines that faded out at his temples, like old trails. He looked damp and pale, not nearly as pink as the flesh-colored frames of his glasses. In fact, he had a cold.

"Lizzie, I think it would be better if you and Peter were not in your brother's room." He sniffled, tugged at his clerical collar.

Lizzie rose from my knees and brushed at herself, as if to shed the imprint of me. "We were just listening to one of Harry's jazz records before Peter left."

"It's nice seeing you again, Peter," the Reverend Burford said.

"Yessir," I said, rising from the chair, wondering if the stiffness in my jeans was as evident to him as it was to me. I stuck my hands in my pockets and looked down at my bootless feet.

"I missed seeing your father at the Humane Society meeting the other night," the Reverend Burford said, taking a handkerchief out of his coat pocket. "Please give him and your mother my regards."

"Yessir."

"How'd you get out of the draft, man?" Red and I were pushing a cartload of hardwood into a storage area. Or rather I was pushing and Red was guiding me across the rutted concrete floor, down an aisle, where the only light was cast by yellow bulbs in wire cages. It was eight-fifteen in the evening, fifteen minutes until dinnertime.

"Student deferment," I said, sliding my safety glasses up my sweaty nose.

"How come you're doing a dumb-ass job like this if you're so smart?" Red came around to the back of the cart to help me push it the last few feet. He was grinning. The reddish-blond stubble on his chin and around his mouth, the beginnings of a goatee perhaps, looked like sawdust stuck to his face, not quite real. As he leaned into the cart, the muscles in his arms flared beneath a cut-off football jersey he'd worn just about every day I'd known him. Six days, to be exact. This was the first time we'd had something like a conversation.

"Must be the money," I said, hoping this would pass for a joke.

"Maybe you can buy some pencils and tablets with it," he said. We walked back down the aisle and into the planing room with its lofty ceiling and broad doorways through which forklifts and the occasional breeze passed.

I didn't know how old Red was. His hard, narrow face suggested he was older than me by more than a year or two. But he had freckles around his eyes, residue from a not-too-far-off boyhood. And his eyes were a mild blue. And his hair—stringy, the color of dried-out red clay—was almost long enough to make me think he might be an ally. There were fewer than a handful of workers in the mill whose hair fell over their eartops.

"How'd you get out of the draft?" I asked.

He removed his right work glove and held out his hand. "The trigger finger doesn't look real useful, does it?" It had been severed at the middle joint. "I can hardly even pick my nose with it." He said he'd cut it in shop class at high school.

He put his glove back on and said, "One more load before dinner." He went down to his work station, singing "Whipping Post," and switched on the machinery. Raw ten- and twenty-foot boards of maple and oak and walnut slid sideways down a canted conveyor and Red guided them into the planer. I grabbed them as they shot across a metal table, all hot and smooth, their grains exposed, and flipped them on to a cart. Red had taught me how to use the table as a lever. "It's like dealing cards," he'd said. "Nothing to it." But I still wasn't in his league. When both he and I worked at my end of the table—sometimes a man named Boyd fed the planer— Red did twice the volume I did.

Red pushed boards toward me at a rate I couldn't keep up with, and in a minute I was buried. I waved at him to stop, but he didn't acknowledge me. He was singing to himself. I started shouting, though I knew he couldn't hear me through the noise of the planer, which was like ten lawn mowers going at once. I watched a batch of black walnut slide past me onto the floor. Then the machine stopped.

From behind me came a voice. "Son, if you make any more messes like this, you're going to have to find another line of work."

The speaker was Mr. Root, the foreman, who was known as Adolph because he bore a passing resemblance to Adolph Rupp, the University of Kentucky's squat, jowly basketball coach. Mr. Root was sitting in his motorized cart, sipping coffee, his round head hidden under a cap.

"Yessir," I said.

"I'll get him to quit playing with his pecker, don't you worry, Mr. Root," Red said. He was helping me pick up the boards.

"You be sure you do, Cloverly." That was the first time I heard Red's last name; I never did find out his Christian name, unless Red was it.

Mr. Root departed. "Sorry," I said to Red.

"Some guy I know died in Vietnam because some fuckup in his platoon didn't do his job right." Red glared at me.

"Sorry," I said, though I didn't see the parallel between the jungles of Vietnam and a wood mill in Kentucky.

"Don't worry about it, Joe," Red said, slapping me on the back. Joe, I later figured out, was short for Joe College. "Just keep your pecker clear of whirling blades."

He grinned, and I grinned back.

"Where are you and Lizzie going tonight, Peter?" Mrs. Burford was tearing up lettuce, dropping the pieces into a wooden bowl on the kitchen table. Some of the pieces were as small as confetti. She was on her second scotch—second that I'd seen, anyway.

"The movies," I said. "Lizzie wants to see this one by Truffaut that Harry told her about. It's at the Crescent." I glanced out the window above the kitchen sink. Lizzie was playing with Miles while the Reverend Burford tended the barbecue grill. She was wearing a sundress, her arms and legs covered by nothing more than smoky light. Watching her throw a ball to Miles quickened my desire for her. The fact that she threw awkwardly, as if her left arm operated independently of her brain, made her only more desirable.

"Harry took me to some Swedish movie at the Crescent just before he went off to boot camp," Mrs. Burford said. "It was all pain and desolation. With subtitles I couldn't make out half the time." Mrs. Burford ceased tearing lettuce and picked up her drink. The bracelets on her wrist slid and jangled. She was a tall, thin woman, nearly a head taller than her husband. She wore her graying hair in a permanent wave, possibly in the hope that it might divert attention from the signs of disintegration in her face. There was darkness under her eyes, which were like glimmers far out to sea.

I picked at the label on my beer bottle. "Do you like musicals?"

"Musicals?" she said, tilting her head, as if there were something hidden in my question and she was trying to shake it loose. In fact, it was an empty-headed question, though I did see now how it might lead her away from the subject of Harry, who was all but present. There were pictures of him on the refrigerator, though none showed him in military dress. In one taken a couple days before he'd been inducted, he had his arms around Lizzie and her friend Evie. Their faces were squeezed together like fruit in a bin. Harry's hair was long, and it fell into his eyes, but it didn't hide his fear.

"Musicals?" she said again, opening the refrigerator and leaning in. "I prefer them to Swedish dramas, if that's what you mean." She emerged with a purple onion and handed it to me. "Why don't you cut this up while I go put something on the hi-fi."

She left the kitchen with her drink in hand. Was I supposed to slice that onion into rings or dice it? Was it for the salad or the hamburgers?

I heard the hi-fi needle land on a record and slide across an acre of grooves before settling on a man's voice crooning darkly about an ill wind. I looked out the window for Lizzie. She was standing next to her father, holding her hair off her neck.

Mrs. Burford re-entered the kitchen, the liquid in her glass a late afternoon color. The music, the solemn voice of the singer and the lush sound of the orchestra, seemed to have made her smaller, overwhelmed her. Then I noticed she'd taken off her shoes.

"I don't suppose you and Lizzie listen to Frank Sinatra much." She took the knife from me and began to dice the two onion rings I'd sliced.

"I hear him on the radio sometimes." With strings swelling behind him, Sinatra sang of having no one to scratch his back.

"I heard him at the Armory in 1941 with the Dorsey band. The place was full of all these young men without dates. Stags, we called them. It was so hot and crowded I could hardly breathe." She looked up from the onions, into, I imagined, the mists of the forties. "Sinatra was just this tough little skinny kid then, a beautiful singer. When he got older, his voice became less beautiful and more interesting. He made this record in 1955, after Ava Gardner left him."

I swallowed the last of my beer. When Mrs. Burford had offered it, she'd said, "If you're old enough to be drafted, you're old enough to drink." I gripped my empty bottle and listened to the record, trying to hear what Mrs. Burford heard. I was a little bit high, which made me receptive. Then I saw her lift her head from her onion chopping. She was crying—whether from the onions or the music or something else, I wasn't sure.

Mrs. Burford wiped her cheeks with the back of her hand. Then she asked me to take the salad to the table on the side porch. There was nothing in the bowl besides the shredded lettuce.

I stood under the slowly spinning fan on the porch and watched Miles run out of the yard in a hurry, as if he'd just caught the scent of something juicier than the Reverend Burford's hamburgers. Frank Sinatra was singing about a man alone in bed. The music seemed gravely wrought, if not overwrought, and I wanted to escape it and go have a cigarette.

When I came back into the kitchen, Mrs. Burford said, "What do you plan on doing if you're drafted?" She was at the sink, washing a head of broccoli. I couldn't see her face.

A year before, in the weeks before my eighteenth birthday, I'd had some notion that I might file for conscientious objector status, though I'd barely cracked the books about pacifism I'd gotten from the library and I knew in my heart I wasn't going to cut it as a C.O. And when the time came to make an appearance at the Selective Service Office, I'd gone downtown and said, in effect, "You can have me when you need me." The clerk, a woman with a Rhine-maidenish tower of hair, had smiled at me through coils of cigarette smoke. A few months later, after I'd gone off to college, I'd received my card and my deferment. I was 2–S.

"I guess I'd go," I said. "Probably." I sat down at the table.

"You don't sound very sure of yourself." Her back was still turned. Her blouse had come untucked.

I touched the glass that held her scotch, then glanced at the pictures of Harry on the refrigerator door. Would I have submitted to the government's call and come home from Montreal? Probably.

Mrs. Burford turned around, the head of wet broccoli in her hands, glistening, dripping on the floor. "I didn't hear what you said." She'd dried her eyes, but her face was clouded and dark, as if there were more bad weather on the way.

"I'm hoping I don't lose my deferment," I said. "My lottery number is kind of low." My number was 43.

"You shouldn't do what your heart tells you not to do." She turned back to the sink. "Harry went because he said some poor kid would have to go if he didn't. He was trying to be noble."

If I went to Vietnam, would Lizzie sleep with me as a parting gift? I thought not. She was a girl with principles.

"Maybe you could take the ketchup out to the porch," Mrs. Burford said. "It's in the fridge. And the horseradish. My husband won't eat a hamburger without it."

I found the bottles and carried them through the living room, where Sinatra was singing to the blue sofa where Lizzie and I sometimes sat, me with my boner, Lizzie with a Coke she sipped endlessly, and Miles at her feet. I set the bottles on the table, and when I looked up, I saw a car stopped in the street, a Falcon like my grandmother drove, with a woman in a golf skirt and visor standing beside it. She'd hit Miles. I could see his black shape a few yards from her fender. I looked dumbly at Miles sprawled in the end-of-the-day haze, and then Lizzie ran by the porch, shouting, and I noticed the way her body moved inside her sundress.

Miles was still breathing. The Reverend Burford wrapped him in a sheet and lifted him into the back of his wood-paneled station wagon, which he'd bought at a discount from a parishioner. Lizzie was weeping, tearing at herself because Miles was her responsibility while Harry was away, and she insisted on going with her father to the vet's. There was blood on her hand, where she'd stroked Miles, and on her cheek, where she'd wiped her hand in despair. Mrs. Burford and I stayed behind. She had another scotch and then excused herself and went upstairs to her bedroom and didn't come back down. I helped myself to another beer and drank it on the blue sofa as the light leaked out of the day, as I felt my desire for Lizzie wane.

"You need to pick up the pace, boy," Red said, "or you're going to get your ass canned." We were on a smoke break, sitting on a bench outside the planing shed, below a huge pile of shavings and other mill refuse. Boyd, who was feeding the planer that night, was sitting apart from us on an overturned bucket, not smoking. It was dark, between ten and eleven.

I was tired and, not for the first time, on the verge of quitting. It gave me pleasure to imagine lying on my bed, listening to Thelonious Monk play the piano, my hand lolling next to a vent that cool air poured through. I could almost hear the air flowing through the duct and Monk doing his odd sprung-rhythm thing. I'd persuaded Lizzie to let me borrow a couple of Harry's LPs.

Red dragged on his cigarette. "You getting laid enough?"

I exhaled smoke and produced a noise like an assent.

"Maybe he's a fairy," Boyd said. Boyd poured the last of a pint carton of chocolate milk down his throat and then let the carton fall to the dirt. According to Red, Boyd was a drifter. He didn't mix with others. At dinnertime, he went out to his car with his vending-machine sandwich and chocolate milk and ate there.

"Fairies get laid, I hear," Red said. "They just go at it different."

"You know that from experience, Red?" Boyd pushed down on the carton with his work boot.

"I know that from seeing you and Adolph get it on in the back of that shit-for-wheels Fury of yours. I asked myself: Why can't they go to a darned motel if they want to do them things? Wasn't I telling you about that, Joe?" Red jabbed me in the shoulder with the stub of his trigger finger.

I nodded in a way that I hoped might be imperceptible to Boyd and then saw him slowly rise from his seat. Boyd was tall and bony, with an Adam's apple that jutted like a crag. His hair receded from a wispy widow's peak high on his forehead. I estimated his age at between thirty and fifty.

Boyd walked past without glancing our way and went into the planing shed and switched on the conveyor and planer.

"Fucking drifting alky trash," Red said. "Don't pay any attention to him."

A couple nights later, when we got paid, I drove Red to a twenty-four-hour gas station after work. The tires on his Camaro had been slashed. He punched the ceiling of my VW and swore, telling me what he planned to do to Boyd when he caught him. (Boyd was long gone; he'd disappeared at the six o'clock smoke break, after the paychecks had come around.) The station wouldn't cash Red's check, so I let him use my credit card and then drove him back to the mill and watched him put the new tires on.

As he tightened the bolts on the last tire, he said, "I know this girl Virgie who has a sister I could fix you up with. I owe you, so don't say no."

I didn't.

I went out with Lizzie the next night, as planned. She was in a cheerful mood. She'd gotten a letter from Harry, who said he was doing fine, "just sitting here on my cot, drinking warm beer, and listening to Johnny Cash on the radio in between choppers flying over." He added, "I wish it was Billie Holiday instead of Johnny, but you can't have everything (ha ha)." Lizzie wrote back to say that Miles was doing O.K. The vet had amputated a leg that was crushed beyond repair, but Miles was now able to hobble around and find his way to the pork-chop bones in the kitchen trash.

Lizzie and I went to see *Jules and Jim* at the Crescent and then we drove to a wayside on River Road and sat on the damp ground under a buzzing streetlamp and watched the river flow by. We talked about the movie, about how the Jeanne Moreau character was too much for either of the men to handle by himself. I said I couldn't see sharing a lover with somebody else.

"You can't have everything," Lizzie said, laughing. Then she asked me to give her my wallet.

"My wallet?" But I did as she asked.

She went through the contents—a photo of her, the combination to my athletic locker at school, my Standard Oil credit card—until she found what she wanted. She held it up to the light and read my Selective Service number and my Random Sequence number and my classification. Then she folded the card into quarters and put it in her mouth. She let it rest against her cheek for a moment, like a plug of tobacco, before she began chewing.

I watched in silence. I was opposed to the war—or, anyway, opposed to having to participate in it myself—but I'd done little to declare my opposition, aside from taking part in a candlelight march at school. There was a whole army of us, upper-middle-class white boys with draft cards in our back pockets, hoping the war would end before our deferments expired.

"What does it taste like?"

"Like paper with typing on it, except for your signature, which tastes kind of inky. You want a bite?" She stuck her tongue out; in the juices of her mouth, the card had been reduced to little more than a spitball.

"No, thanks."

She resumed chewing; she chewed noisily, like a child making a show of her eating.

"You can do time for 'knowingly' mutilating a card," I said. I'd read the fine print on the back.

"Here," she said, leaning toward me. "Be a good boy and swallow." She shoved the sodden wad into my mouth and then kissed me hard. She pushed at the card with her tongue, trying to steer it down my throat, until she started laughing.

I took the lump out of my mouth and put it in my pocket. "I'll tell the draft board my girlfriend ate it," I said.

"Be brave," she said. "Tell them you don't want to fight in their shitty war."

"Would you sleep with me then—before I went to jail, I mean?"

"I'd write you letters in jail." She put her arm around me.

"It doesn't matter. I'm not going to get drafted anyway."

I arrived late for Harry's funeral and found a seat in the rearmost pew, next to the man who'd taught Latin to Harry and (later) me in high school. Mr. Becker had also coached the swimming team, of which Harry had been captain in his senior year. He shared a hymnal with me and sang enthusiastically, in his emphatic Latin taskmaster's baritone. My eyes strayed from the book to look for Lizzie, but I couldn't see far enough forward through all the dark suits and saucer-shaped hats. I'd not seen her since the night she ate my draft card. I'd been going out with Cheryl, Virgie's sister, the girl Red had set me up with.

When the congregation sat for the reading of the lesson, I saw the back of Lizzie's head. It seemed more remote than I had ever imagined it might become. I listened: "Behold, I show you a mystery; we shall not all sleep, but we shall all be changed, in a moment, in the twinkling of an eye, at the last trump." I read, responsively, the even-numbered verses of Psalm 121, and then I went outside into the midday sunshine and took off my jacket and got into my car.

I lit a cigarette. I looked at the white doors of St. Timothy's, the little flourish of a steeple poking at the pale sky, the hearse driver sitting on a fold-up stool in the courtyard next to the sanctuary. I watched cars go down the street—traffic from another world, it seemed. I remembered that when I heard about Harry's death—he stepped on a mine—I was in the bathroom brushing my teeth, getting ready to go see Cheryl. I listened as the bearer of the news, my mother, talked to me through the door. When she left, I finished brushing my teeth and worried a pimple and then wrote Lizzie a note, which, despite its brevity, I flattered myself to imagine was heartfelt. I dropped the note in the Burfords' mailbox on my way out to Shively, where Red and Cheryl and her sister lived. This was my second date with Cheryl, who sold popcorn at the new Movieland on Dixie Highway. On our first, we'd driven around with Red and Virgie, stopping at an all-night auto-parts store where Red wanted to look at tachometers, ending up at a party halfway to Fort Knox. Cheryl had a boyfriend, I found out, who was in Vietnam, and it came as a surprise to me when she took my hand and studied my palm and said, "Don't worry. He won't kill you if we make it."

I saw the funeral-parlor driver get up from his stool, and a couple minutes later the church's white doors opened and six men hauled Harry's coffin into the sunlight. I saw the Reverend Burford without his vestments—he hadn't officiated—and then I saw Lizzie. She was holding her mother's arm, moving unsurely, as if caught off guard by the brightness of the day. She didn't wear sunglasses or a hat, as her mother did. The sun was pouring down, cooking her to her roots, and she leaned against her mother for protection.

I hadn't been the kind of person, I thought, whom Lizzie cared to lean into. What had I had to offer, after all, aside from my worshipful dick, which, like some meddlesome, boorish third party, was always ready to interpose itself? And so, about a week before I would learn of Harry's death, I'd gone to Shively for the first time. The next day I'd left Lizzie a note—I was big on leaving notes—telling her I was "seeing" someone else. I didn't expect her to answer, but she did. On legal-pad paper she wrote, in her jumbly left-handed script, "Happiness is a warm gun, *n'est-ce pas?*"

People got into their cars, and then the hearse, like a great gleaming boat, pulled out into the street and the procession to the cemetery began. I got in line behind the last car, a VW containing Evie and another of Lizzie's friends, but when it turned left, I turned right, toward Shively.

"Don't you know any girls, man?" We were in Red's Camaro, parked across the street from a package store, drinking short boys. Virgie and Red had had a fight, and he was in a dark mood. Cheryl was working at the theater. It was barely seven, the package store neon buzzing in the lingering daylight. When I suggested we pick Cheryl up when she got off work, Red said, "Maybe she can sit in the crack"—he indicated the space between the bucket seats—"and jerk us both off." He smirked at me through the bristly red fringe of his goatee. "I don't know, Joe. I don't think you ought to get too excited about Cheryl. She'd screw pretty much anything with two legs, which is why I set you up with her in the first place. I could see you were in need."

I remembered Cheryl saying, after we'd made it for the second time, "You're so quick." And then she'd kissed me, as if my being quick hadn't mattered too much. This was two weeks ago, the afternoon of Harry's funeral. We'd driven from Shively to the Goshen Motor Court, and afterward had lain on the stained sheets, watching a game show on a TV whose picture wouldn't stop rolling. The air conditioner produced only warm air, and at some point Cheryl had taken a shower and then left the room to look for something to eat. When she came back, with barbecue chips and a Moon Pie and two Orange Crushes, I was overcome by hunger for her. "Whoa," she said, but she was under me before she could take a bite of anything.

I looked out the windshield. A man as skinny as a snake came weaving down the sidewalk. He was wearing an unbuttoned, puffy-sleeved paisley shirt and bell-bottoms that were slipping down his hips and a sashlike belt that fell to his knees. I thought he might weave himself right onto the hood of Red's car, but he slid by.

"Thought that was Boyd for a second," Red said. "Dressed up like a dipshit." He pushed in the lighter and reached for his Raleighs, which were wedged between the visor and the roof. "So you aren't going to introduce me to any of your high-class girlfriends?"

I'd tried to keep from Red—and Cheryl—the fact that I lived in a wealthy East End neighborhood, a considerable distance from the mill and working-class Shively, as well as from the package store outside which we were now twiddling our thumbs. I'd always driven out to Shively or, as on this evening, met Red in between. My economic status had become clear to Red when he'd phoned me and Willie, the maid, had answered.

"OK," I said. "That way." I pointed in the general direction of Lizzie's house.

We swung by my house first. My parents had gone out, and I invited Red in, but he declined: "Wouldn't want to dirty the carpet." I got the two Monk LPs Lizzie had let me borrow and grabbed an unopened quart of scotch from a cabinet. When I presented Red with the bottle, he studied the two Scottie dogs on the label and said, "Woof! Woof!" Then he said, "Now show me where the long-legged women are hiding."

We drove out of my thickly wooded neighborhood, across Brownsboro Road, and over to Lizzie's neighborhood, where the trees were younger and there was less space between houses. I told Red about Lizzie's brother. I said I didn't know if she'd be in the mood to ride around with us.

"Go ring the doorbell, man," Red said. "I'll cheer her up."

I went up the Burfords' brick walk with the albums. In my note to Lizzie about Harry, I'd said she could call me whenever she wanted. In my arrogance, I'd imagined she might come running to me in her grief. I liked Cheryl, I liked the way she held me for those brief moments I was inside her, one hand on my neck, the other at the base of my spine, as if she were guiding me through some country waltz. I liked the frank but uncritical way she gazed at me and the way she said, when a certain C&W singer came on the radio, "Oh, God, I love that man almost as much as my daddy." But I was prepared to give her up in the event Lizzie sought me out—not that Cheryl, if Red was to be believed, would have minded too much. When Harry died, I'd actually imagined that his hold on Lizzie might weaken, that she might see the usefulness of entrusting herself to me, if only temporarily.

It wasn't easy admitting defeat. I liked Cheryl's soft, sweet breasts, breasts between which Moon Pie crumbs could get lost, but I'd set my heart on Lizzie's small, firm ones.

I rang the bell and peered through the screen into the unlighted front hall. I saw Miles lying at the other end, near the kitchen door. He didn't get up. Then I saw Lizzie, halfway up the stairs, gazing at me. Her stillness, the way she sat with her elbow on her thigh and her finger to her lips, startled me. The whole house seemed sunk in stillness, the way a house is when you come back to it from a vacation.

I said through the screen, "I should've come to see you before now."

"Why should you have? What difference would it have made?" She spoke so softly I could barely hear her.

"I brought the Monk records back." Miles was twitching in his sleep, dreaming of chasing a cat on four good legs. "You can keep them," she said.

I ran my finger around the doorknob. "Where are your parents?"

"Daddy went on some church retreat thing in the Smokies. Mom's upstairs."

I heard Red's radio—Eric Burdon singing "Spill the Wine." I turned and saw Red standing beside the car, drumming on the roof. When I turned back and saw Lizzie on the stairs, like a child suspended in some purgatory, her face cradled in her hands, I thought of delivering the apology I'd prepared, or a brief version of it: "Forgive me, Lizzie, for having offered you next to nothing when your brother died." But I was stubborn enough not to, as stubborn as Lizzie had been in her resistance of my charmless attempts to possess her.

"We could go get stoned," I said. "With my friend Red." I nodded toward the street.

"A few nights after Harry died I went out with Evie and got drunk and puked right where you're standing." The recollection of puking where I was standing didn't please her enough to make her smile.

I picked at the mesh of the screen.

"How come you're not out with your girlfriend?"

"She's not really my girlfriend," I said.

"Easy come, easy go, right, pardner?" Red had crept through the dusk to stand alongside me. He had tucked his football jersey into his jeans.

"This is Red," I said, and Red said, "Hey!" Miles awoke from his dream and scrambled to his three feet and hopped down the hall to sniff us through the screen. Mrs. Burford called down to find out who was there, and Lizzie said it was just Peter and his friend. Red told Lizzie he was sorry to hear about her brother, and that he'd had a friend the gooks had killed.

"I played football with this guy," Red said. "We went swimming together all the time at this quarry. Once he bet me that he could stand in this field where grasshoppers were flying around and open his mouth and catch five in two minutes. He won, but he cheated. He had a fuckin' huge mouth."

Lizzie smiled a little. Eventually she went upstairs to tell her mother she was going out. She wore tennis shoes and a sundress and rode in the front seat.

Red decided we should go sit on the Big Four railroad bridge and watch the sun go down. The bridge, which was no longer used, wasn't easily accessible from the Kentucky side of the Ohio River, so we had to cross via a downtown bridge and then drive back up the Indiana shore. Even though Red drove as if our lives hung in the balance, there wasn't much left of the sunset by the time we parked—just a few reddish-purple carcinogenic streaks at the bottom of the sky.

"We can watch the stars come out," Lizzie said, almost cheerfully. She'd drunk half a short boy on the way over. Red and I had passed the scotch back and forth.

"Sounds romantic," I said. A blaze warmed my skull, but it didn't ease my regret for bringing Red and Lizzie together.

"He misses Cheryl," Red said. "The fastest girl in the West." We were walking on the rail bed out to the bridge itself, with its immense steel spans held up by old stone piers. Red was on point, Lizzie was in the middle, and I brought up the rear.

"Cheryl," Lizzie said, turning to look at me. I glanced downward, at the ties and the gaps between them. I could see the glimmer of the river below. Heights frightened me; the fear took the top off my buzz and left me grim.

"We went to the Goshen," I said. I didn't say that I'd registered under the names Harry and Lizzie Burford.

"Motel love," Lizzie said.

We walked to the center of the bridge. The evening was mild, and there was a breeze, which seemed more pronounced up there among all the cables and struts and arcing steel. It licked at Lizzie's dress and hair.

Red sang the refrain from that Eric Burdon song, and then did a spastic boogaloo. He turned to Lizzie and said, "You want to climb up?"

"Sure," she said, as if climbing bridges were as simple as breathing.

"You'll have a much better view of Indiana from up there," I said, trying to light a cigarette, cupping the match against the wind.

"You can wait for us while we go up," Red said. "Play with yourself or something."

All but the last glow of day had been sucked from the sky. The lights of downtown Louisville were on, and there was a sprinkling of lights along the Indiana shore. In the growing dark, the bridge seemed to lose its firmness, to become tracery in the sky.

Red and Lizzie went to the downriver side of the bridge and began to climb a ladder attached to the middle span. Red first, Lizzie second.

I flicked my cigarette away and followed. The rungs were more like handholds than steps—narrow U-shaped bars riveted into the beam. I gripped the rungs, flattened my body against the available steel. Lizzie went up slowly. I stayed close, close enough that the crease behind her knee was within reach. I didn't look any farther up her dress; I didn't want to disturb my equilibrium. Fear was a chastening force. Nor, of course, did I look to either side of her.

"Lizzie," I said. I didn't know what I was going to say, but I wanted to hear her voice instead of the wind, the sound of a boat puttering up the river, Red singing.

She didn't answer.

"Lizzie," I said louder. "What are you doing?"

"Climbing a bridge. Saying to myself that poem the maid says in honor of the Fire Chief." She stopped climbing. We were perhaps halfway to the top. My mouth was at the level of her tennis shoe. She seemed to be quivering, unless it was me—or the bridge—that was moving.

"The men caught fire, the women caught fire, the birds caught fire, the fish caught fire," I recited. "The fire caught fire, everything caught fire." I didn't know I knew the poem until I'd said it.

"You skipped some lines," she said. "'The water caught fire, the sky caught fire, the ashes caught fire.' It's a progression."

"Fuckin' A!" Red exclaimed. He was pleased by the height he'd reached.

I noticed that the right rear edge of Lizzie's right sneaker was worn down, a fact of no importance and yet one that struck me as poignant: she was a girl who wouldn't go through life on the balls of her feet.

"Lizzie," I said. "What could I've done to get you to sleep with me?" The wind didn't carry away the self-pity in my voice.

"You could've doped me up and raped me."

"That would've made you happy?"

"I would've been oblivious, but you would've accomplished your goal."

She continued climbing. When she reached the top, she crawled along the beam to where Red was sitting and smoking, his feet dangling over the side. He held her arm as she unwound her long legs and settled next to him. He brushed something from her knee—bridge grit, I supposed.

"This is scary," she said. I admired her for her honesty.

"Hold on to me," Red said.

She asked about his severed index finger, and he told her how he'd lost it. "It made me 4-F," he said. "Saved my ass from getting shot off in some jungle."

"Good for you," she said. Her tone wasn't bitter, but she let go of him, folded her hands in her lap.

"Shit," Red said. "Sorry."

I gripped a stanchion and looked out rather than down. The dark was almost complete. I saw a drive-in movie screen a mile or so beyond the Indiana shore. The figures on the screen were indecipherable, like bug remains on a headlight. Was the sound I'd make when I hit the Ohio River two hundred feet below like *whap*? *Whump*? But I wasn't going to fall. I was going to crawl back down, slowly, not failing to place my foot where there was a rung.

Humming Back Yesterday

CRYSTAL E. WILKINSON

A native of Indian Creek in Casey County, Kentucky, Crystal Wilkinson grew up, as she has said in an autobiographical essay, among "creeks, one-room churches, outhouses, gravel roads, old men whittling at Hill's Grocery down in Needmore, daisies, Big Boy Tomatoes, and buttercups." She is a graduate of Eastern Kentucky University and has recently participated in various writing workshops throughout the state. A recipient of awards from the Kentucky Arts Council and the Mary Anderson Center for the Arts in Indiana, Wilkinson is a founding member of the Affrilachian Poets, the assistant director of the Carnegie Center for Literacy and Learning in Lexington, and chair of the creative writing department for the Kentucky Governor's School for the Arts. Her journalistic work includes articles, book reviews, and essays in *The Lexington-Herald Leader*, *The Lane Report*, and *ACE Magazine*. Her poems and stories have appeared in *Southern Exposure, Now & Then, Calyx, The Briar Cliff Review*, and *Obsidian II: Black Literature in Review*.

Blackberries, Blackberries (2000) is her debut collection of short stories. Frank X. Walker has noted that Wilkinson's "honest and sensual narrative pulls the reader in like a lover sharing their most intimate secrets." "Humming Back Yesterday," which first appeared in *Calyx* in 1999, depicts a woman's struggle to reconcile her haunting past with her present and future. Using a narrative technique reminiscent of that of Katherine Anne Porter and Toni Morrison, but uniquely Wilkinson, the story is a confluence of pain and joy, fear and comfort, death and renewal.

◆

Aberdeen Copeland was bringing yesterday back from twenty years of hiding. Bringing it back in slow motion. Never mattered where she was, what she was doing—weeding the garden, shopping in the corner store, making love to her Clovis, cooking beets, kneading bread dough—it could come anytime.

She was stirring the soup beans, beginning to wash the dishes. The water was hot, stinging her arms clean up to the elbows. It just came over her again. Came back in still life. A camera taking pictures.

Click. A teenaged Aberdeen in a purple wraparound dress with little green flowers. A toothy smile. Hair wild and bushy like they wore it in the seventies. Wire hoop earrings. A white sweater, knitted in big open loops, draped around her shoulders. Pearl buttons down the front. Her hip jutted to one side. Her head cocked. Hands on waist. Flat stomach. Beaucoup lipstick. Dark pink.

Click. Mama comes in full view. Tall, big boned, big breasted. Shapely. Flawless makeup. Blue eye shadow, Long lashes. Black orchid lipstick. Mouth open. Laughing up some storm. One arm hidden in back of Tommy. The other hand resting on the kitchen counter in the house they used to live in up on Hustonville Street. Tommy is a foot shorter than Mama. His head is right at her shoulders. His spats shiny. Hair slicked back, a skunk streak running through the middle, just a little off to the side. His belly round as a balloon. White starched shirt. Black dress pants, held up by suspenders. No smile. No tie. A cigarette dangling from his lips. One of his big hands snaking around Mama's waist. Fingers big as hot dogs. His other hand spread out on the edge of the sink. His wedding band shining.

Click. God's Witness Church over in Turnersville. Brother Smith up in the pulpit. Black robe. Wrinkled chin. His fist frozen in midair. Tommy's hand is under the coat spread out across Mama's lap.

The humming takes over. Back in her kitchen, Aberdeen is holding her head in her hands. Eyes closed. Elbows on the table. Legs gaped open.

Hum. Tommy's hand is under the coat, his hot-dog-fingered hand moving in some hidden place above Mama's thigh. Aberdeen is watching, though trying not to. She is old enough to know. And old enough to know better. Hum. Brother Smith is sweating. He wipes his brow with a great big white handkerchief. His mouth is moving but there are no words. His arms are moving. Mama's legs are apart. She is moving like shouting. Nobody else notices. Aberdeen watches her head roll back. The coat is moving. Tommy turns his head. Grins at Aberdeen. She turns away but is drawn back.

"Aberdeen," Clovis starts off, "Aberdeen, you got the headache again?" He steps up behind her, places his hands on her shoulders and rubs. He smells of blood and death from the slaughterhouse. A smell that Aberdeen got used to a long time ago, but today it sits in her nose, makes her head swim. Clovis kisses her bent-over head.

"Yeah," she says, coming on back to this side of the world. "Clovis, you member when Mama was with Tommy? Back when we was living up on Hustonville?"

"No, baby," Clovis says, leaning over to kiss Aberdeen's neck, "that was before

I knew y'all. Before we met. I still lived out Boneyville, remember? Need some aspirin? The doctor said plain aspirin was fine."

"Yeah," Aberdeen raises her head, answers only one of his questions, rubs the base of her neck. "Yeah, could you get me some, honey?"

Aberdeen pulls all the pieces of herself back together. "Clovis, I'm awright," she yells in the bathroom direction. "Why don't you go head and take your shower, baby? I'm gonna finish supper."

Clovis hollers back, "Okay."

The sound of running water puts calm in Aberdeen's kitchen. She wishes the past would stay past. Rubs the chill bumps off her arm. Rubs her belly.

By the time Clovis reaches singing stage in the shower, Aberdeen is back at the sink. Dishes washed. She peels Irish potatoes. Discards the peelings in old newspaper. Puts the fresh white potatoes in a pan of cold water. Watches them bob up gleaming like hard-boiled eggs. From the window she can see her garden spot all covered by winter's brown. Come spring she will give it life again.

Aberdeen quarters the potatoes then halves the quarters. She stirs the beans. Drops the potato pieces in a skillet of hot grease. Pulls the milk from the icebox, reaches up, pulls cornmeal from the cabinet to start her hoecakes. Aberdeen, determined to win this fight, keeps on cooking. *Hum.* She turns the potatoes in the grease. Pours the cornbread batter into a cast-iron skillet, making little pancake circles. She slices yellow onion on a saucer. *Hum.* Pulls corn from the deeper freezer. Plops the frozen lump into the saucepan. Frozen straight from the garden. Better than store-bought any day. Cuts half a stick of butter into it.

Hum. "Bitch, you don't know how to cook. Look at this damn cornbread. You call this shit cornbread?" Back on Hustonville Tommy has his thick fingers squeezing both sides of Mama's cheeks. Her face is squeezed together like a fish's mouth painted with black orchid lipstick.

Aberdeen stirs the beans. Flips the cornbread. Tastes the corn.

Hum. Tommy's two sheets to the wind. Liquor on his breath. In his other hand is the piece of cornbread all crumbled in his fist. Tommy eases off a little to see what Mama's got to say. "Aberdeen made it, sweetheart. It's her first time. That's all. You calm down, sugah, and I'll fix some more. Hear?" Mama tries to smile. Tommy gives her fish lips again.

Aberdeen sets the table, trying to sing over the humming in her head. A plate for her. One for Clovis.

Hum Tommy's face is all tore up. Mama reaches over under the table between Tommy's legs. His face changes. He eases his hot dog fingers. Rubs them across her face. Pulls Mama's face up close.

Knives, forks, jelly glasses. Ice.

Hum. Kisses her lips. Aberdeen sees his tongue flitting like a snake in and out of Mama's mouth. "Shhh," Tommy says at the end of the kiss, "it's just her first time." He laughs. "Shhh." He puts his big finger up to Mama's mouth making the hushing sign. Mama laughs. Rubs between his legs some more.

Aberdeen pours the sweet iced tea. Cuts a lemon up in it. Tears off paper towels for napkins.

Hum. Tommy slobbers on Mama's neck. Leaves spit running. Whispers something in her ear. Drags her laughing like a child to the back room.

Aberdeen puts bowls out for the beans.

Hum. The table is still set. Food's still hot. Aberdeen tries to eat her dinner. Tries to ignore the thumping sounds.

Sets the lemon pie out for dessert.

Clovis walks into the kitchen, rubbing his wet hair with a towel, smelling like Old Spice aftershave. His blue terrycloth robe pulled tight at his waist. "Baby, I needed that like you wouldn't believe. Feel good now. Your head still hurtin? You awright?"

Aberdeen is at the counter, pouring the soup beans in a big serving dish.

"Aberdeen?"

She lines a bread basket with paper towels and puts the hoecakes in. Puts the fried potatoes in the big green bowl Mama passed on to her. Notices the white chips around the edges. Notices how big the opening is.

"Aberdeen?" Clovis moves toward Aberdeen, who is somewhere down in the green bowl.

"Huh? Clovis, you say something, baby?" She sticks in serving spoons and moves around him to put the food on the table. Sets out a jar of homemade relish. Rubs her belly.

"Think I need to call the doctor?" Clovis puts a worried look on his face.

"Naw, I'm fine."

"You shore?"

"I'm fine, Clovis. You hungry? Let's eat."

Clovis eyes Aberdeen and goes to town on his supper. Aberdeen watches her man eating what her hands have prepared. Taking up supper in big forkfuls. She smiles. Between bean, bread, and potato, she tries to get a word in.

"Clovis, we gonna have a garden this year?" She keeps talking like it wasn't a question he was really supposed to answer. "I was thinking that we could plant some sunflowers out by the fence row." She takes a bite of beans. Chews. Talks. "How about some morning glories? You know Mama had morning glories all over the backyard up on Hustonville? Had yellow lilies all along the front walk. They always bloomed by Easter and—" Aberdeen feels the humming coming on and changes the subject. "Sugah, you have a good day? Seems like you tired."

Clovis is chewing as fast as he can, trying not to talk with his mouth full. Sips from his iced tea to help it all go down. Wipes the side of his mouth with the paper towel.

"Looks like we gonna need plenty of potatoes if nothing else," Aberdeen smiles. "Every time your elbow bends your mouth flies open. You'll be looking like me fore long." She pats her belly.

Clovis frees his full jaws. Laughs. Sips more tea. "Baby, you better go on and eat now, 'fore there ain't none left."

Aberdeen leans over to her husband. Rubs his arm. "You go on. There's plenty."

"My day was awright, baby. Same Ole, same Ole. Givens says he don't mind if I take some time off from the slaughterhouse. Did I tell you that?"

Aberdeen shakes her head. Gets up to cut the lemon pie. The knife goes in easy. She lifts the pie out with her fingers. Licks the sweetness off the tips.

"Baby, I don't know," Clovis shakes his head as she places it in front of him. "This might be too much. I'm awready bout to bust."

Aberdeen leaves the pie on the table to tease Clovis. Winks at him. Stands behind his chair and runs her fingers through his wet hair. She bends over to smell the clean shampoo scent. Clovis's head falls back onto her belly. Her hands reach out to his shoulders. She rubs. Trying to take the slaughterhouse up outta his muscles.

"Mmm, you put a man to sleep," Clovis says, his brown eyes shut. Aberdeen bends down and kisses him on the lips. Clovis reaches up and holds her there.

Click. Bobby Johnson. Aberdeen's first love. Bib overalls. Barefoot. Down by the creamery. It is a young kiss. A fresh kiss. lips smooth like butter. Bobby reaches up her skirt. Reaches inside her panties. His face like agony. Begging. "Let me finger you, Aberdeen. Come on. Please."

Aberdeen holds on to Clovis. Lets him kiss her long.

"Love you, baby," he says, raising his head up and digging into the lemon pie. He puts the fork up to Aberdeen's mouth.

"Love you too, Clovis." She takes a bite. Chews.

Way up in the night Clovis is sleeping, Aberdeen is tossing and turning, trying to find a comfortable spot. Her dreams roll up like a reel-to-reel across her closed eyes.

She is running up Hustonville Street in a night fog. Being chased. Her heart is beating fast. She hears Tommy's laugh, in between houses, cross the yards, from the trees. There is something, someone, at the end of the road that she must get to before Tommy. The fog grows thicker. The closer she gets, the farther away the something or someone moves. There is no end to Hustonville. Tommy is on her heels. She can hear his breathing. Through the fog she sees arms stretched out to her. Somebody crying. Screaming. She can't make out a face. Tommy is still laughing, gaining ground.

Aberdeen wakes up in a sweat. Sits straight up in the bed. Clovis wakes up too. "Baby, baby, what in the world?"
"Nightmare," she says, trembling through tears.
Clovis takes her in his arms, pulls her head to his chest. "Shh," he says, "shh."
Before morning shines through the window, Aberdeen pulls herself from her safe place in Clovis's arms. Makes her way to the bathroom in a quiet way to let Clovis get his rest. Before she even gets to the toilet, Aberdeen feels warm trickling down her leg and a slight shift in her belly.

Hum. Tommy steps through the brush. Grabs Bobby Johnson by the shirt collar. Punches him in the mouth. "You better git, you little bastard." Bobby runs.

Aberdeen is frozen in the bathroom. The green tile is wet around her feet.

Hum. Tommy grabs her by the shoulders. "You little fast-tail whore." He commences to shaking her hard. Aberdeen cries. Bobby Johnson runs. "Nothing but a whore." Tommy slaps her face. Aberdeen pees her panties.

"Clovis! Lord have mercy. Clovis!"
Clovis is out of bed and by her side. He takes her by the arm. Leads her into the bedroom.

Hum. Tommy has his hand around the meat just above her elbow. Jerking hard.

Clovis sets her on the bed. He washes her face with a warm rag, removes her gown. He washes her up and dresses her.

Hum. Tommy takes her up the road, where his car is parked.

Clovis puts her in the car. Aberdeen rocks back and forth in her seat. "Lord have mercy," she says over and over. "Shh," Clovis says. "Baby, it's gonna be awright."

Hum. "Shut up." Tommy drags Aberdeen in the house. Yells for Mama but she's still at work. "Ain't no daughter of mine gonna be no slut." Tommy slaps her again. "You gonna be a whore, you gonna be treated just like one."

Aberdeen feels sharp pain up and down her back. "Lord have mercy." Clovis reaches over, pats her arm. "Hold on, baby."

The hospital bed is cold. Smells like bleach. Clovis is by her side. Pain hits.

Hum. Tommy takes his hot dog finger and jabs it between her legs. "This what you want? This what you want?" Pain.

Pain.

Hum. "No, it was the first time—"

Pain. Clovis is by her side. Wiping sweat off her forehead. "This is her first time."

Hum. "It's her first time." Tommy laughs. There is a second finger poking away at her insides. "Lord have mercy. " Pain. Tommy is laughing and jabbing. Laughing and jabbing.

Pain. Aberdeen clenches her teeth. Bears down.

Click. Tommy looks old. Thin. Dying. His hot dog fingers shriveled. A cane between his legs. His eyes are yellow. Sad. Mama is dressed in black, practicing being a widow. Hair pulled back. Her shoulders drooped. Worn down. Worn out. No smile. No laugh.

Clovis is purring in her face. "Take it easy, baby, we gonna be awright. We gonna be awright. You ready?" Clovis holds the baby up for her to see. Aberdeen holds the girl child in her arms. The baby's face is that of a moon. Bright. Round. Clovis leans down, kisses Aberdeen's lips. Kisses the baby's head. Aberdeen smiles, says, "You happy, Clovis?" adds, "Me too" before he has a chance to answer. She tries to look forward to tomorrow. Tries to keep yesterday from humming back.

Afterword

CHARLES E. MAY

My introduction to Kentucky writers occurred in the summer of 1960, when, after graduating from high school in the small Appalachian town of Paintsville, Kentucky, I received a scholarship to attend Albert Stewart's Writers' Workshop at Morehead State College. Real authors were there—folks like Jane Mayhall, Robert Hazel, and James Still—authors who read and talked about their work, and wonder of wonders, read my work too.

Al Stewart, who later founded the Appalachian Writers' Workshop at the Hindman Settlement School, has been one of the strongest supporters of writers in the mountains for almost half a century, and I thank him for encouraging my lifelong interest in literature. I still have a copy of a little paperback book he gave me titled *Kentucky Writing*. In addition to fiction and poetry by Hollis Summers, Billy C. Clark, and Wendell Berry, it also contained the wonderful story by James Still, "The Nest." I thought it was a marvel; I still do.

During my undergraduate years at Morehead, I was fortunate enough to take a short story class under Jim Still, who introduced me to Chekhov, Turgenev, and Gogol. I still remember his reading "The Run for the Elbertas," a story that makes the back of my neck itch now when I think of it; you need to read it to understand what I mean. After I left Morehead in 1963 for graduate school at Ohio University, I ran into other Kentucky writers. In a class called "Stylistics," Hollis Summers made me so painfully aware of every word and nuance of syntax I feared I would never be able to write a decent sentence. During my first year of teaching at OU, my colleagues included David Madden and Walter Tevis. I was awed by Madden, who seemed to be the complete professional, always writing. And after reading Tevis's *The Hustler* and seeing Paul Newman in the movie role, I wouldn't drink anything except J.T.S. Brown whiskey for a long time.

In the thirty-three years I have been teaching English at California State University, Long Beach, I have had fewer occasions to be in contact with Kentucky writers. Occasionally, I taught Robert Penn Warren's classic story "Blackberry Winter" or Bobbie Ann Mason's "Shiloh," or used Hollis Summers's *Discussions of the Short Story* in a class. Once in a while, I would run into Richard Day, who taught up at Humboldt State, and we would have a beer and talk about Kentucky writing. He sent me a copy of "The Fugitive" just after it appeared in *The Kenyon Review*, and that wonderful first line still makes me smile every time I read it. Once in a while, my brother Don would send me a book, such as Gurney Norman's *Kinfolks: The Wilgus Stories*. Maxine's final dream of riding away with Wilgus, headed west, always haunts me.

On occasion, I would be asked to write a review of a new book by Wendell Berry or Chris Offutt. In fact, I had just finished a review of Offutt's new collection *Out of the Woods*, when my friend and colleague Morris Grubbs asked me if I would write the afterword to this collection. My most recent encounter with Kentucky writers came when an old college buddy, Lee Mueller, who covers Eastern Kentucky for *The Lexington Herald-Leader*, wrote and asked me if I had read a memoir entitled *Creeker* by Linda Scott DeRosier, who was born up a holler four or five miles from where I was born. It is a fine, honest account that made me as homesick as soup beans and cornbread.

I indulge myself in these homey remarks about my personal familiarity with Kentucky writers because the convention of the afterword seemed to give me permission to do so. Since Morris's preface provides a fine critical and historical context for the stories and Wade Hall's introduction does such an excellent job of whetting the reader's appetite, what, I thought, is left for the "words" that follow "after"? Well, to reflect, of course, both personally and professionally on what I have read. So now that I have essayed the personal, I'll assay the professional.

First, let me lay my biases out. In my opinion, when it comes to the art of fiction, the short story, when done right, beats the novel every time. I am not the only one to say this of course. Jorge Luis Borges once claimed that, unlike the novel, "a short story may be, for all purposes, essential." Russian theorist Boris Ejxenbaum has insisted that whereas the novel is derivative, the short story is "a fundamental, elementary form." Many writers and critics agree. Nadine Gordimer has argued convincingly that the novel cannot convey the true quality of modern human life, where "contact is more like the flash of fireflies, in and out, now here, now there, in darkness." Short story writers, Gordimer says, "see by the light of the flash; theirs is the art of the only thing one can be sure of—the present moment." And Elizabeth Bowen has said the short story, exempt from the novel's forced conclusiveness, may "more nearly than the novel approach aesthetic and moral truth." Most writers seem to agree that short stories do not string together "one damned thing after another," but rather focus on what Maurice Shadbolt has called that "hallucinatory point in which time past and time future seem to co-exist with time present."

Novels are too full of the mere matter I stub my toe on and too puffed up with abstraction and generality for me. A good short story makes me sit up and take notice, for even when it seems to be about matter or one damn thing after another, the stuff seems to shimmer, sometimes almost unbearably, with significance. Short stories, it seems to me, are not just about everyday reality, whatever that is, but the transformation of experience, which we too often take for granted, into mystery. That's why in Jane Mayhall's "The Men," what could have been a mere creative writing exercise becomes a delicate exploration, with no answers given or promised, of the infinite, ultimate mystery of love. And it is why Jack Cady's "Play Like I'm Sheriff" is not childish playacting, but a dreamlike fantasy about pretending, madness, lying, and choosing the imaginative over the merely material.

The large number of Kentucky short story writers represented in this collection may surprise some people. Why, many may ask, are there so many good short story writers from one state? It's risky to generalize about such matters, but a few guesses about the relationship between Kentucky and the history and conventions of the short story may be safe enough to chance.

If, as many have suggested, the short story is an essential, elementary form, it may be that it thrives best in a culture where talk and the oral tale are an important means of exploring and communicating what mystifies us about our experience. It may also be that the short story, with its perspectival view of reality and its freedom from sophisticated social structures, fares best in a culture that prizes the independence of the individual. Frank O'Connor once suggested that the reason the novel did so well in England while the short story was such an appropriate form for Ireland was related to the two countries' attitudes toward society. Whereas in England the view of society was "It must work," in Ireland, it was "It can't work." As in Ireland, Kentucky's largely rural and oral culture and its relative freedom from big-city social structures may make the short story a more appropriate narrative form for the state's writers than the novel.

One of the most basic problems about stories largely centered on place is the danger of the dreaded label of "local color" or "regionalism." In that little book of Kentucky writing Al Stewart gave me forty years ago, the editor James McConkey felt he had to remind readers that it was the "manner" of the writing, not merely the "matter" that was important, insisting that the regional details in the stories were used in such a way "that a greater understanding is gained of the universal human spirit." Hollis Summers, in his introduction to *Kentucky Story*, published at about the same time (1954), also noted that what was at stake was the artist's "what" and "how," not the sociologist's "why" and "where."

Such veneration of the universal and the aesthetic probably sounds "New Critically old fashioned" nowadays, when the trend among many academics is toward the multiculturally exotic, the postcolonially quaint, and the sociologically significant. Although I run the risk of being called retrograde and old fashioned, I once again lay out my biases in favor of form and the universal rather than rhetoric and the marginal. To my mind, the stories in *Home and Beyond* should be read, as Summers said of the fictions in *Kentucky Story*, not as regional artifacts, but as "stories, succeeding or failing on their own merits."

James Still is the quintessential example of how the writing in this collection is both regional and universal at once. For although he has the language of the people of the mountains of Eastern Kentucky "down to a T" and although he knows their customs intimately as an insider, readers who find such regional particularity the main merit of his fiction miss what makes him great. It is Still's ability, without the slightest hint of sentimentality, to magically transform fascinating difference into sympathetic sameness and thus make Nezzie Hargis in "The Nest" break our hearts trying to be "a little woman." There is no "local color" here, no "marginality," no "exoticism," no "social significance"—just pure narrative that is real and transcendent at once.

I feel a little like Jim Still did at the end of his interview in *Conversations with Kentucky Writers*, when Elisabeth Beattie asked him if there was anything else he would like to mention. "No," he said, "I think I have said too much already." However, I cannot resist making one final comment about the short story in the last half of the twentieth century—of which the forty stories collected here are such wonderful examples.

I grow weary of reading reviews of short story collections in which the reviewer avows his or her amazement that a mere collection of short stories could win the National Book Award, the Pen/Faulkner Award, or the Pulitzer Prize. And when a collection of stories stimulates a publisher's bidding war and garners a six-figure contract, reviewers fall all over themselves with astonishment. It happened in the final year of the century when Nathan Englander received a generous contract for his first book, a collection of stories titled *For the Relief of Unbearable Urges*. It occurred again in 1999 when Jhumpa Lahiri won the Pulitzer Prize for her collection of stories *Interpreter of Maladies* and when Annie Proulx returned to the short story with *Close Range: Wyoming Stories* and showed up many "mere" novels published during the year of "baggy monsters." And when John Updike's selection of *The Best American Short Stories of the Century* stayed on several bestseller lists for weeks in 1999, reviewers were astonished that readers might be so interested in the short story.

This amazement that a mere collection of stories could get a big advance, sell a lot of copies, or win a major prize is not a new phenomenon—it was the catch phrase of reviews in the late fifties when Bernard Malamud's *The Magic Barrel* won the National Book Award and in the late seventies when *The Stories of John Cheever* won the Pulitzer Prize. Reviewers still shake their heads over writers such as Raymond Carver, Alice Munro, and Peter Taylor who stubbornly stuck with the short story, and exceeding all critical understanding, captured reality in a more complex way than anyone writing prose in the last half of the century.

Isn't it about time that publishers, reviewers, and academic critics get over that tired old bias that bigger is better, that the novel is the norm, and that short stories are finger exercises in preparation for the big book still to come? New writers should not have to feel pressured by publishers, the press, or the pedants to consider the short story a sort of narrative adolescence to get past so they can get on with the so-called serious business of the novel.

I like the stories in *Home and Beyond*—professionally, because they are very fine examples of the genre I have spent my whole career studying and teaching, and personally, because they make me homesick for Kentucky. I get a great deal of pleasure running across such language in these stories as "the onliest thing," "It's kindly tied with bailing wire," and "He would give a pretty," for they sound like my mother and my father and my brothers and my sisters. I know exactly what it feels like to leave the mountains where you were born, shaking the dust off your feet with relief, but even before you get out of the state, looking over your shoulder and missing those ancient hills. I am grateful to the writers here, not only for contributing to the short story as a genre, but also for taking me back home for a little while. As the character in Jim Wayne Miller's story "The Taste of Ironwater" says, "There ain't a better place to live than down home. People don't put on the dog or nothin'."

Reprint Permissions

Kim Edwards: "The Way It Felt To Be Falling" from *The Secrets of a Fire King* by Kim Edwards. Copyright ©1997 by Kim Edwards. Reprinted by permission of the author, W. W. Norton & Company, Inc., and Elaine Markson Literary Agency. All rights reserved. Appeared originally in *The Threepenny Review* (1993).

Normandi Ellis: "Dr. Livingston's Grotto" from *Sorrowful Mysteries and Other Stories* by Normandi Ellis (Arrowood Books ©1991). Reprinted by permission of the author. Appeared originally in *Southern Humanities Review* (Summer 1989).

Janice Holt Giles: "The Gift" from *Wellspring* by Janice Holt Giles. Copyright ©1957, 1958, 1963, 1975 by Janice Holt Giles. Reprinted by permission of Houghton Mifflin Company and John Hawkins & Associates, Inc. All rights reserved. Originally appeared in *Good Housekeeping* (1957).

Caroline Gordon: "The Petrified Woman" from *The Collected Stories of Caroline Gordon*. Copyright ©1981 by Caroline Gordon. Reprinted by permission of Farrar, Straus & Giroux, Inc. Appeared originally in *Mademoiselle* (1947).

Paul Griner: "Clouds" from *Follow Me* by Paul Griner (Random House ©1996). Copyright ©1996 by Paul Griner. Reprinted by permission of the author. Originally appeared in *Bomb* (1996).

A. B. Guthrie: "The Fourth at Getup" from *The Big It and Other Stories* by A. B. Guthrie. Copyright ©1960 by the author. Reprinted by permission of Houghton Mifflin Company and Brandt & Brandt Literary Agents, Inc. All rights reserved.

James Baker Hall: "If You Can't Win" by James Baker Hall appeared originally in a slightly different version in *The American Voice* (Spring 1986). Reappeared in *The Journal of Kentucky Studies* (September 1988). Reprinted by permission of the author.

Elizabeth Hardwick: "Evenings at Home" by Elizabeth Hardwick appeared originally in *Partison Review* (1948). Reprinted by permission of the author.

Robert Hazel: "White Anglo-Saxon Protestant" by Robert Hazel reprinted by permission from *The Hudson Review*, Vol. XIX, No. 4 (Winter 1966–67). Copyright ©1967 by The Hudson Review, Inc.

Chris Holbrook: "The Idea of It" from *Hell and Ohio: Stories of Southern Appalachia* by Chris Holbrook (©1995). Reprinted by permission of the author and Gnomon Press. Appeared originally in *Louisville* magazine (1995).

Gayl Jones: "White Rat" from *White Rat: Short Stories* by Gayl Jones (Random House ©1977). Reprinted by permission of Faith Childs Literary Agency. Appeared originally in *Giant Talk: An Anthology of Third World Writings* (1975).

Barbara Kingsolver: "Homeland" is excerpted from *Homeland and Other Stories* by Barbara Kingsolver. Copyright ©1989 by Barbara Kingsolver. Reprinted by permission of the author and HarperCollins Publishers, Inc. and Frances Goldin Literary Agency, Inc.

Lisa Koger: "Bypass" from *Farlanburg Stories* by Lisa Koger (W. W. Norton ©1990). Reprinted by permission of the author. Appeared originally in the *Kinnesaw Review* (Winter 1987) and *The American Voice* (Winter1987).

David Madden: "The World's One Breathing" from *The Shadow Knows* by David Madden (Louisiana State University Press ©1970). Reprinted by permission of the author.